Heart of Flesh
Matthew Wolf

©2025 Matthew Wolf. All rights reserved. No part of this publication may be reproduced or used in any form or by any means, graphic, electronic or mechanical, including photocopying, recording, taping, or information and retrieval systems without written permission of the publisher.

Paperback ISBN: 978-1-62660-182-6
Hardcover ISBN: 978-1-62660-183-3

Map art by Flavio Bolla
Book design by Michael Campbell

 MATTHEW WOLF
www.mattwolfauthor.com

Heart of Flesh

Book Five of the Ronin Saga

MATTHEW WOLF

"Wolf has created a richly detailed, complex fantasy universe populated by intriguing characters who will continually surprise readers throughout the briskly paced tale. Gray is a particularly well-developed protagonist, and [the novel] refreshingly allows the villainous characters to change… A strong, confident fantasy novel [and] an impressive, page-turning adventure for fans of the series."

KIRKUS REVIEW

OTHER NOVELS BY MATTHEW WOLF

THE RONIN SAGA
The Knife's Edge
Citadel of Fire
Bastion of Sun
Tides of Fate
Heart of Flesh

Short Stories in The Ronin Saga
Dreams of a Reaver
Visions of a Hidden
Legends
An Arbiter's Gift

THE REALMWALKER SAGA
Skythief

To my Patreons… your support and steadfast belief in me is like an unwavering torch in the dark. And of course, this book is for everyone I've ever met at a comic con. Your enthusiasm is infectious and your love of the Saga—while sometimes surreal—fills me with boundless gratitude. Without you, I'd just be toiling over my keys while reading Amazon and Goodreads reviews.

FARHAVEN

FARHAVEN

De-Grael

The Abyss

Death's Gates

Burai Mountain

The White Plains

Sobeku Plains

The Green Valley
Moonshire

The Silvas River

Burmen's Bank

Koru Vi

Lakewood

THE LO

CONTENTS

THE THREE RULES XV
THE TALE OF THE RONIN XVII

Bickering Guild Leaders 7
An Invitation 32
Pyre 55
The Grand Tournament of Flesh . . . 80
A Council of Dragons 87
To Bow or Not to Bow 91
A Dragon at the Gates 105
Reprisal of Flames 111
Rising Winds 139
A Game of Elements 148
Blood and Dust 161
A Little Less Public 172
Shadows and Mud 180
Smells Like Dragon 194
The Deadmark 203
Curated Creatures 217
Ice Boy 221
The Shadow in the West 235
I Do The Burning 239
Just Another Fan 256
Merrick 266
A Chat with a Thieflord 270
Not This Girl 283
No Holding Back 290
The Wind Watcher 293

Beauty and the Beast	304
Gauging the Competition	310
The Sands Run Red	315
Fire and Ice	318
The Bloody Blacksmith	326
A Long-Awaited Meeting	350
More Drink	367
A Reunion of Fire and Flesh	374
Legends in the Sands	397
Fire and Sun	402
Nalia, the Final Blade	414
Thieflords and Wind	417
A Wolf Among Sheep	421
Merrick's Match	430
Back to The Red Blacksmith	439
Midnight Meetings	453
An Ancient Secret (Part 1)	459
Left Standing	472
A Fleshguard's Fight	487
An Ancient Secret (Part 2)	494
Sun and Water's Retribution	496
Wind's Fury	511
Shadowbane	530
Grand Primus	538
The Covian Legion	550
Epilogue: A Leafbug's Fancy	565
GLOSSARY	577
ACKNOWLEDGEMENTS	589
ABOUT THE AUTHOR	591

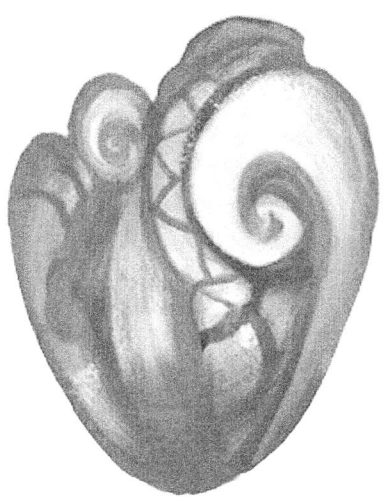

XIII

THE THREE RULES

ONE

Nine kingdoms will be deemed "The Great Kingdoms", those who bear the eternal elements as their sigil: wind, sun, leaf, fire, moon, water, stone, flesh, and metal.

TWO

The warriors known as the Ronin, with nine magical swords, will be bound to the kingdoms — each matched to their elemental power in turn. Baro will be the ambassador for the metal kingdom, Seth for fire, Hiron for water, Aundevoriä for stone, Aurelious for flesh, Dared for moon, Maris for leaf, Onni for sun, and lastly, their leader, Kail for wind. They will be the peacemakers of the land, the arbitrators of justice.

THREE

A prophecy will be forever engraved upon the walls of each Great Kingdom, words to spell the future of the world.

THE TALE OF THE RONIN

Long ago, the world was in chaos. Kingdoms fought for dominion, and blood ran in rivers… until a robed figure arrived. Some say the figure descended from the clouds on a mote of light, others that he walked across the oceans, or appeared in a blaze of fire. Yet all stories agree that the nine were at his side.

The Ronin — nine warriors who each wielded an elemental power: wind, water, stone, fire, leaf, moon, sun, flesh and metal. Together, they saved the world from near ruin. As the ambassadors of each city, the Ronin protected Farhaven, the land of magic. If a king grew unruly or a land attempted to disrupt the peace, the nine legends would unite and with their combined powers end any injustice.

Yet nothing can stay good forever; and if great power corrupts, the Ronin were no exception. The supposed protectors of mankind turned and nearly destroyed the world, or so the stories say… At last, they were stopped behind a great barrier known as Death's Gates, banished to a land without magic. The evil was thwarted but not conquered, sinking back into the lands, seething and waiting to return.

Slowly, the world rebuilt from the ash and rubble. Yet tales floated upon the winds as bards and minstrels spun accounts of the war and the evil sworn to return… An evil known as the Ronin.

Heart of Flesh

xx

Grim was lost. His thoughts brewed like a dark storm, his fingers digging into the well-worn railing, as he stood on the upper deck of *Bloodsworn*, his flagship, staring into the waters below. On the main deck, his sailors shouted as they worked to clear the thick slush of ice, a remnant of the Ronin of Water's power.

"Cursing legends," Grim grumbled, remembering the Ronin of Water and the Ronin of Leaf swooping down on the back of that damned leafbug and laying into his pirates with ice and vine. As much as he hated the Ronin…this destruction, Grim knew, was not their doing. That blood was on Grim's own hands. So many dead…Grim shifted his gaze from his sailors hauling bloated corpses out of the sea to survey the sacked city of Median, once the Great Kingdom of Water.

Or at least what was left of it.

It was a day after the battle to secure the city, and the horror of war was evident.

Fires still burned everywhere, and smoke rose in plumes, darkening the sky. In the distance, stone towers crumbled. The true horror, however, was the dark army of creatures, from troll-like vergs and gangly fox-faced saeroks to misting dark horrors known as nameless, swarming over the ruined city as far as he could see. Vergs lumbered across the docks, while saeroks crawled or loped in the tens of thousands, clogging streets, swarming rooftops, and scaling towers. Median looked like a kicked hill teeming with fire ants. On the docks, creatures piled corpses into a burning pyre. The sickening scent of burning flesh made Grim's insides curdle. The wharf itself was ravaged. Most of it had been crushed by the dark leviathan that had surfaced from the harbor's depths—the sleeping giant, awakened by none other than the Ronin of Water.

Grim fingered the thick scars on his skin beneath his jacket—the thumb-sized indents where the arrows had been embedded. He flinched in memory, remembering the feel of them slamming into his body. That woman with death in her eyes…she'd nearly killed him. If it wasn't for the dark Reaver's magic and his men's aid, Grim would be dead.

Just another bloated corpse bobbing in the water.

"Mistress of Shadows," he muttered to himself with a snarl.

One of the saeroks on the nearby docks spotted him and gave a rictus sneer in return.

A rasping voice broke Grim's somber contemplation.

"Captain…"

Grim turned to see the scarred face of Yaris, his first mate. His white-bearded old friend wore the black and bloodred of the Dragon's Tooth Marauders, Grim's pirate clan. Yaris's white beard, normally dripping with grog, was now red with dried blood.

"Captain…" Yaris repeated, "Are you all right?"

"Twelve," Grim counted aloud in a grave voice, eyeing the red sailed ships with black swords on their mostly tattered sails. He'd come with nearly fifty ships. "How did it come to this? How can a man fall so far? I've led us to our deaths."

Yaris joined his side, hands stained red from hauling corpses. "We had to take a side, Captain…you said so yourself."

"The wrong side."

Yaris shook his head. "But you said if we ignored the summons, we'd have been slaughtered."

"I did." Grim had a memory of that fated night.

He was hovering at Serenia's side, tending to her as coughs rattled her frail body, damping the sweat from her hot brow as a storm raged outside trying to bring down the heavens. "Leave me…" Serenia begged. "I don't want you to see the end…"

In that moment, Grim's heart broke. He'd witnessed a thousand deaths, been subject to endless pain and slaughter…but seeing the love of his life pleading, that look in her eye, sent a wave of grief and sorrow that gutted his very soul. He couldn't hold her eyes, and his gaze flickered to the left, eyeing a portrait of her in a silver frame—a woman so full of life and love…He knew he didn't deserve her. But she never deserved this. Not like this.

"Leave," Serenia pleaded again, gripping his much larger, calloused hand.

Grim growled, squeezing back. "You know that's a fool's ask, my love. I'm not going anywhere, nor are you," *he said, but he felt the lie on his tongue as she gasped, clutching at the sweat-stained sheets. Again, she cried out in pain, and her eyes rolled to the back of her head, as she fought the invisible demon inside her—a sickness that no amount of gold Grim had thrown at it, no knife to an herbalist's throat, had been able to cure.*

Suddenly, a dark pounding on his doorstep.

"Go away!" *Grim bellowed.*

Again, it thundered, rattling louder than even the storm's rumble, enough that he was surprised the door didn't splinter and burst.

Slowly, he rose, consoling her, but Serenia's eyes were clenched tight, and she was lost again in a fever dream. He knew the end was soon.

Again, the door rumbled with a terrible knock.

"I said, go—" *Before he could finish his sentence, a shadow fell upon the house.*

Abruptly, the storm stopped. Not a trickle of rain.

Grim felt terror, but this was something else altogether.

A figure appeared out of the shadows, tall, broad-shouldered, smiling, "Grim Battleborne, is it not?"

"W-who are you?"

Nothing but burning red eyes could be seen in the deep darkness from where the being spoke. "Consider me a messenger of hope. I have a task for you, Grim, leader of the Marauders. Aid me, and you will find your beloved will not die this day, and you will be showered in rivers of gold…Refuse, and all that you care for will wither to nothing."

Shouts drew Grim back to the moment—they sounded from the deck where his pirates worked to drag a man out of the ice. In halves. He'd been chomped in two by the water serpent and his body had landed in the Ronin's ice pile. Grim sighed. "I was wrong, Yaris." He turned to his friend, looking into Yaris's sea-green eyes, which narrowed in puzzlement.

"You said that a river of gold would follow," Yaris said.

"*Gold*," Grim replied as if it were a curse. "Pointless trinkets."

"Trinkets?" Yaris scoffed. "This is just your own guilt speaking. I know this. Your men know this. You won't be speaking this way when we're clad in silks, high in our towers, living like kings—"

Grim interrupted his first mate, turning on him and booming, "You don't get it! Look around, you fool!" He gestured to the pile of dead, the monsters crawling over everything. "What good is gold when all the world is burning before our eyes, and we hold the flame! I lead us into the devil's pit, into the very center of hell. I've doomed us all, Yaris! We are dead men walking, if not in body, at least in soul." His voice trembled with anger at his own folly.

Yaris's eyes went wide.

The men down below stopped their work.

"Doomed?" they whispered.

"*What's he on about?*"

"*We were sent to die?*"

Whispers rose on a swelling tide of fear and anger.

Grim deserved their fury, and more.

A light of clarity, of horror, entered Yaris's eyes, as if seeing the burning city at last, letting the true reality of their situation sink in. Then came the anger. It burned in Yaris's eyes, washing away the years, the decades of loyalty. "You…you lied to us…What could possibly have swayed your heart to doom your own brothers? Your own crew?"

Men strode forth now toward Grim on the upper deck, asking what was wrong.

Yaris snapped over his shoulder, "Back to work! The lot of you. Or I'll flog your hides!"

None so much as shifted.

They all watched Grim, and he felt their anger, their bafflement, weighing on his broad back as he hunched, trying to contain his own indignant fury. "I failed you…" he called, speaking up so they all could hear. "I failed you all."

A few deckhands stepped up—men Grim had raised since they were boys.

Whispers of mutiny rose like a dark tide.

"No," said the cabin boy, no more than sixteen. His blond hair was sweat-slick from hauling bodies. "He's lying. I can hear it and see it in his face. There's something he's not telling us."

Yaris shook his head in disbelief. "How could they convince you to send your own men to their doom—" Then his expression went flat. "Serenia."

Grim looked up, and images of her face flashed in his mind.

"They have her, Cap?" asked Hargar, a burly deckhand with a giant scar from temple to lip.

Grim heaved a huge gust of breath. "A sickness has her. Her life was fading before my eyes when a shadow appeared upon my doorstep, promising a flicker of hope. Said if we fought, he'd heal the sickness." He was ashamed, their eyes weighing on him. "He showed me a hint of proof, and I seized it like a drowning man." His fist trembled at his side, then he looked up. "I agreed to his pact, but this?" He looked up at the ice-filled harbor, the floating bodies, the monsters. "I assumed we'd hold the waters, scout for those fools trying to flee Median, and take them as hostages. I never thought…" His voice broke. "I was a fool." He lifted his hand, eyeing the pinkish scar that cut across his palm. Then looked back to his men—if not good men, at least they were loyal, honest.

"Let me get this straight, Cap," said Kregin, a wiry boatswain with a curly red beard, always two steps quicker to pull a dagger. "You made a deal with the devil, and now we're in the pit of hell?"

"That's the gist of it," Grim replied. "Worse, I do not know the way out."

Others began to whisper.

They all conferred for a moment. Some voices were heated.

Grim remained motionless.

Yaris looked ready to snuff the rising flame of potential mutiny.

Grim held up a hand, stopping him, and sent his friend a message with his eyes and a simple nod: *Let them speak.* He would take whatever punishment they felt fitting. Yaris paused.

When the men were done conferring, the biggest stepped forward, speaking for the lot. "Well, we discussed it, Cap, and you get a pass this time."

Hands edged away from cutlasses.

Gruff smiles creased the men's scarred, rugged faces.

It was a touching moment, despite the hell surrounding them.

Grim frowned. "I don't deserve your mercy."

"Ha!" said another man. "As far as we see it, we've been dancing with the devil our whole lives! Perhaps this is our lot, our purpose. I don't really believe in that load of rubbish, but Farhaven is wisest...After all, only blokes as corrupt as us get close enough to see the devil's neck, in order to cleave it from his shoulders."

Grim understood.

Yaris nodded, joining the others. "Seems you can't push us away after all, old friend."

A third man spoke up. "We're not good men, Cap, but perhaps we can do a good thing."

Grim looked away.

Serenia...Am I dooming her by turning on my pact? He wasn't sure. Part of him didn't care if it spelled his own end, if only they could find some sort of redemption, some glimmer of light at the end of this dark tunnel.

Above, a beam of light broke through the dark clouds and haze, warming the hull of the *Bloodsworn* and touching his hand. His thick fingers dug into the well-worn railing of his ship, each splinter and crevice as familiar as the calluses on his own palm. At that moment, Grim decided. He grinned, turning back to his men. "So be it..." Their ragged faces gleamed with mischievous smiles as they fingered their weapons. "This is our new path. If we're in the pits of hell, then we will slay the devil and rise back out of the depths."

Yaris clapped his shoulder.

The men cheered.

Despite their rallying calls, Grim's gaze panned to the plumes of smoke and fire, to the hordes of monsters...He knew in his soul that if he'd set their fate before, now it was locked tighter than a Landerian seal. There'd be no escaping this, at least not alive.

I will see you, my love. In this life, or the next.

It was time to dance with the devil.

Bickering Guild Leaders

The morning after the celebration, Gray found himself with a host of more than a dozen men and women around a massive table to decide the fate of Seria, Great Kingdom of Water, and to shape the future of Farhaven.

Aside from the giant table of blue marble surrounded by gilded chairs where they sat, the room contained no furniture, and likely it hadn't been used in ages. The room itself was vast, with a fresco of battling titans painted on the high ceiling. The floors were a little dusty from time, though still breathtaking, with blue veins spidering through the white marble. The far wall was open, revealing the verdant city of Seria and its many waterfalls suspended from clouds.

Several large floor-to-ceiling paintings of the Ronin, looming behind Helix, were the room's only other decoration, including a painting of Hiron riding a tidal wave. The current Ronin of Water was unable to keep himself from glancing at it from time to time. For a moment, Gray was lost in thought, wondering how many times the original Ronin had held council here.

A guild leader cackled, then another shouted across the table, and Gray was thrust back into the present moment. He rubbed at his temple. Wind swirled about his fist, and he tried not to flip the massive, likely priceless, table in rising frustration.

"And I say, Seria's wealth is to be shared!" a guild leader spouted.

"Ha!" another leader, a heavyset merchant, scoffed. "Is that so? I find it funny since your version of sharing is coin falling into your own pockets!"

"I told you once, I'll tell you again, if you fund the innkeepers, you fund the people!"

This was the same argument that had been used a hundred times.

By each of them.

It was like putting out fires while living in a house made of straw and ember.

Meanwhile, the Ronin listened…mostly.

Darius, Ronin of Leaf, had his feet kicked up on the table as he cleaned his nails with his arrow-headed dagger. His occasional wincing or eye rolling indicated he was paying more attention than he pretended.

Ayva, Ronin of Sun, had begun the meeting calmly and then inserted sound reasoning at key points in the debate. At this moment, however, she was yelling at a greedy red-haired merchant.

Helix yawned as if he'd rather be anywhere else in the world.

Gray felt them each in his mind—nodes of green, yellow, and blue, representing their elemental powers of nature, sun, and water.

Xavia, Darius's girlfriend and now queen of Seria, sat at the other head of the table, opposite Gray. Attendants at her beck and call stood behind her. She wore a simple blue linen dress, her frosty diadem crowning her head.

Imar was there too, dressed in a black robe that matched his ebony skin.

Imar…Gray had a suspicion the man was royalty of the Great Kingdom of Stone, but he'd had no confirmation so far.

A merchant said something foolish, and Ham, Imar's brother, slammed his fist down, sending cups and plates shuddering. Ham was as big as an ox, his muscled girth spilling over his chair.

Wyatt—the sly thief who had helped Ayva and Gray escape through the bowels of Median—also sat at the table. His hair was freshly slicked back with some sort of paste, and he wore his purple vest. He ignored the chatter, set on devouring all the food piled on silver platters.

Even the leafbug was perched close by on a giant branch outside. The giant lime-green insect might have blended with its surroundings perfectly if it hadn't kept rustling impatiently; its transparent wings fluttered, revealing an emerald web of veins, and its huge multifaceted eyes watched them with curiosity.

"*Shush!*" Darius said under his breath as the leafbug chirped again. "*Al'arasa,*" he added in Elvish.

He was doing that a lot more lately, speaking Elvish.

Bafflingly, the leafbug made a sad, plaintive sound and bowed its huge head, hunkering on the giant branch like a reprimanded hound.

Those who carried the majority of the conversation, and who had the real bone to pick, were the dozen displaced guild leaders from Median—men and women in varying shades of blue. Some skinny as a bone, and a few corpulent from well-indulged lives.

Gray tried to be patient, but they were getting on his last nerve.

Running a kingdom, as he had imagined, was a lot of work…especially a kingdom that had been lost to the ages and overrun with vegetation from a thousand years of disuse. The list of issues needing attention seemed impossibly long: find housing and food for every person, secure jobs, nurse those injured during Median's destruction back to health; even quelling daily little squabbles felt like an endless task for Gray and his companions. After all, thousands of people had been displaced in the battle of Median, and while Seria was more than big enough to accommodate them, the refugees practically a drop in the bucket, the actual maneuvering of who went where was…a lot. Amid all that, these dozen guild leaders were somewhere on a spectrum of magnanimous to utterly self-serving.

This is going nowhere, Gray sent through the bond, a mental link that could communicate thoughts only a Ronin could hear. Its uses grew more varied every day. Though sometimes Gray felt it was just a convenient way for Darius to relay sarcastic comments.

Darius sent back, *You know it wouldn't be hard to bind and gag them all with roots and vines.* Gray noticed the trees outside the windows, near the leafbug, seemed to grow and little vines spread out along the marble floor.

Ayva's fingertips glowed a subtle gold. *Not before I set them all on fire.*

"What of the Scholar's Guild?" Botan, a reed of a man and head of said Scholar's Guild, complained. "Should we all be stupid, but fat as swine?"

Is it me or have they both made that point six times already? Darius asked through the bond.

Aiko Marani, leader of the tavern and inn guild, snorted, "Your guild is pointless, Botan. What need do we have for books if we're all starving!"

"Yet provisions for the common folk are *my* jurisdiction, Aiko," Derigard said. "You just want all these big, fancy buildings to be assigned to you and your ilk."

Aiko's face tightened with disgust. "That's what you want, you fat old pig! I knew you would do this; don't you try to make *me* seem like the greedy one."

Derigard grew red-faced shouting back, and voices escalated across the table as they slung insults.

They rose out of their seats.

"*Enough!*" Gray bellowed. They all looked at him, sufficiently cowed. "That'll be all for today." He hadn't realized it, but he'd threaded a tiny bit of wind into his voice, and it had boomed through the huge council hall.

Eyes fell upon him, mostly those of the guild leaders, but also Xavia's.

"My Lord Ronin," said a guild leader, "this meeting is necessary, is it not? You yourself called it."

Gray sighed. He had and was beginning to regret it. "Yes, I did, but squabbling around a table for hours on end is pointless."

Derigard spoke again. "B-b-but, my Lord Ronin, how else are we to ascertain how goods and accommodations are to be distributed?"

Gray rubbed his brow and answered, "Discuss it among yourselves, then return with a plan."

A few of them had greedy eyes.

Gray added, "Might I remind you, the people come first. Don't disappoint us." He let a little wind swirl around his fingertips, and Darius's eyes blazed green. He touched Masamune as if simply maneuvering the sword to be more comfortable. Even Helix, breaking out of his yawning stupor, let a little ice crawl along the table, near enough to Derigard that the man had to shake some frost from his fingers, his expression terrified.

Ayva merely rolled her eyes, teasing through the bond, *Boys and their swords.*

Still, this quelled some of the ambitious looks of the guild leaders and earned Gray a small tug of a smile from Imar.

Ham added, pounding the table, "Ha! Well said, my Lord Ronin."

The guild leaders mumbled something like an agreement.

Derigard replied in a quick, nervous tone, "It will be as you say, my Lord Ronin."

Aiko, matriarchal as ever, bowed her head. "We shall see it done properly." She made it seem like a command, willing the others with her eyes to stay their greed.

Gray grunted, satisfied. "Good. If that's it, you all may go."

They moved to rise when Ayva coughed and said through the bond, *Uh, Gray? Have you forgotten someone?*

Gray saw Xavia looking at him, her brow raised.

Darius chuckled and put his hands behind his head, looking smug and happy to be out of the line of fire for once.

The guild leaders were moving to leave, sliding back chairs, when Gray called out, stalling them. "That is—" They froze awkwardly, halfway between standing and sitting. "You may go, with the queen's approval…"

Nice recovery, Darius sent.

Xavia directed an easy smile at Gray. "More than acceptable. We've talked long enough about the distribution of goods for the city. I believe we've other important matters to address. All the guild leaders may go. Have the draft upon the morrow, and if it's not as selfless as the Lord Ronin wisely suggested, then know I can always find others to take your places."

"My queen," several of the guild leaders said, bowing, and then they hurriedly took their leave, vacating the Hall of Water like scared mice fearing another swipe from the barn cat.

"Well handled!" Ham boomed, a smile splitting his affable face as he grabbed a leg of meat, ripping into it. Gray wondered what it would sound like if Ham tried to whisper.

"Thanks, but fools like that don't stop," Ayva said, sighing. "Tomorrow, they'll just find other ways to thwart our authority."

"Maybe," Imar replied. "Maybe not. We have seen our fair share of greed and avarice." His words had that strange cadence he always used. It tickled something in Gray's mind—as if recalling Kail's memories. *The accent of a Landerian, Great Kingdom of Stone.*

The Ronin of Leaf wasn't so subtle. Knife still in hand, Darius leaned forward. "While ruling the Great Kingdom of Stone?"

Imar gave a small shrug, and said evasively, "I have served *many* roles."

Darius rolled his eyes and returned to cleaning his nails, mumbling something about "dicing mysterious man."

Imar continued, "Anyway, as for those men and women, I think they just needed to know there was a stern hand to keep them in line. All people need boundaries. This is a first, after all…we are all finding our way as we reestablish a Great Kingdom from the ashes of its past."

Xavia gave a warm smile. "Doing something for the first time is always a bumpy road."

"Wise words," Imar said.

"It's…something my father used to say often."

Xavia's father, Baron Belfont, had died in the battle of Median…a wound that Gray knew hadn't healed, yet she somehow had pressed onward with a sense of conviction and spirit that Gray admired.

Imar replied, "I see…Then his wisdom lives on, and in a daughter so noble that any father would be so lucky to have." And he bowed his head respectfully.

Xavia gave the nobleman a smile. "You are too kind."

Well, I can't follow that, Darius sent.

Wyatt was eating more slowly, as if finally sensing the tension.

Gray and the others had a moment of silence. He could tell Darius wanted to reach out and comfort Xavia, but the moment came and left quickly as Xavia spoke again. "No one ever said it was going to be easy, but we thank you for your counsel."

Ham grunted, juices spilling around his mouth from the turkey leg he was devouring. He wiped it with a napkin the size of a small blanket. "Of course!"

Imar nodded, stroking his fine salt-and-pepper beard. "Gladly given…Barthos couldn't attend this meeting and asked us to fill him in. Not to mention, you've put him in charge of the coffers, and we've some *small* knowledge of handling finances, which provides some aid. That said, my queen, my Lord Ronin"—he nodded to Xavia, then Gray—"we must depart the city, if that is acceptable."

"You two don't have to go," Gray said. "That was mostly for those blowhards."

Ham pushed back his chair, scraping it loudly on the floor, and patted his bulk. "No, no, you've been most accommodating keeping us in the midst of the city's duties. To that end, we must plan our departure, isn't that right, brother? Events are moving quicker than we had foreseen."

"Leaving?" Ayva asked.

"Yes," Imar said, looking out the large windows, past the vines and waterfalls. "North."

To the lost Great Kingdom of Stone, Gray thought, a zephyr of curiosity rising inside of him.

"Can we hitch a ride?" Darius asked.

Ayva cleared her throat. "We've still yet to discuss where we're going, remember, Darius?"

Darius cursed and sent through the bond, *Why are you all being so weird around Imar? You're acting like you're stepping on brittle bones in a bear cave. If he knows where Lander is, we should too. We need to find the city, right? Find the Ronin of Stone?*

In time, Gray sent. *We need allies too, Darius. Imar seems like a good friend, but he still needs time to trust us. In the War of the Lieon, Lander closed their walls, and it saved them. They have been hidden for a thousand years because they trust no one. They don't want to be found. It will require patience and tact.*

I am tactful! Darius shot back.

You're as tactful as a cerabul in a Serian porcelain shop, Ayva sent. *Is that tactful? I'm guessing that's tactful.*

You can't play the village bumpkin any longer, Darius. You're a Ronin. You're eventually going to have to act like it.

Yeah... He shrugged mentally. *Eventually.*

Ayva sent the equivalent of an eye roll through the bond.

Also, you're avoiding the point. I know tact. Seven hells, Helix and I infiltrated the Order of the Serpent!

Helix, who had seemed to be falling asleep in his chair until now, yawned again, and without opening his eyes, he joined in the conversation by sending his response through the bond. *Nope. That was dumb luck. We just put on a few scratchy brown robes and nearly died. Multiple times.*

"Nearly" being the operative word, Darius sent, holding up a finger.

Uh, guys... Gray posed, nodding.

The three other Ronin—including Helix, who reluctantly cracked open an eye—looked to the others standing around the polished blue table.

Imar, Ham, Xavia, and even Wyatt—a piece of cheese in his mouth—stared curiously at the Ronin. By now, most knew the Ronin could communicate through the bond, and while they did that more quickly than speaking out loud, their bickering had still created a pregnant silence.

Gray rose and smiled. "You're free to come and go as you please. Thank you for everything," he said, and meant it—they'd been utterly instrumental in saving the citizens by evacuating the city and helping to open the portal that led them here. "If you ever need us, we'll be there."

Imar nodded, a glimmer in his keen eyes. "Likewise, my Lord Ronin." Then he extended his forearm.

Ordering the guild leader to stop bickering was one thing—in that moment, Gray allowed himself to be "Lord Ronin." Yet hearing it from Imar? Part of him squirmed, as if the title was another's. Or perhaps it was his, yet like a growth spurt, he was just realizing the pants he once wore no longer fit.

Gray accepted Imar's forearm.

He turned to Ham who barreled forth and picked Gray up like a rag doll, squeezing every last puff of air out of him. Rubbing bruised ribs, the brothers said farewell to the rest.

Before the doors closed, Darius called, "Feel free to leave a map next time!"

Gray leaned forward, clasping his hands upon the table, and then looked at the others. "It's time to discuss what we are all thinking."

Darius's chair rocked forward, his feet hit the ground, and he exclaimed, "Okay, now hear me out…might sound a little biased—City of Leaf! That's where we're going next. Who's with me?" He raised his hand and then grabbed Helix's wrist.

Helix slapped Darius's hand away.

"Little biased?" Ayva replied.

"Not at all. A city suspended in the trees? C'mon, you can't tell me that doesn't sound cool!"

Helix said unexpectedly, "I want to find the hidden Kingdom of Stone. I know you said they don't want to be found, but if I'm being honest, that makes me want to find them all the more."

The Ronin of Leaf raised a brow. "I thought you were sleeping."

"Not anymore," Helix replied, sitting straighter, a glint of blue in his eyes. "Great Kingdom of Stone is my vote. I hear there are boulders stacked on top of one another a mile high, and cities perched upon that. And their walls, stories say, are so thick it took from King Darmin the I to King Darnin the V for one section to be completed. Five generations, and each ruled for nearly fifty years. That's nearly three centuries! Plus, I've never seen a dwarf. Not a lot of water there, but I'm sure we can change that."

Ayva shook her head. "Sorry, Helix. I love your enthusiasm, and yours too," she said to Darius, "but there's only one option."

Darius folded his arms in a huff. "And that is?"

Gray replied, "Great Kingdom of Flesh. We need to stop the threat that's coming out of Median. If the army of the enemy is amassing in the west, Covai is the next nearest threat."

"Well, then, why'd you ask us?" Helix protested.

"Because, we decide together."

Helix and Darius burst into laughter.

Gray glowered. "What's so funny?"

"You two always decide for us," Helix scoffed.

Gray opened his mouth to rebut.

Darius held up his hands in defense. "But we're okay with it."

Helix nodded.

Xavia, across the way, smiled and rose.

"Where are you going?" Darius asked.

"This looks like Ronin business." She bowed at the doors. "Safe travels, you four. I expect great things. Know Seria's gates are always open to you…even when we get around to repairing them." She looked at Darius, her brow raised in a way that even Gray could read, which meant Darius was in trouble again. Then she left with her attendants trailing her like ducklings.

"You didn't tell her you were leaving, did you?" Ayva asked Darius.

Darius winced, then held up a finger. "Hold that thought for a second. I'll be riiiight back."

"I'm out as well. I've had enough Ronin and bureaucracy. I think there is a tavern calling my name." Helix slid back his chair.

Gray let them go.

As soon as the door shut, a plate clattered to the floor. Wyatt, who Gray had forgotten about, looked like he'd been caught in the hen house, with a chicken wing in one hand, and buttered bread in the other.

"Wyatt, you can go," Gray said.

Wyatt set down the wing and bread. "Jeez, okay, okay! I'll leave you two lovebirds alone." He got up to leave, then paused and began to say, "You know, you two really make a—" But Gray opened the door, pushed him out, and shut it with a thud using his power.

When it was done, he dusted his hands.

"Not even a little curious about what he was going to say?" Ayva asked. "Also, you're getting pretty good with your power."

"It's coming easier." His hand went to Morrowil at his side, feeling the reassurance of the newly wrapped handle. He admired his sword—white wings for a hilt and a white-gold sheath, with a wind symbol emblazoned on its pommel. Morrowil, legendary blade of wind, formerly held by Kail—the last leader of the Ronin. A sword more famous than any weapon in Farhaven. In many ways, the very bane of Gray's existence as it had been the catalyst for him finding Vera in her room, covered in blood, then led to Ren's death, and then ultimately hers...It had also saved him more times than he could count. It had shattered in Death's Gates but had been reforged by the elves...It looked worthy of its legendary status. Gray's brows furrowed, thoughts storming. "I need to take a walk." He rose and approached the open window.

She joined his side, putting her hand on the hilt of Aurora. The name she chose. It...sounded right.

Gray surveyed Seria, Great Kingdom of Water—once lost, now found. By them.

A churning mass of people stirred below, while waterfalls rained from heavenward clouds. They walked over marble bridges that spanned rushing rivers. The survivors—once citizens of the City of Median—were making this place their new home. Still, the vision of hulking vergs and long-limbed saeroks was a recent memory. Gray saw people jump when he got too close, and they kept swords and axes at their hips—as if anticipating another attack.

For now, they were safe.

The city was running smoothly.

More or less.

Still, Seria was unlike anything he'd seen before. The jungle had done its best to reclaim the tiered city, with ferns, vines, and little trees growing in every crevice, but a magical spell seemed to repel the vegetation from overrunning it, even though there were reports of people still pulling down vines that blocked doors to once-thriving inns and taverns. Some of Seria seemed intentionally built that way—as if all the tiers were meant to be lush, terraced gardens. Only the jungle had other plans. The wild, untamed majesty of it was like a rushing river, its dam shattered.

Just beyond Seria, over the rim of the blue stone outer walls, was the wilds. Towering trees filled Gray's vision, their massive branches and gnarled roots plunging deep into the land. Birds cawed, monkeys howled, and insects trilled in a cacophony of sound, the jungle symphony sifting over Gray and Ayva as they took it in.

Gray's eyes sought farther, however, and he looked beyond the ramparts. This was the highest place in the city, aside from the waterfalls above, and still, he could glimpse in the distance some of the canopy to the Rehlias Desert. As if he could see Farbs, City of Fire, then Eldas, Great Kingdom of Leaf beyond that, raging with the war against Dryan…all of it waiting. "Are you ready?" Gray asked Ayva, her presence a ray of hope.

"I am."

Gray smiled. "Do you sense them?"

She was silent for a moment, so long Gray didn't think she was going to answer, and then…

"Yes. I sense her. Omni's part of me. I can almost feel her eyes on me."

"There is something I haven't told you," Gray confessed. "Kail's last words."

Ayva turned to him.

Gray looked into her eyes. They'd always been a bright piercing blue, now they seemed to have a small halo of gold in them. Both of them changing, outwardly and inwardly. He tried to remember Omni. He thought she might have had the same vibrant oddity in her eyes.

Suddenly, Gray was taken back to that moment. *Kail's white eyes looked into his, as the winds of Death's Gates whipped about them. Kail was dying. Gray watched in horror as the man's body began to disintegrate. "Listen, boy," Kail said in his gravelly tone. "This is not the end, not for you. Not yet. You will be more."* At that moment, looking into Ayva's eyes, he was starting to understand those final words.

She stopped him from going further. "That was meant for you, Gray."

In the corner of his vision, he saw movement on the winding road that led to the heart of the city.

Two elves and one human rode fine silken-haired cormacs. Gray tensed.

"Is that…who I think it is? Rydel? C'mon." She grabbed his wrist.

"Better idea…" Gray tapped into his Nexus.

Darius was with Xavia when he spotted the newcomers. Rydel was easy to notice, even from this distance, what with his stupid, handsomely stoic face, straight back, and air of menace. The kind of threatening aura of "I'll ride alone to face an army," and Darius thought the army might indeed retreat, if they knew what was good for them. Darius liked the guy, even if he gave him a bit of the shivers. He knew there had to be more to him than all hard angles…something soft, maybe a love of kittens? Or at least why he'd gotten so hardened, or how he'd earned the elite warrior status of a Hidden. Without Karil, queen of the elves, to soften him, he was like a sword without a sheath. *Eh*, he thought. All these mysterious pasts were beginning to annoy him. First Imar, now Rydel. Darius snorted. He'd make open-book softies of them all.

There was another elf beside Rydel, a female…kinda pretty too, though it was hard to tell from this distance. The third and last rider was a red-robed Reaver. At first, he dismissed him, then he looked closer…Reaver Finn? His heart leapt into his throat.

Finally, a true ray of light after stewing in this bureaucratic nonsense for weeks.

The cormacs they rode seemed exhausted, breathing hard, slicked with sweat.

Do you all see them? Darius asked through the bond.

We do, Gray sent. *Looks like they have pressing news.*

Was…was it just Darius, or was there a faint sound of wind in Gray's message?

Uh, who are we looking at? Helix asked.

Darius rolled his eyes. *What do you mean? Don't you see the two elves and the human causing all the fuss down below?*

Sure, but I've no idea who they are.

You will, Gray sent.

A Serian guardsman on horseback—one of the few steeds that had survived the destruction of Median—escorted them. He led the group to the platform of stone, a huge, wide altar surrounded by a moat of water, bridges spanning it at several places like spokes of a wagon wheel.

We're going to meet them now, Gray sent.

Ha! Trying to steal the limelight? I don't think so! Darius sent.

Darius hesitated as he looked at Xavia.

When had she started to mean so much to him? He liked how she could always see through him, how she handled herself in front of others with strength and poise, but above all? It was that gleam in her eyes. He inwardly chided himself, knowing how many false paths he'd been led down in the name of "beauty" or "allure." Sure, Xavia had that in spades but…turns out he liked intelligence. Who knew? Of course, if Ayva, or Gray, had heard that comment they'd have a clever quip or two.

Xavia, seeing the commotion below, gave him a small smile. "You know them?"

"Yeah, you could say that."

She squinted. They were still a fair distance away, but even from here, there was an air of urgency about them. "Who's the big elf that looks like he can chew rocks?"

"That's Rydel. Karil's right hand."

"Karil as in the rightful queen of Eldas? You know her?"

He rubbed the back of his neck, chagrined. "Yeah, a little bit."

She folded her arms. "Uh-huh. It's cute when you feign modesty."

He shrugged. "Thought girls liked that."

She rolled her eyes. "Another queen…Should I be jealous?"

He winked. "I don't know, should you?"

She glowered and continued, "Anyway, you have some interesting friends. How do you know the man?"

"He's…come to our aid once or twice. Helped us not die against a horde of evil monsters in the Battle of the Sands, and fought against the Kage, the false Ronin." She raised a brow, and he continued, "The Reaver's name is Finn. We fought Darkwalkers and thieves from Darkeye's clan in the Battle of the Sands to save Farbs." Of course, he'd already told her most of this. Hadn't he?

She glared at him. "You're gonna have to fill me in more later. In detail." The way she said it wasn't a question, but an order.

"Yes, my queen," he said with a bow.

She sighed. "The elf woman?"

He shrugged. "No idea."

"Well, it's settled. Now I'm excited to meet them. If only to prevent you from being whisked off by another monarch. C'mon." She started walking forward and he grabbed her wrist.

"I've a better idea," Darius said, smirking.

"Oh god, I know that look in your eye. I'm going to regret this, aren't I?"

He didn't want to lie, so instead, as he winced he said, "Maybe?" And he whistled. Last he'd seen Leafy, the leafbug had been on a branch a few hundred paces away, begging to get inside their secret conference room. He sensed Leafy closer now, and he was proven right. More right than he intended when there was a rustle from a nearby giant bush and the leafbug pounced on him like an oversized dog, pinning him to a wall that had a marble relief of the Ronin during the Lieon. "Bah! Get off!" Leafy kept nuzzling his face with that giant bug proboscis, or mouth, or something.

Whatever it was, it was *wet*.

Xavia only watched, trying not to laugh but failing.

He shouted in Elvish. "*Endrasa!*"

Down.

Leafy promptly lay flat.

Darius rose to his feet, brushing himself off, and eyed Xavia. "Gee, thanks for the help."

She smirked. "Consider it a preemptive payback." He offered her his hand to help her onto Leafy, but she leapt into the saddle with surprising ease, then looked down at him, raising a brow. "Well? What are you waiting for? I'm assuming you're going to make some sort of childish bet regarding who gets there first?"

He sighed. "Why do I even talk if you can read my mind?"

"Because I like the sound of your voice."

"Oh, that was good." And Darius vaulted into the giant saddle with Xavia behind him. He grabbed the reins, and then he sent through the bond, *Last person down there washes Helix's underwear!*

I am not agreeing to that! Ayva sent.

Hey! I am quite clean, thank you very much, Helix replied.

Gray jumped in, *How about, the last person down there buys the first round of drinks at the next city?*

Deal! Helix sent.

Much better, Ayva agreed.

Darius felt the others burst into action.

But Darius was quicker, commanding the leafbug in Elvish, *"Andarasia!"*

Fly.

Leafy leapt off the nearest marble railing, diving toward the waters below. Xavia let out a small yelp and held Darius's waist tighter. As they plummeted, he saw a figure inside the rushing waterfall to his left. *Helix.* Darius's jaw dropped, seeing his friend encased within a giant hollow water droplet. The raging torrent carried Helix downward, toward the arriving party. The sneaky bastard was literally riding a waterfall!

Oh, no you don't, Darius thought. "Hold on tight!" And he urged the leafbug faster; its wings folded in, and they dove like a shooting arrow.

Xavia let out a few choice—and rather impressive—curse words into his ear, and her arms tightened around his waist, squeezing the air out of him, as if she were trying to crack a rib. Wind blurred his vision, and they raced impossibly fast toward the altar.

At the last moment, Darius called out, *"Etara!"*

Now!

The translucent green wings fanned wide, catching a current of air.

Helix was almost to Rydel and company, riding a wave of water that washed over the platform. Yet Darius landed first, Leafy pulling up short. He helped Xavia off the leafbug's back and called out through the bond, *Ha! I win!*

Not quite, Gray sent from thin air in front of Darius.

Wind rushed over those gathered on the stone platform. Darius was knocked to his knees still a dozen feet from Rydel and the other newcomers.

Seeing a root sprouting from a crack in the altar, Darius delved into his Nexus, a glowing green leaf with silver veins in his mind's eye, and made it grow. Using it as a tether, he held on to Xavia, squinting against the sudden maelstrom. A white cocoon of air appeared, then vanished in a puff, and Gray and Ayva stood in its place.

Gray gave an exaggerated stretch and then yawned. "Oh, were you both racing?"

"You cheating son of a verg!" Darius groused.

Helix, still half-soaked, complained, "Stupid fancy wind vortex." Eyes briefly flickering a deeper ocean blue, he waved a hand, and water misted into the air as his soaked clothes were suddenly bone-dry.

Gray scoffed. "Whoa, whoa, whoa… I used my powers. You used your powers. How's that cheating?"

Helix and Darius looked at one another, a bit at a loss.

"Go ahead, tell him, Helix," Darius said, folding his arms with a huff.

"Me? I mean, yeah, me. Sure, I'll tell you why. Because…" Helix said, scratching his wet head, looking about as if Rydel or the others were going to help. "Because… wind is too powerful?"

"Yeah! What he said," Darius replied, pointing a thumb at Helix. Then he dropped his hand. "Wait, no. I don't like that."

The pretty female elf cleared her throat.

The newcomers' mounts stomped at the ground, feeding off the riders' impatience. Darius felt a strange affinity toward the elven steeds—majestic beasts with long sloping backs, intelligent green eyes, and fine silken hair.

A raised eyebrow from Rydel revealed he was impressed. That was it, one eyebrow. But it was practically an exclamation from him. Rydel was big—Darius had forgotten just how big. His brawny arms made the ties of his vambraces bulge, he had a thick neck and a jaw like an anvil. Hells, Darius thought he could cut his finger on that thing, or on the man's cheekbones. Where many elves had a feminine grace to them, Rydel's features seemed all hammered out. Two swords protruded over the elf's broad shoulders, and as he fluidly leapt off his cormac, they appeared as an integral part of his body.

Darius looked at the female elf. If Rydel was a lion, all raw power, she was a panther, sleek and ready to pounce. Her blond hair was woven into many braids, which accentuated her exceptionally long, pointy ears, and her expression had a tightness to it, as if she bore the strain of years in contrast to her ageless, fair skin. She had looked amazed by their magical arrivals—until her bright green eyes focused on Darius like hot awls.

Reaver Finn was a pleasant contrast to the two elves. He wore a beaming smile, as if in awe at the display of their powers. Darius remembered him. He had a lover, Reaver Meira, a powerful woman and ally in the effort to save Ezrah, Gray's grandfather, from the torturous madman known as Sithel. Sadly, Meira had died in the Battle of the Sands, and Finn had been the one to find her broken body. Darius knew that had nearly killed the man. Reaver Finn had then been sent with Lucky, a small orphaned boy, to Karil with a gift of a chest full of gold in an attempt to give the Reaver a new purpose. *A new start*, Gray had said.

Now, Reaver Finn seemed…different. While he still wore his traditional scarlet robes, he'd altered them, as if to symbolize his new identity. The red robes were split down the middle and worn as an ankle-length overcoat. Beneath it, he wore a pair of black pants and a shirt. He still bore shadows under his eyes, as if he were perpetually tired, but he'd grown out a peppered gray beard that hid the hollowness of his cheeks and gave him a distinguished air. In those eyes, normally kind and intuitive, now burned a new intensity.

Darius ignored the look and waved. "Hello!"

This broke the tension in the air, and they each moved in greeting.

Gray and Rydel gripped forearms.

It was some Devari-warrior thing.

"*Reklah forhas.*"

Darius's mind—his Ronin side—translated it.

With honor, until death.

Stupid Elvish. Well, mostly Elvish, with a hint of…old tongue? His mind was doing that more lately. Knowing words and sayings or picking up on abilities. Yesterday, he knew how to tie a really cool knot he'd never known before. He'd grinned until he'd growled. It was clearly something Maris, the Ronin of Leaf—his predecessor—would know. In one sense, it was kind of cool. In another, Darius didn't like anything controlling him, even if it was helping. Not even destiny.

"It's good to see you. It feels like ages," Gray said, smiling.

"Likewise," Rydel grunted, a small quirk of his lips cracking his stony exterior.

Ayva rushed forward, embracing Reaver Finn, and then Rydel.

They all turned to the female elf.

"Alandra," she said in introduction, remaining mounted, though she added a small bow.

"I must say, that was…impressive," Reaver Finn said, drawing their attention back. "Enough to make a three-stripe green with envy. It seems you three have come a long way."

"We've still a long way to go," Gray replied, eyes steely.

Darius wrapped an arm around his friend. "What old grumpy pants means is that we still need to find the others."

"And your presence is a serious boon," Ayva replied, stepping to his side.

Gray looked at his two friends. "Thankfully, I have translators."

Reaver Finn. Darius looked to the man. He remembered the three-stripe had lost Meira, a powerful Reaver who had been a close ally during their adventures in Farbs. Meira, like Finn, at first had been forced to torture Ezrah—Gray's grandfather—under the direction of Sithel, a corrupt madman. They turned to the side of good and helped the powerful Arbiter escape with Gray's aid. Only, during the Battle of the Sands, Meira had been killed by some dark Reavers. Finn, judging by his bags and hollow cheeks, and the dark glint in his eyes, was still not whole…if one could ever be whole after something like that. But he seemed to warm seeing the Ronin, as if they reminded him of better times.

Rydel looked to Helix. "Speaking of which, I'm presuming you must be the new Ronin of Water?"

Helix had been knocking on the side of his head, as if trying to empty a clogged ear. He looked up and nodded. "Helix," he replied with a small wave, then touched the hilt at his side, like water in motion "And yeah, until they can find another reborn legend to take my place, guess I am."

Darius admitted the Ronin looked rather impressive all standing together with their swords.

Ayva elbowed him, nodding at Xavia.

Darius shook himself and went to introduce her, but Xavia spoke first.

"Welcome, each of you. I am Queen Xavia Hayes, daughter of the late Baron Belfont Hayes. If you are friends of Darius and his companions, then you are friends of Seria, true Great Kingdom of Water."

The newcomers registered this news with differing reactions of surprise and distress. Darius hadn't known the baron well, but he felt a residual burning anger for Xavia's pain. She hid the grief well.

Rydel spoke first. "That is most appreciated, Queen Xavia. We will burden you for only a short while."

"I have to ask," Ayva said, "how *did* you find us? We're supposed to be in a lost city after all."

"Nothing worth finding can stay lost forever," Rydel said, as if quoting someone.

"Elven riddles aside," Finn interjected, "we were headed north to where we heard you were last seen, in Median. However, we hadn't gone very far when we learned a trade route had opened near the Mountains of Soot and its outlying villages. Followed by whispers of Ronin." Finn gave a small whistle, eyeing the thundering waterfalls. "To be honest, I didn't quite believe it myself. The lost city of Seria. Still not sure if I'm dreaming."

"Forgive me," Gray interrupted, "we are truly happy to see you all, but why have you come?"

"Is the coronation of a queen not reason enough?" Reaver Finn replied.

Gray folded his arms. "You said so yourself, you were headed north. Your arrival was just good timing? You came for us. Why?"

"He's right," Ayva said. "Three powerful warriors don't travel for days on end for a greeting."

Reaver Finn dipped his head. "It's true. We have a greater purpose."

And as one, the three directed their focus to Darius.

Darius's jaw tightened. He gave a nervous chuckle. "Uh…what's with the looks?"

"We have much to discuss," Alandra said.

"Yes," Rydel agreed. Then he cleared his throat. "Perhaps there is a place we can talk…away from prying eyes?" He glanced around, and Darius realized hundreds of curious citizens watched from the walkways, and the tiers above, distracted from their work by the mysterious gathering below them.

"But of course," Xavia said, and gestured to the guard on horseback, who inclined his head. "Please escort us to the tavern." She looked at the others and apologized. "I'm afraid my palace is under renovation. I can barely hear myself think there with all the hammering."

"This way, my queen," the guard said.

They took a marble bridge to a nearby tavern whose facade crawled with wrist-thick vines and wicked finger-length thorns.

Darius stepped up.

"I've got this." He cracked his knuckles and summoned his Nexus, then pulled.

Calling on power came easier every day. He was getting stronger, he was certain of it. He still didn't know exactly how the *flow*—the source of the Ronin's power—worked. It was supposed to be different from the spark, the essence of all magic. In some way, it felt like using a muscle—and also like a hazy memory gaining clarity. Again, he didn't like that thought as much. It felt a little too close to the possibility that Maris was living inside his body.

Shrugging it off, he conjured his flow, the innate magic of the Ronin, and "threaded." To those with spark or flow it looked like hundreds of filaments of green extending from Darius's fingertips, floating through the air, like the ethereal gossamer strands of a spider's web, stretching toward the building. To those without the eye for magic, it looked like nothing. Yet the effect was the same. The thick shroud of vines choking the tavern shriveled until they crumbled to dust, and the building looked good as new.

"Well done," Reaver Finn said, raising his thick brows. "On your way to becoming legends quite quickly, I see."

Alandra even looked a tad interested. Wait…maybe too interested? He felt a little sweat break across his brow.

"Show-off," Ayva said.

Darius chuckled nervously, then urged Leafy to wait outside while Rydel and Reaver Finn entered the inn.

"Curious animal you have," Alandra remarked as she dismounted her cormac, leaving the ring in the hands of the guard who held the other steeds. "Leafbugs are quite rare. You know they're worth a fortune, yes?"

"He's a leafbug? I could have sworn he was an overgrown green hound," Darius replied.

She raised an immaculate elven brow and asked, "Was that humor?"

Xavia sighed. "You get used to it," she said, and entered the tavern.

Darius smiled at the elf, trying not to shiver beneath her ice-blue eyes. "Don't listen to her, I've been told I'm endearing."

Alandra looked unmoved. She said nothing. Instead, she moved past him and into the tavern.

"Tough crowd?" Ayva asked, patting his shoulder.

Gray winced, and Darius shot him a look.

"First she looks like she wants to eat me, now she wants to stab me? I don't get it."

"Don't worry about it, buddy," Helix said, putting a hand on his shoulder. "Maybe it's an elven thing."

Darius looked at him. "You think?"

"No, she definitely hates you."

"Gee, thanks," Darius groused, and they entered the tavern together.

Inside, the tavern was nearly bare, holding only chairs, tables, a stage, a long bar, and a staircase leading up to rooms that likely hadn't been used in a thousand years. Somehow none of it had deteriorated much; save for a few cobwebs and a fine layer of dust, it seemed magically preserved.

With a small gust of wind, Gray cleaned off a wide, long table. Ayva raised an eyebrow at him, then lit up the room with one sweep of her arm, throwing light on the table and singeing the spiderwebs that hung from the ceiling.

Gray gestured toward the table, and they all found seats around it, the Ronin and Xavia at one side, and the elves—plus Reaver Finn—on the other.

"First, tell us what happened," Reaver Finn said. "I want to know everything."

Gray and Ayva did most of the talking, filling the others in on events outside of Eldas. Some of which they'd already heard. She started with her and Helix leaving Vaster, City of Sun, to head to Median to find the next Ronin. Darius told of his journey—skipping over the deaths of Drowsy and Alga, the old healer and his wife, for the pain was still too raw, having burned a hole of sorrow and anger in his gut.

He moved on to tell them about Mathelstan, the Thieflord of Water, who had stolen Gray's and his swords. Then some bits about pirates storming the city's port, then saeroks, vergs, and nameless flooding out of the portal. About a treacherous steward, Owen, an evil Ronin, Merrick, and finally, how the city was lost. They'd fled in the nick of time, finding the Great Kingdom of Water in the process.

He took a deep breath when he finished his part, and Gray and Ayva filled in the rest—setting up the city and deciding where to go in their quest to find the next Ronin.

The three newcomers processed all this news with varying reactions.

When they were all done, Rydel spoke first. "I see. The armies of the enemy have been amassing...that they've taken another city means the war is no longer on the horizon, but before us. Yronia, gone, Median, gone..."

"They'll be coming for Covai next," Gray said.

Reaver Finn rubbed his jaw contemplatively. "That's a fair bet."

"It's not so simple," Alandra said, as if they were all village idiots.

Darius folded his arms. "Uh, I'm not a map guy, so correct me if I'm wrong, but Covai is right next to Median, no?"

Alandra pulled out a rolled map, as if she'd been waiting for that very comment, and unrolled it upon the oak table, showing a faded map of Farhaven. She pointed. "The Ker Stream divides Median from Covai. But *stream* is a bit of a misnomer. The river is wide and treacherous. There's an outpost, strongly guarded by Covai, that is the only true gateway toward the Great Kingdom of Flesh."

"Guarded or not, if the enemy can sack Median, nothing is safe. Doesn't change the fact that we need to get there," Gray said matter-of-factly. "Now, are you going to tell us why you're here?"

Again, they all looked at Darius. "Okay, you guys keep looking at me like that. It's kind of making me nervous." He turned to Alandra, trying not to glare. "Who exactly are you? Friend of Karil's? What am I missing?"

Reaver Finn clasped his hands upon the table. "Alandra is an emissary of Queen Karil, and head of the Lando."

"I noticed." Darius nodded to the tiny gold fragment of a crown pinned to her tunic.

"Enough mincing words." Alandra planted a fist upon the table. "We're here for you, Darius."

Rydel grunted affirmation while Finn had a grim look on his face.

"What's she talking about?" Ayva questioned Darius.

He raised his hands. "Don't ask me."

Reaver Finn spoke, "We have orders from Queen Karil to take you back, Ronin of Leaf. The queen needs your help. Dryan has been building his forces, biding his time. Now is the calm before the storm. He will make his move soon, and the queen will make hers."

Alandra added, "The queen wishes you to be at the vanguard, to lead our people."

The weight of their eyes bore into him. A moment ago, he had felt that owning a flying insect was too much responsibility. Now this.

"It makes sense," Gray said thoughtfully. "She's asking the Ronin of Leaf to save the City of Leaf."

Darius shot him a look. "What? You're not helping."

"We will take back Eldas and save our people," said Rydel.

"And why send the three of you for me? Planning to kidnap me if I say no?" He said it with a small laugh, but the three didn't chuckle, nor show any signs of mirth. The laugh died in his throat, and he felt sweat break out across his scalp. His eyes *briefly* scanned for an exit.

"It is your decision," replied Rydel. "The queen insisted that you must come of your own free will." Did the big elf sound upset by that?

"So I could say no, and you would all just, what…leave?"

Alandra glowered and Darius was almost certain he heard her knuckles crack.

He only smiled back.

"You could," said Reaver Finn casually, "but the queen told us to be persuasive."

Leave?

Abandoning his friends, and their mission to find the other Ronin, pained him, but even more painful was leaving Karil in danger. She'd always been kind to him, gifted them cormacs when they'd first journeyed to Farbs, saved them at Death's Gates and plenty of other times. Darius's hand idly brushed the broken piece of gold metal etched with leaves upon his breast…he'd re-pinned it recently. The treasured gift from Karil. A piece of her murdered father's crown. Karil had promised it would be a boon, especially with elves not corrupted by Dryan, and it had. It had gotten him through locked doors, and helped him befriend a tall, terrifying elf named Hadrian. But more than that, it was a promise, a pact.

All around the table, the others watched him.

Darius glanced at Xavia. She squeezed his hand with a slight nod. It was all the confirmation he needed.

"Okay. I'll go," Darius replied. In truth, he had made up his mind as soon as they had spoken the words.

Ayva tried to hide her pain, but he felt it through the bond. He looked at her and she gave him a half smile, nodding softly.

Helix and Gray wore unreadable expressions.

"I'm pleased to hear that," Rydel said. "The queen will be most delighted."

Darius placed his hands behind his head, leaning back. "What kind of Ronin of Leaf would I be to ignore the call of the City of Leaf?" Then he saw the sober-faced Alandra. Her eyes were a crystal clear shade of blue, like ice water fresh from a glacier. "You don't seem excited."

"I'm not."

Rydel placed a heavy hand on Alandra's arm. Clearly, this was a conversation that had happened before. Judging by Alandra's strong-willed gaze and Rydel's naturally imposing presence, there seemed to be a small battle for who was actually in charge.

"I'm coming," Helix said suddenly.

"What?" Gray asked.

"You know I hate that much sand. Ronin of Water and all… Trees and elves sound way nicer."

Ayva leaned forward, gripping his wrist. "We need you to help find the others, and to stop the armies of the enemy."

Helix shook his head. "We need Eldas as a common ally, do we not? Right now, the Great Kingdoms are split. City of Fire and City of Sun are on our side, but Covai? They've always been neutral. They'll be hard to convince. Stubborn and self-serving as Landerians. Or perhaps just greedy. What if they deny us, reject our help, and fall to the enemy? Then the kingdoms will truly be split. Then Median, Yronia, and Covai will be in enemy hands. We have no idea where Lander is and if they'll come to our aid, and Morrow is lost to time. If Eldas falls too? Then what chance do we have? Two Great Kingdoms isn't enough. If that's the case, this war will already be over before it's even begun."

Darius's stomach fell.

There were a lot of unknowns there, but Helix made some convincing points.

"What are you suggesting?" Gray asked.

"I go with Darius. Two Ronin to take back a Great Kingdom is better than one," he said, his blue eyes shining with conviction. Then he swallowed. "Am I wrong?"

Rydel nodded. "Not wrong."

Reaver Finn rubbed his jaw. "Two legends? We would be fools to say no."

Helix continued, "See? Darius and I help Karil, stop Dryan in his tracks, and then we come to your aid. Maybe even wipe out the darkness in Median in one fell swoop."

"And the scourge in Yronia?" Alandra asked. "Those dark mines have been festering with saeroks for centuries. The smoke of their forges billows up in sight of our forests. They are making siege weapons—this war won't be so easily won."

Helix shrugged. "So what, then we have elves on our side. We need every ally we can get. But right now? They need to regain their kingdom, and to do that, they need our help."

Gray shook his head. "I…don't like splitting us up any more than we already are, but…I agree."

Both Rydel and Reaver Finn looked to Alandra, their glares palpable.

Alandra's grimace turned into a smile that *actually* looked painful. "We'd be happy to have you. Both of you."

Why's she so cranky? Darius asked.

Probably because she's going to be riding with the two of you to Eldas, Ayva shot back.

What? That should be cause for rejoicing! Darius sent.

Helix sent, *We are twice as much fun.*

Three times, Darius corrected. *It's basic math.*

Xavia rose. "If that's all, I'm going to attend to some important business."

Darius gripped her wrist.

She winked at him, then leaned in and kissed his cheek. "Don't worry. I'm not going to let you leave without saying goodbye."

She departed, with her guard following like her shadow.

Conversation turned to lighter things: planning their trip, going over details of what to bring, and how they could try to stay in communication while separated across the land. Then a heavy knock came on the door, and all in the tavern launched to their feet and grabbed their swords.

An Invitation

Gray turned toward the sound at the door, and words from a memory returned to him.

I don't think the Kage are going to knock. Mura had said it, long ago, back in the Shining City.

"Enter," Gray ordered.

A messenger strode in, dressed in a red coat, a ruddy orange vest, and tan pants. *Covai messenger,* Kirin, his old self, spoke, again whispering another memory of Farhaven. As Kirin, he'd been training to be a Devari warrior…before he found Vera, his sister, impaled upon Morrowil, dark wings spreading from her back. Possessed, he'd killed his best friend and mentor Ren, and two other Devari, until he'd gained control of his mind once more and fled to Ezrah, an Arbiter, a powerful wielder of the spark, and his grandfather. Ezrah had taken his memories and set him upon an ancient prophecy called The Knife's Edge. That felt like a lifetime ago.

The man who now entered the tavern was from the Great Kingdom of Flesh.

Gray looked at the others, and Ayva gave him a curious look back, as if thinking the same thing he was. The timing felt suspicious. They'd just been talking about the City of Flesh, and the next moment, a messenger from that kingdom arrives? Was it a coincidence? Or the enemy's doing?

No. Gray shook his head.

He was jumping at shadows now.

The evil of their enemies was obvious, destroying whole kingdoms, turning all they touched into darkness and drenching Farhaven in blood. What need did they have for subtlety? No, this war was going to be fought in the open against teeming hordes of monsters.

"You're from Covai," Ayva said in surprise.

The messenger bowed deeply to Ayva, then to the others. "I am, my lady. My name is Ambros. I am a royal messenger to Her Majesty,

Queen Imala. And I come with urgent news." He held up two rolled cases.

Gray reached out a hand, grabbed the cases on a current of air.

"*Wind…*" Ambros stammered, eyes wide as he staggered back looking caught between awe and terror before catching himself on the door. "Rotting flesh, it's true…"

Darius snorted. "If you think he's special…" From his seat, he flitted his fingers, and Gray saw filaments of green. A finger-length root that had broken through a floorboard suddenly grew tall as the man, formed into an arm and hand, then waved at Ambros.

Ambros looked like he was going to faint, and he gulped.

Show-off, Ayva sent.

Ambros looked at the four Ronin, then to their blades, those that he could see, and he stammered, "You're back…"

"In the flesh!" Darius said.

Helix face-palmed himself. "Tranquil Seas, I think your jokes are getting worse…"

Gray didn't join in. Instead, he coolly grabbed the two floating tubes out of the air and examined them. They were a thick white hide that his old self recognized as leather made of belegrun—a huge albino bearlike mount that was a rare Covian beast and worth a fortune. Each tube was no longer than his forearm and stamped with the emblem of Flesh.

Reaver Finn spoke, "Careful, lad. If what's inside is what I think it is, then it's only for the intended recipient. If it wrongly binds to the opener…it's…dangerous, to say the least."

"How dangerous?" Helix asked.

"*Very.*"

"Oh, great, that's fantastic!" Darius said, drumming his fingers on the table, "Gray, I'm not going to hold your hand if you get involved in another blood pact. What are these scrolls about?"

"Hold on," Ayva said, eyes tightening as she eyed the messenger. "One thing at a time. How'd you find us?"

"She's right," Helix replied. "Seria has been lost for ages! You expect us to believe you just stumbled into it?"

Darius put his hand on Helix's back. "Uh, buddy, we're up to four newcomers—not exactly lost anymore. This is turning out to be the worst Hidden City I've ever heard of."

"I didn't find you. I found them." Ambros pointed to Rydel and company. "This?" The messenger gestured to the two-story tavern, though clearly indicating the whole of Seria. "I had no idea I'd end up in the lost City of Water!"

Rydel snorted. "That's a nice story…but I don't leave tracks, so try again."

Ambros licked his cracked lips, opened his mouth, and his dry voice rasped. Gray floated a cup before Helix, who got the idea, rolled his eyes, mumbling something about "Water Boy" and filled it with water. Then Gray floated the cup before Ambros, who took it gratefully and drank deeply. "Thank you…" he said, and tried again. "Sorry, I've…I've been traveling without pause, barely sleeping or eating." He bowed his head to Rydel. "Apologies, master elf. It is true, you don't leave tracks. It was…difficult, I admit. My clue was that I was told you'd be to the south, near the Relnas Forest, preparing a siege against the dark elf known as Dryan."

"We weren't near the Relnas Forest…" Alandra said.

"Thankfully not," Ambros admitted. "I went south and caught a caravan. That's when I heard of an elf his size passing through the small towns and villages below Farbs, heading toward the Mountains of Soot…"

Alandra's ice-blue eyes were practically slits. "And that's when you just happened to pick up on our trail, hmm?"

Ambros replied. "I...I got lucky. I spotted you in the town of Harinas. Then I lost you again."

"Clearly not for long," Reaver Finn said, looking a little amused.

Rydel rumbled, "I don't believe you. You're saying *you* could track *me*?"

"Not you...exactly..." Ambros admitted. "Even average elves are hard to follow, and you two? You were like ghosts. You left no tracks. Thankfully, you weren't traveling alone." They all looked at Reaver Finn, who winced. "He left signs..." He looked to Rydel. "Not big ones, and I could tell you covered many of them for him, but not all...It was hard, but my father trained me to track snakes and lizards in the shifting sands of the Covian Desert. A few broken branches were enough to follow."

Reaver Finn rubbed the back of his neck, wincing.

Rydel muttered something under his breath.

"Great!" Darius said. "We found the world's best tracker, and now know that Reavers are about as stealthy as a cerabul in a porcelain shop," he said, tossing a wink at Ayva for stealing her line, "but what's that have to do with the cases?" He pointed to the two cases Gray still held.

"They are invitations from Queen Imala," Ambros said, cheering up. Yet, despite his excitement, there was a wariness in his tone. "You may open them. I was given two, but I only know one was intended for him." Ambros nodded his head to Rydel and pointed to a case that seemed indecipherable from the other. "That one."

"Well, then, it seems only fair," Gray said, and floated one to Rydel.

Rydel grimaced and set the leather tube on the table, unopened. "I know what that is, and I have no interest. I choose the Right of Innoctus."

"This is getting ridiculous." Helix reached out for the case Rydel had set down.

"No!" Ambros, Rydel, Alandra, and Finn called, almost as one.

But it was too late. Helix's hand grabbed the case, and with a twist he unlocked it. As he did, a faint glow suffused the leather tube, making the already bright room flash—blindingly so. Then it was gone.

"What did you just do?" Gray breathed.

"You're worse than Darius!" Ayva snapped, smacking Helix's shoulder. He still held the tube, wide-eyed and white-knuckled.

Darius squawked. "Hey! I...No, actually I was thinking about grabbing it too."

A trickle of sweat ran down Helix's temple. "It feels…cold…I know that feeling. It's magic."

"You fool," Reaver Finn said. He'd risen in the commotion, a fire in his eyes, and now he smoothed his slicked-back dark hair, and sat again with a breath, eyeing the tube in Helix's grip. "There was a magical seal on the case. It was intended to be opened only by its rightful owner."

"Then how could he unlock it?" Ayva asked.

Reaver Finn sighed. "When Rydel invoked his Right of Innoctus, it released the bind upon the seal…allowing the pact to be taken by another," he explained, rubbing his brow. "Now the contract is bound to our young legend of Water here."

"Contract?" Helix repeated, swallowing. "What do you mean?"

"You're about to find out," Rydel replied, his voice deep and gravelly.

Alandra added, "It's a death pact."

"No," Ambros countered, stepping forward, addressing Helix. "It's a great honor! Many would kill to have the contract bind to them. You are *most* lucky."

"Uh, does anyone want to explain what's going on?" Darius asked. "She says death pact, and he says honor? Those seem pretty different. Can someone speak plainly?"

"Read it, see for yourself," Rydel said.

Helix was still mute. His face was stricken with fear, and he swallowed, hands still shuddering on the tube.

Gray sighed. He'd dealt with pacts before…and while he wanted to avoid them at all costs, the mood of Rydel and Finn, and the awe in Ambros's eyes told him this was a double-edged sword. Whatever Helix had enacted was…dangerous, but also a great honor. Ayva looked at him, tensing, as if sensing what he was about to do. She opened her mouth, but it was too late to stop him.

Gray eyed the second scroll and then cracked the case, opening it.

A shiver of magic traced over him. But it didn't feel cold. It felt…warm.

"Are you serious?" Darius asked. "Didn't we just say that was foolish?"

"I agree with Darius for once. You're both idiots," Ayva said.

Darius folded his arms. "Thanks—wait…for once?"

"I can't let Helix be alone in his stupidity, or potential glory," Gray said. "Besides, you told me I needed to loosen up."

"Loosen up! Not initiate a dangerous pact you know nothing about!" Ayva replied.

"Did it feel cold?" Reaver Finn asked.

"No. It felt…warm," Gray answered warily.

The others narrowed their eyes.

Ambros shuffled forward, eyes wide. "What luck! What an honor!"

Reaver Finn stroked his patch of facial hair on his chin. "Luck is one word. Destiny is another."

"Everyone start explaining!" Helix snapped.

"Sorry, my Lord Ronin," Ambros explained. "You see, if the Ronin of Wind touched it and it felt warm, then that means it was already meant for him." Gray already knew that. He'd felt it. It was for him.

"On a good note, that means you can still deny the contract after you read it," Reaver Finn said.

"Finally! Some good news." Ayva sighed and motioned toward the open case. "Well? Go on. We're this far already."

Gray unfurled the parchment inside and read aloud.

> Dear Chosen:
>
> If you are reading this, then you have been formally invited to participate in the Grand Tournament of Flesh, held in the esteemed city of Covai, Great Kingdom of Flesh.
>
> As is the custom, the seven-day event will feature the strongest, most-revered warriors invited from all over the land. Each Chosen has been painstakingly vetted and picked by the Council of Flesh, and while each of you are at the zenith of your skill and strength, you all originate from very different callings. You are the very best from the land of Farhaven.
>
> As one of the Chosen, you are allowed to bypass the Opening Games and will begin your journey in the later rounds of the tournament. If you succeed, you will pass on to the Finals, and lastly, the Grand Finals, where the winner will be crowned Grand Primus of Flesh. In addition to the regular rewards heaped upon the Grand Primus, including one thousand Farbian gold coins, a rare steed of your choice from the prestigious Royal Stables, and you and your friends will be

granted free access to all establishments of Covai. I, Queen Imala, am contributing an additional reward from my personal treasury.

Alas, the surprise reward will be announced on Opening Day.

While being a Chosen is a rare and grand honor, the recipient of this letter must agree and register their intent to enter below. Simply offer the life force that binds us all.

X. _____

Chosen Gray, Leader of the Ronin
Signed,
Queen Imala
Cosigned,
Reaver Nefrin, High Counselor of Magic

Gray finished reading it aloud, and they all sat in a moment of silence.

Darius whistled through his teeth. "One thousand Farbian gold coins?"

"Really, that's what you take away?" Ayva asked.

Darius scoffed, "Hey! It doesn't sound so bad. Who doesn't love a tournament?"

"Show me yours," Gray said to Helix.

With a steady breath, Helix opened his and laid it on the table, then he crafted two hunks of ice and placed them on either end as paperweights.

Gray and the others all rose and leaned over, taking in the letter.

It read the same, except instead of Gray's name it read:

X_____

Rydel, Warrior of Eldas
Rank: Hidden, Number Two

Yet even as Gray stared at the words, Rydel's name vanished—eliciting a collection of gasps from the others—and was replaced by golden flowing text spelling out the following:

Helix, Ronin of Water

Darius shook his head in disbelief, then clapped Helix on the back. "Well, look at that. A new Chosen! Good for you, bud!"

Helix gulped. "Abyss, take me…"

"He's not a Chosen," Rydel said softly.

"What do you mean?" Darius asked. "Gray's a Chosen, and—" He read who the letter was addressed to. It was blank. Instead, it simply said, *Dear Replacement*. "Oh, well, I'll be, you're right. Sorry, bud, looks like you're riffraff."

Helix had his face in his hands and shook his head.

Gray looked at Helix. "How have you not heard of this? Aren't you from Farhaven?"

"I've heard of the tournament, sure. But I had no clue what the invitations looked like! They're rarer than gold. Oh god," he bemoaned again, cradling his head in his hands.

Ayva consoled him. "It's fine! It says you can decline."

"No," Darius replied, pointing to Gray's invitation, "Gray's letter says as much. But look, Helix's doesn't." Sure enough, Helix's was missing the line that added his signature. Instead, there was a red spot right above his name, like a droplet of blood.

Helix turned his finger over and saw a tiny dot like a pinprick.

Gray understood.

The magic must have accepted his signature as soon as Helix had touched the leather case.

"How the hell is that fair?" Helix squawked.

Rydel rubbed his head, and his words came out as a growl. "Because you agreed by opening it…most people who invoke Innoctus give the scroll to a new person…I would have done that, or simply thrown the invitation away."

Darius sniffed. "It's not all bad! A thousand gold coins? A rare mount? Getting to go to every inn and tavern and rack up a bill as high as you want, then just say 'Yep, don't worry about it, Grand Primus here!'"

"That last prize," Gray said, staring at the line. "Says it's a surprise—that the queen will announce it on Opening Day. What do you think it is?"

"No idea," Ayva replied, "but if it's from Queen Imala's treasury? It has to be good. Covai is notoriously one of the wealthiest of the Great Kingdoms."

"Yes, a wealth built upon the backs of its people, flesh traders, slaves…it's a deplorable city," Alandra replied contemptuously.

Ambros made a face but said nothing.

That raised Gray's hackles, but still…that prize. He felt it had to be special. Maybe it would be something they could use in the coming battle. They needed every edge they could get. More than anything, he needed to gain the queen's trust. On top of that, finding the next Ronin in Covai…Something called to Gray, whispering to him, as if the next Ronin was already there, waiting for them. Though something also told him it might not be as easy as before.

Helix didn't seem to have the same eagerness.

The Ronin of Water cursed, trying to tear the letter apart. "Stupid letter, won't tear!"

"You really thought that was going to work?" Ayva asked. "It's magic!"

Helix sighed and tossed the letter on the table. "Was worth a shot."

"So there's no way to reverse it?" Gray asked, looking to Ambros and Reaver Finn.

"No," Finn said, "he has to participate in the tournament, at least the first round. Once he gets to the later rounds, he can forfeit. But there's one more thing."

Ambros also looked equally grave.

This was what they'd been avoiding.

"What is it?" Gray asked.

Ambros spoke, "As a non-Chosen, the first round is…not ideal."

"Please explain." Gray asked.

Rydel replied this time, "It's a battle to the death. Only a handful are allowed to survive."

"That's…barbaric!" Ayva said.

Gray realized he'd been clenching his jaw so tight his teeth were now grinding.

"What if I just refuse?" Helix asked with a trace of hope in his voice.

Finn shook his head. "No use, I'm afraid. It's a blood pact."

"Our favorite!" Darius said, clapping Gray on the back.

Gray groaned, remembering all too well. His blood pact with Faye had almost killed both of them.

"Too soon?"

"Too soon," Gray replied. Then looked at Helix. "Change of plans. Sorry, Helix. You're coming with us now. Once you survive the opening round, and you move on, you can forfeit." When Helix looked up at him with fear still in his eyes, Gray added, "You know this is only the beginning…right?"

"What do you mean?" Helix asked.

"I mean, we're going to be facing much worse than whatever you find in that arena. I know it sounds like a lot, but you can do this."

Darius put his arm around Helix's shoulders. "What our intrepid leader *means* to say is, you're a Ronin. This'll be easy. Bend a few arms, scare a few people into submitting…boom! Consider it practice for what lies ahead."

"You know we can also try a less…direct approach," Ayva said. "We can talk with this queen, explain the situation, maybe there's extenuating circumstances."

Gray doubted the queen could do anything. Magic was magic. But he simply put a hand on Ayva's, seeing how tense she was, and nodded, then spoke to Helix, "Ayva's right. We'll start there. Maybe she'll see reason."

"If that fails, we'll persuade her," Ayva said vehemently, squeezing Helix's arm for reassurance.

Helix, for his part, was still a little pale and mumbled, "To the death."

Darius stretched. "Guess it's all settled! Can't say I'm not bummed to lose a traveling companion, but hey, I'll aid Karil's rebellion, crush Dryan, and see you guys before you can say 'Where in the seven hells is that charming, affable Darius we love so much?' Or something like that."

Rydel grunted.

Reaver Finn yawned. "Well…if that's all, it has been a hard road…"

Alandra, who didn't look tired, gave a nod. "Yes, we need to prepare for tomorrow. We leave at dawn." Gray offered accommodations and she held up a hand. "This tavern will be fine. I saw a stable in the back. In the morrow, we leave." She eyed Darius again, a lingering look that made even Gray's hair rise, and with that, she set off, back to her cormac where her pack was secured. Rydel rose as well, shaking Gray's arm in the Devari-like tradition, but as he reached the door Gray called out to him.

"Rydel, I need to know…how's Mura?"

"I'm..." Rydel hesitated. "I'm afraid I do not know. The last I heard, he set off with Jiro, attempting to infiltrate Eldas. We...haven't heard from him since." Before Gray's heart could falter, he added, "But that doesn't mean much in regard to your uncle. He's a rock too hard to crack, even for Dryan."

Gray nodded, but his stomach felt suddenly unsettled.

Finn rose and both turned to leave when Ayva stepped up. "I know! Perhaps we can catch up more tonight? It's still plenty light out, and there's going to be a small festival...we can make it a kind of gathering and send-off."

Rydel's bluff face broke with a hint of a smile, and he nodded.

Reaver Finn lifted a hand, flames dancing along his fingertips. "Did someone say fireworks?"

"Dice, yes!" Darius said, using his choice curse word. "That's exactly what this place needs!"

Word spread, and several hours later, the small festival being held for the summer solstice—as a way to cheer up the people—turned into a massive gathering and send-off for the Ronin as well. All were in attendance. Foods of all sorts were served; somehow the once-abandoned kitchens churned out a bountiful harvest of cakes, pies, and sweet crisps.

Lights sparkled amid the waterfalls—Ayva's doing.

Vines and roots had been transformed into hundreds of chairs and tables—courtesy of Darius.

Gray just watched the spectacle from afar, contemplating their next moves.

"So brooding," a voice said.

He knew who it was all too well.

Faye sat on a rooftop nearby, kicking up her legs.

Her companions, Modric and Odaren, were nowhere to be seen.

For Modric, as the Ronin of Moon, that didn't mean much, but the stout, pudgy Odaren? It was easier to hide a boulder.

He looked up at her.

Faye's hair had been chopped off, the long auburn replaced with short, dark red, bordering on black, that fell to her attractive jawline, framing her high cheekbones. She was using a knife to eat an apple, carving a slice, then biting into the crisp skin with her teeth as she looked down at him with a teasing smirk. Dressed in her normal dark leathers, they seemed surprisingly less…bloody. As if she'd found a way to have them cleaned in this city, either forcefully, or just by running them under one of the many waterfalls. She wasn't in her full Yronia dark plate, or Dragonborne armor—only a spiked pauldron and some black metal vambraces.

Gray sighed. "You really know how to spoil a moment."

"Look who's talking," Faye shot back. "*Oh, I'm Gray, always the lone wolf, as I sit mysteriously in the corner, eyes full of purpose while everyone else has fun.*"

Gray grumbled. "I was thinking, that's all."

"*Brooding,*" she said, speaking around a bite of apple.

"What am I supposed to be doing? Partying?"

"Yeah, would it kill you?"

He looked ahead, seeing his friends amid the revelries—Helix danced hand in hand with the cultist girl from Median, while Darius twirled Xavia to the sound of a fast beat. Imar asked Ayva for a dance, while Barthos and Ham seemingly encouraged Wyatt to go talk to a girl. Others ate and drank, happy, but oblivious to what was coming. "I know I should be enjoying this moment…but I can't help but think there is some dark storm cloud that hovers over our heads, and no one is willing to look up and take cover."

Faye sighed, finishing the last of her apple and tucking her knife away. "We can't all just brood and look morose."

Gray protested. "*Thousands have died, Faye.*" In the shadows of the rooftop, he saw his words take hold. Her eyes grew somber, and his heart felt equally heavy. "Worse, I know many more will die, and the Ronin will be in the center of it all. I'm not naive enough anymore to think this is going to be won without sacrifice."

"First off…wow, you really know how to drain the life from a party."

Gray winced. Maybe he had gone too far. "And second?"

She scoffed and gestured to the revelers. "Second, you big buffoon, you don't think those people know this storm of yours is coming? These men and women witnessed their loved ones being ripped open by monsters. They're well aware. They're just doing this thing called 'living.'"

She was right. He wasn't considering all they'd been through. Gray said as much.

"Eh, don't beat yourself up, I'm glad you're finally wising up. Nothing is gained without loss. But seriously, I need a drink, and so do you." From seemingly nowhere, she tossed him something, and with a small gust of wind, he caught it, bringing it to his hand. A bottle of wine? "Well, look at you, aren't you special? Really getting the hang of that wind business, I see." She nodded to the bottle. It had already been opened, but the cork was jammed in the top. "Look, I know you've never heard of the concept of letting loose, or having fun but—"

Gray popped the cork free and drank deeply. The wine was silken, and surprisingly honeyed, with a chocolate undertone.

Faye's gaze went wide with surprise. "Well, then…Who are you and what'd you do with stuffy, white-knight, can't-have-any-fun Gray?"

He shrugged. "I never said I can't have fun…" Then admitted, "It's just been a while. Also"—he hefted the bottle in hand, taking another sip—"not bad, but a bit sweet for my liking."

She sighed. "I know. I'm more of a tart or sour gal."

"I'd never have guessed," Gray replied. "What poor sap did you steal this from?"

"Eh, who knows?"

He corked it and tossed it to her.

She took a swig, then asked, "So you're going to go off and play general?"

"That, and find the others."

"The other Ronin. How exciting. I think I caught wind that you're headed to the City of Flesh?" she asked, throwing the wine back to him.

He took another drink, wiping his mouth with the back of his hand. "Yes."

"You know there's a tournament going on there, right?"

"Oh, well aware now," Gray said, and lobbed the bottle back.

Again, she caught it nimbly, this time freezing. "You're going to compete, aren't you?"

"Not just compete." Gray grinned. "I'm going to win."

She laughed deeply, though the sound of merriment from the festival and the dancing crowds beyond swallowed it. "Look at you. Grand Primus of Covai…leader of the Ronin…Blightseeker Reborn…you're really trying to collect all the titles, aren't you?"

Blightseeker.

It was one of the darkest of his predecessor's titles, gained at the end of his reign when all the world thought the Ronin of Wind was the head of darkness, slaughtering thousands like a thresher through a wheat field.

"He wasn't the Blightseeker," Gray said with a bit of heat, hating that she still got a rise out of him.

She raised her hands. "Jeez, sorry, I forgot it's a touchy subject."

Gray decided to change the topic. "You know this would be a lot easier if your shadow joined us."

"My shadow…" she repeated and huffed a laugh. "Your little Ronin of Moon? If only. You can take them both. Hells, I tried to pawn them off on you. But idiots have an annoying habit of following me." She looked down at him, giving a grin. "Oh, sorry, maybe you don't count. You also abandoned me."

Gray growled. "How long are you going to keep bringing that up?"

"For as long as it keeps annoying you." Faye took another long swig, legs still dangling over the rooftop.

He sighed. "What's your plan then? Aside from continuing to be a thorn in my side."

"Please, if I was a thorn in your side, you'd know it." Then she sniffed. "As for what I plan to do? That's none of your business."

"Typical Faye answer."

"Typical Gray question. Always trying to orchestrate all the world, turn everyone into beacons of light and hope!"

He took a random stab in the dark. "You're going to try to unite the Thiefdoms, aren't you?"

Faye, bottle halfway to her lips, tensed.

Gray pressed, "I thought so. To what end? To become the Mistress of Shadows?"

Her eyes flashed like daggers. "Careful, young Ronin of Wind. That's dangerous territory."

"So?"

"So, other Thieflords would kill you for even touching on their well-kept secrets." Her hand moved to rest almost casually on her blade's hilt.

Gray couldn't tell if Faye was toying with him, as usual, or seriously threatening him. Either way, he was having none of it. He touched his Nexus. In a rush, wind came to his aid—little zephyrs flowing from the ground, over his limbs, until he was like a contained maelstrom. Since he was still in the shadows, partygoers didn't cast him, or Faye, a glance, or else they would have gawked, or trembled. Gray spoke clearly, "I'm not going to balk at your veiled threats anymore, Faye."

Faye's expression as she regarded him, which had been heated, now looked…amused. "That look. How fearsome." Though her tone didn't sound afraid at all. "Quite different from the scared young man I met in that desert."

"That's because I'm not him anymore."

"Maybe…" she said thoughtfully, "or maybe you're just a boy with a bigger stick." Her eyes flared in the light. "Also, a little advice? If you're trying to veer away from your previous title of Blightseeker…?" She nodded toward the crowd, and Gray followed the nod, noticing a few people from the festival had caught sight of him and were pointing and whispering.

Gray sighed. He let the wind drop. "What do you really want?"

"To fight you."

"I don't want to fight you."

Faye pouted. "Hmm, well that's boring. Not even a little tussle?"

"No."

She sighed. "What with that little display of wind, you know how to get a girl excited, then leave her wanting for more. I just want to see how strong you've gotten. To test your mettle." There was a wicked gleam in her eyes, a sinister curve to her lips. Now that she had his attention. "After all, if you're going to be competing in the Grand Tournament of Flesh, being a Ronin might not be enough. It's a tournament of the most powerful from all across Farhaven. Men, women, creatures, and beings who've had centuries to imbibe the spark and hone their strength and skills, each of them hardened by battle. You've had what…a few years?"

Gray reflected on that. She was annoyingly right. He might have the potential to be the strongest of all, but even the largest tree needed time for its roots to develop. He shrugged it off. "I guess we'll find out together, won't we? But your concern is touching."

"Always been told I have a motherly effect."

He looked up at her. "How much have you drunk tonight?"

She waved it off, taking another long swig, then threw the bottle where it would have shattered on the cobblestones, but Gray caught it on a bit of wind. "Protector of the Nine Realms, and Garbage Collector! Yet another title."

Gray muttered under his breath.

"Anyway," she said, brushing herself off and rising, "if you decide to reconsider that duel, you know where to find me."

He realized…he didn't. "Uh, no, I don't."

"Oh, right, I suppose you don't." She shrugged. "Better that way." Then she nodded, and he looked at the people enjoying the night. Darius now made his dancing rounds, while the leafbug intermittently chirped on the sidelines. Helix was with the serpent leader girl, chatting off to the side. Even Ayva toasted with Barthos, while Rydel and the other newcomers watched from the sidelines—Reaver Finn sending up dazzling displays of colorful explosions in the night sky using the spark. "Watch over the nature one, will you? He's my favorite. And my Diaon, she's still rough around the edges, but I see Omni in her."

He didn't need her to say it, but he thought he'd take any agreeable moment with Faye he could. Besides, antagonizing her seemed unnecessary. "I will."

"So you know, I've a gut feeling things are going to get much worse before they get better…"

He felt it as well but had to ask. "How do you figure?"

"You didn't choose the occupation of a baker, Gray. You must stop an evil that has been patient, biding its time for a millennium. An evil your own predecessors couldn't vanquish with thousands of years of knowledge, and skill at their disposal…"

"I won't be alone."

"Yes, yes, you'll find the others."

"And I'll find a way to bend the Great Kingdoms to our side."

"The last Great Kingdoms. The ones not already on the side of darkness, no? Yronia, Median…Lander is anyone's guess. The war is already split. Let's say you can do that—"

"I will—"

She kept going. "Love your optimism. Let's say you can. It will take more than uniting the last of the kingdoms to stop this foe, and more might than the rest of the Ronin. You will have to find a greater power…a power the world has never known."

"What kind of power?"

"Well, I've already kind of explained it with the whole 'the world has never known.'"

Gray gave her a flat look.

"Hey, you're the hero of this story. You've got to find the way when it seems impossible. Well, probably *is* impossible, but *seems* leaves room for hope." She rose, then tossed the apple core. "Welp, drink is out, conversation done, and no fight—which is quite boring, by the way—means I've got to find some other entertainment for the remainder of this evening." Faye gave him a vulpine smile. "Good night, Gray."

With that, she was gone, leaping onto the next rooftops, slipping into the shadows.

Gray grumbled, clenching his fist, watching the festival, seeing Ham win an eating contest against Darius, who was clearly outmatched. *She's right…How am I going to sway the other kingdoms? I don't even know where Lander, the City of Stone, is. Morrow is gone, and Eldas is still overtaken by a mad elf, while Moon is held captive by a Shadow Lord. Yronia is overrun, only the remnants of Water and Sun are on our side…and maybe fire.* Ezrah, Gray's grandfather, was an Arbiter. He wasn't the Patriarch, but maybe he could sway the grand monarch of the Great Kingdom of Fire to join their side. *If only there was a way to convince the others…a way to travel between the cities…*

Why didn't you ask earlier?

Gray's whole body went rigid, and a flush of cold washed over him—a chill that had nothing to do with the cool night air. The voice was smooth and sent directly into his thoughts.

What in the seven hells?

Gray pivoted, trying to find the voice's origin, but there was none. Then he realized the source, feeling a presence, a warmth on his back.

He pulled Morrowil from its sheath.

The sword pulsed slightly with a faint white sheen and his heart raced.

And the voice spoke again, ancient, and faintly amused: *Well? What are we waiting for?*

You can talk? How?

If you're asking how I'm alive and speaking, it's…complicated. Living is perhaps too strong of a word. In many ways, I am simply an extension of your will. I also hold a remnant of Kail's spirit and I can be thought of as an embodiment of wind itself, captured within the folds of my steel. All these things make me...me.

This can't be real...

More revelry and laughter sounded from the party. *We can have an existential crisis over this later. For now, I know how to get you what you want. A way to travel to Covai, to get the other Ronin, and save Farhaven.*

How?

The altar, Morrowil said, indicating the giant stone circle beyond.

The portals? They're broken. I should know, seeing as I broke them.

I can fix that. I just need you to take me there.

He looked over, seeing the teeming mass of people. *And how do you expect me to do that?*

In the morning, when the revelry is over. Tonight, sleep. We've got a big day tomorrow.

Gray suppressed the desire to shiver, stuffing the white gleaming sword away when Darius called his name. He smiled and joined the party, eager for the dawn and...hoping he wasn't crazy.

When morning came, Gray was the first one up. He dressed quickly, cinched his frayed ash-colored cloak, strapped Morrowil to his back, and made his way to the altar.

A hole in the canopy showed the sky above, the predawn with faint glimmers of light promised a clear, bright day. The great falls rained all about, feeding into the moat and waterways that crisscrossed their way up the tiered, lush city.

In the morning, the falls seemed less thunderous, as if magic deadened their uproar, letting the inhabitants of the city sleep in. Which was probably a good thing too, after all the festivities and a fair amount of indulgence.

Alone, and feeling terribly exposed on the altar, in the center of the Lost Kingdom, Gray pulled Morrowil out, waited, and...*listened.*

So what am I doing here? he asked the blade.

There, Morrowil whispered.

Gray followed the feeling, walking toward a large flat paver.

There was a lip to the stone.

Press and pull.

Before he could—

"Whatcha doin?" Darius asked.

The Ronin of Leaf, with his dark hair in its typical disarray, stood there, Masamune slung over his shoulder, the green hilt gleaming. He wore his usual tunic, the color of a deep forest, a cloak, its edges embroidered with leaves, flung over his shoulders, vambraces—also with vines and leaves—and his golden brooch on his chest, a gift from Karil. Leafy, his massive leafbug, was munching on a giant leaf behind him like a dog with a bone. As they approached Gray, Leafy's bug eyes looked up, and Gray could swear the thing was grinning, if it could. He half expected it to slobber and jump on him, and it did wiggle its rear, but Darius shushed the huge bug, then winced, grabbing his head as if in pain.

Gray pinched the spot between his brow, trying not to sigh. "Please tell me you're not hungover."

"That's ridiculous!" Darius said, then suppressed a belch.

Gray raised a very skeptical brow.

"All right…" Darius said with a shrug, "maybe just a smidge. Hey, before you give me that high-and-mighty look, I'm *pretty* sure I saw you talking with Faye last night and handing something bottle shaped back and forth?"

Gray rubbed the back of his neck with a wince. "You saw that, did you?"

Darius grinned, clearly taking a little too much pleasure out of Gray's surprise. "How'd that go?"

"It's Faye, so, as well as you'd imagine."

"Unproductive with a fair amount of veiled threats and some heavy flirting?"

Gray grumbled.

Before he could reply, Darius waved it off. "Anyway," he said, turning to the wide stone platform, "I'm trying to be a little more responsible lately. You know, what with the task of leading the fight into the City of Leaf to liberate the citizens from a tyrannical elf." Nevertheless, Darius's emerald eyes did squint a bit at the light from above, as if he'd rather be tucked in thick blankets. Gray hesitated. Were Darius's eyes *always* that green? "Why are you out here so early?"

"A surprise," Gray said, glancing at the paver Morrowil was urging him toward. "I'll wait until everyone is here."

Darius narrowed his stare. "When'd you get all secretive and intriguing?"

The others arrived, Ayva leading Helix, Xavia, Barthos, Finn, Alandra, and Rydel. In the distance, at the little bridges that led to the altar, hundreds of citizens had awoken, many pretending to go about their business, but really using that as just an excuse to watch the group.

"Well, what's the surprise?" Ayva asked. She wore her normal attire—brown leather pants, supple leather boots, and a gold vest. Only now, Gray noticed a few extra pieces rounding off her look, including a pair of gold bracers and a thick belt cinched at her narrow waist. Aurora—famed Sword of Sun—was at her side, with its elaborate golden hilt and sunburst flaring from the cross guard.

Helix, on the other hand, was just in his typical shades of blue.

Gray glared at Darius. He'd forgotten it was possible to speak through the bond individually.

Darius raised his hands. "Hey, you brought this on yourself. You can't be all cool and mysterious. That's my role."

Ayva cleared her throat. "Boys? Focus, please."

"Right, it's easier to just show you," Gray said, then asked Morrowil, *You sure this is going to work?*

Trust, Morrowil replied.

Gray returned to the stone beneath his feet.

Press and pull, Morrowil whispered again.

He did so. The stone, as big as his hand, pressed in slightly, then he pulled on the lip. As if on oiled hinges, it slid beneath another, revealing a panel of sorts with a symbol.

The Star of Magha.

The others made sounds of surprise, taking in the star. Nine colored gems fit into each of the star's points. Before anyone could say anything, Gray placed the gems in the correct order, then pressed the blue gem. The light within the blue gem dimmed. Then he pressed the whole star. It sank into the ground.

Immediately, all nine pillars rose in a circle about them, each a different color to represent the nine elements. Even the half-shattered pillar of blue rose—the one they'd partially destroyed to disrupt the portals and stop dark creatures from pouring through when they'd first arrived.

"You got the portals working!" Ayva exclaimed.

"I did," Gray said, then saw Xavia's worried look. "Don't worry," he told them, looking specifically to Xavia, "I made sure the portal from Median to here is disabled." Morrowil had already reassured him on that front. "We got you here safely, and I intend to keep you safe."

"Thanks," Xavia said, her furrowed brow smoothing at Gray's words. "I don't particularly like the idea of a horde of monsters pouring through the portals and into my city." She smiled and looked at the budding tiered walkways and bustling activity of the citizens. "Especially when we're just getting started."

Darius stood beside her, crossing his arms and grinning like a proud boyfriend.

"Impressive," Helix said as he ran his hand over the blue pillar. "How'd you know that was there?"

Gray rubbed a hand through his hair. "Uh, I'll fill you in later." He didn't want to unravel the knot that involved the conversation with his sword quite yet. "More importantly, this is the answer to our problems. We may not have an army at our beck and call yet, but now that we can move from city to city at will?" He grinned. "We can start recruiting."

Ayva caught on. "This is how we reunite the Great Kingdoms. Fire, Water, and Sun are with us—we just need convince Flesh and Stone."

"Aaaand once we retake Eldas," Darius chimed in, "that'll put us sitting pretty at six Great Kingdoms." He flipped his dagger, catching it with a flourish, "The shadow won't stand a chance."

Reaver Finn rubbed the patch of hair on his chin, looking a little more doubtful.

Rydel and Alandra wore veiled expressions.

Just then, Imar and Ham walked onto the platform. "Are we late?"

"Just in time!" Darius said, tightening the straps on his pack, the leafbug shuffling on its six legs like an excited toddler needing to go to the bathroom. "Well, what are we waiting for? We go first!" He clapped Gray on the back. "Green portal, please! Eldas here we come!"

Alandra snorted, folding her arms with a look that would have made most men wither. "Not unless you wish to die."

Darius raised his hands. "Jeez, okay, killjoy."

"Alandra is right this time," Rydel said. "Dryan still has total control of Eldas. The portals are definitely guarded. We'd be walking straight into the heart of the enemy's fortress. We could have a thousand arrows pointed straight at our head, and Ronin of Leaf or not, we would be torn to pieces before any of us could lift a finger."

Darius made a strangled sound, then looked at the giant green bug. "Yep, longer road it is, right, Leafy?"

The leafbug trilled and hopped within arm's length to be patted affectionately on its giant bright green head, just above one of its plate-sized eyes.

"Really? Leafy?" Ayva said.

"What's wrong with Leafy? He likes it, don't you boy," Darius said. "Or girl? Hmm. I never really thought about your gender. Leafy is nice and neutral, though." He turned to them and gave a bow. "Anyway, good luck with the whole tournament of death thing!"

Helix turned a shade of green. "You had to remind me. Thought that was a bad dream."

While Ayva bickered with him about "why he touched the scroll" and Helix said something about "having a curious nature," Gray stepped up and opened the Portal of Flesh.

Stone grated.

VWOOOM.

Appearing in the center of the altar, a giant ruddy-colored portal opened. It revealed a sprawling desert surrounding a teeming city.

Gray recognized the city as Covai, Great Kingdom of Flesh. His skin prickled in anticipation.

"Think they're expecting us?" Ayva asked, a trace of apprehension in her voice.

"Guess we'll find out soon enough," Gray replied.

She sniffed. "Don't think you've gotten out of explaining how you figured out how to work the portals on this side."

Gray just shrugged. "I'm cleverer than I look."

"Story of my life. Welp, good luck!" Darius clapped them both on the shoulders, and Gray embraced him. "Not the first goodbye and not the last."

"Well said." Then Gray added, "*Rekhla forhas.*"

"*Etrana morah,*" Darius replied.

Gray raised a brow.

"Same thing, pretty sure it's the Terna or Hidden version, can't remember. Either way, it definitely sounds better in full Elvish instead of your watered-down version in old tongue."

Hidden, Devari, Stoneguard, Lightguard, Moonguard…

In Gray's head, pieces were beginning to fit in place.

Morrowil whispered in his head, *They are not so different.*

Gray sent back his response like a cracking whip. *We talked about this. No talking in my head. Not yet at least. I've enough voices inside my skull. Wait until I get used to the fact that my sword can suddenly communicate with me.*

And with Ayva and Helix following, he moved toward the portal, toward the Great Kingdom of Flesh.

Pyre

Zane had chased Sithel to the ends of Farhaven.

At first, he'd followed the whispers. When the whispers had run dry…he carved his own path.

Though the last thing he'd heard had led him here, to the outside of an apothecary's shop. A small sign above it read "Azimuth's Elixirs".

The sign also read "Closed".

Zane entered anyway.

The door banged open, rattling a chime above, and he took in the shop.

Bottles of every shape and size lined the walls. He heard voices in the back room and pushed back a curtain to see a table surrounded by men. A small, ratlike man sat at the head with a dozen assorted miscreants around him. The ratlike man burst to his feet. "What are you doing here? Can't you read? We're closed!"

Zane sighed. "Are you Azimuth?"

"Who's asking?" Azimuth replied, his beady black eyes tightening warily.

The men all about—thieves by the look of their dirty faces, ragged leathers, and the way they pawed at the rusted shivs at their hips—glared at Zane, a few going so far as to rise out of their seats.

"The man said leave, so leave!" said a thief.

Zane growled. "Go on, get up. Let's get this over with."

The thieves looked at one another, then rose, many grinning ear to ear. "The pair on this one! They must be the size of boulders! Well, suppose I'll cut them off and use them as a trophy."

An older thief missing a few teeth—the rest yellowed or silver-capped—rose. "You must be the least lucky man in Farhaven! What kind of fool willingly walks into a den of thieves," he cackled. "Don't worry, we'll make it quick, take your coin, and dump your body in the river. No need to draw this out."

Zane cracked his knuckles. He let them come.

A good moment or two later bodies lay everywhere, furniture shattered. Their weapons were scattered, but one small shiv stuck out of Zane's chest, buried only into the meat of his muscle. His pain, however, wasn't the focus of his attention. Instead, he focused it on Azimuth, who'd avoided most of the fight save for a few burns to the whiskers on his cheek and upper lip. The apothecary owner gripped a bottle of green liquid, waving it threateningly. "Stay away! Or you'll regret it!"

A dozen vials were at his hip, all sloshing with a similar viscous vileness.

Zane sighed. "You don't want to do that."

"Why not?"

"Because it won't work out the way you want it to."

Azimuth saw the conviction in Zane's eyes, and tried a different tack. He hesitated, his hand holding the bottle lowered just a fraction. "What do you want with me?"

Zane refrained from saying he could have started with that, instead of having his men attack him, but instead replied, "Just a few answers."

"I'm just a simple apothecary!"

Zane looked back at the dozen fallen men and their serious arsenal strewn about the ground. "Right…" He sighed. "I'll say it one more time, before I was so rudely interrupted by your…friends. I'm looking for someone. I was told you might know his whereabouts. That you've had dealings with him before. Tell me where he is, and I'll let you live."

"Who?" the apothecary asked warily, as if seeing a possible way out.

"Sithel."

Azimuth's right eyelid twitched, just a fraction, and in his face, Zane saw a light of recognition. That was enough of an answer. "I…I've never heard the name," he stammered, shaking his head.

"I recommend sticking to the truth. I'm done with lies," Zane replied, knuckles cracking as he clenched his fist at his side, which was bruised and battered, blood from fighting Azimuth's goons still covering it. "I was told you two were friends. Close friends…as close as a demon can get to making friends, that is."

Azimuth licked his lips. "I haven't seen him in years, and even if I did, I would never tell—" He threw the bottle.

Zane tapped into his Nexus.

A burst of fire exploded the bottle, only an inch away from Azimuth's hand.

Searing green liquid poured down the man's hand, melting his first two fingers, and the apothecary shrieked in horror and pain. He stumbled back, crying, gasping, and finally looking up at Zane. He snarled through staggered breaths, "How…how did you…"

Zane pulled the small shiv from his chest and sealed the wound with a bit of fire—the smell of burning flesh mixed with the vile stench of the green liquid that continued to melt the man's hand. Then Zane approached him, still holding the small knife. He made the metal hotter, and hotter, until it was like an iron brand, and he put it before the rat-man's bulbous eye. "I won't ask again."

"A R-Reaver? Here? My spark wards never went off! They're supposed to warn me!"

"Not a Reaver," Zane said, and he knew his eyes flashed orange.

A cold wave of terror ghosted across Azimuth's face, as if he was just beginning to understand. "*Who are you?*"

"A man demanding answers. Now tell me everything."

Azimuth began to stammer, "I told you…the last time I saw him, he was trying to make himself into something more. He let me tinker on a potion for him, experimenting with new concoctions and the like. Some would make him faster, others stronger, but the adverse effects…well…I never quite got it right. Then he left sometime afterward…that's all I know, I swear!"

"Then you're not much use to me," Zane said, letting the now flame-wreathed dagger get closer to Azimuth's skin, drawing sweat from his pores, heat blistering the man's flesh.

"Fine! Fine!"

Zane pulled the dagger back.

Azimuth panted, shaking beneath Zane's grip as the apothecary finally sputtered out, "There…there was one thing he used to rant about…a place of ancient magic that could make him stronger than even the…"

"Than the Ronin?" Zane asked with a hint of amusement.

Azimuth flinched. "Yes…but no one goes there."

"Where is this place?"

At this, Azimuth cracked a hideous, knowing smile, "You know where. A place even the elves avoid…the birthplace of magic, some say…a place where no one who enters ever returns."

Zane did know. He'd been feeling called to it…Something told him that was where Sithel was hiding, where he'd find his answers. Where it would all end. And for the first time his broiling rage faltered, a flicker of fear rising in his chest. But he let the fire burn that too. And breathed the name aloud, "Drymaus Forest."

Azimuth, still gripping the nubs of his burnt fingers, which dripped with the green acid, gave a mad little cackle. "Yes, that's the one." Then he licked his dry, cracking lips. "I…I warned him against it…cautioned him of the dangers! But if there's anywhere he might be hiding, it would be there." When Zane's eyes glinted, the man pressed with conviction. "I'm sure of it! I swear upon my life!"

Zane dropped the dagger, turning.

Azimuth called to his back, "Tell me, what did Sithel do to you to cause such hate, such anger…"

Zane debated not answering. He owed this man, this dark dealer of vile arts, nothing. But something compelled him. To voice the reason, the one driving force that kept him going.

"He took something precious. Something I loved. So I will take everything from him."

Without waiting for an answer, or hearing one, Zane stepped over the dead bodies of Azimuth's men and walked out.

Outside, he mounted his horse, and left the small town of Entroc, weaving through the bustle of people, pulling his hood up to hide his face—after all, he'd left a bit of a wake—and headed south.

When Zane made camp that night, he stared into the flames of the fire, and heard her voice.

Why are you doing this?

Hannah's face…his sister's. He saw her in the flames.

He looked away.

Answer me! she demanded.

Zane let the words slip out through gritted teeth. "I can't do it anymore…I can't control the anger…" His vision blurred with tears.

What will it take to make you let go of your grief?

"You know the answer to that."

More blood, she replied bitterly.

"He stole you from me," Zane snarled, speaking into the flames. She was dead after all. Just a memory. It was happening more of late, talking to himself, but he found the pain was less if he pretended she was still there, though he knew his words met only empty air. "Am I just supposed to let a madman run free so he can hurt or kill others?"

That's not why you're doing this, and you know it. Your hatred grows every day, Zane! You don't see it, but you're becoming more like him.

He said nothing, but the words stung. He looked away from the flames, from the image of Hannah's face.

Tell me, what happens when you get your wish, brother? When your path of vengeance is fulfilled, and you kill Sithel?

"I'll be satisfied," he said, yet he recognized the lie on his tongue as soon as he said it.

You said you were done with lies.

"What do you want from me?"

To stop! Please…I'm begging you. Hatred like this destroys…there's so much more to you, brother. This anger, this hatred…it's a fire you're trying to kill with more wood, with more flames…it makes no sense.

"I don't even know if he's there," Zane confessed to the image of Hannah's face in the fire's flickering light. He knew he was grasping at straws. Drymaus Forest? Sithel could just as likely be in the Abyss, or the seven hells of Remwar. But something pulled him toward that forest, and he looked south, past the fire's light…feeling its draw. All this time…What Azimuth revealed hadn't truly been necessary, it was just another breadcrumb leading him toward the forest. Drymaus was calling to him. Zane took an even breath and looked back to the dancing flames that snapped and crackled. Hannah's face…those soft features, the angle of her eyes. She looked so sad, yet he knew this projection was just his imagination—likely going mad from his hunt.

She said what he was thinking: *It's killing you. This path…even if you aren't killed, you aren't you…this…this isn't you.*

For a moment, the sound of her voice in his head made the hatred, the rage, the fury in his heart diminish. Then he pictured Sithel's face, remembering that day, Hannah's eyes wide with fear, then the moment his anger was unleashed.

Zane rose, turned, and with a swipe of his hand, he snuffed the flames.

Her voice was silenced. Was he mad? His confusion briefly gave him a respite.

He lay in darkness until exhaustion took him.

In the morning, he awoke, his anger burning hot once more—and he lost himself to the hunt.

Days blurred together, and eventually, he found himself before the dark woods of Drymaus Forest—a tangle of vine, mature birch, rowan, pinewoods, and deeper thick-trunked silver roots. Moss clung to everything, and all of it was cast in misty gloom.

At his side, his mount, Mercy, whinnied in fear, backing away.

He patted her flank, reassuring her, and she replied with a soft nicker. "Don't worry, ole girl. You don't have to go in."

He'd taken her from Vaster, from the City of Sun, and in his weeks-long travel, he'd grown close to the steed. When it all seemed darkest, the chestnut mare was at his side.

Now he took the mount's bridle in his hand and slipped it over her head.

"I'm sorry, girl. This is where we part ways."

Mercy nuzzled him, as if trying to warn him against entering the foul forest.

"I'll be fine. This might be that twig-for-brains' domain, but fire isn't afraid of a few stray branches." Though even as he said this, something, a sound, a dread-like feeling—a palpable shadow—seemed to emanate from the woods, washing over him, and even putting a tremor of fear inside of Zane, causing him to shiver.

It was in all the stories...ancient dark magic existed within Drymaus Forest.

He shoved the feeling down. "Go on, now," Zane said, and slapped the horse's flank, and Mercy trotted north, away from danger toward towns and plentiful grazing. A good steed like her would be discovered and taken in.

Zane turned back to the dark forest and muttered, "Into the belly of the beast..."

And he stepped forth, into the woods.

Immediately, a rush of fog poured over him, thick and cloying.

With a growl, he burned it, fire sparking—as if the mist was more than droplets of suspended water—pushing it back so he could see a dozen steps before him. He walked deeper into the woods.

He swore he heard the creaking of trees as they leaned closer, trying to grab him. Zane brushed aside hanging moss as he went, pushing his way farther in. He pulled out his dagger and tagged trees with a small X to mark his passage. He paused, hearing something, and when he looked back at the X he'd just left in a tree's craggy surface, the tree's bark wove together, like flesh healing itself, and his mark disappeared.

"Great," Zane huffed.

He put his dagger away and resumed his trek.

As he went, he took in the forest.

Many-legged insects crawled out of burrows in trees. A cawing over his head alerted him to the canopy above where a bird the size of a small dog perched. It resembled a raven, but when it cawed and peered down at him, instead of two eyes, there were six, and they glowed a vivid red. Hand on his sword, Zane moved onward. A rumbling sounded, and Zane quickly hid. Something lumbered past him, and he remained frozen behind the trunk of a massive oak as the thing moved by, hearing only the slow earth-rattling steps, and catching only the briefest glimpse of treelike limbs, all brambles and thorns. A balrot? He'd heard of trees that had come to life, looking vaguely humanoid and infested with evil. He had no desire to face anything other than the demon who had taken his sister. Just as he thought this, the tree before him uprooted.

Definitely a balrot.

"Fire and ash," Zane cursed.

The tree-not-tree roared, limbs covered in thorns, and faced him—eyes gleaming black and green and full of malice. Thirty feet tall, it loomed over him, a terrible monster. Zane gritted his teeth, pulling the flow—his magical source, and the element of fire—into his soul, and his hands burst with deep red flames. "I'm pretty sure trees burn." But there was something in those green eyes—an inky evil. "I don't think you want to do this," Zane told the beast.

The balrot roared, raising thick, thorny appendages, and attacked.

Zane ducked a swipe that would have caved in his skull.

He sighed. He knew he couldn't reason with it.

It, like him, was too far gone, so he whispered forgiveness and let the flames in his heart rage.

Moments later, he was covered in dark tree sap, panting and ragged.

"If you're trying to kill me, you're going to have to do better than that!" Zane shouted into the abyss of the dark woods.

In hindsight, it was probably the wrong thing to say.

As if in reply, there was a screeching sound, and an insect flew from a tree branch. Zane lifted a hand, and fire erupted from his palm. The creature shrieked. Its momentum was halted, and it fell to the ground with a thud—charred and smoking. Now that he saw it up close, it was like a centipede with a hard shell, a thousand legs, and no eyes. Finger-long fangs dripped with vivid green poison. It had clearly been trying to end Zane, and it got a tad closer than he would have liked.

"Poison," he cursed. "I hate poison."

Briefly, he glanced back over his shoulder, but the pathway was gone, shrouded in gloom. He could try to flee, to vainly hunt for the light of day outside of this dark hellhole of a forest, but Zane had long abandoned that thought. He wouldn't give up. Not until he found the demon that killed his sister or died trying.

He moved to leave, then for good measure sent another jettison of fire at the insect on the ground.

It shrieked again, shriveling more, then lay still, a blackened husk.

He wiped his hands and pushed onward.

After a day of battles, and nearly dying a hundred different ways, by the forest itself or its many different inhabitants, he made camp inside the hull of a huge tree.

Turned out, everything in the damned forest thought he was dinner.

But he'd also found food and was now roasting a creature that looked like an oversized rabbit with claws. There'd been a dozen of the little bastards, and he had to use a few extra tricks up his sleeve. The forest made a thousand and one noises as it came alive at night—chittering and clicking, howls and cries, and even, occasionally, a deep throaty rumble, so low and ominous it could have been the demon inside the belly of Farhaven turning in its slumber. In response to the sound, all in the forest turned silent as the grave. It seemed even the terrible creatures feared it. That, above all, gave Zane chills.

And when the rumble faded, the living night of horrors resumed.

His skin crawled, but he clutched his pitted dagger tighter and eventually found sleep.

Thankfully, in the morning he was still alive.

The next day went the same.

And so did the next.

It began to feel like a blur—attacking, killing, burning, hiding, sleeping. Until finally, covered in the guts and webbing from a spider the size of a bear that lay before him twitching in the throes of death, the creature spewed a thousand terrifying, tiny green baby spiders that charged Zane. He bellowed and spewed fire from his palms until it seemed that half the forest was going to burn.

Of course, it didn't.

The damn forest was unkillable, ancient beyond imagining.

But it certainly was trying to kill him.

When he finally let the flames die, the last baby spider shrieking and popping, he roared in frustration, "ENOUGH!"

The forest answered with silence.

He panted and continued, "You can't stop me! You can try a thousand different ways, ten thousand, throw every damn monster you want at me, but there is no anguish, no horror greater than losing her." A moment of silence. "So…you might as well show me where he is…or you can keep throwing death at me. But I'm not leaving. And if by chance you do kill me, before I die, I swear I'll take as much of you with me as I can." Deep, ominous red flames came to his hands. His voice took on a deeper resonance, as if channeling his predecessor. *"I'll burn it all."*

The heat in his voice alone singed the air, and Zane's Nexus flared.

It was the threat of a Ronin.

Unfortunately, only silence answered.

Zane realized he was talking to a forest.

God, I'm going crazy. Maybe the woods had already won.

No…I'm not crazy.

He knew there was more to this damn woods. It felt ancient, it *was* ancient.

Suddenly, he heard voices.

Laughter.

The woods seemed to shift, and Zane followed the sound.

Beyond a tangle of trees, he saw elves in a clearing, a dozen of them, all jeering, as if poking a cornered animal hidden from his sight.

Zane neared.

He saw what they were: Terma—powerful elven warriors. Until recently, even Zane had thought a Terma was the strongest rank among the elves. That was until he'd been told by Darius about Rydel, right hand to the queen of the elves. Rydel was a secret rank, a Hidden, one of a rare few.

But Terma were still something to fear.

As Zane approached, the elves turned to him, shock rippling through their group.

"What in the Spirit's blessings…" whispered one.

"Who in the seven hells are you?" another demanded.

The elves touched their swords, but he ignored them, focusing instead on the object of their cruelty.

From a distance, based on the cries and huddled shape, and the hint of claws, Zane thought the elves had been toying with and torturing an injured animal. Only now, up close, did Zane see the truth.

The forest had listened and answered.

Sithel.

An inferno of rage welled inside of him.

Sithel lay at the base of a massive tree with a trunk the size of a barn. His nemesis huddled in on himself, in tattered clothes. His body was strange, and inhuman. Back in Farbs, when he'd been playing puppet master, pulling the strings and attempting to seize the Great Kingdom of Fire, he'd just been a man. Corrupted only in heart and soul. Now, his depraved nature manifested itself physically, as if he'd made a pact with a dark god. Sithel was split down the middle, half of him obsidian glass, with the hard angles of a Darkwalker—a creature whose mere touch could sap the spark from one's life—and the other half of his body was flesh, pale and marked with scars from travel and the hardships of the forest.

In Sithel's grip was…something.

A vial?

A moment later, Zane realized a sword was at his throat, and someone was speaking to him.

"*I said*, who in the eternal spirits are you, boy?" asked an elf, not much older than him. While the other elves were all blade slender, this one was bigger, and uncharacteristically wider, as if he'd been bred for battle. His vivid green eyes, the color of a new leaf, looked down on Zane, who was much shorter. Hard lines on his face and a malignant gleam in his eyes were also signs of something…foul, every bit like the dark forest about them.

Zane had heard as much.

Whether through magic, or their own greed, the Terma had chosen to side with a tyrant. They'd turned on the previous king, killed their former captain, and now the elves' home was a den of death and sorrow, led by the mad elf, Dryan, who now ruled the Great Kingdom of Leaf.

Deep down, he felt for the elves, for Karil, daughter of the king, whose home had been ripped away by a bastard hungry for power.

But that was a task for someone else.

For Darius, twig-for-brains, or one of his other companions.

Zane, for his part, had effectively abandoned his role as a Ronin. With so much hatred and rage inside of him, he didn't deserve the title of guardian.

He was no hero.

Glendion—that's what one of them called the big elf—pushed his blade a little deeper into Zane's throat, drawing a thin line of blood. "I asked you a question, human."

Zane turned his focus on Glendion in full.

For a moment, Glendion hesitated, clearly seeing something unsettling in Zane's eyes. The elf swallowed, his sword arm trembling.

"What the blight is wrong with him?" another elf asked, hand on his sword. "He's...he's got death in his eyes."

Another snarled, "Tenla's right. Something's wrong with him."

"Look at his clothes," said another. "He looks as if he's battled death itself."

"Likely has, if he's survived the forest this long."

"Impossible," Glendion said. "How did you make it this deep into the woods?"

Zane still had not spoken. He finally sighed and replied, "I'm going to make this very clear...I have no business with you. I only have business with...him," he said, pointing at Sithel, who looked at Zane with wide eyes.

"You...you came all this way...for me? I'm...touched..." Sithel hacked and coughed, spitting something like blood, only darker, fouler, up onto the leaf-littered earth. Some of it sizzled on the boots of the nearby elves.

"Eternal spirits," one said.

Zane's rage boiled; he took another step toward Sithel.

Glendion's sword bit deeper, cutting.

The elf's arm was a steel bar, ramrod straight. "Another step, and I'll let you bleed out."

"Give him to me," Zane demanded.

The elf smoothed his brow, as if trying to smooth the crease of annoyance out of it, and replied, "I'm afraid not. We found the pathetic creature, so he's ours. We'll bring him back to Lord Dryan. Maybe our lord can find some use for this sickly thing." The huge elf sneered toward Sithel, who was still maniacally smiling, but labored under his own breath. "Whatever he is."

Zane grabbed the blade's fuller, pinching it between thumb and forefinger.

Glendion glared. "If you think moving a Terma's blade will be so simple, you are even more of a fool—"

The sword grew hot—red-hot—until Glendion's skin began to blister.

The big elf dropped the sword, crying out in pain.

"Get him!" Glendion roared in rage. "We'll bring him back to Lord Dryan as well."

The Terma moved like lightning. Out of the corner of his eye, he saw two swords cut for his neck. Zane dipped, and their blades clashed, ringing. Another kicked his leg out from under him. A fist to the side of Zane's head made his ears ring. Another punched, but this time Zane raised a hand and shot a burst of fire, sending the elf flying back. Then, still on the ground, Zane formed a whip of fire and lashed, snatching another elf's ankles and yanking his legs out from beneath him. A flying dagger clipped the lobe of his ear. He snarled in pain.

Two more elves neared, seeking to lop his head off, and Zane rose to his knees, sending bolts of fire. The moment before the fire connected, he let the flame burst—hurtling them backward.

Immediately, they were replaced with other elves, and he nearly lost an arm to an errant sword.

Zane growled. A dozen Terma were too many to fight, and they were *fast*.

Too fast.

More elves charged from all angles.

"Enough!" He roared.

With the power of his Nexus, a billowing flame burst from his core, sending all the elves flying back.

They rose, one by one, quickly and easily.

"A cursed Reaver," an elf griped.

He sighed, rolling his shoulders. "No. Not a Reaver, but I get that a lot."

They all had blades out by now.

"My lord?" asked one of the elves, as if waiting for a command.

"End him quickly," Glendion ordered, rubbing his blistered hand, his superheated sword still lying in a patch of wet leaves, sputtering like a coal from the fire.

"My lord?" an elf female asked again—he'd heard her called Tenla. Like the others, she possessed an otherworldly beauty, slender, with high cheekbones and angled eyes—though that was tainted by her haughty expression. "Surely you're not afraid of one human young man against a dozen of Eldas's finest."

"You will listen!" Glendion snapped.

All the elves turned to him, confused.

He spoke again, composing himself. "He might look like a pathetic child, but he's dangerous. I see it in his eyes."

Zane snorted, summoning more power.

"Oh, you have no idea..." came the words—Sithel's.

Zane's hackles rose, a shiver of fear tracing his spine.

All turned, taking in Sithel, who now stood on shaky legs, and clutched something in his fist that glowed.

A green vial.

It pulsed with supernatural power and screamed danger to Zane.

Words returned to his mind, Azimuth's: *He seeks something to make him stronger, to turn him...an ancient magic...to make him more powerful than even the Ronin.*

"No..." Zane breathed.

"What in the blighted forest..." Glendion exclaimed.

Before anyone could move, Sithel swallowed the liquid in the vial, and Zane watched in horror as it glowed like a firefly inside the man's body.

"What was that..." one elf whispered.

Sithel's eyes flared wide. Suddenly, his arms snapped, bones shifting within as his whole body began to transform. His skin cracked and hardened like charcoal-colored stone, and between the cracks, fissures flowed of molten orange, as if he was filled with lava.

And he grew, and kept growing, eight feet, ten, fifteen...And still he grew.

"Drop him!" Glendion roared. "Now!"

Elves nocked arrows, and let them fly—a few found purchase, but most splintered against Sithel's newly rock-hard skin. His face still held some of its vestiges, and Zane saw a warped smile crease the rock-monster's face. Before anyone could move, he reached for Telna, the closest elf. She backpedaled but was too slow, and she hacked at him. Her sword clattered off Sithel's rock-skin.

He scooped her up in both rocky hands, and then his smoldering eyes met Zane's, and Zane knew what came next. They all did, even Telna, who experienced a moment of horror, her eyes wide with dread, trembling and crying for help as Sithel pulled, yanking her in two—as if she was made of loose fibers, easily torn. The monster spilled her entrails to the ground.

Tossing the two halves of her corpse aside, Sithel roared, dripping orange chaos from his mouth. Zane took in the monster: a towering golem forged from a volcano, he was all rock and lava, on all fours now, with thick arms, squat legs, twin horns, and a slavering mouth.

How? Zane wondered. His limbs felt suddenly heavy. Was this...fear? No, he needed his anger.

All stood petrified for a moment.

Sithel boomed, "COME AND FACE ME, LITTLE ANTS!"

An elf, tears in his eyes for his friend's sudden demise, gave a battle cry. "*Enterius!*"

The elves charged valiantly, and Sithel laid into them with monstrous ferocity.

They ducked, dodged, slashed, laying into the molten golem—in places they scored hits, making Sithel bleed orange blood, but he fought back with terrible power. He smashed an elf into a puddle of blood, threw another into a tree, snapping both tree and elf, and he roared flames, turning several to burning pyres, as they screamed in their final moments. Seeing their dead piling high, the line of elves broke, and the last few fled into the woods.

Zane just stood there, not helping.

Frozen.

Part of him was caught in his own dread, and part of him knew that whatever Sithel was, whatever he had just swallowed, whatever he had just become, made him a threat even Zane couldn't handle. He would fall as well. The monster that was Sithel stood several dozen feet away, breathing hard and transfixed on the dead.

Then Zane saw as well…

Glendion, the big elf, lying amid his dead comrades, shifted and groaned.

Sithel's craggy body, covered in blood and gore, picked up the elf by his legs and eyed him like filth stuck to his boot. "You weak little things…like children picking at the wings of a bug…so high and mighty until that bug comes to eat you."

"Monster…" Glendion cried, trying and failing to free himself from the craggy grip.

Sithel laughed, a deep, throaty, monstrous thing, "Amusing, coming from you!"

Glendion pulled a dagger from his belt and stabbed into the hand holding him, but it bounced off the hard rock. Seeing this, he began to plead, "Let me go! I beg you!!"

"I will…into the embrace of death." Sithel's jaw split wide, teeth like finger-length daggers moving to clamp around Glendion's head and pull, as if dragging meat from a skewer.

Zane cursed to himself, summoned his Nexus, and sent a blast of fire into Sithel's rock-face, knocking him back. Glendion fell from the creature's grip.

"Go," Zane told Glendion with thinly veiled disdain. The elf eyed Zane, stupefied, until Zane shouted again, "Run, you fool!"

The big elf staggered to his feet, stumbling over the mangled corpses of his companions, and fled into the woods.

Sithel let him flee, turning his attention to Zane.

"Well, well, well…we meet again, little Ronin of Fire," Sithel said, chaos dripping from his mouth full of jagged teeth, burning and sizzling all that it touched. "I apologize for the interruption in our reunion. I had to deal with those pests. Now it is just us, two titans on a proper stage."

"I am not a Ronin, and you aren't anything more than a worm…hungering for power."

"Hmmm." The beast that Sithel had become made a sound, as if thoughtful, but Zane saw it twitch in fury at his words. "Not a Ronin? I see. Abandoned your path to become a champion seeking vengeance, instead?"

Zane spat. Why was he talking to this creature? He knew why. Because he didn't know if he had the strength to kill this thing. Even after everything, Zane was afraid. He shoved it down. "You aren't worthy of words. Death is your destiny."

Sithel rumbled a laugh, as if knowing the reason for Zane's hesitation. "Then come, take your vengeance. If you can…"

Zane took a moment to gather his strength, remembering his anger. He didn't need to search very far. Hannah's face came to mind. The terror in her face at her final moment as Sithel callously murdered her still burned before Zane's eyes as fervently as the day he'd lost her.

With a roar, Zane lit the Nexus inside of him, and he attacked with a torrent of fire that collided with Sithel, knocking him back. Sithel recovered and swiped his hand outward, but Zane leapt, using fire to propel him upward and over. He ducked beneath another barrel-like fist, rolled under the creature, and slammed his pitted dagger into Sithel's back leg. Lava spewed out, burning Zane's hand. He dropped the dagger with a cry and then sent out a jettison of fire, barely dodging a leg that was going to crush him. The fire sent him skittering across the leaf-littered ground, and he was a dozen feet away from Sithel when the monster charged with a demonic cry, lava still leaving a trail from the wound in his leg.

Bleed it dry, Zane thought. That was the only way.

But the monster was too fast. Zane couldn't dodge in time. So he staggered to his feet, sending out a crushing cascade of flames. Fire collided with the demon, a conflagration that seared Zane's clothes. Sithel pushed against it, like wading into a deep tide, and Zane sent more, roaring with the effort.

Finally, his Nexus sputtered. It was spent from days on end fighting, and nearly dying, and he fell to his knees, sagging from the effort.

Sithel remained. His igneous skin was a little redder, but otherwise he was unharmed. The demon slammed a clawed hand into Zane's chest, pinning him to the ground, as chaos dripped from his mouth. Sithel spoke, "A shame really…you came to kill me…all this way…only to die yourself."

"You took the only thing I cared about," Zane snarled, but it felt like a boulder rested on his chest.

"And in doing so, you think I made you a monster, is that it?"

"Yes," he growled back.

For a moment, in those glowing orange eyes, there was…hesitation? Humanity from this thing? No…Then it was gone, and Sithel's smile grew. "You are even more deluded than the foolish elves."

Now it was Zane's turn to hesitate.

The rumbling Zane had heard over the last few days returned, making the forest shudder.

What was that?

It subsided.

Sithel's head also swiveled toward the sound, then the demon shook it off, as if it was just an anomaly. "Almost a pity that I have to kill someone so like me, but the truth remains. The strong survive, the weak die." Those words. The ubiquitous evil that was growing, taking good people, converting them to darkness. Zane tried to speak, but Sithel pressed harder, the weight on his chest was too much—crushing his ribcage and squeezing the air from his lungs. Sithel's twin flames for eyes bored into him. "Goodbye, little Ronin of Fire."

A craggy fist rose.

Images dimmed in Zane's vision.

He had failed.

Hannah…He tried to speak. Tried to apologize.

But no words came.

This was it.

"No."

Again, that voice.

Deeper than his own. Both his, and not his.

I will not fail.

Fire roared inside Zane.

Sithel must have noticed the change, because Zane saw a flicker of dread register in the monster's eyes, and he slammed his craggy fist down to finish Zane. A roar slipped past Zane's lips.

Fire, a hot deep red, raced up Zane's unpinned arm and collided with the monster's hand.

Sithel roared in pain. His rocky face burned with bright tongues of crimson and rocked back. Zane seized the moment and rose. Looking at his hands, he felt a strange fire in his limbs, fueling him.

The rock-monster charged, both fists raised for a hammer blow to Zane. He didn't run. Everything inside him wanted to flee the monster, but something more than anger, more than rage, fueled him now—igniting a power in his limbs like he'd never felt before, pulling from a deeper reservoir. He let Sithel come.

Sithel's rocky fists rushed toward Zane, but he reached up and grabbed them.

It felt like holding up a building, and every muscle in his body screamed at him, but he held them.

Sithel's boulder-like arms quaked with fury. "Impossible!"

As if he'd finally pushed himself too far, Zane felt this inner fire stutter. His elbows buckled a little beneath the tremendous weight.

Sithel grinned. "So you are human after all..."

Suddenly, one of Sithel's fingers broke off and smashed to the ground right beside Zane.

Zane released his grip and Sithel staggered back and cried, "No!"

The monster grabbed another vial from his belt, swallowing the entire contents. But something unexpected happened. As the fire flowed down his throat, it engulfed him, and his body began to break down.

"What...what's happening?" Sithel stammered.

The rock that made up his form began to crumble, and it revealed an emaciated body—the true Sithel. Sithel clawed out at Zane, who leapt away, barely dodging the frantic creature before him. In moments, it was over, and Sithel was a scrawny, broken human version of his former self. "My...power...I don't understand..."

Zane knew the spark was inside of everyone. Had heard there was a limit to the "well" inside a person. It seemed Sithel had tapped out that well, or more accurately, he had imploded by overloading his well.

Now, the remnant of a human dragged himself back to the tree trunk where Zane had first found him. Zane approached.

"Please...please...no...I..." Sithel began, then unexpectedly, sobs wracked his broken body. "Mercy..."

"Mercy? You took everything from me."

Zane put his boot to Sithel's neck, which, like the rest of his skin, had burn marks that were spreading like a festering wound, eating away at his physical body.

Sithel knew this, and pleaded, fingers gripping Zane's pant leg, "Please…help me…"

Zane could only stare down, bewildered. "Help…you?"

"Yes! Why not? You're a Ronin, aren't you? A reborn legend, that's what the stories say. You're meant to save…to heal…to protect. I…I never wanted to be what you see now. I only wanted not to be weak…"

"That's your excuse? *To not be weak?*" Zane had trouble containing his rising anger.

Sithel cackled. "And what's your excuse, Ronin? You kill the same as me, and worse, a part of you enjoys it, does it not? You have the strength to end a life, to exert some level of control in a world that's ruthless and callous."

Zane's retort fell short on his tongue.

"Oh, are you surprised? I've seen those eyes before. In the mirror…a monster recognizes its own kind," Sithel said, coughing dark black blood mixed with a strange bit of orange…as if he still had chaos in his lungs. "With your power? You might even be more of a monster than me."

Zane roared, red-hot fire engulfing his fist.

Sithel gave a rictus snarl, showing dark stained teeth. "Do it…if you can't save me…then end me…prove me right…try to fill that void in your soul, and see what happens next."

Zane seethed, heaving, his whole body oddly convulsing. Why was he conflicted? He'd traveled across Farhaven for this, abandoned his friends, left everything he knew behind to get his revenge. He knew it would feel a little hollow, and it would never truly replace her. Only now was he realizing just how true that was. Ending Sithel would do nothing. He could never get Hannah back. She was gone forever…and killing this pathetic wretch of a being? It may or may not prove Sithel right and make him more of a monster, but it served no purpose.

Again, the rumbling in the distance sounded, shaking leaf and bough, then fading.

"What are you waiting for?" Sithel said, reaching up with a gnarled hand and grabbing Zane's orange vest, the man's fingers slick with blood. "Do it! Before you lose your chance, and Farhaven steals your moment." He coughed more black-and-orange blood, then grinned, eyeing the corpses of the elves littering the clearing. "At least in the end, I proved I wasn't the weak one."

At Sithel's words, bile stung the back of Zane's throat. He hated the wretch before him. Yet, looking at Sithel now, instead of feeling anger…he realized what he saw in Sithel. It was the same thing he felt inside himself when he looked too deep.

An emptiness.

Something Sithel's death would never fill.

Hannah's voice echoed in his mind, *I told you.*

Zane sighed and let the flames die out on his hand, then slowly rose and pulled himself free from Sithel's grasp.

Sithel raged, "What are you doing!"

"Nothing."

"Why?"

"Look at you now. You're nothing. You have no power."

Sithel looked down at his frail, bony hands.

"Your sparkwell has imploded. You have days, maybe hours left, and they will be painful. I want you to live powerless." Zane smiled. "Strength is life, weakness is death."

Zane turned his back on Sithel and walked away, dry leaves crackling beneath each step. He didn't know where he was going, only that it was far away from here.

"Coward!" Sithel roared.

Something tickled his awareness, and Zane turned, too late. Sithel had pulled free a dagger with a green tip that looked like poison.

BOOM.

Suddenly, trunks of tall trees snapped, and a behemoth claw the size of a house slammed down, crushing Sithel—stamping the man into the ground and cutting short his cries.

Zane had no time to rejoice. His heart hammered, and his gaze panned up.

There stood a dragon the size of a small mountain, with scales a deep blackish-orange glowing like embers still hot from the forge. The sheer magnitude of the creature was mind-boggling, not to mention the power that radiated from the beast as its chest heaved and the wings crushed nearby trees. The creature was ancient, born at the dawn of Farhaven. Zane didn't think of himself as a person easily afraid—yet now, craning his neck to take in the full expanse of the creature, he saw he was dead wrong.

Terror filled him.

A sound rumbled the forest, jarring Zane's teeth and reverberating inside his skull.

"HMMMMMMMMMMMM."

He realized the dragon was considering him.

"Uh…hello?" Zane said dumbly.

"TWO THOUSAND YEARS I HAVE SLUMBERED AWAY FROM ELVES, HUMANS, DWARVES, DRACONIANS, DRYADS, AND OTHER MORTAL RACES, AND THOSE ARE THE FIRST WORDS THAT GRACE MY EARS?"

Zane swallowed. "Uh, I…"

The dragon lowered its massive maw to level his liquid yellow eye, the size of a boulder, with Zane's face.

Zane was speechless. *Damn it!* He didn't have Darius's slick tongue, Gray's easy charm and knack for appropriate deference, or Ayva's intelligence. So why the hell did this have to happen to him? He tried again to force out words. "Thanks," he said, nodding to Sithel, crushed beneath the dragon's talon. "For that."

"HMMM. THE FIERY ONE THANKS ME, BUT WHY?"

Was the dragon joking? Sithel was clearly dead. His body was broken and at odd angles. "You killed him."

"I DID, BUT I DIDN'T DO IT FOR YOU."

"Why, then?"

"HE STOLE SOMETHING FROM US. SOMETHING PRECIOUS FROM THE ENCLAVE."

Every word in the sentence triggered Zane. Us? And the enclave? But most notably, stole…and Zane understood. "The vial of orange liquid. I knew the bastard took something he shouldn't have."

"INDEED," the dragon boomed. "WHAT HE TOOK IS MORE DANGEROUS THAN YOU CAN IMAGINE. IF IT HAD LEFT THE FOREST, ALL OF FARHAVEN MIGHT HAVE SUFFERED."

"Well, looks like you put a stop to that."

"WHAT IS YOUR NAME, FIERY ONE?"

"Uh, Zane?"

"UH ZANE."

"No, no just…just 'Zane.'"

"HMMMM," the dragon rumbled.

"What's yours?" Zane asked.

"PYRE."

Zane considered the dragon's scales—burnt orange that seemed to shift to a crimson red, then back again. The rest of the creature was equally awe-inspiring: giant fiery claws, trails of smoke puffing from his gaping mouth, even the vague scent of smoke and sulfur from his scaly skin. "You're…you're the fire dragon, aren't you? Not just any fire dragon, *the* fire dragon! One of the nine primordials…" Zane asked, breathlessly. Nine dragons were said to have existed since the beginning of Farhaven, Relnas's offspring—along with the nine titans. Zane thought they were just a myth. Everyone did.

Pyre made a rumbling sound that vibrated Zane's bones. He realized the sound was laughter. "DO YOU SEE MANY FIRE DRAGONS, FIERY ONE?"

"No, I mean…I've never seen a dragon…" He rubbed the back of his head with a nervous chuckle. "Honestly, I haven't seen much of anything, except for the darker side of humans—I've spent most of my life in the sewers of Farbs. I've heard dragons still exist…the drakes in the Burai Mountains, wyverns in the north, and some dragons, bigger ones too, near the coast but…" Zane realized he was rambling. "But you're not any dragon, you're *him*, aren't you?"

"HIM," Pyre repeated.

"Yes, him. All of those I just named, they're your offspring, aren't they?"

Pyre snorted, and steam and fire billowed forth, singeing Zane's clothes. "PITIFUL EXCUSES OF DRAGONS. FALLEN DESCENDANTS. *HALF-BREEDS*. THEIR MINDS ARE TWISTED AND THEY'RE TOO WEAK TO RESIST THE WILL OF MEN. THEY WERE CORRUPTED AND TAKEN BY THE DARKER PRESENCE THAT LIES WITHIN THE LAND."

Zane had no idea what Pyre was talking about. "But…you are him?"

Lips peeled back, showing teeth as large as Zane. Was that…a smile? "YES, I AM *HIM*."

Zane swallowed the hard lump in his throat. "Well, then…I'm probably dreaming…" He certainly felt like he was dreaming, or hallucinating. Why was he sweating so much? "But on the off chance I'm not, thank you for saving my life, Pyre. I owe you."

"I DID NOT SAVE YOU," the dragon insisted.

"What? Sure you did, you…" Zane held his breath as he understood. Heart hammering…sweating…lightheaded. Glancing down to the black cloth on his shoulder, he saw it was ripped, and there was a shallow groove of a wound. Sithel *had* thrown the dagger, and it was poisoned. Why did it have to be poisoned? God, he hated poison. Zane swayed on his feet. "Well, that's not good."

"IT IS NOT. NOT IF YOU WISH TO LIVE."

Zane hadn't…not until now. Or maybe slightly before that.

Hannah's voice whispered in his head, nothing concrete, just a general plea to keep going.

"YOUR INCREASED HEARTBEAT IS SPREADING THE POISON QUICKLY," the dragon boomed. "WE MUST RID YOUR BODY OF THE POISON, AND SOON, OR YOU WILL DIE."

"You're going to help me?" Zane asked. He coughed, feeling the poison coursing through his veins. Fear escalated as the substance burned deeper, permeating his organs and eating away at him.

The dragon made another one of its thoughtful rumbles. "I HAVE QUESTIONS. QUESTIONS THAT CANNOT BE ANSWERED IF YOU PASS BEYOND THE VEIL."

Questions…What in the seven hells of Remwar could he possibly have to say that would satisfy this dragon's questions? That almost made him nervous…but his death and the giant dragon were more impending threats. "That's good, I guess. I'm…beginning to feel pretty faint, should we get going?"

"YES. COME," Pyre rumbled, and turned, the wake of his massive body decimating a whole swath of trees. Huge sections of the Drymaus Forest were trampled by the simple pivot, as he snapped trunks that were thick and wide—likely centuries old—as if they were no more than saplings.

Zane rushed to follow, though it was hard to keep pace with the beast, and each lumbering step jarred his whole body. A stray claw was likely to smash him into paste, but the dragon seemed to be cautious with its steps.

"YOU ARE SLOW," Pyre boomed. "I AM GOING TO REGRET THIS." And without preamble, it lowered its body until its long neck was parallel to the ground, flattening, and scaring creatures deeper into the woods. "CLIMB ONTO MY BACK."

Zane did so, using the red spikes to ascend Pyre's back, and he settled into the ridge of the dragon's spine, gripping the edge of a red scale as if it was a saddle made for a titan. His head felt heavy now, and his chest tight. He pushed away his rising fear and asked, "Are those going to regrow?" Zane looked down on the trees made into matchwood far below.

"YOU ARE ON DEATH'S DOOR, AND YOU ARE CONCERNED ABOUT THE TREES?"

Zane felt a flush that might have been from the poison. He scratched his jaw. "Well, not normally, but this is your home, isn't it?"

"DO YOU PROTECT YOUR HOME?"

"Farbs?" Zane grunted. "No. Well, I never viewed it as much of a home. More like a place to survive. We did stop a horde of Darkwalkers, and Sithel, that...thing you killed. But I suppose that was more out of necessity."

"I SEE. YOU BELIEVE YOU ARE WORTHY TO LECTURE ME ABOUT PROTECTION?"

Zane realized he was being a bit of an idiot, trying to rebuke a dragon that had lived since the dawn of Farhaven and was infinitely wiser than him. Not to mention, when did Zane care so much about that sort of thing anyway? Trees? That was Darius's realm. Gah, that fool was rubbing off on him. "You're right. Protecting those close to me, that's all that ever really mattered to me."

"YOU ARE...A CURIOUS ONE."

"I've never been called that before. Stubborn, idiot, muleheaded, fiery—"

"THOSE ALSO SEEM ACCURATE."

Zane growled. A dragon had just rebuked him? If Darius found out about that, he'd never hear the end of it. "Thanks. Well, I'll accept curious. Sounds like a step in the right direction. You never answered my question about destroying the forest?"

More trees snapped like tinder in Pyre's wake, as if he were an avalanche. No, as if he were a volcano, lava flowing down the mountain. "I AM FIRE AND BRIMSTONE. NATURE WILL HANDLE THAT. AS FOR CONVENIENCE, I DO NOT NOTICE IT, AND MORE IMPORTANTLY, I HAVE SLUMBERED FOR EONS. I WAS AWOKEN BY THE PILLAGING OF OUR SANCTUARY, OUR ENCLAVE."

"Ah, so…you don't get around much."

"DO ALL HUMANS TALK THIS MUCH?"

Zane chuckled, but it sent a pain coursing through his gut, and he caught his breath. He groaned. "You should see this one human. Oh, man, he makes me look tame. I think the poison is making me a bit loopy." Sure enough, his vision began to blur, his heart crashing against his ribcage. "Uh…dragon? Are we almost there? I don't feel so—" Darkness enveloped Zane and he never finished his sentence.

The Grand Tournament of Flesh

As Gray moved to the Portal of Flesh, a voice called, and Imar stepped forth alongside his giant brother, Ham. "A small favor, my Lord Ronin. I should have asked earlier, but do you mind if we take the portal to somewhere else? It would save us much time, and it would be a great boon to us."

Darius sent through the bond, *I'll bet one hundred gold Farbians it's Lander, the "lost" City of Stone.*

Of course it is, Ayva sent back.

Gray read between the lines of Imar's request. *He's going back to the City of Stone…to ask for aid. Wind and spirits, imagine having another city on our side.* "Of course," Gray replied, "just give me a moment with my friends first?" He realized he'd said it more like a command, and he remembered that Imar was likely some sort of royalty. "If that's acceptable," he added awkwardly.

Ham barked a laugh. "Ha! Stepping quite easily into the shoes of a legend and a politician." The goliath of a man clapped him on the back and nearly sent Gray tumbling.

Gray turned to Rydel.

Rydel bowed his head in assent. "Go ahead. We've a few more things to prepare. But be quick." With that, the elves busied themselves with their mounts, packing and making last-minute preparations.

Gray pulled Helix, Darius, and Ayva aside, moving onto one of the bridges that spanned a rushing stream. The waterfall drowned out their conversation, and he instructed Helix to reduce the downpour just a bit so they could hear each other.

Darius interrupted, "Whatever you're going to say, I got it. Stop Dryan, save Eldas, don't die."

"In that order?" Helix asked.

Darius shrugged. "Eh, I figured 'don't die' was obvious. Then I realized it wasn't."

Gray clasped Darius's shoulder. "Whatever you do, get back quickly."

"Wait, that's it?" Darius asked, scratching his wild head of hair.

Gray took a deep breath and replied, "Just…don't delay."

"Righhhhht," Darius said slowly. "Thanks? Look, I know you'll miss me and all, and I'm aware I'm the Ronin of Leaf, but I wasn't planning on vacationing there. I mean, I *thought* about it but, you know, save the world and all. Still, what's the rush?"

Ayva, whose hand was on Aurora's hilt, now folded her arms across her chest. "You're worried about the Nine Stones the evil is collecting, aren't you? We've no idea what they can do when they're all gathered."

Gray nodded. "That, and I think Dryan might be a puppet."

"Like Owen," Ayva said in realization.

"Wait, the king of the Great Kingdom of Water?" Darius asked.

"Water *steward*," Helix corrected.

"Right, steward, sorry," Darius agreed. "That guy was a bad egg."

Gray felt his hackles rise, remembering. Evangeline, Ayva, and he had sought the steward for help, only to be betrayed and held captive in the dungeon. As the city became overrun by the dark army, Owen had challenged Gray to a game of Elements, which revealed the pathetic steward to be only a pawn of a greater evil. Gray had barely escaped by unleashing a new power inside himself. *Blur.* The power to move through solid objects, like shifting, but instead of moving great distances, he could become incorporeal, turning into wind, if only for a brief moment. He was still working out the kinks and had a long way to go to master the power. "Point is, he revealed that someone, or something, is pulling the strings."

"Yeah, head of the snake, I didn't forget," Darius repeated. "But why are you mentioning this now?"

"Because the enemy is cleverer than any of us know. Owen was just the first act. I'm beginning to think Halvos of Moon, Dryan of Leaf, Owen of Water…they're all just puppets meant to sow as much chaos as possible."

"For what purpose?" Darius asked. "Y'know, aside from amassing power to hand it over to their master, who's trying to dominate all life."

Gray felt his brow furrow. "I think the enemy is trying to split us up."

"You're saying I shouldn't go?" Darius asked.

"No," Gray replied, shaking his head, "you have to. Just…be quick."

Darius scoffed, "Why are you playing mother hen all of a sudden?"

"He's right," Ayva added suspiciously. "Splitting us up is dangerous, but is there something else you're avoiding?"

Gray sighed. "It's just a theory, and I know this is going to sound obvious, but we're stronger together."

They all looked at him like he was a fool.

"In other news, water is wet," Darius replied, his brow arched.

"Brilliant," Helix said.

Gray sighed. "No, not just *stronger*, I mean like *a lot* stronger. I think that's the whole reason why the Ronin broke."

"I thought it was because your old buddy Kail went mad," Darius said.

"Yeah, ole Blight—" Helix began.

Gray shot him a look and he swallowed the word.

"No, it wasn't because of his madness," Gray corrected, "it was because Kail was losing his powers. Morrowil had forsaken him."

"So, he wasn't the Ronin of Wind," Ayva said in realization. "And without nine…"

"They were missing some really awesome power?" Helix questioned.

Gray shrugged. "I'm only guessing." But he wasn't really. "When they're—I mean, when *we're* united, we're unstoppable. We've all heard the stories about how the Ronin could lay low whole armies, break down the doors of Great Kingdoms, and carve a path to any throne. There's something complete in our unified power. That's why we *need* to find the others."

"And find the stones," Helix added. "Because if we don't, some nebulous evil is going to collect them all and awaken some world-shattering force of destruction?"

"Yeah…" Gray said. "Basically."

"You're good at guessing, buddy," Darius said, patting Helix's back. Then he raised his hand as if in question. "Sidenote, you know we still have a self-loathing Ronin who abhors the very idea of our existence and is literally evil, right?"

Gray hadn't forgotten. *Merrick…Ronin of Metal.* "I haven't forgotten. I'll deal with him."

"How exactly will you deal with him?" Ayva asked, folding her arms across her chest.

"I'll find a way," Gray said, shrugging. "I have to."

Darius gave a thumbs-up. "Works for me! I'll keep an eye out for any youthful idiots wielding moon, flesh, or stone."

"Uh…" Gray winced, glancing back to the many buildings of Seria, and he spotted Faye on a rooftop with Odaren and Modric, another bottle in her hand, watching them. Seven hells, it was morning. He could just hear her saying something about "a drink for a farewell party." He still didn't know what she was planning. Worse, he had a sinking feeling he'd need her soon. "Well…" Gray began, a little chagrined, "maybe you don't have to look *too* far for the Moon."

Ayva rolled her eyes. "Light above, you can't be serious."

"Are you saying what I think you're saying?" Helix asked, jaw hanging.

"Yes. Our leader here has found another Ronin, it seems," Ayva huffed, planting her hands on her hips and glaring at Gray. "That is what you're saying, yes?"

Gray tried not to wilt under her stare. "Yes."

"*Eldarania!*" Darius cursed in Elvish and gave a low whistle. "And I thought I was a blockhead."

"Ha! Look who's in hot water now," Helix said smugly.

Ayva rolled her eyes. "No, you're still a light-blinded fool, too."

Helix grumbled.

"When were you going to tell us?" Ayva asked.

Gray rubbed his neck. "Honestly? There's just been a lot going on. I guess I just kinda got caught up in it all… I mean, we're about to face a full-blown war. One more Ronin is a pretty big deal, but I figured I could get him to our side, then surprise you all with the good news."

Ayva complained, "We agreed, we'd do things together, remember, Gray? As a team? You know, being the Ronin and all? Not to mention, you just went through a whole rant about how we're stronger together."

"Seriously, though," Ayva said. "You need to keep us in the loop."

Gray took a deep breath and nodded. "I will, I promise. I'll be better. As for who he is, his name is Modric, and he's the Ronin of Moon." He pointed to the rooftop in the distance where the three figures watched them, though it was too far away to make out their features.

Helix narrowed his eyes. "Wait, the pudgy guy?"

"No, the other one," Gray groaned.

Darius strained to see. "Eh, can't see his face, but he looks great! Get him over here!"

"Unfortunately, I tried." Gray remembered Modric's quick dismissal, and his obvious allegiance to Faye.

"Did you tell him the fate of the world hangs in the balance?" Darius asked. "That worked on me."

"I did, but he's got a bit of a…fondness for Faye."

Ayva groaned. "Light and heavens, does everyone have a fondness for that woman?"

Darius rolled his eyes. "Take a number."

"I feel like I'm missing something here." Helix looked confused as he tried to keep up.

"No, just Faye things," Ayva remarked.

Gray knew the two were a little sour about Faye after being handed to her father as a present, then nearly fed to a Darkwalker as a snack. Their bitterness was understandable. He added, "Modric's wary of us. I think he's got some sort of trauma with the Ronin, or at least those in power. He's not bad, but he's not good. Not yet."

"Eh, we'll win him over eventually," Darius said, wrapping his arm around Ayva's shoulders. "Dice! Moon and Sun! Look at that—your counterpart, Ayva! I'm sure you two will get along swimmingly."

Ayva rolled her eyes and looked at Gray. "Is that all?"

"That's all," Gray said.

Rydel, Reaver Finn, and Alandra approached. "We must go. Time is wasting."

Gray gripped Darius's shoulder. "Find the stones, stop Dryan, and get back to us quickly."

Darius grinned and embraced Gray, then pulled away and turned to Helix.

"Don't die?" Helix asked.

Darius snorted. "You're the last one I'm worried about. We're like a lucky set of dice, you and me. Some reason we're always stuck on the one pip…but then, just when you need it…Bam!" He mimicked rolling a die.

"Six pips?" Helix asked.

Darius rubbed his hand through his disheveled hair. "Honestly, I lost the analogy halfway through. Point is, you'll be fine. Charming, handsome ones like us always land on our feet." He winked.

Helix grinned.

Ayva just rolled her eyes. "Oh gods, just go already."

Darius smirked, then with a few last embraces—including a lingering kiss with Xavia—he leapt on Leafy, joining Rydel, Reaver Finn, and Alandra. "Safe travels!" He waved over his shoulder as they rode off into the woods.

Imar and Ham appeared. "My lord—"

Gray held up a hand. "Say no more." He opened the Portal of Stone.

Imar inclined his head, a glint in his eye, "Until next we meet again, my Lord Ronin. I will do all I can to see that Farhaven is not lost to shadow."

Ham neared and picked Gray up, nearly breaking a few ribs with his hug.

After a few last goodbyes, Imar and his brother moved to the bronze portal. But they pulled up short when—

"Oops, sorry! Coming through! Yes, yes, ah, my bad, was that your foot? Oops, sorry!" A stammering ripple in the crowd revealed Wyatt, hair slicked back, wearing his plum-colored vest. "Never seen Lander!" Then he leaned in closer to Ayva and Gray, gave a conspiratorial wink, and said, "Figured I'd be your eyes and ears, if you catch my drift."

"Um, thanks? But how are you going to report to us?" Ayva asked.

"Oh, right…didn't think about that."

"C'mon, lad," Ham said, and they snatched up Wyatt and pulled him along.

With a last wave, they moved into the portal, which showed glimpses of a vast city built on towering pillars of stone, connected by massive rope bridges.

"Whoa…that's Lander?" Helix asked in awe. "Can we go there?"

Gray marveled equally. Devari memories whispered that it was an impenetrable city full of hardheaded folk. Seeing it now…part of him did want to split the party, to try their hand at convincing Lander to join the Ronin. Instead, he let his more rational side speak. "Sorry, Helix, we're limited to conquering one Great Kingdom at a time." Gray moved to the panel. A moment later, a portal opened showing a sprawling desert city with endless clay buildings, thousands of spires and minarets, a golden-domed palace, and…the colosseum.

Helix released a tight breath. "So what's the plan? Straight to the arena of death and start bashing in heads?"

"Queen first," Ayva replied. "You know, to try to get you out of the death fight?"

"Oh, right," Helix said.

From the many bridges all over the city, Gray felt eyes, and he saw hundreds, thousands of citizens watching curiously. Xavia and Barthos too, all of them waiting. "Go on, lad," Barthos called. With a last goodbye, they leapt into the Portal of Flesh.

Gray's whole body tingled, the world going white, then…

Stone beneath his feet.

Quickly, he gained his senses. He was in a vast chamber with torches lining the walls. Helix chuckled. "Well, look at that, we made it with no monsters on our tail!" The other two looked at him. "What? Median Portal, saeroks, and vergs?" He shivered. "This is a lot better, we—"

A moment later, guards stormed into the room, and hundreds of swords and spears were leveled at their throats as a woman shouted at them in a different language. Ayva glowered at Helix. "You just had to say something…"

A Council of Dragons

Memories returned.

Zane awoke in a glade, and he felt the warmth of rays peeking through a vast canopy above as shadows and light played across his face. Then he remembered the dragon, when he was near death, falling off its back... How was he still alive? First, he noticed his surroundings, though he hadn't moved yet — his muscles still aflame: a vast area of vivid green grass with a giant pool in the center, clearly magical. Motes of gold and orange hovered above the pool's surface like steam. Spark? And...something else? All around him were towering trees, impossibly wide and tall. They seemed far older than anything else in Drymaus that he'd seen so far, with deep, wild vines and shimmering silver bark. For that matter, the whole of the glade seemed like a dream, and ancient beyond memory.

Zane began to turn when he felt a gusting breath, hot as steam, on his back.

He rolled over to see Pyre standing in all his majesty, molten red and black, as if made of an active volcano. The dragon's body was so massive he made the gargantuan trees behind him seem small. As he planted another step, liquid fire dripped from his jaws, burning the lush grass beneath him and nearly singeing Zane's leg, though he moved it back in time.

"YOU'RE ALIVE," Pyre intoned, voice booming and rattling leaves from their branches. He didn't say it as if it was positive or negative. It simply was.

Off to a great start, Zane thought. The memories of the poison, the pain, the sick feeling in his stomach rushed back. Sweat broke out on his brow as he patted his body to reassure himself. Sure enough, the greenish-black veins were gone. "How, though? How'd you get rid of the poison?"

"THAT WAS NOT MY DOING."

Earth rumbled and Zane's bones shook. Out of the shadows of trees that scraped the clouds came another massive dragon. It was equally huge, and just like Pyre, as the creature approached, its bony head snapping boughs in its path, Zane had to crane his neck to see it. Instead of fire and flame, however, this dragon was made of flesh and bone. No skin, just red muscle. Bleached white bones protruded from the creature's body—from its shoulders, its giant head, and all down its spine. Bone claws like scythe blades dug into the earth as it stopped paces away from Zane, tilling the soil as it rumbled and lowered itself to hunker down beside its fiery brother.

Zane had to remember to take a breath.

Pyre spoke, "LITTLE FLAME, MEET MY BROTHER...SINEW, MEET TINY EMBER, THE YOUNG RONIN OF FIRE.

"MMMM," Sinew said, lowering its massive head. Its breath smelled like corpses. "I SEE THE RESEMBLANCE TO YOU, BROTHER."

Pyre snorted contemptuously. "DO YOU INSULT ME BECAUSE I WOKE YOU FROM YOUR CENTURY-LONG SLUMBER?"

"LOOK PAST FLESH, BROTHER, HE IS MUCH LIKE YOU. THE FIRE IN HIS EYES MIGHT BE SMALL, BUT IT BURNS BRIGHTLY. I AM GLAD I WAS OF SOME ASSISTANCE TO KEEP IT FROM BEING SNUFFED."

Zane knew he should say something. Anything. Speak, damn it! Again, why weren't Ayva or Gray here, or Darius with his gift for gab. He never had a problem speaking his mind, but...holy hells...

Pyre snorted, and a tiny burst of flame erupted from its nostrils, which were wide enough Zane could likely crawl into them. "HUMPH! MAYBE...I DID WITNESS HIS ATTEMPT TO CONFRONT A FORCE OF THE LEAF WARRIORS SINGLE-HANDEDLY."

"I AM GUESSING BY THE WOUND, HE DID NOT WIN."

Zane, tongue-tied and terrified until now, felt a sudden flame of indignation. "If you're talking about the fight with the dozen Terma, that wasn't a fair battle! Besides...I could've won, I was just...interrupted by another." By Sithel drinking some strange flame-liquid, then turning into a horrifying creature and ripping apart the elves limb from limb, only to be squashed underfoot by Pyre like an unseen bug.

Zane still hadn't come to grips with Sithel's sudden demise. Part of him was relieved…

Part of him felt…empty. Zane hadn't been the one to deliver the final blow. To take out his hatred, his anger on Sithel for all the pain he'd caused by taking Hannah from him. That part still boiled.

Sinew, standing beside Pyre, its massive head lowered so its eyes were nearly Zane's height, laughed. "HA! FIRE INDEED."

Zane tried not to shake beneath the fixed glare of the colossal dragon as it curled its tail around the glade; the girth and size of it was enough to fell the huge trees. Sure enough, Sinew's bony tail whipped like a cat's, and a few trees cracked. "You saved me?" Zane asked the Dragon of Flesh, swallowing.

Again, Sinew made a low rumbling sound that vibrated Zane's bones. "I DID. AT THE REQUEST OF MY BROTHER."

He gulped. "Still, thank you. Both of you."

"DO NOT THANK ME YET, LITTLE EMBER. CONSIDER IT A STAY OF EXECUTION," Pyre added, peeling its lips back to show a glint of its terrifying flame-colored teeth.

"What do you mean? Why save me at all, then?"

"BECAUSE, LEGEND OR NOT, NO ONE GRACES THIS, OUR SACRED ENCLAVE, AND LIVES. WE MUST DETERMINE YOUR WORTH AND MERIT TO FARHAVEN. WHY DID YOU ENTER THE FOREST OF OLD?"

Forest of Old…Drymaus? Zane ventured honestly, "I was…chasing someone."

"WHO?" Sinew asked.

"A man—or more like a demon." His fists clenched at his sides as he looked to Pyre, rage rising. "You killed him."

"HE WAS A BROKEN SHELL OF A BEING. I CONSIDERED IT A MERCY."

"It was," Zane spat. "A mercy he didn't deserve."

Pyre lowered its eye until it was level with Zane as well. Now both dragons were side by side, staring at him, their bulk dominating the vast glade. The primordial Dragon of Fire gave a puff that smelled of sulfur and smoke. "CAREFUL, LITTLE EMBER. YOU ARE BEGINNING TO SOUND LESS LIKE A GUARDIAN OF FARHAVEN AND MORE LIKE THE STORIES ALL THE WORLD FEARS."

Zane's fist shook at his side, and he looked away, into the dark forest. "I'm not like the other Ronin."

"HMMM. IS THAT SO?" This time it was the bony dragon that asked. "HOW SO?" The huge dragon moved closer, as if to hear his side of the story, though a talon the size of Zane nearly destroyed his foot.

He moved a few steps back, looking away again. "I'm broken. There's a well of anger inside of me that I can't seem to heal."

Sinew replied, voice shaking the trees and rattling Zane's brain with its deep resonance, "I SEE. YOU BELIEVE IT WAS BECAUSE YOUR SISTER WAS TAKEN FROM YOU?"

Zane staggered back, reeling. "How did you…?"

Sinew's fleshy lips peeled away in what could have been a smile. Though it also made Zane want to release his bladder. He shoved the feeling aside as Sinew answered, "WITHIN FLESH LIES MEMORIES."

"You already know everything, then. So you know you saved the wrong one."

Sinew and Pyre exchanged glances. "PERHAPS," Pyre said.

"So…" Zane said, terrified, then summoned his nerve. "Are you going to kill me or—"

Sinew smacked his lips. "THE MORTAL MAKES AN INTERESTING REQUEST."

"No, I'm not asking to be killed, I just…What do you want with me? I answered your questions."

"WE WAIT UNTIL THE OTHERS ARE HERE."

This time, Zane's bravado slipped, and he felt his body tremble a little. He gulped again. "The…others?"

A moment later, the forest echoed with thunder.

Out of the trees stepped the others, and Zane's heart seized in his chest.

The Nine Dragons.

To Bow or Not to Bow

Gray was led with the others at the point of spears and swords through a warren of halls filled with Covian guards, messengers, and servants scantily clad in colorful clothes. They finally arrived before a pair of giant hammered-gold doors.

Stay close, and remember, we need to win her over, Gray sent. *Our main goal is the armies.*

Helix cleared his throat. *And helping me not die in a fight called the Bloodbath, right?*

That too, Gray agreed.

The guard pushed back the huge doors, revealing a room of opulence. Gray's eyes went wide. At his side, Helix's jaw dropped, and even Ayva muttered a low exclamation. Rich, loud music from many-stringed instruments filled the room. They were played by three men who sat on cushions in a candlelit corner. Red, gold, blue, and green fabric stretched across the room's expansive ceiling, adding to the lively and colorful atmosphere. Sweet and spicy incense suffused the air, lazily burning from a hundred different reedlike sticks on tables or chairs, or on the ground.

Candles adorned the already well-lit room. Men and women moved around the chamber, lounging on vibrant cushions, or drinking, eating, laughing—all obviously enjoying themselves very much. A woman passed Gray and touched his cheek, giving him a flirty smile and eyeing him as if he were a tasty morsel. She seemed totally oblivious to the dozens of swords and spears that surrounded Gray.

At the far end of the royal chamber sat the queen. Her massive bulk spilled over the sofa. Plates were scattered all about her, and a shine from the greasy food they contained coated her mouth and a good portion of her wide face.

The head guard stepped forward, then put a knee to the marble, bowing his head in reverence. "My queen...I bring the Ronin."

Gray simply inclined his head.

Ayva and Helix gave courteous bows.

When they had first entered, Queen Imala had been mid-bite into a roasted wing of some large bird, ripping off chunks with truly impressive ferocity, yet upon their entrance she dropped the hunk of meat, and a grin spread across her face.

"Your Majesty, we come with urgent news..." Ayva began.

Abruptly, Queen Imala shouted, "Stop!"

The guests froze in place and exchanged fearful looks.

Imala waved for her plate to be taken away, and servants quickly did her bidding as the woman's eyes grew wider and wider. "Bone and sinew," she cursed. "It's true, isn't it?" Her eyes sparkled as she licked her lips. "You're really them, aren't you?" As she scrutinized him, Gray realized wind was flowing over his limbs. Her eyes went wide. "By the gods, it is true! This is wonderful, just wonderful! I must admit, I've been hearing stories about you since I was a little girl crawling at the foot of my father's throne, trying to scramble into his lap. And now you're here, in my court. *Ronin.*" She exhaled the name, as if savoring it. Then, as much as she could in her deeply cushioned lounge chair, she gave an actual shimmy of barely restrained enthusiasm. "Oh my, just saying the name gives me shivers!"

Gray exchanged a look with Ayva.

The queen clapped a hand. "Look at me, I'm an abominable host!" For a flickering moment, rage crossed her face. "Servants!" Dozens of men and women appeared. "Quickly, quickly, see to our guests! Get them food and drink, and some comfortable chairs!"

In a whirlwind, plates of food and cushioned seats were set out before them.

Gray's stomach rumbled looking at the meat, cheese, and fruit, and Helix reached out to touch a golden goblet full of what smelled like spiced wine. Gray held out his hand, halting it all. "I'm sorry, Your Majesty. This is all...very...grand."

"And generous," Ayva added.

"Yes," Gray agreed, "but as the Ronin of Sun mentioned, we've not come to celebrate. We've important news for you."

"But of course!" Queen Imala said, grabbing a leg of meat dripping in sauce and leaning back in her lounge chair. "Who am I to delay such important news? Please, go on, I am listening."

A queasy feeling churned Gray's stomach.

At his side, Helix sent, as if reading his mind, *Why do I get the feeling she's treating us like entertainment?*

We don't need to be friends with her, Gray sent. *We just need to convince her of the coming danger.*

"You must have heard by now, but Median was destroyed," Ayva declared, capturing all eyes with the sudden words. "We were there, fighting, as thousands died…" Her voice broke a little. "Ravaged by an evil that knows no bounds. Now we've come for aid. To stop the rising shadow, before it destroys everything we hold dear. Saeroks, vergs, and nameless… If you could've seen them…" Her eyes took on a haunted look, a glassy sheen, as if she were seeing all the dead filling the streets in Median. "They're monsters. So is the evil that leads them." She took a step forward, fists clenching at her sides. "But with your help, and the other Great Kingdoms, we can stop it. We can save Farhaven."

"With my help…" the queen repeated. She bit into a tomato, the juice spilling down her mouth. "And what say the other Great Kingdoms? How many do you have on your side, hmm?"

"Three," Gray answered, "for now. Median was lost, but we saved what we could of the people and found the true Great Kingdom of Water. Seria is on our side. As is Vaster, Great Kingdom of Sun." Gray thought of Lord Nolan. "They were plagued by sickness from the missing sword, but we came to their aid and gained their trust. As for Farbs, Great Kingdom of Fire, well, we have…connections and helped defeat the Darkwalkers in the Battle of the Sands."

"I see." The queen seemed to mull this over. "So much bravery, saving the Great Kingdoms, and still so young for legends."

She sees us as children, Helix sent.

Gray let wind rise about his form. "We aren't here to entertain your court, Your Majesty. We are here because we need your assistance."

Imala huffed. "My assistance. You mean my army, the Covian Legion." She grew a little prim, as if bristling with pride. "As well as my Reavers, I can only assume. I have over two dozen, you know. Speaking of which, where is Nefrin, hmm?" The queen looked around.

At this, as if waiting for his name, the doors burst open, and a man in scarlet robes entered.

A Reaver.

Immediately, Gray spotted the four stripes upon his cuff.

He had a receding hairline and thinning long blond hair, with a little patch of growth on his chin. His cold eyes filled with cunning, brewing with machinations. Nefrin was tall, taller than Gray even, though stooped, as if he spent hours in dimly lit libraries poring over arcane tomes. As he caught Gray's eyes, however, he straightened, as if flaunting their disparity in height.

Ayva narrowed her eyes. *Know him?*

Gray shook his head. He had memories as Kirin—when he lived in Farbs, home to the Reavers—but the memories were hazy at times. This time, it was crystal clear… he knew all of the four-stripe Reavers. It was the rank shy of Arbiter, of which there were only three: Gray's grandfather, Ezrah; Arbiter Fera; and the head of Farbs, Great Kingdom of Fire, the Patriarch. To say a four-stripe Reaver was rare was a grand understatement. However, Gray had no recollection of this man.

The queen introduced him. "This is my High Counselor of Magic, Nefrin, who advises me on all things. I am curious to hear his take on this most urgent news."

Nefrin bowed his head. "Legends in our midst, how fascinating. Please, don't let me interrupt. Continue."

Gray did this time. "As we were informing the queen, Median has been taken. The enemy has made their first move. We are seeking an alliance to face the coming evil."

Nefrin folded his arms into his voluminous red sleeves. "The enemy, what of their numbers?"

Ayva replied, "It's hard to know for certain. Tens of thousands of saeroks and vergs is what we witnessed, but maybe hundreds of thousands. They never stopped coming."

"Pirates too," Helix added. "Really nasty ones. Tattooed, ugly, with their big red-sailed ships."

"I see," Nefrin said, stroking the small patch of growth on his chin. "Then this would be a force even Covai could not face alone."

Queen Imala scoffed. "Nefrin! You dare to cast doubt upon the Covian Legion?"

"We have to be practical, my queen," Nefrin replied. "We have the largest standing army in Farhaven, but even we cannot contend with the might of an endless horde of monsters."

"Precisely," Ayva said. "That's exactly why we've come. We must stand united, every Great Kingdom together."

"Every Great Kingdom," Imala replied, sounding almost curious. "I wonder about that. You say three Great Kingdoms are on your side, but I actually count only one. Seria, a broken city. Farbs has made no such official allegiance to my knowledge, am I correct?"

Gray's whole body tensed.

At his side, Ayva cursed beneath her breath.

"Oh, and Vaster," the queen scoffed. "Nolan is your friend, I hear, but the City of Sun is ruled by a bunch of incompetent old men! Yes, yes, I hear you saved them, but you must know that people have short memories. Lander is a recluse. Morrow is gone. Yronia is scrap metal, and Narim is lost to the thieves." She waved a hand, fingers still covered in sauce. "I'm afraid I count only one. And now you wish me to join…"

Ayva growled. "They will align, *Your Majesty*." She bit the words off. "Besides, if numbers are what you wish to see, then all will join once the threat of annihilation looms on their doorsteps. Don't you wish to join us before it comes to that?"

Queen Imala shifted her large bulk on her throne as a servant neared. She was offered a plate brimming with plump green grapes. Imala popped a few into her mouth, chewing, thinking. "Yes, you make a compelling argument." With another grape, her face suddenly soured, and she picked the bruised fruit out of her mouth. "Ugh, what is this, scraps from the pigs? Get out of my sight!" She whisked a hand, and the servant—a man with fraying hair and tired eyes—scuttled away in terror as if he'd been whipped by a lash of fire. Gray's teeth gnashed, trying to still his reaction.

He felt Ayva's hand squeeze his wrist. *Remember, Gray. You said it yourself. We need her on our side. It doesn't mean we need to like her.*

Like? Helix scoffed through the bond. *I think we should call it a victory if we don't throw Her Majesty from the balcony.* Helix looked at him. *But Ayva's right, Gray. Don't go all white-knight on us. We need this army.*

Gray sent tersely, *I'm trying.*

In that case, you might want to hide your fist trembling with rage, Ayva sent.

He realized she was right and he unfurled his fist, taking a frayed breath.

Imala nibbled on a piece of cheese as she asked, "Say I agree, who will lead this united force, hmm?"

"Does it matter?" Gray asked, trying not to clip the words.

Nefrin countered, "An army to protect can just as likely attack; not to mention, wars have been fought because of a void of power. Power struggles are nothing to quibble over."

Resolve settled over him, and Gray declared, "We'll lead them."

He felt Helix's and Ayva's looks beside him.

Nefrin raised a brow and began to walk down the dais, his hands clasped behind his back. "Ah…I imagined you would say that." His fine red robes whisked along the cool marble as he neared the Ronin. "Do not mistake me. The Ronin are legends, and I very much believe you are their successors, but you are fledglings, still learning to fly."

Gray opened his mouth to contend, but the Reaver had a point.

He knew deep down he was destined to lead this war. But he had no *real* experience. Sure, Gray had fought skirmishes, like when he'd battled the Darkwalkers in Farbs, or clashed with the foul legions inside Median, but he'd never *really* led any of the armies or battles. Now he was demanding a position he knew little about—he had faint memories as a Devari, where training included knowledge of positioning, fortifying, securing supply lines, but leading and commanding thousands? Sending droves of men and women to their death?

Gray felt their stares. His heart quickened; everyone in the room was watching him. This was his moment, though. He hadn't faltered until now. More importantly, he couldn't entrust another with leading the armies. The Reaver was right. Power corrupted. If he left it to some king or queen, they'd just as likely use it to their own ends.

Gray needed a solution.

At that moment, Morrowil whispered, *Perhaps I can be of assistance.*

Gray nodded and listened. He smiled and spoke again, "To be a Ronin means more than just having a bit of wind at your beck and call. For centuries, the true Ronin fought this enemy. They knew better than anyone how to wage war."

Nefrin narrowed his eyes. "Are you saying you have their memories?"

"Yes."

Ayva spoke through the bond, *Uh, Gray? I'm all for convincing them by any means necessary, but what are you talking about? Omni isn't whispering in my ear—is there something you haven't told us?*

I'll tell you later.

"Let's say I agree." Imala rose from her seat and moved her surprising bulk to a table with carafes of wine, pouring some into her golden goblet studded with red rubies until it overflowed. "And I very much wish to…as I said, I believe you are a gift from the realms above. Still, I cannot commit all the legions without some sort of assurance."

"What kind of assurance?"

"Hmmm, an excellent question! I wonder…" She swirled the wine in the goblet that she held in her outstretched hand, fingers bejeweled with rings, while the other hand rubbed her thick chins.

The queen reached for a plate that had been set nearby with tiny cakes, each topped with an assortment of small berries. She grabbed one, a cake the color of blood, and settled back into her seat, eating as she spoke around bites. "Again, you must know I very much like you three already. How could I not? You are the reincarnations of my girlhood fancies…" Ayva raised her brow and the queen laughed, waving a hand. "Not like that, Lady Ronin, don't worry. I assure you, I was just a girl with a wild imagination. After all, as I grew up, the world told me the Ronin were just a myth. As a result, I was left with a void, a yearning for something out there that was better than death and bloodshed. Two things that are very…common in Covai, I'm afraid. So I began my search for heroes. At first, my father thought me foolish. Luckily, he loved me, and indulged my fantasies, sending couriers far and wide. Yet each time, they returned with another fraud. Some were liars, others cutthroats and miscreants, and some? They were just plain…boring."

She sighed, picked up another cake, this one with a lime-green custard, and popped it into her mouth, then wiped a smear of filling from her lip. "Legends, as it turns out, often tend to be exaggerated. But not you." She grinned. "I always held out hope that the Ronin were different. The greatest story of all time! And here you are…my legends, in the flesh." Her expression was a mask of delight, then her brows furrowed with seriousness. The look seemed strange on her jovial, plump face. She crumpled the napkin and tossed it to the floor.

"So I ask again, how far will you go to obtain my allegiance to this little...alliance of yours?"

"Whatever is required," Gray said.

"Now that I like," Imala said hungrily, licking her lips.

Both doors to the room opened, and a figure entered.

"Ah! Perfect timing..."

In walked a woman with such deadly grace that Gray's breath was momentarily caught in his throat. Both sides of her scalp were shaved, revealing intricate tribal tattoos, and her thick black braid was long and fell to her back. She bore a few piercings in her nose and ears. Perfectly sculpted muscles on her arms showed striated muscle that rippled as she walked. Gray's eyes were drawn to a sword at her side—a malevolent red light issued from it even sheathed as it was. Her presence was like a bonfire, drawing his eyes but also making him want to look away, as if he would get burned if he got too close. She stalked past the trio to stand at Queen Imala's side.

Unable to help himself, Gray reached out with the ki—but immediately found a wall impossibly high and wide.

The queen intoned, "May I present to you, Nalia, Grand Primus—four tournaments running. Nalia, look who it is, the Ronin have come to pay us a visit, and they are entering the tournament! I guess they are your competition."

Helix audibly gulped, though only loud enough Ayva and Gray could hear.

Ayva sent, *I don't like her. She appears like Faye, but way worse.*

Helix snorted. *What's to like? It's like hugging a blade. You're just going to get stabbed. Please say I don't have to fight her in the first round.*

She's Grand Primus, Helix, Ayva replied. *Unless you get to the last rounds, you won't even see her.*

Gray was silent.

Nalia was staring into Gray's eyes. She hadn't said a word. He could tell she was sizing him up, scanning him. Not the ki, or anything magical like that. In fact, he wasn't even sure if she had magic—just a terribly large spark. No, she was just reading him with a warrior's keen eye, as if she'd been in countless battles and saw every weakness and every strength within him laid bare. He forced himself to not look away.

Ayva was wrong, Nalia was not like Faye, or Jian, or Dalic, or any of the other impressive warriors he'd faced in his life. No, this woman was different. If those men were swords with sheaths, Nalia had no sheath. She was all blade.

Imala's smile was wide. "Won't this be a sight for the ages! Now, as for your offer to lead the armies, I have one issue, why would I not choose my own Grand Primus to lead? Nalia is my champion and has no equal…"

"Then I'll win the title, and prove to you I am the worthy champion of your armies, the more rightful general," Gray replied.

"Good," the queen said. "Then I propose this: fight in the tournament, Ronin of Wind and Ronin of Water, and if you win? Well"—she spread her hands benevolently—"then I will accept your offer and join your alliance, and together we will face the coming darkness."

"Beneath our banner?" Gray asked, heart pounding.

"Indeed!" she said cheerfully. "That is…" She turned to the stone cold-faced Nalia at her side. "If that's acceptable, my champion?"

Nalia, with a faint hint of a smile, inclined her head without words.

"Splendid!" Imala intoned.

At Gray's side, Ayva stepped forward. "Before I ask the price, how can we even trust you?"

"Flesh and bone," the queen cursed, smiling and gesturing broadly. "If you win, I'll ride out behind you on my prized flesh belegrun myself! I'll swear it on whatever oath you wish."

"And if we lose?" Helix asked with a gulp. "What's the catch?"

Imala's eyes tapered, and a shadow seemed to form in their recesses as she leaned forward, collapsing her hands together, voice smooth as honey. "Why, you join me. Under my banner, as my personal…*guard*." She laughed, shivering with delight. "After all, what could possibly sound more grand than that? The Ronin at my beck and call!" She grabbed a bell and rang it for effect, giggling.

A cold wave crawled down Gray's back. "A moment to confer with my friends?"

"Please," Queen Imala said, waving a hand. "Take all the time you need."

Gray looked at the others, moving a bit away. *Well, what do you think?*

Helix spoke first through the bond, *I say yes.*

Gray and Ayva looked at one another, flabbergasted. Gray expected Ayva to agree, and Helix to eventually be cajoled, most likely by twisting his arm, but not to suddenly say yes.

Helix shrugged. *What? As much as I really don't like the idea of being anyone's slave, let alone that woman's, what's there to debate about? We need their army. Besides, we're going to win anyway, right?*

Agreed, Ayva sent.

Gray nodded. *We will win.*

Exactly! And if not, we're her groveling slaves... Helix gulped, face growing pale. *Tranquil Seas, we better win.*

Gray turned. "We agree."

"Splendid!" The queen's eyes had a gleam as if she knew they'd agree to the terms all along, and she clapped in delight. "As a sign of good faith, I've something else for you three. Something I think you will be most pleased to see." She looked toward Nefrin, her grin spreading on her face. "Show them."

The Reaver's hands danced. Threads of stone floated through the air, and the floor shifted—dancers and other servants had to step back as a giant casement of glass rose from the ground. Inside were the queen's treasures, and there was a small collection of gasps from those in the room, including Gray.

Weapons, jewelry, and armor filled the case that spanned a good part of the room.

Swords, axes, hammers, maces, each gilded or glittering with gems. There was a Devari blade in there too. Most glowed, emitting a strong sense of magic. There were other items: little trinkets...a necklace, an earring, a dark blue belt, a white leather pouch with gold thread accents, each seemingly made of forgotten material. The collection was odd at first glance—from priceless weapons to others that appeared worthless. Gray knew they were anything but.

He felt pulled toward them.

"Is that...I mean, are those what I think they are?" Ayva whispered.

Gray asked the same of Morrowil.

Some of them, the sword answered. *That leather pouch was Kail's. Some of those weapons are Hiron's, Seth's, and even Dared's, but many are fake. Nonetheless, it is...an impressive collection.* The sword almost sounded nostalgic.

Queen Imala leaned her bulk forward in her chair. "Oh, that's but the start. This is my true collection."

Another stone shifted, more people had to move, and a new case rose out of the ground, smaller than the first, housed behind an even thicker pane of glass.

Gray marveled, stepping nearer...

He touched the glass that protected a polearm, white with gold trim, a gleaming blade with impossibly intricate symbols of wind etched across its surface.

Mistral, that was its name.

A memory sucked him back in time, just a fragment—

An ancient forge, poised on the top of a hill, at the height of Morrow's power. When there was such a thing as peace. A hammer pounding away. Day after day, deep into the night. Until, one morning, Arogath called for Kail.

Kail met the man, still in his blacksmith's apron, soot covering his body, his thick muscles cording as the bloodred sun greeted them. The polearm lay in Arogath's well-calloused hands.

Kail had marveled at it, even back then.

"Sorry it took so long. I know it's no Morrowil, but it's the finest Yronia metal. It took some convincing to get a dozen Reavers to infuse it with bloodstone, as well as darkstone, but...it should do the trick. Consider it a small token for saving my son," Arogath had said.

"We are at peace, my old friend. Why now?"

"I make weapons of war, Lord Ronin. Not jewelry."

Kail gave him a stern look. "Yet that's not why you made this, old friend."

Arogath had looked out on Farhaven, a glint in his eyes, as he confessed, "Men are a violent lot. I would not be in business if it were not so. I fear this peace is too good to be true...that it will not last."

"You worry too much, but it is better than an earring," Kail admitted.

Kail's old friend smiled.

The memory snapped.

Gray shook himself.

A memory…from Kail? Was it his own, or did Morrowil send it? Was it from simply being near the polearm?

He eyed the silver-white weapon again.

Ayva gasped, and Gray followed her gaze.

On a mannequin's head was a white shroud.

Omni's.

"Oh, I thought you'd enjoy that one," the queen said wickedly.

Ayva put her hand to the glass, then looked to the queen. "That is mine. It rightfully belongs to me. These relics are all ours."

Even Helix tentatively touched the glass where a faded blue cloak, frayed at the edges, draped a stand. The cloak was stitched with water glyphs and symbols.

The queen *tsk-tsk*ed. "Come now. Don't be that way. I like you three—I think it's fair to say I idolize you, hence, my collection before you. Very few have even laid eyes on this. I can't just give away my treasures. Some of these have taken years, decades even, to acquire and more gold than you can possibly imagine."

"They are not yours to covet and possess," Ayva replied, heat in her voice.

"They are mine!" the queen snapped back, rising halfway out of her chair, her bulk and many chins quivering with her sudden flare of rage. Guards behind them readied spears. "Do not believe my idolization of you will stop me from ordering my guards to run you through for your insolence!"

Ayva's body glowed with sun.

Ice crawled up Helix's arms.

Gray took a deep breath and sent to his friends, *Easy, you two.*

Helix shook himself, letting the ice dissolve and took a step forward. "Your Majesty, if I may, to aid us in the tournament, allow us to borrow the items in your collection out of your infinite benevolence."

She snorted. The room was tense; guards gripped their swords, as if readying for the inevitable clash. Imala eyed Helix warily. "You speak of benevolence, but why should I aid you, Ronin of Water? Especially when *you've* acted so rudely."

Helix shrugged, spreading his hands. "Simple. Because you love a spectacle, don't you? A show." He moved near the glass case. "I've heard stories of the Ronin of Wind and that"—he pointed to the wind spear—"or the Ronin of Sun using that shield." He knocked lightly on the casement, toward a gleaming golden shield with symbols of Sun. "Well, then, what better spectacle than to see the Ronin using their abilities and their items like the heroes of old?"

As soon as his speech finished, a silence followed.

Imala's face, still slightly flushed from her outburst, was pinched with disdain.

Helix gulped.

Finally, her scowl broke and a deep grin spread in its place. "Ah, it was said that Maris, Ronin of Leaf, had the gift of the golden tongue. Whoever thought it'd be the Ronin of Water!" She looked to Nefrin, who gave a fractional nod of his head, and she smiled. "Fine, as a gesture of my goodwill, I will allow you to borrow an item or two from my collection."

Gray released a breath he didn't know he'd been holding, the tension suddenly dissipating.

The queen, straining with effort, rose out of her chair and raised her chalice. "A toast!" Gray and the others were handed drinks. The rest of the people in the room raised their glasses. In that moment, Nalia leaned to whisper something in Imala's ear. The queen nodded, and the Grand Primus took her leave. Her eyes said everything as she passed Gray like a cold gust of wind. *I will see you in the arena.* Then she left the room, with all eyes on her. The queen cleared her throat, drawing their attention back. "A toast!" she repeated. "I do hope you win, dear Ronin, but I also hope you lose. To have you as my personal guardians"—she gave the same wicked smile—"how splendid that would be."

You will find that leash difficult to hold, Gray thought inwardly. He raised his own glass. "To finding a worthy champion."

"And saving Farhaven," Ayva added.

"And to a new alliance, cheers," Nefrin said, raising a glass.

They drank.

Gray raised his mug to his lips, but didn't sip. He lowered it and pointed to the case. "Our items?"

Imala waved him away. "Don't worry, I'll have them delivered. Now, enough with the serious talk, I—"

Just then, the double doors burst open once more and a distraught servant, sweating and exhausted, called out, "*My queen! There's been an emergency at the gates!*"

"Well, what is it?" Imala snapped.

He stammered, terror in his eyes. "S-something is coming...our Reavers have detected a m-magical anomaly."

Gray's blood froze. *No...So soon. How'd the Ker Stream get crossed?*

"From the west?" Ayva breathed.

"No, my Lady Ronin," the servant said, "the south!"

"What is it?" Nefrin asked this time.

The servant swallowed. "I...it's a...a..."

"Spit it out!" Queen Imala commanded.

A sudden roar cracked the air in the distance.

Gray, with Ayva and Helix at his side, dashed out to a balcony that overlooked the desert city and looked south, and his blood ran cold.

A Dragon at the Gates

A moment later, the whole of Covai was stirred into action. The streets were alive, and Gray, Ayva, and Helix had been given mounts and were now rushing through the city. The queen had remained, but Reaver Nefrin was at their side. Somehow, the Reaver had quickly recruited the half a dozen other Reavers at his flanks.

Now they galloped through the desert city, toward the gates.

Helix called out over the rush of wind and the sound of galloping horses as they wove through crowds, "What the hell is going on? Why here, why now?"

Gray shook his head. "Your guess is as good as mine, but whatever it is, it's no coincidence."

"Do you think it's the enemy?" Ayva called back.

"No," Gray said. "I don't know why, but it feels…familiar."

Helix yelled, "Familiar? What are you talking about? It's a bloody dragon!" There was true dread in Helix's voice, and Gray felt it from everyone else too.

He understood all too well.

His memories of Farhaven were returning to him.

A red dragon.

No, *the* red dragon.

The Dragon of Fire. One of the nine primordials, an ancient being said to have been born at the time of Farhaven's origins. As the stories went, Renalin the Creator, the father of all things, had two children: a son and a daughter. In a spectacle to impress their father, they had created the nine titans and nine dragons. The titans were lost, said to have bled back into the land.

Dragons…

No one had seen one, not for a thousand years.

Sure, Gray had faced dragons when fighting at Death's Gates, but he'd later learned those had been wyverns and drakes mostly, turned—and tainted—by the enemy to become shells of their former selves. Dragons, the nine, were said to be the oldest of races, cunning and ruthless beyond measure, and now, seeing this one…he realized how wrong he'd been. Even from this distance the dragon was…massive, almost blotting out a part of the sky, like a globe of fire challenging the sun—and coming fast.

"It's headed for the bazaar!" a guard shouted abruptly.

They veered left, down another pathway, past stalls and wide-eyed men and women in colorful clothes, all with terror etched on their faces.

Finally, they reached a giant open pavilion.

Shops filled the area—from small stalls with colorful awnings to worn-clay buildings that had been there for centuries. At this hour, with the sun high in the sky, the marketplace was teeming with people. Some were fleeing, and others cried out and pointed at the sky.

Covian guards shouted for the people to clear the area.

Despite the wide dirt streets, the citizens were bottlenecked, falling and crawling over each other in their desperation to get out of the city.

Gray cursed, trying to help, pulling people up with wind or stopping others, but his attention was directed above.

Soaring closer now was the giant red dragon, its scarlet scales glimmering in the high noon sun as his huge leathery wings beat a steady rhythm. It was terrifying and majestic all at the same time, but mostly otherworldly—the size of it seemed impossibly big.

Helix called out, "Why do I get the feeling it's coming straight for us?"

"Because it is," Gray said.

For now, it was still beyond the walls, but it was moving fast.

So many innocents.

"There's too many people here," Ayva said. "We need to get them to shelter."

"Too late for that," Gray said. Calling on his power to gather the wind to enhance his voice so it would be heard over the panicked crowd, he cried, "Get down! All of you!"

Gray watched the creature pass over the outer walls.

Cries from archers on the ramparts sounded, and the sky darkened. A hail of arrows and thick javelins from wall-mounted ballistas flew, aimed for the red-winged creature. Gray watched and held his breath with the others. Yet, at the last moment, with surprising nimbleness, the massive red dragon twisted, evading the majority of the onslaught. Arrows that found their mark bounced harmlessly off platelike scales.

"Oh gods," Helix said.

"It didn't attack the guards on the wall," Gray whispered in realization. The creature flew onward, deeper into the city—toward them—while Covian guards scaled rooftops and Nefrin prepared his Reavers into a defensive line in the heart of the open bazaar. Gray shouted to his friends, "Don't attack it."

Helix, wide-eyed, gripped the reigns of his mount, the horse bucking and threatening to throw him. "What?" he asked as he struggled to control the horse. "If this is because you think it's your friend—"

"No. I told you. There's something more to all of this."

Ayva bit her lip. "I couldn't agree more, but are you certain?" She let the golden glow in her hand dim as she gripped her terrified horse's reins in the other. "We might be the only thing that can stop it…"

Gray dismounted his horse, as did the others, all while keeping their eyes on the behemoth dragon now blocking out the sun. The three horses bolted in fear.

"They're attacking it," Helix said, pointing to the archers on nearby buildings and the Reavers a few paces away. Reaver Nefrin's lips were twitching, as if eager, and his clay-colored eyes were squared on the approaching dragon. Gray saw complicated threads of moon materializing at the Reaver's fingertips.

Gray replied, "Yes, but they aren't us. We're the Ronin, what we do is symbolic."

Ayva smiled, that rare smile he got from time to time that tugged at one corner of her mouth and touched her eyes—a smile he was quite fond of. "Well, if we go up in smoke and ash, let the record state, I wouldn't choose to be anywhere else."

"Speak for yourself. I rather like my body without a crispy shell." Helix let the ice at his fingertips melt.

The beast appeared impossibly large in the sky.

A dozen paces from them, his voice quivering with anger, Reaver Nefrin shouted, "Bring the beast down! We can't let it beyond the inner walls!"

From the buildings, archers loosed more volleys of arrows.

This close now, they couldn't miss.

The beast's maw opened wide, and it breathed forth a stream of scarlet flames. Gray felt terror. He readied wind and was suddenly afraid he'd made the wrong decision. They were about to be burned to a crisp. Sure enough, heat rushed over him, but that was it. The inferno reached no farther. Ash from the burnt arrows and glowing red metal hunks fell from the sky.

He was right. The dragon was merely defending himself.

The massive red dragon descended like a rock into the center of the square. Guards rushed forth at Nefrin's command with swords bared. Spells of flame and ice, shards of stone, and spears of moon were readied at the Reavers' hands.

The dragon's massive yellow liquid eyes fixed on him.

The warriors raised swords and the Reavers' spells nearly collided—

"*Enough!*" Gray bellowed, his power making his voice boom. He flung out his hands.

Torrential threads of wind issued forth. They shoved the charging warriors flat to the ground—as if stamping a giant hand on top of them. With another swipe, he cut the onslaught of spells from the air. The hardest of them was Reaver Nefrin's, but the massive globe of undulating moon vanished before it touched the dragon. The beast hadn't even flinched.

Gray moved between the dragon and the men. "Lay down your weapons," he said and then he eyed the Reavers at Nefrin's side. "And release your threads. I will not let a single one of you harm this creature."

Reaver Nefrin sneered, looking over his army of tan-clothed warriors, many of whom were already rising to their feet. The dozen Reavers too, after recovering from the display of power, were weaving spells.

"You, and what army?" Nefrin asked in a cold sneer.

As soon as he spoke, ice began to climb from the street, coating the guards' feet, rising higher until they were rooted in place. Meanwhile, brilliant flares of sun burned like a hundred tiny fireworks all about. As it did, bowstrings snapped, bows cracked, and several swords turned lava red as men and women cried out and dropped their searing-hot blades.

Ayva and Helix joined Gray's side.

"This army," Ayva said.

Both their eyes were glowing.

Helix's were icy white-blue, and Ayva's were burnished gold.

Whispers spread among the crowd, a susurration of fear and awe, words murmured like a refrain:

"Ronin…"

"They're back…"

Reaver Nefrin suddenly raged, "You are fools! Fools of the highest order. That beast cannot be trusted. Do you know who that is? Haven't you heard the stories? Flame and ash, his name is Scarlet Death. He burned half the world. He's going to kill us all!"

"I don't listen to stories," Gray said. "They have a tendency to be wrong."

"Yeah, he looks pretty calm to me." Helix glanced over his shoulder at the dragon two dozen paces away, but Gray saw him shiver a little before quickly looking away. "Besides, you're the ones who attacked it."

"Fine, I'll do it myself." Reaver Nefrin readied spells, thick threads of moon, ice, water, stone—

Before he could cast anything, Gray saw the shocked looks of the crowd.

Gray turned. A figure—hidden by the dragon's massive head—slipped from the creature's back. His eyes glowed faintly, not white, gold, or blue, but orange.

That familiar face.

He looked the same as ever.

Youthful, but years on the street as a thief had given him a darker, hardened edge—something in the set of his jaw, and a faint crease at the corners of his eyes. He wore a deep red tunic, like before, though there looked to be a bit more dried blood on it. Black pants, belt, and faded boots completed his thief-like attire. He was still as broad and muscular as ever; though his spiky black hair was now a wavy tangle down to his jaw, and his deeply tanned skin was darker. Gray noted a few more scars than he remembered gracing his face and arms, but that unquestionable fire in his eyes…that remained the same.

Zane, Ronin of Fire.

Flames danced on Zane's fingertips, hotter and redder than Gray remembered. Zane *tsk*ed softly, eyeing Reaver Nefrin with a dangerous light in his gaze. The Ronin of Fire seemed oblivious, or uncaring, of the hundreds of eyes on him—the warriors, the archers, the Reavers.

"I wouldn't do that," Zane said to Reaver Nefrin.

Ayva's breath caught, and Gray sensed a gamut of emotions from her through the bond—relief, confusion, sadness, and a hint of fear. As if she was afraid of what came next.

Through the bond, Gray also sensed Helix's anger.

The Ronin of Water had a dark, hooded look, fingers unconsciously moving toward the scar on his cheek, and his eyes took on that same icy gleam. *Zane*, Helix uttered in a low growl of distaste through the bond.

Gray would have to deal with that tension, and soon. For now, a smile broke through his shock at seeing Zane at long last.

Reprisal of Flames

Zane took in the spectacle. He'd asked Pyre to drop him in *front* of the city. Dragons were...dragons, as it turned out.

The actual primordial Dragon of Fire was the most "dragon" of them all.

When he'd asked Pyre to set him outside the city, the dragon had just roared and let loose a jet of fire, smoke blowing back into Zane's face. He wasn't sure if that was laughter or anger. He hadn't pushed the dragon further. The jettison of flames had, of course, caused a wave of panic inside the city.

Zane had felt a moment of hesitation when the arrows had started to rain...

Now here he was.

He took in Covai. He stood in the center of a bazaar, much like Farbs's own central hub, but this one was bigger, grander, and more...fitting for the City of Flesh. Massive creatures—bison-like beasts, six-legged cerabuls, and other hulking creatures—were pushed to the corners of the square.

Zane then took in his friends.

Gray and Ayva...Helix, who he knew now as the Ronin of Water, was there too.

Tan-clothed warriors stood all about, hands on blades.

Reavers in red robes with one or two stripes on their cuffs made a line in the center of the square.

One man in particular caught Zane's attention—a man with a gaze that displayed arrogance and entitlement, all the things Zane hated.

"Reaver Nefrin, should we attack?" a Reaver amid the line, a young two-stripe, asked.

Reaver Nefrin held up a hand, as if assessing this new piece on the board.

Zane turned his attention back to Gray, who was calling his name.

"Zane..."

He might have said it a while ago, judging by the look on Gray's face.

"Gray." Zane inclined his head.

Gray spoke excitedly, "You're alive... what happened, how—"

He was interrupted as Ayva rushed forward and wrapped her arms around Zane and held him in a tight hug.

Zane felt something tug at his heart.

Ayva had been there. Had been the closest person to him other than Hannah, and Father. She had been there through everything. Together, they'd traveled to the Nimue Everglades. She'd sacrificed so much, bled, fought at his side, and been there when Hannah had been killed.

Despite the hundreds of people watching—the Reavers, the warriors, the Covian townsfolk—Ayva acted as if it was only him and her. As if all the world mattered not. In that moment, Zane hadn't realized in his driven quest to find Sithel how alone he'd been. How terribly lonely.

Still, he moved to push her away. But Ayva squeezed tighter. Her words came deep and full of resounding empathy. "Zane... I'm so, so sorry."

The words he didn't expect. The simple truth of them seeped into his heart and threatened to break the wall he'd built to protect him from what he feared.

The pain.

Zane felt his barrier crack, his jaw grit.

The tight knot in his chest... loosened, and he felt his eyes grow moist. *LET GO*... a voice whispered. They were Pyre's words. Zane reached out to return Ayva's embrace, to hold her as he wanted to do, as Hannah would have held him, and—

He stopped.

A growl rose from the ground and filled his body as Pyre, still waiting behind him, spoke again, "LET GO, BOY. GIVE IN, FOR THE FIRE OF RAGE DOES NOT BURN HALF AS BRIGHT AS—"

Zane shut out the dragon's voice. "Enough!"

He'd learned he could do that when Pyre spoke in his mind.

They were the same words that Pyre had already told him on their journey here. Words that held deep truth, and also promised pain. So much pain. He wasn't ready for that.

So instead, he focused on the image of Hannah once more.

Rage burned away Zane's tears—a rage as pure and incarnate as the dragon behind him.

Ayva must have sensed this because she pulled back, but didn't leave.

Zane took another step away and spoke to Reaver Nefrin. "I've come to compete in the queen's tournament. I was told there's a prize. I want it."

Silence answered him.

Then laughter.

Reaver Nefrin's, echoing over the crowds and warriors.

Gray's eyes were narrowed, as if trying to read Zane.

Trying to see if I'm evil? Zane wondered. *Always the arbiter of truth.*

Reaver Nefrin spoke, "You...you're one of them, aren't you? So you enter the city on a dragon, causing uproar and panic, more upheaval than in the last three centuries, and you wish to join the Grand Tournament of Flesh?"

"Yes," Zane said, "is that a problem?"

"A few issues," Reaver Nefrin answered calmly. "Ronin of Wind, do you side with your friend?"

Gray joined Zane's side. "I do." Then he whispered under his breath to Zane, "Quite the entrance. You really didn't want to just, y'know...use the gates, like a normal person?"

Zane shrugged. "No."

Helix joined them but faced the Reavers and the warriors, his back to Zane and the dragon. *Just so everyone knows, I'm not over what you did.* He shot a glare at Zane and rubbed at his scarred cheek. *Being an angry Ronin isn't a pass, it's a piss-poor excuse. I should know, seeing I was one not too long ago. Angry, that is.*

Helix...is this really the time? Ayva asked. *Besides, you above all others should know we all deserve a second chance.*

No. He's right, Zane replied through the bond. *Fair enough. You can be angry at me.*

Helix snorted. *Good. I will be. Wait—*

Gray cleared his throat and sent, *Maybe we can talk about this later?*

"I see..." Reaver Nefrin said, stepping forward, only a dozen paces away—spark swirling at his fingertips. "So you're all together..."

Zane saw the man's hand twitch, and read the look on Nefrin's face. He knew what came next. He called, "No. They're not with me! I am not one of them. Not anymore." Over his shoulder, he looked to Pyre, and the dragon seemed to understand.

Pyre rose a little, bulk shifting where—aside from the occasional puff of smoke—he had been quietly watching the exchange.

Cries sounded with the dragon's movements.

Instead of breathing fire, or eating anyone, Pyre simply lifted a giant claw, then stamped it down—separating Zane from the others, and causing Ayva and Helix to leap back.

Gray merely eyed the trajectory of the massive cart-sized black-and-scarlet claw and held his ground, though it nearly smashed him into the hard-packed sand.

"They are not my friends," Zane said clearly. "I speak for myself."

Reaver Nefrin seemed amused. "I see. Then you abandon the title of Ronin? I did not know such a title could be so easily forfeited."

Zane grinned. "Was riding in on the Scarlet Death not proof enough?"

Reaver Nefrin, along with others in the crowd, flinched at the title—a name nearly as embedded into the subconscious of humanity as "Ronin."

The Reaver's dark eyes narrowed. "Regardless, your reckless behavior cannot go unpunished. You will come with us to be placed in custody. Your friends will remain guests of the queen, but I will inform her of your *allegiance*. The dragon, however, must be bound and placed in the dungeon." Then he showed teeth as he shouted, "Seize the beast!"

Immediately, chaos erupted.

Reavers who had been readying threads of moon flung them outward.

Zane and the others reacted.

Pyre was quicker.

Much quicker, and much more terrifying.

Opening a maw that could have swallowed a few draft horses, the dragon roared, dissolving the threads of moon with flames that scorched the air. Pyre then turned in a full circle, whipping his giant tail and sending everyone to the ground, including Nefrin and his Reavers.

As the flames vanished, Pyre boomed, "FOOLISH MORTALS! DO NOT MISTAKE MY SILENCE AS MEEKNESS. SINCE YOU DO NOT SEEM TO KNOW WHO I AM, I WILL TELL YOU. I

HAVE BEEN KNOWN BY MANY NAMES, ONES YOU HUMANS HAVE UTTERED IN TERROR, TREMBLED AT WHEN YOU HAD GOOD WISDOM. AMONG THESE ARE A FEW YOU MIGHT REMEMBER: DRAGON OF THE NORTH, SCOURGE OF ETHARON, BANE OF UTHER, THE CRIMSON CURSE, AND SCARLET DEATH."

Pyre took thundering steps, his massive bulk filling the vast bazaar. People cried and shuddered. His enormous tail cracked and smashed vendors' stalls with precision as his declaration continued. "I HAVE LIVED A HUNDRED LIFETIMES, WITNESSED SIGHTS THAT WOULD BREAK YOUR FEEBLE MINDS. I'VE SEEN KINGDOMS CRUMBLE TO ASH, THE GREATEST KINGS AND QUEENS HAVE KNELT BEFORE ME AND MY BRETHREN.

"YET TODAY, I AM MERELY PYRE. I AM SIMPLY HERE TO ESCORT A FRIEND."

Pyre neared Reaver Nefrin, who still lay flat against the ground.

"YOU…LITTLE REAVER. BE THANKFUL, I PROMISED THAT I WOULD NOT EAT ANYONE, AND A DRAGON DOES NOT BREAK ITS WORD. DO NOT TEST ME. I CAN STILL TURN YOU INTO ASH AND CINDER WITHOUT BREAKING MY PROMISE."

Reaver Nefrin craned his neck as Pyre opened his cavernous maw. Teeth the size of the man chomped down an inch away, and the Reaver cowered.

Satisfied, Pyre sent out a puff of smoke and returned to Zane's side.

"MUCH HAS CHANGED IN THIS WORLD, AND MUCH REMAINS THE SAME. AS ALWAYS, MEN'S HEARTS ARE EASILY CORRUPTED…" Pyre spoke to Zane alone, and his massive molten yellow eyes squinted, as if seeing far into the distance. Toward Median? He spoke again, "THE DREADED SHADOW IN THE WEST LOOMS. WAR IS COMING."

He looked back at Zane.

"ONE MORE THING, LITTLE EMBER. I SEE YOUR FRIENDS CARE FOR YOU, AND THEIR HEARTS SPEAK WELL OF THEIR TRUE NATURE. MY COMPANIONS WILL BE PLEASED TO HEAR THIS. I'M CERTAIN THEY'LL WISH TO MEET THEIR COUNTERPARTS SOON. YET THIS PLACE, THIS CITY…"

The dragon's nostrils flared, wide enough Zane could fit his whole leg inside. Then Pyre shook his massive head as if inhaling something foul, and the movement sent a young couple hiding behind a pile of crates shrieking. "EVIL. IT IS RIPE IN THE AIR. I SMELL IT. LURKING…A KINDLING WAITING FOR A SOLITARY SPARK TO BECOME A WILDFIRE, ONE THAT WILL SPREAD AND DEVOUR ALL THE DESERT. BE WARY OF WHO YOU TRUST, LITTLE EMBER."

You're worried about me? Zane sent back—somehow able to also speak to the dragon through his mind. A Ronin thing he knew, or something to do with his connection to the Dragon of Fire.

Pyre replied with a puff of smoke that blew back Zane's hair. "I WOULD NOT WISH FOR YOU TO DIE BEFORE WE CAN MEET AGAIN. WE HAVE…MUCH…TO DISCUSS."

Much to discuss.

Great, Zane thought, growling inwardly.

They had already talked once, and it left a bitter taste in Zane's mouth. That had nearly broken him, and he pushed down the very *difficult* memory for another moment.

Yet, at the same time, the thought of Pyre leaving felt wrong.

He felt a kinship with the primordial being—like a lost part of himself—or like he was a lost part of the dragon. As he most definitely knew by now, there was no changing a dragon's mind. Especially not this one. It wasn't like he could have kept Pyre in the nearest twelve stables while feeding him half of Covian's livestock.

Zane nodded and replied, "I'll do my best to stay alive, but no promises."

"GOOD," Pyre rumbled, as if this was most acceptable.

Then, with the crowds still pressed to the ground in fear of being burned to a crisp, the dragon lifted its head. He issued a roar that Zane was certain shook all of Farhaven and sent the most terrible, awe-inspiring pillar of fire into the air that reached to the heavens. Men and women cried out. Then the dragon, with a giant beating of its massive wings, ascended. Several stray arrows ricocheted off its gleaming scarlet scales as it flew southeast once more—back to Drymaus Forest.

Gray drew a deep breath, sending through the bond, *Okay.* He turned to Zane. *You and I are going to have a very long talk about what just happened here.*

You mean about how he just befriended the primordial Dragon of Fire? Ayva asked.

Yeah, that, Gray sent. *Zane?*

Zane was already walking away. "I told you. I'm not one of you." He still felt the weight of hundreds of eyes, but he strode quickly, trying to slip away.

Zane! Ayva called out. *Please don't go…*

Though it pained him, he ignored her too, pressing his way through the crowds.

Over his shoulder, he saw Reaver Nefrin. The red-robed man had risen and was still watching the skies, as if he half expected the Dragon of Fire to return to finish the job. Once Pyre flew out of sight—faster than anything had a right to—the haughty gleam in the Reaver's dark eyes returned.

Zane knew what came next, but was hoping he'd avoided it.

"*You!*" Reaver Nefrin's voice snapped like a whip. "Forsaken Ronin. Stop right there!"

Zane didn't stop, but he was suddenly forced to.

Tan-clothed guards surrounded him. He sighed.

Now, without the giant dragon at Zane's back, the Covian warriors were more confident. Most wielded spears—as was the way of the desert tribes, even the civilized ones—but some bore scimitars or their smaller curved brothers, shamshirs. A woman with caramel skin, tattoos on her face, and alluring dark eyes put her scimitar to Zane's neck, pressing hard enough to draw blood.

Zane said nothing, a faint hint of a smile in his eyes.

The woman must have seen it. She grinned, shaking her head. "Don't try it, *car'an*. Move and I will separate your head from your shoulders. It would be most unfortunate for one so pretty." Her words had that Covian clip to them, rich and husky.

Zane opened his mouth, then closed it. Wait…did she just call him pretty? That was a first. All thoughts of what he was going to say fled his mind, but Reaver Nefrin drew him back to the moment.

The four-stripe Reaver practically foamed at the mouth. "Enough of this madness! I demand order and respect! You, Ronin"—he pointed at Zane—"you will answer for what has transpired here! If it were up to me, I'd slice your belly open and leave your innards for the vultures, but I will leave your…fate in the hands of Her Majesty, Queen Imala.

Pray she's more forgiving." Now Nefrin's slicked-back hair was in his face, and a vein throbbed in his forehead. "You three!" the Reaver shouted, turning on Gray and the others. "If you even attempt to interfere, Ronin or otherwise, I will have my men cut you down where you stand. My patience has limits, and you have seen it stretched too thin!"

Wind danced at Gray's fingertips, but he hesitated and sent through the bond to Zane, *Why?*

Zane looked away. *Stay away. I told you, I'm not one of you. Not anymore.*

Gray let his hands drop, relenting.

What are you doing? Ayva asked Gray. *We finally got him back! We're just going to let him go?*

Gray said nothing, clearly trying to read Zane, their eyes locked.

Ayva snorted and sent, *Fine. This is stupid, but I'll play along.* Then she said aloud for all to hear, throwing a glare that threatened to turn Nefrin to ashes, yet also letting it pass over the warriors, archers, and other Reavers, "If you harm him, any of you, you will have to answer to me, and you will regret it." Golden light bloomed around her hands—Nefrin and the others squinted against the sudden flare like a second sun.

But it was more than that.

It was her voice.

She had changed.

The authority in her tone made even Zane swallow.

Reaver Nefrin huffed but answered, "He will not be harmed, lesser Omni. Not yet. He will come, willingly, or otherwise." Then he turned to the warriors surrounding Zane. "What are you waiting for, you fools? Bind him!"

Zane smiled slightly and offered his wrists, almost mockingly.

The husky-throated woman looked down at the gesture as if it was a trick, as if his hands were snakes and they were going to bite her at any moment. Yet, at the same time, a wolfishness filled her gaze, an eagerness—as if she welcomed him to try. A big Covian guard slapped iron manacles into her hand and she shackled Zane. "These will hold even you, fire one." Spears prodded Zane and he was pushed out of the bazaar, leaving the other Ronin behind.

He tried to shove thoughts of them from his mind.

He had a feeling Ayva wasn't done with him. Hopefully, the others didn't have any foolish plans to try to save him. Before he'd been removed, he saw Gray's face one last time over the heads of other Ronin, and he knew he was wrong. He hadn't shoved the thoughts away hard enough.

He had a plan for that too...

That is, if he wasn't killed or locked away in some dungeon by a power-hungry queen.

Gray sent a message, for him alone: *You're one of us. No matter what you say.*

Zane merely snorted and turned away, blocking Gray from his mind.

As he was led like a slave, Zane took in the sights and spectacle of Covai, Great Kingdom of Flesh. With the sun high above, he felt like clay in the kiln, baking beneath the hot dry air.

Huge beasts shambled past. One was a giant mountainous goat with red antlers. Large, slanted horizontal eyes passed over the denizens of the streets. A Farin goat, Zane knew.

Next, two belegruns passed by pulling a giant wagon—they were bearlike creatures with scales, long claws, curved snouts, yellow teeth, and burning eyes. One had black scaly skin, the other was the color of smoke. Their barrel-sized heads swiveled as they made baleful growls at any man or woman who got too near. Thick paws the size of Zane's head clawed deep furrows out of the hard-packed street as if the beasts groomed the ground for new seed. Chains around their necks rattled with each step. Zane knew there was nothing life-giving about these beasts...they were born for war, for killing.

Then he saw strange desert beetles the size of draft horses pulling another wagon train, and he tried not to gawk at their long, clacking mandibles. On their spindly legs he spotted dewdrops. Zane had heard of these creatures. They had a shell meant to absorb water so they could easily survive in this harsh climate.

The animals all kicked up plumes of dust.

Teeming wagons with crates and carts rattled by, filled with a myriad of other strange creatures, from long-furred jackrabbits to large lizards with two tongues and three tails. And...so much more.

Zane, despite his dour mood, couldn't help but marvel.

Covai, city of man and beast indeed.

People in vibrant clothes, loudly hawking items for sale, began to resume the normal hum of a busy city. He passed stands selling greasy meat pies, bins of vividly colored spices that smelled so strong it burned his nostrils, brightly colored silk scarves, and gaudy bangles of all kinds. Still, the vendors at each stall would go silent and watch as he passed.

In many ways, Covai felt like Farbs, like home.

Even the people, most wearing tan or ruddy clothes—but many others colorfully garbed in vibrant hues of vermilion, blues, greens, and shades of gold—reminded him of Farbs. Scents of food wafted in the air, making Zane's stomach growl, reminding him how long it'd been since he'd eaten.

Chains rattled on his left. He turned to watch as a coffle of slaves was hauled along.

Here lay the one significant difference between Farbs and Covai.

Zane took in the chained line of men and women. Out of the dozen linked slaves, there were only two strong men. The rest looked very young or old and frail. A young boy, no more than twelve, with large, haunted brown eyes peering out from his dirt-smeared face, was shackled to a withered gray-haired woman, her skin tanned and leathered.

The slaver was a fat man, his bulk straining against a threadbare shirt. While they walked, the man ripped into what looked like a raw piece of meat, letting the juices drip down to soil his shirt and congeal in his hairy chest—which already looked matted from fat and grease. All the while, he spat harsh Covian insults to his prisoners, his whip lashing at their feet.

Zane snarled, feeling his blood heat, fire rising.

Yet a voice spoke at his side, breaking his trance.

"You're not from here," said the husky-voiced female guard.

Zane glanced over at her, trying to slow his breath, to cool the fire in his veins.

She stared at him, dark brown eyes judging.

The other warriors weren't as close. When had they backed away? They now made a giant ring around him, their hands still on their hilts, muscles tense, all standing like coiled springs ready to release if Zane made a wrong move.

Zane debated letting the rage win.

He imagined melting the chains on his wrists, grabbing the slaver's whip, and choking the life out of the fat man, ridding this world of one more piece of filth.

Then he took a breath, letting it go.

Not here, not now, he told himself.

Hannah's face was there again.

You wouldn't approve of that, would you? he asked her.

Choking the light out of a man? Hannah's words sounded in his head, really just a figment of his imagination and further proof of his slipping sanity. It was a welcome voice. *What's become of you, brother?*

I know I've failed you up to now. I know vengeance is wrong. I have something in mind…something I think you'll be proud of. Ahead, in the distance, over the clay buildings and colorful awnings, he spotted it, or at least the crest of it.

A massive structure, imposing with its many arches, a feeling of life and death emanating from it even from here.

The colosseum.

What are you planning? she asked.

You'll see. Perhaps all the death, all the chaos, all the anger…it'll have a purpose.

Hannah said nothing.

At his side, the woman guard cleared her throat.

Her eyes still took him in, as if she could read the layers of his past on his face, though he knew all she could read was a mask of anger, thinly veiled. Zane studied her more closely. Her skin was a deep bronze, and the black tattoo swirled from her cheekbones to dot across her forehead. Her eyes weren't as dark as he'd originally thought. When the sun hit them they were more light brown, like…cinnamon or wheat. Zane had never taken much notice of such things in the past. She wore armor like the other Covian warriors, yet her steel plates had intricate engravings, swirls and tribal-like patterns much like her tattoo. The armor wasn't bulky—more like a seamless second skin. Underneath she wore tan cloth tightly wrapped around her lithe frame. It reminded Zane of more sophisticated Algasi armor, and he wondered how close Covian blood was to that of the nomadic desert warriors.

Either way, those intense eyes kept prying even as he remained silent.

"Do you not speak?" she asked. Then, wearing an impish smile, said, "Did I imagine you with a tongue?"

"I speak…" Zane started. He watched as her warriors continued to usher the crowds aside. Men and women were still pointing and staring at him and his procession. "…when it's necessary."

She mused, "You're not from Covai."

"What gave it away?"

Her broad shoulders shrugged. "Everything." She moved a little closer to ensure the other guards couldn't hear, yet her hand still rested on her curved scimitar. He could tell it wasn't just for show. "They said your name. Zane, was it not?"

He grunted.

"I am Leanna." She put one hand on her chest.

"Leanna, no offense, but…I'm not looking to make friends."

This only made her smile. "Clearly not. You rode in on a dragon, and you tried to spit in the face of an already bitter Reaver, little *yvrana*." Zane couldn't speak Covian, which was closely related to Sand tongue, but he recognized that last word. *Spark user*. He was pretty sure it had…a very *unfriendly* connotation.

Reaver Nefrin rode ahead, looking pompous as ever as he yelled at people to get out of his way. Zane's eyes were still on the slaver and his slaves.

Suddenly, one of the older slaves in the front, a balding man in dirtied, once-white rags, tripped.

Rage twisted the fat slaver's face and, spit flying from his mouth onto the fallen old man, he bellowed, "*Harlavs!* Get up! Move, you worthless piece of trash!" Snarling, he threw his piece of meat and raised his whip.

Zane's rage boiled over, and he pulled upon the flow. Fire danced in his soul, ready to burn the stout slaver to cinder. He knew he'd be cut down, but he didn't care. Quick as lightning, however, Leanna was there. She had somehow crossed the distance and caught the slaver's whip.

The fat man looked back over his shoulder, incredulous. "You filthy wench! Covian guards aren't to interfere with slave work. I'll make sure you pay for this!"

Still holding the whip's end in one hand, Leanna pulled down the collar of her tan cloak, as if revealing something. Unfortunately, from this angle, Zane couldn't see what she showed the slaver, but whatever it was got a reaction. The fat man's eyes grew wide. He choked, biting off whatever he was about to say.

Leanna dropped her end of the whip and replied back coldly, "There are rules, slaver. You know this. Even from *Sunha* to *Diaon*. Don't push them." Then she pointed to the old man, still on hands and knees. "Now, help him up."

Grunting, the fat slaver gestured to two of his vassals. "You two!"

"No," Leanna said, folding her arms. "*You* help him."

Grumbling, the slaver looked like he was going to protest—his eyes searched the crowds, which had now formed a small throng around the scene, but he saw no sympathy from them or Leanna's warriors. Finally, he shoved the whip into his belt, then helped the struggling man to his feet. Before Leanna could order him about more, the slaver cursed under his breath, and pushed his gang down another side street, away from Leanna's watchful gaze.

Zane felt eyes on him.

He turned to see Reaver Nefrin watching, a slight quirk to the man's greasy face. The look was clear. He'd seen Zane's reaction to how the slave was treated, and he was stowing it away.

They moved onward.

"Thanks for that," Zane said after a moment to Leanna.

She shrugged. "Eh." She gazed up at the glaring bright ball of fire high above beating down on the citizens of Covai. "Bit like pouring water on the sun. Not sure how much good it'll do." Then she smiled a little. "But it was fun."

"Whatever you showed him clearly did the trick. What was it?" Zane asked.

She eyed him sidelong. There was a flicker of pain in her glance, before her face became a mask and she looked ahead once more, past the crowds. "We all have our secrets, *car'an*. More importantly, you should be more careful here."

Zane hefted his chained hands. "It seems that ship has already sailed."

She mused, "Oh, the queen won't kill you. Everyone knows she has a soft spot for your kind."

"My kind?"

"Ronin."

He snorted. "You mean she'll want to make me her pet. A slave." He spat into the dirt—the dry sand just soaked it up. "Like the rest of this cursed kingdom."

She snorted. "Likely she will try, but will you let her?"

He looked at her, all fire—his jaw clenched and his eyes bored into her.

Leanna smiled. "That's what I thought." Then she laughed. "I like you, *car'an*, I truly do. That fire, it burns inside you. Allow me to explain my caution…" He opened his mouth to argue, but she continued. "I will offer wisdom, even if you will not take it. This city is different." She eyed the inhabitants, men and women of all ages, many of whom pointed at him, whispering—he heard a few murmurs of "dragon rider." He rather liked that. "Reputation is everything. Kill someone powerful, and people fear you, respect you…you can do what you want. Food? Fame? Women? Men? *Strength*. That is all people care about here. Show your strength, and you can get whatever you want in this city. That is why the Grand Tournament of Flesh means so much. Those who survive the first round, they no longer want for food or drink. Second and third? They are minor royalty. Fourth and higher? Kings and queens. The Grand Primus? He or she is a *god* of Covia. That is, if you survive."

"What's your city's twisted power hierarchy have to do with me?" Zane asked.

She snorted. "You're a Ronin, you fool, the most powerful of all."

The truth of her words sank in.

He saw people watching him, not just with curiosity, but with…hunger.

She went on. "You especially, with that fire of yours. It will get you far. But let it burn too bright, and it will attract others like wolves to the smell of blood. A grand beast to be taken down. To prove they are *worthy*. That is, if your fire does not consume you first." She snorted. "*Aratas*. I can sense it from you. So can others. At this rate, you're going to draw the anger, and the hunger, of this whole city."

Sure enough, a group of thieves lingering in the shadows of a dark alley eyed Zane, and even with his impressive entourage, they touched blades as if they planned to cut him down right there. "Let them try," Zane said, sneering at the group, lunging and rattling his chain. They flinched, practically leaping out of their skin.

She sighed and rubbed her brow, cursing in Covian. "You truly are a fool."

Suddenly, a memory sifted back.

Zane staggered into the Underbelly, clutching his gut.

"What have you done?" she cried as she neared. Then she pulled his hand back and gasped.

"Not good?"

The memory got a little patchy after that—likely from his near-death wound—but the next thing he knew, he was lying near their cot, Hannah kneeling over him. Her hands glowed as she frantically wove threads of flesh to stem the tide of warm blood. After nearly an hour, when at last the wound was sealed, she lay back against her cot, sweating, tired. Words slipped past her lips that Zane still remembered to this day, that still afflicted him: "I don't get it. You see yourself as worthless. As a tool to be used and thrown away. How? How many people have to tell you differently until you see the truth of it yourself? You are...more...so much more...so live, you big idiot."

Zane grunted. "For you."

"No, not for me. For yourself."

Zane shook himself, realizing Reaver Nefrin and the others had stopped.

He'd been in a bit of a trance. Now he looked around.

The street behind him was wide, flanked with what he could only assume were statues of former champions of the tournament—each twelve feet tall. The thoroughfare was oddly sparse of citizens.

Ahead sat the true spectacle.

The Palace of Flesh.

Shiny things usually only meant more money when Zane was a thief. But this...the sight took his breath for a moment. The overall structure was massive, with parapets, fluted spires, and crenulated ramparts. In the center of it all, and what they stood before now, was the central palace, topped with an enormous golden dome that was practically blinding in the high noon sun.

Ahead were giant golden doors, each seemingly heavy enough to require a team of cerabuls to open. Beside the doors stood guards, and despite the heat, they wore heavy plate armor and layers of royal regalia. Reaver Nefrin was the first to leap off his dark mare. The doors opened and Zane's retinue entered under the scrutiny of the stern-faced guards. Inside was a giant hallway branching off to dozens of different rooms, but the main path was covered with colorful carpets and seemed to lead toward the heart of the palace, where he was certain the queen awaited.

The doors slammed shut behind them with a resounding clang, and as they did, Nefrin turned to face Leanna, Zane, and the warriors.

Strands of his black hair had fallen, and he slicked them back and donned a smug smile. "Well, I must thank you for the escort, Guard Captain Leanna. It was most appreciated. We can take the prisoner from here. After all, I'm sure you have more pressing matters."

Leanna's jaw set. "We will accompany you."

His smile cracked a little. "As I said, that is quite unnecessary. He is in capable hands," he said, gesturing to the dozen other red-robed Reavers at his side.

Leanna didn't flinch. "I beg to differ. He is a Ronin."

"A fledgling one," Reaver Nefrin said through gritted teeth.

Leanna's jaw tightened further. "Still, I—"

"I said *that is all*, Guard Captain," Reaver Nefrin said, no longer hiding his disdain, as his lip twitched. "You may go. *Now*."

Leanna looked to Zane.

He smiled. "It's okay. I'll be fine." Zane knew Nefrin's type. Seen them a thousand times while thieving. The Reaver had been demeaned, and now he was trying to exert what little power he could.

Still, Leanna hesitated a final moment before at last nodding stiffly. As she moved to leave, she grabbed Zane's arm and whispered in his ear, "Do not let your fire burn you alive before I see you next, *car'an*. You are far too pretty to die yet." Her warm breath sent a trickle of excitement down his spine. Without giving him a chance to reply, she made a gesture and her warriors smoothly formed columns and took their leave. The massive doors slammed shut behind them.

"Well?" Zane said. "Lead on. I'd rather like to see this queen who holds your leash."

Reaver Nefrin sneered. "I think not."

The other Reavers fanned out in front of Zane in the wide hallway.

Zane sighed. "You really think this is going to work out well for you? Trying to kill a Ronin in the middle of a palace full of witnesses?"

"Oh, little Ronin. I don't think you quite understand the reality of your situation."

Sure enough, the people ahead who were watching suddenly scurried away—taking side corridors, or moving into rooms—like mice fleeing the barn owl.

Zane growled. "Seems you've sunk your claws deep into this place." He heard the pulse of his pounding heart in his ears, and he knew he had to attack first.

Before he could, dozens of threads of flesh slammed into him like a thousand cuts. One buckled his knees, another sent searing pain through his muscles, spasming his arms. A final one smashed his face into the stone floor. Ringing filled his head, and he tasted blood.

Another sharp blow made his mind succumb to darkness.

Time stretched, and he struggled to cling to a faint ray of consciousness.

He felt hands dragging him.

His eyes fluttered, visions flickering.

Hallways and dark corridors.

Servants whispering, "Ronin," then flitting away.

"*The boy's still conscious,*" said a voice.

"*Quickly, we have to get him away from here—the other Ronin will find him.*"

He tried to fight, his anger a dim pulse in his mind, but his muscles wouldn't respond, and through his blinking vision, he saw the dozen Reavers circling him.

Zane lunged, putting his manacles around the neck of the nearest Reaver when—

Nefrin snarled, waving a hand, and sudden darkness took Zane like a blow to the back of his head. When he came to, he was in an alley, sand beneath him and the high sun still glinting above the edge of the clay buildings. It was a wide back alley, wide enough that the Reavers surrounded him—but it was sealed on both entrances. Nefrin stood over him.

Zane still smelled the sulfur from the blacksmith's forge that they'd passed.

He was certain they hadn't gone far.

The four-stripe Reaver was grinning. Ruddy-tan and red filaments danced from the vile man's fingertips. The other Reavers, in a ring around Zane, had arms extended, each threading to keep his muscles locked, while others readied spells of fire, water, moon, sun, metal, and leaf.

Zane didn't care.

He tried to rise, tried to let his power fill him and—

It felt like running into a brick wall.

His power was there, like a deep roiling river of magma inside his soul, the pressure rising. Yet he couldn't move. His arms…they felt…strange…as if they were cut off from his body.

Zane looked down at the shackles in sudden horror.

Black metal with veins of scarlet red.

Zane tried to touch the flow again, and the manacles glowed a sinister scarlet.

"Bloodstone fused with Yronia iron…" Nefrin explained, the sun high above making him a silhouette to Zane's eyes. "I made sure the Captain did one thing right, at least. I plan to use them on the others of your kind, but you make a good test subject. For an average Reaver, that much bloodstone touching their skin would likely kill them. For a Ronin, it will at least keep you from using your power."

Zane remembered Leanna's words.

These will hold even you, fire one.

A sinking feeling made Zane suddenly sick to his stomach.

He'd never been cut off from his power before.

Nefrin's cocky smile grew. "Oh, how I love that look…that despair…after such arrogance. It's almost sweet."

Zane roared, yanking against his invisible tethers, but the Reavers kept his muscles locked tight, issuing more threads of flesh that were visible in the air as tendrils of tan and red. "Why?" he snarled. "Why kill me? Why are you so afraid of me meeting the queen? If it's because you're afraid I'm going to expose you as a pathetic coward hiding behind his men, I'm sure she already knows that." He eyed the Reavers.

"Silence!" Nefrin snapped and punched Zane hard in the jaw— sending a wave of pain that rattled his whole skull.

Nefrin's eyes were full of rage, but then the man took a slow breath, and something in his eyes…*shifted*. The impetuous fire was replaced by a placid, almost bored look. What in the seven hells? The Reaver sighed and eyed the gore on his fist. "Look what you made me do. I hate bloodying myself." Coolly, he knelt and wiped his hand on Zane's already red tunic. He spoke differently now—no snide edge to his voice. Instead there was an almost eerie calm. "You know, Zane, I may despise your kind, but I almost feel sorry for you. You were born a Ronin. You didn't choose it. Like me and this city. I didn't choose Covai. I was forced here against my will twenty years ago. I loathed it when I first arrived. The people, the baseness of it all…" His lip curled, his face souring as he stared up at the sun high in the sky. "A hot, hellish prison. Their ideals rankled me. They kill each other for nothing! Coin and food. Then I realized, there was something beautiful in their depravity. Their simple way of blood, sweat, and toil taught me the most valuable lessons." He scooped a handful of golden sand, letting it sift through his fingers. "Flesh, bone, sinew. That's all we are, and our suffering makes us human…makes us realize we're truly alive, wouldn't you agree?"

The last of the sand ran out of his palm. As it did, Nefrin snapped his fingers and sudden agony coursed through Zane. His muscles felt ready to burst, and he screamed against it, staring into Nefrin's cold eyes. It felt like tiny filaments of glass needling into Zane's skin, sinking into his bones. Tears poured down his face as he fought the agony.

After what felt like an eternity, Nefrin let the power drop.

Zane gasped for breath, nearly falling into Nefrin, who moved enough so that his face hit the sand instead.

"No, no, look at me…it's only polite." He twisted his fingers, making Zane's muscles stiffen. "As I was saying, our time in Farhaven is just sand in an hourglass, yet we all have different amounts." His voice was sweet, almost crooning. "Yours just happens to be less…this city has taught me that we must embrace the chaos, the randomness of life. We need to *seize* it."

He gripped Zane around the neck, nails digging into his throat, and again he sent a jolt of terrible pain into Zane's muscles, making it feel as if he were ripping the tendons out of Zane's body with his bare hands. Zane cried out as Nefrin continued, "You are standing in my way, simply a fruit to be plucked and eaten. That is Covai's great truth…almost poetic in its simplicity and unerring veracity. As for the people, you see brutes, rough men and women who are slaves to their own desires, who put others in chains. Yet I see free people…men and women who understand the simple truth of this world: that whatever you can carve out of this life is yours. Kill or be killed. Take what you can. Beautiful, is it not?"

Nefrin let him go, and the pain abated.

Zane sagged against his invisible bonds, sweat streaming from his face. He'd never experienced threads of flesh used in that way. On his tongue was the sharp metallic taste of blood. If it had gone on much longer, Zane wondered if the agony alone might have killed him. "Rationalizing your depravity is all I hear. You're mad."

Nefrin shrugged. "I admit, in the hunt for true power, I twisted and tugged a few threads in my own head. I wanted to see the extent of the mind's abilities. To see if I could carve out a more perfect me. Alas, it had its…*consequences*. I don't regret it. It made me who I am," he said, eyes mixed, as if warring with two people in one mind—one man eerily calm, and the other an insane, short-tempered zealot.

Zane looked to the other Reavers, many of whom watched with some alarm, as if seeing a new side to their leader. "You all…" He felt sweat trickling into his mouth, tasted salt and blood. "You're willing to follow this madman? To kill and torture a chained man in broad daylight?"

One of the Reavers, a young woman with curly brown hair and a round face, scoffed, "Don't act as if you're some innocent nobody. You're an abomination. A broken relic from a forgotten time. The Ronin don't deserve the power of a god."

"Let me guess—you do, I suppose?"

Her eyes burned with hatred and hunger. "More than you."

"Korella's young," an older two-stripe Reaver said, as if excusing her. A peppered white beard tried to hide a burn mark on the old man's cheek—Sons of Flesh? Zane had heard of them. They were a religious cult of Covai who valued self-mutilation to feel closer to Renalin, the Creator. The old man had deep-set, haunted eyes. "She doesn't understand that power isn't everything. Yet, one thing is certain—this world is broken, boy, and it needs saving, but not by your kind. By someone who promises true change. A new order is coming…one that will take us into the light."

Zane gave another bloody smile, turning his head as much as he could under his bonds to stare down the dozen red-robed Reavers who circled him. "You all believe the same? A new order?"

"The Lightbringer will save us from your kind," Korella said with venom.

So he had a name. It made sense that Nefrin was only a puppet.

Zane snorted. "You can spout whatever twisted reasons you want, but the truth is, you took a solemn oath to protect Farhaven—for what? Him?" He eyed Nefrin, who was only smiling. "For some nameless evil?"

They looked uncertain.

Nefrin said nothing, however, merely watching, as if letting it play out.

Zane tried to seize on their trepidation, still tightly bound by their magic. "I might be the heir of fallen legends, but at least I'm trying to be different. *Really* trying." He growled. "You don't have to do this, you don't have to follow him."

Korella's sharp, derisive laughter cut through the silence. "Is that all you've got? Pitiful. You're just a pathetic rat, drowning in a bucket, looking for a way out. No one is coming to save you."

Zane eyed her. "Thanks."

She snorted. "For what?"

"Now I won't feel bad for what comes next. You'll die first."

Korella's smug face wavered. She swallowed, hands extended, still sending thick threads of flesh, now looking far less certain.

"Are you done trying to turn them? A truly valiant effort," Nefrin said.

Zane snarled. The man had known it'd be futile, that their hearts were already too dark. He was playing with him. "What do you want, you bastard? If you wanted me dead, you would have done it already."

"Cleverer than you look," Nefrin replied. "Tell me—your sword, have you found it yet?"

So that was it.

The Sword of Fire.

Zane's blade, Seth's sword.

Heartguard. That was the sword's name.

Zane hadn't discovered it. Not yet. He couldn't tell Nefrin that... If the man thought him useless, then he was as good as dead. There was something in the twisted Reaver's gaze, as if he deciphered the truth in his words. So Zane threaded the needle. "Even if I did know, I'd never tell you."

"Wrong answer," Nefrin replied. He grabbed one of Zane's hands, still in manacles. Then threads of flesh slammed into Zane's pinky and with a sharp crack, his finger snapped. Zane clenched his jaw against the blinding pain, swallowing a cry. Nefrin continued, "New plan. I break one finger at a time until you tell me the location of your sword."

Zane continued to gnash his teeth, smiling.

Nefrin, face calm, snapped Zane's middle finger.

Zane roared, every muscle on fire. When he caught his breath, he panted, "My friends are going to end you…"

"No, they won't." This time, Nefrin slowly bent another finger until it snapped, and Zane grimaced, fighting back the sudden flare of pain. Three fingers. He had only two left on his right hand. "Now tell me, where is your sword?"

Zane pretended to croak something.

Nefrin leaned in. "Come now, you'll have to speak up."

Zane lunged, biting Nefrin's ear and tearing it away from his head.

Nefrin screamed, scrambling back. Blood poured from his ear. His sudden calm vanished, and those crazed eyes returned. "You imbeciles! I told you to keep him in place!"

One of the Reavers, a young man, replied, "We're trying! He's stronger than—"

"I won't hear excuses! You're a dozen Reavers, he's one boy!" He worked threads of flesh to knit his ear back to whole. "Wait…I see…" The madness in his eyes grew bright. "You don't know where your sword is, do you? Then this is a waste of time. I'll disappoint the Great One, but hopefully your head, along with the heads of the others, will be enough to stay his rage."

He twisted a thick thread of flesh, making Zane's heart suddenly seize.

Zane gasped as pain made him see spots of black. The feeling was different and terrifying. Nefrin crooned as his fingers continued to send threads of flesh into Zane—the man's eyes dancing with delight, as if he savored each new level of pain on Zane's face as he twisted the knife deeper. "Funny thing, *flesh*. Did you know, it's one of the more difficult elements to work?" Nefrin's fingers tightened into a fist. Zane's heart squeezed, feeling as if it was going to implode inside his chest.

Until now, Zane had held back, not willing to give the sick creature before him, or his cronies, the satisfaction of crying out in full. Now Zane couldn't keep it down, and a moan of rising torment escaped his lips. Nefrin continued, undisturbed, "You can stop a man's heart with enough threads of flesh. It's not…efficient, nor easy, but it is fascinating to watch."

Zane writhed, trying to force his mind to think straight.

He was going to die here by the actions of a madman no different than Sithel. That alone made his blood boil and his power flare—only for the shackles to glow brighter, and his arms to grow cold, as if dunked in an icy lake, blocking his power from surfacing. In the corner of his vision he saw the other Reavers, all working hard to hold him in place.

This was it…

He was going to die.

After everything, before he even had a chance to redeem himself, he was going to die on these dusty streets in this hellhole of a city. The pain radiated higher as Nefrin visibly worked harder, twisting more threads.

"You are something…aren't you…perhaps not as pathetic as I thought…still, your legacy is tainted. You are just a relic from bygone days…" Nefrin said, sweat trickling down his temple, making his slick black hair stick to his forehead. "This power…it should never have been granted to you…"

Zane felt his heart, like a ripe melon, slamming against his ribcage.

"Now *die!*"

Nefrin's hands worked more feverishly, weaving thick threads of flesh that filled the air with their ruddy-tan aura—a spell clearly powerful enough to end Zane.

At the same time, Zane's muscles contracted as if a mountain of power begged to be used and was blocked.

Blocked.

Not gone.

Nefrin's words echoed in his head: *Your power is still there.*

A faint memory from long ago resurfaced.

He and Hannah as children, no more than five or six. Just taken in by Father, a benevolent old man who oversaw the Underbelly. Zane, in an attempt to help—despite Father's warning that he was too young—had stolen. The older thieves had punished him by tying a band around the hand that had filched. It was supposed to be a lesson, but the band was too tight, and now his hand was completely numb and he was scared he was going to lose it. Meanwhile, Hannah was trying to use her power to burn the cord off.

"Hold still, you little numbskull. I can't concentrate when you're wriggling like a fish out of water!"

"Well, I'd do it myself but they took my pocketknife!" His hand was ghost white, and it had stopped hurting a while ago. "Am I going to lose it?" He tried not to sound scared.

She paused to flick him in the middle of the forehead.

"Hey! What was that for?" He rubbed his head. "Now two things hurt!"

"Because you're being a dummy. Your hand isn't going to fall off!"

He huffed. "Fine, if you're so smart, then where'd the blood go?"

She snorted as she worked. "Didn't you listen to Mistress Tana?"

Zane looked away. Mistress Tana had been awful. She'd beaten them in a halfway home before Zane had finally grabbed Hannah and fled. He took her to a place where only misfits went, under the city of Farbs. That's where they'd met Father and the others, and found their new home in a place called the Underbelly. "No. I hate her. I wish I could scrub my mind of anything she's ever said."

Hannah sighed. "Well. The point is...magic, or spark, and blood, it's all the same, they're tied. If it's cut off somewhere, your spark doesn't just dry up! Mistress Tana said it's like a river behind a dam. Once something's blocked, it finds other paths." She concentrated and finally the band snapped from a little sizzle of fire. She rejoiced. "Ha! Success!"

Zane rubbed at his wrist, watching the color return and with it a wave of pricks and sharp pains. He looked at his sister and grinned, rising and rubbing her blond head of hair. "When did you get so smart?"

She huffed this time. "I always was. You're the dumb one," she said slyly, making him smile.

Zane returned to the moment.

Blocked.

His power still wanted a way out. He felt it coursing through him

Nefrin's eyes were bloodshot, his face quivering as he finished the final threads of the intricate spell to kill Zane.

Distantly, Zane was aware he was still screaming.

Zane might not have been Pyre, but in that moment, he channeled the dragon's instincts—all his rage and fury, all his passion. Nefrin's eyes went wide, as if confused by the sudden change in Zane's facial expression.

The air suddenly crackled with earth-rending power.

Nefrin's spell vanished. "Kill him!" the mad man cried out, backpedaling. "Now!"

It was too late.

The power in Zane's soul listened, finding a way out.

Zane roared.

Fire bellowed from his mouth. Thick, violent, and white-hot orange that rivaled the sun's brilliance. Somehow, he knew its name and what it was. *Everburning Fire.* A fire that wouldn't extinguish until it consumed everything it touched. An ancient spell that drank deeply from the well of his flow. In the last moment, Nefrin attempted to erect a shield, only for the white-hot fire to devour it, sending him up in flames, ensuring his end.

At the same time, the other Reavers sent killing spells.

Zane turned his roar upon them.

Not as white-hot, but a scarlet inferno that consumed their spells. He sent it farther, breathing red tongues of fire that seared two Reavers, burning their faces, and they dropped their threads entirely. Korella, her eyes wild with fear and fury, was nearest to him. She screamed, summoning all of her spark. Straining, she dislodged part of the building and hurtled a hunk of stone the size of a draft horse toward Zane's head. Stone. He couldn't melt stone that quickly. So he rolled beneath the stone toward her and it skimmed his scalp. She raised a fist, threading a thick torrent of fire. "Die!" she screamed, terror and anger still contorting her soft features into a vile, depraved mask.

He grabbed her fist. "Wrong choice. Fire is mine."

She cried out, "You stupid little—"

He sent the fire back up Korella's arm and into her, erupting her spark in the core of her body.

She had only a momentary flicker of terror before it happened.

There was a burst inside the woman—Zane felt it—and a puff of orange essence escaped past her mouth. The last of her spark. Her eyes rolled back into her head, and she collapsed like a puppet with her strings cut.

From behind, more spells assaulted him in a wave.

He turned and roared again.

Spells of ice, metal, stone, moon, and sun all melted beneath the terrible red flames—that actually flickered from white to tongues of blue. A heat so strong it made the nearby brick and clay run. Reavers screamed, two more being burned alive. Yet they fought back, creating an onslaught of defenses as they'd been taught. Several Reavers threw up a six-foot-tall wall of stone, while others sent a hail of metal and ice that bombarded Zane. He burned these, too. The manacles on his wrists glowed red-hot. Damn it! He realized they still sapped his power, draining him. More than that, his "roar" was his only attack. It was a powerful spell, but not versatile. Not against this many trained Reavers, most of whom had decades of experience using the spark, especially now that they'd gained their composure.

The truth became clear: Zane *might* win, but he'd just as likely die trying.

More spells rained down on him, and he burned them from the air with small blasts of flame-breath, barely able to burn one before another came. Suddenly, he staggered to one knee as the next flames sputtered from his mouth, more smoke than actual fire. Thankfully, he'd vanquished the spells, but in their place a thick, acrid smoke filled the space between him and his foes.

More! his rage demanded. *Burn them all...*

It sounded like Pyre's rumbling boom.

But it wasn't Pyre, Zane knew.

It was him. His own voice, his own rage.

Zane squinted, peering through the haze. He'd spotted the Reaver's bulwark of stone when a figure staggered into view—blackened by his flames and wavering on his feet, but not dead. *Alive.* Zane seethed. Nefrin's eyes fixed to Zane with a madness, a fury that was no longer bound to sanity. His body was mangled—smoke still smoldered from his burnt and tattered robes. It was his once-tan, almost handsome, if arrogant, face that was the most altered. Where there had once been flesh, now the entire left side of it was a ghastly mix of red muscle and tendons—as if half his face had been flayed. Down the side of his neck were bubbling blisters. His hair was gone, seared away. Those eyes—they were red from popped blood vessels, and seething with hatred. *How is he alive?* Zane was certain he'd sent enough fire to kill Nefrin. He remembered the man's words: *I'm skilled with flesh.* He realized Nefrin, or the other Reavers, must have excised the skin from his body to stop the Everburning Fire. Nefrin was threading, and Zane heard the air crackle—the man was summoning enough spark to level the whole building.

Everything inside Zane told him to run. Hamstrung as he was, he was no match for this many spark-wielders, nor a four-stripe Reaver threading with his full power. Despite this, the dragon inside of Zane hungered to watch Nefrin's blood boil. Demanded that he hold his ground and "roar," defiant.

Burrrrnnnnn them alllll, it rumbled again.

Zane gave in to the rage, preparing to make his last stand, when another voice whispered in his head.

Live...please...

Hannah.

The Reavers were regaining their footing, and a wave of spells flew toward him, more deadly than even the last barrage.

Zane barely ducked a chunk of stone that would have taken his head from his shoulders. A shard of metal flew toward his chest and he burned it to molten slag that dropped to the ground. Again, he staggered, catching himself on the building. Though his flow still roared through him, the manacles were too much. Snarling in anger, he made his decision. With the last remnants of his restrained power, Zane roared fire in an arc.

White-hot flames rose ten feet high between him and his enemy.

He knew the name of this one too.

Firewall.

It wouldn't hold for long—not with that many Reavers working together. They'd shatter his spell shortly, but he only needed a moment. So with flames hot on his back, and despite everything inside him shouting, demanding that he finish Nefrin, Zane turned and ran, Hannah's voice echoing in his head.

You are...more...so much more...live, you big idiot.

Rising Winds

Gray maneuvered through the streets with Ayva and Helix as they followed Zane and his entourage.

Well…Helix lagged behind a little bit.

"Gray, slow down! Abyss take me, gads!" Helix called out, struggling to keep up with him and Ayva through the crowds of Covai. The streets were untamed, packed with people and beasts, the city toiling as the hot sun beat down from above.

Zane and his entourage finally came to a halt, and Gray pulled up with the others behind a jewelry stall. Why had Zane's company stopped? Then he saw the reason. A group of slaves. Men and women, young and old, chained together while a big crude-looking slaver with a haunch of meat made a scene. Gray's jaw clenched. He'd known Covai was rampant with slavery, and it was on his list to abolish—right next to not dying at the hands of a dark army, and finding the rest of the Ronin. Judging by the tense look on Zane's face and the way he spoke, he was pretty certain Zane was letting his opinion be known. The Guard Captain, however, smoothly stepped in and grabbed the slaver's whip.

Gray tapped into his flow and with threads of wind he crafted a spell he hadn't used in a while. Catching the vibrating air before their lips, he pulled the words to his ear in a stream and caught her name.

Captain of the Guard Leanna.

"Can someone tell me what we're doing?" Helix asked, panting. "Why are we following them?"

"Because we said we would," Ayva replied. She waved away the jewel vendor—a rotund man with a thick, curly black beard who was trying to sell her cheap pieces of "farlas," or rubies, which even Gray could tell were just chipped colored glass. "Besides, Zane's one of us."

Gray watched Nefrin, who seemed content to let the little spat play out. A cruel, dark look appeared in the Reaver's eyes whenever he thought someone wasn't watching.

He knew the man was trouble—Gray didn't need the ki to read that—so he would have to be wary. Nefrin seemed a favorite of the queen, and he had power in this twisted city. Luckily, the Guard Captain seemed…different. With the ki, he sifted through her, and she did nothing to wall up her emotions, which radiated off her clear as day—duty, honor, and…arousal?

Wait, what? Gray shook his head, growing flushed, and against every instinct telling him *not* to, he caught more words from Zane's conversation with her.

Did…did she just call Zane pretty?

Through the ki, Zane seemed just as perplexed. Well, beneath the mountain of anger that always boiled inside the Ronin of Fire.

"What are they saying?" Ayva asked, tugging on his arm.

"Uh…" Gray began, "you know, Zane stuff—short, terse, fiery."

"*Harkas, mira!*" the fat jeweler growled, shoving a blue "jewel" into Ayva's face.

"I said, 'no thank you,'" Ayva replied, more through clenched teeth than anything. She tossed a few coppers on the man's stand, and he just glared at them. "We just need another minute here, then we'll be out of your way, all right?"

The man huffed and crossed his arms across his barrel chest.

Helix folded his own arms. "I don't get this. Zane may be a Ronin, but he's not one of us—"

Ayva rounded on him. "Helix, just stop! You don't understand him. You don't know what he's been through!"

Instead of backing down, Helix's blue eyes blazed. "No, I don't, but do you? Does Zane even understand himself? Men like Zane use their anger as a tool to push others away, as a means to feel strong, but deep down, they're scared. That fear? It's going to burn us. Abyss take me, the way he is right now, how is he any different than Merrick, Ronin of Metal, who's trying to kill us all?"

The jeweler now resorted to yelling. He shoved a yellow glass shard at Ayva.

"*Hatas!*" Ayva shouted loudly in Covian at the pudgy man, eyes blazing golden. The heat from them melted the glass in the man's hands. He cried out, stumbled backward, tripped, and nearly upended an apple cart. Gray tapped into his Nexus and caught both apples and cart with wind, quickly righting it and apologizing to the apple vendor, who was now red-faced as his goods. At the same time, he threw a few more coins to the jeweler—the last of what he had—who was still sitting on his rear in the dusty road, stunned and mute. Gray then grabbed his two friends and dragged them away.

"Time to go," Gray said, pointing to Zane and company, who were starting to move again through the wild tangle.

"He was a con artist!" Ayva replied as he pulled them onward.

"Sure, but we were occupying his stall, and I think everyone in this city has a different moral compass than we do."

"Gray, that doesn't make it right," Ayva scoffed.

He shrugged. "Fair enough."

"I guess I'm just a little worked up still," Ayva said as they pushed back into the flow of people. "You know, what with facing a light-blinding dragon…"

"Tell me about it," Helix replied. "Did you hear it? It said 'the others want to meet us.' Is that as terrifying to you guys as it is to me?"

"Terrifying? More like exciting," Ayva said.

Helix fixed her with a stare as they shoved through a group of men haggling over a jug of water that inadvertently fell and shattered, spilling precious water on the sands. That set the group into a frenzy, and the squabble looked like it was about to break into a full fistfight. Gray looked to Helix, who rolled his eyes but caught on. Without breaking stride, Helix tapped into his flow, issuing threads of water into empty jugs at the men's feet. Helix pointed to the jugs. "Try those."

The ragged, thirsty looking men all looked inside the jugs to see sloshing liquid, then stared at Helix, grinning ear to ear and talking animatedly.

Ayva smiled at Gray with that narrowed gaze that meant: *I see what you're doing.*

Helix acted like nothing had happened and continued his point to Ayva. "So let me get this straight. Meeting a dragon, the most ancient of beings, who the stories say hates everything and everyone—*humans most of all*—and can wipe out whole cities…and you're just excited? Like, hanging out with an ole pal?"

Ayva bit her lip. "Well, maybe a *tiny* bit terrified."

"Thank you," Helix said.

The words echoed in Gray's head as they wove through the bustling streets, following Zane and the guards and keeping an eye on the man's broad back.

THE OTHERS WILL WANT TO MEET YOU SOON.

That's what Pyre had said.

The other dragons.

He should have been terrified, and a part of him admittedly was. Like Ayva, his heart thrummed in his chest, but his mouth was also bone-dry in dread. The nine primordial dragons were the most powerful creatures in all of Farhaven, and the Dragon of Wind was the strongest of them all. Well, aside from the titans, Renalin's children, and Renalin himself—but they were more myth. Still, the Dragon of Wind!

Some called him by his elemental name, Zephyr—much like Pyre, the elemental name of the Dragon of Fire. Yet most myths and legends knew him by his true name, one given by the elves in the ancient tongue. *Mali'cor*. Mali'cor wanted to meet him. Visions of the Dragon of Wind came to his mind. Mali'cor was said to be invincible. That no blade could pierce his gleaming scales, that he could disappear and reappear on eddies of wind, as well as level kingdoms with his hurricane-like squalls.

His gaze passed over the heads in the throngs of people and rose to the massive building in the distance.

The colosseum.

It jutted above the city like a bronze crown, its thousands of arches and columns all gleaming in the high sun. Gray half expected to hear the roar of the spectators and the cries of battle, even from so far away. *That's where all eyes will be,* he knew. *Where I have the chance of finding the rest of our kind.* It was time to move out of the shadows and into the light. Time for all the world to see that the Ronin were back and what they could do. Of course, if they won the tournament, the Covian Legion would be theirs to command—which would be necessary if they were going to win this war.

So again, he whispered under his breath, "I will win the tournament. I will unite us all."

"What was that?" Ayva asked at his side.

Gray eyed the colosseum again. "Nothing, just planning."

"Speaking of which," Helix said, "has anyone come up with a plan for how to get me out of the first round? You know, that whole brutal fight to the death?"

Gray put an arm out to stop Helix from being nearly run over by a team of giant cerabuls. They snorted and grunted, kicking up massive plumes of dust as they hauled a huge wagon filled with…some strange meat that Gray couldn't identify. "Let's try to keep from dying beforehand, deal?"

Helix swallowed. "Deal."

"As for getting you out of the lower rounds, I have some thoughts," Gray said.

"Oh, great, I'm all ears! You know, while I still have them…and a head."

Gray paused. "Yeah, I'll fill you in. First, Zane."

Helix grumbled.

Zane and company were just turning ahead, moving onto a grand thoroughfare filled with people. Here, along with the normal bustle of trade and vendors, giant statues lined the wide streets—towering, majestic forms of men and women. Many wielded an assortment of weapons, spears, shields, swords, and flanges, while some were barehanded, or held simple staffs. Their expressions fascinated Gray the most—from proud and imperious to wild and almost animal-like. True enough, one man looked more bear than human, with ragged furs covering his body and claws affixed to his massive hands. Scars covered every inch of his exposed muscled arms and legs, and the sculpture captured him mid-roar, mouth filled with…fangs?

"These are all Grand Primuses of the Grand Tournament of Flesh," Ayva whispered.

Most of the swirling masses in the street seemed to pay no mind to the statues, as if they'd seen the Grand Primuses a thousand times. Still, here and there, a passerby would touch a statue's feet and whisper a quick prayer before moving on.

Gray noticed gifts, food, and flowers at the base of many statues. Despite the corrupt, barbarous nature of the city, he had a feeling none would dare steal the offerings.

They're treated as gods, Gray realized.

Helix gulped. "You sure these were people? They look more like monsters."

Gray sighed. "I don't think they were all actually ten feet tall, Helix."

Ayva read a placard on the statue of the nearest Grand Primus—a man like a vision of death himself who had a giant sickle strapped to his broad back. In his hands he held a claymore the size of a man. "Anderous Moravosu. The Thresher. Grand Primus XXXI, of the Second Age. Forty-two wins in the games, zero losses. Eight feet tall."

"Eh, I'm sure they exaggerate," Gray said.

At the bottom of the inscription was a quote in Covian from the Grand Primus: "Ataras cwarla I blun. Ataris miras, hua seem. E tora wan fa li o fileras mo ataras eno"—Anderous Moravosu.

"Oh, look at that, something that guy liked to say. I'm fairly certain I don't want to know," Helix said.

Ayva read it, paled, and winced. "Yeah, probably not."

Helix sighed. "Tell me anyway."

"My Covian is a little rusty, still working on it, but I think it goes... *My currency is blood. My music, human screams. I long to watch the light of life flicker and fade from my enemy's eyes.*"

"Well, at least he was eloquent," Helix said, shivering. Then he pointed. "Look, they're taking Zane into the palace. See? He's safe. Can we go now?"

Sure enough, Zane and company were moving up a wide set of stairs leading to the hammered-gold doors of the palace.

"I don't get it," Ayva replied. "Why are you so dead set on abandoning Zane?"

Helix's jaw set. "Better question, why are you so dead set on trying to protect someone who doesn't give a damn about us?"

Gray joined in, clearing his throat. "I seem to remember another individual who didn't want anything to do with the Ronin when we first met him."

Helix folded his arms. "That's not fair."

"Sounds like the definition of fair," Ayva agreed.

Helix rubbed a hand through his short blond hair, watching the crowds who continued to bow and pray before the statues, and they moved a few feet away, behind the shadow of a graceful little champion that seemed a lot less venerated. "Look, I was different. I also wasn't—"

"Angry, with a chip on your shoulder?" Ayva finished.

Helix fixed her with a stare. "Fine, maybe I was a little like Zane. I *wasn't* violent. I was maybe distant, removed... scared. Not *scary*.

Zane's got so many demons, and you think he can vanquish them, but I've seen men like him. People who have that much hurt always end up hurting others," he said, then pointed to a small scar on his cheek. "Or don't you remember when he nearly killed me?"

"We've been over this," Ayva said, teeth gnashing, clearly losing her patience. "He didn't mean to. He'd just watched his sister die, and he sent out a wave of fire. You stopped him, but he was seeing red. It wasn't you he was trying to hurt. He was just…lost…traumatized. You know that."

What he'd suffered…

Ayva was just skimming the surface.

Zane had lost everything.

Hells, and now Evangeline was dead—did Zane even know about that? Gray doubted it, and he was terrified of how the man would react if he knew. The two were close, more than friends. Fate had dealt Zane a losing hand, but Gray would make sure Zane would rise above it.

Then he looked to Helix and read his friend with the ki. He hadn't grown as close to Helix as he had to Zane. Darius was the one who had spent more time with the Ronin of Water, and they'd been rubbing off on one another. Gray wasn't exactly sure that was a good thing. Two Dariuses was a lot. The ki delved into Helix, and emotions streamed into Gray. Surprisingly, he sensed duty, the calm of a dormant volcano, and beneath that, impatience. Anger like a waterfall, barely restrained.

Helix feared the part of him that was like Zane. A part of him that was wild, impulsive. Gray knew that because he feared it himself—a side that could be like Kail. With the bustle of the city surrounding him, he placed a hand on Helix's shoulder. "Zane's one of us, Helix. Just like you. I'm not going to abandon him…I think you know better than anyone that this power that's inside of us…it's not easy to control, like a raging river, and I know you're also afraid that if you let it go, it'll consume you, or worse—destroy those you care about."

Helix's eyes grew suspicious. "How…"

Gray smiled. He didn't mention using the ki, but instead told a half-truth, "I know, because it's my same fear. I'm telling you now, I'm not going to let that happen. Not to any of us. If I'm wrong, and you fall into despair, I'll pull you back out."

Ayva wiped at a tear that traced her cheek. "Gray…"

"Sorry, too much?" he asked, rubbing a hand through his hair, watching as Zane and his escort ascended the final steps.

"No," Helix said, smiling, "just enough. Hells, where's Darius to lighten the mood and say something stupid like—"

"'Gods, I got some sand in my eye…'" Gray posed.

"Yeah, or 'We're not supposed to cry until we win. Way too soon, guys,'" Ayva added in a Darius voice.

Gray paused, watching Zane and company for a moment longer. "I think Helix is right."

"I am?" Helix asked.

"Not about abandoning Zane, it's just there's no point in following him now. He's going to see the queen—she's a bit twisted in her motives, but she won't harm Zane."

"Nefrin?" Ayva questioned. "I don't trust him."

"True, but as long as he's with the Guard Captain, Zane is safe."

Ayva raised a brow, curious.

"I can sense her motives. She's good."

"'Good'? That seems subjective in this city. How are you so sure?" Ayva asked.

Gray delved into Ayva with the ki. Emotions assaulted him. *Anxious, proud, defiant.* Deeper still, he felt something…there was a light inside of her, growing every day. Not just hope but also a reservoir of strength, a sun's energy so powerful that it almost frightened him. For a flickering moment, he understood why the world feared them. Ayva was growing strong. Gray wondered if he was truly the most powerful of them.

Finally, he answered Ayva's question. "You're afraid for Zane, but it's deeper than that. You think if he can't be redeemed, that it'll affect me. That I might never overcome my fear of being the 'Blightseeker.' You're also worried because you think Zane's hiding something, which I'm sure he is. I'm not certain that what he's hiding is a bad thing."

Ayva folded her arms. "I hate you. I always forget you have the ki."

He shrugged. "If it's any consolation, I'm not sure I like having it."

"Okay, fine," Ayva said, looking out on the crowds of men and women, all seemingly caught up in a strange fervor. "Then what are we supposed to do? Just sit down in a tavern, drink, and wait?"

Gray turned to Helix.

Helix waved his hands. "Hey, don't you dare read me with the ki."

"Trust me, I try to stay away from you and Darius," he lied, not admitting he'd just read the man. Then he turned. "More importantly, we need a plan to get you out of the first rounds. Also…these crowds…something is going on."

"What do you mean?" Helix asked, eyeing the wagons and people, where a volatile, excited energy hung in the air.

"There's something off…the ki, it reads energy, and it's telling me something is about to happen."

The people, beasts, and wagon loads of goods were all heading in *one* direction, north. Toward the colosseum. Moreover, most of the people looked dressed for an occasion. Gray grabbed the arm of a passing man. The man had a bright orange shirt and loose tan pants, and judging by the ruddy hue to his sunburnt face, he looked deep in his drink already. Gray had actually interrupted him mid-swig from a sheep's bladder. "What's going on here?"

"You haven't heard?" a big man beside him asked, flabbergasted. "It's Opening Day!"

And the pieces clicked together.

"Oh gods, I think I'm going to be sick," Helix groaned, paling, until Gray was certain he was going to pass out.

Then the horns sounded.

The tournament had begun.

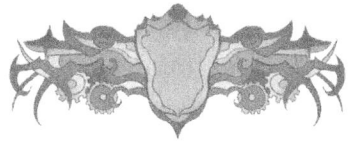

A Game of Elements

Merrick, Ronin of Metal, strode through the Citadel, ascending through the black stone corridors and heading toward the Upper Halls and the Patriarch's chambers, for he'd been summoned. After all, one never refused the Sovereign of the Citadel and Ruler of the Great Kingdom of Fire…or as he was known by his hidden title, the Dark One.

As always, the Citadel was thriving, a hub of men and women wielding the many elements of Farhaven—the green courtyards teeming with exhibitions of magic, while inside vaulted rooms and great chambers instructors taught everything about spells, incantations, the history of magic, and even fundamental herbology. Merrick hated all of it.

Magic, he spat, feeling the taint of it like slick oil on his skin, something which he could never rid himself of despite his every attempt. He set the loathing aside, aware of the many eyes following his every movement, as if he were a wolf among the sheep.

Countless Neophytes, young and old, in their clean gray robes and Reavers of various ranks in their renowned scarlet robes cast him furtive looks as he passed. Merrick was dressed in black, with Osmium on his back. Osmium, once called Iridal, also known as the famed Sword of Metal, was Merrick's constant companion. Merrick could transform the metal at will and now kept it as a bow on his back, his favored weapon. What many thought of as a simple black bow was something far more than they could ever imagine. In the right light, Osmium's surface gleamed, an iridescent glow unlike any other known metal.

He'd discovered the sword within the heart of Yronia when he was only a small boy, afraid of who he was, afraid of everything.

Now Merrick's fear had been recast into resolve.

A single-minded desire to end the world of magic and bring justice to those who had nothing—no more strength versus weakness. That meant drinking from the poisoned well. Yet, ultimately, the end would justify the means, or so he hoped.

More eyes followed him as he took another hallway up, knowing an impossible power waited for him.

They fear me, he said to Osmium.

The black bow replied, *Yes. People always fear authority or what they don't understand.*

Merrick took an even breath. *You'd think I'd be used to it by now,* he said as a group of Neophytes came into view. They'd been scurrying to their evening meals, or to run one of their countless errands, as they gossiped about one thing or another, when they turned a sharp corner and bumped into him. The three, noticing who it was, looked as if they'd seen a nameless in the flesh and cast their eyes down. One, a smaller girl, whispered to the oldest, "I-it's him, Evelyn…"

The oldest girl, likely his age, nearly twenty, with flaxen hair and wide blue eyes full of fear, elbowed the smaller one into silence and spoke up. "M-my Lord Merrick," she stammered, "we didn't see you there, a-apologies, we—"

He interrupted her. "It's all right."

They stood frozen, not knowing what to say, or how to extricate themselves, trembling in fear.

Merrick alleviated their distress. "I assume you have places to be?"

They looked as if he'd just saved them from the headsman's axe. "Yes, Lord Merrick! W-we do. Headmaster Anicia will be most cross if we keep her waiting again. Apologies once more," Evelyn said. The other two mumbled a quick apology, and they darted away, practically running from him.

Merrick sighed. *I didn't ask for this.*

Osmium answered dryly, *You did, Lord Merrick, when you chose this path…*

Are we on this again? Trying vainly to sway me to 'the path of good'?

No, Osmium replied. *I have made my thoughts clear already. I am…patient. There is good ore inside of you. I know you will discover it when the time is right.*

If I don't? Will you abandon me? Merrick asked, taking another dark hallway. He passed through a shimmering red force field that would have killed him if he didn't have his level of magic. It was just one in a myriad of protective measures on the way to the ruler of the Citadel.

I have chosen my path, as you have chosen yours, Osmium replied.

Merrick snorted. *Anyway, I wonder why he had to call me here now. There's other places I could be. Overseeing the forces in Median, for one. They are in shambles after the Ronin's actions. Those cursing fanatics are as likely to turn on us as aid us, and without someone there to watch over them...*

Osmium mused, *They're pirates, what did you expect?*

Merrick growled. *I suppose. Still, ash and brimstone, I would have been happy staying in Yronia.*

With the thousands of saeroks and vergs who also want to eat you?

They don't want to eat me.

They also fear you.

Fair, he said and walked on, passing a few three-stripe Reavers. He ignored their obvious disapproval. *At least with them there's no false niceties. They're direct. I prefer that.*

Literally evil creatures, not to be esteemed.

Yes, some would say I fall under that category as well, he said. He reached a door two-stories tall, made of hammered gold. Despite himself, he turned Osmium into a sword, then moved it to his hip. In close quarters, a sword was easier to swing.

Worried you'll have to defend yourself? From your own master?

I am simply cautious, he said, feeling the bite of bile in his mouth as he moved to open the door, only for it to swing wide on its own. It revealed a room, a vast library of sorts, and on the far end was the man himself. The oldest living mortal in all of Farhaven.

The Patriarch.

Instead of sitting behind a grand desk, he sat at a simple chair near a towering window that occupied the entire wall, revealing all of the Citadel—and the sprawling desert city of Farbs beyond that, a teeming mass of people, oblivious to the true nature of the man in the tower.

The Patriarch was playing a game of Elements on a simple glass board.

A figure was behind the Patriarch.

The leader of the nameless, the general of the armies.

A young girl, a Neophyte, shivered in the corner, holding a tray of wine.

The Patriarch, engrossed in his game, spared a look up.

Merrick's heart froze.

That look. The power, the knowledge, the wisdom it possessed...Despite Merrick facing dark spawn from hell itself, being unafraid of nearly dying a thousand times over, the look terrified him to the core and nearly sent him running. Every fiber in him said the Patriarch was no mortal, no mere man. *Yet, he is a man*, Merrick convinced himself. *And like all men of power, he must fall so humanity can rise again.*

The Patriarch made a gesture, and Merrick strode across the enormous room—another sign of vanity that should crumble—and came to kneel before his master, placing a fist to his chest.

"Welcome, my dear boy," the Patriarch said, his voice dry and crisp, like leather scraped with a knife, and full of unquestioned authority. "So good of you to make it."

Merrick kept his head bent, "My lord?"

A snort sounded above him. "Dear boy, you're among friends. No need to play the part of a humble servant." Merrick looked up to see the Patriarch scrutinizing him. It was impossible to know how old he was, but he was drawn to the Patriarch's eyes of fathomless gray, something between ash and smoke. "After all, we both know better than that. Were you thinking about my demise again, boy?"

Merrick's jaw tightened. He hesitated, his emotions roiling inside of him. He was conflicted. The Patriarch had found him at a young age, had saved his life when all the world felt pointless. He'd even given him meaning again. Much of who Merrick was today was due to the Patriarch's apparent benevolence, his constant direction. In many ways, the man was like the father Merrick never had. He who sat before him—a mortal of insurmountable power—clashed with Merrick's true purpose. Much like Merrick's own being conflicted with it. At last he answered, "I make no claim to hide my true feelings, my lord. While I never want to see you hurt, I do want what you promised me all those years ago. What you swore to me."

The Patriarch's eyes tightened, the creases deepened at the corners as he took in Merrick, "Yes, our little deal…the end of magic. Fear not, my dear boy." He looked back to the board and made another move, the glass clinking as he shuffled the fire piece forward. "I have not forgotten. I have summoned you for other reasons…"

Behind the old man, the huge nameless gave a long, hoarse sound that forced Merrick to suppress a shiver as its words grated like the rasp of a dying man's last breath. *"The stones…"*

The Nine Elemental Stones.

Merrick asked, "We have seven, do we not?"

"Yes, but I desire them all," the Patriarch said calmly, making another move, shifting the glass bauble of sun to the left. He was playing the game against himself, and from Merrick's cursory glance—quite experienced as he was with Elements—it was a close game, many moves ahead considered and then countered.

Merrick was familiar with the Nine Elemental Stones. Stories said they were powers given to kings and queens to help them counterbalance the Ronin's powers. Or that they were created by Renalin's daughter and hidden away from the Ronin, her father's gift to the world of Farhaven.

Merrick knew where the seven stones were kept, deep in the ancient vaults of Yronia. It was the most protected place in all of Farhaven, ancient safe rooms created by powerful Reavers and smiths during the height of the Ronins' power. The steward of Median had attempted to steal the stones, and Merrick had killed the man. "So you want me to get the two remaining stones?" he asked. "Is that all?"

"Yes…and no."

Merrick's eyes tightened. "My lord, I am but a humble servant, I might need further explanation."

The Patriarch issued a dry laugh. "Please, do not use the words 'humble' and 'I' in the same sentence. You are anything but, and I have taught you not to hide the furnace of your passion, but to let it burn." Glancing up at Merrick with a small, cunning smile, he added, sighing, "As for your duties, I want you to get *one* stone. One stone is still hidden. I have yet to uncover the location of the Windstone. It was sealed away like Morrow, hidden by the Ronin in their inexplicable wisdom to protect the future generations…from me."

"The other?"

The small smile returned as he continued to move pieces on the board. "Have you heard of the Grand Tournament of Flesh?"

Merrick huffed a laugh. "Yes, everyone has. It's happening now. The fools are fighting in frivolous little matches while the world crumbles around them."

The Patriarch, holding the figure of wind, paused, his eyes tightening. "Not as foolish as you may think. Your fellow…companions," he said, and Merrick tensed, "are cleverer than you give them credit for. They know they need armies, so they have gone to sway the queen and get the Covian Legion under their banner. More than that, the arena is a place of unique magic that, if they succeed, will make them far more formidable in the coming war."

Merrick frowned, then a sneer formed on his lips. "It still won't matter, I faced them before. They are weak. I can face them again and—"

"DO NOT UNDERESTIMATE THEM!" the Patriarch boomed, rising from his seat in a rush that sent the board, the pieces, and table flying—the room abruptly darkened ominously as if storm clouds gathered above, and the bookcases rattled and the floor trembled, as if the Patriarch could break the world in two beneath Merrick's feet. His power and ferocity made Merrick stagger back as if struck.

He fell to his knees, breathing hard, teeth grinding as silence reigned.

"Apologies, my lord…" Merrick breathed.

The shadows receded, and Merrick saw the Patriarch's fingers dance and everything returned as it was, floating back into place: the board, the table, the books.

All the while, the nameless hadn't shifted an inch.

Merrick knew it was staring at him from within its cowl.

The serving girl in the back, whimpering and cowering, had dropped her platter, and even that hovered back to its original place as she opened her eyes.

The Patriarch resumed his game as if nothing had happened, moving another piece on the glass board.

Merrick swallowed, licking his lips, his voice a little more cautious as he asked, "Then, my lord, if I might be so bold…why don't we move on them now?" He tried not to sound impertinent despite his rising restlessness.

"Because," the Patriarch replied with eternal patience, "I need the Nine Stones. What you don't see, my dear boy, may indeed kill you. The dagger in the dark." Slowly, the Patriarch lifted the element of fire again, moving it beside the element of moon. "As we speak, there is a second force moving in the shadows. The Thieflords are making their move."

"The Thieflords?"

"Yes, but fear not, I have a plan to deal with them as well."

"Then what about the Great Kingdoms?"

"The Great Kingdoms are broken," said the man with a wave of his hand. "Stone is a recluse; Wind is lost to time; Leaf is ours—held firmly by Dryan; Water is shattered, a shell of its former self; Moon, now that the Shadow King has been dealt with, is in my favored servant Leah's hand; Metal's dark forges are ours, Fire…well, Fire is of course mine. Only Flesh, Sun, and a fragment of Water still have the potential to stand against us now. I am fairly certain Vaster, in the hands of Lord Nolan, will side with the Ronin when the time comes."

Merrick shook his head. "My lord, if they band together and gather the Great Kingdoms of Water, Sun, Flesh, and Stone…that's their four kingdoms to our four. Even weakened, that is formidable."

The Patriarch held that same slight smile. "You are basing that assumption on the belief they *will* be able to unite the other kingdoms."

Merrick opened his mouth. "I saw them with my own eyes. I was wrong before. They are…relentless."

Cautious, the Patriarch made a move on the board.

Merrick's eyes narrowed.

He'd been taught Elements from birth; he was good, by some measures even a master. But the Patriarch was leagues beyond that. A living legend, most would say. Still, the elderly old man had made a mistake, as clear as day.

The Patriarch continued, speaking as if nothing had happened, sighing in a paternal way. "Yes, it is in their blood…I'm sure you can sense it in yours. A duty to protect. Something I admire. All these years, my young boy, where do you think you learned this sense of wariness…of caution…"

"You, Father," Merrick answered at last, saying the word he had not uttered for years.

"Yes. And I am nothing if not patient, my son."

Merrick eyed the board, his hand impatient.

The Patriarch gestured. "You want to make a move, do you not?"

Merrick did and moved the metal piece with his power, shifting it with a slow gesture of his fingers to land it three squares forward—a killing move with no downside, taking the piece of fire.

"You see, dear boy," the Patriarch said slowly as he methodically made his move, one that…wasn't at all what Merrick expected, "there is one thing that wins against the power of tenacity." He gestured to the board, and Merrick's heart raced.

He was cornered, backed against the wall, until…there! He saw a way out. A slim chance with a few other moves. He moved again. Sweat trickled down his brow as his mind focused on the board.

The Patriarch didn't touch the board, but waved a hand, and a piece that Merrick had never expected moved, landing two squares from his most valued figurine. Merrick's heart skipped a beat, his breath taken.

Just like that…

He'd lost.

"How…"

The Patriarch rose, moving to the tall windows, staring out north—as if gazing toward Covai, the Great Kingdom of Flesh. "I have not lived, not planned for a thousand years simply to take risks now. Assuming they can gather the four Great Kingdoms, and find their blades and the rest of their kind"—his voice was a harsh grate now, full of venom and raging fury—"it will mean *nothing*. Many will fall, but we are stronger than they know. Even you know."

"Then what do you fear? What's moving in the shadows?"

Eyes narrowed, the Patriarch replied, "You must go to the Great Kingdom of Flesh." With a wave of a hand, the nameless misted out of existence, then into it again and slammed a paper down on the desk. Merrick stepped nearer to see what it was. A contract. No, an invitation to compete in the tournament, signed with his name. The Patriarch stood with his back turned. Merrick could still feel his grin widen as if he were positioning the final pieces on the board of life. "It's time, my dear young man, for you to win a tournament."

After the man left, the Patriarch remained standing at the window of the Citadel. He looked out over his city, its black ramparts with hundreds, if not thousands, of Neophytes and Reavers who trained, walked the halls, or scurried to their next chore or class. All the while, he felt their magic, tiny sparks like a thousand fireflies in the dark web of his mind.

He didn't disparage them for their weakness. No. That would be pointless and petty. Nor did he pity them. Instead, he…saw them as seeds, some yet to grow into small saplings, some never to take root in their lifetime. Others, however, like Merrick…their seeds had the potential to grow into something truly wondrous.

Hands clasped behind his back, he felt his age. He picked up a piece from the board—a figurine of wind—and rolled the smooth piece between his aged fingers as he watched Devari spar below, blades flashing. "You believe he will win the tournament?" Isilnar asked in a deep guttural rumble, deep enough to rattle his old bones with its gravelly rasp. Just hearing his voice would make men break lines in war and run

The Patriarch continued to watch the grounds. "Perhaps. But it matters not. He is merely meant to distract the Ronin and keep them out of my way."

"I thought you trusted the boy."

"I do," he replied honestly. Far below, a two-stripe Reaver was instructing a group of Neophytes on the intricacies of using flesh as an element, triggering pressure points in their friends and on a simulacrum dummy. "He is…special to me. His heart was darkened long ago. Turning him will be more difficult than the other Ronin can possibly imagine." Merrick's past was…complicated. Of course, he knew all about it. After all, it only made sense that he would. "But as I told him, I have my plans."

Frizzen Marauders to the west.

The Thieflords' feeble attempt to find a Master of Shadows—one that he foresaw and could easily thwart.

The battle in Eldas led by his puppet Dryan against Karil, the daughter of the previous king, and her forces.

And of course, his armies amassed in Yronia and Median.

The Nine Stones.

All these plans and more Isilnar knew of, and behind the Patriarch, the powerful nameless's discontent was palpable. The Patriarch turned to face his old friend. The room, his room, was expansive. A steepled ceiling spiraled upward, impossibly tall, large stained glass windows thousands of years old, made before he was even born, let in diffuse light. Towering bookshelves with endless tomes filled the walls. Artifacts, ancient objects, all powerful and invaluable, sat on a hundred different stands, pedestals, and shelves all about the room. Some items were from his predecessors, though most were his.

The truly valuable relics, however, were housed elsewhere.

A painting on the wall showed two ancient men with hoary beards and too-keen eyes, each similar, yet as different as could be.

His…predecessors.

There'd only been two Patriarchs before him, first-rank Arbiters. They had lived long lives as well. Though none so long as him. After all, they didn't have the same tenacity, the same resources…the same undying passion that would shape the very fabric of reality. The rest of the room was as expected. A large white desk carved out of a single giant silverroot, a species that was rarer than bloodstone, with elegant gold trim. The floor was an exquisite geometric pattern using rare marbles, while rich rugs from Aster cushioned his feet.

All priceless. But all worthless in his eyes.

Save for the game below him, a relic he'd found long ago. The little figurines were more priceless than any knew. He was down to the last six.

Isilnar, a few paces away, and avoiding the light from the window in the shadows, stood like a giant sentinel. The nameless's hood was deep, but the Patriarch saw within it. Flesh clung to his bony face, stretched out across the bones like webbing. Unlike other nameless, who had no eyes, Isilnar was unique. Dark, pitiless orbs filled his haunting skull. The Patriarch was a tall man, broad-shouldered—not that that mattered. No one was intimidated by him because of his stature. That would be like…burning alive on a cross and fearing the splinter. Yet Isilnar was taller, wider than him. "Speak your mind, old friend."

Soulless eyes fixed on him, and Isilnar's dark voice rasped, deep and demanding, "Merrick is young, so he does your bidding, but he should have asked. Why are you not going yourself? Or sending me?"

With a wry smile, the Patriarch replied, "Median was sacked, your blade tasted hundreds…is your thirst for blood not quenched?"

Isilnar's eyes burned. "Not until we are finished. Not until our pact is fulfilled."

Their pact…a bond, a promise, a vow. One they'd made nearly two thousand years ago. "Yes, and it's coming to fruition." He turned back, looking at the grounds once more. So many of them…like a thousand little ants. The Patriarch watched as a young girl running across the courtyard with books in her hands tripped, dropped the stack, and then scrambled to pick them back up. "So many small lives, yet each trivial moment is so important…it is all they know."

"I ask again, old friend, why not you?"

The Patriarch sighed, eyes tightening. "Because, I am being watched."

In his peripheral vision, Isilnar's face showed shock, as much as it could. "Who could you possibly fear?"

"An age-old opponent, and clever adversary. One who remains close, yet beyond my reach. He knows far too much already. If I make a bold move now, he will know, may interfere, perhaps even disrupt so many of my well-laid little pieces," he said, eyeing the board of Elements again, all perfectly arranged. Then he fixed Isilnar's dark, merciless eyes with his own. "I cannot have that, Isilnar." He held his old friend's gaze, a burning fire slowly rising inside of him. "*I will not have that.*" A dark storm churned inside the Patriarch, and he knew despite the terrifying menace in the soulless man's eyes, his own were far more pitiless. Finally, under the heat of that gaze, Isilnar was forced to look away.

"Forgive me." Isilnar bowed his head, casting his eyes to the marble floor. "I was wrong to question your wisdom."

The Patriarch sighed, moving closer. He put a weathered hand to the shoulder of his closest companion, feeling the dark cloth covering it, but also beneath the cloth to layers of tough sinew, tendon, and bone. Power roiled inside of Isilnar, and while the Patriarch did not have the ki, he understood what burned inside the soulless man, for it raged inside of him too. "You were not wrong, old friend. Simply impatient. I know what you sacrificed. I know all too well," he said, as Isilnar looked up once again with empty pitch-black eyes. They were once so full of life. They still held the same conviction. But they'd been blue once, so long ago, a shade like the Abyss—turbulent and deep. He still remembered it, and those days, when the only way out was *through*.

He smiled, his grandfatherly smile that softened so many to his side. That made many let down their defenses. "But do not fear." Then he held up the wind element in his hand, eyeing the clear glass bauble in the light. "Soon, I will be able to make my move."

"How soon?"

"Very soon," he said reassuringly, "and when I do, the world will know." His grip tightened around the glass figurine. "Every piece that I have set up will fall into place, one after another." Now he touched it, a seemingly bottomless well that stretched for ages—his power. Unlike others, he didn't just conjure threads to manipulate water, moon, sun, leaf, stone, flesh, or metal. He breathed the elements into life—understood every facet that comprised the tiny shard of glass in his hand, the filaments of water, of stone…he knew them to his bones. With the faintest trickle, he sent out a fragment of his magic.

The young girl—seemingly forgotten in the corner—who until this moment had listened to everything, watching all the while in terror and still holding a tray and glass pitcher of water, whimpered as the Patriarch turned to face her.

"So, dear girl, you've heard much…do you promise to say nothing of what you witnessed here today?"

Her head bowed low as she practically sobbed the words, "Yes, Patriarch. I vow it, I swear it on my life." And she meant it. Raising his hand, the magic spiraled into her, cutting, just a quick snip that sealed the binding words.

"Good. Then you may go, Neophyte," he told her, waving a hand.

"Y-yes, Patriarch." The girl got up and attempted to shove the tray and glass pitcher onto the table, but only managed to place them halfway on. They teetered and shattered to the marble floor. She gasped, looking as if she was going to die of fright, as if he'd turn her to ash. Only he smiled thinly, and waved it off. She stammered an apology and fled.

"You simply let her go?" Isilnar asked. "The girl will tell others."

"I put a spell on her. If she seeks to spill our secrets…well, then, the pact she made will bind her throat and she will die before the words leave her mouth." He snorted. "As for why? Ezrah is cunning and seems to know what I'm doing. I am hoping to root out where his eyes and ears are. If she's one of his little spies, then she'll help squash these little nosy insects who hear too much. If she's innocent? Well, she will live with a very interesting story that she'll never be able to tell."

Once she was gone, the Patriarch held up the tiny clear figurine of wind, and the glass crumbled into nothing between his fingers, vaporizing into the air—not ash, or smoke, or soot, or molten glass. No remnants of the object remained.

It was gone.

The Patriarch grinned, looking north. "One by one, all will fall."

Blood and Dust

Gray stood before the massive colosseum. Dust stung his eyes, his mouth was dry, sweat rolled down his back, and cries from the crowd filled his ears. Throngs of people pushed at his sides. Many were shoved to the ground in the thick tangle. More than once, Gray had to help someone smaller to their feet. As his power grew, so, too, did his senses, and the smell of sweat, blood, and roasting meat filled his nostrils. But the strongest was that of impending violence.

He viewed the double-wide stone doors, so tall that he had to crane his neck. They let in the flood of people—Covian guards in leather and tan cloth yelled for order. His heart raced as the colosseum loomed larger and larger with each successive step.

"I don't like this," Ayva said, speaking his thoughts aloud as she helped up a woman who had been shoved to the ground.

"What was it?" Helix asked. "The bloodlust in the air, or the people being nearly trampled to death?"

"All of it," Ayva said.

Nearby, food vendors shouted, *"Harkas untari!"* as they moved up and down the lines with steaming trays of meat kebabs, savory-smelling pies, and haunches of meat.

Ayva raised a brow. "Is there anything that's not meat in this city?"

Gray turned to see Helix exchanging coin and grabbing two skewers slathered in a thick brown sauce.

They both looked at him.

"What?" Helix asked.

"You don't even know what type of meat that is," Ayva said.

Helix shrugged. "I don't want to know, so please don't tell me." He took a bite, groaning and speaking around a mouthful. "Mmmm, wow, that flavor…smoky, sweet, but also a bit of tang? Mock Covai all you want for its very questionable morals, but they do grub right."

Ayva raised a brow. "Yeah…I'll take your word for it."

He offered her one. "Here."

She waved it off. "No thanks."

Helix shrugged. "Your loss. Gray, mysterious meat kebab?"

Gray smiled a little weakly. "As appealing as you make that sound, I'm good."

Ayva tucked a lock of blond hair behind her ear, squinted up at the sun, and said, "Helix, I'm pretty certain you have a fight today or tomorrow. You know, that death match you unwittingly signed up for that you *need* to win?"

Helix looked a little green. "Don't remind me."

"Exactly, so are you sure you want to be gorging yourself on mystery meat? Isn't that a recipe for disaster? Fighting and suddenly having to... release your inner demons?"

Helix eyed the skewer for a moment as if debating whether the snack was friend or foe, then shrugged and took another bite. "Don't worry so much. Besides, this'll prolly be my last meal, so I oughta enjoy what little time I have left."

Suddenly, fingers like a vise grabbed Gray's shoulder and a voice rumbled, "You're in the wrong line, friend."

Gray turned, readying threads of wind, only to see a giant of a man with a brimming smile. His long black hair was braided close to his scalp, and his heavily muscled black arms were marred with tiny scars from thousands of fights. The man's size and presence reminded him of Golgath, the warrior he'd fought in the pit of Median, and his heart hurt for a moment, remembering the man. Golgath had died protecting the city. "Wrong line?" Gray asked, a little tense. "I didn't see a sign anywhere or..."

"Relax, friend, I am only chafing you. I'm Drega," he said, putting a hand to his broad chest. "Pleasure to make your acquaintance, Ronin of Wind."

Gray nodded, a little taken aback. "Pleasure..."

Then Drega looked to Helix. "You're Water, I presume?"

Helix just nodded, his mouth full of mystery meat.

"You're smaller than the legends say, but there's cunning in your eyes." He grunted. "Your foes will be sorry if they take your stature as a measure of your strength. You will do well upon the sands."

"Thanks?" Helix said, wiping his mouth.

"Are you," Ayva began, "the leader of the Fleshguard?"

"I am. You must be the Ronin of Sun, as intelligent as you are beautiful." He bowed deeply. "Your foes will equally tremble."

Ayva actually blushed at this.

How'd you know? Helix sent.

Fleshguard cloak, two bands of blue on his swords, like the spear of Dalic, the Algasi leader.

"Are we actually in the wrong area?" Gray asked.

Drega grunted. "Indeed. The tournament is about to begin. I've been informed you're a Primarian, my Lord Ronin, so your match is not until later, but on the other hand, you are a Noxii…" He turned, grinning at Helix. "Yours is about to *begin,* my Lord Ronin. Come now, no need to enter via the commoners' entrance." He put his arm around Helix's shoulder, ushering him onward.

Um, help? Helix sent, glancing back over his shoulder.

Gray and Ayva looked at one another, shrugged, and ran to catch up. They quickly navigated through the crowds.

Helix gulped, "About to begin? Like now?"

"Yes!" Drega said enthusiastically, guiding them through the throng, though most of the crowd quickly parted from his tall stature and intimidating face, or perhaps they glimpsed the Fleshguard attire. "Can you not hear it?" He cupped a big hand to his ear.

Gray suddenly did. The thumping feet, the boom of the crowds, and a roar of cheering. "They're warming up the arena," he said in realization.

"Indeed, the Bloodbath is about to begin! You can't miss your opening day, my Lord Ronin!"

They were led past a long line of rough-looking warriors that hailed from all over Farhaven. Many snarled as they passed, until they realized who was leading them and then they quieted like dogs whimpering beneath the lash.

Helix asked, "So uh, what's the first battle about? I don't have to fight you, do I?"

Drega boomed in laughter, startling those nearest them. "If only! Gods, what I wouldn't do to be a Noxii and fight in the Bloodbath."

"What is a Noxii?" Ayva asked.

"Well, criminals, degenerates, the lowest of the low, of course!"

Helix looked like he was going to faint.

As Drega led them into the warrens of the colosseum, more Covian guards dipped their heads in respect to the Fleshguard leader. As they moved through a training ground filled with wooden dummies and men sparring, Gray caught glimpses of the arena through slits in the wall, and the sights beyond stole his breath.

Thousands of people filled the stands, and Drega pointed to the expansive sand arena below. "Ah, flesh and blood I remember those days…" His eyes grew misty. "Fighting within an inch of your life with nothing but your bare hands, clawing and scraping like an animal…I've never felt more alive." Drega shook himself and actually wiped away a tear, returning to the moment as if remembering where he was. "Anyway, no, I'm afraid. As leader of the Fleshguard, they've forced me into the later rounds. I'm a Primarian-hadus, just below my Lord Ronin here." He clapped Gray on the back, then patted the hilts of his two swords, one at either hip. "With luck, and if the gods favor me, I'll have the honor of my swords crossing both of you."

Gray took them in more closely. As Ayva had noted, there were two bands of blue on the hilt of each sword, and symbols of Flesh emblazoned into each pommel. Their grips had literal indents from the man's fingers. Drega's swords had a distinct air of rarity, though he was also aware that the man coolly cast an eye more than once to their own swords.

"But first, you must survive the Bloodbath as a Noxii, my young Ronin," Drega continued. "Then the ranks are Primarian-basaeri, Primarian-hadus, like me, then Primarian, your leader here, and of course, you must know the last two, Primus and the Grand Primus."

Then Gray processed what the man had said. *The leader of the Fleshguard, one of the most elite warriors in all of Covai, is a Primarian-hadus, and I'm a Primarian, one rank above him?*

Helix clearly had the same thought and sent, *Uh, Gray, if this guy is a Primarian-hadus, who the heck are you fighting as a Primarian?* Helix was actually sweating. *Are you sure they don't have you confused with the original Ronin?*

Honestly, I'm starting to wonder that myself, Gray admitted. Then he glanced at Ayva, who was oddly quiet, staring up at Drega's imposing figure until she nearly bumped into a Covian guard. Gray used a zephyr of wind to correct Ayva's path.

You're welcome, Gray sent.

Huh?

"Anyway," Drega said, clapping Helix on the back again, making him cough, "look at me, chatting your ear off like we're old drinking buddies when you have people to grind into dust or beat into a bloody pulp! Ha, ha, ha!" His booming laughter scared a few serving girls carrying pitchers, making one of them stumble.

Gray caught the silver pitcher on a cushion of wind, guiding it back into her hands.

"Ronin…" one whispered.

Both wore diaphanous gowns of pink and yellow, and they blushed at his smile as they moved on. Gray looked back over his shoulder for a moment and caught their gaze, and they giggled together, covering their mouths with their hands as they batted their eyelashes coyly.

Gray? Ayva sent. *Less mooning over pretty girls, more saving Helix?*

Gray rolled his eyes. *What? I…never mind,* he grumbled, not deigning to give her a response as they returned to the moment. A boom of cheers and the stomp of feet practically bowled them over. As he watched Drega move a few steps ahead, his thoughts spun like a maelstrom…planning how best to win the tournament, stop an ancient evil, and find the others.

Morrowil rattled at his side, as if the sword were eager, hungry to cut through all opposition and find a way to victory.

The sword whispered, *The greater the challenge, the greater the reward.*

Gray sighed. *I don't like it when you can read my thoughts.*

Not your thoughts, just the emotions behind them. I can only hear your thoughts when you speak to me directly.

The roar of the colosseum resonated in Gray's heart. *Then tell me, if you're so smart, how do we win this?*

You already know the answer. Your Devari training will provide you with a practical battle plan. Use your ki to understand who is friend or foe in this city—there are many deceptions. As for gathering the other Ronin, you will have more luck if you assemble the others. Bring the Ronin of Fire to your side, and the rest will be found.

I will bring them all together. I will win.

An admirable zeal, young Ronin. Your predecessor would be proud.

"Well, here we are!" Drega boomed abruptly. "The tournament's waiting chambers." Two double doors were thrown wide as they entered a bowl-like room. At the far end was an iron gate that revealed the colosseum arena.

The chamber was packed with fifty or more rough-looking warriors of all sorts, the dark room lit by flickering torches that cast the men in an eerie, almost moody light. The scent of sweat and fear assaulted Gray's nostrils.

He didn't need the ki here…nor would he want to try.

Brutality and death were the only things on anyone's mind.

"What is this place?" Helix asked.

Drega answered, "Think of it like a waiting room…for death. For the first round here you'll find all your fellow Noxii combatants, who hail from all over Farhaven, quite a lively lot."

Sure enough, several men in the room wrestled or shoved each other, while others brooded, backed against the clay walls like caged beasts. Covian guards with whips watched over the fighters, likely keeping them from running away or starting brawls.

"They seem…unsavory," Ayva said, wrinkling her nose.

"Ha! An apt word! The first round has the habit of attracting the most depraved, dark scraps that lurk in the shadows…but also a few rough gems just waiting to be born again into something more. Word of advice? Try not to make too many friends. You may have to kill them later." Drega gestured as one man grabbed another and bashed his head against a pillar. In another part of the chamber, three group of men were at each other's throats in a wild scramble. A handful of guards leapt in, trying to break up the mad tangle. "Well, they're in a cheery mood! Destiny awaits!" Drega boomed, again slapping Helix heartily on the back.

Helix gulped, watching as the men were pulled off one another and forced to different parts of the darkened room. One man in particular—wrapped in belts, blood smeared across his face, and red painted over his chest—took four guards to subdue. "Oh gods…"

"Fear not, the gods will surely be on your side, my Lord Ronin! I'll leave you three for parting words. Once you're done saying goodbye, you two can accompany me to the Upper Terrace." With that, the leader of the Fleshguard moved down the hall to converse with a few Covian guards, who looked terrified in his presence.

Helix gulped. *"Goodbye?"*

Gray grabbed Helix's shoulders, pulling him into an alcove a few steps away from the chamber. "Helix, listen closely. You've got this."

"I do?"

He smiled. "Like it or not, you're a Ronin. You're not going to die here."

"Here? I'd rather not die at all…"

Gray shrugged. "Well, I might be able to help with that… I'm still working out the details of a bigger plan. Before we left Seria, I learned some things that should help. First, the bad news is I don't think you can use your sword in the lower rounds." He nodded to the sword at Helix's side. "Weapons are only permitted after the Bloodbath."

"Can we stop calling it that?" Helix gulped as a bone-shattering crack and a bloody cry sounded through the walls, followed by more cheers.

Gray winced. "Right, sorry. Anyway, I didn't have a lot of time to do more digging. Apparently, the tournament has existed for almost a thousand years, so the rules are pretty ironclad." In truth, most of what Gray learned was from Morrowil. But he wasn't ready to unveil his chats with an inanimate object just yet.

Helix growled, "Great, so what about the whole 'to the death' thing?"

Gray explained, "The first round is a free-for-all. From my Devari memories, I know that means if you engage first, you'll be targeted. Looks like there's at least fifty or so gladiators in there. Even if they allow you to use your full power—"

"Wait… are you saying I can't use my magic?" Helix asked, wide-eyed.

Gray winced. "No, you can use the flow but it will be limited—you can't just put everyone in a giant icicle."

Helix's face grew a little more ashen. "Great. No sword. Hamstring my power. What else?"

"Pretty sure you'll still be the strongest which usually means they'll be aiming for you."

"What if I hide?" Helix asked.

Ayva planted her hands on her hips, "And how exactly are you going to do that? You know, in an arena with a hundred thousand eyes?"

"Fine, hiding is out, so I just try to avoid all conflict and wait for opportune moments?"

"I'm afraid it's not that simple." Gray took a deep breath and added, "I didn't say this before, but…there's something else. As a Ronin, it's not about just winning, but the *way* we win."

Ayva narrowed her eyes, as if catching on.

Helix raised a brow. "I thought I was just trying to survive. Now you want me to be flashy?"

Gray answered, "If we're going to spearhead this war, we need to demonstrate we're worthy to lead." He fixed Helix with a look. "That's why you can't hide, or play cat and mouse. We need to show the world the Ronin are back. Like it or not, you're the first Ronin many have seen outside of reading about them in storybooks. This is our chance. Show them who we really are and what we're capable of."

Another thunder of applause sounded from within the arena. Helix wiped a bead of sweat from his forehead, then glanced into the dimly lit chamber as men clambered toward the iron gate, readying themselves. "Right, anything else?"

Gray nodded then lowered his voice. "Find an ally. Someone strong. You may have to fight each other eventually, but at least you won't kill each other right away. Lastly, when inside the arena, stick to the walls to keep your back from being blindsided."

Helix nodded. "Got it. Strong ally, back to the walls, and flashy win." He shrugged, despite looking a little pale. "Easy, I can do this." Suddenly, another bloody cry resonated through the thick walls—the cry continued until it was suddenly cut off. This was followed by a storm of cheers loud enough to drown the world. Helix turned ghost white. "Oh gods, I changed my mind. Yep, definitely not doing this—" He took one step, then froze. "Gray, don't look now, but I think you're glowing."

Gray looked down, following Helix's gaze as bright red light flared beneath his sleeve. He pulled back the cloth to reveal a symbol slowly etching itself in red ink onto his arm, resembling scarlet flames.

When it was finished, Ayva whispered a curse.

It was three red swords with cross guards, all in a line, like claw marks.

Mark of the gladiator, but yours signifies the mark of a Primarian gladiator, Morrowil explained in his head.

Gray somehow knew something like this was coming. *This has to do with the contract, doesn't it?*

Correct, Morrowil sent. *It'll keep you near the colosseum until you fulfill your pact. Each stage grants the gladiator more privileges, both within the arena and without—not limited to wealth. It provides access to restricted areas, and social standing in Covai. The Ronin of Water will attain his first sword if he wins this next battle.*

Gray echoed aloud the sword's words, though refrained from adding the word "if."

"How do you know all that?" Ayva asked.

"Read about it," Gray lied. He looked at Drega at the end of the hall, still chatting with the guards, but he couldn't make out the man's inner forearm from this angle. He hadn't noticed the arm of the queen's right hand, Nalia, though it might have been covered. He'd be sure to look for it now.

"Helix?" Ayva asked. "Are you...are you okay?"

Helix said nothing, looking at the chamber beyond. "I...I don't know if I can do this..." he said, a tremble in his voice.

"You're wrong," Ayva declared.

Helix looked up, frowning.

She continued, "I'll be the first to admit, when I first met you I didn't think you'd turn out to be anything more than a thorn in my side." He frowned, opening his mouth, but she continued, her tone shifting, "Then you fought beside me in the glades...then what you did in Median...Helix, light and ash, you brought a water serpent to life! As if that wasn't enough, you faced hordes of saeroks and vergs to save countless people. Then you helped us find the lost city of Seria." Ayva pointed to the chamber. "So you're wrong. I know you're afraid, but if you ask me, they should fear you."

Helix rubbed a hand through his short, shaggy blond hair. "Well...when you put it like that..." Then his eyes changed, a hard, resolved glint entering them that reminded Gray of Helix's predecessor, Hiron, the first Ronin of Water. "You're right," Helix said, then looked to Gray. "Let's win this thing."

Cries reverberated through the halls. The mark was clearly a theme through the colosseum. The Ronin of Water grinned, a sudden bright look in his eyes, and said, "*Anyway*, thanks for the pep talk. I'd love to stay and chat, but I gotta mingle with some likely murderers and cutthroats! Of course, try to become best friends with a giant, who I'm sure would rather crack my bones and use them for toothpicks. Hey, maybe some of Darius's charm has rubbed off?"

Ayva rushed forth and hugged Helix fiercely, then pulled away, eyes glassy.

Gray gripped Helix's shoulder. "I'd say good luck, but we make our own."

Helix mused, "I like that. Sounds very Darius-like. Now get out of here, Primarian. See you in the upper matches." With that, the Ronin of Water tossed them a wink and dipped through the doorway and into the chamber.

Drega abruptly appeared. *"Friends!"* he boomed. "Have a good chat with your companion? Sure you did! Ha! Shall we continue?" He wrapped his heavy arms around their shoulders, leading them on without waiting for an answer. "We ought to hurry—don't want to miss anything!" With that, they followed the big man through the massive structure that was the colosseum—passing all manner of people—while the stomping of feet, and the beating of drums thundered in Gray's head like the march of war.

Ayva put a hand to her stomach. "Is it always like this? I'm not even competing and I feel like I'm going to lose my breakfast."

"That's the nerves!" Drega said, looking over his shoulder and grinning. The hallways grew more crowded as they went deeper into the colosseum. With Drega's broad-shouldered frame, his tan Fleshguard cloak fluttering behind him, people made way for the trio. "Ah, I can feel it in the air! Makes you feel alive!" He winced. "Or lose your bowels. Far less pleasant. Alas, everyone reacts differently!"

Ayva sent through the bond, *I don't like this.*

Gray looked over at her. She was biting her lip, her usual nervous trait, yet at her side, her hands were balled into fists. *Because Helix is about to fight in a battle called the Bloodbath? Or because you're not the one fighting?*

Ayva snorted. *Both? It's ridiculous that they won't allow women unless you're already seeded into a later round!* She sighed. *It's more than that. I don't like how little we know about the tournament. The queen is offering us her legions if we win, but I think she's got something up her sleeve.*

I agree, Gray said as he passed more serving girls who tittered at him. Gray shook his head. What was happening? That was the second group of women who seemed bashful and blushed at his presence.

What? Ayva questioned.

It doesn't matter. Images of his grandfather's face—Ezrah—came to his mind and he added, *A wise man once told me 'We can only do the best with what we've been given.' So, she can throw whatever she wants. We'll win regardless.*

Ayva nodded, a glimmer in her blue eyes.

"This is your stop, my Lord Ronin! My Lady Ronin will follow me to the Upper Terrace."

Ayva wrapped her arms around his shoulders, then pulled away. "You got this."

Gray winked. "So do you. Watch over the queen."

She nodded, and with Drega at her side, chatting amiably, his voice booming, they disappeared down the corridors. Gray turned and opened the doors to his new chambers, and his jaw dropped.

A Little Less Public

Zane ran for his life, pushing his way through the wild tangle that was Covai, sprinting from Nefrin and the chaos he had just sown. He didn't know if he was still being followed, so he kept running, not willing to risk it. The manacles at his wrists attracted unwelcome attention. Covian guards shouted. One slaver, a putrid, gangly man, grabbed his arm, but the fury in Zane's eyes had the man stumbling and tripping over himself. He left them all in his wake, finally dipping into a side alley. There, he slid down the cool clay wall and sat, his breath ragged. He looked down at his fingers on his right hand. They were still mangled and twisted—the pain had subsided, just a dull throb now, and he took a slow, even breath, grabbed his index finger, and…twisted.

Pop.

Sharp pain lanced through his fingers as he set them, one at a time.

When it was done he tried flexing his fingers. They moved, but the pain was still there, and his hand was weak. *Not likely to hold a sword with it anytime soon*, he thought. *Doesn't matter.* Standing, he looked up and over the heads of the crowds.

Before him sat the colosseum, its many arches filled with statues of Grand Primuses. A tumultuous mass of humans clamored to get inside, and he could tell from the fervor the tournament was starting soon.

I have to get in there.

Zane, don't be an idiot! Hannah, or his imagination of her, whispered to him. *Your fingers are broken and you're still wearing manacles that are cutting off your power.*

I have to join, he snapped back as he watched the crowds shuffling in.

Do you have to die?

Zane spotted a young woman stalking a Covian guard.

A thief.

Zane got up and slid into the mass of people, following her. The woman was tall and slender, in tan and red clothing like the rest of

Covai. The fabric wrapped around her face hid all but her eyes—a surreal light brown hue, so light they were almost the color of sand, and framed by her lush black eyelashes. Just as she went to snag the keys dangling from the guard's waist, Zane, his chains rattling, snatched her wrist.

She turned and, quite unexpectedly, backhanded him across the face. Hard.

Zane's whole head rocked, but he shook himself. Looking down into her eyes, he cursed., "Well, that wasn't very friendly."

She moved to follow the guard.

Again, he grabbed her wrist with his good hand.

"Let go!" She tried to hit him again, but he avoided her fist.

"I think once was enough," he growled.

She looked back at the Covian guard, who had slipped back into the folds of the crowds, and continued to shout at people to maintain order. "You let him get away!" she protested.

"I let you keep your hand."

She narrowed her intense pale eyes. "What are you going on about?"

"See for yourself." He spotted the guard through a gap in the crowds—she followed his gaze as Zane channeled flame through his upper body. He blew a stream of hot air. The spell wasn't elegant, but it was enough to thread filaments of flame across the distance and heat the key at the guard's side, which triggered the spell. There was a small explosion like a firework at the guard's waist. Crowds shrieked, but it wasn't enough to hurt anyone. The guard snarled, scanning for the culprit, but the key remained on his waist.

The young woman looked back at Zane, perplexed. "A Fleshward?"

Zane grunted in affirmation. "Triggered to go off if anyone but him touched it. Or used magic, in this case."

"So what are you? A Reaver?" She looked at the chains on his wrists. "A criminal?"

"Not exactly to the first. As for the second question? Well, that depends on who you ask."

"But you threaded fire."

Zane hesitated. "It's complicated. Now, mind if we talk somewhere a little more private?" She twisted out of his grip, breaking the hold by going against his thumb, and Zane raised a brow. "All right, you've some skill, I'll give you that. Can we please talk somewhere a little less…public?" People were beginning to cast them sidelong glances, a few whispering about Zane's shackles. She hesitated. "I did just save your hand."

"Five silvers buys you two minutes." She held out a palm.

He protested. "Really?"

"Really."

"Fine." He awkwardly nodded to the coin purse at his side. "Little help?"

She pulled the leather pouch off, dumping coins into her hand. "That's all? Four silvers? Wow, you looked a little rough, but…I almost feel bad taking this from you." He opened his mouth. "Not bad enough to give it back. Four silvers buys you one minute."

He rolled his eyes and gestured for her to follow, moving into the alley he was in before.

"Okay, you got me here." She pulled down her scarf to reveal a face that was…just as striking as her eyes. Narrow, sharp chin, and thin pink lips, but somehow it fit her perfectly. He took in the rest of her. The tan cloth wrappings were tight around her narrow waist and upper arms, revealing lean muscle. She was relatively tall—almost as tall as him. Not to mention, she had a dagger at her side with a well-worn hilt. A huntress's gaze bore into him, and she tossed the red shawl over her shoulder—using it as more of a cloak now. She folded her arms. "Time's starting, brooding eyes. Start talking."

Zane shook himself. *What am I doing? Gather your thoughts! You're not Darius, for fire and ash's sake.* He was certain the Ronin of Leaf would have given his little smirk to charm the woman to his side, which could have worked, or just as likely failed. He cleared his throat and found his tongue. "The name's Zane. You're not really going to keep time, are you?"

"Fifty-eight, fifty-seven, fifty-six…"

Zane growled. "Seriously?"

"Get to the point, handsome."

"Fine. You were planning on stealing the key to get in. You asked what I want? I want in, too."

She shrugged. "So? What's stopping you?" She gestured to the crowds still pushing to get inside the colosseum, while the drums thundered louder, making Zane's skin crawl in anticipation.

"Not to watch," Zane clarified.

"Ah, a fighter? You have that look about you." She pursed her lips, then said almost reluctantly, "Raina." He raised a brow. "That's my name. If you want to fight, then just go up there and tell them. You're a man, and a criminal by the looks of it. I'm sure they'll welcome you with open arms." She waved a flippant hand to the huge arena. "You're perfect for the opening death games." Then she raised a sculpted brow. "Practically destined to spill your blood and die on those sands while a bunch of jeering morons with slavering mouths cheer you on."

Zane snorted. "Not a fan of the tournament, I'm guessing?"

For a second, she looked a little embarrassed by her rant, then her dark brows furrowed and she folded her arms again, showing the lean, striated muscles of her forearms. "The tournament is fine. I'm not a fan of bastards putting those who are weak or defenseless into the games against their will. However, if you want to die, be my guest, by all means."

"You can't fight, because they don't allow women. Is that what you're so upset about?"

"Wrong again," she said, flipping back a lock of raven-black hair. "I don't want to fight."

"Then why are you so upset? Why would you—" he began. Then his eyes opened, the pieces clicking. *Those weaker.* "Someone you care about, someone you love is being forced to fight, and you're trying to get in to stop it. To save him or her?"

"Not as dumb as you look," Raina said, then held up her thumb and forefinger, "by a small margin."

"Who is it?"

"Why do you care?" she snapped.

"Because I *do*."

She snorted. "No, you don't. No one does. This city is brutal." Then she scoffed, "That cursed mantra, '*Strength is life, weakness is death.*' It only serves you if you were born privileged. If not, your life is practically worthless." Her eyes narrowed. "Someone like you wouldn't understand."

He shrugged. "I think you'd be surprised. Try me."

"Time's up anyway," she said, turning to leave.

Zane sighed, and said quietly, "I do understand."

She didn't turn. "How could you…"

"Because, like you, someone I cared about was also put in harm's way. Someone who wasn't strong enough, someone who wasn't able to fight back…" He almost said more about Hannah, but he held his tongue, choking against the emotion in his throat. Raina turned to face him and he continued, "Because I also hate bastards that put those who aren't their version of 'strong' down, just because it makes them feel superior. So, yes, I do understand."

Tears welled up in Raina's eyes. "My brother, Sasha," she admitted, smiling. "Younger brother, to be exact. My only sibling. Well, the only one left, that is. The little idiot is of age for the tournament—just turned sixteen—and my father's debts needed to be paid. I work three jobs, but Treckis—that's the slaver who holds our title—is a bastard of the highest order. Covai pays a hefty bit of coin if you send 'good fodder' into the Bloodbath. So Treckis enslaved my brother to cover our debts. He planned to send my sixteen-year-old brother, who's scrawnier than a reed and softer than a kitten, to die on the sands. Fortunately, or unfortunately, for my brother, he caught the eye of the noble lady of the House of Hisan Viper. She is known to wager on young pretty boys in the Primarian-basaeri round. It makes for a more interesting fight, she says. If anything, it's worse than the Bloodbath." Tears streamed down her face now, but she didn't wipe them away. Instead, her face was harder, more set. "So yes, I was trying to steal from that guard who is also a jailer. I was fairly certain it was a key to Sasha's cell."

"I see," was all Zane said, and he did. "Okay, so you get the key. Then what? Are there guards before Sasha's cell?"

"Maybe…" Raina said, then admitted in a grumble, "Yes. Too many to count."

Zane snorted. "Right, and say you get past them. How would you have gotten him out?"

"I'd find a way."

"Perhaps you would," Zane said, not doubting her for a second. "It's risky. Risky enough to get you both killed. Maybe the key wasn't even to his cell. Worse, I think even if you got in, you might be too late. From what I saw, they were gathering all the fighters together in one place. He might not even be in his cell."

"What other choice do I have?"

"Help me. And I'll help your brother."

She scoffed. "Are your muscles taking too much of your brain power? I told you already." She pointed to the arena. "Just go in if you want to fight, you big brooding idiot."

"I did have a bit of blood loss," he admitted. Thinking back now, he'd broken four fingers, rode a dragon across the plains for days on end, nearly died fighting a bunch of Reavers, expended a massive amount of his flow, and still had shackles on his wrists that were restricting his power. Yet he felt fire in his veins. "It's not that simple. I—"

The crowds scurried as guards appeared—a dozen of them marched into the square, quickly followed by a familiar face that sent a torrent of anger swirling inside of Zane. *Nefrin.* His scarlet robes were still seared off at one arm, revealing scorched skin. His scowl showed a face split down the middle, one half still tan and unscathed, the other half inflamed red from his encounter with Zane.

Rage and hatred filled Nefrin's eyes as he scanned those gathered and ordered, "Spread out, find him! Don't let him get away!" The teeming mass was too big for an orderly search, but eight Reavers and the dozen guards pushed out through the throngs, looking for him.

Zane cursed, pressing his back against the wall.

"Ahhh," she said, "a wanted criminal indeed."

"Ash and fire," Zane growled.

"Oh, look at that nasty wound on his face. Was that your doing? Who are you? You fought a four-stripe Reaver and lived?"

Urgency fueled Zane, and he felt the window of opportunity to enter the tournament slipping through his fingers as the Reavers got closer and closer to the main archway. He knew in a moment they'd be scanning every face to ensure he didn't get in. "It's too late…I need to go, I can't lose this opportunity—"

He only took one step before she grabbed his arm. "You know that won't work. Even if you can slip past that bastard, you know they'll find you. Nefrin is a well-known weasel, but he's not an idiot. He'll have the other guards spread word, lock it down, and keep an eye for someone with your description."

"Then what do you suggest?"

She grinned. "I have an idea, but you're going to have to trust me."

"Anything," Zane said.

"Oh, careful what you wish for, brooding eyes. Put out your hands. First things first, we gotta deal with those shackles of yours. Can't beat up too many people if your power is restrained by some Yronia bloodstone."

"You could tell?"

She nodded. "It's what they use for higher-rank spark-wielders. I'm surprised they used it on you…" She looked at him, and he just shrugged, so she sighed and placed her palms on top of his. "Now, this is going to feel strange, and definitely hurt…sorry in advance. Just stay perfectly still, or it could go horribly wrong."

Zane opened his mouth to ask a question, but then simply nodded. "Just do it."

Raina's eyes flashed, and thick threads sank into his skin. *Crack.* A bone in his right hand snapped. Then another. He wanted to lash out, to strike back, to pull his hands away, but he trusted her. The agony was sharp, and continuous, like someone slowly taking a grinding stone to his bones—stabbing pain radiated all the way up his arm, and he suppressed a cry. Sweat streamed out of his pores, and he watched in awe and anguish as…the manacles slipped from his wrists, as if all the bones in his hands suddenly disappeared. "Ash and fire!" he cried out.

"Relax!" she said. "I'll make them whole again. Don't move, or they might heal at odd angles." Sweat also beaded across her brow as she focused. Zane tried desperately to control his breathing while she murmured something under her breath—almost like a chant. He heard it: *"Flesh be kind, flesh be new, flesh be remade, when a heart is true."* *Pop, crack,* followed by more shooting pain, then…His hands gained structure, and a moment later, Raina released a heavy breath, wiping sweat from her face. "There, that should do it."

Zane had one eye closed.

"Well, don't be a big baby, give it a try."

Slowly, Zane flexed his hands, and sure enough, they worked. No, not just worked. All the pain in his recently broken fingers was gone. He felt as if he could crush stone with his bare hands. They felt…remade. "What…what did you do?"

"Eh, I used a bit of spark to regenerate ligaments, tissues, nerves…" She must have seen his look. "Too much explaining?"

He shook himself. "No, I just…" She was powerful. Incredibly so. "How did you learn that?"

She shrugged. "Taught myself. Had to. Was always stitching up my dad from his drunken brawls, or gambling mishaps, or my siblings when—" She shook her head. "Doesn't matter. Point is, you're good as new. Now you can go fight and save my brother. I helped you, you help me, that's the deal, right?"

Zane extended his newly formed hand. "I swear on my life, I'll do whatever I can to save your brother."

Raina shook it. "I'll hold you to that."

"I'd expect nothing less. But…" Zane glanced back out the alleyway, to the colosseum. Nefrin and his goons were getting closer—the guards had now thoroughly locked down the entrance. There was no way he was getting in, and his heart sank. "How in the seven hells are you going to get me in?"

"Oh, that's easy," Raina said. "You're *sure* you want in? Certain?"

He glared at her. "I *need* in." Redemption was inside those walls.

She sighed. "Fair enough, just had to ask. Then are you ready for a little more…discomfort?"

Zane's heart thrummed in time to the rising drums in the distance and he nodded. "Do your worst."

Raina grinned. "You sure know how to please a woman, brooding eyes." Her brows knit, and she placed her hands on his face, and Zane lost himself to a maelstrom of pain.

Shadows and Mud

Helix moved in the dimly lit chamber with its flickering torch light. A sweaty bare-chested man with thick arms roamed the center—the girth of his round belly strained against the leather belt that held up his wide, voluminous black pants. With a whip in each meaty fist, he stalked the chamber, lashing out at any man who was too slow to move out of his way. "Welcome to the Bloodbath, scum! Name's Malgar, but you can call me the overseer. If you survive today, you'll see me again! If not, well, consider yourself lucky that you get the honor of seeing my pretty face before you descend to the depths of hell! Now, sit tight and wait until the final horn sounds." He pointed, "Quazy here, my good little pet, will come by and paint you like pretty little dolls. Until then, wait quiet like, or I'll have your heads!"

Almost as soon as Helix entered, he was forced to relinquish his sword. A Covian guard eyed it, jaw dropping. "Flesh and bone...where did you get this?"

Helix held Frostfall's hilt for a moment longer, not letting go. Inwardly, he wrestled with himself, not wanting to give it up. When had he grown so attached to his sword? He'd gained it in Median when he dove into the watery chasm and found it sticking out of the water serpent.

Frostfall's blade, with a hilt that looked like shards of ice, had a sharp, straight edge. The sheath was iridescent and, depending on the light, seemed to morph from a deep abyss blue to a pale green blue almost like seafoam. Waves in motion were etched across the blade and the scabbard. Helix knew if he took it out it'd likely blind those nearest with its brilliance. The famed Sword of Water was as beautiful and striking as it was deadly. With it, Helix felt infinitely stronger. To lose it...well...it was like losing a limb.

In that moment, he tapped into his mind.

Slowly, painstakingly, Helix placed Frostfall inside the huge chest, and the man locked it away. "Keep that safe, or it'll be your head."

The guard, who normally would have told Helix off, gave a nod. "Won't leave my sight," he promised. Then he shook himself, as if remembering he was talking to a slave. "Now get on with you."

"I wouldn't try to unsheathe it either," Helix warned. The guard sneered. "Actually, on second thought. You can try it if you want." Then he turned to the chamber.

The room was like a pit, and Helix walked down into it, until a huge man stepped out of the shadows. It was the same giant of a man who'd smashed another ruffian's head into a pillar earlier. The giant was big enough that his head nearly scraped the ceiling. Red paint had been slashed down his chest. Now Helix saw that all the men in the room were shirtless and bore red paint. Why? He didn't have time to question as the giant took another step closer, until he was a handbreadth away, looming over Helix. Tattoos covered bulging muscles, the black-and-red ink marred by thick ragged scars. Most of the tattoos were just knives, daggers, maces—one or two showed a brutal scene of what Helix imagined was the big man himself killing someone. Helix heard another man whisper his name: Jivran.

Jivran snarled down at Helix, a growl that shuddered his bones. "Say, Jivran, any chance you want to team up? You know, seeing as we're the two strongest ones here."

A few men overhead this and cackled.

"Did you hear that, Gaius? Strongest ones here! Ha, ha, ha!" jeered a sly, scrawny man who had a lisp and bug eyes. His tongue practically flicked as he talked. "What a heavy pair on the boy! I can't wait to cut that tongue out and wear it as a trophy."

Other men laughed loudly at this—save for the bigger, brutish man with a thick beard that had been addressed—Gaius. Clearly a ringleader of sorts. One eye was an empty socket, but the other, bright blue, glared into Helix's soul. "Oi, I heard him, Ahna. There's cocky, and then there's just dimwitted nonsense."

"Or maybe he's mad! Not the first time they brought cracked ones to the Bloodbath," Ahna guffawed.

"I really don't like that name," Helix said, more to himself than anyone.

Gaius neared, standing beside Jivran, staring at Helix. "So, which is it? Are you something special"—his mouth soured—"or is it just the pitiful, desperate plea of a man who's destined to die?"

Helix tried to keep a small smile. "Gaius, is it? Having a conversation here, do you mind?"

Gaius's one eye narrowed, and Helix was sure he would have jumped him if it weren't for the overseer watching nearby with a bemused smile, hand on his whip, or the dozen guards at the entrance. "I do mind," snarled Gaius. "You see, this lot here is mine"—he gestured to the milling group of rough-looking men scattered about the room—"and you come in here, acting tough. They're going to wonder if you're something special, or if you are cracked, like Ahma suggests. I look at you and wonder…fancy clothes, clean face…tell me, which are you? Cracked or something special?"

Helix felt stuck at a crossroads. He could tell the man he was something to be feared, but Gray had specifically said to avoid the spotlight. If his power was going to be hamstrung, he couldn't gain the ire of all these foul men. He took a deep breath, and luckily didn't need to reply.

Jivran growled to Gaius, "You go. Me talk. Not you."

Gaius was big, a hand or two taller than Helix, but he was forced to crane his neck up to the giant. A tense moment passed, as if he debated taking on the colossus. Then he gave a fake smile and barked a laugh, slapping Jivran's back. "Have at it." As he passed Helix he snarled, "Careful, boy. I'm watching you."

Helix tensed and swallowed, but when Gaius was gone, he looked back at Jivran, who still loomed over him. "So as I was saying, whaddya say, big guy?" Helix asked. "I promise not to disappoint. These guys will definitely stab you in the back given the chance. Me on the other hand? Not a backstabber. I may have to kill you, but I'll announce it way beforehand." He was trying to channel Darius, hoping his nerves didn't show, but his right hand shook. He stilled it, making a fist.

Jivran's upper lip twitched, and he growled.

"Uh…is that a yes?" Helix asked.

The giant bent down and spoke, *"Ikllyoufirs."* It was one long, slurred word. Covian?

"Sorry, uh…I didn't get that?"

Snickers broke out among the crowd, until one man clarified, "He says he'll kill you first!"

Jivran nodded, and accentuated the point by dragging his thumb across his neck and baring his teeth.

"Yeah, thanks, got it now."

The room exploded in laughter, sharp and snide.

Jivran lumbered away, and Helix took a deep breath and moved into the corner. Well, it was a round chamber, so just closer to the gate, trying to get a glimpse of the crowds and sands. The arena lay beyond the iron gate, and the frenzied crowd made his muscles tense and heart skip. However, mostly he was trying to avoid some of the attention he'd just garnered and the fifty pairs of blood-hungry eyes that he felt on him.

"Well, that could have gone better," Helix muttered to himself.

A familiar, husky voice whispered from the shadows, "Well, look who it is…" The words were laced with amusement. "Quite the bravado you had there. You're starting to remind me a little of the Leaf one. He's fun, I miss him. Cute too, if a tad disheveled. Though he doesn't hold a candle to the Fire one." The person made a throaty sound. "Mmm, brooding and damaged, just the way I like 'em. I heard he rode in on a dragon? Now *that's* an entrance. Impressive, though I'm more of a cloak-and-dagger type: arrive in the shadows and leave without a trace."

Helix squinted, peering into the shadows, heart pounding. Whoever was talking knew about Darius and Zane, which meant they knew he was a Ronin. Helix decided to play dumb. "Huh? I've no idea what you're on about. Do I know you?"

The person sat on the ground but leaned forward to slide into the bleak light coming from the gates, as if offering him a better glimpse. Helix took in what he could: the stranger's physique was far less bulky than most of the men in here—built more like a blade. A face, rather shapely, was oddly wrapped in bandages, as if burned, revealing only penetrating dark almond eyes rimmed in black kohl and lips bearing a faint, bemused smile. The look was almost sultry? Helix shook himself, forcing himself to take in the rest, trying to understand: the man's clothes were of the Farbian style, with dark umber and orange accents and a patch of a bloodshot eye on the shoulder. "Hello, Helix."

A *Darkeye thief*? His throat clenched. "Who are you?"

The figure in the shadows sighed. "Am I that forgettable? It's a shame, we keep meeting in really the most undesirable scenarios. Well, undesirable for *you*. I'm fine. This is kind of my element, no pun intended. How about this…if I kicked you in the head, would it ring any bells?"

Suddenly, the voice, the memory, the kicking in the head…she'd done that when they'd been on the *Pride of Median*, and he'd been tied to the mast, and Captain Xavvan had—it all came back in a rush. "Faye?"

Faye pulled some of the cloth wrappings aside to reveal her face: beautiful as ever, and totally not Helix's type—more the "probably stab you after they kiss you type," which seemed to be Gray's sort of thing.

But he liked Faye. Quite a bit, actually. They'd saved each other when he'd gotten himself too deep into Narim, the Great Kingdom of Moon. He'd been tied to the *Pride of Median*'s mast as a stowaway while searching for the true Great Kingdom of Water, and Faye had watched over him more than once. He didn't know a ton about her. Gray and Ayva had filled him in that her father had been Darkeye, the Leader of the Darkeye clan and Thieflord of Farbs, Great Kingdom of Fire. She'd inherited that title, and apparently been the one to kill her own father…a fact that made her terrifying all on its own.

Helix knew something was happening among the Thieflords; Gray and the others had all discussed it after hearing the rumors. The Thiefdoms were uniting—all the rulers vying to be lord of all the thieves—but it seemed Faye didn't want anything to do with it, despite her legacy. The only other thing Helix knew about Faye was that she had been all about trying to save her sister. Now she was here.

Helix gawked for a moment. "You can't be serious…how are you here?"

She shrugged. "You think a few Covian guards are going to stop me?"

"Yes, well, yes I do," he said, and feeling eyes on his back, he knelt at her side and lowered his voice. "Also, it wasn't just a few guards—we passed like a hundred Covian soldiers on the way here. You know, with weapons? Lots of weapons, and there were locked doors."

She leaned back, reclining on her elbows, as if the dilapidated damp chamber was a sandy beach. "No door is truly locked if you have the right key."

He glared at her.

She sighed. "*Fine*, a few guards owed me some favors. You're ruining my mystique over here, Water Boy. Anyway, it was annoying. I'm a Thieflord of Fire and I didn't get an invite? It just didn't seem fair. Figured it got lost by carrier pigeon or something, so I let myself in."

The drums were getting louder. "But…it's men only for the first round."

An apple flitted to her fingers from seemingly thin air and she took a crisp bite. "So?"

"Right," Helix admitted, "suppose that wouldn't stop you." Helix looked about at the rough-looking men. All whispered and eyed him from the shadows. He could feel their hatred, and he listened to the drums, seeing the bright sands beyond the gate. "I'm going to die out there, aren't I?"

She replied around a mouthful of apple, "It's not looking great for you."

Helix growled, "You're supposed to give me confidence!"

"Whoever told you that lied. I'm honest if nothing else."

"Team up with me," Helix said.

She scratched her jaw. "Eh, no thanks. I don't do well with teams. Your friends should have told you that much."

It was true. Faye had left Darius and Ayva in a pit to die at the hands of a Darkwalker, or murdered by her father, Darkeye. It…admittedly was a pretty awful move. One she'd tried to make amends for by saving hundreds of lives in the Battle of the Sands, but still. Helix wasn't naive enough to believe Faye was good, not like Gray. She wasn't evil either, just complicated. "Well aware, but I know you better than you think I do."

"You do, do you?" she mused.

"I do." He grinned. "You like to win. And I can help you with that." He let a little ice crawl up his hand, making sure the other warriors didn't see.

Her eyes widened, and she looked almost ready to agree, but hesitated, appearing suddenly worried for him. "About that…"

A hunchbacked man hobbled about while carrying a tin bucket in one hand and a brush in the other—as he went up and down the lines of men he'd bark an order and the men would grudgingly take off their shirts, or turn to face him, then he'd splash their bare chests with red paint. The hunched man approached Helix and Faye and muttered something in Covian, jabbing a finger at their chests.

"Do we have to?" Helix asked.

The gibbous-shaped man barked again harshly.

He looked at Faye, who merely shrugged.

Helix sighed and took off his shirt, exposing his body.

While he'd gained some strength in his travels with the others, he wasn't built with heavy muscle like Zane; nor did he have Darius's lean and agile frame; nor was he athletic and broad-shouldered like Gray. Helix looked down at his pale body, and was surprised by a few more abs than he remembered. That wasn't a Ronin trait, was it? Slowly inheriting their musculature, their physiques? Eh, he doubted it. More likely just a result from all the training, riding, and nearly dying with Gray and the others.

Faye let out a low whistle and he glared over his shoulder at her.

Cold paint slapped against his body in one quick, practiced swipe. "What's this for?" he asked the hunched man.

The man answered in a slurred common tongue, *"Dead mark."*

Helix felt a chill of fear.

The crookbacked man hobbled toward Faye, grouching a garbled order at her.

Faye growled, "Bring that bucket near me, and I'll make sure every part of you fits inside of it by the time I'm done." If not completely understanding her words, the man clearly understood the fire in her eyes and the tone in which they were said. Ducking his head, he practically ran away from her.

Helix sighed, sitting back down next to her again. "Do you know why?"

"No idea," she admitted. "I'm sure it's something twisted." She reached over and slowly slid three fingers across his chest, and Helix's every muscle tensed as he reflexively grabbed her wrist. She smiled up at him, a seductive pucker to her lips. "Oh, sorry, never been touched by a girl before?"

He let her wrist go. "I'll not dignify that with a response."

She huffed in amusement. "That's a no," she said as she dragged the paint across her eyes and mouth in three lines of red, like claw marks.

He glared at her. "You're just trying to get a rise out of me."

"Did I?" she asked, her gaze briefly moving down to his trousers.

Helix grew red-faced. "Why are you really here, Faye?"

"The truth?" She lowered her voice. "I've got some ears on the inside. Hear there's a special prize this year. Something to make the thousand gold coins seem paltry."

"I heard the same. Know what it is?"

She rolled her shoulders, watching the warriors warily. "No idea. I'll be happy to take it and be on my way. I'm not particularly fond of this city. Blood and dust are all fine and well, but too much subjugation of the masses for my liking, and people whipping themselves." She shivered. "Not my cup of tea."

Helix raised a brow, glancing over at her. "You sure? Gray and Ayva told me some stories about you…holding people against their will under the threat of violence seems kind of your thing."

She narrowed her eyes. "When did you get such a backbone? Also, don't listen to everything you hear. Gray takes the weight of the world on his well-defined shoulders. Ayva is an insufferable know-it-all who can't help but find the good in every single person, dog, bug, or inanimate object. *'I have hope for them'!*" she said, as if quoting Ayva. And then, using her voice, she added, "Some people are just destined to disappoint."

Helix snorted. "Tell me about it. If Gray wasn't so humble, it'd be annoying."

"Are you kidding? That's the most annoying part!" Faye replied. "At least the Leaf Boy has the good sense to have some bravado. I mean if you're going to be a reborn legend who can level mountains and lay waste to armies, what's the fun if you can't be a little swollen-headed about it? As for Ayva, that whole cute, hopeful bright-eyed thing is…well, it sounds exhausting."

He didn't disagree. He wasn't nearly as hopeful as Ayva. It's partly why it'd taken her so long to convince him to join and do something that was other than self-serving. But something else had been nettling him about Ayva. "I don't think Ayva's realized her power quite yet…"

"Probably not," Faye admitted. "Good thing too. Can still lord it over her."

He snorted. "Yeah, for now. I don't know what it is, but something tells me there's something she's afraid of, something holding her back. If she let that go…" He shivered. "The stories of Omni were something else."

Faye looked over at him. "I say that's true for a lot of us. We're afraid not of our inadequacy, but that we're more powerful than we can possibly fathom." Her face soured. "Ugh, imagine that, countless people tapping into their truest and highest selves to change the world for the better? Sounds like Ayva's dream." She gagged *and* shivered. "Thankfully most of us will run from our potential until we die. What about you? What do you want, Water Boy?"

"To live through today."

"You worry too much. I'm sure you'll figure a way out. Hells, you're a reborn legend—a thousand-year-old myth that's come to life." Her eyes lit up, and she said the next words with mysticism and a hint of teasing: "A *Ronin*."

"As I keep getting reminded."

"Well? Then act like it," she said, yawning and rising, stretching out her lithe muscles. "After all, can't you just channel your predecessor?"

"If only it was that easy," Helix said. "I'm learning my powers more and more every day…" Even now, Helix didn't get a full picture of what he could do with water. "I can remember fragments of what Hiron could do, like seeing a map, with half of it covered in fog. Or like a puzzle, and only knowing a few moves. Every once in a while, a new section will open up, or a piece on the board fits into place and I can do a new spell. Usually it's only under duress."

"Well, perfect!" she said, waving to the mass of snarling men who stalked the chambers. "Duress central!"

Helix growled. "This is different. Gray said my power is dampened. And I think you're hiding something, too. So fighting in hand-to-hand combat like this? I'm not a fighter! Maybe Hiron was, but…this? I'm not a warrior, like you."

"You're going to become one today."

"Teach me. I'm a quick learner. Help me get out of this, and I'll do anything."

She bit her lip, as if seeing the fear in his eyes. "You're asking a lot."

"Oi, you lousy lot! Line up!" Malgar roared.

Pushing and shoving, hate in their eyes, the ruffians gathered at the iron gate.

Helix's heart hammered. "It's too late…"

Faye growled. "*Haras*," she cursed in Sand tongue. "Quick, take this." Up against the wall, sand and water on the ground had created a muddy sludge. She slabbed a bunch of it into Helix's hand.

"What in the seven hells is this for?"

"You want my help? Then do as I say. Rub it in your hair, your face, quickly," she said under her breath, as two Covian guards approached, clearly looking to force them in line.

"Two in a row!" Malgar ordered. "Move it! Quicker!" He lashed a man who was too slow to move, a bloody groove slicing into the man's back, while Covian guards shoved others with the tip of their swords, corralling the unruly throng of rough warriors.

Frantic, Helix shot back, "I think they already know who I am!"

"Don't be so sure. Their memories are short. Besides, in the heat of battle, things mix together. All that matters is who looks like prey and who doesn't. Judging by your face…" She winced, as if the rest was self-explanatory.

Helix glowered. "What's wrong with my face?"

"I mean, you're cute—not my type, obviously—but you look like a choir boy who decided to become a legend. Clean hair?" She tousled his blond locks. "Smooth face that hasn't ever seen a blade yet." She ran a knuckle down his cheek. "Clothes that don't look rummaged from the trash?" She eyed his blue trousers. "You look like a bunny rabbit trying to blend in with a pack of wild dogs."

The nerves returned. "Oh gods…I'm going to die, aren't I?"

The guards neared, shouting at them. "In line, you two, now!"

Faye's eyes glared at him, urging him to do it.

Helix growled but did as she said and slathered the mud in his hair, feeling the cold, wet muck slide down his scalp.

"What in the seven hells is he doing?" a guard asked in a growl.

Faye replied, hooking her thumb at Helix, "Oh, him? Thinks he's a pig."

The guard leveled his sword to Helix's throat. "Enough, swine. In line, now!"

Helix, now slathered in mud, was shoved beside Faye to stand in the center of the chamber while the drums thundered, beating in time to his racing heart.

"How do I look?" he asked Faye, trying to hide his fear.

Faye closed one eye as if examining a painting, then gathered some muck from his hair and smeared it on his face—the mud was cool to the touch against his hot skin. She leaned back, admiring her handiwork. "I don't want to admit it, but with those bright, shiny eyes of yours and the mud? It's working for you. I'm not going to say *fearsome*, but…maybe tough with a hint of imposing."

"Thanks," he said, just as the overseer bellowed.

Then Faye's eyes caught the mark on his arm, a giant burned X. He reached to cover it with mud, and she grabbed his wrist. "Don't. We use any advantage we can get." She chuckled. "Seriously? You should know by now that I'm the last person to judge another for the sins of their past."

"It wasn't a sin," Helix muttered. "My father—" A flash of memories tried to overwhelm Helix, memories of his father reaching out, grasping his shirt, hands covered in blood, and he shut it all away, shaking his head.

"Oh, father issues? I can relate. I'm listening."

He growled. "I'm not talking about it. Not with you, not with anyone."

"Not a problem, but channel that anger."

"*Line up, scum!* The Old One will read your magic now!" Malgar ordered.

From the chamber's entrance, an old woman in thick brown robes doddered into the room, escorted by several guards. When she moved under the light of the flickering torch, Helix realized the woman wasn't just old, she was *ancient*. Her face and hands bore a web of wrinkles and brown liver spots. In her palm, she cradled a crystal orb no bigger than a fist.

Helix looked to Faye. "What is that thing?"

The Old One and the guards moved to the iron gate near the entrance.

Faye rubbed her neck, chagrined. "Yeah…it's what I didn't want to tell you before. That thing in her hand is a magical artifact that reads one's innate magic. Your magic, while powerful outside these walls, is not the advantage you think it's going to be…not really fair if you can just shoot out a thousand shards of ice and kill all these fools." She shrugged. "Doesn't make for much of an opening round." She looked up, as if able to see through the dank, torchlit chamber to the stands above, toward the queen, or perhaps the rabble that was deafening now in their roars. "They want their spectacle, *their blood.*"

Abyss take me, Helix cursed. Gray had mentioned hamstringing, but this? He grabbed her arm. "What does it read? Spark or flow?"

She arched a brow at him. "What do you take me for, an Arbiter?"

Helix prayed it could only sense spark. If that was the case, perhaps it couldn't detect his flow. Flow was a different magic, after all—the essence, the soul of the world, something only ancient or primordial beings were infused with, or could touch. Its origin was in Renalin, the Creator of all things. In essence, the life force of a god. Spark was the lesser magic Renalin had passed on, which became the life force of humans, animals, and all creatures. It was said perhaps a tiny flicker of flow existed in all people—their soul—if only they could learn to tap into it.

Helix whispered in terror as he was shoved forward, eyeing the collars in the guards' hands—they were smooth black metal, with a faint red glow. "Those collars, what are they?"

"Bloodstone fused with Yronia metal," Faye explained. "From what I heard, it dampens one's powers relative to how much magic you have. Even fight and all."

"Yeah, real even," Helix growled.

The iron gate opened with a grating rumble and the roar of the crowds swelled, almost a physical thing as it washed over them. Helix sensed the stench of fear and anticipation among the milling gladiators.

"One at a time, maggots!" Malgar ordered, lashing at their feet. "After you're read, you'll be shoved onto the sands. Find your footing, and no killing one another until the drums stop! Remember, only five survive." A cruel smile alighted on his face, revealing the man's rotting teeth, black, as if he chewed tar. "Try anything and archers on the upper rows will find your heart and end your chances of victory."

The first man was read.

The crystal sphere remained dormant.

The Old One's beak of a nose wrinkled in disgust. "No magic," she crooned. "Next!"

One after another, they were tested, then thrown out of the iron gate, onto the sands—each time to the roar of the crowd. A few men made the orb flicker, but the guards made no move with the collars. *Not strong enough to be handicapped,* Helix guessed. Then it got to one man: the wiry, rat-faced-looking warrior called Ahma, who snickered as he approached. As he got within a foot of the old woman, an iridescent orange glow grew—extending about a finger's width past the crystal sphere.

"Him!" the Old One ordered.

Malgar shouted, "Cuff 'im!"

Ahma struggled, but it was pointless as two Covian guards clapped the dark black metal collar about Ahma's neck, then shoved him onto the sands. Men like Ahma, Helix knew, were called Untamed— those who could thread the elements, but weren't trained under the

Citadel to become Reavers. Some learned on their own, while some just suffered, having abilities but never knowing how to truly harness them. Helix made a mental note to be wary of the rat-faced man.

The next, a big man with an unruly black beard and savage eyes, snarled, shaking his head. "Nice try, witch, but you won't read me with that! I'd rather die!" The bearded man lunged, reaching for a guard's sword still in its scabbard. Only another guard was quicker, and interceded, stabbing the warrior through the throat. Blood gurgled from the fatal wound and he fell to the floor in a heap.

"Idiot. Wish granted," Faye murmured.

Helix swallowed, watching as more were tested, none lighting up the orb, then thrown out of the gate. Until Gaius came forward.

Gaius, the ringleader, glared at the crowd with his one eye. His thick torso was covered in black tribal ink that now had a smear of red—his hateful gaze passed over the Old One and the guards. As he neared, the crystal sphere burned suddenly, enough that the Old One winced at the light.

"*Powerful*," she muttered, and stabbed a finger toward Gaius. "Him!"

Gaius's lips curled, and he looked ready to fight, but he let two guards snap a collar on him and thrust him out onto the sands. A dozen more men gained collars, but none were as powerful as Gaius or Ahma—most only made the crystal sphere glow.

Until Faye and Helix were shoved forward.

Faye was read first while Helix's heart thundered.

She took two steps nearer to the Old One and the orb was dormant for one second, then two.

Nothing.

No glow.

"Well, could have told you that much—" Faye began.

Then, like tinder to flame, the sphere abruptly roared to life.

So bright, it started to burn—the blaze suffused the whole of the chamber, banishing all shadows, as if the room was illuminated by a bright sun. The Old One shrieked, flinching beneath the sudden brilliance. Yet the sphere continued to radiate brighter. The guards, Malgar, and the last remaining gladiators covered their eyes with their hands. "It's him!" the Old One cried, shaking a crooked finger at Helix. Then she squinted at Faye. "*Or both.* I—I can't tell, it's too strong! Quickly, bind him! Restrain them both!"

Bathed in orange, Helix froze. The light wasn't blinding to him. Part of him wanted to make a run for it.

The rest of him was oddly at peace, seeing them all shy away.

He embraced the moment, breathing it in, and just like that, all fear was gone as he glimpsed the seed of what lay inside of him.

I am a Ronin.

Then the moment was shattered by the overseer's cruel shout.

"Clap 'em both!" Malgar ordered. "Now!"

Faye snarled, looking like she wanted to fight the dozen armed guards, but she relinquished, and they snapped dark metal collars around her neck, then Helix's. "Great going," she muttered.

Helix had opened his mouth to reply when a guard broke from the others and slipped something into Helix's hand.

"A gift, from Her Majesty," said the man in a low whisper, and Helix had no time to reply as they were shoved onto the sands, into the arena, into the realm of death.

Smells Like Dragon

Zane moved through the warrens of the colosseum, the stamping of the crowds beating a rhythm above his head, as Raina led them toward the opening chambers. Raina had been true to her word. The pain of "changing" had been excruciating. Now he could barely see over the tip of his nose, and he couldn't help but touch his pockmarked face and sunken eyes.

"Stop doing that," Raina hissed as they passed a group of pretty serving girls roughly his age who were eyeing him. "People are going to think you're crazy."

Sure enough, the three scantily clad young women shot him strange looks, as if he were a lecherous old man. Well, he was. He passed a statue with shiny armor, and in its mirror he saw his reflection. Curved long nose, pock marks, and liver spots. What teeth he wasn't missing were so yellow they looked like kernels of corn. "I can't help it. It feels unnatural being in someone else's skin." He tried his rugged smile at the girls. Immediately, a very bad idea. Their faces curdled as if they'd just drank soured milk. Dust and sand, one actually *gagged*!

"*Ew...*"

All three skirted *far* around him, practically dashing down the corridor.

Raina cackled. "Now that was smooth. Real smooth."

"Ugh, ash and fire! Did you really have to make me this hideous?"

She snorted. "Oh, I'm so sorry that not everyone swoons when you smile now!"

Zane groused, "I wasn't asking for swooning. I'd settle for not fleeing in terror."

"Uh-huh."

"What?"

She raised a brow. "Oh, we're playing the 'I'm tough and rugged Zane, and I don't know what you're talking about' card?"

He glared at her. "I don't know what you're implying."

"Please, you're as obvious as a fart underwater! You're just so used to being handsome, that this *kiiiiiiillls* you, doesn't it?"

"I..." Zane began. "No, I'm not, and...no, it doesn't."

"No, you don't get flirted with? Oh yeah? Sure, I believe you. Then tell me, when's the last time someone flirted with you? Has it happened this week?"

Zane actually felt his cheeks heat. "I'm not answering that."

"Oh gods, it happened today? Who was it? If it's a guard, I'm leaving you here in chains."

He growled, but admitted, "I *think* she was flirting, I'm not sure."

"Who?"

He winced. "Captain Leanna?"

She stopped walking. "You can't be serious."

Zane threw up his hands. "I don't know. Maybe she was just being polite! C'mon, we can't stop." The crowds were growing louder, and Zane's heart was thundering in anticipation.

Raina sighed, catching up and pulling him along. "Fine. What'd she say?"

"Something about me being far too pretty to die? She kept calling me the *ca'ran*, whatever in the ash and shadow that is."

"Hells, Zane, women aren't that hard to understand..." Raina said. Then she hedged, "Well, unless you're a clueless man. To other women, we are painfully obvious with our intentions. If she said, 'you're far too pretty to die' and called you the *ca'ran*, which means *Chosen* by the way, and you're questioning if that falls under the category of flirting? Well, you might actually be an idiot. A hopeless idiot." She shrugged and sighed. "But still cute."

He grunted. "Thanks? Anyway, now she'd run from me."

"No," Raina said, waiting for a servant to pass as she led them down another corridor, "I'm pretty sure she'd stab you in the heart to put you out of your misery. You *are* hideous." She wrinkled her small nose.

Zane protested, "I don't smell!"

"True, but you give the impression you do—the mind is a powerful thing." She leaned in a little, sniffing him. "Actually, no offense, you definitely smell."

Zane sniffed himself and recoiled a little. "Gods..." How long had he been traveling on that dragon? Did he smell like dragon? Was that a thing? Was it from traveling through the woods, chasing Sithel? He'd taken a bath or two on his vengeance-fueled mission...well, mostly just dipped into a cool stream, or beneath a waterfall. He'd been pretty consumed with killing Sithel.

"Eh, don't worry about it," Raina consoled, dragging him up another winding corridor, past halls filled with people celebrating. "You're going into a Bloodbath, literally. Maybe your stench will be a secret weapon, though probably not. Pretty sure your fellow combatants all smell the same or worse."

Zane eyed the halls leading downward, past less and less lavish rooms and more sordid guards sporting stubbly beards. "Are you sure we're going the right way?"

She smiled. "Yes," she said, then pointed to the corridors lit by torches and lined with archers' slits that showed glimpses of the sand arena. It made Zane's heart pound. He just needed to get out there. He could solve it all. "If I remember correctly, the holding chamber for the Bloodbath is just up ahead. It's where all the fodder from the first round usually go. Sorry, no offense."

"None taken," Zane said, "you just need to get me in. Speaking of which, what's the plan again?"

"I told you, I'm a healer," she said, tapping the healer's emblem that was stitched into her outer flaxen coat—a symbol of a snake curled about a staff. "As a healer, I'm escorting a recently healed gladiator back to the Bloodbath."

"Where'd you get the uniform again?"

"Well, that's just rude. You think I steal everything?" She huffed, touching the flaxen coat she now wore that she'd pulled from her pack. Her fingers flitted, little bits of tan threads dancing above her palm. "It's real, for your information," she said, admiring her own attire. "I passed the healer's test. I'm quite good too."

Zane cast her an eye. "Right, what then?"

"Then you go into the Bloodbath, kill everyone, or whatever you have to do to survive."

"Uh-huh."

"Then in the next round—the one my brother is competing in—you'll get access to his cells." She glared at him, almond eyes the color of honey suddenly turning more sinister. "If you hurt my brother, I'll hunt you down and torture you for all eternity..."

He raised a brow.

"Once you're in the same cells, you'll have to find a way to get him out of that dungeon. The other Primarian-basaeri are allowed to leave, but nobles' slaves are still owned by those royal bastards. They don't get their freedom. That's where you come in. Can you do that for me?"

Zane nodded.

She smiled. "Good. I have our bags packed already. We flee the city and never come back. If none of that works, then once you're inside—after you survive this round, of course—you find my brother, and we plan a prison break."

Zane rubbed his bulbous eyes. "You're starting to sound like my friend."

"Well, she sounds smart."

"Try naive," Zane corrected. "Have you seen how many guards are around us?" Sure enough, as soon as he said this a dozen guards passed in Covai uniforms bearing the symbol of flesh on their armor and tan cloaks. "See?" One of their ilk, a taller man, entered the corridor. Immediately, Raina pulled Zane aside and into an alcove, away from the guard's eyes. "Uh, hello?" he asked her in the cramped niche. She smelled nice, like vanilla, and something else he couldn't put his finger on, which made him all the more aware of his smell.

"Yes, hello. Sorry, just saving your hide."

"From him?"

"Yes, him."

"Who's he? Someone special?"

"You could say that. That's Drega, the leader of the Fleshguard. He seems affable, and friendly, always smiling and laughing, making friends with everyone, but there's stories that he's death with a blade. Most say he'll make an equal match for even Grand Primus Nalia this year. That is, if you and your Ronin don't show off your legendary skills…"

"How did you know…"

"It's written all over your face. Well, not now it isn't. Whispers are abounding all over town. First, I heard someone landed a damn dragon in the city! That's a rumor that's going to be told for the next century. Also, that your friend, the wind one, is a Primarian? That's never been done before, at least for an outsider. Guess being descendants of thousand-year-old legends gives you some clout. Why aren't you with them anyway?"

Zane looked away. "Long story."

She shrugged. "Suit yourself. As long as you can get my brother out, you could be nameless for all I care."

The huge man, Drega, had stopped to converse with a few guards. Zane read the man quickly. He seemed…intimidating. Tall, with jet-black hawk-like eyes that were deeply set, and a jaw Zane could have honed his blade on. Twin swords at his hip looked…well used, their leather worn to the nub. Drega's eyes roamed the corridors as he laughed and clapped men on the back, but the moment he looked away, a coldness like a frozen river entered his gaze. After living most of his life as a thief, Zane could usually sense a man's motives. Unfortunately, he wasn't sure if it was evil, or something else, but Drega was someone he'd rather not face in the first round.

"I don't think you'll make it to the Grand Primus tournament, but if you do, avoid Drega at all costs."

"Thanks for the vote of confidence." Finally, after Drega passed, they moved onward. Zane offered, "Why didn't you pose as him? You could probably get your brother out yourself."

She snorted. "Doesn't work like that. I need enough flesh to make the proportions right. I mean…I think I could do it, but then you'd have to kill someone for me, or slaughter a cow, any flesh will do really—all of which requires time, a luxury sorely in short supply. Worse, I'm…" She winced. "I can't do the voices yet. As soon as I try to speak and sound like this? I'm pretty sure they'll kill me on the spot."

Zane opened his mouth to reply when above them, in the stands, the thundering grew louder. His heart began to race. "We're not going to make it…We need to run."

She yanked him away, holding him back as he startled a few messengers, and said, "If we start running through the halls, disguises or not, people are going to catch on." They then hurried through the corridors until they came upon the Bloodbath's entry, a huge round door guarded by two men.

Hearing the crowd's enthusiasm suddenly swell, Zane's pulse skipped a beat. The queen began to make a speech. Zane's heart fell. "No…we're too late."

"We have to try," Raina said, pulling him toward the two door guards.

One was a plump, shirtless man with two whips at his hip who looked like a pit boss—the type who handled rough gladiators. He had stringy black hair that clung to his oversized melon of a head, bulging eyes, and missing teeth. Even if the man wasn't nearly as hideous as Zane, he had a vileness to his laugh and a hateful gaze in his eyes. His whips were stained with blood—though Zane doubted it was from men who'd had the chance to fight back. The other man was a simple Covian guard in leather and mail. Both men cackled and laughed, until Zane and Raina approached and then their expressions turned sour.

"I need—" Zane began.

The guard growled, "I'll stop you right there. You're hideous enough to kill your opponents with that face of yours, but it's too late. No one goes into the Bloodbath once the tournament has started. Missed your turn, old man. Maybe next year you can die." The two men chortled a laugh. "However, if you're really that ambitious to spill your blood, I can do it for you here." The guard cleared his sword from his scabbard a little, and grinned. "I hear there's an army in the west. You can go try your hands on some of those foul beasts." Then he snorted. "Now get lost! Ain't got time for you!"

"Well, that's rude," Raina said. "He deserves his chance to die on the sands. After all, I just healed him up. Why split him open here and make all my hard work for nothing? Can't you make an exception? You know, just kick him out the gate with the others?"

"Did I not make myself clear?" the guard said and touched his blade threateningly.

Raina turned, but the plump pit boss caught her wrist. "Hold on, Agras. No need to be so hasty to our guests." He made a lecherous curl of his lip. "You know…you can stay, if you want…dump the old man and come with Malgar," the fat guard said, licking his lips as his eyes played over her body with a hungry look. "I'll take care of you, lass. Not enough fat on the wing, but at least enough to suckle on."

Raina's eyes flared. Zane knew she was going to use her power. His Nexus roared as well, fire and flame, as he prepared to kill both men right then and there—

Hannah shouted in his mind: *Stop!*

Zane froze with the fire churning in his palm hidden behind his back.

You wanted to win, didn't you? Then you have to be better. You have to be patient.

That means?

You can't die here swarmed by a hundred guards. We have to win.

Zane's eyes hardened as he stared at the two men. Then he clenched his fist, snuffing the flames within and without. At least…for now.

Raina opened her mouth. "Well, since you seem to value your—"

Zane grabbed her, cutting her off, and Raina scowled, her eyes full of a very familiar fire. "Why'd you pull me away?"

"Trust me, no one wants to make ash piles out of those two more than me—"

"The world would be better for it," Raina huffed.

"That's not why we're here. You need to save your brother, and I need to get inside to win this damn thing. Murdering a few guards doesn't get us any closer to either of those goals."

As they took strides down the stone-paved corridor, her eyes narrowed, doing that thing women do when they're seeing into you. He…didn't love it.

"What?"

"Nothing," she said. "Just learning. One second—" She paused at the end of the corridor, glancing back to see the two men cackling in the distance. Malgar was grabbing his crotch in a crude manner, and Raina's hand danced. Then she looked back at Zane. "Okay, I'm done. Shall we?"

He raised a brow and they turned into another hallway. There was a shriek from behind them, sounding as if Melgar had just been castrated.

"What'd you just do?"

She sniffed and, keeping her voice low as they joined the crowds of people in a busier hall, said, "Oh, it was nothing serious. I just made his manhood a little less…*manly*. That's all men care about anyway, right?"

"Y-you can do that?" Zane said, a little less smoothly than he would have liked.

She glanced down at Zane's crotch, then winked at him. "Don't worry, you're safe. Though I'd suggest staying on my good side." More shouting chased them from down the corridor, and Raina pulled on him harder. "I'd also suggest we move quickly. That fat oaf probably won't put two and two together, but better to be safe than sorry." They continued on, passing groups of people.

"How long does that last? Is it"—he cleared his throat—"*permanent?*"

She shrugged. "Don't think so? Kind of like dipping into freezing water, I hear. Never been around to make sure."

"Right," Zane added, shaking it off. "Anyway, you know as well as I that the games have already started, so there's no way we are getting in. We need another plan, and a good one." Pulling the hood of his cloak up a little more, he tried to ignore the disgusted faces people gave him as they passed down the torchlit hallways.

Raina sighed. "There is no other way! The Bloodbath is the entry and—"

She froze mid-stride.

They were in a four-way intersection of corridors. Messengers, guards, and mostly servants in colorful clothes swarmed about, and the light of an epiphany came to Raina's eyes.

"What is it?" Zane asked. "How do we get in?"

She grinned. "That's just it, we don't get into the Bloodbath. You're not Noxii material, you strike me as Primarian-basaeri. So that's what we are going to make you."

"Primarian…what?"

She rolled her eyes. "You idiot. There are rankings. Noxii are the lowest that fight in the Bloodbath, and if you're one of the five that survives that, then you move up to Primarian-basaeri, followed by Primarian-hadus, Primarian to Primus, and finally, Grand Primus."

Zane sighed. "Right, but I haven't earned that rank. How in the seven hells of Remwar am I supposed to enter a later round?"

Raina's eyes glittered with mischief. "That's where I come in." She grabbed his wrist, tugging him down the passage through servants, and nearly bumping into a Fleshguard. "Come on, this way, quickly!"

Zane didn't protest as they snaked through the hallways that now descended into the bowels of the colosseum.

They reached a pair of double doors.

Two guards stood watch.

"No way around them," Zane growled, stepping forward. "I got this—"

"No, I do," Raina said, and with a deep breath she sent out tendrils of flesh.

The guards' eyes grew heavy-lidded, and both men collapsed, swords clattering to the stone.

"How'd you…"

"Easy," she said, giving a small shrug. "Slowed their heart rates." She stepped over the two men's bodies, swiftly unhooked a jangling key ring off one of the guards' belts, and unlocked the door with a click. Glancing back over her shoulder, her almond eyes shining in the gloomy dungeon, Raina tossed him a smile.

Zane's mouth worked silently. In that look, he felt like he was staring at a flame, and the closer he got, the hotter it seemed to burn—a heat, a passion…something inexplicable that he couldn't quite look away from.

"Well, are you coming, Fire Boy, or just going to stand there all day and stare at me? They won't be out long."

He shook himself, "Yeah, I'm coming, just—"

She didn't wait.

Zane grumbled, following.

Within the dungeon it was even darker; a smoldering brazier shed light, revealing some reed bundles for torches lining the wall. Grabbing two bundles, Raina moved to light them in the glowing embers, when Zane snapped his fingers, and the torches roared to life.

She raised a brow at him. "Right, forgot about that."

Zane looked ahead, peering into the incredibly dark passageway beyond. "All right. Why does it feel like we're headed toward the heart of hell? Where exactly are you taking me?"

Raina bit her lip and pulled him onward. "Well, you see, the next round that my brother is in, they're not all *common* entries. Sometimes, the gladiators face more…unconventional foes."

"Unconventional?"

"Sure, you know, like demons and beasts."

"Demons?" Zane echoed. "You can't be serious."

They passed cells and Zane peered into them.

Abruptly, a gaunt and wild-eyed thing snatched the bars of its cell, hissing. In the torch's light, Zane saw milky bloodshot eyes, a sunken face, and long fang-like teeth as the thing swiped for his arm holding the torch. Zane didn't flinch. He merely let the torch's fire roar to life, so bright it was blinding. The creature hissed and scuttled back to the shadows.

Zane turned to Raina. "Now are you going to explain?"

Raina shrugged. "I told you, demons." She snatched his wrist. "Now c'mon, Fire Boy, that's not our goal."

The Deadmark

Helix entered the arena with Faye next to him to the roar of the crowds. It was like a wave crashing down on him from all sides. After the dark chambers they'd just exited, the sun was practically blinding, and he squinted against it, taking in the spectacle. The stands were filled with men and women—nobles and commoners alike—many on their feet, cheering or jeering.

"So many," Helix breathed, turning in a full circle to take in the masses. "So many just to watch us suffer and die…"

Faye set her shoulders, first eyeing their fellow combatants who gained their senses, and then coolly glancing to the thousands in the stands. "Ignore them," she said. "First things first, what'd that clumsy guard give you?" He opened his mouth to question, but she interrupted. "Before you ask how I noticed, I'm a thief, remember? Not the first time I've seen sleight of hand." She shrugged. "Helps that he was about as sly as an archwolf in a bunny hutch."

Helix unfurled his fist. In his palm rested a blue-and-white ornamental band…a bracelet? "*A gift of the queen*," the guard had said. It all clicked. Queen Imala had agreed to give them artifacts from the previous Ronin. *Hiron's*. His heart skipped a beat as he examined the trinket more closely. It was made of a material he'd never seen before, hard and flat like metal but with a slightly rough texture, almost like clay. There was a carved scene of deep blue and hoary foam-capped waves inlaid with jewels, so realistic it appeared as if the image were moments away from splashing into his palm.

"Jewelry?" Faye asked. "That's…romantic. I didn't know you had a suitor. He didn't really seem your type—you know, with the thick beard and all."

"It's Hiron's," Helix breathed.

"The previous Ronin? So…legendary jewelry?"

"There's more to it." Something about the band called to him, like a phantom limb he'd been missing since an injury. He tried to feed some *flow* into it. A sudden restriction on his power made Helix choke, and he remembered. He touched the cold steel collar about his neck. A shiver traced his spine, but willfully, he set it aside for later, and focused back on the object in his hand. He fed it a trickle of power and the band grew *colder*; flakes of frost spread across its surface. "It's definitely magical. I just wish I knew what it did, or how to unlock it." He went to put it on his wrist, then hesitated. He knew exactly where it should go. Moving it to his bicep, the band snapped open, then cinched perfectly around his arm.

Faye mused, "Well, then…a sentient bangle. Learn something new every day."

"It's an armband," he mumbled.

She ran a finger down her jaw, taking him in. "Eh, it actually does kind of suit you, but we have more pressing issues…" She nodded to their fellow combatants, who were listening to the thundering drums, each waiting, watching. All vehemently aware that with the last beat, the Bloodbath would begin. Their hands flexed at their sides. "Looks like our friends are a little more…eager. Think your new toy can take out fifty warriors for us real quick?"

"Let's not count on it," Helix said.

Helix… Ayva sent.

Helix looked up and spotted Ayva on the Queen's Terrace. Ayva's mouth was parted. The bond felt…faint from here, her words like a whisper: *Wow, Helix, you look…Is that really you?*

Can't talk, little busy now.

Right, but I'm here if you need me.

You just win over the queen, make sure we're not going to get stabbed after I win this thing.

Right, will do. Speaking of, I think the queen is about to give a speech.

Sure enough, the queen rose and moved to the edge of the balcony, and her words suddenly boomed over the crowds.

An amplifying spell, Helix knew.

The drums continued, quieter now, a low thundering.

"Welcome, Covai, my darling subjects! I welcome you all to the Two Hundred Twenty-Eighth Grand Tournament of Flesh!" More horns sounded, and cheers followed, practically deafening. "Once every four years we gather here to witness a truly amazing spectacle…Yet, I believe this year is to be the most auspicious, most pivotal tournament ever to grace these lands. Today, you will witness warriors fighting and dying for your entertainment…but more than that, in these hard times, these dark days, champions arise…victors we need more than ever. We must have the strongest to defend us from the shadows that encroach. To that end, and to encourage the strongest of warriors to participate from all across Farhaven, I have added a very special prize." She waved a hand and a chest rose from a pillar in the arena, higher and higher, until it was three dozen feet in the air. The chest opened, with the guidance of a Reaver's hand. "I give to you the Earthstone! One of the Nine Elemental Stones, said to mimic the powers of the Ronin of old. It is rumored the one who collects all nine is gifted a power the world has never seen before."

Faye's jaw dropped.

The other gladiators on the sands whispered, eyes wide, practically drooling.

A few Reavers waved hands, and a crystalline matrix surrounded the pillar—a spell—some sort of warding?

The queen continued, words reverberating, "Some might wonder, why a tournament now? When the world stands upon the edge of a precipice? When the shadow in the west grows? I would answer: What better time? When else would we prove ourselves, show our might? From these sands, we will forge the strongest warriors for the coming war."

Helix sniffed. The queen wasn't as foolish as she seemed. She was addressing the war, and using the tournament as a platform, a way to provide even more legitimacy for her reign. He felt his gaze narrow. Up there, the queen was having her own battle. Sure enough, Helix noticed stands full of nobles with different emblems on their clothing: a gryphon, a giant bear, a desert snake, and a few others. Many of the cheering or politely clapping nobles in these gilded balconies were now sneering. Their power was being thwarted by the queen.

"Now," Queen Imala continued, "I am pleased to—"

Faye neared, speaking to him over the woman, "All right, we got the gist. While Her Majesty prattles on, listen up. Game plan. Our real threats are Gaius and his little runt of a pet." Her eyes flickered to Gaius and Ahma. "Even hampered by the collars, their spark is an unknown quantity, especially since you won't be able to wield your full power." A dozen warriors slowly gravitated to the other two, forming a sudden tight little group. "Seems like they've gotten themselves some friends, so the plan is—"

"Gaius is mine," Helix said suddenly.

She shook her head. "What? No, I wasn't finished. That's *not* what we're doing."

Helix looked into Faye's hard brown eyes, rimmed in red paint. "Gaius goes down first."

She folded her arms. "Exactly how many battles have you been in?"

Helix counted quickly on his fingers. "A dozen? Before you say anything, I know you've been in more…"

"More than you can count."

Undaunted, Helix added, "I also know what you want to do, even if I can't do it."

"Oh, you do, do you? Please, enlighten me, oh wise Ronin," she said, as the queen announced something that elicited another roar from the crowds.

Helix nodded to the other forty or so rough-looking warriors. "I'm guessing you want to let the others whittle Gaius and his crew down, but not so much that they become the dominant force. In the meantime, you want to pick off all the weaklings from Gaius's group. Then when the moment is right, and while they're still distracted with the other men as fodder, you want to take down the head of the snake."

Seeing Faye's mouth open in surprise was worth it. "What is this? What are you doing? Can you read minds? Is that a Ronin thing?" Her gaze narrowed. "If you're in my head, Helix, so help me—"

Helix raised his hands. "Whoa, whoa, whoa, I can't read minds. I don't know how I knew…maybe sensing battle plans is a Ronin thing? You know, being generals of the Lieon and all. It just seems logical. While it's a great plan, really, I'm going to take out Gaius first." He looked up at the crowds, fists clenched at his sides. "Gray told me we have to prove ourselves, to not hide."

"This is how you're going to do it?" She arched her brow. "This suicidal plan of throwing yourself at the strongest opponent you can find with your incredibly limited hand-to-hand fighting experience?"

Helix shrugged. "Precisely. It's gotten me this far, hasn't it?" She gave him a flat look. "Anyway, I got you on my side. The badass Thieflord of Fire, who slayed a hundred men in the Battle of the Sands."

"Yes, with *weapons and armor. Nice weapons*, I'll add. I'm very good with weapons."

He grabbed her wrist and raised her fist. "Look at that, you got weapons!"

She rolled her eyes, pulling her hand away and folding her arms across her chest. "You're an idiot." She sighed. "Fine. Gaius and Ahma it is. Just know a battle plan is only good until the first swing of the sword, or in this case, fist. Just stick close." She glared at him. "And you *will* listen to my calls, Water Boy, or I'll choke you out with your own hands."

Helix nodded. "Deal." Then he cleared his throat. "One other liiiiiiiittle problem." He nodded to Jivran. The giant just stood there— two dozen feet away, chest heaving with anger. If he could snort steam, Helix was sure he would. Even worse, Jivran had a collar on. *Great, he's got magic.* Thankfully, a hundred archers positioned upon the walls with arrows at the ready held the giant's ire in check. "I think he might go for me first."

Jivran made another throat-slitting gesture at Helix, practically shaking with rage.

"You think?" Faye whistled through her teeth. "Yeah, he wants to kill you *real* bad. What'd you do to him?"

Helix swallowed. "Honestly no idea."

She clapped him on the shoulder. "Don't worry, I'll handle the big guy. Now get ready…I think Her Royal Windbag is coming to an end…"

Helix's heart thundered.

Amplified by the spell, the queen's snide voice echoed throughout the arena, her words clearly building to a crescendo. "…When only one of you remains, one *fateful* soul, bloodied and triumphant, standing in the heart of the arena after vanquishing the most powerful of Farhaven, only then shall you earn your rightful crown! A title all the world covets…one demanding fear and awe: the one and only, *Grand Primus of Farhaven!*" Cheers shook the whole colosseum at this, rattling Helix's bones. "It will be this fated individual who shall lead us in the coming war! Beneath their sword, our enemies will tremble!"

Another roar of the crowd, and this time, the queen's silence grew.

"Now…warriors of Covai, of Farhaven…"

Drums thundered and Helix's pulse raced.

Thud.

Thud.

The tension mounted. Helix could see Gaius's eyes tighten as he stood among his men.

Meanwhile, the other forty or so fighters all spread out, their muscles and tendons taut, eyes flickering from one to the next, waiting, the fervor of blood, the hunger of battle all-consuming.

To the death, Helix knew, and he could hear the thundering of his own heart in his ears, so loud it nearly drowned out the rising beats of the drums. Meanwhile, the crowds had gone still, the whole arena captured, on the edge of their seats, holding their breath…waiting.

"It's almost that time," Faye whispered, looking up at the hot sun above. "It wouldn't be a bad day to die."

"We're not dying," Helix said. "Not today, anyway. Are you ready?"

Faye grinned. "Y'know, you're beginning to grow on me, Water Boy. Suppose I can live a little longer." She hunkered down at his side, lowering her head, and her knuckles cracked. "Ready as I'll ever be."

The queen, who was grinning at the corner of Helix's vision, suddenly cried, *"Begin!"*

Just like that, the drums stopped.

Helix, Faye at his side, burst into motion.

Fighters roared, laying into one another.

Helix ignored them all, his gaze set solely on Gaius. He charged. Jivran bellowed, running to intercept him, as predicted. The giant's steps practically rattled the arena as he barreled toward Helix.

"Faye!" Helix called.

"Relax! I'm on it!"

Suddenly, an apple core flew through the air and collided with Jivran's face. It wasn't enough to slow the giant's momentum, but it did stun the man enough so that Helix ducked and rolled to the side of his outstretched arms. Jivran pivoted, but Faye was there. She leapt, swinging her legs around his neck. Jivran grabbed at her, but she twisted like a snake, and with the power of their combined momentum, she sent him tumbling forward.

Faye tried to untangle herself, but Jivran clutched her tight and she went down with him. Their bodies sent up plumes of dust as they slammed and skidded across the sands.

Ahead, Gaius's back was turned, and Helix spotted an opening to take him out. Yet he couldn't abandon Faye—not when she was literally fighting the giant who wanted Helix's head. So, with a string of curses, Helix ran back to Faye.

A group of warriors from the main group broke off, chasing Helix. He ignored them.

Faye slithered out from beneath Jivran, where she'd been briefly pinned. Crowds cheered as Faye slid under a punch that would have bent iron.

Helix arrived, pulling flow and sending what was supposed to be an ice pick. The collar grew cold around his neck, and instead, he sent a jettison of water that splashed the back of Jivran's head. The giant touched his soaked, bald skull and sneered, "Oh gods…"

"Good going, Water Boy, you just gave him a bath!" Faye called. "Maybe towel him down now and tuck him in for a nap?"

Jivran turned to face Helix and his eyes grew wide, hungry. He swung.

Faye cursed and dashed in front, pushing Helix aside to deflect a punch that skimmed off her forearm. They both slid across the sands. She winced, clutching her arm, shaking it out. "Damn it, that really hurt. Definitely gonna leave a bruise. What in the seven hells are you doing, you idiot! I told you, I got this!"

"Helping!" Helix said, gaining his feet.

"Oh, really? Is that what you call it?" Faye shouted, then her eyes grew wide. "Shit, incoming!"

Jivran roared, charging.

She pushed Helix out of the way again and slipped a kick toward the man that would have shattered ribs.

Helix saw an opening. He ran and leapt on Jivran's back, wrapped his bicep around a trunk-like neck and squeezed, choking the giant. For a moment, Jivran struggled, scrambling to grab Helix—his massive bulk restricting his movement. "Now!" Helix called, and Faye ran forward, striking, trying to bring the giant down. Then Jivran's hand finally grasped Helix's ankle and yanked. *Oh no...* Helix was flung like a discus, smashing into Faye. The two rolled across the arena's sand as crowds laughed and cheered.

She rose to her feet, brushing herself off with a growl. "Why are you here again?"

"It looked like you needed some help!"

"Well, I didn't! I don't ever need help, and you're supposed to get Gaius!" She pointed to Gaius, who was fighting in the distance with his men. "You're letting our chance slip away!"

"Gaius can wait," Helix shot back, watching as Jivran turned on the warriors who had been chasing Helix, grabbed two, and smashed them together like dinner plates. The crowds cheered. "Look, Jivran's got magic. *I* have magic. You said it yourself, you don't have your weapons."

"I don't need weapons, I just need to figure out how he's not taking any damage."

"Magic," Helix repeated again. "Besides, he wants me, not you."

"Uh, maybe you didn't notice, Water Boy, but we're in a death match!" Faye gestured to the dozens of men fighting, crashing, and crying out. "They *all* want us dead! And I can handle a towering muscle-bound idiot."

"Listen to me, my instincts say Jivran first, then Gaius together."

Faye grimaced, watching Gaius and his group lay into the other warriors, cries echoing across the sands. "Fine, but we better make this quick—we're losing our opening."

Six men lay in a heap around Jivran, unmoving, one or two groaning.

Two scraggly-looking warriors snarled, "Forget this! I just wanted to kill the weak boy, not fight this monster!" The two men fled.

Jivran turned back to Helix. "You…fight me…"

"Gladly," Helix said.

Faye took a step forward. "Us," she corrected. "You fight us."

Jivran's face contorted, eyes full of confusion. "Why? Why protect him? He weak, small! *Nothing*. You strong."

Faye sniffed. "I don't need a reason, you big idiot." She folded her arms. "Maybe I just don't like you."

Helix felt a sliver of hope for the first time.

Ayva sent through the bond. *You can do this.*

"Fine," Jivran said. "Kill you both. Steal spark."

Steal…spark? Helix wondered. *What in the Tranquil Seas is he talking about?*

Jivran abruptly beat his big barrel chest, then charged. For a flicker of a moment, Helix saw something, some magic…faint threads in the air, but then it was gone, and Jivran was upon them. They both leapt to the side. Helix, drawing on his Nexus, formed a shiv of ice and, as he rolled, jabbed it into Jivran's calf. The man howled in pain, swinging. Helix was too slow to dodge, and a huge fist clipped his skull. Pain exploded, blotting out his vision, and he tumbled and rolled along the ground.

Helix growled, staggering to his feet as Faye laid into the giant.

For a moment, all Helix could do was watch her, and his jaw dropped.

The crowds were silent.

She moved like a panther, full of grace, yet with ferocity and violence as she punched, kicked, and dodged. Faye expertly ducked a punch that would have taken a chunk out of a boulder, letting it scrape across her hair as she dipped inside and smashed an elbow to the Jivran's knee, eliciting a howl of pain from the big man.

"Need…you…shorter!" Faye shouted.

Jivran grabbed Faye's arm.

Before he could do anything, Helix slipped in the gap and slammed a spike of ice into the back of the man's hand, forcing him to let go. Faye tore into the man like a lumberjack whittling away at a tree trunk. With a last swift kick to the back of Jivran's leg, the giant collapsed to his knees. Grinning in triumph, Faye spun and delivered a roundhouse kick to the man's temple with a bone-crunching crack.

It should have been a finishing blow.

Only it wasn't.

Jivran's head barely twitched, as if his girthy neck was made of stone.

The spectators gasped.

The giant grinned and snatched Faye's throat. "Fast wench, but soft strikes…"

Not good, Helix thought, and seeing an opening, he barreled into Jivran—making the giant drop Faye as they rolled on the ground. Jivran's weight and size, however, were too much as he pinned Helix and began pummeling. "*Weak!*" Jivran boomed, as a heavy cross slammed into Helix's temple. It felt like being struck with a hammer. Pain exploded in his skull. Through blurred vision, he saw another fist hurtle toward him. Helix knew if he got hit with a punch like that again, he'd die. By sheer instinct, he pulled more, demanded more from his flow. Grudgingly, it listened, and this time the collar grew painfully frigid on his neck. *Hot and cold?* It must have something to do with his power of water. Thankfully, a shield of ice formed in front of Helix's palms, and Jivran's fist crashed into it, creating a long fissure in the frozen liquid. Again, the giant struck, and with each successive punch he bellowed, "Weak!" Jivran roared. "Small!" *Smash.* "Like…" *Smash.* "My…" *Smash.* "Father!"

Helix strained, his muscles burning, attempting to keep the shield between him and the terrifying giant.

The ice shield cracked again and again, ready to collapse.

It would shatter any moment.

Helix! Ayva sent.

Helix felt the crowd's eyes, the world watching.

He remembered Gray's voice: *A shadow is coming. The world needs us. We need to prove to them we are worthy of the mantle.*

I can't be weak, Helix whispered in his mind. *I can't be weak…I can't be—*

The shield cracked a little more, fissuring down the middle and his arms trembled beneath Jivran's powerful blows as the man continued to bash and shout in a blind rage. In that moment, as Helix knew he was about to die, a single phrase he had been hearing again and again repeated in his mind, searing his tumultuous thoughts—spoken by Gray, by Ayva, and finally by Faye:

"*You are a Ronin. Act like it.*"

The clarity, the simplicity of those words—the unerring truth—struck Helix to his soul.

Finally it made sense, and he believed it.

I am a Ronin.

Through a transparent spot in the ice, Helix saw Jivran cock back another fist, roaring, and Helix let the ice shield drop. The fist came flying through. Only this time, Helix wasn't there. He shifted his body and the fist smashed into the sand where he had been only a moment ago. Helix pulled, drawing deep within the core of his soul, demanding power. Immediately, the collar sent stabbing pain throughout his body. He ignored it. *More*, he demanded. While the collar grew frosty, feeling as if it was burning his skin off—Helix's power listened. Overlapping plates of ice flowed over Helix's arm, the frozen armor suddenly making his limb feel…*stronger*.

The giant, still on top of Helix, pinning him to the sands, snarled and swung again, looking to end the one-sided battle.

Helix snatched the man's fist with his ice-coated palm, stopping it in place.

Jivran's eyes split wide.

Before he could react, Helix swung again, punching up at the man. He saw blue veins in his arm, as if his blood was filled with ice, and he slammed his fist into Jivran's square jaw. The blow connected. Where Faye's strike with all its power had barely shifted the man's head, this time Jivran's skull rocked. Blood sprayed. The giant's eyes rolled in their sockets as he tried to orient himself, tried to shake away the pain.

Only, Helix wasn't done. Jivran still pinned him, so he drew more of his power and coated his legs in that same frozen-blue armor. Crying out, he shoved. Despite the man pressing down on him like a two-ton draft horse, Jivran flew, landing on his back on the sand.

Gaining his feet, Helix ran and leapt.

The giant regained his senses, grinding his teeth as he threw a punch, stronger than any before, powered by sudden thick threads of ruddy magic. Helix was ready for this. Flinging a hand, he sent out ice: thick and hoary. It coated Jivran's arm—freezing it in place. As he flew through the air, Helix bellowed, drawing more power. Conjuring a five-foot-long spear of ice to his hand, he rammed it into the ground, a finishing blow that sent a ripple across the sands.

The crowds went silent.

Then roared.

Helix had missed the giant by a hair's breadth, burying the ice spear right beside Jivran's head.

Slowly, the crowd's fervor rose, and a chant sounded.

"*Kill!*"

"*Kill!*"

"*Kill!*"

Helix turned his wrath on the crowd.

They silenced.

Huh. Didn't expect that to work.

He looked back to Jivran as the ice melted, dripping onto the giant's bald, tattooed brow. Jivran stared wide-eyed at the spear, then squinted up at Helix, clearly confused. "Why not kill?"

Helix rose, letting the spear dissolve to water. "I'm not going to make a long speech, but I think I got you wrong. You're not evil." Helix pointed across the sands to the other warriors, to Gaius, who lifted a spike of stone and jabbed it through a man's eye, slowly, painstakingly, while grinning. "*He* is evil. He is weak. That's who our real enemy is." He looked back down at Jivran, then smiled. "Join us."

Jivran eyed his outstretched hand, then gripped it. Helix grinned, helping the big man to his feet with the power of his enhanced right arm—thankfully, since there was no feasible way he would have been able to pull the giant up without it.

Faye joined his side, wiping her hands. "Did I miss anything?" Dust coated her face and some of her bandages were torn, revealing more of her pretty, if terrifying, features. Blood covered parts of her body. "It's not mine." She planted her hands on her hips, looking up at Jivran, who stood at Helix's side. "Well, look at that, we've got a giant. And ice armor," she said, admiring the blue ice still coating Helix's arm—the one that didn't have Hiron's band on it. She whistled. "Looks cool…very Ronin-like."

Helix raised a brow. "Thanks, but I could have used your help. Where were you?"

"Me? Just house cleaning. Besides, weren't you going on about 'something, something, I need to prove I'm a Ronin'?" She gestured to the crowds, who roared, chanting, but Helix couldn't quite make out their words. "Looks like you made a decent start."

Helix looked away from the spectators. He'd almost forgotten they were there. "Not done yet," he said, turning toward their true threat.

Gaius and Ahma. They weren't alone. The dozen warriors at their side had become more than two dozen. They'd somehow swayed a large cluster of the gladiators to their side. Gaius grinned, blood covering his face. Ahma, the ratlike man, picked a piece of flesh from his black sleeve and joined his leader's side, showing a haughty curl of his lip. His collar glowed red-hot with use

"You two with me?" Helix asked.

At his side, Jivran grabbed the ice pick that was still sprouting from his hand, then pulled it free with a trickle of blood. Flesh knit as his wound quickly healed, and he grunted, staring ahead. "With you. We kill."

Faye shrugged. "If the big guy says so, lead the way. Besides…"—she stretched her lithe muscles, then cracked her neck and bounced lightly on her toes—"that was a decent warm-up, but I could use a real fight now."

Jivran rumbled, "I no warm-up. I crush you."

"Sure, sure." Faye patted the man's trunk-like arm. "Whatever you say, big guy. We'll call it a draw."

Jivran growled. "You saved by him!" He pointed to Helix.

Helix rubbed his brow with his ice-hand. "Guys? Really, not the time."

Faye sighed. "Right, right, big evil group of men while tens of thousands are watching us…I gotta know, big guy…I overheard something when you were punching Helix. What was that all about? Helix reminds you of someone?"

"Father. Weak man. Small man. Whip me, hit me…I wrong. Helix strong. Not weak."

Faye's jaw dropped, and then she chuckled. "Oh, that is priceless. So let me get this straight. What you're telling me is that you have a troublesome past with your father"—she looked to Helix—"and so do you…" She chuckled again. "Renalin, the Creator himself, knows I do. Oh lords, we are quite the trio. Good job Helix, you know how to pick 'em."

Gaius marched toward them, while two dozen men at his side spread out as if to encircle the three, their eyes full of hunger, hate, and unslaked bloodlust.

Faye's nose scrunched in disgust. "What's wrong with them? Seven hells, you'd think we killed their favorite pet."

"Look off. Not human," Jivran grunted.

Something did seem off with the rough-looking warriors…from their bloodshot eyes to the way they ground their teeth. Some sort of herb or drug? No, it was something else. Helix shook his head. "Doesn't matter. We just have to win."

Thud. Thud. Thud.

The thousands of spectators took up a steady rhythm, beating their feet against the stands.

Helix looked to his friends. "Let's bring the fight to them, shall we?"

"Couldn't have said it better myself," Faye said.

And together, they stalked toward Gaius.

Jivran grunted. "Five survive."

Helix said, "Well, let's make sure we're among them."

And to the roar of the crowds, they charged.

Curated Creatures

Zane, Raina at his side, reached an intersection with many more cells. Creatures thrust their claws through the bars as they drew too near. "Raina," Zane said, "I'm going to need more of an explanation for what's going on here. If you're worried I'm going to back out, I'm not. I just want to know what I'm getting myself into." Who was he all of the sudden, Gray? Since when did he want to know what he was getting himself into? Normally, he'd just break enough fingers and burn enough things, to get where he wanted to go.

In his mind, Hannah smiled. *You're learning.*

I'm trying.

"That's fair," Raina admitted, thrusting the torch out as a clawed hand grasped at her sleeve from within a cell. "This is the queen's little den of iniquities," she said, passing a cage with a strange beast. Horns sprouted from its head, something between a goat and a wolf. It rumbled with a guttural snarl as they passed.

"Yeah…I heard she likes rare things."

Raina snorted. "Sure you have. Even more certain she'd love to throw you and your little legends into these cages."

"Where does she find them?"

"The queen scours the lands of Farhaven and places the most twisted and bizarre creatures she can find in here. I heard some were found in far-off places like the Mountains of Soot, or the enchanted woods of Drymaus…but I think some are just men who've sold their souls." She looked over at him, raising an eyebrow. "This world is full of all sorts of evil, brooding eyes. You should know that by now."

Zane was all too aware. He banished images of Sithel and Reaver Nefrin from his mind as flames burned in his fist and made the torch's flames rise. "Fair enough, but how is killing some demon going to get me into the next round?"

The hallways grew darker still, casting long shadows from their guttering torches, and Raina's eyes glinted. "You'll see," she said, her breath heavy. "Let's just hope you're as strong as the stories say you are, Ronin of Fire."

"How do you even know about this place?" Zane asked.

"I was told about it from someone who'd been in charge of feeding them. Some of them seem to like...human flesh."

"Of course they do." They reached another door.

Written on the steel face were the words: *Second round creatures.*

"Well, there we go. We're here!" Raina lifted her keys, trying one after another. "Damn it, one of these has to—"

Zane seared the lock off with fire.

"Right, I keep forgetting."

He strode inside.

Inside were six cells, and a few creatures crept forth from the shadows to peer at them. A fox-faced saerok with long gangly arms and talons had been clearly bred with a man. It chittered, and its fangs snapped at the air as it hissed, "Oh, little humanssss...come clossssserrr so I can tear the flessssh from your bonesssss."

"Shhh, quiet, creepy thing," Raina said, then turned to Zane. "So here's my plan—"

"I take one of them out, and then you use your incredible and kind of eerie flesh powers to make me look like one of them. I'm guessing these things are going to be in the next battle?" She gave a nod. "Well, there we go, just like that I'll be in the second round. Only...on the wrong side. Still, I don't think the crowds will care. I just need to win...and I will win."

She mused, "Yeah, that's pretty much it."

Zane stalked the cells. "Now the only real question is which one do I want..." He thrust the torch out and saw an assortment of vile faces, some creatures, some men, but all looked like they deserved to be locked up.

"Remember, my only limit is that you have to be roughly the same size."

One after another, Zane passed.

A giant with claws for hands. "No." A half-man, half-birdlike creature, with a beak for a nose. "No." A green goblin-like creature sprouting a dozen small horns. "No." Then Zane froze before the next cell, and a grin creased his features. "This one."

"Uh-huh, and what about something that's not going to rip your head off?"

"This one," he repeated.

"Are you sure?" Raina asked. "I mean…that's…are you *sure*?"

"Positive."

She took a deep breath and faced him. "All right, like last time—"

"It's going to hurt. I remember." He smirked. "Now will you stop stalling? I need to win this damn tournament and save your brother."

Bright almond eyes took him in, and with a faint twist of her lips, Raina smiled. "Right. One last thing…I'm not going to be able to change you back until I see you next. With this level of magic, it could last a long time. You're going to be stuck like this…for a while." She shrugged. "Or an incredibly short time. Honestly, I have no idea, first time I'm doing anything on this level." He raised a brow and opened his mouth. She held out a hand before he could retort. "I'm not trying to talk you out of it, just warning you."

He nodded and grabbed her shoulders gently, but firmly. "This isn't going to sound as convincing when you change me, so I'm going to say it now…I'm going to save your brother, Raina. I swear it. You can trust me."

Tears came to her eyes, and she nodded, wiping them away. "I…um…" She seemed to swallow a knot in her throat. "You know, if you didn't look like a creepy old man that was going to try to grab my backside, I might just kiss you."

Zane grunted. "See? Twice in one day. Guess I'm not as hideous as you said."

"No, you *really* are."

He huffed a laugh. "Right. Okay, I'm ready."

She nodded, and pain consumed Zane. He cried out, the sound even making the men and creatures in the cells step back. When it was done, he felt his old, lecherous man form had shifted to something entirely different, and wholly…unholy. Zane turned to face the prisoner within the cell, and it stared at him, as if gazing into a mirror. "Amusing," the prisoner said in a low rumble that shook the hall. "You think because you look like me, I won't kill you?"

"No. Quite the opposite." Then to Raina: "You might want to step back."

She did, surprisingly with no quips. Zane snapped his fingers and flames melted the lock on the prisoner's cage into molten slag, which dripped to the cold floor. "Well? What are you waiting for?" Claws clacked as the prisoner shoved the door wide with a creak. Its hollowed eyes gleamed as the prisoner inside the cage attacked.

Fire consumed the hall.

ICE BOY

Gaius, Ahma, and his group looked stunned—they hadn't expect them to attack. Helix, with Faye and Jivran at his side, advanced on the twenty rough-looking warriors.

"Kill them!" Gaius roared.

The gladiators charged.

Helix responded with a wave of ice.

Gaius erected a barrier of stone, and most of the ice shards collided with it, yet a few found their mark, taking out men here and there. Jivran roared and barreled into a group of bare-chested gladiators. He snapped a man's neck with a twist using his huge, bare hands, then threw the man's body at a group of warriors, as if bowling. In the corner of Helix's vision, Faye moved like a specter, slipping in and out of the ranks of men, striking with brutal efficiency and grace—so much so that Helix was transfixed for a moment.

Thank the gods she's on our side.

A voice drew him back to the moment.

Gaius shouted, "Kill the boy. He's their leader! They will crumble with the Ice Boy dead!" He pointed at Helix, and six warriors broke from the main group and surrounded Helix.

Helix rumbled, "If you knew what's good for you, you would turn and run."

The six men cackled. "Don't listen to him!" said a sunken-chested man with a snaggletooth. "He's just a bloody Untamed!"

"That arm, though, Godwin, that doesn't look like no common Untamed..." said another, pointing to Helix's ice-coated arm with its wicked spikes.

"He bleeds like anyone else!" Godwin said, gesturing to Helix's brow.

Helix wiped the blood and shrugged. "Fair enough. Well, come on, then, let's do this."

The six men attacked.

Helix created a patch of ice and slid beneath the first two gladiators, stabbing long ice picks through their feet, rooting them in place. The remaining four rushed him. Helix ducked a strike, but then took a blow to his chin that dazed him. He tried to dodge, but Godwin, the snaggletoothed thief of a man, kicked his knee, almost tearing ligaments and tendons. Helix roared in pain, legs buckling. He blew all four back with an icy blast.

His anger flared.

Not again. Not ever.

He had to prove himself.

The refrain returned in his head:

I am a Ronin.

Godwin was the first to rush in, eager. Helix, still on his knees, saw it coming. The man kicked, aiming for Helix's head. This time, Helix caught the man's boot, and with his enhanced strength, *twisted.* A pop sounded as the ankle snapped, and the snaggletoothed warrior howled, writhing on the ground and clutching his ankle. The other three men hesitated, looking like they wanted to run. Helix didn't let them. A man punched, and Helix pulled, popping the man's arm out of its socket, then smashing him with a headbutt that he reinforced with ice. Another tried to sucker punch him, and ancient instincts whispered:

Be water...

Helix ducked the haymaker and drove an ice spike into the side of the man's temple. The last two charged, and Helix drew on his Nexus, conjuring fist-sized chunks of ice that he shot out, smashing teeth and knocking the two out cold. It was over as soon as it started, and they all lay motionless, bloody, and silenced.

Suddenly, Godwin garbled a vile curse. He rose and pulled a hidden shiv from his boot, and stabbed Helix's exposed back. *Be water...* the voice whispered. Somehow, Helix moved *with* the strike, turning ever so slightly so the blade glided and barely missed severing his spine. As he dropped, he gave a sharp elbow to Godwin's temple, and the thief collapsed, dead. Only...Godwin twitched, not in the throes of death, but with something else. Something unholy, as if he were possessed. It all clicked when Helix turned to watch Jivran fight six men. They piled on the giant like monkeys climbing a tree, wild and frenzied. The dozen gladiators fighting Faye were equally demented, enraged, eyes bloodshot. They practically foamed at the mouth. Then Helix saw it: faint red threads in the air.

Across the sands, and away from the fighting, Ahna stood, hands flitting as if puppeteering. The right hand of Gaius chanted, a scarlet fervor in his eyes, and a ruddy spell flowed outward, sifting into the two dozen men or so under Gaius's control.

An old memory, both his, and not his, whispered to him: *Bloodfrenzy.*

"Great," Helix growled. "That's why they're so damn tough to take out." Then he shouted to his companions, "Kill Ahna! I think he's possessing the others, putting them into a frenzy!"

Faye replied, backflipping over half a dozen men who tried to surround her, "We're well aware, Water Boy! Kill that one-eyed bastard now!"

"Yes!" Jivran roared. "Kill leader!"

I can do that. Helix turned his ire on Gaius and stalked toward the one-eyed man as the crowds chanted.

Now he understood what he was hearing.

Wa-ter.

Wa-ter.

Gaius's one eye was wide and bloodshot with rage, as he ordered a huge man before him, "Get him! Get him now, or I'll flay your hide!"

The brute, while not as tall as Jivran, was still a monstrosity—wider, with a scarred chest and black eyes. He was the final barrier between Helix and Gaius. A mark of a Covian guard was burned into his muscled arm, and he sneered at Helix, "Don't be afraid, little man…I'll kill you real quick, and your friends can—"

Helix flung out a hand. A spike of ice slammed into the man's neck, and he gurgled blood, falling over, lifeless. "Sorry, I can't waste too much energy, or time."

Gaius's muscled chest heaved with rage. "You…" Stone formed all across his body, thick plates of armor like a second skin, as Helix advanced. "Why won't you die?!"

Helix bellowed, and his ice-blue fist collided with Gaius's stone gauntlet, the sound of it like a thunderclap. Gaius flew backward. The stone armor crumbled, no match for Helix's own power, and the man coughed, spitting scarlet, viscous blood to the sands.

At the same time, Helix's collar blazed hot to the touch, scalding his neck. He'd been ignoring it up until now, fighting all those men.

At the sound of a crack, Helix looked down to see his ice-arm shatter to a thousand pieces. He tried to call it back, but he couldn't.

Fear traced his spine, then it dawned on him.

I used too much…

Helix began to understand.

I can push past its restriction if I can withstand the pain. Like a river, the wider I open it, the more flow I can use. Yet there's a limit…

If he pushed to widen the river of power too fast or hard, the collar would kill him. He could damage his own power. Like a muscle, it grew with resistance, but it could also snap. That's why the ice-arm had shattered. *I have to push it, but I also have to be careful.* As it stood, he didn't think he'd ruptured or shattered his sparkwell, only bruised the hand that reached for it. He felt it returning even now, but he couldn't use magic, not yet.

He needed time to get his power back.

He needed to stall.

Gaius gained his feet, his face stained with blood that mixed with the red paint splashed across his broad chest. His dark eyes raged as they fixed upon Helix.

The crowds stomped in rhythm, as if sensing imminent death.

For the crowd, anyone would do.

Helix hated that he was giving them entertainment, but he also needed them…needed the world to see what the Ronin were capable of doing. Gaius seemed like just another broken man corrupted by power, but then he cackled. Not as much from loathing, but rather pity. "You fool boy…you don't get it, do you? You think you're special?" Gaius seethed as Helix stalked forward. "Do you know how many men thought they were destined for greatness, only to have their blood spilled upon these sands? There is only one rule in Covai, one truth! The strong survive, and the weak die. There is no strength to be found on these sands…not while *they* hold all the cards." He pointed to the nobles in the higher stands. "They watch us from the safety of their luxurious balconies, sipping their chilled drinks in the hot sun while little ants dance about on a stage for their entertainment. You and I? We're *nothing*."

Helix needed to bide his time. "If you're so set on proving them wrong, then don't play their game. Stop fighting us!"

Gaius gave a small, sad, almost disgusted shake of his head. "There is no winning this, no avoiding our fate!"

The words struck Helix like a lightning bolt, and memories assaulted him.

Helix looked down at his small shoes and tiny frame. He was eight—he'd just had his birthday. His father was there, and they hid in a dank alley, the smell of fish guts and ocean salt heavy in the air. They were in the Fishmongers' Ward of Median, near the wharf. It was a moment they'd been planning for weeks, a moment Helix had dreaded, but he had come all the same. His father's face was clear and memorable as ever: every wrinkle, every hard angle, down to the snow-white whiskers of his beard, and the deep frown lines at the sides of his mouth.

This was the moment that had changed Helix's entire life.

"It's time," his father had said.

"I don't want to do this…" Helix pleaded yet again, gripping his father's sleeve. "Please don't make me do this?"

His father's face grew hard, unyielding, bright blue eyes piercing into Helix, then it softened, as if Helix was simply too young, too foolish to see the truth before his eyes. "You don't get it, do you, boy? There's no avoiding our destiny. My father was wretched and poor, and I was determined to rise above, only to be pulled back into the same muck. Even if you gain riches, and power…life will find a way to put you back where you belong. In your station in life, men can never truly rise above. This…this is your fate."

Helix severed the memory with a growl and returned to the moment to glare at Gaius. "No."

Gaius looked flabbergasted. "No?" he simply repeated.

"Yeah, that's it. I just disagree, that's all. Say we prove it to them." Helix reached out a hand. "Only five can survive, right? So join us, and we can fight back against them, *together*. We can change that status quo, change our fate." His jaw tightened. Helix felt a whisper of power return, the Nexus coming to his mind's eye. It wasn't much, but it was something. "I swear it."

Gaius looked hesitant for a moment, his one eye squinting, his hand trembling as if it wanted to take Helix's. Then he shook his head and gave a thin smile. "You almost made me believe…no, I'll never bend a knee. Not to you, not to *anyone*." He roared, sending out a thick spike of stone from the ground beneath Helix's feet.

The spike would have impaled Helix if he hadn't felt the ground rumbling beneath him a moment before. He leapt to the side, sending a blade of ice that caught Gaius in the leg. The man cried out, but sent another spike of stone upward. With his limited power, Helix shattered them as quickly as he could, but it was clear the man was going far beyond the threshold of his power. Gaius would rupture his spark soon, or the collar would kill him any moment, but it didn't look like he cared as long as he killed Helix first.

Suddenly, Ahma broke from his chanting, the warriors losing some of their fervor as the rodent-faced man sent thick threads of red and tan. A spasm of flesh coursed through Helix, sending him to his knees. Then the pain vanished, and Hiron's armband grew cold on his bicep. *It absorbed the spell…* Yet, Ahma's meddling had done its job. Struck to his knees, he couldn't dodge in time, and another of Gaius's earthen spikes shot up from the sands. This time the sharp stone stabbed Helix through his shoulder. He gasped from the knifelike agony.

Helix, no! Ayva leaned over the railing as if preparing to jump into the arena to save him.

Don't, Ayva! They'll kill you too!

I…I can't watch you die!

Helix could only flash her a small, weak smile. *Good thing I won't.* Helix reached for his power and…it came up empty. The collar was scorching on his throat. *Abyss take me…*

Gaius drew nearer, chunks of stone floating around him. The crowds stomped in a rhythm:

"*Kill!*"

"*Kill!*"

"*Kill!*"

In the corner of his vision, Faye and Jivran, overwhelmed, were slowly losing to the frenzied gladiators. Even with all Jivran's might and Faye's skill, it was clear they'd be dead soon.

Gaius muttered in disbelief, "I won…" He cackled, his one eye growing wide. "I beat a Ronin!" Seeing Helix's surprise, Gaius barked a cruel laugh. "Oh yes, I knew your little secret, young Ronin of Water. Who else could cast that much water and ice? Yet, to beat you...I suppose the stories were just that, *stories*."

Helix snarled, trying to rise, but the stone pinned him. He needed time. "I will not fall here...I cannot fall here!" He tried to pull himself off the earthen spike that impaled him, but Gaius curled his hand, and shackles of stone enveloped Helix's feet, holding him in place.

"Something to prove, banished boy?" Again, Helix's whole body went stiff. "Oh, I know that too. After all, I should know that mark well..." Gaius unwrapped a cloth from his forearm to reveal a giant black X.

Even pinned as he was, Helix breathed, "The banished mark..."

"We're not so different, little legend. I am you, only I see the whole picture."

Warm blood ran in thick rivulets down Helix's arm. *Too much*, Helix knew. *Focus! I just need my power!* Yet it felt like dipping his hands into a bowl of water, only to come up with dry fingers. *Tranquil Seas, I need time!* That was the one thing he was out of. *Why hasn't it recovered yet?* "What whole picture?"

Gaius stalked toward Helix as the crowds chanted a chorus—their anticipation heightening. "I've had the luxury of time to see the way the world is spinning. A darkness is coming."

"The shadow in the west..."

Gaius smiled. "No, something else. I admit that evil is something foul, but this is a threat much closer than you expect...an evil you won't see until it kills you, kills us all."

Helix fought back the pain in his shoulder and demanded, "Wh-what are you talking about?"

"Your Thieflord friend knows," Gaius said, nodding to Faye, who barely slipped another strike. "You think Thieflords have sat quietly this whole time? '*Strength is life, weakness is death...*'" Gaius quoted, then snorted. "It is more than a simple phrase muttered by fools or criminals. It's high time we ended this." A stone sword formed in his hand.

Helix struggled, his heart beating faster. "You don't have to...do this..."

Gaius knelt and snarled his next words into Helix's ear, "Our hands are forced, little brother. Shame, though, really...I was beginning to like you. Goodbye, little Ronin." He thrust his sword toward the hollow of Helix's throat.

I don't want to die, Helix thought in panic. *Not here. Not now. Not yet.*

He grasped for his power.

Nothing.

The sword descended.

Give me my power!

Nothing.

Death descended.

Then he remembered.

Water, both wild and tumultuous as a waterfall, was also calm as a placid lake. It was the key to his Nexus, and perhaps it was the key to understanding the collar. So he released a deep breath, closing his eyes and accepting whatever came next.

In that moment, a glimmer, a faint vestige of his power flickered in the corner of his mind, and Helix seized it. Inside, he was both calm and wild. The floodgates opened wide, and the torrent of water in his mind returned, rushing back into the empty reservoirs, the dry rivers roaring with his renewed *flow*. Bellowing, Helix broke the stone holding his legs, then grabbed the spike in his shoulder and pulled it free. He dodged Gaius's killing blow, the sword skimming his neck. The man's one eye went wide and he tried to redirect his blade, to hack into Helix, but Helix *was* water: turning, twisting, fluid. The stone spike danced from his left hand to his right as he rotated in a full circle beneath Gaius's blade—avoiding another killing strike—and at last, he let the spike descend, stabbing Gaius through the chest with his own weapon.

It all happened in an instant.

Breathing hard, Helix stepped back to witness what he'd done.

Gaius gasped, eye wide in shock as he took in the stone spike that rose from his broad chest. The man staggered back. Blood flowed from the fatal wound, running down his painted abdomen. More blood trickled from Gaius's mouth. The stone sword slipped from the man's grip, falling to the sand.

Then his single eye glinted in realization, and unexpectedly, his lips twisted with a faint smile. "Destiny…"

He collapsed.

The crowds roared.

The warriors fighting Jivran suddenly fell to their knees as if their strings were cut. Helix looked over. Across the sands, Faye held Ahma's decapitated head by its matted black hair, breathing hard. Ahma's ratlike face was frozen in an expression of loathing and surprise. Faye grimaced at the gory trophy before tossing it away and coolly ambling to Helix's side, wiping her hands. "Well, look at you. You survived!"

Helix put a hand to his wounded shoulder, feeling a little faint, but remained upright. "Yeah, I guess so, mostly. So did you. You took out the Flesh threader, nicely done."

She snorted. "Yeah, about bloody time. That mousy bastard was a real pain in the ass, making all those guys bloodlusted, or whatever." She sighed. "I was *trying* to go for that effortless, almost bored look for the Bloodbath. You know, really impress the crowds with my apathy." He raised a brow. "Don't give me that look. Good apathy takes work. Anyway, that rat-faced little creep really put a cramp in my style." Then she looked at all the warriors who had been under Ahma's spell. The men stood, sat, or knelt, dazed, hands to their heads, moaning or staring into space. "Huh. Creepy. Cutting the head off the snake is usually just symbolic, but guess not this time." Then she eyed the blood oozing from Helix's shoulder. "Also, you don't look so hot. You gonna live, Ice Boy?"

"Ice Boy…" Helix quirked an eyebrow. "I thought I was Water Boy."

"Promotion," she said, eyeing Gaius's body. "You did well. I mean, took you a little while, but you got there."

Helix cursed. "I had to wade through a half-dozen men, thank you very much!"

She rolled her eyes. "Boo-hoo, I had *two* dozen, and mine were all crazed from that stupid Flesh threader."

"So were mine! Also there were only twenty men in total!"

"Are you doubting me, young Ronin?" She scoffed. "Shame on you." Then put a hand on his shoulder and inspected his wound. "I'm ganna' chalk it up to the blood loss and let it slide this time." She ripped a length of cloth from her bandages and tied it tightly around Helix's wound.

Jivran joined them, lumbering over to stand at Helix's side. The big man looked down at him, then to Gaius, who lay in a pool of blood that swallowed up the sands. Jivran grunted and clapped Helix on the back. "Good job." He nodded to Gaius. "Evil. Dead."

Helix nodded, but wasn't so sure himself. A tremor of uncertainty and guilt spiraled inside of him. So much of what Gaius said was wrong, and yet much of it felt far closer to the truth than he'd like to admit. The banished mark—

Shaking his head to prevent himself from going down that rabbit hole, Helix looked away from Gaius's body, then smiled up at the giant, the smile only a little forced. "Thanks, big guy. You did well, too!" Blood covered Jivran's tattooed, red-painted body, but Helix saw no actual wounds. He hoped he wouldn't have to face Jivran again, for multiple reasons.

Then a spike of fear shot through him. The banished mark on Gaius's arm played on Helix's mind again, and guilt twisted his insides. Gaius had understood him, at least a part of him. Sure, the man had been misguided and he'd chosen the wrong path, yet...Helix understood how that could have easily happened. He even felt some of Gaius's pain. Being sent to die, shunned by your own people. Worst of all was the last thing he said, about the Thieflords, and Helix looked to Faye. She was cleaning her makeshift weapon on a dead man's cloth pants. "Wait, is that...a chunk of bone? You made a bone into a shiv?"

Faye shrugged. "Told you I'm good with weapons. So, do we run off or...What's going on? Why's no one called an end to this thing yet?" A chant rose from the masses in the stands. "Oh, seven hells take me, I always speak too soon..."

The crowds grew louder and louder, all echoing the same word:
"*Kill!*"
"*Kill!*"
"*Kill!*"

Faye eyed the dazed and confused men, who continued to either wander about the sands or remain in place, simply staring. Helix squinted. Whatever the spell had done, it seemed to have broken something in their weaker-willed minds, exhausting their bodies beyond their natural limit. A few simply fell over, convulsing. Faye's mouth made a hard line, and she looked to the crowds, a dark expression entering her eyes—an expression Helix hadn't truly seen from her yet. He knew what it was.

It was the look of the Mistress of Shadows.

"You aren't seriously thinking of killing them are you?" Helix asked.

Her look melted, and she arched an eyebrow at him. "Seriously? How evil do you think I am?" She shrugged. "No, I'm not that messed up. If anything, I'm thinking about how to kill the crowds."

Helix snorted, but his blood was hot as the chant continued, rising in vehemence.

He felt the monarch's eyes on him from the Queen's Terrace, waiting, pressing, urging.

Ayva stared at him too, brows furrowed, her blue eyes filled with worry.

"I should have said this a while ago," Helix said, and he turned to the crowds, grabbing Faye's bone shiv.

"Hey, that's mine!"

He moved to a gladiator, a blue-eyed man staring up at nothing.

"*Kill!*"

"*Kill!*"

"*Kill!*"

Helix knew he'd have to sacrifice a part of his soul to win this thing. Yet something Gaius had said rankled him. He lifted his hand, raising the bone shiv high, and the crowd's fervor peaked as the gladiator—the blue-eyed man with a shaved head—stared up at him, trembling as if scared, or perhaps broken, and…

Helix tossed the weapon to the ground.

The crowds gasped.

"No more…" Helix called.

The simple words echoed throughout the arena.

Whispers from the tens of thousands spread like wildfire, and Helix witnessed the monarch's eyes flare from the Queen's Terrace, her jowls quivering with rage.

Helix shouted to the masses, "A true champion shows mercy!"

Suddenly, a figure on the tall wall of the arena leapt off and landed in the sands with perfect grace, rolling only to rise to her feet. She didn't stop. Helix recognized her. Nalia. The current Grand Primus of the tournament, yet she looked nothing like the Nalia he'd seen before. Now, with fire-like eyes, a shaved head, and muscles that were hard and taut, she moved like death. With feline grace, she pulled a spear from seemingly thin air and stabbed one dazed gladiator through the neck. He fell to the sands, burbling blood. "These men must die.

Finish them, or I will finish them myself." She spoke simply, her voice a dark rasp, as if stating an unequivocal order.

Faye eyed the woman, looking more fearsome suddenly, as if Nalia's mere presence drew something out of the Thieflord of Fire. "Now *you* look like a fun challenge…"

Helix sensed Nalia was very dangerous.

Terrifyingly so.

Nothing like the woman they'd first encountered.

He whispered to Faye, grabbing her arm, "Don't try it."

Faye snorted. "Really? You have that little faith in me? After I just saved your hide a dozen times over? Relax, I'll be quick—" she said, stalking forward.

Helix opened his mouth when archers drew back bows. "No!" he shouted, waving a hand, cutting down a swath of arrows from the sky with a barrage of ice. But there were too many, and arrows fell like hail, the men suddenly riddled with thick bolts. Helix, filled with rage, looked to the balcony to see the queen raise her hand, a thin smile on her lips.

Yet her eyes blazed with fury; she was clearly enraged by Helix's defiance. He understood. He'd tried to ignore the rules, and by doing so, made her look weak. Abruptly, Queen Imala's voice boomed across the colosseum. "Congratulations to our winners of the Bloodbath! As per the *honored* rules, the arena demands that only five remain standing…and it seems we're left with three…A truly momentous fight, one that will be hailed for years to come."

Cheers accompanied this, but there was no mirth in Queen Imala's eyes.

Only cold, calculating fury.

Helix eyed the bodies littered across the sands. "They didn't even know where they were…" The waterfall of rage rose higher. "They were defenseless, harmless…"

Faye's eyes were tight, and she put a hand on Helix's shoulder. "I know, and she'll pay, Ice Boy, but you're going to have to harden that heart of yours…It's only going to get more difficult from here on."

Helix opened his mouth to reply, but then he felt something.

On his wrist, a single red sword formed.

The mark of a Primarian-basaeri.

Before he could say anything, all the nearby bodies suddenly began to glow. *The deadmark*, Helix remembered. The dull red paint on the dead men's chests turned a vibrant scarlet that almost burned his eyes.

A collective sound of awe from the crowds washed over them as the bodies began to turn to ash, disintegrating into the winds, leaving only a strange orange essence that floated into the air.

Helix breathed in and the spark filled his lungs. Immediately, he gasped—his skin tingled, hairs rising as if he'd just been struck by lightning. "What in the Tranquil Seas…" He felt more alive than ever, as if he could punch through a brick wall unscathed. Helix tapped deep into his Nexus—feeling the raging waters—and flung out his hand, and while the collar grew hot on his neck, ice shards shot from it. Sharp spikes like dragon's teeth appeared in a long line across the sand.

At that moment, the voice whispered again. Not words, just an awareness, and he knew the spell's name: *Ice Barrage*. Orange spark also flowed into Jivran and Faye at his side, making the two glow as if they'd just swallowed a bunch of magical fireflies. Jivran punched the air. "Feel strong."

"Tell me about it," Faye replied, flexing her hand.

"How is this even happening?" Helix asked.

"Deadmark power," Jivran replied, touching the paint on Helix's chest.

"Yeah, I get it's from the paint, big guy," he replied tersely. "How does it work? Can anyone just steal our essence now?" He summoned water, ready to give himself an impromptu bath to rinse the paint off.

Jivran grabbed his wrist. "Not work like that. Paint symbol."

Faye, meanwhile, was lost in awe. "Ash and shadow, I…I thought it was just a rumor. I've never witnessed the tournament in person." She knelt and put a hand to the sand, while the crowds cheered, watching the spark rise into the air. "There's some ancient magic here; I can sense it."

Helix pulled his hand back from Jivran. "Faye—"

"Jeez, will you relax? You already know how it works. Within the arena, and while bearing the paint—which clearly has some magical component as well—a conquered foe's spark can be imbibed by the victor."

Helix narrowed his gaze. "So we're eating our enemies' spark when they die…"

"Well, when you put it like that, it sounds a lot more morbid. Yes, that's basically it."

"I don't want it—" Helix protested, scratching at the paint on his body.

"Don't be an idiot," Faye snapped, grabbing him. "First off, did you forget they're watching?" Her head nodded to the masses, and little bits of spark that hadn't been absorbed by Helix and company were fading in the air. "Don't do anything stupid. Second, they were already dead, Helix. You don't get squeamish when you eat a carrot do you? Spark returns back to the soul of Farhaven. It would have happened anyway. Even then we'd all get some…just…an infinitesimal amount. That's why we can use magic. It's the essence of life. This arena and its spell allow us to get more of it directly." She squeezed her fist. "A *lot more*."

Meanwhile, Helix had forgotten about Nalia, who watched them. He understood.

How many had she imbibed the same spark? "The more we kill as we advance, the stronger we get."

"Thus the Grand Primus becomes very, very, very—" Faye said, eyes dancing with fire.

"*Strong*," Jivran finished, also watching Nalia, who just stood there, as if she knew they were connecting the pieces. Completely uncaring. Finally, with only the faintest hint of a curve to her lips, Nalia turned and stalked off the sands. A metal gate opened as if in response to her sheer presence, then slammed closed behind her.

"Thus concludes the first round!" the queen declared with a sweep of her hand.

Helix half expected more bolts to riddle their bodies, but instead, guards rushed out of the gates and corralled the three of them, ushering Helix, Faye, and Jivran at sword point toward the gate. Only Helix's eyes lingered on what they left behind, and he watched as servants rushed out to haul a figure off the sands. *Gaius.* He hadn't turned to ash? How? Was he not dead? The red-attired slaves dragged Gaius's limp body out of the arena.

The dead were gone, as if they'd never been there.

Helix's rage didn't diminish. It grew, thundering like a waterfall. In that moment, a part of him understood Gaius's mad rant. *You and I? We're nothing. Just little ants that dance about on a stage for their entertainment.*

Helix met the queen's cold gaze and matched her intensity.

With his eyes, he sent: *You will pay for this.*

The Shadow in the West

Gray witnessed it all as he stood on the balcony watching Helix's fight.

A little while ago, he'd bid Ayva goodbye as she went off to "watch over" the queen and try to keep the monarch from plotting their demise. Drega had escorted him to his room, and his jaw had dropped upon seeing his new accommodations. The room was bigger than Mura's entire cabin. When the roar of the crowds had grown too much, he'd rushed to the arena and found a small balcony with an unobstructed view to witness the first round. He'd taken it all in: the revealing of the Earthstone as the queen's main grand prize, the bloodfrenzy that had enchanted the warriors, the use of spark…all of it. He even knew who fought at the Ronin of Water's side.

Faye.

Gray's pulse quickened.

It'd taken a moment to realize who it was beneath the bandages. He remembered those moves. He'd been on the receiving end of them firsthand. He gave a small snort. *Of course she's here, and in a round that's only supposed to be men.* Still, how? Last he'd seen, she was in Seria. Had she followed them through the portal? What was she after? He smirked at her tenacity.

The most impressive spectacle, though, was Helix.

Standing in the center of the sands was the Ronin of Water. Helix had just delivered the final blow to the one-eyed man who had threaded stone. Meanwhile, Faye held the head of the ratlike man who'd threaded flesh. Now the thousands of Covians were chanting something.

"Wa-ter?"

Gray huffed a laugh. *Well done, Helix.* He sent to Morrowil, *I knew he could do it.*

The infamous sword at his hip replied, *Is that why your palms were sweating?*

Gray protested, *You can't actually sense that, can you?*

No. An educated guess, yet your concern for your friend is more than understandable.

Good. It's strange enough I'm chatting with my own sword. Even stranger that I'm starting to get used to it. Gray eyed Helix as the other two, Faye and the giant, joined his side. *He remind you of someone?*

A little shorter. Yes... Helix took in the adulation, and his hard blue eyes held a tempest. That storm only vanished when the giant, the man who Helix had somehow converted mid-fight, clapped him on the shoulder, making his friend smile. The coldness was gone. Morrowil continued, *He has the potential of Hiron, perhaps even more.*

Gray grunted. *At this rate I'm going to struggle to keep up.*

Perhaps... Or maybe true metal is only forged under heat and hammer.

His eyes hardened as he surveyed the arena. *Are you saying what I think you're saying?*

If you think I'm saying you should fight, then yes. That is what I am saying.

I couldn't agree more. However, there's something I need to do first...

Gray had turned away when there was a cry.

In the arena, arrows rained from the heavens. Helix attempted to block them with an icy blast, but there were too many, and the arrows riddled the remaining warriors—all save the giant, Helix, and Faye. The queen, shaking with rage on her terrace, the nobles at her side, stared venomously down at Helix. Gray readied wind, preparing to—

What are you going to do? Morrowil asked. *Kill all the guards? Murder the queen? Rash, I think.*

Gray thought about it, and he saw the look in Helix's eyes, as if he wanted to tear down the whole colosseum, too. He growled and released the wind about his hands. *It's wrong.*

Of course it is. Yet, you're the leader of the Ronin. You have to temper your zeal, show patience, even when everything inside you demands action.

Then what? Gray questioned.

We wait to make our move. For now, let the queen think you're being played, until you move your pieces against her.

I hate waiting, but you're right, as always.

Did you expect differently? I am nearly two thousand years old.

Oh yeah, I keep forgetting that.

A gasp escaped the crowds, and Gray looked down to the arena to see the arrow-riddled bodies turn to orange mist.

Spark, Gray realized, as his fingers seized the cold marble banister. "What's happening?"

An ancient magic, Morrowil answered in reverence, *older than even I... If stories are true, it's a spell created by one of Renalin's children during the birth of the Great Kingdoms, when the titans roamed the land.*

"The sands are releasing the spark from the bodies."

Indeed, upon the sands, the victors receive the conquered foes' essence, their magic, their life force.

Doesn't that seem cruel?

It is the opposite. A hunter does not kill to simply leave its prey's carcass to rot in the hot sun, so why let the spark vanish? In a very real way, your conquered foe's spark—their essence—lives on inside of you. More importantly, I think you know what this means for your odds...

Gray did and he answered, *If I wait to fight in the final round, then every combatant before me is going to get stronger.*

Much stronger. You know what you have to do, don't you?

Turning, Gray's gaze panned west, over the colosseum walls, over Covai's sprawling buildings, toward Median. The city they'd lost. Like Yronia, Great Kingdom of Metal, the city now swarmed with saeroks, vergs, nameless, and other foul things, all with one purpose: to destroy Farhaven. Despite the necessity of the tournament, that evil weighed on Gray's mind. It was coming. It was only a matter of time.

If I can gain even a scrap more power to stop what's on its way, I'll do it.

Morrowil agreed. *If not for you, then for those you care about.*

I must, whatever it takes. Memories, images, faces came to his mind. Hannah. Reaver Meira. Evangeline. Mathelstan. So many more. The list of those who had fallen was too long, and it was seared into his mind. Gray's jaw clenched painfully, and he understood. He needed to get stronger, much stronger, and he had just the idea. On his wrist, he saw the red swords tattooed with the magic of the arena. Three of them. It named him a Primarian.

But not for long.

Helix was being hailed as a champion, yet his gaze was fixed on the queen, the message in his eyes clear as day: *You will pay.*

Gray grinned and echoed his friend's sentiment. *We will do what we must and the queen will regret this day.* He moved back into the colosseum, stalking down the halls.

Now where are we going?

Gray grinned. *You said you wanted me to get stronger. Well, now's my chance.*

You know they're not going to just let you march on the sands.

Oh, they will. I've got a plan.

Morrowil groaned.

I Do The Burning

Standing on the Queen's Terrace, Ayva watched in awe as spark, orange essence, floated into Helix, making her friend glow. The crowds oohed and aahed. Beside him were his two companions, the giant and Faye.

Ayva wasn't an idiot.

Faye's bandages were starting to loosen, and Ayva saw through the disguise. After suffering as the woman's Diaon—more loosely translated as "apprentice"—Ayva knew Faye well. Perhaps too well. She watched as Faye tried to cool Helix's ire, but he ignored her, his gaze fixed on the balcony.

On the queen.

Who had ruthlessly killed the remaining gladiators.

Ayva had tried to stop the monarch, only to be met with resistance in the form of the queen's guard. While she'd considered more *forceful* measures, killing the queen seemed rash. Besides the fact that there were half a dozen Reavers on the balcony with her, let alone hundreds of guards positioned all around the colosseum, clearly ready to act at the queen's whim…now wasn't the time. This fight was bigger than her, than Helix's retribution. *Patience*, she told herself, as her grip tightened on Aurora's handle, her famed blade of Sun. The smooth gold hilt was a comfort in her hand, even now. She pictured Omni, and a calm came over her.

"Well, that was impressive," the queen remarked through a sudden breath. She turned to face Ayva, and although the woman's dark eyes still glared with violence, her whole demeanor shifted like a sudden breeze as her thick-painted red lips smiled widely. "Quite the turn of events, wouldn't you say?"

"Indeed!" said a young noblewoman with an orange falcon, the color of flames, embroidered on her dress.

Ayva stilled her rage and scanned the faces on the spacious balcony as if surveying a battlefield. She found a forum filled with snares and deception, otherwise disguised as gaudily dressed nobles surrounded by a host of servants.

The Queen's Terrace was expansive. It was a terrace in name only, more of a balcony, yet the only balconies Ayva had seen before in Farhaven included the one in Lakewood that could barely fit two people. The Golden Horn had one, though it was purely decorative. Still, all the town had oohed and aahed when her father had installed it. This? The landing could have fit a small house, or even a medium-sized one. Elegant silver tables and chairs and cushions of all sizes and shapes filled the space. A long banquet table in the back held a literal feast, and attendants circled it, trying to be discreet while holding pitchers of wine and platters of food. Ayva expected flies, though she saw the food was rotated out repeatedly for fresher steaming plates. At the front, overlooking the arena, an elegant engraved-marble railing surrounded the balcony. As she looked closer at the railing, she saw the engravings were marble skulls stacked on one another.

How very City of Flesh, Ayva thought.

A dozen guards in mail and chain stood at the back wall. Reavers in red robes, mostly one- and two-stripes, sat quietly nearby, as if keeping the peace. They were the queen's personal guard, aside from Nalia, Grand Primus, who had leapt off the damn balcony to enforce the queen's rules. Ayva was certain the Grand Primus would be back at any moment to emanate her intimidating presence, like an angel of death.

At the entrance to the terrace, were a few more Covian guards, as well as a silver-haired old man the queen had called Howard. He seemed to be presiding over the schedule of events. The rest of the balcony, aside from a few musicians, was filled with nobles and their entourages, each sorted into their little groups as if in some sort of popularity contest. Servants, trays and pitchers at the ready, flitted in and out as soon as a noble swirled their glass or gave a lofty, impatient glance.

Ayva counted four groups of nobles, each in fine silks of gold, orange, red, or green. The men's layered coats and the women's embroidered dresses, heavy with lace, were so gaudy Ayva was tempted to burn her own eyes. But it was their sigils that caught her attention: a gold bear with scales, an orange-tailed falcon, a desert fox with red fur, and a green two-headed snake.

Ayva remembered Faye's training long ago.

Faye sat before a campfire, breaking twigs, flames dancing in her eyes. "Covians are a brutal, nasty lot, and that's saying something coming from me. They only value two things: strength and flesh."

"Strength is obvious enough," Ayva said, warming her hands on the fire, "but flesh?"

"Flesh in the form of their native creatures, many of which they work to death, ironically enough. Which is also very Covian," she said, snapping another twig, "You can identify them by their individual mascots: the beloved belegrun, a nasty bear from the heart of Drymaus, the two-headed Hisan Viper, the Red Fox, and finally the Copper Falcon. That's the order of their houses too, from most powerful to least. House Belegrun is a rich, fat clan with a slob at their head, but it's the Hisan Viper I'd be wary of; true to their namesake, they are just as slithering and awful." Faye shivered and tossed the twig, flames crackling as Darius let loose a snore nearby. "Now, we should get some sleep too, it's—"

"What are their names?" Ayva asked.

Quirking a brow, Faye replied, "It's late, girl."

"Please," she insisted.

"Why? Plan to take down the Covian nobility one day?"

Ayva shrugged. "You never know."

With a sigh, Faye had told her.

Armed with Faye's knowledge, Ayva returned to the moment and looked over the nobles. "The Ronin of Water is quite the warrior," said Howard, the attendant near the terrace's entrance. He had a Cloudfell look about him with his blue eyes and white hair, and he held a quill and pad of paper in his hand. Instead of looking at the queen, he watched Ayva; then the keenness in his eyes vanished as he smiled and nodded his head like a doddering old man.

Others chimed in, nobles echoing their agreement in a chorus of sycophants.

Ayva silenced them all as she faced Queen Imala. "You didn't need to do that. You didn't need to kill those men."

The queen's countenance grew stern. "I'm afraid I did, my dear."

An older fat man with a huge gold bear on his coat—Otto Gromin, head of House Belegrun—and his feet kicked up on a tasseled ottoman, suddenly snorted. "Rules are rules, my Lady Ronin," Otto proclaimed with all the confidence of a man who governed his house with an iron fist. "Surely a Ronin should understand that."

"Rules can be relaxed," Ayva replied, eyes locked on the queen. "Those men didn't need to die. They were defenseless." Ayva had touched her Nexus, and power and authority entered her voice.

Queen Imala sighed as if she were a patient mother. "Yes, I know. I hated it. You must understand, the rules must be followed precisely. If not, the very nature of the tournament lies in jeopardy, and as the leader of this fair kingdom, I must ensure its continued existence."

"What does any of that have to do with you killing defenseless men?"

Queen Imala snapped, shouting, "It has *everything* to do with it!"

The nobles all tensed.

The servants looked as if they wished to be anywhere else.

The queen took a calming breath, and at her gesture a goblet of wine was brought to her. She took a little sip. Gaining her composure, she looked over the nobles, attendants, and guards on the terrace, then with a forced smile, she resumed her seat on the gilded throne. "Come, sit," she told Ayva. "Take Hakeem's seat."

Hakeem, an older man wearing the orange falcon on his elegant umber robes, opened his mouth to protest. The queen's whole face tightened, and she bared a hint of her yellowed teeth.

"Please," Hakeem said, feigning a smile as he rose and gestured to his seat.

Ayva didn't move.

The queen spoke through her clenched jaw, "Sit, girl. *I insist.*"

Guards nearby shifted, readying themselves.

Ayva released a tight breath and sat.

The tension persisted until Queen Imala waved a hand. "Well, what are you all gawking at? The first games are done, enjoy yourselves, let us celebrate!" Slowly, awkwardly, those on the balcony resumed their conversations. "Music!" the queen demanded, and the three musicians in the corner began playing an upbeat song on dulcimer, lute, and drum. The queen breathed a sigh as she relaxed. "Dear child, don't you see? I adore you and your kind, but what you view as simple is anything but." She gestured to the nobles, who were again engrossed in their small talk—gray-haired men and women, jovial by all measures, but their eyes watched Ayva and the queen with haughty disdain. She lowered her voice. "These men and women may bow to me, but that power hangs by a thread. You see how they look at us, do you not?"

"I do," Ayva said thinly.

"Covai is like the desert that surrounds it," the queen said, plucking a sliced pomegranate from a platter that was whisked before her and biting into it. Juicy red pulp and seeds spilled from her mouth. "It is a place of brutal honesty. If you show strength, you rise; if you show weakness, you fall. So you see, if I had let your friend simply trounce the rules of this honored game, these vultures you see around me would think me weak. With any signs of weakness, comes boldness, even treason…I can't have that." The queen looked at her, a smile donning her face, which was caked in layers of makeup in an attempt to conceal her ruddy, cratered skin. "I am not the demon you think I am. I am merely practical."

"Practical," Ayva repeated through clenched teeth. She had…many more thoughts on the matter. First, why would anyone permit a system that perpetuated cruelty instead of simply changing it? Ayva knew why. In the same way she knew this was a fruitless conversation that would only engender the queen's wrath and gain her nothing. So she changed tactics, speaking directly to the older man who had the quill and pad. "My good sir. Howard, was it?"

"Yes, my Lady Ronin? How may I be of assistance?"

"Do you know when the next match will begin, and how it will work?"

The queen's eyes tightened; she was clearly annoyed at being ignored.

"Oh, my Lady Ronin, an excellent question!" the old man said, as if relieved she'd steered the conversation elsewhere. "Wondering when your courageous friend will have to fight again? Mmm, let's see here." He examined his notes. "The next round will be broken into six individual fights. The fighters will take the main stage, two at a time, again in a battle to the death or surrender, whichever comes first."

"This is the round that gets exciting, when betting is allowed," said Teras, a quiet woman and head of House Copper Falcon. As the weakest house, with merely three others standing together on the balcony, they seemed a subdued group, watching over the other nobles like hens amid foxes.

Otto, head of House Belegrun, bellowed a laugh. "Finally when things get exciting!" The fat man jiggled a bag of coins in his hand. "My wager is on the boy of Water!"

An axe-faced woman, Jima'ra, head of House Red Fox, spoke while sipping on her drink, "Don't lie, Otto, you have coin on them all." As the third-most powerful house, House Red Fox made their fortune in selling weapons. Faye had described Jim'ara as cunning and reserved, the latter being uncommon for a Covian noble. Jim'ara was lavishly dressed, with a red fox pelt wrapped around her shoulders, and her crest upon her sleeve.

Otto chortled, his eyes giving nothing away. "Well, I like to win, what can I say?"

"Who's Helix fighting?" Ayva asked.

"That depends," the queen replied.

"On what?" Ayva's tone grew steely.

Howard interjected, "It is a simple system of ranking. Let's see here…his collar ranking, plus his standing, counting his wins and losses, which is one, and…" The old man's eyes lit up. "Yes, he should be fighting…" He swallowed. "Ah, well, um…"

"What?" Ayva asked, rising. "Who's he fighting? Why are you hesitating?"

"Please, sit," the queen said. "There's no need for theatrics."

Ayva slowly sat, but asked again, "Who is Helix fighting?"

Howard licked his lips.

The queen gestured to him. "While it is normally frowned upon to reveal some of our secrets to keep them a surprise for the next match, Ayva's interest is a special case. Go ahead, Howard. You can tell her."

A noble named Larissa, wife to the head of House Hisan, sniffed. Unlike the others, the two-headed snake was embroidered all over Larissa's green dress, as if she flaunted her status. She spoke eagerly, almost ravenously, her dark eyes like black orbs. "Don't tell me. It's one of the Depraved, isn't it?"

Ayva felt a chill run down her spine. "The Depraved?"

"Oh, you don't know about them, my Lady Ronin?" Larissa asked haughtily as she delicately bit into a pastry from a passing servant's silver tray. "Oh, they are truly wretched! Each more vile and disgusting than the last, but they are a sight to behold. Our dear queen here is a curator of sorts. She has gathered creatures from all over the realm, and among these, only the most barbaric of beasts are reserved for the second-round fights. Some have even killed Primarian-hadus!" She practically tittered with excitement.

Ayva wanted to melt her face off.

From within their group of snakes, Omar, her husband and head of House Hisan, spoke, "Larissa, you've frightened the poor girl. She may be a legend, but she's still only a child!"

"Oh, dear girl, I apologize profusely!" Larrisa said, her slender hand—gilded and jeweled as it was—touching her green-adorned breast in feigned sympathy. "I forget sometimes, a thousand-year-old legend is a lot of responsibility for someone who is barely more than an adolescent."

At this, the queen gave a thin-lipped smile.

One or two of the nobles from the other houses snickered.

Howard's eyes watched Ayva, curious, discerning.

Larissa locked eyes with Ayva, her face wearing a faint smirk as she put the goblet to her lips again. Ayva sighed and touched her Nexus;

she twirled her fingers and sent a thread of sun into the goblet, heating the liquid within just as the noblewoman sipped. Larissa's green eyes went wide as she spat out the scalding wine, soaking her fine clothes, and some of her husband's, while more dribbled down her chin.

Larissa gaped, then glared at Ayva.

Others on the balcony recoiled and gasped.

Ayva didn't so much as flinch. "Is the wine soured? Or too strong for your taste?" She grabbed a passing goblet, then took a sip. "Hmm. Tastes fine to me, though I'm only an adolescent," she said. "Anyway, I'd be more worried about your little group of Depraved, Your Majesty. A Ronin just bested two dozen fighters in the first round without breaking a sweat."

At her side, Queen Imala tensed.

Ayva smiled back. "I mean, you did want a good fight, did you not?"

"Of course," the queen said.

A huge man, bearing a falcon on his coat, laughed in his little group of four. "The Ronin of Sun has some fire in her! I like it!"

The queen's smile was indulgent. "I do, too. Just be careful, child, fire often burns."

"I *am* the Sun, Your Majesty," Ayva replied, "*I* do the burning."

The queen grimaced. "Yes, well…shame you won't be in the tournament, and you'll just have to watch. No burning for you, I'm afraid." Ayva felt as if she'd been smacked, and the queen's smile tugged at the corner of her waxy red lips. "Fear not, you have the best view in all of Covai!"

Ayva felt her blood heat, and she replied as coolly as she could, "Yes, Your Majesty, the view is…amazing." Staring out at the sands as they were cleaned and prepared for the next round, she continued, "I mean, if only the company could match the caliber of the contestants, I'm sure it would be impossible to beat."

A few nobles tittered. One gasped.

"Impudent child, I—"

Howard interjected, "I must say, while Lady Ronin's fire is commendable, she might be reminded that this was only the Bloodbath. An opening round." Then his sharp blue eyes fixed her. "One must temper their enthusiasm." His look was clear as day, basically shouting *stop taunting the queen, please, for your own good.*

The queen made a little hiss.

"Yes, Your Majesty," Ayva said quickly, dipping her head just a little. "Sorry for my frankness. My father always told me my tongue was quicker than my brain. He also told me that I'd rule the world, so he's to blame for my big head. Sometimes I have to temper myself. I'm used to doing it for other people," she said, thinking of Gray, Darius and Helix, "not so much for myself."

"Forgiven, dear child. You are young, and ambitious, qualities I love so dearly. You remind me of myself." She lifted her glass and sipped on her wine, eyes just above the rim. "That said, I am eager, almost ravenous, to see the Ronin's gifts on full display." The queen plucked a berry from a plate, her yellow teeth biting into it, and Ayva shuddered in disgust.

"Speaking of gifts," Larissa said, still blotting the wine from her dress, dropping all fury with a false smile. She then clapped her hands. "Aterias!" she snapped at a young long-haired servant.

One of the other servants nudged him, as if he was new.

The young man stumbled forward, looking at Larissa. "Yes, m'lady?"

"How brazen! Lower your eyes when you speak to me!" Larissa hissed.

Aterias prostrated himself, forehead scraping the ground at the feet of the noble. "Please accept my deepest apologies, m'lady! It won't happen again, I swear it! How might I serve, m'lady?"

Ayva's hackles rose and sun readied at her fist. *Would it really be so bad to burn the woman to ash right here and now?*

Howard glared at her. *Patience.*

Ayva sighed, releasing the glowing ball of sun in her palm, and sent to Howard through her eyes, *Fine. But she's on borrowed time.*

"Much better," Larissa said as her sickly smile grew. "Now, please, be a dear and bring out our *present* for our beloved queen." Aterias ran off, and a few other nobles commanded the same of their servants. Ayva narrowed her gaze, fearful of what spectacle awaited her now. Larissa had finished wiping her face. "I do hope Her Majesty is prepared for her selection, as I have personally handpicked our participant this year."

"I am most eager," Queen Imala said, sounding aloof as she sipped her wine.

"Oh, I'm certain you all may try to outdo me this year, but I'm afraid you'll fall short yet again," Jima'ra said.

Larissa's smile was vulpine. "We shall see, my Lady Jima'ra."

Otto Gromin guffawed. With his sizable girth, many chins, and bulbous nose, Otto looked Covian through and through. In one hand he gripped a silver chalice, and in the other a smoldering pipe that he puffed religiously. The smoke smelled of sweet cinnamon and curled about his retinue, all of whom looked well-habituated to the haze. "Ha!" Otto exclaimed. "Your little rivalry this year is most entertaining, but bicker all you want, none of you will hold a candle to my participant. He is built like a bear, which of course is the most noble of creatures, and twice as fierce! His slaver told me he killed his former master, then ate the man's heart. His heart!" Otto boomed a laugh while gesturing for a meek serving girl with large amber eyes to fill his chalice once more.

Ayva cleared her throat. "Your participant?"

"My, my, my, Lady Ronin, you are new to this world, aren't you?" Jim'ara said with only a hint of snideness. "How splendid! You, our guest, will get to witness something special today."

Larissa's eyes expressed danger as she feigned sudden distress. "Oh, but wait, you showed such concern over the dead gladiators. With such a kind, *soft* heart, perhaps you should skip this next event?"

"Perhaps not," Ayva said, matching the woman's provocation. Yet she thought there might be a note of truth in Larissa's words. Well, not softness, but goodness. She gritted her teeth, knowing that if this next event as unpleasant as Larissa's smug expression indicated, she would have to try *very* hard to restrain herself.

A moment later, the guards returned, followed by the slaves.

Six men were marched to stand like fruit on display before the nobles as they whispered and bantered among themselves about their "wares."

Ayva left the railing where she'd been standing and moved to an empty chair next to Larissa for a better view of the slaves. She ignored the snide expression the noblewoman gave her.

Each slave looked more feral than the next—carved from tooth and nail, wearing pelts, and caked in dirt. Their wild eyes peered at them, each contestant looking like they wanted to rip the heads off every noble. The guards were ready with swords.

The first man was muscular, with red, hateful eyes and a beard to his knees. He bore a bear on his cloth armband. "I forgot to mention, he has the spark!" Otto chortled from his seat.

"What kind of spark?" asked Jima'ra.

Otto scoffed, "Bah! Who knows! Some sort of barbarian flesh nonsense."

Another noble snickered, "Perhaps that's why he had a fondness for meat!"

The others chuckled.

Ayva looked to the next man…a replica of the first, wild and draped in furs, only smaller, a red fox displayed on his armband.

The next three men in the middle were undoubtedly thieves; they had darting eyes and cruel expressions.

It was the last slave who drew Ayva's attention.

He wasn't a man at all, but a youth who couldn't have been older than fifteen. The boy trembled in his chains, watching the nobles as if they were moments from breaking out a fork and knife to eat him.

"Oh, a scared one!" said a noble.

"Larissa," Otto boomed, "why'd you choose such a pip-squeak? Flesh and bone, he doesn't have enough muscle to lift an empty bucket!"

It was true. He was scrawny and dirty, with bright blue eyes and tangled blond hair. The boy was attractive, effeminate, his features soft and refined. He wore a coat two sizes too big for him, his head nearly drowning in it, like a turtle peeking out of its shell. The boy licked his lips and pleaded, "Your lords and ladies, please have mercy on me…I don't want…I don't want to fight…My sister, she's the fighter. I can barely harm a fly!"

A few nobles laughed at this.

Others looked disgusted.

"A good thing you don't have to harm a fly, but rather kill a man!" said Otto.

"Please, I—"

"That's enough out of you," a guard snarled, his sword clearing an inch of its scabbard.

Ayva saw a green snake on the guard's armband.

"Do you like my choice, my Lady Ronin?" Larissa asked, leaning forward in her chair to whisper in Ayva's ear. "As I said, I picked him out especially."

Ayva felt sun come to her hand.

Kill them all, or just kill her? she asked internally.

Patience, the voice of reason told her.

As did Howard's stern look.

The queen rose and walked up and down the line of men as she tapped her pursed lips, pondering. "Most interesting..." she mused, and without any fanfare, she picked the giant with the wild, hateful eyes, the bigger of the two with the bear symbol. "This one shall do nicely."

"Ha! I knew it!" Otto exclaimed.

A few of the nobles grumbled.

"You must pick two, Your Majesty," Howard said. "Only two."

"Well, it only stands to reason that I am next," Jima'ra, the axe-faced woman, said.

Ayva knew where this was going, and she tried to suppress her rising anger and concern. She gripped her chair's arm and sniffed burnt wood glowing beneath her fingers.

The queen stopped before the young boy. "What's your name, boy?"

"S-Sasha," the boy muttered, breathing fast, eyes wide.

"Sasha," she said and lifted his chin, moving it side to side to examine him. "You are quite pretty for a boy. Almost too pretty. There is something else to you, isn't there? What could it be?" With a bejeweled hand, the queen traced the high collar of Sasha's coat. "Your sister's I'm guessing?"

Sasha nodded, trembling. "Y-yes, Y-Your M-Majesty. S-she gave it to me."

Sun roared in Ayva's mind. *Patience,* she demanded.

Howard was practically glaring at her.

Casually, Queen Imala peeled back the high collar of Sasha's coat to reveal a bright red Yronia iron and bloodstone collar. "Ah, there's our little surprise. Quite the spark on you, isn't there?"

The boy swallowed. "I...I don't know...It comes and goes. I don't really have control over it. Sometimes it's powerful, sometimes not. It won't help me on the sands. Please, I—"

Queen Imala held up a finger to the boy's lips, tutting. "Shhh. Bravery is its own reward." Then her eyes danced with delight as she tapped Sasha on the chest. "Him."

Larissa's grin widened. "An excellent choice, Your Majesty."

Ayva rose, hiding the sun in her fist. "I won't allow it. He can't participate."

The queen's eyes narrowed gravely. "Careful, girl…I excused your first outburst, *Lady Ronin*," she said, almost mockingly, "I will not excuse a second."

A few guards tensed, readying themselves.

Reavers stood.

Ayva didn't care at all. "Look at him!" she yelled. "He's just a boy! He'll die to those monsters out there, for what purpose? For your entertainment? I understand fighting and dying when there's a chance, but this? This is evil." Ayva's words echoed across the balcony. Now that she was closer to the boy, she sensed magic…something in Sasha that seemed…strong. Even if his eyes spoke only of terror as he stared at her, as if she were a lighthouse in a raging sea—the only thing keeping him from being sucked into the Abyss itself. So Ayva demanded, "You cannot do this. I will not allow it."

Reavers stepped forward, spark coming to their hands.

"Yet, it is already *done*," Queen Imala grated, biting off every word.

"By done, she means dead," said a noble in the back.

Nobles cackled at this, while a few bickered at the queen's choices, resenting that their offerings hadn't being selected.

Queen Imala held Ayva's gaze a moment longer as Ayva's whole body seethed…

"Let's liven things up, shall we? Bring the Fool," Queen Imala commanded, and a few moments later a man was dragged onto the balcony. He wore jarringly bright baggy pants, colorful paint upon his aging face, and a jester's hat. A court fool, Ayva knew. Imala eyed the man. "We often reserve the slaves for later rounds…It's more entertaining. The cards we will draw today give them an opportunity to survive a little longer. Why not let them decide, my Lady Ronin?"

Ayva fumed.

Queen Imala glared, and the Fool quickly procured a handful of cards. She reached to pull one, then stopped. "Actually, after you, my Lady Ronin."

Ayva spoke through gritted teeth, "I will not play your twisted games."

Queen Imala's eyes glared with rage. Then, quickly, she stilled her features and spoke evenly, "Perhaps I shall simply kill all these offerings?"

"You don't want to do that," Ayva replied with cold confidence.

A few nobles laughed, then swallowed.

"Please, calm, my Lady Ronin! It is just a—"

Ayva let a flare of sun come to her hand. "Go ahead, say it's just a game again."

Reavers stepped forward.

Imala snorted. "Come, girl, think! You would start a war with Covai over slaves?" The whole of the balcony was gripped in suspense. She scoffed, waving a hand as if it was a foolish, childish whimsy. "You are young. Do not let your emotions rule you."

Ayva felt her body tremble with anger. "My emotions? You're the one that's being petty enough to rush a young boy to his death"

"Hardly!" Queen Imala sniffed. "If anything, I'm being more fair. Fool, please explain to our guest my magnanimity."

The Fool bowed. "It is as Her Majesty says," he said, revealing a handful of shiny gold cards. "Five cards, my Lady Ronin. One for each round." He showed five cards, each with a number: A two. A three. A four. The last two cards were blank, no number on them. "Two for a chance to free those before us. Whichever you pull, I shall fulfill."

"So whatever number I pull, that's the round they enter," she said, nodding her head toward Sasha and the other slaves, "but if I pull a blank, they get to go free?"

The Fool flourished the cards. "Indeed! Simple as can be! You've got a keen eye for the aim. Now shall we play the game?" *It must be rigged,* Ayva thought. As if reading her mind, the Fool kindly gave a smile that looked almost tired. "If you are thinking it's a trick, I can assure you it is not that slick. You can examine them again for yourself, my lady, so you can be sure." He spread the cards out once more. Sasha hopefully eyed the two cards that had no number. Nearby, the nobles made a few snarky comments, though mostly simply watched. Then the Fool shuffled them and turned them over once more. "Pick one, my lady, and see if the gods favor you…"

Ayva hesitated, the tension mounting. She looked at Sasha, who watched her with terrified eyes. *I have a chance to set him free, right here, right now.* She loathed the idea of playing the queen's game. Did she even have a choice?

Larissa began to rise. "Ugh! If the coward girl is too afraid, then I—"

Ayva pulled a card.

The Fool's green eyes looked almost sad.

He showed it. A number two.

Second round. Sasha would have to fight this round.

The others laughed. "An early death it is!" Larissa remarked.

All the color drained from Sasha's face as he muttered in fear.

Meanwhile, the other Chosen grew grim-faced.

Smiling, the queen resumed her seat, and the slaves were marched off.

A noble griped, "Ah, folly! I was certain my offering would be picked this year!"

Otto boomed, clapping the man on the back, "Ha! The bear always wins!"

Other nobles continued to bicker, laughing loudly, as Ayva remained frozen, grip trembling, trying desperately to restrain her power, but it was rising. The haughty laughter grew in her mind. Hope was dwindling. *I should end them all. I should—*

A honeyed voice broke her rising anger. "A refill, my Lady Ronin?" Howard.

He'd moved to her side.

Ayva disregarded him, power swelling, and—

He gripped her arm, whispering quickly as the other nobles carried on with their bickering, "You cannot change this, my lady. Worse, the more you show interest in that young man, the more the queen will use it against you. You must bide your time." The stabbing truth of this nearly sent Ayva into a fit of rage. But he was right.

Still, what could she do?

"I can't just stand by," she hissed back.

The sun in her hand begged to be used.

Hope felt like a flickering thing, until—

"There is always another way," Howard whispered as the nobles continued to squabble.

Another way…Ayva's eyes tightened, and she gave a cautious smile, resuming her seat. *Sasha*. As he stepped off the balcony, the young man gave a final look over his shoulder, eyes finding Ayva, until he was spurred around a corner, and out of view.

"Oh, my Lady Ronin! You should have seen yourself." Larissa huffed a laugh, breaking the moment. The other nobles stopped their quarrels to listen. "With such a squeamish stomach, I do not think you would have fared as well on the sands as your brothers."

Ayva sighed. "You know, Larissa, just because you are a common snake doesn't mean your forked tongue needs to slither out of your mouth each time you speak."

Larissa's mouth was agape.

A few nobles gawked.

One even spat out his wine.

The queen's eyes only danced with mirth.

Howard, who had resumed his station at the terrace's entrance, shook his head.

Ayva knew she should hold her tongue, but light and heavens, she was a Ronin! Not a meek, tiptoeing scullery maid. "On second thought, Larissa, you don't even need to speak at all. That was my father's principle. Nothing nice to say, keep it to yourself. I'd add to that, however. For you, Larissa, if you've nothing clever to add, you should definitely keep your lips sealed, for fear of everyone finding out what a glaring imbecile you might be." She shrugged. "Just my two coppers." Then she looked at Howard and asked with her eyes: *Too much?*

Howard sighed and his eyes replied: *Yes, my lady, far too much.* Only to add a begrudging smile, as if to say: *but well done.* Meanwhile, Larissa's face was beet red and she gasped like a fish out of water. "Y—y—little—" She raised her hand as if to order her guards.

Ayva's eyes were golden like the sun. "Do it. Try me. Give me an excuse."

"Oh, I like her," Jima'ra said, shivering. "I like her a lot."

"Yes," the queen agreed and sipped her wine again coolly. "Me too." Then to Larissa, "Sit down, girl, and do not act more of an imbecile by doing anything foolish. You flew too close to the sun, and you incurred the consequences. After all, she's a Ronin, you idiot, not some milkmaid."

Larissa, still fuming, was fully aware of all eyes on her, and none were on her side. She slowly lowered her hand and, still quaking with rage, glared venomously at Ayva.

Ayva was over it.

The woman could choke on her rage for all she cared.

Thinking of Sasha, Ayva moved to initiate her plan when—

A horn sounded.

The beginning of the second round.

"Ah, just in time," the queen said, grinning.

Drums reverberated through the colosseum. New spectators entered, adding to the deafening cheers as excitement built once again.

An announcer spoke, his voice, enhanced by flesh and sun, echoing across the colosseum. "Welcome—" He introduced the next fighter, some brutish-looking man wearing a boar's head who took the sands with an axe and flail in hand. *Weapons…?* Ayva thought. *Well this is going to get interesting.* A moment later, as if to drum up the crowd's enthusiasm, two red-striped tigers were released from side gates, and they rushed the boar-headed man.

With ease, the man cut the beasts down, to mixed acclaim.

Ayva glared. "Coward," she snarled, "those tigers were half starved…"

Behind Ayva, the nobles began their wagers, which turned her stomach. She tried to pay them no mind. The announcer spoke again. "In our west corner…" His voice trailed off. "Uh…what is this? It doesn't say? What are you talking about? How could he not say who he is?" Fumbling as he realized he was still speaking to the masses with his echoing, magic-enhanced voice, the announcer cleared his throat. "In the west corner, a mysterious newcomer!"

Ayva's heart raced in anticipation, her breath stolen away, as she watched a figure stepping onto the sands. "Gray…"

Just Another Fan

After the Bloodbath, Faye was separated from Helix and Jivran and led down a dark hallway by a group of guards. She'd questioned the decision at the time, and Helix had tried to stop it, but she'd told him to stand down and went along with it. But now, as she found herself in a dank little cell in the bowels of the colosseum, she regretted not letting the Ronin of Water turn their escorts into ice sculptures.

For a brief while, she'd used the moment to relax, tossing up her feet and fondly recollecting particular highlights from her recent fight. She glanced at her wrist, saw the single red sword had formed, and made a little amused sound. *Another mark to her collection…* However, the smell of mold and the constant drip of water in her cell were getting old.

Faye rose and held the bars, calling out to the guard who watched over her from the entryway. He was a trollish bald man who clutched his cudgel as if it were his baby. "Say, handsome," she purred, "how about you come over here and use those big keys of yours to let little old me out of this big scary cell. In return, you might find yourself with a heavier coin purse… I don't have the coin on me now, but I promise I'm good for it."

"Shut it, you!" the guard shouted as he neared and whacked her cell bars with his cudgel. "That's enough out of you. They said you'd try to weasel your way out of here, and I'll have you know, I don't take bribes. Especially not from scum like you."

Faye groaned. "An honorable guard, great, figures I'd get the only one in all of Covai. Well, how about this, you open this cell, or I'll kill you." He gave a little laugh, then she smiled widely, a gamey grin that showed no hint of amusement. His mirth wilted like lettuce in the sun. She added, "You know, as the Thieflord of Fire and all."

Suddenly, all color drained out of the man's face.

Oh… I'm onto something here, Faye thought.

"Y-you can't be…" the man stuttered.

With a quick gesture, she removed the rest of the bandages that had obscured her face, and his jaw dropped. "In the flesh." She gave a little flourish.

He gulped again, stepping back. "No…there's no way…"

Faye sighed. "Fine, need more proof?" She peeled back her leather armor on her shoulder to reveal the burned insignia of a Darkeye officer. "Well? I didn't just stumble into a branding iron, you idiot. Now, are you going to open this cell, or am I going to have to make an artistic design out of your entrails?"

"I…oh gods, it *is* you!" the bald man said, eyes wide. "M-M-Mistress of Shadows! Oh, ash and dust, I-I didn't know! How was I to know?"

Faye raised a brow.

"I'll get you out of there right away!" Stammering, the guard fumbled for his keys to open her cell. "Oh, ash and dust, bone and marrow," he cursed. "My lady, Irasa would have my head if she knew I kept a fellow Thieflord under lock!"

Ah, Irasa…of course, the Thieflord of Flesh.

Faye had a love-hate relationship with the only other female Thieflord. Come to think of it, Faye had a love-hate relationship with *a lot* of people. That was more their fault than hers, she was pretty sure.

"Well, that's convenient," Faye mused beneath her breath. Of course, also not terribly surprising. One never knew where they had sunk their talons, fangs, tentacles, or *whatever* apt analogy you envisioned for the nine dark Thiefdoms that ruled the world in the shadows of the Great Kingdoms. "Easy, easy," she told the man as he dropped the keys in his rush. "Don't have a heart attack over it. Don't wanna ruin the moment."

Frantic, the guard finally slid the key in with a click and pulled the door wide.

Faye exited. "Ah, much better. What's your name?"

"Maligard, mistress," he muttered, eyes downcast.

"Good name and great job, Maligard. Now, I left that arena with some idiot friends, a big guy and a little guy," she said, gesturing to their heights with her hand. "Where are they? Also, why was I separated from them?"

Maligard mumbled, "I-I don't know, I was only told that you were dangerous—"

"Accurate and appreciated. And my friends?"

Maligard rubbed his bald head as if trying to think. "All Primarian-basaeri are free to go, mistress. I don't know where they are. They could be anywhere."

"So what, I was just an exception? Locked away because I'm so scary?"

He winced. "I think so?"

Faye felt her pride swell a bit. "Well, then, you know how to make a girl feel special, Maligard. Now, why don't you use that big brain of yours," she said, grabbing his weak chin in her fingers, "and if you just *had* to guess, where would you say my friends would be?"

Maligard's whole face scrunched in thought, then his eyes went wide in realization. "The Primarian Feast!" Faye raised a brow for him to continue and he stammered on. "Queen Imala holds a gathering after the Bloodbath in the Flesh Hall for all Primarian, the upper-tier warriors. I imagine they might be there? You know, since the queen seems to have—"

"An obsession with the Ronin? Yeah, I heard. That's an understatement." Faye took another step forward, until she was nearly right on top of Maligard. Slowly, she reached down toward his belt and pulled a dagger from the man's sheath, raising it, and the man winced, as if expecting to die. With her other hand, she patted him on his bald head. "Thank you, Maligard. That's a good boy. You've been very helpful. I promise not to kill you when I bring down this city from the inside."

Maligard just shivered from her touch, backing away.

Sliding the dagger into her boot, Faye made her way out of the dungeon and through the halls, and the clamor of the crowds washed over her. The next round—for Primarian-basaeri—would be coming up.

Well, I'm sure I have time to watch a quick match.

Mixing with the Covian citizens that flooded in, Faye joined the throng. Vendors moved up and down the stands selling a variety of treats from baskets. Faye filched a crimson scarf from one of the baskets and wrapped it around the collar on her neck. A rather plump-looking merchant was enjoying three chargrilled lizards on a stick. Faye slipped the skewers out of his pudgy fingers, leaving his mouth agape.

Smiling, Faye found herself a nice little spot in the stands as more and more men and women gathered upon the tiered seating. Thankfully, she knew the winners of each match got a small respite before their next fight.

With a slow, rumbling grind, the iron gates opened on the far end of the arena.

Out stepped a man attired in mail and leather, his chest smeared in red paint and wearing…a giant boar's head? Blood still dripped from the severed head, as if recently killed and the insides scooped out. *Well, that's a fashion statement,* Faye thought. He was otherwise burly, with a thick chest, arms, and a bulging gut like he'd swallowed a barrel. In one hand the man wielded a wicked battle-axe, and in the other, a spiked flail. The boar-headed man roared, trying to garner the crowd's favor.

The masses cheered with each wave of his flail.

Faye bit into her lizard, and her eyes split wide. Sure, there were quite a few burnt, charcoaled bits but the meat itself was flaky, tender, and surprisingly delicious.

Huh…who knew?

Abruptly, two more gates opened, and red-striped tigers raced across the sand for the boar-headed gladiator. The man waited until the last moment to step aside from their swiping claws and then laid the flail into the first tiger, sending it smashing against the wall to lay still. The other tiger attacked, and the boar-man hacked its claw off. The beast howled, limping.

Faye's stomach churned.

How very Covian.

The boar-headed gladiator turned his back and motioned to the crowd, trying to get them to cheer, pretending to be oblivious to the tiger behind him. It was all a very stupid ruse, but it worked on the hungry, gaunt tiger. Seeing an opening, the enraged red-striped tiger lunged, clawing at the boar-man's exposed back. Only, before the strike could land, the boar-headed man turned in the nick of time and buried his axe in the tiger's skull. The tiger collapsed in a puff of sand, lifeless.

The crowd applauded.

Not all of them, however. Many in the tiered stands seemed less than impressed, perhaps because of the man's sheer brutality, but more likely because they *also* knew the beasts were barely more than skin and bones—it was far from a fair fight.

Faye ripped off the next chunk of lizard with a bit more fervor. Meanwhile, the boar-man raised his hands up and down, attempting to rally a cheer.

Only a scattered few did.

What a fool. It was like gloating over killing caged livestock.

Then... the idiot kicked the tiger's lifeless body.

The skewer snapped in half in Faye's hand.

Seven hells, do I wish I was down there.

The boar-headed man roared, smeared his body in tiger's blood.

To hell with the rules...

She moved to rise, ready to leap into the sands when—

The announcer, his heavily tattooed face pierced with bone, metal, and other decorative objects, declared, in his theatrical voice, "Now for the first battle of the second round"—*Covai*, Faye muttered to herself—"I give you, in the east corner..." He pointed to the boar-headed man. "From the Ander Forest in the east, where even bandits fear to adventure, with five kills and two surrenders... *Tamiran the Barbarian!*"

The crowds gave another mixed cheer.

"And in our west corner—" The announcer fumbled for words, saying something about a mysterious newcomer as the gate grated open on the west side.

Gray walked out.

Faye smirked and sat back down. *Well, suppose I can let him have some of the fun.*

The crowd went quiet, then men and women whispered, 'oh gods, he's just a young man!' and 'He's going to be slaughtered', even a few, 'The matchup... it's not fair."

They were right.

The matchup was lopsided.

The boar-headed man roared, taunting Gray, and Faye watched as Gray's gaze took in the two starving, dead tigers at the man's feet. The boar-headed man charged without warning, his axe and flail raised. He threw the axe end over end. Gray had a collar around his neck, but he lifted his hand, and a thin, purposeful gust of wind rushed outward from his palm.

Controlled by the wind, the axe flew back at the man and embedded itself in his skull. The man staggered on his feet, groaning, and then... he slumped over, dead.

Welp, that was expected.

After letting the orange essence flow into his body, Gray turned, fury in his eyes, and stalked off the sands. The gate he'd come through in the first place hadn't even finished closing yet. With a swipe of his hand, the Ronin of Wind opened it again and left before the crowd could even react. There was a pause, as if they were all stunned. Then the whole amphitheater erupted in cheers and thunderous applause.

Ro-nin.

Ro-nin.

Faye sighed. *Tough act to follow. Well done, Wind Boy.* She still had her other skewers of grilled lizard when she noticed a woman with a heart-shaped face and a single scar down her left cheek seated next to her, with a young boy, likely six or seven. He cheered madly at the turn of events. "Here," she said and offered him the skewers. "Enjoy. "

"Thank you, that's so kind. What do you say, Rayan?"

"Oh, wow, we can never afford stuff like this," the little boy said. "Thank you so much!"

"Eh, don't mention it."

The young boy bit into the lizard. "Oh, wow, this is amazing!" Sticky sauce dripped onto his small hands as he offered her some. "Sure you don't want any, miss?"

"Eh, I'm good, thanks. Not really hungry before a fight anyway."

"Fight?" the boy's mother asked. "Are you fighting?"

"Uh…no…" Faye lied. "More a figure of speech. Anyway—" She moved to leave.

"Who are you cheering for?" the boy asked.

Faye paused. "That's a good question," she said, as if trying to be thoughtful. *Myself,* she answered inwardly, and then asked aloud, "Who are *you* cheering for?"

His eyes went wide as Farbian gold coins. "I like the Ronin of Wind! Did you see what he just did? That boar guy was mean! And he beat him fast!"

Well, "beat" was one word. Dead was another. This was Covai though, there were probably worse sights on the local streets. Seven hells, taking her son to the tournament was probably a light, happy outing in comparison. Faye snorted. "He's okay. What about that…" She coughed. "*Man* from earlier, the one with the bandages?"

"Oh, wow, he was amazing too! He moved so fast! Those other guys couldn't even touch him!"

Faye grinned. "He was pretty good, wasn't he?"

"Not as good as the Ronin of Water, or Wind!" Rayan said, bouncing in his seat.

Faye grimaced, folding her arms. "Magic powers, that's pretty much cheating, no?"

"No way, not with the collars!" The young boy started swiping and attacking, using his lizard skewers as imaginary weapons. "They had to be fast, too! Oh, man, I wish I could thread wind or water!"

Faye cursed under her breath.

"I think the Ronin are going to win as well," said the mother. Faye took in her ragged clothes and her fingers, stained from the tannery. "The Ronin represent hope," the woman said excitedly. "A change, something that is going to take this city out of the mire and muck it's been in…" Faye tried not to roll her eyes. *Thank the Abyss, Gray isn't here for that to go to his head.* The woman's big blue eyes fixed on Faye. "I mean, you saw them, don't you think so? They can bring change…can't they?" She looked so hopeful, as if Faye's next words could lift her out of the cesspit that was Covai.

Faye winced. "I, uh…"

She was interrupted.

Behind her, a man barked a laugh. "Ha! Ronin as saviors! Foolish woman, you think those little whelps for legends can win, let alone save us?" Faye looked over her shoulder—a man holding a thick drumstick, grease spilling into his black beard and brown skin peeling from the harsh sun, sneered down at them. Then she saw his attire and the symbol of a bleeding hand with a sword through it.

Great, Sons of Flesh. Just what I need, a zealous cultist to round out my day.

She opened her mouth to put him in his place when—

People nearby began to chime in.

A skinny man, his red hair tucked into a turban, exclaimed, "My coin is on the Ronin of Water, did you see 'im? The boy fought like a belegrun!"

Another a few rows down barked her opinion. "Mine's on Coile Grovewarden! I hear her powers are something otherworldly!"

"Have you all forgotten about the Grand Primus?" said an old man to the left of Faye, gripping a cane with his gnarled fingers. He gazed upon the sands as if he were seeing Nalia in the now-empty arena.

Others voiced their agreement.

Faye's blood grew hot thinking about that woman.

Part of her was afraid, but most of her was eager to test her mettle against a woman like that. Not entirely fair based on how much spark the woman had likely consumed, but still…Faye's knuckles cracked in anticipation.

The Sons of Flesh member with the curly beard said, "Old man's right! Some Dryad or pathetic legend might look strong against these nobodies, but when the Grand Primus takes the stage?" He scoffed. "Nalia will break their bones and suck their marrow."

"Colorful," Faye muttered.

"There's no way she can win it three times in a row! Egrin the Barbarian, Nefrin's champion, that's who my coin is on!" said a man a few rows back.

"Bah!" said the Sons of Flesh zealot, rising to confront the man. "You're a fool! You're all fools if you think Nalia will lose!"

A man with a beak of a nose and a piercing in his lip spoke, "My money is on that Moonguard fellow—saw him stalking into Covai the other day. You would have thought he owned the place! Moved like shadows, he did. Had hate in his eyes like he wanted the whole world to burn." He shivered. "Carried with him a sword that caught me eye. Dark purple, like the moon on a violet equinox. Ain't natural, and that sorta thing has got an edge in these games."

Faye hesitated at this...Moonguard fellow?

She had a bad feeling about that one. Fire and ash, she prayed it wasn't the maniac who had laid waste to Median.

"How are you all not talking about our very own leader of the Fleshguard, Drega!" said a woman who looked like an off-duty city guard. "Sure, the man seems friendly enough, but the whole Covian Legion gets shaky knees when he walks by!"

"You're all wrong," said a smaller man at the Sons of Flesh member's side, clearly his companion. He was dressed in rags that looked more like a pile of refuse, and spoke in a snide voice. "That *woman* is going to win it. I'm sure of it! She moved like the Dark Lord himself!"

The Sons of Flesh member smacked the small man upside the head. "I thought I told you to shut it with that nonsense, Jemin! That ain't no woman, no way a woman could move like that! Just like the Ronin, she's destined to die. The sands always know who."

"You're wrong," said Rayan. "They aren't weak, you are! And you're a bully!"

Just leave, Faye told herself. *You can leave now, and not get involved. Just leave.* She stood up. *See? Simple.* She started to walk away.

"Ha!" the Sons of Flesh member said. "Backbone for a little runt. Did your whore of a mother teach you that? To talk back to your betters?"

Keep walking, Faye said. *Just keep walking.*

She took another step, moving a few people aside.

"I did," said the boy's mother. "And not only are you the furthest thing from his better, but he's right." Glancing over her shoulder, Faye saw the woman raise her fist, and despite the dark shadows in her eyes, a spark of hope entered her voice and her face softened, looking younger, less tired. "The Ronin are going to win. I'm sure of it, and they're going to change this city when they do. Then we'll be rid of bastards like you, once and for all."

The Sons of Flesh member laughed cruelly and said, "Aww, poor woman, what's wrong? Ain't like the way the world works, do ya?" He leaned in, and the woman cringed. "I know what you need, just someone to cuddle you at night. Your loins yearn for some tender meat, do they?" He laughed. "The Ronin of Wind and Water, is it? They're barely older than your own welp." He leaned nearer, his stout finger moving to stroke the woman's cheek. "Forget them. How about a real man?"

Faye sighed, stopped walking, turned, and threw her dagger.

It landed in the man's throat. His eyes went wide, and he gurgled blood before collapsing, dead.

Faye fetched her dagger. "He really picked the wrong day to be…" She shrugged. "Well, I guess to be who he was."

Jemin, his small companion, was wide-eyed, as were most of the onlookers.

Faye rubbed the back of her neck and told the crowd, "You know, you all have some pretty interesting takes on who's going to win next, but…" Horns sounded. In the corner of her vision, she saw that guards had been alerted to the commotion and were coming her way. "There's only one of you who had it right." She winked to the snide-looking little man. "Really, you should choose better company."

The boy and his mother looked at her, eyes like saucers. "Wait, you're—" the woman said.

"The soon-to-be Grand Primus," Faye answered, grinning. Then, as guards encroached on her from all sides, and before they could get a good glimpse of her face, Faye backflipped over a railing into a stairwell and slipped away to prepare herself for the next round.

Merrick

Merrick rode into the city of Covai, Great Kingdom of Flesh, with Jian, the leader of the Devari, at his side. Jian's cloak held its telltale crossed swords, attracting looks from citizens, though not as many as Merrick's black bow upon his back, looking as if it were absorbing all light.

The leader of the Devari hadn't said more than a handful of words to Merrick. The Patriarch had commanded. The man, bound by duty above all things, had simply bowed his head and obeyed. Now his eyes scanned his surroundings as they passed into a bustling bazaar with colorful stands displaying a host of wares. Many citizens cast fearful glances at them. "Well, we're here. What's the plan?" Jian asked.

Merrick sank deeper into his cowl and answered, "Find accommodations. Our round starts in two days. Meanwhile, I need to make a visit." He eyed the crest of the colosseum in the distance.

Jian lifted his reins, but Merrick grabbed the man's wrist.

The leader of the Devari glanced down to the hand that held him, utterly unfazed. Then his eyes looked up to meet Merrick's with a cold, steely indifference. Merrick knew the twin bloodstone Devari blades on Jian's back could be drawn quicker than one could blink—it was his famed move, and while Merrick wasn't afraid of this man, he was…formidable. "We aren't going to have a problem, are we?"

Jian gave an even breath and replied in an even voice, "I'm just here to win a tournament, my lord."

So Merrick let go. "One of us will. I am curious, though. Are you at least a little hungry for a rematch? I heard you fought the Ronin of Wind once before."

Jian's jaw clenched. "I did."

"You lost."

A weak smile graced the man's rugged face as he replied, "Were you there, my lord? Or were you busy destroying the last vestiges of Median, the once City of Water?" Merrick tensed. He hadn't realized how much Jian knew…clearly more than was ideal. Jian continued, "And you must be desirous to fight your own Ronin?"

It was Merrick's turn to snort. "I am."

"I would be wary of Gray, my lord. He is more than he seems."

"So am I," Merrick replied.

"Ha!" Jian said, breaking the tension, his face more relaxed. "Good, I like that fire. Truthfully, I'm glad I was asked to join the competition. It has been a while since I've found a worthy fight. Something to stretch my muscles at last." He rolled his shoulders. Then he grew serious and grated out, "As for my allegiances, I wouldn't worry. I will do what I must for duty's sake. All else is second."

"Good," Merrick said.

"If that's all, my lord? I'll go see about those accommodations," Jian said, easing up a bit. "Think I spotted one on our way in. Not too opulent, but with enough cheer and chatter. My kind of place." He gave a small smirk. "Ash and sand, with any luck they might even have something other than warm piss at the bar."

Merrick snorted, then gave a nod.

Jian dipped his head, trotting in the direction of the inn. Merrick rather liked Jian. Which said something, as he didn't like…almost anyone.

It was obvious the leader of the Devari was a conflicted man, caught between his duty and his own sense of what was "right." While the Patriarch's motivation for sending him was a bit of a mystery, it didn't matter to Merrick.

All that mattered was for him to win.

And win he would.

After a short ride, he found himself before the grand colosseum, which admittedly was rather impressive. It towered over most of the city, taller than any other building aside from the golden-domed palace in the distance. Primus and Grand Primus statues watched over Merrick as he made his way through the east entrance, and he caught a glimpse of a statue he knew all too well. The forty-foot monstrosity depicted a warrior in glorious armor, with a symbol of Flesh on his cloak and eyes the color of blood. Somehow the artist had captured the warrior's rage and an otherworldly calm as the figure summoned spikes of bone at the base of the statue.

Merrick's fingers lightly grazed the inscription as he passed.

AURELIUS, RONIN OF FLESH.
HARBINGER OF THE NINE SANDS BATTLE.
COURIER OF THE UNDEAD.
ALSO KNOWN BY HIS LESSER TITLES: BONEHEWER, FLESHRENDER.
LEGEND OF THE LIEON, FIRST AGE, CIRCA XXXIII

Of course, Covai was the only city that would glorify such legends... Another thing this city had gotten wrong, but Merrick would set it right. Passing thousands of citizens still waiting in line for the next round, Merrick caught snippets of conversation here and there about a young man, a giant, and a graceful man taking the first entry round of the Bloodbath. This was followed by whispers of the Ronin of Wind thoroughly vanquishing his competition.

Good, Merrick thought. He didn't want the battle to be one-sided.

So you're still planning on killing them? Your own brethren? Osmium asked. The blade's original name had always been Iridal, but Merrick had renamed it after a god of metal in ancient folk legend—it was his sword after all.

You knew that was the plan.

When you see them? What will you do then?

Merrick breathed tightly as he moved through the crowds, making his way to the inner structure of the massive colosseum. *What do you mean?*

You slaughtered thousands in Median. They will want your blood.

They can try, but I've a feeling their dear leader is still naive enough to believe he can turn me to the side of good, maybe even use me as an agent to stop my father.

The others will not forgive so easily. Innocents died, thousands, you promised not to turn a blind eye to—

His muscles tensed as Merrick pushed into torchlit hallways, passing messengers, guards, and servants, climbing higher into the colosseum. *I am not ignoring anything. Median happened. I did what I thought was right to take back a city from a corrupt king, and to put an end to magic. Besides, "innocents" is a strong word. Most of them were soldiers.*

Whatever mollifies your conscience.

Why do you antagonize me now? We've been over this.

I simply wish to know what your plan is. Do you think the Ronin will just let you enter...

No, Merrick thought, feeling a grin come to his face. *They're not going to have a choice.*

Merrick made his way through the halls until he came to a pair of grand double doors.

The Flesh Hall.

A Chat with a Thieflord

Now that the Bloodbath was over, the second round had officially commenced.

Ayva glared at the nobles as they laughed, drank, and wagered.

"Primarian-basaeri!" an announcer shouted again. "Fight!"

She turned her attention to the arena, ignoring the nobles. Gray's battle had been the first and most interesting thus far. There were notable exceptions, and she studied each combatant's strengths and weaknesses…preparing.

Women entered at this stage of the competition, mostly thieves or the criminal sort, hoping to gain advantage by rising in the tournament's ranks. More magic was used in this round. Currently fighting in the arena were a pirate and a one-stripe Reaver, whose face and body were marked with red paint. The announcer called the Reaver Vivian, and she reminded Ayva of Meira, the three-stripe Reaver who had been instrumental in saving Ezra, Gray's grandfather. Meira had gone from torturer to savior, redeeming herself in the end. She died in the Battle of the Sands, and her death had been devastating to Reaver Finn, her partner.

"How curious," Jima'ra, the axe-faced head of House Red Fox said. She coolly plucked grapes from a platter, popping them into her mouth one at a time while waving away Otto's lingering pipe smoke. "That's one of those cutthroats who sold their swords to the shadow in the west to help sack Median."

"Ah, yes, what was their name again?" asked a noble.

"Dragon's Tooth Marauders, my lady," Howard said from the entrance.

"Dragon's Tooth *Raiders*," Jima'ra corrected.

"Ah," Howard dipped his head. "Forgive my blunder, my lady. You are as keen with the history of the land as ever."

"Do I look like a biscuit, Howard?" Jima'ra asked, popping another grape into her mouth. She leaned back with her legs crossed on the balcony's railing.

Howard replied, "Of course not, my lady!"

Jima'ra sighed. "Then why do you butter me up so? You did that just to make me sound smarter, but I don't need your aid to run circles around these fools."

"Oh, you just astound us with your wit," Larissa said as a servant fanned her. "At least you have one asset to compensate for your other less than favorable liabilities."

Jima'ra barked a laugh. "This again? Please, Larissa, if you wish to favor looks over intelligence, we all know you've won in that department. Alas, I'd rather be uglier than a verg. At least I'm twice as smart as you." Larissa scoffed. "Besides, I know you're just upset that you're about to lose your wager on that Reaver of yours," Jima'ra replied, biting into another grape.

Ayva stood watching as, upon the sands, Vivian roared and sent a globe of molten fire at the pirate.

The cutthroat, wielding a cutlass infused with bloodstone, slashed at the molten globe, dissolving it into whispers of smoke. Then he charged. Vivian caused roots to grow from the sand, but the pirate cut them away. He slashed at her, and she suffered a gash across the belly that parted her red robes. Vivian cried in pain, clutching her stomach, and sent a frantic spray of sand toward the pirate. He recoiled, momentarily blinded. Seizing her chance, two thick roots shot out of the sand and grabbed the man's ankles, then another wrapped around his neck.

Vivian's face was full of fury as the pirate gasped, face turning red.

"You were saying, axe-face?" Larissa asked Jima'ra snootily.

"Yes, I'm going to win!" another noble said excitedly.

"Ha! I told you," Otto exclaimed, puffing smoke. His feet were still kicked up on the tasseled footrest. "Always bet on House Citadel! The Patriarch's entries are as safe as gold!"

Ayva wasn't so certain, however.

Vivian's collar was growing red-hot about her neck.

"She's going to lose," Ayva said in realization.

Queen Imala, from her throne in the midst of the nobles. Her hand rested on the cushioned armrest and she raised a brow. "Nonsense!"

"Watch," Ayva said.

The pirate's face turned red, then purple.

On the verge of victory, Vivian grinned, but her power was waning, her grip slackening.

It was all the opening the pirate needed.

With the last of his strength, he threw his dagger.

Vivian blocked it with a chunk of stone, but having expended all her spark, the rest of her spells dissolved as she fell to her knees. The pirate caught his breath, then rose and stalked towards the woman. Vivian scuttled back on the sands, pitifully trying to send shards of stone, or threads of flesh. The pirate simply cut them from the air, finally moving to stand over her. The cutthroat whispered something, maybe an apology, and with a quick slash of his dagger, he opened the Reaver's throat to the cheers of the crowd.

"Aww, seven hells of Remwar!" Otto groaned, bulk rising out of his chair. "I had two thousand Farbian golds on that woman, *and* a priceless Serian vase!" He shot a look over his shoulder at the other six Reavers guarding the terrace. "I thought you were supposed to be the elite of Farhaven!"

An older female Reaver with gray hair and two stripes snorted, "Vivian was brash and a one-stripe. There's a world of difference between her and me."

Ayva watched as the pirate breathed in the woman's spark.

Another noblewoman tittered, "How fun would it be to see an Arbiter on the field?" She looked to Ayva. "I hear rumors that Arbiter Ezrah, second only to the great Patriarch, is the Ronin of Wind's grandfather. Can you attest to this, our little Ronin of Sun?"

Ayva saw no reason to lie, so she nodded, and said, "It's true."

"How fascinating," Jima'ra said contemplatively. "With such a lineage, perhaps he will win this year. Imagine that, Ronin of Wind *and* Grand Primus. I can see why you admire them so, my queen."

Queen Imala gave a smirk. "Who wouldn't?"

"What say you, our dear Grand Primus?" a nobleman asked as Nalia stalked back onto the terrace. "You are the favored this year, but are you worried the Ronin of Wind might take your spot? He is a legend, after all. He might even be immortal!"

Nalia's face could've been carved from granite for all the reaction it showed. "All men die." Then she turned to the queen, whispering something in the woman's ear, and the queen waved a jeweled hand. Nalia whisked away.

The nobleman swallowed. "Did I upset her? Flesh and dust, that's a terrifying notion."

"Ha!" Otto exclaimed. "If we find Yorin's head on a pillow tomorrow absent a body, I think we will know why!"

"Why the paint?" Ayva asked suddenly. "Is that what enables the arena to absorb magic?"

Judging by the bored faces, the workings of magic was a line of questioning the nobles didn't seem to care about. Thankfully, Howard answered. "Purely symbolic, my lady," he replied, his keen eyes lowering as he spoke. "The crowds like to see the Noxii and first-round combatants covered in paint, a not-so-subtle representation of the blood to come. After that, we dispense with the formality."

She squinted, curious. "So the arena doesn't require paint to absorb spark?"

"No, it does not," Howard said. Imala watched now, taking a sudden interest in their little back and forth, as if Ayva pried too deeply. Ayva didn't care. "To my knowledge, the arena is curiously perceptive. It knows the winner and loser, and any who enter are subject to their spark being 'absorbed' as you say, upon defeat of course."

She thanked the man, who dipped his head, and the nobles returned to their bickering. Fascinating. The arena seemed oddly intelligent. Too intelligent. As if alive. She'd need to pry deeper into that. For now…Ayva cleared her throat. "I'm afraid I must excuse myself as well."

The queen snorted. "Where must you go?"

Ayva lifted her glass of wine.

Queen Imala gave her a shrewd, discerning look, then snorted and waved in dismissal.

Ayva passed Howard, pausing to hand him back her chalice. She leaned in as she did so.

"Third-rank dungeon, second to the left," Howard whispered.

She thanked him with a look.

Above, the roar of the crowds shook the walls. The clashing and clang of metal and cries of men urged Ayva to move faster. She knew time was wasting. Sasha could be summoned any second. Winding through the crowded halls, Ayva reached a set of metal doors just as Howard described, guarded by four burly men in armor.

She cursed. She could kill them, but the hall behind her was crowded.

Was there another way in?

"Something you're looking for?" a voice asked.

Captain Leanna stood behind her. She had an athletic build, muscles well-honed from a decade of training and skirmishes. The woman's smooth skin was colored a deep clay from the harsh sun, with only a few stern wrinkles at her mouth and the corners of her eyes. Leanna's blond hair fell in a utilitarian cut to her shoulders, and tattoos swirled up her cheeks and across her forehead. Otherwise, she wore thick leather armor, tooled with engravings, that tried to hide her lithe frame. Her whole aura was one of efficiency. Ayva was certain, however, if Leanna wanted to look less like a blunt object of war, she'd make heads turn.

"You..." Ayva remembered her as the woman who'd escorted Zane with Reaver Nefrin to the queen's side. "I was," she said, clearing her throat, scrambling for a reason, "wanting to see the conditions of the dungeons."

"They're dungeons," Captain Leanna said flatly. "They are dark, dank, and smell of mildew."

Well, that was an obvious answer. Think! You're supposed to be good at this. Ayva wasn't a fast-talking charismatic charmer like Darius or good at lying like he was, righteous and noble like Gray, full of a "do it or else" attitude like Zane, or just lucky like Helix. She was...Ayva, so she was honest. She took a breath. "Can you get me in?"

The woman looked her up and down. Then she smiled, moving toward the dungeon.

I'll take that as a yes? Ayva thought, and followed.

Leanna nodded to them, and the two guards stepped aside. The number of guards, with more armor and crossed halberds, increased as they went deeper. Upon seeing Captain Leanna, though, they relaxed. Ayva followed closely behind her until Leanna came to a stop. "Just ahead are the second-round prisoners the queen uses for the Primarian-basaeri battles. Deeper down are some creatures you don't want to face." She looked Ayva over again, noticing the light in her eyes. Ayva had a feeling they were slightly glowing in the dim light. "Well, maybe you do."

"Where are the prisoners escorted?"

Leanna pointed to a hallway. "That corridor leads to the arena. On the off chance you're waiting for someone, they'll have them in a holding cell until the next match starts. You might have to wait." Her eyes briefly glanced to a nearby alcove with a large statue of a previous Grand Primus. "I suggest a good hiding spot."

That was…surprisingly helpful, yet again. "Thank you," Ayva said honestly.

Leanna dipped her head, as if moving to leave.

Ayva had to know. "Why are you helping me?"

Leanna turned back. "Because I'm a believer in the Ronin," she said and grinned. "I saw your fire friend. He wants to make a change for good. I like that." She glanced at the cold stone walls and cells inside. A smell of pitch and mildew filled the air. "Besides, it's the dungeons, not the queen's jewels."

Ayva shrugged. "That's fair."

"If that's all?"

Ayva nodded.

"Good."

Leanna turned to leave, and Ayva called out, "You're right, by the way. This city, this world…all of it needs to change if we're going to survive."

Leanna gave a small snort, eyeing her. "Yes, and you might just be the one to do it. Word of advice? The queen has more up her sleeve, and Nefrin cannot be trusted. Keep your friends close, *Kin'ara'ni*."

Kin'ara'ni. Ayva knew just enough Sand tongue to know that was…*Sun goddess?* No. "Divine one of Sun" was the more literal translation.

Leanna sighed. "Now I'm afraid I have a few loose ends to tie up myself. Good luck." Without another word, the Guard Captain marched back into the dimness of the dungeons, leaving Ayva alone.

Ayva waited for Sasha, remaining hidden in an alcove that housed a giant statue of a previous Grand Primus. He was a man with a bald head and he carried strange hook-like weapons she recognized as *tiras*, or hook swords from nearly a thousand years ago. *Glad you're just a statue, because I feel like you'd smell.* As time passed, she grew worried. Had Leanna set her up? Nodded to an alcove and then flitted off to inform the queen? Ayva wondered what Imala would do anyway.

Replacing Sasha was a bold move, but Ayva was a Ronin. How far could she push that?

Finally, thoughts churning, she settled on trusting Leanna. Then she heard voices carry out of the dim shadows. The first was pleading and full of fear. "Please… I don't wanna die! You don't have to do this!"

Ayva's heart leapt: *Sasha*.

"Listen, boy," said one of the guards, "we don't want to do this either, but it's your head or ours!"

Ayva waited until the voices grew louder, and two guards marched by trying to shush the terrified boy as they gripped his arm in his large white coat. Sasha continued to beg and plead. Once or twice he tried to shirk or slip out of their grip, but the guards held him tight. Ayva trailed them until they took her where she wanted to go. She needed to make sure she was at the right gate.

The thrumming of the crowds grew louder.

The three arrived at a wide, round portcullis. Beyond, the metal grate revealed the bright sun and sands of the arena.

"Please, you don't have to, you can let me go!" Sasha pleaded.

One guard fumbled with Sasha's chains. "Gah, I can never find the right keys!"

"You don't think this seems wrong, do you?" said the other guard again, tugging worriedly at his beard. "I mean, he's only a boy. He's scared enough, he's practically wet himself."

The other guard threw up his hands. "What do you suppose we do, let 'im go? Then the queen will string us up for all to see. I don't know about you, but I'd rather keep my head attached to my body."

Ayva stepped into the center of the hallway. Sun glowed in her hands and fed the fire in her eyes. "Put down your weapons," she ordered.

Both guards looked at her, confused. "My Lady Ronin…"

Ayva sighed. "Look, I don't wanna fight, and clearly you don't want to either, but here's what's going to happen. You're going to let that boy go and say you did your job, just as instructed—"

"If we don't?" one guard asked tremulously.

Sun roared in Ayva's hands. "Well, I thought the alternative was kind of obvious."

Both looked at the other, pulling out their blades.

Ayva sighed. "Always the hard way. Close your eyes," she shouted to Sasha. He did so, and the Nexus filled her mind's eye—a glowing sun. She instilled herself with *hope*. It wasn't hard now, and the flow responded with ease as she sent a flash of brilliant light. Both guards cried out, blinded.

They stumbled around. "I can't see! Ah, you damn witch, where—"

They swung swords, hitting walls and nearly each other.

Sasha ran to Ayva's side, clinging to her.

"Huh, that worked better than intended," Ayva said.

"Wh-what are you going to do with them now?" Sasha asked.

Ayva wasn't sure. She had spells to kill and blind, but nothing to incapacitate. But then…Aurora whispered to her, something ancient and familiar. "Close your eyes again," she instructed Sasha. "I'm going to try something." Sasha did so, and Ayva sent out another ball of light. Only this time, much, much smaller. *Start small*, the sword gave an urgent message—*especially with such a confined space.*

The two guards scrubbed at their eyes, cursing her out. Only this time, as the pin-sized ball of light floated between the two men, Ayva reached inside and pulled a thread loose. Just a single thick cord in the core of the ball of light, and it collapsed. Then it expanded, suddenly, violently, instantly.

Boom.

The whole hall shook. Ayva was sent flying, and her back hit the wall. Dazed, ears ringing, Ayva saw Sasha. He was knocked on his backside, looking equally stupefied. "Are you all right?"

Sasha checked himself, then nodded. "I-I'm fine."

Ayva looked up to what she'd just done. Dust filled the air. Both guards lay on the ground, helmets dented. Blood ran from one's temple, and the other's arm was broken. Ayva stumbled to their sides and checked their pulses. "Alive," she announced, "just unconscious."

"How did you…" Sasha asked, eyeing the dusty air and chips of stone all about them.

"It just came to me." Ayva glanced to the legendary blade of Sun at her hip. *Did you help me with that?* She knew the sword had taught her the spell, or…retaught her. Light and heavens, thank the eternal spirits she'd done it that small. Then her pulse raced. How big *could* she do it? Ayva knew that it wasn't a ball of light. It was a star. That knowledge was foreign, yet completely familiar, as if Omni's wisdom had been passed down to her. A star…a miniature one at least. By pulling on one thread, she'd taken away its power source, which had made the star collapse in on itself. Under such pressure, it was forced to rebound, the star matter literally bouncing back, the explosion ripping through the star's outer layers. She shook her head in wonder, and then she turned to Sasha. "We're almost out of time. I think your round is about to begin."

"I'll do whatever you say. What's the plan? You want to pose as me, don't you?"

Ayva nodded. "First, we need to figure out how to get that collar off you." She searched the metal band, but it was smooth, seamless, no latch or even keyhole.

"Well, this is curious," a woman's voice said.

Ayva turned, hoping and dreading who she'd find.

It wasn't Leanna, or Faye, or…anyone she knew.

A Covian guard was at the woman's side—a bald man with a few sparse hairs—who took in the scene slack-jawed.

The woman, on the other hand, was completely unperturbed. She was tall. That was the first thing Ayva noticed. Taller than most women, with a few faint scars on an otherwise handsome face. Thick ropes of blond hair twisted down over her lithe, strong shoulders. Ayva had seen the custom before—common of Covian nobility, or Cloudfellian men. Her hair was matted, and filled with silver jewelry. A tan-colored vest exposed her impressive arms, heavily bronzed from the sun, with lean, hard muscles and covered in gold bands. Her bangles looked like they were more than fashion—as if she could use them to stop a blade.

The woman took in the scene with an all-too-perceptive gaze, as if she stumbled across two stunned guards, an explosion, a Ronin, and a captive all the time. Wait…Ayva did know her. Faye had described the woman now before her in equal notes of jealousy and grudging acceptance of her prowess, admitting the woman was *impressive*. "You're Irasa, the Thieflord of Flesh, aren't you?"

"Yes, and you're the Ronin of Sun. Now, we can sit here making acquaintances all day, only I'm pretty sure"—Irasa paused, as if listening to a faint alarm in the distance—"you're about to be captured and hauled away, and this…swap? I'm assuming? Well, it's not going to work. You need a collar to get on that field." She tapped her mouth in thought. "*And* something to hide that face of yours. The boy is pretty," she admitted, eyeing Sasha, "but he's not a girl, and he doesn't have your freckles. I mean, you could probably get away with showing a bit of eyes, nose, or cheekbone, but not the whole face."

Ayva unwrapped the scrap of white cloth that was tied about her arm. She had received it from Dalic, leader of the Algasi, who had ties to Vaster and Omni. He'd given it to her after everything they'd endured in the Nimue Everglades, a final parting gift, and Ayva had kept it with her all this time.

Irasa snorted, eyeing the white cloth. "Well, isn't that convenient."

"Now, can you help get this off?" Ayva gestured to the smooth collar on Sasha's neck.

Irasa tossed something, and Ayva caught it: a small metal object with strange glyphs carved into the side. *Old tongue?* It was an ancient dialect used during the Lieon, by the Ronin, said to have its origin dating back to the titans.

"Is this what I think it is?" Ayva asked, feeling the cool metal in her hands.

"If you think it's an ancient artifact created by Reavers of old? Then, yes."

Ayva used the device on Sasha's collar. Hearing a click, the boy gasped as if he'd been underwater breathing through a straw all this time, and now was he able to take a deep breath. *Great.* Ayva wasn't looking forward to that same feeling. Sasha rubbed his neck as Ayva held both the collar and the metal tool.

Irasa cleared her throat. "I'm going to need that back. It's worth a small fortune. The queen herself only has two of them, and I've a feeling I might need it soon."

Ayva threw the tool to her. Then, with a deep breath, she snapped the collar on her own neck. Immediately, she felt its cold restriction on her power. She turned to Irasa, who eyed her coolly. "Thank you."

"You're welcome. One thing, you can't take that with you…" She nodded to Aurora. "Weapons are permitted in the second round, but not famed magical blades of untold power. I'm afraid they'll either confiscate that or shoot you on sight."

Ayva looked down to Aurora, the legendary Sword of Sun. The golden sheath was etched with white-and-honey-colored scrollwork. The cross guard was formed in the shape of a resplendent sun, golden flames fanning out from it, and the handle was white leather-like material that had been lost to the ages, probably from a creature that no longer existed. If cleared from the scabbard, she knew the blade would glow like the sun itself.

With a breath, her fingers lightly grazed the sheath, releasing the bond on the blade. She marched forth and handed the famed sword to the Thieflord of Flesh. "Take it. Keep it safe."

Irasa's eyes fanned wide, then she blinked in confusion as she regarded the famous weapon in her hands. "You can't be serious…" she whispered in disbelief. "You're just giving me the Sword of Sun? How do you know you can trust me?"

Ayva shrugged. "I don't, and while I'm not Gray, with the power to sense others' true intentions, I don't think you're bad. For starters, someone who wanted to steal the blade wouldn't question the gift."

"Maybe I'm just daft."

"Hardly. I've heard stories about you, the Keen-Eyed Thieflord of Flesh and the Web-Weaver."

Irasa rolled her eyes. "Never much liked 'the Web-Weaver,' too spidery for me. Surely, you have another reason to trust me with this."

"I do. You were down here to see Faye, Thieflord of Fire, weren't you?"

"I was…" Irasa said slowly. "Only someone set her free. Isn't that right, Maligard?" The Covian guard at her side shrank back, his bald head recoiling, as if he were a turtle trying to disappear into its shell. "And yes, Faye's an…old friend. What does she have to do with all this?"

"She's in the center of it, isn't she? There's a war happening beneath the surface, with the Thieflords, isn't there?" Irasa's eyes narrowed. It was all the confirmation Ayva needed. "We've been hearing whispers for weeks of the other thieves gathering power. Mathelstan knew it too, didn't he?" Again, a clenched jaw from the woman. Ayva continued, "Only, Mathelstan wasn't the strongest Thieflord. That's why he tried to use us to protect Median." She shook away the painful images of Median's destruction, of Mathelstan, the Thieflord of Water's death. He gave his life to create a diversion that saved them all. She pressed on. "Mathelstan wasn't a rightful heir, so he couldn't claim what you and the others are vying for, some sort of object or title? Whatever it is, it's clearly something powerful."

"My lady," Maligard said at her side, "we can't stay. If the guards find us here—"

She shushed the man. "Go on, girl. I'm listening."

Ayva read the woman's eyes. A mixture of eagerness, uncertainty, and hope struggling to climb to the surface, despite a mountain of worry. Ayva knew that look well. "You can't claim it either, this power, can you?"

Irasa this time didn't look away. "Other Thieflords would kill you for knowing far less, girl." Her eyes were cold daggers. "What are you after?"

Ayva's jaw clenched, and she looked up, toward the hallways above. She knew their time was dwindling. Footsteps would be echoing down the corridor any moment. She replied, "If I'm right, even if we get the other armies, we still may not stand a chance against this enemy…" She looked back into Irasa's eyes. "The Thieflords won't be able to sit this one out. They're going to have to choose a side."

"If we don't? Or if I decline?"

"Aside from likely needing our help in this little power struggle of yours?"

"Yes, aside from that."

"That one's easy," Ayva said. "Becoming some dark god won't do you much good if the rest of the world is destroyed. Look, I'm giving a sword to a literal thief—"

"Thieflord," Irasa added.

"I'm trusting you. Take it as an act of good faith. A first step toward a possible alliance."

Irasa snorted. "'*All the libraries of Morrow and Vaster couldn't contend with the Sun's wisdom,*'" she said, as if quoting from something. Then she added her own bit, "You are as clever as they said you are."

"Well, we'll see," Ayva said. "Say that again after I make it out alive. Word of advice, though?" She nodded to the sword in Irasa's hands. "Don't try to remove it from its sheath."

Irasa's eyes tapered. "Why? What'll happen?"

"Let's just say you don't want to find out." Unsheathed, none but a Ronin could wield the Sword of Sun; they would die trying. Irasa only nodded at this, looking a little more wary of the sword now. "Just to be clear, you're not going to tell anyone, are you? Me taking Sasha's place, that is."

Irasa chuckled. "Who'd believe me?"

Ayva glowered.

The woman waved away her concern. "Relax. We have a deal, not to mention, *a lot* more to discuss. You've piqued my interest, girl, and that's no easy feat."

Ayva put a hand to Sasha's arm. "You can get him out of here, right?"

Irasa scoffed. "Please girl, I can sneak the Dragon of Fire into the queen's bedchambers in broad daylight." Well, if that wasn't clear now that she knew all about Zane and the dragon, Ayva didn't know what was. A cheer sounded from the crowd in the colosseum. The gate on Ayva's left ground open. "Now you have a fight to win."

She nodded and turned to Sasha. "You're going to be safe now."

Sasha sniffled, then threw his arms around her. "Thank you for saving me. I can never repay you."

Tears were hot against Ayva's cheeks—whether they were hers or Sasha's, she wasn't sure. With a final squeeze, she pulled away, smiling. "No need. Just live. That's repayment enough. Besides, I have some frustrations I need to vent and some wagers I need to ensure are lost."

The crowds roared again.

"I think it's about time," Irasa said. "They're waiting...*my Lady Ronin.*"

That title seemed special coming from Irasa.

"One more thing," Ayva said, nodding, "I'm going to need your coat."

Sasha glanced down to his oversized white coat with a high, flared collar; the breast and sleeves were embroidered with delicate gold swirls. His bright blue eyes widened in understanding. Quickly, he took it off, and she slipped it on. It was still warm from Sasha's body heat. Glancing down, Ayva saw it hid her form nicely—not that she had Faye's curves, but still. She made a decent boy. *Now to complete the ensemble.* Ayva wrapped the cloth about her face until only her eyes and some of her blond hair peeked out.

Irasa's dark blue eyes gleamed. "Spitting image of Omni herself."

With that, Ayva strode onto the sands, a miniature sun burning in her fist.

Not This Girl

Zane sat in the dungeon, his back to the cold, mildewy wall. Above him the drums thundered, and he waited for his turn to live or die. A cry sounded, one he knew all too well: the blood-curdling howl of a man dying. "It's just about that time," Zane announced.

"Well, don't sound so gloomy," Raina replied. "You're about to win and save my brother." She tossed a pebble in the air as she leaned against the wall outside his cell, then added belatedly, smirking, "Also yourself, I suppose. That's good too."

Zane lolled his head to the side to look at her directly. In the shadows, her eyes were an iridescent golden brown, even more striking than before. "You know you don't need to be here."

"And I told you I want to be." She tossed the pebble up again and caught it. "Besides, where else would I be? Fretting in the stands among the rest of Covai?"

"Yes."

"Well, too bad." Raina stretched, yawning. "Honestly, it's kind of cozy down here. You know, aside from the murderers and monsters in the cells all around us. Or the smell," she said wrinkling her small nose. "Or, well…a lot of things." She sighed and folded her arms, sitting cross-legged, hunkering down. "I suppose I'll head up there once the fight is about to begin. Not much of a view down here. Until then…you can stop pestering, because I'm not leaving."

Zane held up his clawed hands in defense. "Just checking!"

She glowered. "What? You don't like my company, Ronin of Fire? You *want* me to leave?"

He opened his mouth, then answered honestly, "No. I'm glad you're here."

She seemed taken aback. Was there a hint of color in her cheeks? Then it was gone, and Raina gave another huff. "Good. That's the right answer. I am pretty great company, aren't I?"

"Incredibly humble, as well."

"Oh, you're one to talk," she shot back. Zane grumbled, but didn't disagree. Tossing the pebble up and catching it again, Raina replied more seriously, "Sasha hates it. My *bravado* as he calls it, or confidence. We're opposites that way."

"That happens a lot with siblings," Zane said. Raina opened her mouth, looking like she wanted to ask him a question he feared, so he pressed forward before she could. "So, if I'm saving this kid, what's your brother like?"

"Sasha? Oh, he's amazing. He sees the world through this pure lens. You know, the kind who meets even horrid, unredeemable people, and sees a glimmer of good in them. Then that goodness grows. Sometimes I wonder if the goodness was always there, or if just being around him—someone who sees the world full of light and life—makes you want to be better." She looked over to him, eyes shining in the dim light. "I don't know, maybe that sounds dumb. Probably is..." She chuckled. "Maybe the fumes of this place are getting to me."

After a moment of silence, Zane replied, "I had this man who believed in me once. I called him Father. I used to nag him with the same dilemma. I'd tell him he chose the wrong person, that there was surely someone else more deserving."

Raina's bronze-colored eyes narrowed thoughtfully. "What'd he say?"

"Said we all deserved a chance, including me."

She snorted. "He sounds smart."

"He was."

"Did he..."

"Killed by the previous Thieflord of Fire..." Zane said, fist clenching, remembering the Underbelly alive with flames. The horror of that day still haunted him. He'd discovered his home torn apart, Hannah kidnapped. Zane had seen red, and he'd headed straight to the Shadow's Corner, the darkest part of Farbs, and to the nefarious tavern known as Maris's Luck. It was there he'd stumbled upon Victasys—the scarred Devari—as well as Gray, Darius, and Ayva, who'd helped him save Hannah, and ultimately Farbs. "But before he died, he told me that the only thing that matters is finding my own peace." Zane scrubbed a long claw across his furry scalp. "Still trying to figure out what that means"

Raina answered, "It's funny how these people come into our lives, sharing their light...I'm not really a person who believes in fate, or whatever. Especially with all the cards I've been dealt in this hellhole of a city, but, I don't know…maybe there is something more guiding it all. Like you helping me."

"Maybe," Zane mused. It felt right, helping her, and being here. Only, Zane had witnessed so much wickedness. How could there be a purpose to bastards like Nefrin or Sithel or… He shut it out and found Raina's words had struck a chord. A purpose, a guiding hand, like Renalin's own. Zane thought of the Creator, the shaper of Farhaven, according to the stories. *Wherever you are, and if you are real, I could use you now.* Maybe the pieces on the board would start to make sense.

If he could only win…

Raina looked lost in her own dark thoughts, brow furrowed. He guessed she was worried about her brother.

"Tell me more about Sasha," Zane requested.

She gave a small chuckle, shedding some of her concern. "Where to start? Sasha's different from me in so many ways. He's kind, inquisitive, often quiet, with a softness surely, but also an openness…He sees the world the way I wish I could." She snorted. "If a thief stole my brother's last copper, then tripped trying to make a getaway, Sasha would be the first one to rush to his side to pick him up." She shook her head. "He's too pure for this world, like one of those purple lotus flowers amid the muck and mire. You know what I mean?"

Every word both burned and somehow…soothed. How were they so similar?

"Did I say something wrong?" Raina asked worriedly.

Zane realized he'd been silent for a long moment and said quickly, "No. Tell me more."

Raising a brow, Raina looked as if she was trying to understand him, and continued, clearly happy to be talking about her brother. "I don't know…siblings are weird. You don't choose them, but they're this core part of you, yet so different. Almost like they're trying to make up for your deficiencies, and you for theirs. Hells, I'd take Sasha's deficiencies any day." Then she paused. "Sorry, I'm rambling…I guess I'm just worried about him."

"Don't be," Zane said.

"Worried? Or sorry?"

"Both," he replied. "Sasha is lucky to have you."

"You don't have any do you? Siblings that is."

Don't shut down, Hannah's voice sounded in his head. *You have to trust someone.* Pushing back the coldness, Zane answered in a quiet voice, "Yes." Then he added, "I did, a sister."

"Oh…" Raina said as she looked at him, eyes full of sympathy and a true understanding. There was a long pause. "I'm so sorry, Zane."

Zane gave a shrug. "It's fine."

"No, it's not, you idiot. I'm sure she was pretty special. What…what was she like? If you don't mind me asking."

"Like your brother," Zane replied. "Too pure for this world. She saw the good in everyone. Her smile was like…" He pictured it again. "Like the warmth of the sun on a cold day. She also always knew what to say, like some sort of ancient prophet in a sixteen-year-old girl's body."

Raina smiled. "Sounds—"

"Annoying," Zane replied, and she chuckled. After a moment he found his voice again. "When Hannah died," he said, voice hoarse, "I didn't think I had anything to live for. She was the only good part of me, and the only thing keeping back my rage. Then I stumbled upon…" He cut off, remembering the dragons, their words that had driven him here—had encouraged him, lit the flicker flame of hope inside him—not to mention how they'd brought him back from the brink of death. Zane owed them dearly, and he would repay that debt, no matter what. "I'm not fully recovered, but I'm a long way from what I was."

"For what it's worth," Raina said, shuffling a little nearer the cell, "I'm glad you didn't die."

"Not yet."

She threw her pebble at him. He caught it, crushing it to a fine powder. "None of that! You're not going to die," she said, even as the crowds roared. Clearly they were taking the bodies away, or something else was happening as they prepared for the next round.

"I was meaning to ask you about the form of this body you gave me," Zane said, eyeing the powder in his clawed hand.

"You mean, why are you so strong? It's all that muscle and tendon. You should be about ten times stronger. That's the good news."

"What's the bad news?"

She winced. "I haven't found a way to make it last. The bigger the transformation and stronger the body, the shorter the flesh holds its form."

"It just needs to hold long enough," Zane replied.

She narrowed her gaze. "Are you going to tell me why you're fighting, brooding eyes? Or are you going to make me guess. You know why I'm fighting, it only seems fair to share."

"It's…complicated."

"Try me."

"Would you believe me if I told you it's for a dragon?"

She mused, "Well, if that's a lie, it's a good one. Also no, I don't believe you."

Zane laughed. "Why not?"

Raina shrugged. "Why not? How many dragon riders do you know? Also, if it's true, you should have led with that—you'd make any girl swoon with stories like that."

He felt his new body's brow rise. "Girls like guys who ride dragons?"

"Are you messing with me? You've got to be."

"What? No, I just…I don't know. Dragons are scary to most people."

"Scary and *amazing*."

Zane made an amused sound. "You know, you're not like most girls."

She snorted. "Then you're hanging around the wrong ones."

For a moment, Zane thought of Evangeline and grew subdued. Evangeline, daughter to Lord Nolan, the steward of Vaster…the memory of the woman returned, drudged up from before his path of vengeance, before he'd lost himself. *Was she alive?* He'd heard about the battle in Median. When he'd gone to hunt down Sithel, Zane had given everyone up for dead. Nothing had mattered. Yet Zane liked Evangeline. She was special to him. The time they'd spent together had been nice…even in what felt like his darkest hour, her company and touch had pushed back a small bit of the shadow. He hoped she was safe.

Raina spoke, her light, almost "annoyed-to-be-explaining" tone bringing him back to the moment. "Yes, for the record, a dragon-riding Ronin? Yeah, incredibly attractive. Totally the thing you'd lie about to get with a girl."

Zane chuckled. "Why would I lie? I'm about to be sent into a duel to the death!"

"You serious? That's the best time to lie! There's no repercussions if you kick the bucket." Zane shot her a look. Raina held up her hands, adding quickly, "I said *if*. I saw what you did to that creature." Her eyes flicked, and Zane specifically tried not to look at the thing's body that filled half the cell with him—or at least what was left of it. Raina had been forced to use a fair amount of the monster to "add" to Zane's form. "I definitely wouldn't want to face you."

He'd left the beast a mangled corpse, prying the collar off its decapitated head. Then he'd placed the huge metal collar on his own neck to rest like a beer-barrel hoop on his shoulders. When he'd grown in size, and his new neck had gained its trunk-like girth, the collar had cinched tightly.

More cries sounded from men and women on the sands as an announcer spoke. Zane heard the word "demons."

They both knew it was about to be his turn.

Raina spoke, as if to cover up the sounds, or to distract him. "But seriously," she said, looking up at him from the shadows, her bright almond eyes shining, "if you were trying to be smooth, then as far as first dates go…" She looked about at the dank, dark cellar, wincing.

"Not so good?" he asked.

"I've had worse."

"*Really?*"

"No, not really," she replied. "I can't tell if that's the smell of blood, vomit, urine, or just the pleasant mix of all three. Also, you look like a terrifying beast, demon thing."

Zane grimaced, then looked to his clawed hand. "Can't argue with that. Not something girls are into?"

"Not this girl." She took him in, eyeing his form in the dark light. "I mean, gods, look at you."

Zane glanced at his thick arms covered in fur, feeling his muscles roil with unbridled strength. "What about it?"

Raina gulped in the darkness. "Don't get me wrong, it's impressive, but mostly incredibly intimidating. Ash and bone, if you tried to hug me, you'd shatter every bone in my body. Anyway, I'm sure when you *unbeast* yourself, you'll clean up real nice." The crowds thundered again, and Zane knew he'd be announced any moment.

Zane felt a tug at his heart as it beat faster, and he took the risk. "All right."

"All right what?"

"All right," he said slowly, "when I get out of this, I'll take you on a real one."

In the dimness, she gave him an amused expression. "One a little less dungeony?"

"I didn't know you were such a princess—" he began, and she looked like she was going to throw some muck or dungeon slime at him. He raised his clawed hands. "Okay, okay!" He hesitated, then spoke quietly, "There…is this one place in Farbs. It's a little hard to get to, but it has the best view in all the city, maybe all of Farhaven." He squinted into the darkness, as if he could see the place again, feel the heat of the flames and the cold desert air. "You can see for miles, a city of light and life, alive with spark, and beyond that the cold, endless dunes. If you time it right, during the Festival of Fire, it's something else. Reavers display their arts and spark, lighting up the night sky with all the elements. They say the flames can be seen from Vaster."

Raina's eyes danced, as if she could see the magic as well. "You know how to paint a picture, brooding eyes. I'll be honest, though, I was already sold on no dungeon. It sounds…beautiful."

Zane chuckled and gave a wistful smile. "It was a favorite of Hannah's. Whenever I couldn't find her, she was there." He felt her eyes on him, and saw she was studying him curiously, as if seeing deeply into him.

Finally, she spoke. "Now I'm really honored. So it's settled—you save my brother, win the tournament, fulfill your mysterious purpose, then a visit to a magical view of Farbs."

"Deal."

Drums rumbled as Zane's door grated open.

He rose to his full towering height, head brushing the cell's ceiling, and turned to Raina. "You'll head to the stands now, where it's safe? Promise me no acts of heroism, no matter what happens."

"What could I possibly—"

He cut her off. "Promise me. Please."

Raina opened her mouth preparing to say something sarcastic. Then, seeing the candor and intensity in his demonic eyes, she closed it. With a half smile, Raina crossed her hand over her heart. "Promise."

Satisfied, Zane nodded and moved to the door.

She called, "We have a date, brooding eyes! I won't accept death as an excuse."

Zane snorted, nodded his hoary head, then turned, stalking out into the arena.

No Holding Back

Faye strode onto the sands, able to keep the dagger she'd pilfered from Maligard. Looking about, she saw pillars, like a titan's craggy fingers, rising out of the sands. Six of them, each a stone monolith roughly a dozen feet tall, and wide enough that four men with arms outstretched might not touch. The pillars hadn't been there during the Noxii battle, and she saw why: they held weapons. Axes, hammers, spears, pikes, quarterstaffs, flails, swords of all types—from cutlasses and longswords she could scarcely imagine trying to heft, to a hundred other rare weapons from all over Farhaven.

On the far end of the arena, the gates rolled open, and a huge man walked out.

Her whole body tensed.

Jivran.

Cursing hells, Faye thought, teeth grinding.

Jivran looked equally annoyed, his eyes hard, lip curling.

"I really don't want to kill this guy," Faye called into the stands. The crowd's cheering just overrode her. "Sure you don't want to send someone else?" Her gaze panned to the Queen's Terrace, spotting the monarch. The woman wore a cruel expression, and the other nobles seemed to be laughing at her expense. Clearly this whole thing was set up. "Figures," she muttered. What she wouldn't give to face the lot of them. *Shouldn't have shown I liked the big guy.* She'd broken her own creed again, revealing stupid emotions. They always caused more trouble than they were worth.

She turned back to Jivran, strode forth, and they met in the center of the arena.

The crowds, who had been roaring until a moment ago, made confused chatter as neither raised a hand to attack.

Jivran gripped an axe and cracked the haft over his knee, then dropped it to the sand.

Boos rained down on them, many in the crowd shouting obscenities.

"No want fight you," Jivran rumbled, his voice like rocks tumbling.

Faye sighed, rubbing the back of her head. "Me neither, big guy. Unfortunately...." She glanced at the hundreds of archers around the colosseum's upper wall. "I think they're going to make us. Guessing you don't have a way to stop a hail of arrows that can blot out the sky?"

Jivran shook his head glumly.

"I figured," she said, taking a deep a breath. "Well, in that case, it's surrender or death."

The giant grunted, his eyes hardening. "I no surrender. I must fight."

"Me too." She patted his muscled arm, which felt like solid rock. "But I'll try not to kill you."

He snorted. "I try not to kill *you*."

"Yeah, that's what I just said."

Jivran glowered. "No, *I* say it."

Faye opened her mouth to make another quip, then stopped. "Can I say something?" They were both ignoring the bombardment of slurs and shouts from the tens of thousands of Covians all around them. At the same time, Faye could tell the queen grew angrier by the whole "jowl quivering" thing she was doing. Any moment now they'd likely be pierced like pincushions with arrows. "I'm actually kind of glad you're not surrendering. Doesn't seem like you."

"Nor you." His frown broke into a smile. "I no hold back."

"Me neither, big guy," Faye said, shaking out her limbs and cracking her neck. "You ready for this? Let's give 'em a show."

Jivran grinned and then neared the closest pillar. He ripped off two great axes that would have been two-handed weapons in a normal man's grip. Instead, he made them look like overgrown hatchets. Jivran swung, slicing the air in an intimidating show of skill. He easily had enough force and speed to fell a mature oak. His collar turned a faint tinge of red; he was clearly using a small bit of his spark to wield the axes with such ease and force. She'd forgotten he was stronger after imbibing all the spark from the Bloodbath, just like her.

At Jivran's display, the jeering from the masses changed to thunderous applause.

Faye released a breath. *Well, this might be harder than I expected.* "On second thought," she called, "you can go a little easy—"

Jivran roared, charging.

Faye swallowed the rest of her sentence and grinned. Then, flipping her dagger to hand, she shouted a battle cry as she launched herself at Jivran.

The Wind Watcher

After Gray's match, he'd gone off to find the others. That had proven…unsuccessful. So he'd decided to watch the next fights. First, he'd returned to his room briefly to make sure Morrowil was safe in the chest.

His rooms were immaculate, as usual.

The central room was large, with colorful chairs, sofas, and gilded furniture. Several bookshelves and a few paintings of the other Great Kingdoms adorned the walls, and pedestals held Serian porcelain. Beyond the room was a central balcony that overlooked Covai. A dining area was to the left, and on the right were double doors to the master bedroom that held yet another balcony. It was all…far grander than he could ever imagine. But he was only here for his sword.

Once he saw Morrowil was safe and secure, he'd moved to leave, then turned and—

Came face-to-face with a woman.

Gray took her in, standing only paces away from him.

She was dressed in simple Covian livery, but her clothes did nothing to hide a shapely, slender form. Curiously, her head was shaved, showing only a faint bit of dark growth. Dark brows matched her hair, and she had a dapple of freckles, like Ayva's, but more of them. The woman had a strong, angled jawline and full lips. Bright olive-green eyes took him in. If he was being honest, she was beautiful. Breathtaking, even. If anything, her shaved head only accentuated her nearly perfectly symmetrical features. Unfortunately, however, she wore a stone-faced expression that bordered somewhere between "bored" and "annoyed"—so much so that he was afraid he'd offended her.

"Uh, can I help you?"

She dipped her head. "I am Hati, my lord. The queen has sent me to watch over you and ensure your every need is met."

Gray suppressed a sigh. *To spy on me, more likely.*

He watched Hati walk to a small dining table laden with bowls of food. She pulled out the chair and motioned for him to sit. "Perhaps you'd like to start here? The kitchen has prepared a meal, and I'm sure you're famished. While you're eating, I will draw you a bath."

"That's kind of you, but I'm in a bit of a hurry."

"The games are not going anywhere, my lord. You must be hungry, and you have an image to present, do you not?"

Gray felt offended. "What's wrong with my image?"

Hati's olive eyes panned up and down his red-slathered body and wild hair, and she raised an eyebrow. Her nose scrunched in disgust.

He sighed.

She ushered him over to the table, and when he smelled the intoxicating aroma of food, his stomach rumbled. *Storms take me, when's the last time I had a good meal?* So, grudgingly, Gray took the chair she held out for him and piled a plate high with chunks of warm bread and slabs of pheasant and roast duck, and then he ladled a dark gravy on the meat. As he dove in, almost ravenously, he realized Hati still stood at attention at his side.

She watched him.

Gray, wincing, grabbed a napkin, wiping his mouth.

This seemed to be a trend that continued through his meal. He would do something, and a mere look from Hati would make him feel like some backwater bumpkin. After another few bites, still feeling her eyes, Gray sighed. "You know, you can come sit." He turned and saw her olive-green eyes narrow. "I mean, there's plenty for us both." He chuckled. "If I were Darius, that'd be a lie, but I don't mind sharing."

"I…am not going to eat your meal, my lord."

"You're not eating my meal. You're eating with me," he said around a mouthful of roasted potatoes. He looked over his shoulder.

Hati seemed torn, her whole body reflecting her indecision, and she eyed the food. "It is not proper. A servant does not eat with a lord…" Then she added belatedly, "My lord."

"Also, about that," Gray said, "you can call me by name. It's Gray."

Hati immediately neared and sat, making herself a plate.

This time, it was Gray's turn to raise a brow. "I thought you didn't want to eat with me?"

Hati said defensively, midway to grabbing a hunk of herb-crusted bread, "I am most definitely not calling you by your first name, my lord. So if I have to choose between your requests, this is the more preferable option."

Gray tried to hide a smile as he shoveled another forkful of candied carrots into his mouth. Then, seeing her look, he let a few of the carrots drop to his plate and took a smaller bite. *Small victories*, he thought. They ate in silence for a little while, until he realized she was only eating the bread, so he placed a bit of roast pheasant on her plate. "You have to try this."

Hati scrutinized it, but brought it to her lips, chewed, and…she actually let out a little moan. Immediately, her cheeks reddened, and she glared at Gray as if it was *his* fault somehow.

Gray chuckled. "I'm guessing that means it's good?"

Hati covered her mouth as she chewed, then she poured herself a glass of milk. "Good," she admitted. "Thank you for asking, my lord." He almost grumbled about that, but she asked, "Before, you said something about Darius? Who is he?"

"My friend, also the Ronin of Leaf, and a voracious eater." Gray shook his head. "I swear, I don't know where he puts it." He chuckled, remembering. "One time an innkeeper bet Darius he couldn't eat his famous 'Giant's Mutton Stew.' Said if Darius could finish it, *anything* on the menu was free. When the innkeeper brought out the bowl, it was *big*," Gray said, gesturing with his hands, "I couldn't believe my eyes. Aaaaaand then *six* mutton stews later, the innkeeper changed his tune. On the tenth bowl, he kicked us out. Sweating and red-faced, the man swore and said Darius was 'eating him out of house and home.'"

As he delivered the last line, Hati was mid-drink of her milk, and she snorted. Milk shot out of her nose.

Gray burst into laughter.

At first, Hati turned beet red, clearly caught between mortified and galled by his reaction, but after a moment, she laughed along too. She took the napkin he offered and wiped her mouth. They ate the rest of the meal in comfortable silence, and when they finished, Hati rose smoothly and bowed. "I will finish drawing your bath, my lord."

After a quick bath, Gray returned to his bedchamber to don his normal clothes. He found them folded on his large four-postered bed, looking freshly washed. He paused, still wrapped in a towel. "How did she…"

Hati spoke, startling him. "Does my lord not prefer clean clothes? If so, I can head to the nearest sty and sully them once more. I think they might still be cleaner than they were before."

Gray protested, "No, it's not that. I want to go watch the next matches, maybe see if I can get a good seat in the stands, but I'd rather not go as the Ronin of Wind."

Hati whisked to the nearby wardrobe, a massive thing that took up the whole of the wall opposite the bathroom, on the other side of his bed. Opening one panel after another, she revealed more clothes than Gray had ever seen in his entire life. Most of it was finery in shades of Covian red, but as she kept opening panels, he found himself thoroughly corrected. *Light and wind, I can dress up as an Asterian noble, or a Cloudfellian barmaid.*

Hati pulled out some simple brown pants and a white shirt, then a lightweight beige cloak with a red symbol of Flesh on the back. "Will this do, my Lord Ronin?"

"That's...perfect. One more question, where's the best place to see the games?"

She glanced at the two crimson swords on his forearm, the marks he'd gained from finishing his second round. When he'd started, he'd had four. Then he'd been reduced to one by renouncing his Primarian status. Now he was climbing his way back up, one sword at a time. "For my lord, I would suggest the Lower Primarian balcony. It's reserved for all combatants who are Primarian-hadus or below, or those rich enough to pay for quality seating. Unfortunately, the best seats—aside from those for the noble houses or the Queen's Terrace—are found at the Upper Primarian balcony, which is reserved for Primarian, Primus, and Grand Primus."

Gray thanked her, then looked down, realizing he was still only wrapped in a towel. His wet hair dripped onto the likely priceless rug beneath his feet, making Hati raise an eyebrow once more. "I'm going to get dressed now."

Hati didn't move.

"Alone," he added.

Hati's expression was tight-lipped. However, he was fairly certain he spotted a flicker of mirth in her eyes as she bowed her head. "As my lord wishes. I shall remain in the antechamber should you need anything."

Thanking her again, Gray breathed a sigh. Then, donning his simple clothes, he paused, fumbling with some strings near his collar. Did he…tie those? Shrugging, he left them loose, then turned and found himself standing before a mirror. The reflection that came back surprised him a little. He was taller than most and broad-shouldered, so the clothes fit him a little snugly, but he looked almost halfway Covian. More than that, he'd grown a little stubble. He'd borrowed a razor from Barthos back in Seria. They'd stayed in the lost City of Water for a bit of time, but clearly some of his beard was growing back already. Had it really been only one day since they'd arrived in Covai? So much had happened.

His hair had grown too, now reaching nearly to his jaw. A few faint scars showed here and there, likely gained during the siege of Median. Green-gray eyes, like his grandfather's, stared back at him, a little harder, a little less naive then he remembered them. It was strange. He knew himself better, felt more at home in his skin than ever, and he also felt…like he should have been looking at the softer, confused boy who'd wandered into the Lost Woods, stumbled upon Mura's cabin, and trained beneath a waterfall. Mura…his heart panged. How he missed the man. His jaw clenched. Had his cheeks grown a little more hollow? As if all baby fat had been rendered from him. In a way, it was a little strange seeing the shell of his past cast off. In another way, a greater way, he was grateful. He'd need to be hardened if he was going to save Farhaven.

Gray shook his head, returning to the present. He thought he struck a rather fine image. He made his way to the antechamber.

Hati stood patiently beside the door.

She took him in, eyes scanning him up and down.

"Good?"

She gave a faint nod. "Better."

Gray grumbled, "Thanks, I'm flattered."

Hati gave a discerning look, then looked to his chest. "If I may, my lord?" Gray followed her eyes. She was pointing to the loose strings he had left to dangle. "Covian attire has them in a knot, like this," she said, slowly tying them up, her fingers lightly skimming his chest as she worked. "As for your looks, we already know you're handsome, my lord. You just needed to shake the dirt off so we could see the man beneath the layer of filth." Her olive-green eyes looked up at him from beneath long lashes. They were faintly kohl-rimmed to make the color all the more striking, and up close now, he saw there were notes of yellow in them, like flecks of gold. A lump formed in his throat. She continued, "A word of advice, my lord. The tournament is not the only grounds of danger."

Well aware, he thought, but asked, "Is there something I should know?"

She opened her mouth, then closed it, tying the last knots. "Finished." She pulled away. "It's nothing. Forget I said anything."

"Hati," Gray said, stepping forward, holding her shoulders gently, "what is it? I can see you know something." She bit her lip, looking away. He continued, speaking honestly, "I…I'm doing the best I can, but this tournament, the war, finding the next of my kind? Honestly, sometimes it feels like I'm swinging a sword in the dark. If you could shed even a little light…"

She blurted, "I saw another…he looked like you."

Gray felt a cold chill. "What did he look like?"

Hati shivered. "His eyes were cold…the color of steel. As he took me in, he felt evil, and a sense of conviction so deep I nearly drowned in it." She seemed far away, then shook herself. "There was a bow on his back, a soul-sucking black that seemed to absorb all light as he passed. I could have sworn the torchlight dimmed."

Merrick.

"Do you know who he is, my Lord Ronin?" Hati asked.

"Yes," Gray said. "He's one of us. Or at least…he will be."

Hati shook her head. "That man, you cannot face him."

"I know what you saw, but he isn't evil," Gray said. "He's just afraid, like we all are."

"There was no fear in that man, my Lord Ronin, and if there was, it was buried so deep you cannot reach it."

Gray took a deep breath. How could he tell her he needed Merrick? That without him, all was lost? That Gray himself had been lost, had thought himself evil, and had found a way back. That Kail, the blightsworn, the breaker of the world, was his "supposed" destiny. He needed to believe that no one was without redemption. So he gave a nod and let it drop. "Thanks for telling me. Still feel in the dark, but at least I'm not alone."

She nodded. "Well, at least in the dark no one can see your bad manners."

He chuckled. "Fair enough." He made his way to the door.

"Be careful, my lord," Hati called from behind him.

He looked back over his shoulder, saw her worried olive-green eyes, and gave her a small smile and a nod.

Then he headed to the Lower Primarian balcony. It was large and filled with an assortment of characters, from combatants to wealthy merchants and everything in between.

Gray watched the next fights.

The first was Faye's.

She walked onto the sands to face the giant she'd fought beside in her previous round.

Jivran, the announcer called.

Gray snorted. Of course. He looked to the Queen's Terrace. The scheming monarch watched the battle with keenness, sipping from her chalice made of bones. Clearly they'd seen the bond between Faye and Jivran then, so they had set up Faye to face her ally in this round.

However, Faye and Jivran surprised the whole arena by having a little *chat* in the center of the colosseum, all eyes on them. This resulted in a chorus of boos and heckling from the masses…but suddenly the crowd changed their tune. Faye and Jivran had clearly worked out some sort of agreement, and now they clashed blades on the sands to the adulation of thousands. Both fighters were impressive. Gray had a hard time taking his gaze away.

He glanced up to the Queen's Terrace to see that Ayva was no longer there. Where'd she gone? She'd seen his battle, he knew, and had sent a message, but he'd been…sort of lost in the moment.

Below, Faye danced away from Jivran's strikes, which could have cleaved a boulder in two. She struck blows, drawing blood here and there, but the huge man's wounds kept healing. At this rate, even with Faye's speed and agility, it might seem the fight favored the giant. That is, if one didn't see Jivran's collar growing a slight tinge of copper, as if heated beneath slow-burning embers.

He was expending too much spark, whereas Faye…

Wait, why was Faye wearing a collar? Could she manipulate her spark? To his knowledge, she'd never shown any affinity toward an element. She didn't need to. She was just…Faye.

The battle continued—a fierce back and forth.

Jivran's muscles flexed as he thrust a kick that would have killed a man. Faye sideslipped it and used his own momentum to grab his leg and throw him across the sands like a rock skipping across a lake. The crowd roared. Jivran rose, charging like an enraged cerabul. Faye had to backpedal beneath his sudden fury of attacks as he wielded the giant axes with devastating power. Faye bided her time, waiting until his collar grew red. When he slowed his attacks and paused to catch his breath, Faye struck, swiping his legs out from under him. Jivran toppled hard in a puff of sand. As the big man fell, he kicked, and his huge boot caught her square in the chest. Faye flew, rolling across the sands to lay sprawled out by a nearby pillar.

There was a momentary pause in the fighting as both groaned.

Gray realized he was leaning forward.

Seven hells, this is a closer fight than I anticipated.

Jivran was impressive.

Faye was…Faye. Something changed in her eyes, as if she was finally taking this seriously, whereas Gray was pretty certain Jivran had been fighting all out since the beginning.

Wiping blood from her mouth, Faye rose. She neared a pillar, then grabbed two daggers from it. With a cry, she charged. Jivran had also gained his footing, practically snorting steam. Dipping, ducking, Faye laced him up like ribbons. The giant growled, swinging, but Faye was too fast. Again and again, Jivran healed, bloody gashes miraculously closing. But not quickly enough. The collar grew deeper and deeper red.

A flying roundhouse connected with the giant's jaw, with a crack all the arena could hear, and dazed, he dropped one of the giant axes. Faye seized the moment. With the flat of her blade, she smacked his other hand, disarming him completely, and after a subsequent flurry of kicks to his legs, Jivran collapsed to both knees.

Faye raised her blade for a finishing blow.

The crowds roared, hungry for blood.

Jivran grinned and nodded, accepting his fate.

Faye plunged her dagger—back into her belt, adding a little flourish.

Then flicking sweat from her brow, she offered Jivran a hand.

The giant looked at it for a long moment, then made a sign with his hands, putting them up in prayer, and bowed his head.

"Victory by surrender!" the announcer boomed, the same older man as before, covered in tattoos, bone and metal piercings riddling his face. His voice echoed across the stadium. Instead of disappointment, the crowd's applause grew even louder.

Seems they have favorites.

And then Gray remembered something Drega had said before dropping him off at his rooms: *Win the crowd, win the tournament.*

I will, he thought.

For the next fight an elf—a Terma—took the sands. He had long, fine blond hair and pointy ears, and with a haughty expression, he surveyed the crowds, who gave him a mixed reaction. The Terma wore the typical forest green armor of his rank. Red paint coated his arms, looking as if he'd dunked them in blood.

Gray's teeth ground together.

Beside Gray a man snarled, "Bastard elf, thinks he can just show up here while his kin slaughter innocent elf-kind!"

Others on the balcony muttered similar things, but a few shot back support for the Terma.

Gray ignored them. He wasn't here for politics—he wanted to keep an eye on his competition.

From the opposite gate, a man in dark purple and midnight-black garb, his face bearing the red paint, stepped onto the sands. He and the elf both stalked forward, grabbing swords from the pillars, then turned to face one another as the announcer shouted.

"I give you a Terma, an elite warrior of Eldas…As a close right hand to Lord Dryan, King of the Elves, this very Terma was instructed to fight for the glory of the Great Kingdom of Leaf…an elf who, alone, has felled a hundred men and never suffered a single scratch! I give you Qinlar Swiftblade!"

Then the announcer gestured to the opposite end of the field.

"In the west, a man who wishes to be known by title and solitary name alone…I give you a Moonguard, the most elite of Narim, Great Kingdom of Moon!"

The Moonguard's hood was up, but Gray felt as if the man was smiling.

Tension mounted.

"Fight!"

Qinlar was fast, dashing across the open space. He cut, dipped, and sliced with elven grace, barely parrying a thrust to his abdomen, then deflecting a blow to his head, redirecting his own sword's momentum to cut at the Moonguard's shoulder. Then the Moonguard stepped into the shadow of the pillar and vanished.

Whispers of surprise rushed through the crowd.

No, not vanished, the man was still there—he just seemed to turn *faint*, as if he was a silhouette. From the shadow, the Moonguard struck again, cutting a deep gash in Qinlar's shoulder, and the elf cried in pain, backpedaling. Something wild entered Qinlar's eyes then—he pounced again, sword moving faster. All the while he seemed to be shouting a long string of Elvish curses. The Moonguard slowly retreated under Qinlar's flurry of blows. The crowds shouted Qinlar's name as if he was approaching victory.

They were all wrong.

Gray's Devari training told him the Moonguard was just waiting for an opening. Then it happened. After shoving Qinlar back and creating enough space, the Moonguard took a deep breath. A purple shadow coalesced on the steel of his blade. Qinlar's eyes went wide. He raised his own sword as a slash from the Moonguard's blade caused a purple arc to carve out the air. It slammed into the elf, sending him flying.

The crowds were shocked.

Qinlar, however, as if powered by some dark force, slowly rose, using his sword as a crutch. His eyes were swirling inky black pools. A string of curses poured out of his mouth, but Gray didn't think they were Elvish. Qinlar charged, sword raised. However, a dozen paces away, the Moonguard slashed again. Not once, or twice, but thrice.

Three waves of purple burned through the air, oddly both drawing all light and blinding to the eye. On the balcony around Gray, people winced, covering their eyes briefly as the three arcs of deep violet tore through the space between the two. Qinlar tried to react, but was too slow. One arc sliced off the Terma's red-painted arm. Then another his leg. Finally, before his body could drop to the ground, the last slice severed his head from his shoulders.

Walls reverberated with the spectators' collective cheers.

Gray's gaze narrowed as he watched the Moonguard soak in the dead Terma's spark. He realized the Moonguard had been showing off, building anticipation.

Winning the crowds.

The next few matches were less exciting, but equally brutal in a way that made Gray's stomach turn. Two criminals conspired together to climb the pillar in the center of the arena that housed the glowing Earthstone, the relic and grand prize. Using rope, armor, and large shields on their backs, they blocked a good majority of the hail of arrows, but some pierced their weaker joints until, like spiders crawling up a waterspout, they were shot down. *What in the seven hells was their plan?* Gray thought. They'd have to get out of the arena and...He shook his head as both of their bodies went to spark and evaporated into thin air. This fight was followed by a one-stripe Reaver who tore apart an Untamed from Taerian, a city to the east of Vaster.

Gray was almost ready to leave, to search for the others again, when the announcer called out, "And for our next match, in the west, sold to our very own House Hisan Viper and now fighting for your entertainment, a young man with hopes and dreams. Fear may seize his heart, but a hidden ember of spark lies within! Can he unleash it? Or will he be cut down far before his time? I give you the underdog, Sasha Evenwood!"

A figure stood in the arena wearing a white veil that hid all but his blue eyes and blond hair.

"To the east, witness a creature from the queen's own dark dungeons, one of six beasts so hideous, so dreadful that it has slayed the last dozen of its opponents in brutal savagery...I give you...a Vile One!"

Then, opposite Sasha, a twelve-foot-tall gate, the largest yet, ground open like a dragon opening its maw, drawing all eyes. And from out of the darkness strode a monster.

Beauty and the Beast

Stepping onto the field of battle, Ayva found herself facing off against a monster.

Whatever it was, Ayva had heard the announcer refer to it as a "Vile One," one of six equally terrifying monsters. This one was covered in mottled green scales from head to toe, except for its thickly muscled chest, which was smooth, taut skin. Strong legs lumbered forth as the beast stooped, scraping its head on the twelve-foot-tall gate. Its talons dug into the sand, creating divots. With a snout and a long reptilian tail that dragged along behind it, the Vile One looked like a massively overgrown human who had been turned into a lizard. Ayva blinked, remembering a conversation with Faye in Farbs.

"Tell me about Drymaus," Ayva had said. "You said dragons live there?"

Faye flicked a hand. "And other things."

"Like what?"

"Oh, all sorts of scary, nightmare-inducing creatures. Let's see, if my children's-tale lore is current... You've got balrots—towering, tree-like creatures, relatively friendly but they can harbor a temper. Herkas, dark demon creatures that can smell fear, and have no eyes. Then..." Faye listed a dozen more, until she snorted, "What you really oughta fear, however, are the twisted beings, or Vile Ones, choose your favorite evil name. They're more than just creatures. They're us, well, pre-"us," I suppose. Created long ago by Renalin's children, they were the first mortal races, crafted after the immortal titans and dragons."

"First... mortal races?"

"Bred with dragon, or bird, they are sort of... an evil version of humanity. Scarier, taller, stronger... Think of them as the trial version. You know, if you believe in children's tales."

Ayva returned to the moment as the Vile One's orange eyes, like hot glowing coals, fixed on her. The first mortal races. The being seemed curious, and it tilted its lizard-head as if examining her, trying to understand what it was seeing. But there was a hunger in the creature's eyes, almost a humanity—clearly sentient. It was studying her. Suddenly, flames danced on its fingertips, though it held no collar.

That's…not ideal, Ayva thought. *How much magic could it thread without a collar to hold it back?*

The announcer was speaking, and Ayva caught the last bit of his word. "…as always, the rules are simple! A fight to the death or surrender, whichever comes first. Let it be known, with surrender, no spark gained, no advantage accrued."

The Vile One's expression was unmistakable as it stalked forward.

It would not surrender, nor allow her to.

The only outcome of this battle was death.

Heart pounding, matching in time to the drums that echoed through the vast arena, Ayva took a slow, steady breath, calming her nerves. One thought resonated through her, like the light of a single star in a dark night.

Hope.

As soon as the announcer had finished his introduction, he bellowed: "*Fight!*"

The drums stopped.

The Vile One threw the ball of flame floating above its clawed palm.

Muscles tensed as Ayva pulled a bit of sun and sent a thin razor of light that cut the molten orb in two, causing both halves to spiral to either side and burning black lines in the sand. The collar on her neck grew warm. *Conserve*, she told herself.

Eyes dancing with flames, the Vile One charged.

It moved with lightning speed as it raced across the sand. *Hope*, she thought and power filled her. Again, an icy-hot grip—somehow both cool and scalding—radiated from the metal collar around her neck and it turned a faint rust color. She felt as if she were surfacing from the ocean, gasping for air, only to be plunged back into the water. The glowing ball of sun in her hand sputtered. She forced herself to keep it alive. Yearning to throw the orb, she refrained. An inner voice told her she'd have to preserve her power; she was afraid to push the collar too far and suffer the consequences.

The gap between her and the Vile One closed.

Eighty paces.

Sixty.

Forty.

Twenty.

The creature, all scales and claws, with eyes full of fury and hunger, was nearly on her. Flames enveloped its dagger-like claws as it slashed. *Now!* Ayva thought. She sent the ball of light, and it slammed into the creature's smooth chest. Ayva pulled the thread in the center, but with the collar clouding and restricting her magic, her concentration slipped. She pulled a thread, but the wrong one. The orb of sun burned the creature, sending it back a dozen paces and stopping its charge, but the orb didn't explode.

The Vile One's claws dug into the sand, slowing its skid across the arena, and she saw its scales and chest were merely blackened. *What is this thing?* Its skin was like dragon's armor, and it seemed to have some sort of resistance to fire.

Ayva cursed as the Vile One eyed its unharmed body, shook its reptilian head in fury, then attacked again. Only this time… it *shifted*. One moment it was twenty paces away, the next it was on top of her, knifelike claws seeking to spill her innards upon the sands. The first claws struck, scratching across her arm, tearing through the coat, and the pain of it was excruciating. Ayva cried out, clutching at her arm and falling to the sand. The Vile One loomed over her, and its claws descended, seeking to finish her.

Ayva raised her hand as the beast fell upon her. A long spear formed in her grip, one of sun. She planted the butt of the spear into the sand in the nick of time, and the Vile One slammed into the spear's tip. The creature looked down at the wrist-thick spear of light piercing its belly, burning a hole in the creature's abdomen. Then orange eyes fixed Ayva with fury as it *leaned* forward, seemingly uncaring of the beam of light melting a hole in its center. Saliva dripped onto her cheek as its claws reached out, trying to rip her face.

Ayva's mind frantically tried to think of an escape.

Only there was none.

How had it come to this?

She was going to die, right here, right now, in front of tens of thousands.

Distantly, she heard a voice. Gray? Somewhere from the stands, he was calling to her, pleading with her. But she couldn't spare a moment of concentration. Holding the burning spear, pushing the limits of her restricted power, was hard enough alone.

How? Ayva thought again. All this time, she had been *certain* she was stronger… How had she failed? Failed… as the Vile One's eyes filled with conviction, she understood. There was no questioning, no reservations in the beast's eyes. It knew what it was. It knew what it had to do. *Doubt.* That was it. Her flaw wasn't real, it was only fear. A thin veneer of doubt on her mind, she realized.

At that moment, the pieces clicked.

She had to stop thinking of herself as Ayva *wanting* to be Omni.

Instead, she was both.

She was Ayva.

And she was Omni.

As the Vile One's razor-sharp claws reached out, nearly opening her throat, Ayva took a deep breath, finding her center. The crowd's swelling noise turned to a muted rumble.

The world dimmed.

Hope.

Ayva did the only thing she could. She pulled a thread of the spear. This time, she'd pulled the right thread, and a bigger one, a thicker thread that held the spell together. The spell unraveled and burst. *Collapsing Star.* At the same time, and in the moment before the eruption, Ayva created a thin golden shield before her face that absorbed a large portion of the explosion. Still, the force of the blast was a hundred times bigger than before, and it sent her flying across the sands. For a moment, there was darkness. Then all she heard was the ringing in her own ears and the dull thunder of the crowds, chanting, crying out. She forgot where she was, breathing in dust, smelling only sweat, fear, and the hunger for blood. Slowly, Ayva's vision cleared—or she forced it to, looking up from her hands and knees.

Across the way, a creature, the reptilian Vile One, lay in a smoking, charred heap.

The crowd roared until…

The Vile One twitched.

Not dead.

Ayva pulled herself to her feet, stumbling to the nearest pillar.

The Vile One made a crooning groan—something between a howl and a cry.

Snatching a sword off the pillar's iron rack, a long, straight blade vaguely resembling Aurora, Ayva touched her power. The collar had grown cool, but touching the Nexus made the heat return, her neck burning. She ignored it. The creature was stirring, beginning to rise. Patches of scales had been blown off in the explosion, revealing bloody skin beneath. She walked by chunks of its flesh, a few thick claws, even the whole of its tail. But it was still alive, and she could feel its rage, even from here, like a blazing furnace. It wouldn't stop, not until she was dead.

Running two fingers along the fuller of the steel, Ayva staggered forward as the creature attempted to rise. It saw her. Flaming orange eyes fixed her, full of rage, hunger, and even a hint of sorrow. For a moment, Ayva hesitated. She saw in it, twisted and tormented as it was, some vestige of...if not goodness, or humanity, *something*.

The first mortal race, Faye had called it.

Suddenly, the vertical slits of its pupils danced with delight, as if it had caught her in its trap. Now she saw it, in the corner of her vision. A spiked tail had been regrowing. The needlelike thing hovered over her shoulder, ready to plunge into her back, to sever her spine and kill her.

"Cannot...lose..."

Only, Ayva was quicker.

She stabbed it through the heart, the sword burning like a hot iron poker. Hot as the sun, it didn't just burn, it consumed. Like parchment put to flame, the white-hot sword ate away at the beast as the Vile One howled and shrieked until nothing was left but teeth, bones, and a pile of ash at her feet.

For a moment, the crowd was silent, gripped by shock and awe.

Then the tidal wave of unified voices rushed over her, the sound of it nearly knocking her from her feet. Orange bits of spark floated in the air before her, and she breathed it in, the rest of it sinking into her skin. A lightning bolt of energy coursed through her veins. Ayva's breath was ripped from her lungs in amazement, and she felt more alive than ever. Not to mention stronger. Quicker.

The sun in her mind blazed.

My magic...It just grew, like a reservoir deepening in her soul.

Huh, Ayva mused…always she assumed spark and flow were two different entities. Clearly, as the golden Sun in her mind seemed to pulse with energy, there was some deeper connection here.

The Vile One must have been strong.

She looked up at the crowds, feeling the strength enter her bones as the tens of thousands watched her, curious what she would do next. Ayva decided to add a little flourish.

She sent a spire of sun into the air.

They cheered.

"Winner! Sasha Evenwood!"

She looked to the nobles, to the Queen's Terrace, and saw the fury, the cursing and bickering filling the balcony, felt the hot hatred of Larissa's eyes on her. From behind her cloth veil, she smiled.

Ayva thought, *I could get used to this.*

Then she felt something on her arm and looked down to see two thin crimson swords etch themselves on the inside of her forearm.

A voice in her head sounded, *That was…impressive.*

Gray? She turned to see him on the Lower Primarian balcony. He was dressed in simple Covian-beige clothes, with what looked like a Sons of Flesh cloak. *You look different.*

So do you, he said, smiling down at her. *Omni indeed.* Then he nodded his head as guards came out of the gates to escort Ayva off the field of battle. *Meet me?* he sent. *You know, after you're done soaking in the adulation of the masses. I have to tell you something.*

Oh, we have lots to discuss, Ayva sent.

Gauging the Competition

Gray was waiting in the Lower Primarian balcony when someone sat down next to him and cleared their throat. He didn't turn — he'd sensed her presence before she arrived — but he quietly smirked. "Well, look who it is. Greetings, Sasha Evenwood. You know, they were chanting 'Champion' for a while after you left the sands."

Ayva sighed, glancing about at the others on the balcony. "That's a little premature. Should we find a more private area?"

Gray got her meaning, and they moved to a part of the stands, higher up, away from the other combatants or lesser nobles, to the highest stone seat in the tiered balcony. People still cast them glances, but being over two dozen feet away allowed them a bit of privacy.

"So," Ayva continued, "are we going to talk about your stunt? You know, the one where you jumped onto the sands in the Primarian-basaeri round and ignored your Primarian placement?"

"I had to," Gray replied. "I'll explain everything." He took her in fully. She still wore her cloth scarf wrapped around her face, hiding all but her bright blue eyes and wisps of blond hair. "That outfit is really something. It's kind of eerie."

She pushed a strand of hair off her forehead. "Is it too much?"

He smiled. "I like it. Very Omni."

"I think you mean 'very Sasha Evenwood,'" Ayva teased, eyeing the spectators too far away to hear.

"Oh, right, forgive me. Guessing he was someone who needed saving?"

"Something like that," Ayva replied. Then she looked to the Queen's Terrace in the distance. "I think you can guess who was pulling some strings that needed to be cut. Besides, if I spent another moment on that terrace full of snakes, I'm pretty sure I would have leapt off to my own death."

"Real snakes, or figurative?"

"Both."

Gray nodded.

She took him in. "Look at you, I'm not sure I've ever seen you look so—"

"Covian?"

"Well, I was going to say clean, but a little of that too. It looks good on you," she said, tugging at the sleeveless leather vest that exposed his arms. Then she lowered her voice. "Now are you going to tell me why you sacrificed your Primarian position to start near the bottom? You know we need to win this tournament, right? Not just for the Covian Legion."

Gray nodded to the Earthstone on a pillar in the center of the colosseum. "I know. Trust me. Very aware." One of the Nine Stones. He knew evil was searching for them, too. "Just as I'm aware the queen didn't offer up the Earthstone for no reason."

On the sands, a new match began. Two men who looked like thieves, one from Narim, Great Kingdom of Moon, and the other from Farbs, Great Kingdom of Fire. *A Darkeye officer?*

The crowds gave half-hearted cheers.

"What do you mean?" Ayva asked.

"I mean," Gray said, "the queen's agenda. She was trying to attract someone else to the tournament." Ayva's eyes tightened and Gray answered the question in her gaze. "Merrick is here. I think the stone drew the evil, the true Dark Lord, out of his hiding."

Breathless, Ayva added, "Now he's sent the Ronin of Metal to win it…If you think Merrick is entering the tournament…"

Gray sighed. "Not *if*, when. The only question is who's going to face him."

Light blossomed around Ayva's fist.

He put a hand over hers, and the sun dimmed. "Careful. It's good no one knows who you are. I think that'll give us an edge if you have to face Merrick. As for why I gave up my position, I need to get stronger. Spark is the only way. There's something to this arena…something peculiar going on, and I need to figure it out."

"Oh, you mean the spell that allows us to take another's life force? You think that's just a little strange?"

Down on the battlefield, the Darkeye officer, after suffering a few cuts to his arms and legs, dipped under a strike that would have taken his head. Then he thrust his sword into the other thief's belly to a chorus of applause. He inhaled the man's spark.

Gray snorted, then hesitated.

Morrowil whispered, *Tell her.*

"It's ancient," he said. "The spell, that is. I think that might be the other reason Merrick is here. It has something to do with the Ronin. I think…"

Ayva finished his thought. "If the dark evil can access a way to absorb spark at will, outside of the tournament, he'll be unstoppable. Even if he doesn't get the Earthstone. We have no idea how many stones are missing, how many he already has." She looked ahead, watching as the Darkeye officer raised his hands, soaking in the adulation. "I hate how everything we learn opens up a path of ten new questions that we can't answer."

"It's okay, I have a plan."

"Is it winning? I think I got that covered."

Gray felt her power sitting next to him, like the radiant flames of a furnace, despite the black band around her neck. "What happened?"

Ayva glanced to her palms, feeling the radiating sun. "Nothing in particular. I just feel like I'm finally getting the hang of this. This collar, it's teaching me how to access my power more readily. The spark from that creature was surprisingly powerful…"

"The first mortal race," Gray said.

"How'd you know that?"

He tapped his temple. "Devari memories, but that's about all I know."

Ayva sighed. "I almost felt guilty killing it."

Gray's eyes fixed hers. "Hard things are coming, Ayva. You know this war is only the beginning. If we're going to win, then difficult decisions like that…we're going to have to make a thousand of them."

Her eyes were just as flinty. "I'm well aware, Gray. That doesn't mean it has to be easy. If I were you, I'd be careful of that line of logic. If we allow ourselves to become too calloused, or use our actions to justify 'because we had to'? Well, that's a slippery slope to becoming the very thing we're trying to stop."

Gray took a deep breath. As much as he didn't want to agree…Ayva was right. Still, though, up until recently, he felt as if he'd been soft in many ways. Cautious. Careful. Now they didn't have such luxuries. Sacrifices were going to need to be made. He couldn't be naive. She knew this too, so instead of harping on the point, he simply nodded. "You're right."

On the sands, the Darkeye officer was escorted away.

Gray sensed Ayva giving a smile beneath her cloth mask. "I know."

He chuckled. "Oh, so humble, too."

Ayva turned to face him, her brows furrowing. "Wait, you didn't answer why you abandoned your Primarian role yet. Was it just for more spark?"

Gray looked down at his wrist with the two thin red blades. "No, it was more than that."

"Explain."

He sighed. "It's only a guess, but I think the queen is trying to kill me."

Ayva sniffed. "I wouldn't put it past her, but why do you say that?"

It was Gray's turn to add a little heat to his tone. "Primarian, Ayva? As an entry? I didn't even have to fight."

"You're the leader of the Ronin."

"Still, there's only one other who entered as a Primarian without having to fight."

Ayva's gaze narrowed. "Nalia…"

"Exactly, and she's won Grand Primus four times."

Ayva shook her head. "So what. Let's just say you're not worthy of it. How does—"

"If I entered the arena with no idea of how to use my power because of a collar that restricts my *flow* and then was thrust into a fight with the Grand Primus herself? The very person who has, for the last several tournaments, been killing and imbibing the spark of dozens of warriors?"

Ayva breathed in realization. "It's a death sentence." Again, she shook her head. "Why? It doesn't make any sense. The queen's infatuated with us."

An old memory resurfaced in Gray.

A tenant of the Devari, of the Hidden.

One Morrowil had whispered when they'd put the pieces together. *With hero worship also comes fear.*

Gray turned to face Ayva and said softly, "No, it doesn't make sense. Unless she's afraid of something else…"

Cold dread entered Ayva's bright blue eyes. "You think she's…" She hesitated, then more cautiously sent through the bond, *You think she's sided with the shadow? With evil?*

Gray's jaw clenched at the thought of that. "I don't know. Possibly. It would make sense. But either way, I wasn't going to win being thrown into the lion's waiting jaws. This way, at least, I have a chance. Hopefully, more than a chance."

"If what you're saying is true, we obviously need a plan to take the legions when she decides to renege on her deal."

Gray looked over at her. "I missed you. It's easy to forget how much we're on the same page."

Ayva smiled. "Of course you did, who else would keep your feet on the ground and prevent your head from becoming so swollen you can't fit through a door?"

"Faye?"

Ayva glowered, punching his arm. "Too far."

"Hey, just teasing!" Gray said, wincing. "But honestly, I don't know what I'd do without you."

"Well, it's a good thing I'm not going anywhere anytime soon." She grinned. "After all, we have a tournament to win and a kingdom to save…" Just then, the drums thundered and the gates opened.

Gray's heart seized, muscles tensing, and he watched as two *very* unexpected contestants took the stage.

"Oh gods," Ayva muttered.

The Sands Run Red

Helix took to the sands. He'd gotten a little time to eat some food, of course, but now he was thrust back into the arena. Only this time, he was ready. His rage over the queen's act still burned inside him like a flame that couldn't be snuffed, and he felt sorry for whoever he was about to face.

Helix had witnessed Faye fight Jivran. Granted, it had gone as well as it could have, but he still felt bad that Jivran had lost. He'd tried to catch the giant after the fight, but was shoved to his gate in preparation for his match.

Now he was here.

On the terrace, he saw the queen, watching with her cruel eyes and red-painted lips.

You're next, he thought.

The announcer was finishing his introduction. "…in the west, a warrior who showed great promise in the Bloodbath. We witnessed his attempt to block a hail of arrows from finishing men destined to die…Now he must use that same strength and conviction if he hopes to survive! I give you, in the west corner…a legend, a relic, a myth come to life, the greatest wielder of ice in all of Farhaven…*Helix Kirvas, Ronin of Water!*"

The crowds roared.

Helix only scratched his temple. Lathered in red paint and mud, it did itch. But mostly, he was curious. *They know my last name?* Then he felt a spike of ire. Prying into his life, unearthing secrets he wished would lie buried. *Tranquil Seas, is nothing sacred?*

Unconsciously, Helix moved to cover his banished mark, but he stopped himself.

No one here cares.

This was a tournament of death, of criminals, where the more debased you were, the better. So Helix raised his forearm, flaunting the giant X of his banished mark, then sent a jettison of ice skyward to a chorus of cheers from the rabble. He eyed the queen again, seeing her waxy lips twist with distaste, and smiled wide.

"In the east…I give you the most twisted and foul of all the Vile Ones yet. It took six Reavers and two dozen Covian guards, led by our very own Fleshguard leader, Drega himself, to capture this beast. Even then, nearly all of them perished." The announcer's voice echoed with sinister intent, the crowds had gone silent—which was even more poignant. The tens of thousands waited with bated breath, leaning forward in their seats, hanging on the announcer's every word. "A beast so wicked that he was to be put in the next rounds. The very bars of his cell needed to be reinforced with Yronia steel and bloodstone to keep the monster within contained…"

Helix gulped.

No, he reminded himself, *I will not be daunted*. Touching his Nexus, using the power of anger and tranquility, water's innate attributes, to touch his flow more deeply, his collar grew that strange warm chill. Helix pushed his Nexus wider. Now he had a decent grip on his strength. He felt as if he'd unlocked nearly half, if not more, of his true potential. Moreover, his *flow* felt stronger. As if under the pressure of the collar his spells had grown more dense, more *powerful*.

From the opposite end, a giant gate rumbled upward, showing darkness within.

Steaming-hot breath issued forth as a massive monster walked out onto the sands.

Despite a desire to take a step back, Helix held his ground, feeling his jaw tighten. The monster was huge. Easily eight feet tall, and *wide*, built with strapping muscles that bordered on obscene. Most notable was the fur. A thick brown pelt covered the creature, and its torso was that of a brawny giant, but the rest of him was clearly a bear. Its head was a bear…*and were those antlers?* The beast made Jivran look small. Its shoulders practically scraped the walls of the entrance, and each fist was the size of Helix's head. A leather belt with tooled engravings cinched his waist. A giant collar sat around his neck, as well as a broken chain. It looked like someone had attempted to enslave it, and it now used the shackle as a badge of honor.

The crowd audibly gasped, once again.

Helix had heard of such a beast. *An Ursa, or Bearfolk*. This one seemed bigger than even the stories. Tales said they kept to the enchanted forest of Drymaus, along with Dryads and other strange creatures, but they sometimes lived among humans and elves.

The announcer reached a crescendo, "I give you, Brambos Bear-borne, the Vile One!"

Brambos's huge clawed palms—somewhere between paws and hands—suddenly lit with terrible red flames. *It can wield fire? Great,* Helix thought. Its eyes, the color of red flames, fixed on Helix. Instead of taking a step back, this time, Helix's fist tightened. *I didn't come all this way to stop now.* He grasped the swirling water droplet in his mind. Ice flowed up his arm, and he felt it enter his veins, turning his sight a haze of blue.

The crowds reacted, and the creature seemed to hesitate.

Helix sent a hail of ice.

Fire and Ice

Zane knew who he was facing as soon as he stepped into the arena. Helix, the Ronin of Water, stood in the center of the sands, eyes filled with a cold, icy fury peering out of the dark mask of mud. More dark clay slathered his body, along with a slash of red paint. His blond hair was wild and longer than Zane remembered. Much of the youth and naivety he remembered had been weathered away. Was this the same moody young man who'd wandered wide-eyed into the Nimue Everglades?

For a moment, Zane stood there, conflicted. He saw a tremor of fear in Helix as the young man's eyes witnessed the monster before him. *Ash and fire, this isn't the way it's supposed to go.*

Zane wanted to win. Needed to win. Yet, not like this…

Do I tell him?

Zane hesitated.

Unfortunately, the two of them hadn't left on the best terms. Last he'd seen the Ronin of Water was when Hannah had been murdered. Zane had gone into a blind rage, and nearly killed Helix. He wasn't sure if telling the young man who he was would soften his fury, or do the opposite. Helix's eyes tightened. *Does he know who I am?* The bond was an unspoken connection between the Ronin—an ability to both communicate and also sense their kindred.

Zane shook his massive, bearlike head, growling.

What am I doing? This wasn't like him. *I said I wasn't a Ronin. I gave up the claim, yet why do I feel so conflicted?*

Helix, however, held no such reservations.

"Fight!" the announcer shouted.

Helix summoned thick shards of ice that flew toward Zane. Zane had taken the collar from the beast in the cell, and now as he tapped into his own Nexus, he felt that strange warm yet cold sensation around his trunk-like neck as the collar cut into his power. Once before, Zane had been shackled by Yronia and bloodstone. Nefrin's attempt to kill him had actually been to Zane's benefit, as he'd grown somewhat accustomed to the collar's restrictions. The ice flew. With a swipe of his hand, Zane melted the shards to steaming mist.

Snarling, Helix let more ice crawl up his arm and then charged.

Zane sighed, then let the fire roar inside of him and with his thick bearlike legs lumbered to meet Helix in the center of the arena.

Their powers collided, element meeting element.

Fire and ice *boomed* like a thunderclap, shooting sprays of water and gobs of slush into the air along with red-hot flames. The crowd's roar was deafening. More fire and more ice appeared until… *Too much*, Zane groaned, and he was forced to fall back before the icy onslaught rushing from Helix's fist. Tiny shrapnel of blue ice, as sharp as a sword, flew by Zane's face. It cut dozens of thin, bloody grooves across his ragged fur, and he howled in pain.

Helix advanced, and the crowd loosed a wave of surprise, followed by a roar of approval. In the back of Zane's mind, he heard a voice. Ayva. *Zane! Stop this!* It was all he could do to not be torn to ribbons by Helix's sudden devastating power. Raina's face and the thought of her brother's life hanging in the balance sent the sputtering flame in Zane's heart to roar anew.

Helix summoned a javelin of ice resembling a dragon's fang, slamming it down on Zane, as if the Ronin of Fire was a shark darting beneath the ocean and Helix was attempting to pierce him with a giant harpoon. *Power*, Zane demanded, and the metal about his neck glowed red, burning him. He rejected the pain and waves of fire coursed up his arms. Zane grabbed the massive lance of ice, and his heavy muscles flexed. His backpedaling stopped.

The giant icicle, held above Helix's hands and angled toward Zane's face, halted in midair.

Helix's eyes fanned wide.

Zane! It was Ayva. *Stop this!*

He pushed her voice away.

Only, Helix wasn't done. The young man's shock was quickly replaced by a tidal wave of the same cold fury Zane had seen before. Was this really the same Helix? It was not possible. Was it? Ash and flame, the man's torrential fury matched his own. Zane knew he was strong, just below Gray, Ayva, and Darius. At least, that's what the stories always said. Only now, seeing the power of water, the ice floating in the air all about Helix...Zane suddenly questioned the stories.

"I won't lose," Helix seethed.

The white javelin above the Ronin of Water grew in both his hands. Zane held the spearpoint of the icy harpoon in check as it tried to crush him into the ground, growing thicker, wider, and longer until it was like a spear crafted by a god.

Even in this strange, hulking bearlike form, it was too much. Zane's muscles ripped and tore beneath the immense strain. The fire had already been lit. "Neither can I..." Zane snarled back, and he roared. Fire consumed the icicle, then he kicked with a burst of fire, sending flames toward Helix. The Ronin of Water blocked the flames, but they distracted him for a minute, and he let the ice spear crumble, slamming like falling boulders onto the arena sand, sending puffs of dust into the air to the crowd's thunderous acclaim.

Helix wasn't done, and he rose and advanced. This time sending ice, like frozen hands, to grip Zane's heavily muscled legs. Zane was rooted to the ground. At the same time, Helix flung out his hands over and over, shooting thousands of icy shards. With bursts of fire—legs still frozen—Zane batted the icy shards out of the air like annoying flies, though some sliced into his thick pelt. *Enough of this.* He hadn't truly tapped into the power of his new body, and so using the power of his heavy muscles, Zane leapt, shattering the ice about his legs.

Helix had no time to dodge.

Zane landed on the Ronin of Water, pummeling the young man with punches.

Zane, you can't do this! Ayva cried.

Gray shouted in vain.

Zane couldn't stop...he had to win. Not just for Raina, but for Pyre's sake. A promise that would change the world. His huge fists scored a blow or two on Helix as he tried to grind him into the sand, but he felt...ice. Ayva's dread was presumptive. Helix had created a shield. Suddenly breaking through the blue ice was a giant icicle. It would have gutted Zane, but he'd sensed something was off, and he reacted just in time. Sharp pain exploded in Zane's raised arms as Helix tore chunks of flesh from them. Zane slammed down a fist of fire. It collided with ice once more, creating an explosion that sent both skidding across the sands. Now they both knelt, several dozen feet away from each other, catching their breath.

The crowds went wild.

Hand to the sand, Zane caught his breath and spotted the queen on her balcony in the corner of his vision. Round eyes and sharp, judging brows glared down at them as she gripped the railing, leaning forward, almost salivating. Was she wanting Helix to die? Or…

He had no time to question.

Helix bombarded him with a thin razor of ice that sliced Zane's cheek again, scoring a painful gash that ripped away more flesh. More and more he sent. Helix created a sword of ice—or something like ice, made of a deeper, radiant blue. So Zane followed suit. He took a deep breath, pushing the channels of his power wider, and held out his hand. A sword of pure fire formed in his grip.

Helix's blade arced down, smashing with Zane's fiery sword. Sparks of fire and shards of ice flew with each strike. Zane's strength was greater, though, and with his next downward slash, Helix's blade went flying. The Ronin of Water was sent tumbling across the arena. Helix rose, wiping blood from the corner of his mouth, eyes wild.

"I…cannot…lose…" Helix bellowed.

This was wrong. He was killing Helix. If he didn't kill the man, he'd die first.

This isn't why he came here…

Zane dropped his fiery blade.

A hush fell over the crowd, then they turned unruly, as they jeered, shouted and yelled for the fight to continue.

Helix's anger faltered as he wavered on his feet.

Zane sighed and called out, "I'm not who you think I am."

Helix's eyes tightened, a small smile forming on his lips. "I know who you are." Then Helix sent through the bond, the words echoing in Zane's head, *Ronin of Fire.*

Zane's throat went dry, and he stepped back in confusion. Then he sent back, *You knew the whole time?*

Of course, Helix replied.

The crowds protested, and the queen looked enraged, but Zane ignored them all. *You knew, and you kept fighting?*

Helix barked a laugh. *You realize how foolish that sounds, right? You also knew.*

Zane cursed. *I have to. I can't lose.*

Good. Neither can I. Helix's eyes burned, and currents of water flowed about his arm.

Zane growled. *Enough!* he shouted through the bond.

Helix hesitated.

Gods, Zane thought inwardly. *Why am I the voice of reason?* Then he sent through the bond, *this is wrong. We can't kill each other, Helix.*

Why not?

Because…we're Ronin.

Helix's rich laugh echoed openly across the sands, and he wiped away an imaginary tear. *Oh, that's just great, and incredibly convenient. Ronin, a title you already admitted giving up just this morning?*

I may not be a Ronin, but you are.

So what?

So the world needs you.

Helix snorted. The crowds were growing irate. Food was being thrown onto the sands as they remained locked in a standstill. *How compassionate. The world needs me, but not you?*

Zane looked away. *I've done too much. I'm not deserving of that title any longer.*

Helix protested, *You really are a light-blinded fool, aren't you?* Zane hesitated and Helix continued, stepping forth, now only a dozen paces away. *You think any of us feel deserving? Do you even know what I've done?* Helix held up his X-marked arm.

Whatever you've done, it pales to what I've done, Helix. A Ronin can't be—

Helix cut him off. *Can't be what? Can't be a killer? Can't have fallen to darkness? What about murdering your own father?*

Zane froze, then sent, *I…*

Don't! Don't try to empathize with me now. You know nothing of who I am.

Zane shook his head and stared into Helix's eyes, which were glassy with passion, the young man's whole body shaking with restrained fury. *You're right, I don't. But I know you hate me because of that day.*

Helix laughed. *You Abyss-cursed fool, that's not why I hate you!*

Zane shook his head. *Then why?* Something was happening on the balconies above. He realized archers were getting into position. Gray called out to him, but Zane pushed his voice to a muted whisper, gaze fixed to Helix.

Helix stalked forward as he replied, *I hate you because you abandoned us. You abandoned Farhaven. Despite that, Ayva and Gray still try to pull you back to us. To get you to see reason, to give you another chance. Again and again, you throw that away… you spurn them. That's why I hate you! Because you can't think beyond yourself and your own rage and grief! We've all lost, Zane. We've all suffered. You lose yourself, cut yourself off from us, from the world, and everyone suffers for it!*

Zane staggered back. Every word cut deeper than any ice Helix had sent so far.

The crowds had gone from crying out to jeering, and now looked on the verge of storming the arena grounds. Guards, hundreds of them, held the wild masses back. Just then, from the balcony, the queen's voice echoed, "Enough of this! You will fight and finish this match, or I will end both of you!"

At this, a fierce-looking woman leapt down to the first wall.

Nalia, Zane knew. He'd heard of her.

The Grand Primus.

Archers pulled back bowstrings.

Zane ignored it all. *You're right*, he told Helix. *What do we do?*

Helix gave a faint smile, blood staining his white teeth as he nodded to the faintly burning sword in the sand at Zane's feet and replied, "We finish what we started."

"I told you. I don't want to kill you," Zane said.

Helix grinned. "Good thing you won't."

Zane's gaze tightened, and he rolled his boulder-like shoulders. "You say that now."

Helix dipped his head, gesturing toward the archers on the walls. Zane was acutely aware of the bowmen. *Ash and fire, I can practically hear the creak of their bowstrings from here.*

"Well?" Helix asked. "What are you waiting for? Think it's that time. Do or die." Ice coated his arms and he grinned. "Literally."

Zane knew his friend was right. So, with a growl, he attacked. He flung out his bearlike hands, unleashing a river of fire. This time, Zane held nothing back. Helix wanted his full force?

Then he'd get it.

Water issued from his companion's hands like a flood. Helix's collar grew bloodred from the exertion of power. Fire and water collided, hissing billowing steam, and the crowds, who had been on the verge of a riot, suddenly shifted their mood. The colosseum shook with their fervor. Roaring, Zane sent more fire. Helix matched it. Glimpsed through the torrent of water and flames, Zane saw the look in Helix's icy eyes.

A conviction.

Is that all you've got? Helix taunted.

Both nullified each other's spells as quickly as they came.

I told you not to pull your punches, Helix sent through gritted teeth.

Straining beneath the icy fist, Zane grinned back, finally feeling alive. *I never do.*

They exchanged blows like this, fire and ice erupting. Zane deflected an icy fist that would've caved in his skull, and a growing realization took hold in his mind. Despite the flames in his soul, he felt the collar grow too hot. Deep down, he knew he hadn't had enough time to adjust to his magical restriction, to understand how to push his *flow* further.

It was clear Helix had.

Picturing Pyre, Zane tapped into that primal spot within, and flames roared forth, shooting out of his hands like orange spears as he leapt.

Helix didn't move.

In the last moment, diamond-like ice shot from the Ronin of Water's palms, impossibly fast. Somehow, deep down, Zane knew that strange crystalline ice could punch a hole straight through his broad chest. Zane's fist, fueled by fire, raced toward Helix's head, but it wasn't enough.

In the very last moment, that spire of ice veered, just barely, as if Helix's concentration had slipped. The ice buried itself deep into the earth, creating a shockwave. Sand erupted. Having evaded Helix's final strike, Zane's fiery fist found its mark, but he pulled his strike short, stopping it an inch from Helix's skull.

The crowds held a collective gasp.

Helix put up his hands in prayer and bowed.

The announcer, who clearly forgot he was dictating the events of the arena, spoke in a breathless declaration, "In a surprising turn of events, our challenger from the west, legendary Ronin of Water, gives the act of submission."

The crowd cheered, but seemed torn.

It was clear Zane hadn't been the favored champion.

Abruptly, his stomach gurgled, and he shed his thick layer of fur, watching it fall to the sands. Then his body was next, shrinking. No pain this time, gratefully. When it was done, he was draped in oversized clothes. The large chain necklace hung heavy around his neck. The crowds sounds of awe again as his transformation completed from Brambos Bearborn, to Zane, Ronin of Fire.

Then Zane looked down. On his wrist he saw another sword form in red ink.

Two swords.

The announcer finished his declaration. "…winner, leader of the Vile Ones, Brambos Bearborne—" He stuttered, at a loss for words. "Or whoever our mysterious combatant truly is, warrior of fire!"

Zane shook his head, knowing what had just transpired.

Helix looked up, bloody, soot-stained, and wearing a small smile. "Congratulations. Now don't mess this up."

The Bloody Blacksmith

After Helix and Zane's battle of fire and ice, Gray and Ayva left the stands, rushing to intercept the two. However, crowds suddenly swarmed the halls. "Well, this isn't great," Ayva said.

"The second round has ended, and I think everyone's going to celebrate," Gray said.

"See the victors and losers march!" a man added from the crowds.

They pushed their way through the throngs to a long, wide gallery that led to the city proper. The Western Gate, Gray realized, judging by the setting sun. He spotted a statue he hadn't seen before. A twenty-foot-tall figure with a fierce gaze, threading flesh — a thick row of bone spikes as tall as a man.

Gray felt a chill.

"Is that..." Ayva began.

"Aurelious," Gray finished. "Seems strange to see a Ronin venerated when all the world usually fears us."

Ayva agreed. "At least they got one thing right. I think it has to do with them valuing strength."

"Who's stronger than the Ronin?" Gray posed. He pushed and shoved through the crowds, hearing their excitement building, watching as guards made defensive lines, keeping the masses at bay. On either side of the long pathway, the walls of the outer colosseum rose high, balconies positioned to watch over the pathway. Each was filled with nobles and other rich merchants, once again spectating in leisure. On one of the balconies, high up and in the center, he spotted her again.

Nalia.

"Who is stronger than the Ronin?" Ayva repeated, eyeing the woman. "You mean currently or potentially?"

Gray knew what she meant. "I'm afraid you might be right. Something about her…" Again, he eyed that strange blade at her hip, which glowed with a malevolent crimson light. Nalia stretched her neck, revealing taut tendons, and Gray took in their future competition more fully. As before, her tribal tattoos emblazoned on either side of her forehead were intimidating, though they now seemed to swirl, as if alive. Was that his imagination? The only thing that had noticeably changed about her was that black kohl now rimmed her blue eyes, running in streaks down her cheeks. Those eyes…He suppressed a shudder. Even from here, he felt her power, and he knew it was the spark of a thousand warriors trapped within her.

Ayva snorted. "She gives me the shivers."

"Me too," he admitted.

"Can you read her with the ki?"

Gray shook his head. "Too far. Though I think I can make a decent guess."

"Sunshine and rainbows?" Ayva asked.

"Doubtful."

"More like enough anger and hate to drown a belegrun," Ayva agreed.

"What I want to know is why does she still bend a knee to that woman?" Gray tossed a nod to the queen, who watched the gathering procession with thinly masked disdain. "She could have her freedom, but she remains a slave."

Ayva fixed him with a look. "Light and heavens, please don't tell me you're trying to fix her. We have enough angry, unpredictable women in our lives."

Gray muttered. "That's—"

"Totally fair," Ayva said, but added quickly, "If it means not fighting her, I agree. I don't like puzzles I can't solve." The crowds pushed and shoved. "Like a book without an ending, it doesn't feel right."

Then Nalia's smile deepened, showing teeth.

Gray sighed. "I've a feeling we're going to have to fight her."

"That's fine, too. I can take her."

Gray looked at Ayva. With all this time in the sun, her freckles had grown darker and more pronounced. Some of the youthfulness in her face was gone, showing the woman emerging. "You?"

"Well, one of us." She shrugged, folding her arms. "But probably me."

Gray snorted.

More watching eyes made his skin crawl, and he looked up to the balcony to take in Imala, the monarch of the Great Kingdom of Covai. From upon her balcony, Her Majesty gazed down her nose at the gathering crowds. Some of her black eye makeup had run due to the hot day, streaking her rutted skin, but she seemed as unperturbed as ever.

"I don't like what she's up to," Ayva said. "If I had my way, we'd throw her to the sands. I'd like to have a go at her." Ahead, guards pushed men and women back, keeping the lane open for the coming procession. Ayva glared at a man who shoved her aside, and he practically soiled his pants at her reaction. Then he slipped back into the folds of the crowd, looking for a different vantage point.

"If only," Gray replied. He knew their battle with Imala was through Nalia, and through something deeper… The mass of citizens called to Gray. They needed to win *them* over. *Win the crowd, win the tournament,* he heard again in his mind, when there was commotion. "Here they come."

"I give you the combatants of the second round!" the announcer called.

At this, a group of men and women filed out from the mouth of a dark tunnel. Gray's eyes quickly panned over the group: the pirate, a Dryad woman, a Fleshguard, a three-stripe Reaver, and a dozen others.

"Shouldn't we be among these guys?" Ayva asked.

Gray shrugged. "Let them have their day."

Then… Helix appeared.

Worn, ragged, but resolute—a glint of power in his eyes.

Gray found himself taken aback by Helix's transformation. When had the fearful young man become… this? Helix was still covered in dirt, blood, sweat, and red paint. It made him look fearsome, but it wasn't just his outward appearance. The Ronin of Water's shoulders were set. His stride was smooth and long as he took in the crowds, as if looking for the next fight. Pride swelled in Gray's heart.

Helix spotted them and broke from the procession. People and guards parted, grudgingly, and Ayva threw her arms around the Ronin of Water. "Helix! That was *amazing*! You were amazing. That spell you cast… that was something out of the storybooks."

Helix chuckled. "Ayva, you're going to make a guy blush, but you do know I lost, right?"

"Speaking of that—" Ayva punched Helix's shoulder.

He griped, rubbing his arm, "*What was that for?*"

She planted fists on her hips. "Why'd you let him win?"

Helix looked aghast for a moment. "I've no idea what you're talking about." He looked to Gray for help, but Gray fixed him with a look, and Ayva folded her arms. Helix rubbed his neck with a wry chuckle. "I figured you two wouldn't buy it."

"What in the light and shadows were you thinking back there?" she asked. "You guys were actually trying to kill each other, weren't you?"

"Uh…maybe? I mean, we had to make it look real."

Gray cleared his throat. "This is great and all, but we should really find a place a little less…open?"

The three looked about.

Crowds gathered around them.

A young woman with a fiery mane of copper hair, her face sun-kissed with a warm olive glow, approached. "You're the Ronin of Water, aren't you?"

Helix remarked nervously, "Last I checked."

An older woman with a swaddled infant neared. Fine lines at the corner of her eyes deepened as she asked, "Can you bless my baby?" She pushed the newborn at Helix as it cried. "You can give him powers, which will protect him from the evils of this city!" Helix raised his hands, but before the Ronin of Water could say anything, or Gray could dissuade the woman, the crowds turned on them in unison.

Shouts from the nearest masses rose like a chorus.

"*Icebreaker!*"

"*It's the Ronin of Water!*"

A big man with a tattoo across his bald head grabbed Helix's collar. "You! I had you as my champion! You lost me a lot of coin! I oughta bust your skull and hope I find gold inside!"

Ice crawled over the big man's hand, making him blink and swiftly let go.

Others only swarmed around them.

"*Is that Sasha Evenwood?*"

"*Look at that man's eyes,*" one said, pointing at Gray. "*That's the Ronin of Wind!*"

Crowds pressed in, trying to touch them, suffocating Gray. The fervor was shifting from the procession to their trio. This wasn't what he'd intended. With a sigh, he tapped into his Nexus, letting wind swirl over his limbs and pulse outward—air rushed over the crowds. Gasps escaped from the people. Then he sent through the bond, *I…think it's time we found a little less conspicuous place to chat.* Ayva and Helix nodded vehemently. *C'mon this way.* They pushed out of the stunned throng, away from the momentum of the crowd, and back into the colosseum. Some tried to follow, but when they reached an inner corridor, guards held the citizens back. The three found themselves resting against the cool wall of a quiet hallway.

They collectively breathed a sigh of relief.

"That was…unexpected," Ayva said.

"Unexpected?" Helix replied. "Abyss take me, we were nearly mobbed. I guess that's the price of fame."

Catching her breath, her back against the clay wall, Ayva tucked loose strands of hair behind her ear. "Light! We're only in the third round! How bad is it going to be when we get to be at Primarian, or Primus?"

"Oh, that's easy," Helix said. "Much worse!"

"A double-edged sword," Gray replied. *Win the crowd, win the tournament.* "This fame is the lifeblood of Covai." There was a part of him that knew the notoriety, the respect, the admiration, all of it was a key to something greater, but all he said was, "It's going to open doors I've a feeling we'll need soon."

Ayva nodded. "Agreed."

"Same, but I'm not kissing any babies," Helix said. "Anyway, what's the plan now?"

"First," Gray said, eyeing his sweaty, bloody friend, "I think we should get you cleaned up." They followed Gray to his room where they found Hati reading a book. Ayva and Gray made conversation as Helix bathed. Gray busied himself by restrapping Morrowil to his side, but all the while he felt both Hati's and Ayva's eyes on him. Well, vacillating between tossing glares at one another, then him. *Wind and spirits, what's taking Helix so long?* At last, Helix threw back the double doors, grinning from ear to ear. Not only was he absent of blood and sweat, but he'd found new clothes and armor. He now wore a shirt the color of the deep Kalvas Ocean, with stitchwork of sky-blue waves, and a flared collar. He wore one vambrace. His other forearm was absent a bracer, revealing the banished X mark Gray knew he'd once tried to hide, now finally embracing it. Deep brown leather pants and thin leather pauldrons completed the outfit. Of course, there was Hiron's armband too. Gray admitted Helix looked impressive. "Ah, good as new! Save for this cursing thing." He pulled at his collar on his neck. "Abyss take me, I forgot to get it removed by the guards. Remind me when we get back to the colosseum, will ya?" He gestured to his new attire. "More importantly, whaddya think?"

Ayva's brows rose. "Where'd you find all those clothes?"

"I found them," Hati answered at her writing desk, slowly closing her book. "My lord, the Ronin of Water, requested traditional Waterbearer attire. I know there's no such thing anymore, but I managed to cobble together some pieces that match the stories' descriptions."

"I see," Ayva said. "I'm guessing you based it off the works of *Lord Mariman's Tales of the Nine Elite Warriors*? Or perhaps *Jenrar's Heroism*?"

Hati shook her head. "I'm afraid not."

Ayva tried to hide a smug smile. "Ah well, it still looks great."

"Thank you, my Lady Ronin. Alas, I was forced to use other sources, seeing as Lord Mariman's writings are historically inaccurate, due to General Silvara's verified retellings. Jenrar's tales are…" She winced. "A tad childish. Both of which I'm certain you knew."

Ayva stammered.

The tension was palpable.

Before anyone could say anything, Gray cleared his throat and opened the door with a wave of his hand. "Well, thank you, Hati. We'll be going now."

Once in the hall, Helix burst into laughter. "Oh, man, I'm going to be trying to retell that burn to Darius for ages."

"I'm certain you'll mess it up every time," Gray replied.

Ayva, instead of retorting back, just sighed as she walked at his side. "No, I was being foolish. Hati's clearly incredibly smart and well-read. I fear I've just been battling with so many arrogant nobles, I was starting to become one myself. I bet Hati can be of aid when this whole city implodes on itself."

"Not a bad idea," Gray replied. "Now, c'mon, this way." After a few twists and turns they made it back to the streets of Covai to find it still mid-swing in celebration from the finale of the second round.

"Are they still all worked up over your fight?" Ayva asked Helix.

"Over *all* our fights, I think," Gray replied.

Taverns and inns had a never-ending stream of patrons, each bustling and booming with jaunty music and raucous laughter, windows already fogged with the heat of bodies, while a river of men and women filled the streets and moved through the city, vanishing into a thousand tributaries.

As they navigated deeper into the city, Gray marveled at Covai by night.

Above, the infamous angry yellow sun in the sky, now the color of rust, had moved to the distant horizon, peeking above the many clay buildings. The moon was rising to take its place, skulking behind a tapestry of inky clouds. Its milky-white light bathed the city. The city felt different to Gray, like he could almost feel it with the ki. While the people were still bustling and talking animatedly, they seemed less bloodthirsty, satiated by the day's violence…at least temporarily.

Each member of the trio took in the city with a newfound appreciation while they chatted, trying to catch each other up. Huge beasts lumbered by. One had elk-like horns but the body of a bull—a cerabul crossbreed? A wagon with a cage full of chickens rattled past, but as they neared, forked tongues slithered from their pointed wide beaks. Gray even spotted a noble's carriage led by two belegruns, Covai's famous hulking scaled bears, one of nature with curling vines and leaves for fur and massive branching antlers, the other sporting spines of bone and showing red layers of muscle—flesh? Gray gawked, before Helix pointed and *another* belegrun appeared from a side street as if made of shadows and mist, with dark violet fur and bright purple eyes. Its head swiveled as it roared, showing rows of teeth as big as Gray's fingers, its massive paws oozing a purple light. It neared patches of darkness between the streetlamps and seemed to disappear. Nearby, men and women gasped—the crowd stopped to watch, in awe of the rare spectacles.

Ayva dragged the gaping two of them along.

After a few turns, while talking the whole time about the creatures, they landed at a tavern.

There were several signs, each reading: *The Red Blacksmith*, one of which depicted a huge man with crimson skin and an enormous hammer before a red burning furnace. But Gray was pulled to the vine-covered sign, drawn by the verdant growth in a city of dust, sweat, and blood.

At the door to the inn, a young man with curly hair and bright amber eyes, dressed in colorful patches all stitched together, lured in patrons with bawdy jokes and sly charm. Spotting them, the minstrel called out, "You three! You look like you're seeking a good time, and as luck would have it, you've just stumbled upon the finest tavern in all of Covai!" Then he cupped his hand by his mouth as if whispering, but then stage-whispered, "And Farhaven's best kept secret." He shrugged. "I might even be able to get you half off your first drink if you mention my—"

Gray cut the man off and pulled back his sleeve to reveal his forearm.

Ayva did the same.

Two slashed swords.

The minstrel gawked, then stammered, "Primarian-hadus! Gods, why didn't you say so? My lady, my lords," he said, including Helix, clearly not willing to risk assuming his rank, "please come this way!" He led them inside the inn to a chorus of cheer.

Inside the common room, music washed over them. The minstrel chatted nervously, signaling the innkeeper who worked the bar in the lively establishment. Grumbling, the innkeeper navigated through the many chairs and tables. He was portly, with a thick beard that was a mix of auburn and streaks of gray. An untidy pile of hair sat on his head that could have been fake. As he neared, he mopped at his sweaty face with a dirty rag. "What's the big deal, Riven? I told you to stay outside and earn your keep! Your tab isn't going to pay itself! If you brought in another bunch of vagabon—"

Riven was clearing his throat, head vigorously gesturing to Ayva's and Gray's forearms.

Finally, the innkeeper noticed, and his eyes went wide. He changed his tack. "By the gods, why didn't you say so, you fool! Back to the street, Riven!" He bowed his head and his flop of hair fell forward to expose his bald head. Then he rose, placing a hand to his dirty apron. "A thousand apologies for my rudeness! I'm Archibald Brinwall, but you can call me Archie. This is my establishment, and you are my honored guests. Primarians of all ranks are most welcome! How can I be of service?"

"Just looking for a table and some drinks," Gray said.

"But of course, as Primarians, my lord, I have a special table just for you. This way—"

Gray felt eyes on them from all around the common room. Even the musicians on the side stage played a little more slowly, as if distracted by the newcomers. Others stopped what they were doing and whispered to each other. He realized using his title had gained him a little more attention than intended.

He stopped Archibald and pointed to a table in the back. "Actually, we'll take that one."

"My lord," the innkeeper said, eyeing the gilded table near the stage, "but you're Primarians…"

"That one will do," Gray insisted. "Thank you."

Leaving the stammering innkeeper in their wake, they found their table and the patrons resumed their normal chatter and liveliness, thankfully only giving them the occasional glance. Once seated, they caught each other up with all they'd missed: from Ayva assuming the identity of Sasha Evenwood to Gray relinquishing his Primarian title, then winning his first fight. Ayva told Helix about Faye and Jivran's fight. Helix cursed at the queen setting the two up because they clearly liked one another.

Ayva gripped her cider with both hands. She stared into its depths as if the dark liquid could answer her troubled thoughts. "Light and heavens, there's so much at stake now. The Earthstone for starters. We have no idea how many stones the enemy has, or what they can even do when they gather all nine. We need to win that." Helix ticked off a finger on his hand as Ayva spoke. "Then the Covian Legion? That's the obvious one. If we're to have any chance against the shadow in the west, we need to build our forces, and fast." Helix ticked a second finger. "Then our swords…" Helix ticked off a third. "Let's not forget about finding the rest of our kind." He added a fourth. "It's a tad overwhelming."

Helix looked at his four fingers. "Four missions. Oh yeah, I'm going to add 'not dying' in there for good measure." He ticked off a fifth.

"How can we possibly accomplish them all?" Ayva said, gripping her mug.

"Easy," Gray said, leaning back in his chair and causing it to creak as he did.

Ayva and Helix looked at him.

"We all know what we have to do…"

Ayva said it first. "Beat Nalia."

Gray nodded, hand clenched on his mug. "Exactly. That's how we win. The other rounds are going to be difficult, and we should talk about the weaknesses and strengths of those that are left, then come up with a battle plan to ensure one of us makes it to the Finals. But Nalia is the linchpin. She's strong."

"More like terrifying," Helix replied. "Glad I don't have to face her."

Gray rubbed his chin, remembering her eyes from the balcony, a feeling of something like veiled loathing. Every aspect of her was forged in blood, hardened by battle. Not just a mere gladiator, but a harbinger of death. "I felt her aura from a hundred paces away. It was a small inferno. As much as it pains me to say it, she's too strong." The others watched him worriedly, and he looked up, meeting their eyes. "We need a way to beat her."

Ayva nodded, looking thoughtful.

Helix raised a finger. "Riiiight. One little question. Let's say we do find a chink in Nalia's terrifying armor, and by some small miracle, one of you achieves Grand Primus. What then? You know the queen is going to want to betray us. She'll never give us the legion."

Ayva sat back, gripping her cider like she wanted to strangle it. "He's not wrong. She's awful. I can't promise she's going to stab us in the back, but we'd be fools to think otherwise."

Gray sighed. "I know, and I have an idea for that, but something tells me becoming Grand Primus is bigger than Queen Imala."

"Whaddya mean?" Helix asked.

Again, the phrase echoed in his head. *Win the tournament, win the crowd.* Maybe it wasn't just winning the crowd. The crowd…the people, the city and its shadows…there was more to it. "I'm not exactly sure, but my gut says winning the tournament would mean something for us as Ronin, and Covai as a whole."

Ayva raised a brow. "Mysterious, care to elaborate?

"I…don't know, it's just a feeling," he replied.

Helix snorted. "Okay, Ronin of Moon. So veiled and murky."

"Anyway," Gray continued, "we need to advance for another reason. You both felt it, right?" He flexed his fist, feeling wind rising in his palm. "Since the tournament started, we've jumped leaps and bounds ahead. We're stronger than ever." Gray looked to the Ronin of Water in his fine Waterbearer attire, which seemed made for him. "Speaking of, that legendary ice spear was something else." Helix grew a little rosy about the cheeks, though that might have been the ale. "And Ayva, I saw that thread you pulled—" She'd described it to them, but Gray had witnessed it as well, watching the yellow-golden globe fizzle, then combust with awe-inspiring force.

"Collapsing Star," Ayva replied, eyeing her hands as if seeing them in a different light, "Even thinking about it now makes my palms sweat. I can't tell if it's excitement or fear. Whatever it is, I think what we witnessed was just a glimpse…Something tells me Collapsing Star can be even more powerful."

Taking a pull from his mug, Helix laughed. "Uh, more? How is that possible? It already seems like it can blow up the whole colosseum if you let it."

"Maybe." Her hands worked a little ball of sun in the air as she spoke, "It's hard to describe. It's like a knot." The ball rotated in the air. "Currently, I can only understand a mere fraction of those tangled threads. But one day, if I can unravel the whole thing?" She shivered, then let the light diminish.

Helix gulped at the light, sweat on his brow.

Gray realized his grip was tighter on his mug too. No one in the inn seemed to know the danger of what she'd held, though they were tossing them plenty of looks.

Ayva shrugged. "Anyway, for now, I'm satisfied at only being able to unlock a sliver of it's real power. Honestly, I kinda hope I never have to discover its true potential."

The woman musician in the group on the side stage switched to another tune, dropping her lute in favor of a dulcimer, and her partner took up a pair of drums. Feet began to tap in rhythm to the music, and laughter erupted from a nearby table. She sang and her voice filled the common room, enchanting and ethereal, weaving a cozy, almost otherworldly ambiance in The Red Blacksmith. Gray spoke, "Look, the point is, there's a thousand threads, but they all tie together at the same point: becoming Grand Primus. If we win the tournament—"

"We may not succumb to a terrible darkness that wants to swallow the whole world?" Helix posed.

"I was going to go a little more positive. Something like, 'we'll save Farhaven,'" Gray said.

Helix shrugged. "Eh, to-may-to, to-mah-to." Then he settled back, adding a shiver. "Okay, so we have to win. But what if Nalia's a nut too tough to crack?" Ayva and Gray both raised a brow. "Yeah, you're right, I can do better. A storm too wild to sail? An ember too hot to hold? I got plenty more of these, you should probably stop me now."

Gray realized Helix's humor was an attempt to conceal his worry. "You heard something."

Helix sighed. "Just rumors from the other gladiators. But they're terrifying." He gripped his mug tighter, and frost coated the pewter, as if Helix was unconsciously catching a chill himself. "Nalia used to train with our elite Fleshguard buddies…that is, until she started killing them in practice. Not out of malice, mind you. Apparently her strikes are just too strong."

Gray grunted. "That it?"

"No. They said a whole bunch of other stuff about what she can do, from punching holes in stone walls with her bare fist, to her headbutt cracking a man's skull in two like an overripe melon."

"C'mon, Helix. That's classic gossip," Ayva snorted

Helix shrugged. "Maybe. But rumors aside, she's won four tournaments. That's dozens of battles, imbibing the spark of some of the strongest warriors in Farhaven year after year. How do we defeat someone like that?"

"With knowledge," Ayva answered. "Everyone has a weakness. We need to understand her tactics, fighting style, her background... everything."

"How do we do that?" Helix asked. "I doubt we're gonna find a Nalia baby book." He shivered. "Ugh, I can't even imagine her as an infant. Probably was still headbutting and stabbing people."

"I know someone," Ayva answered. "He's the right hand to the queen, Howard. He pretends to be a senile old man, but he's keen. I've a feeling if anyone knows Nalia, it's him."

Gray narrowed his eyes. "What's his loyalty?"

"I know what you're thinking. Right hand of the queen, but he's different... When I almost burned the Queen's Terrace to the ground, nearly starting a war between us and Covai, he stopped me." She unconsciously touched her arm, as if remembering. She looked up, blue eyes burning with conviction, "I think he can be swayed to our side."

Gray eased a breath. "A good start. See what you can find out."

Ayva nodded.

Helix raised a hand as if asking permission to speak.

"Yes, Helix?" Gray said, arching a brow.

"One big question: Who should win the tournament? You know, should we pick favorites? Maybe draw straws?"

"No need," Ayva said. "I'm going to win."

Gray huffed a laugh. "You sound pretty confident."

"I am," she said, leaning back in her chair. A little globe of sun spawned, then rolled across the back of her knuckles. "I think you're in trouble, old man."

Gray growled. "You're older than I am! Also, you are aware I'm still the leader of the Ronin, right?"

"Kail was the leader of the Ronin," Ayva said, shrugging. "Does that mean Wind is destined to lead? Who knows?" At first, Gray felt attacked, even hurt. Then as he thought about it, he wondered... could she be right? Distantly, he realized he was white-knuckling his handle. Ayva put a hand on his, drawing him out of his thoughts. "Light and heavens, Gray, relax... I was just teasing! Sure, history has a way of changing, but you're our leader. I didn't know you were so sensitive about it, though," she teased with a wink.

He breathed a sigh. "Honestly, I didn't realize I was, either." He was only now realizing how much pride he'd put in being Kail's progeny.

Ayva continued, "Anyway, as for who's going to win, I just figured we'd all fight our hardest. Primarian-hadus, the third round is next. That'll be tomorrow, at dawn. After that, we have no idea who we're going up against. It's best if we keep our odds up by trying to get as deep into the tournament as possible."

"Agreed," Gray said.

The musicians took up a different tune. It was an upbeat song that his Devari memories faintly remembered. Gray's heart tugged and he remembered why.

It was one of Vera's favorites…

Gray shook his head as if to dislodge the memory "There's one more thing…" he added, and Helix and Ayva turned curious looks upon him. "I've been having…"—he coughed into his fist—"conversations with someone unexpected."

Ayva clutched his wrist. "You can talk with your sword too?"

"Wait, Aurora speaks to you too?"

Ayva hedged. "Well, sort of. More like she sends me impressions, and just a few times so far. But like the bond, I can sense it strengthening. Is Morrowil the same?"

Gray rubbed a hand through his hair. "Well, he says a little more than that."

"You can't be serious. Are you having full-blown conversations?" Ayva asked, grip tightening almost painfully on his wrist in her wide-eyed enthusiasm.

He chuckled and nodded.

"What's the sword been saying?"

Gray told her about the altar and a few other insights.

"Why haven't you said anything until now?"

He shrugged. "I've been meaning to mention it, but I was trying to wrap my head around the whole thing myself and make sure I wasn't crazy. Now felt as good a time as any."

Ayva's zealotry didn't diminish as they debated the nuances of their swords conversational abilities, until a slammed fist cut them short. Both turned to Helix, who was slack-jawed. "What in the Tranquil

Seas... are you serious? Your swords chat with you guys! That's so cool *and* totally unfair. Why hasn't Frostfall said anything?"

Ayva gave a small smirk. "Probably because we're stronger."

Helix glared, looking like he was going to flip the table.

Gray jumped in before he could. "I wouldn't worry. If I had to wager a guess, it's because you got your sword later and it takes a little while to form a bond."

Helix growled. "Uh-huh. That sounds... reasonable. Still, I'm going to have a stern one-sided chat with that hunk of metal when I see it next."

Ayva asked, "Gray... do you think it's Omni and Kail speaking through the blades?"

Gray scratched his temple. "Morrowil said something about being the Spirit of Wind, as well as having memories of the others."

Six barmaids arrived with an array of bowls and plates containing snacks like honeyed dates, nuts, and fruits. Then came three heaping plates of food, each piled high with roasted chicken, buttered potatoes, green stalks sprinkled with a savory pepper and spice, and thick roasted carrots that melted upon the fork's touch. Gray wasn't hungry before, but now he salivated in anticipation. *Winds take me,* he thought. It felt strange being waited on as if they were lords—and in a way, he realized, they were. But it wasn't their Ronin title gaining them the food. Instead, he looked about and saw the inn was busier than when they'd entered. Sure enough, as if whispers of their appearance were spreading, more patrons entered The Red Blacksmith, casting them looks.

I guess we really do bring in the coin, Gray thought.

"One more thing I just thought of," Helix said, finishing his plate, which he'd been practically licking at this point, scraping the last morsels onto his fork. "What if you two have to fight each other? Or Zane?"

"We don't forfeit without a fight," Gray said. "Agreed?"

Ayva nodded. "Agreed. We fight and at least give them a good showing."

"See? You both gave me so much grief for fighting Zane."

"Because you were trying to kill him!" Ayva glowered.

"Only at first!" Helix said. "Oh, final question, what if you have to fight Faye?"

"Assuming Faye doesn't try to kill any of us?" Ayva asked, pushing her empty plate aside. A servant suddenly appeared and whisked it away. "Which, before you say anything, even if she seems good now, please remember Faye threw me in a pit to die by both a Thieflord and a many-limbed, obsidian-skinned monster." Gray remembered well the Darkwalker pit and Faye's betrayal, and he opened his mouth, but Ayva held up a hand. "I know, Gray, she's also helped. I know I'm still a little bitter, but that's not my point. The fact remains that Faye only does what Faye wants. She can't be trusted."

Another plate of food was brought before Helix, again towering with meat, slathered in a rich brown sauce, and this time, a roasted peach with some caramel-like sauce on it.

"Compliments of Archibald," said a barmaid as Helix dug in.

Gray sighed. "Ayva, I know you don't like it, but I think we'll need Faye before this is all done. And for a reminder, she might have thrown you to Darkeye and his monster, but she also was the one who cut off his head in the Battle of the Sands." Gray remembered seeing a glimpse of that amid the tumult of the fighting, only to discover that Darkeye was Faye's own father.

"Oh, so she's basically acquitted of any guilt because an evil woman killed an evil man?"

"No, I'm just saying, if she's as important to Farhaven as my gut tells me, you might have to let go of some of your bitterness. Also, hells, she even helped Helix survive!"

Helix choked mid-bite on a chicken leg, grease spilling down his chin.

"Don't wrap Helix into this," Ayva replied. Helix nodded vehemently, mouth still full. "Besides, she used Helix as much as he used her. If there was any real threat, she would have thrown him away like an old bone."

Helix shrugged, though he looked doubtful.

Gray sighed, trying to keep his patience. "I'm just saying—"

"That you've a crush on a madwoman. We get it."

He growled. "And you've got a thorn in your rear so deep you don't know how to pull it out!" He continued, seeing the ire in her eyes rise, "Look, I'm just trying to see the bigger picture. Faye's not all bad."

"And she's far from good. Anyway, enough of this. Faye doesn't need you to defend her, Gray."

"Aww, but I like when he does that. Really fits with his whole noble theme," said a voice. In the back of Gray's mind, he'd heard the door to the inn open and smelled a baffling, if familiar, scent of blood, leather, and a hint of spice. Caught deep in their conversation, he'd dismissed it. Now they all turned to see Faye striding through the scattered tables. Patrons muttered, watching wide-eyed, whispering something about "tyrant" and "it's her." Behind her trailed Jivran, the giant of a man now wearing slightly more clothes. Faye wore her typical attire, with a few more pieces of her Dragonborne armor. More than that, she'd shaved one side of her head, which lent her an even more fearsome appearance...as if she needed it. Faye grabbed an empty chair and flipped it around to sit in it backward. A vulpine smile grew as she took them in. "Greetings, Diaon, Ice Boy, and Overly Righteous Leader of Legends." She dipped her head at each name. "I hear you three need some help defeating Nalia? Relatively pointless since I'm the one that's going to fight her, but I'd be happy to help." She plucked the roasted peach from the plate in front of Helix, who complained. She popped it into her mouth, then wiped the juices with the back of her gloved hand. "Oh, that's delightful. I'm getting some sort of roasted caramel note that I can't put my taste buds on...smoky...sweet with just a tang of—"

"Faye—" Gray said.

"Hold on..." She raised a hand. Then she *tsk*ed. "See? I lost it. That's going to kill me. Well, not literally. If anyone can, that will probably be Nalia."

"How did you find us?" Helix asked.

Faye shrugged, throwing her dagger onto the table so it wouldn't catch on the seat as she flipped the chair around to sit normally. "Oh, that's easy. I followed you. Kind of impressive if you ask me, considering I was dragging around a twelve-foot-tall giant," she said, hooking a thumb over her shoulder at Jivran, who was admittedly huge. Gray had seen him on the sands and thought he was big, but standing there now? The man had to lean to one side to avoid a chandelier that was fitted with dripping candles. Even then, when Jivran grunted and nodded in greeting, his head did bump the thing, and hot wax dripped onto his burly neck. He didn't even flinch.

Archie appeared. "What is—"

Faye flashed her two swords.

The innkeeper began stumbling over himself. "My lady Primarian—"

Faye silenced him. "No groveling, just drinks. Six of your strongest and best."

Archie bowed and rushed off to fill her order.

"I know what you're doing, Faye." Ayva's eyes were intense and she leaned across the table. "You have some plan, and you're going to try to ingratiate yourself with us. When we agree, and after the plan goes awry, we'll find out it was unabashedly self-serving and we were played as fools. I'm not your fool any longer."

Faye mused, nodding her head at Ayva from across the table, "You are changing, aren't you, Diaon?"

"I am not your Diaon," Ayva said with heat in her voice, eyes churning gold.

"Oh, someone's getting a hang of their powers. I'm impressed."

Ayva cursed.

"Ayva," Helix jumped in, "Faye's not all bad. I mean, she just bought us drinks, that's gotta count for something, even if they're free."

Faye sighed. "Who said those were for you?"

"Six drinks for yourself?!"

Faye shrugged. "Jivran can hold his own, too. Can't you, big guy?"

Jivran just grunted.

By now, Gray realized a good portion of the inn's patrons were staring at them. He sighed. "Let's all just take a breath, all right? Jivran, take a seat, please," Gray insisted to the giant. "Think we've had enough eyes on us for one day."

Jivran took two seats, smushing a pair of chairs together. He specifically moved Faye aside enough so he could sit beside Helix, who greeted him warmly. They exchanged what sounded like a one-sided, grunty, monosyllabic conversation, but both seemed happy. Gray drew them back to the moment. "Nalia," he said. "What do you know, Faye? Or are you just posturing?"

"A little of both," she admitted, taking a bite of Helix's chicken leg. The Ronin of Water grabbed his plate and dragged it back to his side, trying to hoard it. She put the leg in her mouth, and tore the rest of the meat off, then spoke around a mouthful and gestured with the drumstick. "She's got magic. Not sure exactly what kind, but Jivran here thinks it's flesh threading. Turns out they're from the same tribe."

"Tribe?" Ayva asked.

Jivran grunted. "*Hiras Ugra.*"

That language… something like Sand tongue. Gray had heard of the Hiras Ugra. A tribe that lived to the east of the desert of Covai. They'd once been nomadic but had established roots, building a rather impressive desert city that held its own much smaller Grand Tournament.

"You're Hiras Ugra?" Ayva breathed. "No wonder you fought so well. They're mighty warriors, much like the Algasi, though apparently they favor more brute force to agility and nimbleness."

Jivran grunted with pride. "Rat dodges, lion fights."

Faye cleared her throat. "Big guy, if you're going to hold a grudge against me, we can go another round. Maybe move these tables back and clear the area?"

For a moment, the giant seemed to consider it, then he laughed, clapping her on the back. "I know limit. You strong and fast. Worthy of Hiras Ugra. I should know."

"Why's that?"

He shrugged. "I am Hiras Ugra king."

"*King?*" Helix exclaimed, choking on a bite of potatoes.

Faye also gawked. "*What?* You tell me this now?"

Jivran shrugged. "When else? You no ask."

"Yeah, same!" Helix squawked. "How was I supposed to know you were a monarch of a powerful tribe?"

Jivran shrugged, then placed a huge hand on his broad, muscled chest. "Jivran Falla. Third son of Horkas Falla, my father known as Greataxe. Famous. Very strong. Used flesh. Reavers wanted tame him." The giant's expression spread with a smile. "Would not be tamed. I came here fight. No title. Prove Hiras Ugra are strongest. I wrong." He said, eyeing Helix, then Faye. Then he smiled. "Happy loss. Strong warriors."

Gray rocked back with this news.

"Well, King Jivran, that's good to know," Ayva said.

Jivran grunted. "I learn common language. No good. My tongue Siras Higra."

"What's that?" Helix asked.

"A Sand tongue dialect," Ayva said.

"*Desert Tongue*," Faye replied, "that's the direct translation, but yeah, she's right. Obviously why our big guy here is a little rough around the edges."

"Everyone assume I dumb. I not."

"Because it's your second language," Helix said in realization.

"Third," Jivran corrected, and reached for Helix's drink, draining it in one go, wiping his mouth with his sleeve.

Helix threw up his hands. "Great, just steal all my food and drink!"

Gray steered the conversation back. "Nalia. We need to know everything you know."

Jivran's whole craggy, strong-featured face took on a more dour look as he replied, "Hiras Ugra have strong flesh powers. She heal quick. Move quick. Big spark."

"Is that everything you know?" Gray asked.

Jivran shrugged. "She leave when young. Taken by Covai as slave. I only know she Hiras Ugra. We fight kill. No surrender. Battle means life." Faye opened her mouth. Jivran growled, "I surrender, yes. I king. I have duty."

"Aligns with what I heard," Faye said as she nibbled at the remaining morsels of meat on the bone. Her six drinks arrived, and she drained the first one. "Can't wait to fight her."

"Okay, lots of spark. How do we take her down?" Helix asked.

"Well, one cut at a time won't work," Faye remarked. "She'll just heal from that."

Gray understood. "It has to be an attack she can't block, heal, or stop."

"The only way to do that," Ayva continued, "is with something so large and powerful, it might tear a hole in the side of the colosseum."

"So we need a spell that can take down a titan," Gray remarked, feeling hope rise like a flame burning in his chest. He thought of Helix's translucent spear, and Ayva's Collapsing Star. Ancient spells from the Lieon—ones that made the Ronin the legends they were. Ayva's smile told him she was thinking the same thing.

"I love where your head's at," Faye said, popping a grape into her mouth and smacking her lips. "Only one problem with that. She's fast. Incredibly fast. You need a way to pin her down." She raised a hand, stalling them. "Before you say you can hold her in place with fancy wind spells, you want to consider her weapon."

"Her weapon?" Helix asked.

"Oh, I didn't mention?" Faye said as a barmaid took Gray's plate, flashing him a smile. "Surely you saw it? A crimson-and-deep-blue sword?" Gray had seen it; Morrowil had even seemed to react to the sword. "Forged during the Lieon, they say. Seems you all have something in common." She nodded to Morrowil and Frostfall. Ayva explained Aurora had been left with the Thieflord of Flesh so she could enter the tournament. "Point is, in the later rounds, bloodstone-infused blades are allowed, and it's said Nalia's can cut through an Arbiter's magic."

"Great," Helix groused, throwing up his hands. "It's like a game of cat and mouse, and every time we catch the cursing mouse by the tail, the tail falls off."

Gray felt his hand form into a fist, his resolve hardening. "There is a way. I know there is." He looked to Ayva. "Your new friend, Howard, is a good start. Let's begin there. He just needs to find a weakness, even a strength, that we can exploit. We will win this thing."

"I like your optimism!" Faye said, draining her last mug. She tossed a few silvers on the table for a tip. "On that note, I think it's time I take my leave." Jivran pushed back his chairs, and the two rose.

"Where are you going?"

"People to see, people to kill, you know how it is!"

Gray rumbled. "Faye…"

"I like that anger of yours, Gray. I think more of it will need to come out before we're all said and done here. You know, the Kail side of you," she said with a little wink. "And you,"—she turned to Helix—"I forgot to tell you, but I'm quite pleased you didn't die. You know how I said the Leaf one was my favorite? I think I have a new one. But really, pulling your blow? I taught you better than that."

"First, thanks. Second, you didn't teach me anything! You just told me to rub dirt on my face!"

"It worked, didn't it?" She turned to leave, Jivran following.

Gray rose, pushing back his chair. "Faye, wait—"

She stopped and glanced back over her shoulder.

"You know if this whole thing goes south, we're going to need you and the Thiefdoms. Everything hangs in the balance. You can't hide this time."

Faye's face gained a cold mask of indifference. "My *Daion* was right. Don't count on me. I've my own hides to flay."

Gray growled, his hand clenching into a fist.

Her eyes glinted with amusement, eagerness. "There it is…You've grown a little saintly lately. I miss the Kail in you. You're two steps away from unleashing something truly…Well, hopefully we'll find out, won't we?" With that, she turned, and spotting a back entrance, she and Jivran stalked out of the tavern.

Gray was quiet for a moment, suddenly lost in thought. He knew his predecessor's past was complicated. Kail had betrayed mankind but not to the degree that everyone thought. The stories said he'd ravaged all the lands, sending tempests and storms that leveled cities. The name "Blightseeker," and Kail's scarlet eyes—once white—had become embedded like a thorn in the collective conscience of the world.

Was he evil?

Vague memories, like faint dreams that Gray could barely remember upon waking, told him that wasn't entirely true. He'd need to ask Morrowil more about it. The sword, cold at his hip, was clearly not feeling it had anything to contribute.

"Gray?" Ayva said, breaking him from his trance.

He shook himself, seeing his friends' worried looks. "Sorry, I—"

"You don't need to explain, I know better than anyone that she knows the right pressure points," Ayva said. Then she put her hand on his wrist, and he felt her warmth. "Just so you know, you'll never be Kail—at least not the version you're afraid of becoming. Besides, we all have our demons." She looked away and for a moment Gray was tempted to read her with the ki, but refrained. He had a feeling he knew what she was thinking. The fire at Lakewood and the death of her father.

Garmin had been an innkeeper of The Golden Horn. He'd been killed during the Kage's—the false Ronin's—arrival. Ayva's hand tightened on his wrist, her jaw clenching with the painful memory, eyes growing glassy. Gray reached just a thin tendril of ki and blinked, suppressing a gasp from the weight of Ayva's sorrow, guilt, and…surprisingly…anger.

They waited for her to speak.

"My father was a good man." She gave a small laugh. "'*Too smart for his own good,*' people would say. It was the same phrase he'd tell me. People say I was like my mother, but I was my father's daughter through and through. With a nose buried in a book, he was a bit of know-it-all, too. He *always* saw the best in people. Even when they treated him poorly." She shook her head. "I remember once, he sold half his rare books just to keep a rival inn afloat. '*A man doesn't let his neighbor drown simply to see himself rise.*' I swear, he could have filled a book with his little 'adages.'" Gray just listened, as did Helix, captivated by a glimpse into Ayva's past, into her pain that she'd kept secret for so long. "I loved him dearly. He was also the world's greatest fool. When my mother died, he changed. He was still a good father: kind, caring, and attentive. Yet a shadow fell over him, as if he couldn't see forward, couldn't see the light beyond. The inn became his everything. Some say that was because he and my mother had built it, others because he was afraid to face the outside world." She paused at this part of the story, as if gaining courage. "When the Kage came…my father refused to leave. The stubborn mule of a man decided his own inn, a pile of wood and nails, was somehow more worthy to die for than his own daughter was to live for…"

"Ayva…"

She looked up at Gray, tears glistening in her eyes

and gave a little choked laugh. "Sorry." She took a shaky breath, wiping a tear from her freckled cheek. "What I was trying to say is that my father was stuck in the past, but you don't have to be."

Every word struck a chord in Gray. She was right. He was Kail's legacy, not the man himself. He had his own destiny to forge. As he gripped his mug, staring into the dark liquid, he couldn't help but feel…*Why do I feel like there's some aspect of Kail that I'm missing?*

Helix scrubbed at his eyes. "Oh, man, dicing onions at the table." The Ronin of Water shook himself, then picked up his mug. "Here's to conquering our fears and letting go of the shadows from our past!"

Quickly, the conversation then turned to other pressing topics.

Ayva, as it turned out, had learned a fair bit about the other combatants. She listed them off:

A Dryad.

A pirate.

A three-stripe Reaver.

Egrin the Barbarian, Nefrin's champion.

Drega, their good friend and leader of the Fleshguard.

She continued with a host of others.

"Don't forget Zane," Helix said and snorted.

Gray added in his knowledge of what he'd seen. Armed with this, they decided to plan their next battles, rehearsing tactics, strategies, and what spells to use in order to get an edge. Gray's Devari knowledge came in handy as well. "Something tells me the next battle is going to be stacked against us," Gray said. "We need every advantage we can get."

"Right," Helix said, leaning back in his chair, arms behind his head. "Either the queen's going to plot to murder us because we're becoming too much to handle, or the terrifyingly strong combatants will do that for her. Well, you guys, I'll just cheer real loud from the sidelines."

Ayva snorted. "I better be able to hear you."

"Oh, you will," Helix said, rising to stand in his chair and taking a deep breath, as if pretending to shout—

Everyone in the room looked at him.

Ayva yanked on his blue sleeve to pull him back down, and Helix tumbled with a laugh, knocking over his chair.

Just then, the door opened, and a presence fell over the inn like a cold, dark wind. A young man entered with charcoal skin, a white shock of hair, and piercing eyes. On his back was a pitiless black bow.

A baleful dark mist surrounded him.

Merrick, Ronin of Metal.

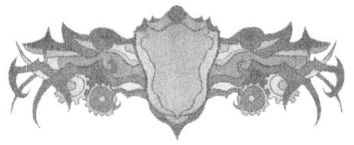

A Long-Awaited Meeting

Merrick entered the inn of The Red Blacksmith. As the door shut behind him, he felt the mood shift. Perhaps it was the faint black mist that coalesced around the bow on his back, his unnerving steely gray eyes, or his overall aura. All these were things he knew well about himself, but the common room reacted as expected. Old men played dice at a nearby table with a pile of bent copper in the center. Upon his entrance, their eyes, filmed with the fog of age, suddenly widened. Weathered hands that gripped cards tensed. A few swallowed and muttered curses, making the gesture of prayer—the "Sons of Flesh" invocation of protection—a simple gesture, tapping forehead, then heart. Barmaids delivering drinks stopped where they stood. On the stage to Merrick's left, a woman was doing a retelling of *Maris's Fall*, but as the door thudded behind him, her fair voice faltered.

Merrick snorted and gave a small smile as he observed the effect he had on the room.

I'd like it more if you didn't seem to relish their fear, Osmium replied.

How is this relishing?

You came in with shadows, with anger in your heart, and you expect them to react warmly?

No sermons today, sword.

One day you will see the irony. You hate power so much, the influence of fear, of terror, yet look at these people, the sword warned, referencing the common room seized in dread. *It is the very tool you wield so openly. You can be so much more.*

Merrick's eyes turned to the true reason he'd come here.

Three individuals sat in the back corner, away from the rest.

Nodes of white, gold, and blue. They burned in his mind, calling to him, even now. This alone set Merrick's blood to boil, as if Farhaven was forcing him toward the others, urging him to join.

Your destiny, sent Osmium.

I make my own destiny, Merrick replied.

As the common room regained its composure like a dancer stepping back into rhythm, Merrick strode across it, purposefully ignoring the patrons' stares. He stopped short before Gray and the others. "Greetings."

Gray watched as Merrick strode toward them. At first, he prepared himself for battle. Then he saw the others at his side. Ayva's eyes burned with a strange mix of sorrow and anger. A faint gold glowed before her palms. Meanwhile, ice flowed up Helix's arm, little chips flaking off, as if melting from Helix's anger. The Ronin of Water's clenched jaw looked ready to bite through thick leather.

For Gray's part, he felt conflicted. Anger burned inside him, too. Merrick had slaughtered innocents in Median, had attacked them with impunity, and had even killed Baron Belfont—Xavia's father. Despite all of that, he was a Ronin. If Gray could find redemption from his own past, then so could Merrick.

I will unite them all.

Merrick stopped before their table.

Gray took him in once again.

On his back, his black metal bow was unmistakable.

Sword of Metal—Gray knew it could change shape. He kept it as a bow. That was a good sign, at least. Using a bow in close quarters was not ideal. Then again, Gray had no idea the extent of the Ronin of Metal's powers. He'd seen those metal arrows fly without the pull of a string.

Merrick's expression was aloof. Dusky skin contrasted sharply with his snow-white hair, but it suited him. A strong jaw, and tired steel-colored eyes that burned with resolve. It was clear the Ronin of Metal would be attractive to women in the same way that Faye was attractive—undeniable in their allure and aesthetic appeal, but equally terrifying at the same time.

Helix snarled as he stood, chair scraping back, as ice crawled higher, coating his fingers, wrists, and the lower part of his forearm.

Merrick snorted, folding his arms across his broad chest. "Sit, Water. No need for such formality."

Gray rose as well, Ayva at his side.

"We don't take orders from you," Ayva said.

"Why are you here, Merrick?" Gray asked.

Helix added, "Give us one reason why we shouldn't shackle you in chains of wind and ice."

"Because you're 'good.'"

Helix growled, the white ice on his hands and forearms gaining spikes like frozen thorns. "Define 'good.' If that's the case, and you're evil, we'd be doing the world a favor."

"Then perhaps this is reason enough." Dark mist swirled about Merrick's body. "You don't like bloodshed, do you? Not unless it's necessary." Merrick glanced over his shoulder. Gray looked about the common room filled with people. He was right. If they fought here, there's no way he could keep everyone safe. How many would die from the sheer collateral damage of their powers? Merrick sighed. "Relax, I've only come to talk."

Helix scoffed. "What could we possibly want to hear from a murderer like you?"

"Come now, is that the way to talk to a fellow brother?"

More ice crawled up Helix's arm. "You're not our brother. Ronin do not kill innocents."

Ayva calmed Helix with a hand on his shoulder.

Gray sighed, rubbing his brow. "Enough of this. Sit," he commanded, pointing to a chair. "I'd rather not have the guards called. We're getting enough eyes as it is." Sure enough, a few people at the nearest tables muttered, and the innkeeper behind the bar washed a mug with a dirty rag. For the third time. "If you try anything," Gray said, jaw tightening, "you will regret it."

Merrick smiled. "My, my, my, you are sounding more and more like Kail. Guess we can't resist our predecessors' fates."

At that moment, Gray wasn't sure what he did, but he sent a mental command into Merrick's bond—sharp and quick. Suddenly, Merrick's knees buckled, and he sat in the offered chair. Merrick's eyes fanned wide. For a moment, Gray was equally perplexed. Then he realized.

He'd sensed that swirling silver node in his mind. It had been open, and he'd sent that mental command.

"That's an interesting trick, but don't do it again," Merrick growled, the dark steely mist coalescing about his body.

"Why are you here?" Gray asked again. "It must be more than simply to antagonize us."

Merrick flitted a hand to a nearby barmaid who walked by with a tray of drinks. One of the pewter mugs floated to his hand. He didn't really care for mead or wine—it slowed one's wits, but it was more for effect than anything. He felt Osmium's scorn of his demonstration without the sword even saying anything. Merrick observed the others' stunned expressions. "I've come to tell you that I've entered the tournament, and I'm going to win."

Helix snorted.

Ayva just glared.

Gray's face was blank, eyes unreadable. "If you're so certain, then why are you here?"

"To advise you to forfeit," Merrick said, taking a sip of the sour drink. Their reactions were equally shocked and unmoved. "I don't know why, call it some twisted mercy, or perhaps these hooks that Farhaven has dug into me, but I don't want to kill you. Not if I don't have to."

"That makes one of us," Helix said, a dagger of ice coming to his hand.

Ayva made a face of disbelief. "You expect us to just forfeit? Because of some misguided notion of compassion? Not to mention, what in your right mind makes you think you can take all the rest of the competitors?"

Merrick knew his gaze, just over the rim of his mug, held a conviction that would have made a nameless cower. "Because I can."

Helix sent through the bond. *Can I stab him now? Please?*

Gray sighed. "You didn't come all the way here just to tell us to forfeit. Not when you know we'd never comply. You may be many things, but you're not a fool. You must know that this is wrong. All of it," Gray said, jaw tightening as he leaned forward. "Don't you see? Can't you feel it? Fighting us, fighting Farhaven? This isn't who you're meant to be."

"Don't tell me who I'm meant to be!" Merrick bellowed. "You say you fight for Farhaven, but have you ever considered you're in the wrong? You unwittingly fight for those in power, while humanity is a broken, ragged thing." Merrick dug his fingers into the metal mug, and it bent beneath his grip. "Look beyond your ivory towers and you will see how much pain Farhaven is in! How many suffer, how many are cast aside? While those in power get rich and fat. The evidence is everywhere. This city is ripe with it. Slavery, nobles feasting in their high balconies while watching as others are gutted and die on the sands. Meanwhile, the masses are kept oblivious. Their lives are pitiful. All they care about is slaking their thirst for blood."

"So, you're just gonna burn it all down?" Ayva asked.

Merrick's words burned with conviction. "You can't build a house upon rotting wood." He melted the mug into a puddle of slag. Then with a wave of his hand, he formed rolling hills, mountains, rivers, and small towns, all out of metal—a miniature model of a new world, but one without cities and high towers with lofty lords and ladies. No magic. "It won't be perfect, I'm well aware, but it'll be far better than this diseased state we know now."

Ayva protested, "You have to realize how insane that sounds!" She gripped the table, looking as if she wanted to flip the heavy, splintered piece of wood. "How many have to die until you think this world is cleansed?"

"Just those on the top and those with magic."

"*Magic*," Helix scoffed. "You do realize you have magic, right? That you're literally one of the strongest magic users in the world?"

He sighed. "That's why I understand. That's why it must be me." Now he sounded a little more self-righteous than he'd like. His blood was hot. "Magic is a stain upon this land."

Gray, however, watched him curiously. Not angry. Not resentful, simply inquisitive and…sympathetic? As he stared into Merrick, he whispered words, as if not intended for Merrick to hear: "*What made you this way?*" Something penetrated Merrick, like thin tendrils, then sifted back into Gray.

A Devari ki?

At first, Merrick tried to resist, to slap the sensation aside, but it wasn't threads or simple magic. It was something else.

Suddenly, the common room disappeared and he was lost in memory.

A memory he thought he'd escaped after eight years.

Neveaha called to him, "Merrick, wake up…"

Merrick blinked and remembered where he was. Twelve years old again, in a dungeon in the heart of Yronia. The smell of sulfur, coal, and death still lingered in the air. The metallic taste of blood was still present on his taste buds. His tongue was swollen. He remembered. He'd attempted to chew off his own tongue so he wouldn't speak a word, but they'd promised to kill her if he tried that again. Tight manacles of iron had long ago cut into his ankles and wrists, the blood adding to the smell of decay. Time formed scars that repeatedly bled, until he could barely feel them now.

Neveaha's voice drew him back to the moment.

She was a dozen paces away, also shackled to the wall.

"Merrick…He's coming…" she whispered, large blue eyes flickering up to the door that would spell the beginning of an endless day of torture. "You have to end it now."

Merrick looked at her. "I can't move, I—"

"Your power," Neveaha said, "I know it's come. I saw it. You can do it."

The bloodstone and Yronia metal about his wrists said differently. He'd already tried. Even if he could…He looked at Neveaha again, truly took her in, like a thirsty man drinking in the last sip of water from an empty waterskin. She was perhaps twenty or thirty, much older than him, though she often called him an "old soul." She always treated him as if he was far older than his age. Her kind, soft cheeks were now hollowed. Her eyes sunken. Her body was frail and emaciated. A thin gray rag of a dress clung to her, bones practically protruding through the threadbare fabric. Scars laced her body. The most recent ones were on her neck. Even those were healing slower now. As if her body was giving up. Beauty was there, too. A faint wisp that still clung like a rose desperately grasping onto its final petal. She was dying, they both knew, and there was no bringing her back.

"I can't," Merrick begged.

"You have to," Neveaha pleaded. "I think I hear their footsteps. I can't go on like this. Even if I could go on, I fear you'll break, and you can't tell them anything. You mustn't."

Merrick's heart broke.

She was right.

Days, weeks, months, it had gone on like this.

Endless torture.

Dried blood at their feet was a painful reminder of what they had endured.

A tremor of rage tried to overwhelm the sudden, unbearable sorrow. "I...I don't understand. You promised it would end! You said there was still hope," Merrick said, trying to stifle the tears. "You promised."

She gave a sad smile. "There is hope. For you." She watched him, and the thin ray of hope to which he had clung for ages faded, like the last shaft of light before the sun dipped over the horizon. "Let's start small," she said, then nodded to a dagger, one of the many cruel implements they used on a nearby splintered table. "Pick up that dagger with your mind. I know you can do it."

Footsteps sounded outside.

They were coming.

"Quick!"

Terror wormed its way into Merrick's bones.

Out of instinct, he tried to tap back into that swirling power in his mind, to unveil the cloak.

Merrick forcefully severed the flood of memories as if cutting a chain. His world rocked, and he was thrown back into the present. Back to the cozy amber-lit inn and the subtle tones of a dulcimer playing a melancholy song. It took a moment to regain his composure, seeing Gray and the others across the table. The Ronin of Wind looked horrified. Something told Merrick that Gray hadn't seen anything, but he'd felt the intense emotions from back then. "I'd love to get into a touching backstory," Merrick said. "We don't have the time. And if your goal, my supposed leader, is to unlock some hidden pain and find the Merrick that will join your cause of righteousness, you won't. My sword has been trying that for a decade, rather unsuccessfully, I might add."

Gray's eyes went wide at this. He unconsciously touched his own sword.

Merrick huffed in amusement. *So Morrowil is talking to him, too?*

Through the bond, Merrick felt the others' equal surprise, even more than Gray. Had they not unlocked the power to speak with the relics yet? *Enough of this,* Helix sent through the bond. *He's evil, Gray.*

Whatever he's plotting, we can stop it by taking him here. I'm not into murder, but if it means saving thousands? Or even just keeping him away from whatever nefarious plans he's scheming, it's worth it.

Gray sent back, *I won't take you against your will. Especially not here.*

Helix looked surprised.

He can use the bond, Helix, Ayva sent.

She's right, Merrick sent.

Helix glared at Merrick. *Oh, I know, I just figured that was more subtle than choking you with my bare hands.*

Merrick made a thoughtful sound, leaning back in his chair. *Ronin of Water, I destroyed your home. I can see why you'd be angry. Know I was only a tool in that fight. My only goal was Baron Belfont.*

Helix shook his head in disbelief. *That wasn't my home, but those were my people. What the hell kind of excuse is that, only killing an innocent man?*

He was far from innocent, Merrick sent. *If you only knew.*

Helix complained, *This is idiotic. You realize there's three of us and one of you, right?*

Three of you, yes…but all of you don't want to kill me. That will dull the edge to your attacks. I don't have that disadvantage.

I think you have me pegged wrong, Helix said as jagged ice crawled across the table, an eerie dark blue that seemed powerful to Merrick.

Gray warned. *Helix…*

In response, Merrick didn't move, but Osmium did. The black bow transformed, sliding from his back to his hip, becoming a long, sleek metal blade complete with a black metal scabbard—which also seemed to suck in the nearby light, like an obsidian star. It had only taken a simple mental command. The others' eyes widened at this. Merrick's face was impassive. *If they think this is something, wait until they see my true trick.* In the corner of his vision, he was aware that a decent portion of the inn, who up until now had been furtively casting looks their way, now openly gasped at his bow's transfiguration. Old men cursed, and barmaids shivered, stepping back.

Try it, Metal Boy, Helix sent, ice creeping higher, his eyes full of power. *See how far it gets you.*

Enough! Gray sent through the bond like a whip. The mental command somehow actually pained Merrick, and apparently Helix also. Both winced against it. Merrick saw his vision cloud for a moment.

Only a moment.

Long ago he'd learned to tap into the true nature of his Nexus, his source of the flow. It'd been accomplished the hard way, forged in the hottest fires. Fires he never wanted to face again. He doubted the others had done or risked the same. As a result, Merrick had discovered almost all of his Nexus. Now he pulled back a good portion of that veil to reveal the full sight of his power: a swirling ball of molten, silvery metal in a field of black. A thick steely gray mist swirled about his arms. At once, the pain in his mind from Gray's command suddenly disappeared. *Curious,* Merrick sent, eyes darkening. *I was hoping to wait until the sands for all to see, but I suppose we can test your mettle here.*

This is not what you promised, Osmium scolded. *You said we only came to talk. I would not have agreed if I knew you were here for violence.*

Merrick wasn't certain what Osmium would do if the sword refused him outright. He rather liked the blade and hadn't wanted to push it too far. His blood was on fire. His hand itched. Part of him felt like this was wrong, as if it was taboo to fight his own kind. Part of him felt calm, but most of him? Most of him *wanted* to fight. *Why?* he wondered. *To prove their ideals wrong? Or to prove myself the strongest?*

The very thing he fought against, the very thing Osmium warned him about.

Gray's fist slammed down on the table. Wind burst out from it. Ice shattered, and the dark coalescing mist scattered. "I said, *enough.*" His eyes brewed with storms. "You're mistaken. I'm not fighting you." He looked at the others. "*We're* not fighting you. You're one of us, Merrick. I know you can sense it. You talk about purpose, this is it," he said, eyes burning into Merrick, pleading, urging. "Farhaven needs us. Join us. I know you're more than just destruction."

If Osmium could smile, the Sword of Metal would have.

For a moment the conviction in Gray's gaze, in his voice, moved Merrick. Something stirred inside of him. What was this feeling? Was it another power of their leader? No, it wasn't magic. He understood. It was simply the passion of a man who believed in a cause. There was a noble honesty within Gray. No lies...not like the Patriarch with his ancient thousand-year-old schemes—schemes of a monster, unfolding in the dark, waiting for the time to strike. Merrick winced against the feeling as a splitting headache erupted. He grabbed his head, meeting Gray's eyes once more as he snarled, "What then? I join the side of magic? Become some great power that inevitably grows corrupt just like our predecessors?"

"That's not what happened," Ayva said heatedly. "The stories were wrong, the Ronin weren't the true evil."

Merrick gave a hoarse chuckle. "Oh, I know all about the Kage. The Ronin's darkness. How do you think that shadow was created? Without the Ronin, there would be no great evil."

Ayva snorted. "What, so any time good arises, it's to blame for an equal and opposing evil?"

"I thought Omni would know our history better."

Ayva floundered for words.

Gray stepped in. "Look, I don't know what happened to you, but magic isn't the enemy. The demon that's sending countless slavering saeroks, and hulking vergs to slaughter thousands? That's the evil. How can you not see that?"

Merrick heard everything they were saying. Saw the logic in it, and for a moment, his mind warred. He shut his eyes against the pain, a literal burning in his mind, as if convictions were tumbling down, and the mind he'd built to be an impenetrable fortress of steel like Yronia's walls, was suddenly crumbling. "I…"

Gray continued, seizing on this, "Magic isn't evil. You know that. It's how it's used. I know you're afraid of what we can do, but we will be different. I know it."

Magic. In that moment, Neveaha's face stood out in his mind. Her pain. Her suffering. Their pain. It was connected, and there was one sole root. Merrick understood. His path was the lesser of two evils. "Different… That's what they all promise." He felt his face darken, his conviction reforging to tempered steel once again. "No. You may believe what you're saying, but that's how it always starts. Eventually, power corrupts. I'd rather watch the world burn than let it languish in shadow for all eternity."

Ayva snapped, "You're a fool! Spark is in everything. You can't abolish magic without abolishing life!"

Merrick's eyes blazed. "Watch me."

"You're wasting your time," Helix grumbled. "He's too far gone."

Gray released a heavy breath. "If you won't see reason, at least tell us who the evil is."

"Oh, you'll find out soon enough. I don't think he wishes to hide for much longer."

Ayva shook her head. "So you admit he's evil, yet you still work with him?"

"Yes," Merrick said. "An unfortunate necessity."

Her look was almost sad. "When is dealing with the devil ever a necessity?"

Merrick snorted. "Says the trio who duels to the death, when their supposed mantra is saving all life."

The Ronin of Sun looked as if she'd been slapped.

Helix snarled, "I'm done bickering with a madman." With a wave of his hand, the ice that had become a thick sheet across the table suddenly flowed up Merrick's forearms in thick shards of azure, locking him in place, and a deep bone-cold sank into the Ronin of Metal.

Merrick looked up, feeling his dark gray eyes cloud white-gray. "You shouldn't have done that."

Ripples of wind flowed over Gray as he uttered, "Merrick, don't—"

Ayva glowed gold.

Merrick reacted first.

Tapping into the unveiled Nexus in his mind, he sent thick, complex threads of metal. They slammed into the metal collars around the necks of the three Ronin across from him. With a mental command, he squeezed. The collars tightened, constricting, and the red bloodstone inside reacted to this—the touch of magic within it restricted their powers even more. Gray must have been trying to summon a hurricane down on Merrick's head, but his channels were thin as a needle now. A white storm could be seen in his eyes, and every muscle was tense, the tendons in his neck strained. Ayva was the same. Her golden eyes burned with an inferno, ready to combust the whole inn. So too were Helix's, enough to bury the world in an avalanche. None of them could thread a trickle of power.

The ice rooting his arm melted. "Curious collars, don't you agree?" Merrick said, shaking his hand free of the now slush. "It took a while to learn how to manipulate Yronia steel. Aside from the bellows of Yronia, it's said only Baro, my predecessor, or an Arbiter, or a hundred Reavers working in tandem could change its shape. But I have learned what you haven't…" His voice grew a ragged edge. "I have watched enough death and torment for a thousand lives, and it has forged me into this." He squeezed his fist, and their collars constricted even tighter, faces turning crimson as they gasped, clawing at the collars about their necks. The three abandoned magic, and reached for their weapons when—

Something slammed into the back of Merrick's head.

Pain erupted as his world fuzzed.

When he looked up through blurred vision, a figure stood over him in a dark red vest, with burning orange eyes. Merrick knew who it was.

Zane, Ronin of Fire.

Flames danced in Zane's fist. Even through those crimson fires, Merrick saw scarred knuckles and a face of pure, if tempered, fury that easily matched his own. Zane snarled, "You're going to regret that."

Zane had followed Gray and the others. He'd sensed them in his mind, leading him to The Red Blacksmith. That's when he'd felt the dark node of silvery black through the bond. He'd burst into the common room, saw the fear in the patrons' eyes, and witnessed a man choking the life out of his friends. He'd put the pieces together quickly.

Ronin of Metal.

The man was sitting, but his hands were outstretched, fingers curled as the metal about his friends' necks burned red-hot.

Zane charged, grabbing a chair, and smashed it into the back of the man's head and shoulders.

Zane, no, Gray sent, gathering his breath as the others recovered. *Don't fight Merrick!*

Merrick…So that was his name.

Gray, being Gray, wanted to convert him. Save him.

Noble, and it's what he liked about the Ronin of Wind.

It was the very thing keeping Zane from the edge of darkness, but also terribly misguided. Zane knew evil, and what knelt before him was the epitome of it. He might have thought the man was too far gone, but his steel gray eyes full of apathy held a deep-rooted pain, a seething hatred—a fire that the Kalvas Ocean couldn't snuff. Zane could, though. He sent a fist, smashing it into the man's jaw. It felt like hitting a brick wall. Even brick crumbled, though. So he did it again.

This time, Merrick snarled and caught Zane's fist in a black gauntleted hand.

When had that formed?

Fire burned in Zane's other fist, and he swung, hoping to crack Merrick's skull.

Merrick deflected it in the nick of time with another shield of metal, then roared, turning the shield into another metal gauntlet. Merrick slammed his black fist into Zane's gut. Zane could have dodged, but he took the blow. Agony, sharp and visceral, made him gasp as he felt ribs crack. Merrick's surprise was evident. The man's steely eyes widened, as if to say, "Why would you suffer a strike like that?" Then he saw Zane's hands. They were held above him, clenched in a fist. Burning crimson engulfed Zane's hammer blow as he brought it down. It would demolish everything.

Merrick formed a bulwark of metal, thick and wide, and—

—vast, sudden threads of white wind abruptly shot out, wrapping around Zane's body, locking him in place. Golden bands wrapped Merrick's arms to his sides. Ice slithered up the Ronin of Metal's legs and arms. Helix leveled Frostfall to Merrick's throat, blade cutting skin and drawing blood. "Move another inch, Metal Boy. Please. I beg you."

In that moment, however, Zane realized the thundering sound he'd been hearing wasn't a storm. On the bar, a yellow globe had been shattered. Huh. Farbs had those too, at least in the nicer establishments.

An alarm.

The innkeeper must've broken it awhile ago.

The inn's door burst open, and guards rushed into the tavern. Somewhere in their clash, many of the patrons had fled. The rest cowered in corners or hid under tables as the common room was flooded by Covian guards in tan leather and mail, swords and spears bared. Before anyone could react, the guards parted and a man entered, followed by a dozen red-robed Reavers. He wore a crimson robe, four stripes upon his cuffs, and his face was partially scarred and pink from recent burns Zane had given him.

Reaver Nefrin.

He had a feeling the rat would come out of hiding sometime.

Nefrin eyed Zane and the others, looking happy to be back in a position of power.

Blood boiling, Zane tried to temper his rising fury.

Hannah whispered, *Control it. You're stronger than your rage.*

Zane... Ayva sent, as if clearly seeing his anger.

Right. They hadn't seen what Nefrin had done.

Zane took a few deep, calming breaths, feeling his hot blood cool. *I'm good.* Gray looked wary for only a moment. *I promise.*

Their leader nodded and gave a small smile. *Glad to have you back,* Gray sent, with a clear dual meaning.

Zane grunted. *Looked like you needed a little help.*

Helix rubbed at his neck. *Bastard cheated. Which reminds me, I need to get this damn collar off.*

Guys, there's a lot we need to catch up on but, Ayva said, *I think we should deal with the four-stripe Reaver in the room first.*

Nefrin approached, interrupting, "What do we have here? Primarian gladiators making a ruckus in our fair city! You are aware you are guests here, yet you sully Her Majesty's hospitality with your rabble-rousing. How very Ronin."

"We didn't start this!" Helix snapped, pointing to Merrick. "He did!"

Merrick rose to his full height, remaining silent.

A guard with a thick, wild red beard and sharp eyes stepped forward. Zane saw he was a lieutenant by the knots of rank on his leather pauldron. "What say you, gladiator? What happened here?"

"I simply came for a talk," Merrick replied.

Nefrin's eyes danced with delight. "See, Lieutenant Hezos, there you have it. As I suspected. The Ronin find a way to cause chaos wherever they tread."

Zane sighed.

Ayva rolled her eyes. *Should have figured Merrick would get in league with Nefrin and the queen. That means the shadow is even closer than we think.*

What do we do? Helix sent.

Zane weighed his options as well. He could kill Nefrin and Merrick now, but he doubted he could take a hundred guards, or however many flooded the street. Besides, after his fight with Helix, killing aimlessly felt wrong.

"Let him go," Nefrin said of Merrick, who was still bound in sun and ice. "He is a guest of Queen Imala, as are you."

"But he—" Helix began.

Gray shook his head and sent something to Helix specifically that Zane couldn't sense. With a grumble, their spells evaporated. Gray spoke, raising his hands, "We meant no ill will. Things got out of hand, but no one was hurt." Nefrin opened his mouth with an eye to the shattered table and chair. "We'll gladly pay for any damages."

Gray… Helix sent.

Gray replied, *He's got nothing on us. Let Nefrin say what he wants. We fight the battles that matter.*

"Figures… Well, I'm sure the innkeeper will…" Nefrin began.

The innkeeper neared. "My Lord Primarian, there's nothing to apologize for. I was simply worried things would get out of hand. A broken table and chair is nothing! Your mere presence in my inn will bolster the coin for weeks!"

Nefrin muttered under his breath.

Zane knew Nefrin was bold.

But Nefrin wouldn't kill him here.

Nor could he kill Zane alone, and he had little chance against all four of them.

Nefrin sighed. "I suppose if no damage was done, you can go," he said to Merrick.

"Him?" Helix exclaimed. "He's literally the worst offender here!"

Nefrin's lip curled. "Is that so? I saw only a man in shackles."

Merrick bowed his head, only slightly.

Evil recognizes evil, Helix sent through the bond.

The Ronin of Metal turned to them. "Thanks for the chat." Then he sent through the bond to all four, *I look forward to facing each of you upon the sands.* He eyed them in turn. *There we can finish what we started.*

Zane let a bit of fire come to his fist. *You'll melt the same as any, pretty boy, but do me a favor will you? Toss the bow when I do. I'd rather not turn a legendary weapon to slag.*

Merrick's eyes flared with rage, taking the bait.

Take your leave, Gray sent before violence sparked to a full flame. *Know this isn't finished. I'm not done.*

A bemused expression on his face, Merrick dipped his head, then slipped through the throng of guards and out the door. Nefrin, his Reavers and guards at his side, rounded on Zane and company. "As for you all, I will be watching. That is, if you survive the next rounds.

My champion Egrin is most eager to face you three. I wonder what you'll do against a true opponent."

"Unlike you?" Zane asked.

"Tempt me, boy, I dare you," Nefrin seethed.

Zane chuckled. "You already tried to kill me once. You can try again."

The other guards reacted in shock.

"Oh, you haven't told the guards that you dragged me into a back alley with a dozen of these cowards," he said, nodding to the red-robed Reavers, "only to fail? That is against Covian law, is it not? Cold-blooded murder?"

"What is the boy talking about?" Lieutenant Hezos asked. "You tried to kill him?"

Nefrin scoffed. "Preposterous! I've no idea what he's on about!"

Zane grinned. "How'd you get those scars?"

Nefrin smiled back. "A training accident."

He's lying, Gray sent.

Ayva reacted, her worry and anger conveyed through the bond. *Light and heavens! You can't be serious! I knew we shouldn't have let you go alone. Zane, I had no idea…If we knew…*

What could you have done? I pushed you away, remember? Don't blame yourself. He shrugged. *Besides, I survived.*

Still, I knew Nefrin was foul, but this? Ayva sent, shaking her head. *This is bad.*

Then we put an end to Nefrin, right here, right now, Helix sent.

Gray looked ready to reply.

Zane was quicker. *No.*

No? He tried to kill you! Helix said, face twisted with anger.

Right. Zane looked over to Helix. *You are aware it's his word against mine.*

Ayva added, *Even if he is a bastard who deserves death, I've been flirting with danger with the queen already. Killing her closest advisor in cold blood is going a bit too far.*

Helix muttered, *Sometimes I don't like being the good guy.*

Lieutenant Hezos seemed caught, but finally breathed a low guttural sound and barked, "Ah, flesh and bone, I've had enough of this! There's more disturbances and fights to quell tonight. You all watch yourselves. If I hear about any more trouble from you four, I'll throw you in the cells, Primarians' favored sons or not." With a gesture, the guards filed out, leaving the inn.

They were left with Nefrin and his twelve Reavers.

Nefrin snorted, eyeing Zane. "Seems there's no need to lie now. I tried to kill you, yes, but for a greater good. You escaped, now go ahead, take your vengeance."

Spark brewed in Nefrin's eyes.

He was goading the Ronin of Fire.

Zane doubted Nefrin could initiate a fight with all these people watching, but if Zane attacked first? Gray stepped forward, clearly ready to say something that would end this petty squabble and get them to their true task. Zane stole the moment. "I won't kill you here. I'd rather you watch our rise to inevitable victory. Only then will I find you and flay the skin from your bones, perhaps make a nice pair of gloves out of it."

Nefrin breathed heavily through clenched teeth.

The other Ronin joined Zane's side.

The twelve Reavers had, a moment ago, looked quite confident; now, they seemed suddenly less so as ice, sun, wind, and fire made faint appearances around each of the Reavers' forms.

Clearly seeing he couldn't bait Zane, or perhaps worried if he did, he'd lose, again, the four-stripe counselor to the queen smirked. "Take your short-lived victory. I will have the last word when your blood stains the sands. The age of the Ronin is dead. A new age is coming, and I will lead it." With that, he turned on his heel and stalked out of The Red Blacksmith with his Reavers in tow, and the four were left alone, with a scattered array of confused, terrified patrons, and an innkeeper who still looked half dazed.

Gray cleared his throat. "Think we should let these fine people have their night…" The four threw what little coin they had on the table, and took to the streets.

More Drink

Jivran at her side, Faye moved through the streets teeming with revelry. The citizens of Covai were celebrating, drunk off the spectacle of the games. Or just intoxicated. She'd seen her fair share of debauchery, but Covai exceeded anything she'd ever witnessed. People drank, laughed, ate, snuck away into dark corners, and not-so-dark corners. Silhouettes of people tangled in each other's arms, emitting moans, clearly "losing themselves" to the wild night.

Brawls broke out here and there.

To the left of Faye, two men slugged it out while others cheered them on.

She snorted.

Pound for pound, the only place that could put the City of Flesh to shame was the Dragon's Tooth, a famous pirate enclave where ordering a drink often came with a side of stabbing.

Jivran drew eyes as they walked. He was tall, and lumbered like a balrot. His heavily tattooed chest, bald head, broad shoulders, and twin chipped axes on his thick leather belt were a sight to be seen. For her part, Faye was less distinguished, though she also garnered looks as she was still attired in half of her Dragonborne Yronia armor. Its spikes and dark metal faintly gleamed in the dusky light that bathed the city.

They both ignored the looks.

"What now? More drink?" Jivran asked as they pushed their way through the masses. Well, he didn't really need to push. He was kind of like a giant ship cutting through icy waters.

Faye sighed. "As enticing as that sounds, and it *really* does—I barely wet my whistle back there with those lightweights—I'm afraid there's something more pressing."

"More important than drink and celebrate?"

"Afraid so."

Jivran grunted. "You won. Celebrate. Life short."

She snorted. "Maybe shorter than I'd like, than we'd all like, if I don't make this visit."

Jivran made a thoughtful sound. "Lead."

Faye ducked a wild punch from two drunk men fighting. One man had been facing the wrong way. "Thing is, I don't exactly know where it is."

"Then where we going?"

She gave a small smile, moving out of the way of a slow-moving team of massive Farin goats. The animals were a sight to be seen, with large, horizontal pupils, and twisted crimson horns that wouldn't fit through a doorway. They were pulling a wagon filled with melons. A moment later, revelers leapt onto the cart, thieving the ripe green fruits as the wagon driver shouted. Faye looked back to Jivran. "I may not know where we're headed, but I know who does."

Jivran grunted, as if this was enough explanation.

Faye took another street, distancing them from the crowds. "You know you don't need to follow me, right?"

Jivran rubbed his brick of a jaw thoughtfully as if trying to find the right words. His dark eyes became a light of understanding as he explained, "You flame. Draws all. Like moth."

Glancing up at him, neck craning, she remarked, "You're one big moth."

He protested, "I not moth. I listener."

"Okay, now I'm confused, I thought you just said you were a moth."

"No. You draw many moths. I want watch how…what you do next. Important for Farhaven."

"Uh-huh. What's that have to do with listening?"

Jivran's face became serious as he tried to find the words. "I Farhaven listener. Farhaven curious." Then he shrugged, admitting, "I curious, too."

She paused in the middle of a slightly less busy street, looking up at her giant friend. "Farhaven speaks to you?"

Jivran grunted. "Yes."

"What's she saying?"

"She?"

Faye shrugged. "Sure. Expansive, curious, life-giving. Seems logical."

He snorted. "I see. She," he said, with a smile, "says you are chaos and order, death and life. How you say…"

"Duality? Means two opposites."

He grunted. "Yes. Du..al..i..ty"—he pieced out the word—"that you."

"What about my duality?"

"It save or doom Farhaven."

Faye froze for a moment in the center of a less packed street. An inn's glowing windows and music of a lute filled the road. Those words. A frigid numbness ran down her spine. They sounded eerily familiar. Something about them tickled the back of her mind. Whispers of the past, of something her father, Darkeye, said. *"You will save or doom us all."* No, she was probably just making that up. Shivering and shaking it off, she said, "Well, do me a favor, will you? Tell Farhaven that I'm pretty sure she's got the wrong person. That's a lot of responsibility I definitely don't want."

"She always listening. No need I tell her."

Faye sighed.

A little man with a plump body and ritual scars on his face approached. "Flowers for your love, my giant friend? Only two coppers!"

Jivran dug into a pouch at his waist.

Faye rolled her eyes. "No, thank you," she said, grabbing Jivran's arm. "Not here tonight for a lover's stroll, Jivran."

He shrugged. "Why no? They pretty flowers."

She sighed, and they slipped down a narrow alley into a rougher part of Covai. Her stomach rumbled, and she stopped at a nearby vendor's stand. With a bit of sleight of hand, she slipped two skewers of green peppers off a bed of hot coals.

"Your friends, good friends. Kind. Nice," Jivran grunted.

Faye had been mid-bite into the green, lightly charcoaled pepper when he spoke. "*H-h-hot*," she said, blowing steam out of her mouth into the cool night air. "Wait, what? Oh, Gray and company? Eh"—she rolled her shoulders—"'friends' is kind of a stretch."

Jivran snorted. "You like them. Not fool me."

She glared at him as they moved north, away from the crowds. "Bah, I don't even know if I like you."

Jivran raised a furry brow that resembled a giant caterpillar.

"Don't give me that look. I should be mad at you. You didn't tell me you were a cursing king."

Jivran shrugged. "King, peasant, what matter?"

She blew on the skewered peppers and took another bite as they slipped by more revelers, heading farther away from the crowds. "That's…a decent point."

"Also, you no tell me you Thieflord. That king, too."

"Also fair," she admitted, then turned down a side street. The crowds were thinner there. She offered her second skewer to Jivran. The big man recoiled. "What? They're not half bad."

"I no fool. Those Lurai Peppers. Hottest pepper all Farhaven."

"Bah." Faye waved dismissively. "Like all things, stories tend to embellish." She bit into another crisp pepper, the heat burning, but the sweet tangy sauce dampened the sting. The charcoaled bit was a nice touch, too. "Now this one time, I was trekking in the Burai Mountains and found a Purple Snowpepper. That was hot. Smaller than my pinky," she said, holding up a finger, "but gods, the thing could've probably liquified metal. I wouldn't wish that one on my worst enemy. Well, maybe I would. Death by pepper? Sounds entertaining to watch."

"You crazy."

She glanced up at him, brow raised. "What gave it away?"

Finally, they made a turn, heading beneath an arch that read "Merigon's Alley".

Jivran made a sound as the dingy, seedier setting revealed itself, and grumbled, "Too cheery name for such dark place."

Faye took in the men and women in rags huddled in corners near small fires, or beneath the roofs of dilapidated inns. "True enough," she said, smiling at a missing-toothed thief, making the man scurry away in the shadows. "Most don't call it by Merigon's Alley. Pickpocket Lane is more common, I hear, and even that's a tad friendly in my estimation."

Eyes followed them, and figures moved in the dark spots of her peripheral vision.

"Evil lurks here," Jivran said.

She sighed. "Tell me about it. Feels like home."

Several men warming their hands before a fire of burning rubbish eyed them and whispered to one another. A surly man smiled, revealing a mouth full of missing and decaying teeth. The eyes of several of them were bloodshot with red. "Red eyes," Jivran said. "Seen before…"

"*Hiras Mira*," Faye explained. "A potent, if toxic, herb. I hear it's a Covian favorite. Helps them relive their cherished memories."

Jivran snarled back at the men, and their dull gazes recoiled at the threat of the huge man.

Though not with as much fear as they should have.

Faye pulled Jivran into a back alley. There were a few broken boxes, bones scattered on the ground, and what looked like a corpse beneath a tattered rag.

"What we doing here?" Jivran asked.

"Getting directions," Faye said, yawning. After a little time had passed, and nothing happened, she sighed. "Really?" She threw her weapons to the ground, then gestured for Jivran to do the same. Rolling his eyes, the giant did so, dropping both axes to the muck.

Out of the shadows stepped six thieves in dingy clothes with greasy slicked-back hair.

Each brandished a dagger.

Their leader, a gangly man, stepped partially into the light of the moon. He had a hooked nose, stringy black hair, and a long horselike face. "Look what we have here, boys."

"Sorry, I'm sure you were about to make a terribly intelligent, even pithy, speech, but I'm going to make this quick, since I've done this a few times." She pulled back her sleeve, first showing the Primarian-hadus mark, which made their eyes widen. They whispered in fear. Then she showed the mark on her shoulder of a Darkeye officer, the scarred imprint of the single bloodshot eye. "Now you know what you're dealing with. I'm not against killing you six, but we just need directions to the Thieflord of Flesh."

The leader hesitated, then grumbled, "Darkeye brood has no power here."

She sighed. "Your name?"

"You can call me Neral." He approached, raising a pitted dagger that gleamed in the light, his eyes full of lust. "See, you might be something special in Farbs, but this ain't the City of Fire, girl. Covians are stronger and hungrier," he said, and his thieves chortled, licking their lips, "and you're looking like a fine snack—"

Faye stabbed the thief under the chin, through his still-open mouth, into his brain.

"Right, I guess I forgot about that weapon," Faye said, wiping the dagger on her pants, then flipping it and folding it back into her sleeve.

Neral, for a moment, didn't realize he was dead.

Then he gasped, gurgled, and slumped over, lifeless.

"Not smart," Jivran said.

Faye looked at the other thieves, still grouped together at the entrance to the back alley, their daggers now held in shaky grips, eyes alert but red-rimmed. She rubbed her brow, smoothing the crease that was forming. "Look, unless you want Jivran to crush your bones into a fine powder, I'm going to ask again, the Thieflord—"

She didn't finish before they were all pointing.

Over the crest of the buildings.

"See? Not so hard. C'mon, Jivran. Games start bright and early. Time for a quick visit."

No sooner had they stepped back onto the dusky street when two dozen thieves dropped silently from the rooftops, encircling Faye and Jivran.

"Quiet," Jivran grunted.

"Yeah, I think they are a *little* higher caliber." Each thief was dressed in the tan cloth of the House of Flesh, with the symbol of their element emblazoned on their shoulders. She realized the street—with its ragtag inns and homes of decaying brick and wood—was now empty. Not that it had been bustling before. "Huh, word travels fast."

A voice sounded behind her. "You know, you're a rather difficult one to track down."

Faye smiled, turning to see the speaker, finding what she expected: a woman with long, twisted, and matted locks of blond hair that draped her strong shoulders. She wore a tan vest, and gold bangles covered her arms, but they couldn't conceal her toned and well-muscled limbs. Her face was handsome, strong, and resolute. Though now it bore an amused expression. Brown tribal tattoos marked her cheeks and crawled down her neck.

"Irasa," Faye said with a toothy, eager smirk, "this big brute at my side is Jivran. Apparently, he thinks I can change the world, so he's tagging along. Jivran, might I introduce you to Irasa, better known as The Spider, The Weaver of Webs, and of course, the infamous Thieflord of Flesh."

Irasa sighed. "You know, I never liked those first titles. They always sound so ominous. But you would know, wouldn't you, Mistress of Shadows, Tyrant of the Tournament, and fellow Thieflord of Fire."

Faye shrugged. "I find the more you try to avoid them, the more they seem to stick."

Irasa snorted. "So it seems. Come." She gestured to them. "We have *much* to discuss."

A Reunion of Fire and Flesh

After their run-in with Nefrin, Faye, and Merrick, Gray found himself in a strange mood. He expected to feel more conflicted, more overwhelmed with all they had to do. However, he wasn't. Instead, he felt like an arrow notched for flight, resolved and with a clear aim of their goals.

We just have to win. Failing is not an option.

The cool night air of Covai greeted them as they stepped out of The Red Blacksmith.

"Well, what now?" Helix asked, yawning.

Zane's gaze panned north, toward the colosseum. "I…have somewhere I need to go."

Ayva's brow furrowed. "But we've only just gotten back together, you're leaving now?"

Zane rubbed at his neck. "I want to stay. I do, it's just…I promised someone."

"A girl?" Helix asked, ribbing him with an elbow.

Zane grunted.

"Oh, it is a girl," Helix said, "well that's good."

"A girl, Zane?" Ayva questioned. "Now of all times?"

"Hey, don't rib the guy for a little romance in this dark in depraved world… Hells, if Farhaven is really on the brink of collapse, when's a better time to find some warm—"

Gray held up a hand, stopping Helix. "I think we got the visual." He looked to Zane. "Who is she? She must be rather important."

"She is," Zane replied unequivocally.

Gray read the undertone and saw the pinched expression on Zane's face. "What's wrong? Is she in trouble?"

"Her brother was thrown into the arena, forced to fight against his will. He'll die if I can't help." Fire appeared around Zane's fist. A few people passing in the street remarked in fear, pointing, but Zane ignored them. "I won't let him die."

Gray exchanged a look with the others.

"Uh, are you all thinking what I'm thinking? Same girl?" Helix asked.

Gray nodded. *Too much of a coincidence. The strings of Farhaven.* "Zane, you're going to want to hear what Ayva has to say."

With a concerned expression, looking toward the colosseum, Zane relented.

Pulling them out of the heart of the busy street into a little abandoned stall that looked like a fruit seller, Ayva explained. She told him everything as concisely as possible. From her meeting with the queen, taking the place of Sasha *as Sasha*, wearing her cloth mask. She pulled it out of her pocket for emphasis. Coming finally to her fight against the Vile One. She reassured him Sasha was in safe hands with the Thieflord of Flesh. As soon as she finished, Zane's whole demeanor—which Gray had sensed was a flame ready to burst into an inferno—shifted. He breathed a sigh of relief. The fire, the worry, and the uncertainty in his eyes dimmed.

"Burn me," Zane cursed, "that's good news… Feels like the first piece in a long while." He ran a hand through his now shoulder-length, shaggy brown hair, which framed his sharp jaw with several week's growth. He eased back to lean against the cold clay wall, and his shoulders slumped in relief. He admitted, "I couldn't let another innocent…" He swallowed the last word, but Gray knew. They all knew that he was talking about Hannah. "Not again," Zane swore vehemently.

"Sasha's safe," Ayva reassured him.

"With the Thieflord of Flesh…are you sure?"

"Certain," Ayva said. "Well, as certain as we can be about anything now. She was after Faye, something about uniting the Thiefdoms."

Gray made a thoughtful sound. "I expected as much."

Helix replied, "Sounds like Faye's going to be helpful as long as we can survive."

"I…" Zane began. "I still need to tell her. Tell Raina."

"Raina, that's her name?" Gray asked.

Zane gave a single nod.

Gray read something there. However, the swirling cloud of uncertainty in Zane's gaze and his tight-lipped expression showed the Ronin of Fire would give no more information. After all, they'd only just brought him back into the fold. No need to push it.

Helix picked up a leftover pear, a wrinkled thing that'd been left in one of the baskets. He bit into it, and said around a crunchy mouthful, "Well, Zane's going to go have a little lover's reunion. What are we doing now? I'm exhausted, but…" He eyed the shuttling clouds, like molten pewter spilled into a black cauldron, spreading across the sky. "The night's still young."

"I'm going to bed," Gray said. "Remember? Ayva, Zane, and I have a fight to the death tomorrow."

"Oh, right," Helix chuckled, scratching his head. "Speaking of, where am I sleeping anyway?"

Ayva smiled. "Oh, about that. The queen might be evil, but she's not uncivil. She has humble accommodations for you, Helix, sorry. Zane's might be a tad more luxurious due to his new status."

"I'd fight that more, but you are the ones that have to fight to the death tomorrow," Helix said, yawning. "Try to get some sleep!" He left them, sauntering down the corridor.

"You don't even know where your rooms are!" Ayva called to his back.

Helix waved over his shoulder. "I'll figure it out!"

"Well," Zane said, eyeing Gray and her, "I guess this is—"

Ayva rushed forward and wrapped her arms around his wide frame. She pulled away and he chuckled. "I was just going to say goodnight."

Ayva smiled. "I'm glad you're back, and thanks for coming to our aid before."

Zane gave a bit of a sheepish, almost guilty look, then smiled. "It was nothing. I'm…sorry I was such a wool-for-brains for so long. Can't promise I'll be as open as I'd like, but I'll try."

Gray gripped his friend's shoulder. "Take all the time you need."

"As long as you don't leave us again," Ayva said, glaring, and planting her hands on her hips.

"I don't plan on it. Hannah would never forgive me." Then he bid them good night, asking a servant to guide him to his new rooms.

Ayva, however, lingered in the hall for a moment.

"Ayva? Something wrong?" Gray asked.

"Things are about to change quickly, aren't they?"

It didn't seem like the question she'd wanted to ask as she bit her lip, looking away. "Am I missing something?"

She looked up at him as if wanting to say more, then she shook her head. "It's nothing. I'm fine. Probably just need some rest. Don't think we've gotten proper sleep in a few days, so I might be going a tad loopy."

"Yeah." He rubbed the back of his head with a laugh. "I suppose sleep before a giant tournament to the death is a good thing."

She smiled at his attempt at humor. "Good night, Gray." Without another word, she left him standing in the hall.

Gray scratched his head. *I really don't understand women. How about you, Morrowil? Any chance they get easier to figure out?*

Morrowil sent a mental shrug. *Kail asked similar questions, so I can only assume no.*

Zane made his way to his rooms. The servant who showed him the way, a young woman, kept glancing over her shoulder at Zane, as if making sure he was still following. The halls were quieter now save for a scattering of attendants in red-and-tan livery, a few couriers, and a handful of guards roaming the halls with tired expressions, stifling yawns. Abruptly, the girl spoke, timidly, but mustering her voice as she slowed down to allow Zane to catch up. "Are you really...are you really the Ronin of Fire?"

"I am," Zane said.

Big brown eyes flickered away, avoiding his gaze. "I...I cheered for you."

"When I was a monster?"

She giggled. "No, when that disguise fell. You didn't seem like a monster anyway."

They took another corner. "Thanks," he said.

"You're my favorite," she blurted.

Zane chuckled, eyeing her. She was smaller, likely sixteen or seventeen, with curly brown hair. "Is that so? Not the Ronin of Wind? Or the Grand Primus?"

She shook her head. "Grand Primus Nalia? She scares me."

"I don't?"

The serving girl shook her head. "No. You're not evil."

"That's good to hear. Not everyone shares your opinion."

Then she spoke again as they turned down a torchlit hallway. Pausing, she wrung her hands, asking nervously, "Are you...are you going to save us? Save Covai?"

The door to his room opened, and Raina was there. She leaned against the doorframe, her arms folded across her chest, giving him that characteristic flirty, slightly aloof look as she took in the two of them. She was dressed in her well-fitted tan-and-brown cloth. Half of her head was shaved, the rest of it was black that cascaded in gentle waves to her slender shoulders. Wait, black? Had it always been black? Or this dark? Her small nose wrinkled in amusement, seeing them. Her sun-kissed skin seemed darker today. He forgot she could change that, could change *anything* really. However, the essence of Raina was the same and seemed immutable.

Raina's light, expressive wheat-colored eyes took him in, and they sparkled with mirth, scanning him up and down—for an injury? Then they flickered between him and the servant girl. "Did I interrupt something?"

Zane opened his mouth to answer first, but before he could, the young woman mumbled a quick apology, then bowed low. "Your quarters, my Lord Ronin. I wish you luck in the games tomorrow." Then she scurried away.

Zane was left scratching his head.

Raina chuckled. "Lords, Zane, how many women are you trying to collect? She's a little young, don't you think?"

He began to protest. Seeing her, the sound fell into a laugh. "How did you find me?" Then he remembered. "Raina, Sasha is—"

"Back at home. Funny thing, I went to look for you, but a strange, sort of terrifying woman found me first. Turns out she was the Thieflord of Flesh? Sasha was with her. He's safe, thanks to you."

Zane laughed. "I wish I could claim I had a part, but that was all Ayva's doing. I just unceremoniously got handed a win."

"I saw your fight. Only it didn't look as one-sided as you're saying." She flipped a lock of hair off her shoulder. "Anyway, if your friend hadn't saved Sasha, you would've." She looked him up and down.

"What's with the furrowed brow? You look like you just had a run-in with a devil."

Zane glowered, thinking of Merrick. The man was a demon. Worse, he'd matched blows with Zane. That hatred, that seething, cold savagery. Merrick needed to be stopped, and Zane wanted to be the one to do it, if only to prevent him from hurting any of his friends. "It's a long story."

"I'm not going anywhere. Heard you got some fancy accommodations, so I decided to come soak up some of your lavish lifestyle." She rapped her knuckles on the door behind him.

"How did you—"

"Thieflords," Raina explained. "Turns out they're fairly well connected."

Zane was bone-tired, but the notion of spending time with Raina sounded nice, and despite his exhaustion, the thought got his pulse racing a little and his blood hot.

Raina nudged the door open wider with an elbow, revealing the ornate room within, and gestured for him to enter. "Don't worry. I know you've got an early day." Then she gave him a mischievous smile. "I'll try not to keep you up all night." Then she shrugged. "No promises."

Gray retreated into his rooms, finding them empty. Hati was nowhere to be seen. He took only enough time to unstrap Morrowil before he flopped onto the crisp sheets of his bed. He released a tired breath, then his head hit the pillow and the embrace of deep sleep took Gray.

His dreams were fitful and vivid.

Images of Covai under siege, of battles on the sands, and of Queen Imala's cruel expression as she watched from her balcony. Merrick, the Ronin of Metal, had a prominent position in his nightmares, often shooting the black metal bow and killing him, Ayva, or Zane. The Earthstone altering whole swaths of land, and Nefrin, the red-robed Reaver, burning and cackling.

A hundred different dreams. Well, mostly nightmares.

Gray woke in a sweat, gripping the sheets. With a sigh, he sagged back into bed, urging sleep, knowing he needed it. But it wouldn't come. The room was stuffy, so he opened the double doors to the balcony, letting in the cool night air. For a moment, as he looked out, he was captivated by the sleeping city. Some lights still flickered across the desert kingdom, and he needed a brief respite from his thoughts to reassure himself that this was reality. His nightmares of fires burning everything in sight, of saeroks, vergs, and nameless descending on the kingdom like a dark shadow still lingered. So instead of returning into his room, he slid his back down the balcony wall, gaze unfocused. The flickering lights of the city, the smell of the desert, the cool air, and the faint breeze lulled him back to sleep.

When he awoke in the morning, he found himself back in his bed. *How did I...*

Shaking himself, he dressed, this time in his traditional off-white shirt, dark pants, black belt, and boots. Finally, he grabbed Morrowil. Leaving his bedroom, he found the table in the center of his chamber filled with an assortment of food: sliced and peeled fresh fruit of vibrant colors, a bowl filled with scrambled eggs, and a big plate piled with buttered bread, and slices of crisp meat from an animal Gray didn't recognize.

Hati appeared from a side room carrying a pitcher of water. She wore a fitted white dress with gold embroidery around the neckline, and she looked stunning. The dress fit her body perfectly, revealing the subtle curve of her slender waist and her hips, and it had a neckline that, while not plunging, drew the eye and made Gray's throat tighten and his pulse race.

"Hati," Gray said, surprised, choking on a piece of bread he'd just bitten into.

She gave a small curtsy. "My Lord Ronin. I've been waiting for you."

A curtsy? Normally, she just dipped her head in greeting. "Me? What'd I do?"

"I am your servant, or have you forgotten?"

"Right," he said, clearing his throat. He sort of had. He didn't really view her as his servant. That seemed too strange. He eyed her well-fitted white dress. "I like your outfit. You look nice this morning."

She raised a brow.

Gray clarified, rubbing the back of his head, "I mean, you always look nice."

Her brow lifted higher.

"That is, I know I haven't known you very long, but…what I mean to say is, you're dressed well." She just stared at him. "Gods, that sounds awkward, doesn't it? I mean, not just your dress, you are—"

She held up a hand, saving him. "Message received, well and good."

"Thank the gods. That surely has to be worse than anything I'm going to face on the sands today." She chuckled, breaking into a smile. "You know you could have spared me that torment, right?" Gray said, picking up an apple from the table. "Literally, at any point."

"I rather liked watching you sweat," she said. "Speaking of which, I've requested to watch the games today." A grin broke out on her face. "The answer was 'yes'." She clasped her hands in front of her. "I'm eager to see you compete."

Gray rubbed a hand through his hair. "I'm sure the fights today will be something to remember."

"I'm more excited to watch *you*," Hati said directly.

"Oh…well," he said, rubbing the back of his neck and smiling. "I'm honored."

Hati gestured to the table filled with food.

Gray pulled out a chair. "Only if you join me."

Hati, a hint of mirth in her pale green eyes, inclined her head and sat.

They ate in comfortable silence, stealing small looks at one another, and then through the thick walls, the drums of the tournament echoed.

Gray's heart hammered, blood stirring.

Hati's hand tightened on the spoon in her hand, and she looked up, gazing in the direction of the arena.

"It's time," Gray said.

"So it seems." Hati wiped her mouth daintily, then approached a table with a canvas backpack on it. She grabbed the bag, handing it to Gray. "I made this for you. You will be hungry. It has plenty of food and anything else you might need." He rooted through it quickly, noticing bread, hard cheese, dried meat, as well as poultices, and even a few sheafs of paper. "For notes." She shrugged. "Analyzing your opponents."

"Helpful." Then he pulled out one of a handful of shiny green and red apples. There were easily six or seven of different shades and varieties. "That's a lot of apples."

Hati rubbed her arm, looking self-conscious for the first time. "I…I noticed you like them. Was I wrong?"

Gray eagerly bit into one, grinning. "Not wrong at all." Swiftly, he strapped on his cloak and Morrowil, as well as his Devari blade. It was given to him in Farbs by Dimitri, whose brother had fallen in the Battle of the Sands. He'd yet to fully unlock the sword; mostly he'd carried it around in honor of his Devari brother. Something told him he might need it today. Finally, he shouldered Hati's pack, then moved to the door.

Hati glided forth like a breeze and opened it.

"Thanks, I probably could have done that myself, but you—"

Hati rushed forward and wrapped her arms around him, cutting him short.

Gray just stood there, frozen.

Before he could do anything, the woman pulled away, composing herself by smoothing her dress and taking an even breath. She bowed her head. "I will cheer for you. You will find me in the eastern stands."

"I'll look for you."

Hati opened her mouth, closed it. Then she opened it again. "There is more we can discuss when you get back."

More… Gray thought. Curious, and puzzled, he gave a slow but firm nod. "Gladly. As long as it's over food." Then, with a little swagger, he added, "Don't worry. I'm not that easy to kill."

She gave a small nod and smiled, then looked up, hearing the drums grow louder. "Go now. They're waiting."

With a final nod, Gray slipped out the door and followed the bond, finding Ayva and Helix on a private balcony. No Zane, however.

"Well, look who it is, Mister Sleepyhead!" Helix proclaimed.

Gray stretched, feeling a vigor in his bones. "Hati made me breakfast *and* made us this"—he held up the pack—"to stay well nourished." He tossed Helix an apple that the Ronin of Water caught with a thin spear of ice. Gray offered one to Ayva.

"*Us* a bag, or *you* a bag?"

He shrugged. "Same thing?"

"Uh-huh."

After finishing his apple, Helix pawed at the pack. "What other snacks?"

Gray offered the backpack to him. "So what'd I miss?"

They all sat facing the sands, feeling the suspense building.

Ayva shrugged. "Nothing really. I don't think we're up for a while."

"Good. We watch," Gray said. "Learn."

"Okay, Jivran," Helix remarked, gnawing on some dried meat.

"Helix, don't eat all the food!" Ayva chided.

"What? I'm hungry."

"You're not even competing!"

He shrugged. "Hey, watching is exhausting."

The fights scheduled next were lower seeds, with rumors that a Lightguard was going to fight.

Leading Gray to remember that day he'd met Lord Nolan, when they'd all ventured into the Great Kingdom of Sun. Of course, Gray had been a little… preoccupied at the time. He'd been slowly dying from an unresolved blood pact with Faye, the result of not learning *Si'tu'ah*. Leaving the others, Darius and he had flown off to find Faye, stumbling upon the woman in Farbs, where Gray had finally resolved the pact made in blood moments before he'd kicked the bucket. Meanwhile, Ayva and the others had embarked on a mission to save Vaster from a plague—one tied to the missing Sword of Sun, and the diminishing power of the Sunroad. After a long, hard-fought battle, Ayva, with Zane's help, had recovered the famed blade.

Now Gray saw Ayva bore Aurora at her hip, the gleaming weapon with its golden sheath, the cross guard in the shape of a sun, and a small burning star in the pommel. It was a sleek weapon, elegant and resplendent—truly the work of a legendary craftsman.

"Your sword, you got it back?" Gray commented in surprise.

Ayva snorted. "Found it in my room. Delivered with a note." She handed him a folded piece of parchment, words scrawled in a quick, fluid script.

We will meet soon.

—Irasa, Thieflord of Flesh

Pieces of a puzzle, so many of them, he thought, *slowly coming together.*

"So, rumor on the street is that a Lightguard is in the next match. What's the deal with them, Ayva?" Helix asked, nibbling on some dates drizzled with honey, which made his fingers sticky so he'd periodically have to lick them.

Ayva seemed to be trying not to look, but couldn't seem to pry her eyes away as honey ran down Helix's forearm. "Helix… c'mon…."

"Imma keep doing this until you answer my question," he replied, offering her a sticky date.

She rolled her eyes. "Fine fine, you win. But what do you mean? You know as well as I that Lightguards are elite warriors from Vaster, like Fleshgaurds."

"Right but what's their special ability? Moonguards can disappear into shadows, Fleshguard like Drega can withstand pain far past the limits of a normal mortal, and heal wounds quicker, too. Hidden are… we'll they're just terrifying." He shivered.

Gray knew Helix was speaking of both Rydel and an elf named Hadrian, someone Darius had mentioned. Gray had heard whispers of a third Hidden. Somehow it was tied to the war in Eldas. A war that even involved Mura. Gray felt like his heart was in so many places, but he shook his head, focusing.

"Then there's Devari," Helix continued, motioning to Gray and his cloak with the crossed swords emblem. "With your odd ability to sense others' emotions. Since they're from the Great Kingdom of Fire… you'd think they could use fire, but maybe they forgot?"

"Soulwed blades are their closest connection to fire," Gray replied, touching the blade on his back.

"Soulwed?" Helix asked.

"Turning a Devari blade aflame," Gray answered. "I can't do it yet, if you're wondering. It's what separates me from a full-fledged Devari."

"Oh, that's a great trick." Helix raised his hand, trying to flag down a vendor selling food.

"Really?" Ayva asked.

"What?! I worked up an appetite!"

"You've just been watching… "

"And it's exhausting." He waved. "Ohh, I think he has those sticky honey glazed ribs—"

Drums cut him off and the announcer took the balcony beside the queen and nobles. After taking a deep breath, he spoke, his voice thundering across the vast arena. "Welcome all, to the third round of the Great Tournament of Flesh! Today is a momentous day. As our challengers are culled, those that remain are ever stronger! Today, for our first fight, let's welcome your two combatants…"

Two men stepped onto the sands.

One a barbarian, wearing thick pelts.

On the other side, a Lightguard, armored in a shimmering yellow plate, all of it engraved with symbols of Sun and elegant scrollwork.

"To the west," he said, gesturing to the Lightguard, who stood solemnly, hands together in prayer, "a famed warrior. Lightguard are among the nine elites of Farhaven—their prowess matched only by their brethren! It is said a Lightguard can fight longer and harder when the sun is high in the sky. No one can match their stamina, speed, and ferocity as long as the day is bright! Renowned for never losing hope, I give you…Titus, Lightguard of Vaster!"

"Oh, right, there's your answer about what makes Lightguard special," Ayva said. "Sorry, I guess we got a little sidetracked."

"Huh. Fight longer and full of optimism. That checks out," Helix replied, popping another date in his mouth.

Titus raised his sword, and it reflected the sunlight.

"Nice touch," Gray said, then glanced to Ayva and smirked. "Taking notes?"

Ayva smiled. "Oh, we can save taking notes until my fight."

Helix clapped them both on the back. "This is great! You'd think you both weren't going to your possible doom soon!"

They both glared at him.

He shrank back. "What? Don't look at me like that! If I was really worried about you, I wouldn't jest!"

The announcer turned to his left, his tattooed, bony hand gesturing grandly. "To the east," he said, gravitas filling his deep voice, taking it down to a more ominous tone, "a deadly barbarian from the Wilds of Teras. Famed for their brutality, for their ruthlessness, and for their depravity." The announcer's voice dripped with malevolence. The barbarian breathed deeply, his chest rising and falling, as if going into a battle trance. "It is said, even among the most fearsome of his tribe, all fear the beast who has no soul." That man's eyes were black, devoid of any humanity. Gray wondered, was he turned? Darkened?

Ayva sent a mental note, *Is he like the Terma we saw before? His eyes…*

Gray shook his head. *Not sure. We'll need to watch him carefully.*

The announcer was building to a crescendo. "…having killed every one of his opponents, countless warriors said to have been cleaved by his great axe or smashed to a pulp by his giant war hammer…I give you, the terrible monster, the vicious beast, the ruthless savage from the east…Egrin the Barbarian!" he bellowed.

Egrin roared, a deep primal outcry that echoed through the stands. It even stifled the crowd's applause for a moment, like a rush of wind, which redoubled with twice as much force.

Ayva put her hands to her ears. "Please let this guy lose this match."

"The bad ones never do," Gray said.

Helix stuffed more dates into his mouth. "So true!"

"He's back." Gray gestured, directing their attention to the queen's balcony.

Nefrin stepped forward on the balcony, showing himself. His half-pink face and his hair, slowly growing back across his scarred scalp, was still a shock to see. He was mostly healed, but Zane's damage had left its mark. Nefrin acted unaffected. If anything, he seemed to relish their reactions. The four-stripe Reaver grinned. "Can I face him in the arena?" Ayva asked.

"Feels like that's more of a job for Zane," Gray said. "Also, at this rate, first the queen, then Nefrin. I think you want to face everyone."

"Just the evil ones," she replied, then admitted, "Which is pretty much everyone."

Helix snorted in laughter as he licked his fingers.

Ayva rolled her eyes. "Do you really have to do that?"

"What? They're sticky!"

"You know you have a way of cleaning them, right?" Gray posed. "You're literally the Ronin of Water."

"Oh yeah," Helix replied, and aptly sprayed a thin jettison of water that washed his hands; he let the rest drip to the floor and then stuck out his wet hands. "Sun? Wind? Mind drying them?"

Ayva glared at him, folding her arms across her chest. "No way. I'm not your towel."

Gray sighed, waving a hand, and a bit of wind rushed outward.

"Gray! Don't indulge him. You're a Ronin, and he just reduced you to a glorified hand dryer."

"Consider it an honor," Helix said, bowing from the waist. Then he sniffed. "You two weren't complaining when I made your drinks cold."

True enough; they both had chilled drinks at their side, courtesy of Helix.

Gray shrugged. "If I no longer have to watch sticky-fingered Helix lick them, it's a small price to pay."

Ayva nodded in concession. "Fair enough."

"Hush, hush," Helix said pointing. "The match is about to start!"

The thundering drums, a constant echo, slowed, building the anticipation, the tension.

Thud.

Thud.

Thud.

The final strike, then silence.

Both warriors with eyes locked and every citizen poised on the edge of their seats.

"Fight!" the announcer bellowed.

The two charged.

Egrin right away ran and leapt, hammer coming down with a strike that would have crushed a boulder to pebbles. Titus raised his sword, but in the last moment, he must have realized he couldn't parry a strike like that and leapt back. The hammer smashed into the ground, thundering, creating a divot in the hard-packed sand much deeper than it should have.

"Magic?" Ayva asked.

Gray nodded.

The crowd roared.

Egrin wasn't done. He swung again, and the Lightguard dodged it, then cut with his sword. The strike caught Egrin, grazing fingers and drawing blood, and the hammer slipped from his grip. Titus advanced, seeing his opening. He slashed using a perfect series of sword forms that seemed terribly familiar to Gray. *Lightguard moves must have some similarity to Devari forms.*

He knew the next form before it happened, seeing the way Titus set his feet.

"Thresher Cleaves the Grain meets The Adder's Bite," Gray guessed.

"What?" Helix asked.

Ayva also cast him a perplexed look.

He pointed.

Sure enough, Titus delivered a curving side slash that the barbarian evaded, which set up perfectly for Titus's thrust. A thing of beauty. It clipped Egrin's side, cutting his thick muscled torso, making the man roar.

"How did you…" Helix began.

"Devari memories," Ayva guessed.

Gray nodded with a smile. "They come and go."

"Seems like our barbarian friend is about to go," Helix said.

The crowds roared as Egrin lost his balance, falling backward.

Titus advanced, marching with cool, calm, collected steps, still in a partial Low Moon crouch.

Gray's blood boiled, now he *wanted* to fight Titus, to test his mettle.

For a moment, he was taken back, a flashing memory to a battle on the ramparts between two men, where he leapt off a merlon, landing on Ren, making their swords clash, and—

Egrin was suddenly on his feet again, roaring.

He grabbed two axes from his belt that had been covered by his thick pelts. They were huge black blades, with keen edges that glinted in the light. Egrin charged. With a fury of strikes, he laid into Titus with uncanny speed.

"Is he faster?" Helix asked, leaning forward.

"I've heard of this," Ayva said, "blood curses, or blood magic… Maybe a flesh spell someone cast on him, or cast on himself? When they're hurt, they go into a sort of frenzy. Berserker, some call it. It has its downsides, though. You run out of energy quicker. Worse, if it's not your own spell, you expend more of your spark, shortening your life."

"I don't think he cares about that," Helix said.

Here and there, Titus scored a flick of a strike, cutting a shoulder, or forearm.

This proved to be a mistake.

Egrin roared, moving faster still.

The crowds thundered, chanting his name.

Titus dodged a slice to his throat, then waved his hand, and a ray of sun flared from his palm. It was blinding.

Egrin's relentless attack halted.

"That's cheating," Helix said.

"It's sun magic, not cheating!" Ayva shot back.

Titus used the moment, crying out as he raised his sword to slash Egrin, who was covering his eyes. It was over. The sword descended.

Egrin, still half blind, threw his axe.

A blind toss.

Hurtling end over end, it sliced across Titus's face. Not a killing blow, just a graze across the Lightguard's cheek. Yet it saved Egrin's life.

Blinking against the flash, Egrin's eyes fixed on Titus, all fury, bloodshot, and full of overpowering rage. Titus raised his sword, and gestured with his hand, as if to cast another flash of light. Egrin's other axe flew. It connected, slicing the hand off at the wrist. Titus roared in sudden agony, falling to his knees.

"Oh gods..." Ayva remarked.

The crowds' roars grew to a feverous pitch.

As if all hope was lost, but true to the announcer's spiel, Titus pressed his hand against the bloody stump, searing flesh and cauterizing the wound. Then he picked up his sword once more. Luckily for Titus, the axe hadn't taken his sword arm. Casually, almost calmly, Egrin moved. He didn't reach for another blade. He just turned to the crowds, a giant grin across his ghastly face. Looking closer now, Gray saw the hollowness in his cheeks, his flesh taut against his bones. The once tanned flesh now looked a little more ashen, as if a good portion of his spark, his life force, had been drained in the last few clashes alone. He didn't seem to care.

"He's not picking up a weapon..." Helix remarked. "What's he doing?"

"Winning the crowd," Gray said.

Sure enough, the masses responded, eating it up, the colosseum shaking with their approval.

Titus just bared his teeth, and blood still lightly dripped from his now-burnt stump of a wrist.

In his eyes, an unbreakable determination.

The Lightguard roared, charging.

Titus raised his sword, sun gleaming off the bright steel.

Egrin remained turned, clearly watching, though, from the corner of his eye.

"No…" Gray said, seeing the move before it came.

Egrin read the man, as if he knew the Lightguard forms. With their back turned, a fighter has a few moves, the most common being Fisher in the Shallows, to Waning Sun. A slicing strike to the body—a feint—which the foe attempts to parry, only to redirect the blade into an overhead strike, cutting downward. Egrin knew all this. Titus's sword lashed out, aiming for Egrin's torso, but it was too slow, the momentum clearly intended to redirect for his head after the attempted parry.

The parry never came.

Egrin pulled an axe from beneath his thick pelts and swung it overhead, in Waning Sun.

The arcing strike found its mark, cleaving Titus from head to groin.

The man fell over, parted in two, blood spilling.

The crowd erupted.

Helix gaped, dropping his food.

Ayva covered her mouth, but didn't avert her gaze, forcing herself not to look away.

"You don't have to watch." Gray muted the crowd's roar with a wave of his hand, and with a hard edge to his voice said, "This isn't necessary."

Slowly, she removed her hand from her mouth and straightened. "Yes, yes it is," she said after a moment. "Worse atrocities are soon to be committed by an evil far greater. I don't have to like this, but I can't shy my gaze away." Titus's bloody corpse disintegrated into orange vapor, and Egrin spread his arms wide, breathing it in. He was still growing stronger. Gray knew he'd be a formidable opponent. Especially if he knew Devari and Lightguard forms.

After that fight, the next one was far less climactic.

The contest matched two powerful Fleshguard, a muscle-bound man and a lean one. After a dazzling display of swordsmanship, the bigger man surrendered when a sword found the nape of his neck, and the other advanced.

"All these fighters are so strong," Helix said. "I wonder who is next."

As he said this, the gates opened, and out stepped a three-stripe Reaver.

"My coin's on her," Helix said. "Three-stripe Reaver with the look of death in her eyes? I feel sorry for her opponent already."

"Don't," Gray said, as from the opposite gate emerged a woman, stunning enough to make a lump form in his throat. Her face was almost too perfect, and she had soft brown skin that was vaguely bark-like in its patterning. Green leaves for hair fell to her lithe shoulders, and a delicate floral crown graced her head. Her pointed, elven-like ears looked dipped in gold. The rest of her flowing garments were a strange mix of spider silk and woven gold leaves that fit a too-graceful frame; thicker bark coated her hands and arms. Emerald eyes danced with the luminescence of the woods, surveying the arena, the stands—all with an otherworldly calm.

Ayva exhaled in wonder. "Is that…a Dryad? Light! I knew they were real, but here, in the tournament?"

Helix's mouth gaped, and some of the skewered meat he was eating fell out. "Abyss take me, she's beautiful."

Gray remarked, "I saw her walking around the upper halls. I didn't know she was a combatant." He'd heard tales as well. Stories of powerful magic users, denizens of the Drymaus Forest. A place where no human dared to enter. It was said they could rapidly make any living thing grow at their will. Due to their attunement to nature, they made a Reaver look like a toddler playing with the spark. While that might be true, Gray also knew that only being able to wield one element was perhaps her weakness.

"She can only wield one element," Helix said, as if reading his mind. "Won't she still lose to a Reaver?"

"*You* can only wield one," Ayva said.

"Yeah, well, we're different."

She snorted. "How so?"

"More powerful of course."

The Dryad, wreathed in vines, stepped farther onto the field, and where she tread, flowers bloomed. "We're not just more powerful." Helix continued. "We can create magic from nothing. Beyond that, a single element can have infinite complexity. I don't think we're going to see only the usual nature- or leaf-based spells in this fight."

"To the west," the announcer said, pointing to the Reaver, "a fighter who hardly needs an introduction. However, she is a powerful wielder of magic from the famed black-spired Citadel! A three-stripe Reaver, a spark user whose rank is rarer than gold…It is said many spend decades to acquire a single stripe. Yet she has gained three stripes faster than any in her class, a pupil of our Lord Nefrin himself! I give you, Reaver Yira!"

Reaver Yira flung out a hand and fire erupted from it.

The crowd cheered.

"To the east"—the announcer's bony arm pointed grandly—"a denizen of the famed and terrifying Drymaus Forest, a place where no living man or woman dares enter! A place of magic and mystery. Alleged to be the very home of the dragons." The crowd stirred at this. All remembered the red dragon that had recently appeared within their walls. He was playing off that fear and awe. "She is a Dryad, a creature that is more magic than human. Made of bark, moss, and vine, she manipulates these with ease.

"Yet despite being pleasing to the eye…" he said with a smirk, to which the Dryad didn't even react, "she is a force to be reckoned with…having never lost a fight, a warrior with cunning in her eyes, she is a Warden of the Woods, and the strongest of her clan! I give you, Warden Eras Barkblood!"

A Warden…

Gray had heard of those, a powerful clan, much like Reavers, but an ancient sect of magic users that honed their nature skills.

"Think Darius will need to learn a thing or two from her," Helix said.

At first, there was silence, and then the crowd whispered. Gray could feel their judgment mixed with their fear, without needing the ki.

"*Drymaus…*" some whispered.

"*Dragon's den…*" came others.

Then came shouts, sporadic, but harsh and jeering. Others shouted obscenities. It was clear the crowd was prejudiced against her skin of bark and mossy eyebrows.

"Are they really booing her?" Ayva remarked, aghast, "This, the very City of Flesh, with every variety of man and beast?"

"I'm having second thoughts about saving this kingdom," Helix remarked.

Win the crowd, win the tournament. Gray shook his head. "Don't let a few bad apples spoil the lot."

"There's hundreds of bad apples, Gray," Ayva said.

"It's a herd mentality," Gray replied. "People follow, you know that. The majority are remaining silent. They're more afraid than anything."

"Of her?" Helix asked, pointing at the Dyrad. "She's breathtaking! They're not afraid of the giant who salivates for blood, or the strange, terrible monsters we've been killing?"

"She's unknown and from the most terrifying woods in all of Farhaven." Thankfully, the Dryad, Eras Barkblood, didn't seem to care. She walked on the sand as if entering an enchanted glade, oblivious to the crowd's derision.

"Fight!" the announcer bellowed.

The two clashed, not wasting any time. Fire met a wall of giant vines. The flames burned the roots, but were immediately replaced with more green, thick tubers.

"She's on the defense," Helix said.

"No. Look at her eyes," Ayva remarked. "They're calm and collected. I think she's got something up her…bark sleeve." Sure enough, her green orbs for eyes were narrowed, calculating…concentrating. A moment later, roots burst out of the ground, grabbing the Reaver's ankles and tugging. Slipping, the fire vanished from Yira's hands. Using ice, she slashed, cutting the roots holding her legs.

Before she could rise, Eras's eyes tightened more, and she raised a hand, summoning something powerful. At once, a thousand roots erupted from the sands like a giant kraken bubbling forth from the Abyss. The many roots grabbed the Reaver's legs and torso, wrapping around her, squeezing. Frantic, the Reaver cried out, shrieking as they ripped at her body, at her clothes. Gray saw there were thorns on the roots, and blood sprayed into the air. In a mad attempt to save herself, Reaver Yira abandoned her own defenses to attack the Dryad, creating a thin, shimmering oval of moon in thin air. Gray knew what she was doing. *Moon can be used to make portals…* Sure enough, Yira sent a fireball into the moon portal, and another portal appeared behind the Dryad. From it, an orange ball of fire burst as the Reaver sought to turn her opponent to ash. Only, in the last moment, Eras Barkblood waved a hand, and a cocoon of protective vines enveloped her.

The blazing fireball charred the erected barrier, yet the shimmering magic of the vines seemed to diminish the globe of destruction until it was a tiny flame, and then vanished entirely.

The cocoon unfurled like flower petals.

Eras Barkblood walked out, unscathed.

Lying on the sand, clothes ragged, blood streaming from a thousand tiny cuts, the Reaver attempted to redouble her effort, screaming as she flung out a hand. Eras sent her own magic. A dozen more vines shot out, grabbing the woman and wrapping around her neck.

Then, with a sharp twist…

Snap.

Yira lay on the sand, neck broken, eyes glazed.

It was over.

"Winner!" the announcer shouted to the roar of the crowds. "Warden Eras Barkblood!"

The crowds first reacted in confusion, stunned at this turn of events. Then as the woman absorbed the orange spark and turned to leave the sand calmly, the crowd erupted in cheers.

"A fickle bunch," Helix muttered.

"She's impressive," Ayva said. "Her nature is on another level. Darius could learn a thing or two from her."

Helix snorted in agreement. "Right? What was that shimmering vine? Almost like the spell itself was infused with some sort of bloodstone that nullified magic. That blazing fireball should have definitely ended her."

"Another person to be wary of," Gray said.

After that battle, the next few went quickly and were also less impressive.

A pirate versus another Reaver, a two-stripe. The pirate won.

The Moonguard came out again, and put down a giant bear of a man with ease.

Two more fights came and went.

All the while, Gray's eyes watched the central pillar and the cerulean shield that guarded what lay within: the Earthstone.

"You know, we were supposed to get our other items," Ayva said, eyeing the band on Helix's arm.

"Hati said we were supposed to get them before our fights, but considering yours wasn't a fight as a Ronin, and mine was…preemptive…Still, apparently the queen will be sending them to us soon," Gray replied.

Helix snorted. "We know how often she keeps her word."

"She likes a spectacle," Gray said again. "I think we'll get them."

A moment later, a Covian guard arrived on the balcony, accompanied by a familiar face, Drega, and a second, Captain Leanna. The three Ronin rose and greeted them.

"Ah, no need to rise for me!" Drega said, slapping Gray on the back with a hand. Gray rubbed his now-bruised shoulder blade and noticed the leader of the Fleshguard was a tad more armored than before. Thick, layered leather snugly fit his wide door-brushing frame, though it did nothing to impede his movements. His sonorous, rumbling voice filled their small balcony, as if he were speaking to a crowd preparing for war—rather than their small trio. "You all look like you've fared well! I even heard you had a bit of fun in the districts last night."

Captain Leanna raised a brow. "I heard about that, too. Something about fire and metal clashing?" Gray took Leanna in more closely. The woman wore leather armor, engraved with tribal-like etchings. He considered her practical haircut, as if she'd chopped it with a knife, and armor that hid her curves, along with her stern expression, Gray imagined the woman viewed her beauty as a nuisance. Gray could read just a faint hint of amusement and a bit of boredom coming from her. There was clearly far more to the woman, layers of buried emotions, and the ki sensed a restlessness.

Gray came back to the moment. "Right...should have figured you'd hear about our tavern altercation."

Leanna gave a surreptitious nod to Ayva.

Ayva returned it.

What was that about? Gray asked through the bond.

Ayva sent back, *Oh, just a little help from a friend.*

Leanna spoke, asking coolly, "Where's your other friend?" Gray detected a suggestion of interest in her tone as her gaze panned across their balcony—as if she expected someone could be hiding beneath one of the few tables and chairs. "The one who speaks fire. The *ca'ran*."

Ca'ran? Gray spoke a small bit of Sand tongue. *Does that mean...Chosen?*

Ayva echoed his thoughts. *Chosen? I think our Captain Leanna might have a crush on our Ronin of Fire.*

Who doesn't? Helix complained. *Zane's got to teach me how he does it.*

"Zane's...preoccupied at the moment," Gray answered.

Leanna's thin dark brow arched again. The only emotion on her otherwise emotionless face. "Is that so?"

Ayva sighed. "Honestly, it's like wrangling cats. You get one Ronin, and another sees a ball of yarn, starts batting at it. Swear, Farhaven could have chosen toddlers and I'd have more success in bringing them together."

"Hey!" Helix exclaimed. "That's old Helix."

Gray groused, *We're not that bad.*

No, I suppose not. You used to be! You running off for the blood pact, hiding your curse, Helix gallivanting about Median, and Darius being…Darius.

Looking at their past, Gray admitted Ayva had a point. *I think now Darius would probably defend himself and say he'd turned over a new leaf.*

Leanna snorted. "Sounds like you've got your work cut out for you."

Drega, a warm smile gracing his well-defined features, nostrils flaring in mirth, boomed, "Ha! You all are just as entertaining as ever! Tell me, how have you been enjoying the fights?"

"Bloody," Ayva said, taking a sip of her drink.

"And spectacular!" Helix added, offering Drega a skewer of meat.

Drega declined it warmly. "Too kind, young legend of Water! Alas, I do not partake in food or drink before a fight. A rule of mine. My only appetite will be what wets my blade."

Ayva asked, "Wait, is it your turn?"

"Oh, better than that," Drega remarked, his dark bristly brows furrowing with delight. "It's *our* turn."

As if to echo his point, the drums of battle thundered.

LEGENDS IN THE SANDS

With Gray and Helix at her side, Ayva followed Drega and Captain Leanna into the bowels of the colosseum. Drega and Ayva would be fighting next, but not necessarily against each other. She wouldn't know who she was fighting until the gates opened. Apparently, for this fight, they all stood at their respective entrances until the announcer called their name. As they reached the depths, Gray cleared his throat. "Mind if I have a moment with Ayva?"

Drega and Leanna exchanged a look.

Helix sent, *What am I missing?*

Nothing, Gray sent. *Just some quick advice before her battle.*

"Be quick, young legends," Drega cautioned. "The next match will begin at any moment!"

Gray pulled Ayva aside. He gently placed his hands on her shoulders and gazed into her eyes. They looked unusually tired, with dark circles under them. He worried how much sleep she'd gotten. "Ayva, what's going on?"

She rubbed her arm. "Nothing."

He leveled a look at her. "Ayva…I don't need the ki, or the bond. I know you. What is it? You tried to ask me last night, but avoided it. Now I want to know."

She sighed. "Are we really doing this? Fighting each other, that is."

He nodded, turning earnest. "We have to."

"We don't just surrender?"

"No," Gray said.

She leveled him with a look. "Gray, I'm not going to kill you."

"Oh, so you think you can?"

Ayva planted her fists on her hips. "I'm serious."

Gray dropped his hands and sighed. "Nor I you, obviously." He paused, and looked up and out to the stands. He'd been doing that more lately, seeing the citizens as if they were a key to all this. "We can't fake it, Ayva. Or just surrender immediately. We have to win the crowds."

"So we fight for real."

He gave a roll of his shoulders. "No other way than to truly test our limits."

She heaved a heavy breath, her resolve solidifying. "Okay. Let's give them something worthy of applause."

Gray nodded, a glint in his gray-green eyes. "Couldn't have said it better myself."

A moment later, after walking onward and reaching the arena's gate, Drega asked for a moment with Ayva. He stood before her with his thick, dark brows furrowed. Then he grabbed her hands in his and gently placed something within her palm. She looked down, eyeing a golden ring. Her heart leapt. Magic. She felt it. The flow was coursing through the ring. "I believe this is yours," Drega said.

Omni's ring.

She'd heard stories of it, a famed magical artifact crafted by Renalin's own son, a being of light.

"You know I might use this against you…"

A wolfish smirk was Drega's answer. "I'd love nothing more and expect nothing less. Do you know how to use it?"

Ayva touched the sun in her mind, sending a ray of light into the gold ring. It bloomed a brilliant, almost blinding luminescence. As she did, she felt the well of her magic deepen. Her magical reserves were growing. Before, her power might've felt like a giant golden lake that she could dip her fingers into, but she was slowly learning to cup more and more, and drink deeply. Now, that lake grew wider and deeper as if becoming a sea, and one day an ocean. Glancing down, she saw that a faint golden radiance wreathed her limbs.

Drega's dark eyes narrowed. "A wise man should rightfully fear giving the ring to you."

She looked up at him. "And you? Do you fear me?"

He smiled. "If ever there was one to fear, it would be you." His eyes pierced her. A small part of Ayva wanted to blush. Only she met his gaze. "Good luck," he told her.

With final words and embraces, Ayva moved to her gate, watching the others go.

Alone, standing before the portcullis that led into the arena, she gazed down at her hands and saw they were shaking. She clenched them into fists. Ahead, two men fought on the sands—the match before hers. A blow was struck, and the crowds roared. Glancing back, Ayva saw her two Covian guards. They stood at attention at the mouth of the tunnel, watching her fearfully.

Ayva breathed in. *I got this.*

Purpose filled her heart.

The last match ended, and she saw the winning warrior imbibing the spark of the fallen before being escorted off. The rusty iron gate slowly grated open. Wrapping her cloth mask about her face, Ayva stepped into the arena to the roar of the crowds.

Her fear was gone.

The drums beat to the rhythm once more.

Ayva spoke the words aloud, as if to breathe life into them, "I will give them something worthy of praise."

Gray and Helix followed Captain Leanna and Drega to his own gate. There, Leanna took up a post with a few of her Covian guards. They chatted amiably, discussing the tournament, though Leanna's eyes followed him as she waited patiently.

Gray still wondered what Captain Leanna's place was in all of this. Somehow he knew she'd play a pivotal role before the end. Meanwhile, the giant leader of the Fleshguard took a few steps back, standing like an enormous obsidian statue before the tunnel to the sands, letting the Ronin of Water have his moment.

Helix cleared his throat. "I'm not very good at inspirational speeches, so…don't die?"

Gray chuckled. It was a line that was a Darius favorite. The two were more alike than Gray ever expected. Water and Leaf. He supposed it made sense. They were also far different. He marveled at each of their true natures now slowly rising to the surface. Finally he replied, "I'll try not to."

Helix grinned and stepped back, letting Drega take his place.

The huge, broad-shoulder man squeezed Gray's shoulder, fingers casually digging in like a dragon's claw. Gray winced, but was certain the man had no idea regarding his own strength. "Ha! Young legend of Wind! You truly are a fascinating one. I still can't believe you abandoned your position of Primarian. Never has that been done before. It was a brave move."

Gray smiled. "One man's bravery is another man's foolishness."

"Ha! Very true!" Drega replied. "However, I've seen enough to know the difference. As well as the truth of a man's heart. You are wise. In doing so, you've begun to gain the crowd's respect and mine."

Judging by the firm set of Drega's jaw and his direct gaze, the man seemed honest. The ki sensed a moment of worry? Was his ki off? He didn't think the man could feel fear—nothing but an overwhelming enthusiasm for blood and battle. Then it was gone. "Whatever happens in the coming days," Gray said, "I am honored to know you and I consider you a friend and an ally."

"Ha! You talk as if you have already paid the ferryman!" Drega snorted, his grip tightening on Gray's shoulder. "Did you not know? Legends never die, my friend. They simply grow in their retelling. And yours? Yours is a story for the ages." Drega had a canvas sack slung across his chest and he removed it, opening it now. "Of course, a hero needs his legendary items, or the bards will have to embellish." He pulled out a pair of white leather bracers, handing them over.

Gray took them reverently. The leather was firm, yet supple and smooth. After a thousand years? How was that possible? His fingers lightly grazed the markings: a symbol of wind flowing with curling zephyrs.

Curiosity compelled Gray, and he channeled some wind into the bracers.

The leather transformed to a silver metal. It wasn't steel. No, it was stronger, harder, and lighter. More wind patterns and symbols were masterfully etched into the brilliant metal, and they burned with an ethereal silver-white light.

"Bone and ash," Drega cursed, his affable nature replaced by one of awe.

The nearest guards, Helix, and Leanna also all stared in amazement.

Kail's bracers.

Helix huffed. "Well, now I'm jealous."

Gray looked up, pointing to the wave-band on his arm. "Helix, you already have Hiron's armband."

"Oh, right!"

The drums thundered.

"It's time," Captain Leanna said. "You must wait at the tunnel's entrance. You might be the next match, or the one after. The queen has instructed all combatants to take their places." She looked at Drega. "That includes you."

"Then I guess this is farewell for now," Gray said, looking away from the tunnel, back to the unlikely trio of Helix, Leanna, and Drega. He gave a deep breath. "Wish me luck."

Helix chuckled. "With that gear?" He nodded to the silver wind bracers. "Whoever you're about to face in the arena needs all the luck they can get. They'll be quaking in their boots as soon as they hear 'Kail's progeny.'"

Leanna added, "Don't lose. I've got coin on you."

"Really?" Gray asked.

She shrugged. "To be fair, I've more coin on the Ronin of Sun. So in that case, do lose."

Gray raised a brow. "Well, thanks for the vote of confidence."

"Wait, you can bet?" Helix asked. "That's not cheating?"

Leanna snorted. "I'm the Captain of the Guard, not a slave. I put silver on you, too."

Helix gave a chagrined chuckle. "Ah, well, sorry about that."

Leanna shrugged. "Don't be. It took odds on your loss, won me a fair bit of coin."

Helix grumbled.

Drega barked a laugh, wrapping his arm around Gray's shoulders, "Ha! Whatever the outcome, I'm sure you'll make a grand showing. Now go on, lad, I might be facing you soon!"

Gray nodded in thanks and headed down the tunnel to take his place.

The crowds beyond roared.

Helix's words echoed in his head.

Kail's progeny...

Fire and Sun

Ayva stepped out onto the battlefield and found, on the far end, the last person she wanted to face.

Zane, Ronin of Fire.

She took an even breath. Of course it was him.

Why us? Zane sent.

Watching from their balcony, Helix sent, *Guys? I think she knows...*

Ayva and Zane both turned to follow Helix's gaze.

The Queen's Terrace. On that balcony, filled with attendants and nobles, the queen sat on her throne, a wicked smile gracing her makeup-caked face. She'd chosen a bloodred lipstick this time, and had yet to smear it on the silver chalice in her grip.

That look in her eyes... Ayva understood. *She's figured out who I am... How?*

As if in answer, walking up to the queen's side was a familiar face that curdled Ayva's stomach.

Merrick—Ronin of Metal. He stared down, meeting Ayva's gaze in particular, those steely gray orbs holding a faint ray of mirth, though mostly an obsessive intent. The rest of his expression was simply boredom.

Well, I think we got our answer, Helix sent. *Ole Ronin-with-hate-in-his-eyes must have watched our fake Sasha battle and clued the queen to Ayva's real identity.*

Zane growled. *That bastard. I want to face him, not you,* he sent, looking to Ayva.

Don't we all? Helix sent. *Well, except for Gray.*

The bony announcer, laden with tattoos, his nostrils with thick metal piercings flared as his hands went wide, said, "Welcome all, to the third-round, upper-tier contestants! In these rounds, our most powerful contestants clash for a chance at more spark and advancement! Today, of all days, I give you something *special*. A treat, my dear citizens of Covai! A once in a lifetime spectacle... Two legends. Two mythical warriors. Their elements are so closely tied that their souls are practically wed. Today they will fight. How can one kill their own brother, or their own sister? Yet, fight they must."

A palpable tremor of tension swept through the crowds.

Whispers filled the air.

Ronin…

Legends.

The announcer, his ebony eyes—injected with ink like the rest of his tattooed body—gestured toward Ayva. "In the east corner, feast your eyes upon one of the most powerful threaders of sun to ever live! A woman who lives in the shadow of greatness. Omni the Wise. Omni the Hopeful. Or known by her less favorable title…*Omni the Destroyer*…Her legacy is one of blood, death, and power! A name revered throughout all the land, which bears many titles: Lightbringer, Dawnshard, Hope Incarnate, and if stories are true, second only to the legendary leader, Kail, Ronin of Wind…For your entertainment, I give you Ayva Yuni, Ronin of Sun!"

The crowds shouted in hysteria, wild with enthusiasm.

This was clearly a change in events, Ayva thought.

Well, no use hiding now. Ayva took off her cloth veil with a flourish to reveal her face. Which elicited another roar from the crowd.

"But wait!" the announcer cried, pulling the crowd's attention back. "In the west corner, a man who already defeated the Ronin of Water. He is a warrior of fire and flame…known by his titles in ages past as the Inferno, Incendiary, Blazeborn, Firebrand, and many others! He is an arsonist who has set the world and our hearts aflame with his raw strength! A man whose temper and fury know no bounds, I give you…Zane, Ronin of Fire!"

The crowds reacted with equal fervor.

Ayva sent to Zane, *Are we doing this?*

Zane eyed the tens of thousands in the stands, on their feet, cheering, calling out their names, then he looked back to her. *I have to fight, Ayva.*

Why? What are you even after?

It's…complicated, but I need to become Grand Primus.

You know we'd help you, whatever it is.

I swore I'd do this myself. To repay a favor. A debt of gratitude to one who saved my life.

She sighed. *That's fair, but light and heaven, I really don't want to fight you.*

Zane shrugged his heavy shoulders. *Well, then imagine it's not me.*

Ayva pictured Nefrin for a moment, his cruel half-burnt face, that black-hearted expression, and eyes full of malice. *I can do that.*

Zane grinned. *Don't hold back. I can take it.*

She heaved a deep breath. This was wrong. To just get him back, then to attack him. Clearly, though, Zane didn't want her to go easy. Then she remembered Gray's words. *Win the crowd.*

Gray was right.

So be it, she thought. The drums rumbled, their pace slowing one beat at a time, and then—

"Fight!" the announcer boomed.

Zane charged.

Ayva let him come.

Zane loosed a battle cry as he sent a column of fire racing toward her. She fell flat to the sand, flames moving above her body. The heat raced across her back, searing, scorching. She cried out in pain and rolled on the sand, putting out the flames, then rose to her feet as Zane forced more fire into his palms and sent, *You're going to have to move faster than that.*

More flames shot out from his hands.

Growling this time instead of trying to evade, Ayva sent a concentrated beam of sun to oppose the flames—hotter and brighter. The funnel of fire burst, dissipating to tiny little flames that vanished in the desert air. *Huh. Should have done that from the start.* "You call that hot?" she called.

Zane sent another torrent of fire—this time, far hotter and the color of blood.

Something told Ayva she couldn't extinguish this fire. So she erected a golden shield like a buckler. Instead of taking the attack full force, she angled her gleaming buckler, and the flames collided, then ricocheted, smashing into a nearby pillar that bristled with axes, swords, flanges, maces, and spears. Abruptly, the stone column exploded, sending weapons and stone shards into the air. The thirty-foot column groaned and crumbled.

"Was that hot enough?" Zane asked, a smirk forming on his face.

Ayva glared, picturing Nefrin. She sent a burst of light. She reached to pull the thread.

Only Zane's attack came first.

He sent a long thrashing cord of burning orange like a whip. It wrapped around her ankles. He pulled, but she formed a blade of light, severing the whip. She sent a shackle of light. He tried to sear the manacle from the air, but the golden arc flew through his flames. Zane rolled to the side, barely dodging it, then, still holding his flame-whip, he lashed.

At the last moment, Ayva formed a gauntlet of sun and snatched the whip from the air. The crowds gasped. Zane's eyes went wide.

"Nice move but…"

He tugged hard. He was stronger than her physically, and she was pulled forward, her arm nearly wrenched from its socket. She released the whip and ran at him, ducking another fireball.

More. She needed to push him more.

With her sword of light, she cut for his ankles. Zane leapt, but too slow, and the blade slashed, cutting a shallow groove into his calf.

It was only a nick.

She was trying to draw more out of him, keep his momentum of magic going.

Zane, ever the hothead, obliged.

A ball formed in his hands, not fire as much as lava. Growling, swirling with a deep ochre glow, Zane roared and hurled the meteor of fire. It was hotter than anything he'd conjured so far, and it scorched the air with malevolence. Ayva was forced to abandon her next attack. Transforming the sword of light into a gleaming gold shield once more, the globe of fire slammed into her. The shield strained, yet held. She cried out in pain from the blow, feeling as if she'd run her shoulder directly into a brick wall. Heaving, she let the molten fireball slough off her shield and fall to the sand where it lay in a burning heap of rock and lava. She looked up.

Zane's collar was scarlet red, so hot it must have been burning his thick neck.

Good. Just a little more, she thought inwardly.

Ayva, what are you doing? Helix sent, sounding worried. *Zane's killing you out there!*

Yeah, well…looks can be deceiving.

No, not in this case. You are obviously getting destroyed! I mean, I know you don't want to hurt the guy, but can you at least scuff him up a bit? I think he's seeing red. At this rate, he is going to kill you. I know I surrendered to him, but you're making this—

Ayva protested, cutting Helix off, *Just, wait! Okay?*

Zane pulled more fire.

Ayva felt the ring in her pocket. She still hadn't put it on.

Not yet…It's only a matter of time, she told herself. *I just have to push him a little further.*

She knew that on its own, a deeper magical reserve meant nothing if the collar restricted how much she could use. Thankfully, she was beginning to get used to the collar's constraints. She had stayed up all night practicing spells, determined to get the hang of it. When it blocked one of her main channels, she found she could redirect her *flow* through others. The collar was made by ancient Reavers—strong as it was, it wasn't intuitive. Equally interesting was the more magic she used, the more her channels widened. While her late-night session had gained her baggy eyes and quite a few yawns the next morning, hopefully it had paid off.

Returning to the moment, she saw Zane staring at her, fire in his eyes. She could tell he was trying to act tough. Raised on the streets of Farbs, he'd gained his fair share of scars, both outwardly on his tanned, well-muscled frame, and inwardly. A shadow in his eyes told her it might not all be an act, as if he was slipping back into the man they'd once called "Shade." Fire blazed in Zane's upturned palm. *What's that look for? Don't tell me you lost your nerve.*

She grinned. *Hardly.*

Good, because I'm just getting started. He bent down. A sword had fallen near his feet from the exploding arsenal and he picked it up, hefting the heavy claymore with ease. Calmly, he ran two fingers along the fuller. Where he touched, crimson flame danced. Something about that fire…It was deeper than what he'd threaded before. The crimson light seemed violent, ominous. Ayva vaguely remembered childhood tales about Seth, Ronin of Fire. Something about him having different types of magic…Three different levels of intensity. If she was right, Zane was approaching the hottest of his fires. There was only one beyond. It was impressive. Even over a dozen paces away, she could feel the heat of those crimson flames.

As Zane maintained the flames, however, the collar grew its deepest red.

Ayva grinned. *Finally.*

This is what she'd been waiting for. It was time to stop holding back. She breathed in and slammed her hands together with a Thunderclap Sun. Light erupted, shooting forth as thick bands of gold.

Lightshackles.

One shackle, then two, then three, then four.

Zane's eyes went wide, and he cursed. Rolling and ducking, using his agility, he dodged the first, then second. The next he couldn't evade. So he sliced it out of the air with his crimson sword. The last golden shackle flew too fast, and it slammed into his chest, sending him flying, landing hard on the earthen floor.

She looked up to Helix on the balcony, who cheered wildly.

Well? she sent to him.

Helix, grinning from the balcony, replied, *I stand corrected.* Then he frowned. *Wait, should I be cheering for only you? This is very conflicting.*

The Covian masses held no such reservation. Ayva heard and felt their adulation as the colosseum rattled with their enthusiasm. She stalked over to stand by Zane, who struggled on the ground, now bound in a wrist-thick gold band of pure light that pinned his muscled arms to his side. Looking up at her, he stopped his growling and grunting. In those orange eyes she read a strange mix of emotions. Anger, annoyance, and also pride, and eagerness. As if he was truly in his element.

"Mind loosening this up? They're a little tight."

Ayva rubbed her jaw. "Sure, right after you admit defeat."

"That was a nice move," Zane said through gritted teeth, the bonds constricting his chest, "waiting until I expended a good portion of my power. Then, before I could regain my strength, you attacked with everything you had."

"Well, maybe not everything I had."

He snorted. "Even more impressive."

She shrugged, then rubbed her bruised arm. "I did have to get beaten around like a rag doll by your flames." Ayva reached out a hand to pick him up. "It was a good fight."

Then something glinted in his eyes. "Good fight?" he asked. "Oh, you're mistaken. I'm not done."

Ayva rolled her eyes and planted her hands on her hips. With thick threads of sun, she lifted him up onto his feet like a mummy, his arms still bound, trapped to his side. "Zane, I love the bravado, really, but you look like a bundle of muscled carrots bound by golden twine. What could you *possibly* do?"

"I'm a Ronin, Ayva," he said, the words sending a chill down her spine. She took an unconscious step back, but he was bound. She was sure of it. It was her strongest Lightshackle, and it held tight. "Besides, you're not the only one who got a trinket from the past."

A calm fell over Zane's features.

Trapped as he was, Zane felt a strange mix of emotions: boiling anger, annoyance, and pride. Pride because of Ayva. Ash and brimstone, he knew she was strong, but this? She'd been clever too, waiting, biding her time. The annoyance was transparent enough. All his life, he hated feeling controlled or constricted. Bound by rules meant to subjugate the weakest… Something about the bonds brought back that same anger, that same annoyance. Trapped. His whole body shook, needing to be set free, to break his confines.

A memory took him.

The Dragon of Fire had said there are three things that compose fire's true power: anger, passion, and love. Love and passion, he was beginning to understand. For now, he delved deeper into the first principal, feeling anger to his core. The impotence of being bound. It was symbolic of all that he had suffered. Or at least he told himself that to dredge deeper.

Ayva watched him as he tapped into something primal.

The Nexus in his mind. Now he saw the more of it, it'd been only a vague silhouette, a ghost of its true power. He pulled back a strange veil—a cloth that exposed the burning flame beneath. Not all of it. A portion. Some of the cloth was stripped away, and in its place, a quarter of his flame—his true power—revealed itself.

Power flooded him.

While his channel burned, Seth's necklace helped with that. The pendant with the orange flame rested upon his chest. He'd been given it just before this match, and it allowed him to bypass that limitation.

Seth's pendant.

Something rumbled in his core.

Flames burst forth and out of his mouth. Ayva blocked them with a shield of light.

A few wisps of fire smoldered on her white shirt, creating holes. She ignored them, letting them burn as she glared at him. "A nice trick, but if you think that's enough to stop me…"

Only that wasn't what Zane was trying to do.

It was just a byproduct.

Dragon's Breath had its roots in something else, something deeper. A deep hum rose, reverberating from the depths of his soul.

Ayva watched in awe and a little dread as flames licked up Zane's feet, his calves, his legs, rising higher still, over his arms and chest. She stepped back from the heat, shielding her face from the intensity.

What's he doing? Helix sent.

Ayva had no idea. She still had him bound.

The hum grew.

With it, the flames rose higher, burning hotter, until Zane was a living torch. His hum turned to a growl, then a roar. As his voice grew, cracks formed in the golden shackle. *Impossible.* His roar reached a crescendo and the thick bond holding his arms in place shattered. Golden fragments of light fell toward the ground, then vanished into thin air before touching the sands.

Zane opened his eyes. They were no longer a shade of orange, but a deep crimson like the sword he'd been wielding. "Now we fight." Still covered in flames, he attacked. Fire rained down on Ayva from all sides. Frantically, she erected shields of light from every angle, faster, and faster, trying to block. Fireballs crashed against them. More came. Between her shields, she sent beams of light, searing hot, but his living torch absorbed all her attacks. It was useless. She needed something stronger, and at this rate, Zane would burn her alive. An idea came to her. Collapsing Star? No, she dismissed it just as quickly. She didn't have time, or the concentration, to pull the thread inside another orb of light and cause another Collapsing Star. If she could find a sliver of a moment between Zane's relentless attacks — but they just kept coming.

Fireball after fireball.

Distantly, she heard the crowd, and their cheers nearly drowned out the flames' roar.

Ayva felt Imala's gaze.

Merrick's.

Nalia's.

Helix sent, *Abyss take me...*

Fire streaked past Ayva, one she didn't block in time with a golden shield, scorching a bubbling line across her shoulder. She screamed in pain. Only, Zane didn't relent. What was happening? Was he lost in his rage?

No, they'd promised to go full-out.

This was a fight to the death.

There would be plenty more before Farhaven was saved, if it could be saved.

So she lost herself as well.

I will show them something worthy of cheering.

Hope — a thick thread spiraled inside of her.

The Nexus came to her mind, and she realized, all this time, it'd only ever been an outline. Now, like the sun lighting up the moon, half of her Nexus was revealed. Half of an orb of sun. True power flared inside of her. Zane's fireballs came faster. However, instead of sweating, and erecting last-minute shields, she waved a hand and a golden sphere of light enveloped her. The fireballs bounced harmlessly off it. Zane extended a hand. A tongue of flame grabbed his crimson sword, pulling it back to his grip. As he did, Ayva spotted a pendant with a flame on it around Zane's neck.

She knew whose it was.

Seth... the previous Ronin of Fire. Zane's collar was red. *Had* been red. He was pushing through it. Was that his item's ability?

With the crimson blade in hand, Zane slashed, cutting into the sphere like cleaving through a chrysalis, parting it in two. Ayva used the moment to slip on the ring in her pocket. Her reserves deepened. The gauntlet of light she'd formed before came again, crawling over her right arm, then her left.

Golden armor flowed over her.

She caught Zane's blade, and while it burned, she didn't let go.

Eyes like flaming embers, Zane snarled through the flames surrounding him, "You've fought well, Ayva, but you've no weapon. This is my fight!"

Ayva sent. *"That's where you're wrong! I am the weapon."*

She held the crimson sword in one gauntleted fist; in the other, she raised an upturned palm, as Zane had done before. Only hers held a tiny, perfect golden globe of light.

He swallowed. "You wouldn't…"

She pulled the thread.

Boom.

In the last moment, she dampened the blow by using a thin shield of gold around it. Still, the force was violent and deafening. Immediately, her golden armor was stripped away. It absorbed the majority of the blast, as she shielded her eyes from the brilliant explosion.

For a moment, Ayva simply stood there, breathing hard, trying to wrap her mind around what she'd just done.

The crowds were stunned into pin-drop silence.

Then…they roared.

Ayva looked about, frantic. She spotted him. Zane lay a hundred paces away, still and unmoving—his red flame armor now extinguished.

*Oh gods…*Ayva thought, putting a hand to her mouth in horror. She ran to him, tears streaming from her eyes. "Zane, please tell me—" She rolled him over and saw he was covered in smoldering ash, his orange vest singed and blackened in a dozen different places. Both of his sleeves had been burned to a crisp—revealing his soot-stained thick arms. Squinting, Zane looked up at her, groaning, "Did…did I win?"

She gripped him tightly, stifling tears. "You big oaf! You didn't need to go that hard!"

She pulled away as he groaned again, holding his ribs, staring up at her with an impish smile. "You didn't either…"

That was totally fair. Ayva gave him a guilty look. "Yeah, guess I got a little carried away, too."

"Ash and brimstone, Ayva," he said, looking up at her, "were you trying to kill me?"

"I was only trying to match you."

He snorted. "Match me. I think you did that and then some. Burn me, you are…really strong." Then he smiled.

While many in the crowds still cheered, a hush fell over most.

She understood. It wasn't over.

Zane looked up and sighed. Then he made the sign of defeat, hands together in prayer, bowing his head. Now a truly thunderous roar took the people by storm, rushing over Ayva like a gust of wind. Zane smiled. "Well fought, Ayva. Well won."

"Winner, Ayva! Ronin of Sun!" the announcer boomed.

She looked down at her wrist as a third sword materialized beside the other two, faintly burning with a crimson glow.

Guards marched onto the sand, including several Reavers. They mended her, knitting the burned flesh on her shoulder to make it smooth once more, and healed Zane's—apparently many—injuries. She adamantly protested that they were *all* from her.

"How can you have that many broken ribs and not be in agony?" a one-stripe Reaver muttered.

Zane just shrugged.

Rising with Ayva's help, Zane reassured her, "I'm good now, promise," and together they walked off the sands, returning to the balcony with Helix, who greeted them with overwhelming exuberance. The Ronin of Water practically danced on his toes about their small terrace, recapping the entire fight to them blow by blow, before Zane explained that they knew seeing as they'd been a part of it.

"Oh, right, still…you two didn't want to save some of that for the shadow in the west? Seven hells!"

"Only one way to get stronger," Zane replied.

"Testing our mettle," Ayva agreed, and the phrase she'd stolen made her look across the colosseum to Merrick. The Ronin of Metal was still on the Queen's Terrace, arms crossed, black bow on his back. He'd witnessed the whole thing. Far away as he was, she still felt his gaze.

"Think our Ronin of Evil is quaking in his boots now?" Helix asked.

"Hopefully," Zane replied. "I'll admit, I'm…disappointed I won't get to fight him."

"You mean beat him to a pulp?" Helix asked.

"Same difference."

"Yet, I'm also glad it'll be you or Gray…You'll put him in his place."

"I think you might still get your chance before all this is over," Ayva replied. "Wait, if he's up there, then who's Gray fighting?"

After a moment, things calmed down again, and the next fight was about to begin.

"Tranquil Seas, I forgot about that! Is Gray up next? I think I need a breather," Helix said, putting a hand to his heart. "You two scared me half to death."

"I was scared too," Ayva admitted.

Exhausted, she slumped back into her chair.

At the same time, she was elated. Her fingers kept turning the gold ring on her hand, and she tried to hide a smile, wanting to reach back into her mind and touch the swirling half-lit golden ball of sun. For a long time, she'd dreamt of becoming a Ronin. Little hints of sunshine, but now? Now she felt the full warmth of it on her face. Or at least the beginning of something more. She wasn't Omni. She was Ayva, that alone was enough. A Ronin. It wasn't just pride in her newfound power, but in what it meant. Farhaven's redemption didn't seem that impossible now.

"Wait, where's Nalia?" Helix asked.

The announcer spoke grandly, "What can possibly top that match, my fair Citizens of Flesh, but our beloved victory, champion of champions, and warrior of warriors…With no further introduction, I give you, Grand Primus Nalia, The Final Blade!"

Nalia, the Final Blade

Ayva had heard thunderous applause before, but this time... it was deafening, as Nalia, Grand Primus, walked onto the sands to an uproar that could have awoken the dead. So loud was it that Helix clapped his hands over his ears. "Abyss take me! What is happening? You'd think she was Renalin's daughter!"

Nalia slowly turned in a circle, taking in the adulation.

Ayva appraised her. The red blade was no longer at her hip, clearly restricted like other magical blades. Instead, she wore a simple gladius—a gladiator's sword. Striated, broad shoulders rolled. As before, her head was shaved except for a strip of long braided black hair down the middle. She was a sight to behold, her beauty buried deep beneath her fearsome and wrathful nature. Intricate black tattoos, a hallmark of her Hiras Ugra heritage, were inked on either side of her scalp, while the kohl around her eyes, once black, was now a deep red, streaking her cheekbones down to her jaw.

The crowds' applause continued until—

Nalia swiped a hand through the air.

On command, the masses went silent.

Helix audibly gulped.

Zane's eyes were steely.

A power like that over the people... Ayva sent.

Helix replied, *Wasn't Gray saying we need to win them? I think that's a lost cause.*

"No," Zane said. "They don't love her. They fear her."

Ayva knew the Ronin of Fire was right. The unease and tension in the air was thick enough she could cut it with a sword.

"In the west corner," the announcer spoke, now that it was quiet enough to hear his voice, "an elite of the nine Great Kingdoms—from a warrior tribe who have been holed up behind their great walls—said to have armor and hides thick enough to take a sword's slash and shed no blood…I give you, Balgar Battlefist, Stoneguard of Lander!"

Out stepped a man of sizable girth, decked in thick layers of brown plate mail. Most wouldn't be able to move in armor so cumbersome. Balgar strode with ease out of the gates to the sound of cheers. After Nalia, it sounded almost pitiful, like a few gratuitous shouts. Balgar didn't seem to notice or care.

"Does…does he remind you of someone?" Helix asked.

"I was just thinking that," Ayva replied. "Is that…he looks like he could be Ham's brother."

Zane brought them each a glass of water from a nearby stand. "Ham? Who's he?"

They explained, filling him in quickly on Ham and Imar, the two very different brothers from Lander. They told him about Median, how the two men had come to their aid and became valuable allies. Now they hoped they were spreading good news to the reclusive city of Lander about the Ronin's upcoming visit. "He looks intimidating," Helix said, seeing the two massive hammers in Balgar's meaty fists.

"I'm not sure it matters," Zane said, wearing a dark look as Nalia stalked forward.

The way she moved…there was something uncanny about it.

Too confident, too practiced.

Superhuman, as she marched onto the sands in long, smooth strides, her tall frame erect. She moved toward the center of the colosseum.

Balgar, until that moment, had been waving his hammers—gaining cheers from the crowd. He turned. The crowd became silent and their eyes expressed their confusion.

Nalia strode across the divide, and he looked baffled.

The drums were still thundering.

"The drums haven't stopped…" Helix posed. "What in the seven hells is she doing?"

The Grand Primus didn't slow.

Balgar's eyes narrowed; he faced her, raising his massive engraved hammer.

The announcer started to say, "Fi—"

Nalia dipped under a strike from Balgar that would have cracked Yronia steel.

She grabbed the man's neck and ripped, pulling out his throat. Nalia threw the skin, muscle, and windpipe to the sand.

She turned, leaving the huge man briefly standing, gasping for air, bleeding, and gurgling.

Then he fell over, dead.

The spectators hushed, stunned to silence.

For a moment, Nalia tilted back her shaved head. Balgar's body disintegrated to dust, then spark materialized. She breathed in, and the orange mist filled her. As it did, her eyelids fluttered, and she moaned, imbibing his nature, the essence that had been Balgar. Then, regaining herself, she turned and stalked off the sands as the announcer called her name, declaring her the winner.

"Oh gods," Helix muttered. "She didn't even unsheathe her sword."

Thieflords and Wind

Gray stepped out onto the field of battle, not knowing what to expect, but ready for anything. His gaze panned across the tiered stands, watching the tens of thousands of spectators as they began to chant:

"Wind!"
"Wind!"
"Wind!"
"Wind!"

He looked east, searching, scanning. It took a moment, but finally he spotted her, standing in a spot slightly less packed with people, beneath a flag with the symbol of Flesh. Hati. Their eyes locked. She waved, expression full of excitement, and he smiled back.

Then Gray turned to his friends, seeing Ayva, Zane, and Helix.

Did…did he just notice somebody else first? Helix sent.

Gray felt his cheeks heat. Gods, he was about to face a battle to the death, and he was getting distracted by a servant girl?

He definitely did, Ayva agreed. *Who's up there?*

No one, Gray sent quickly. *Anyway, are you three going to tell me what happened? I missed a battle, it seems, and I need to know what happened.*

Oh, you missed a lot. It was amazing, Ayva—

We'll fill you in, Ayva cut in. *Please focus on not dying first.*

Gray snorted, though he nodded. He had a feeling he knew what happened, judging by the faint feelings he'd felt through the bond, and the looks on their faces—including Zane's, a sort of resigned, if proud, expression.

Ayva was growing stronger, much stronger. *Could* he *even beat her?*

Gray turned back to take in the arena.

The sands were empty, just the six pillars—five now, one of them having crumbled in the last battle. The pillar on the far end, before the Queen's Terrace, still held the Earthstone. It floated, suspended in the air, surrounded by that strange, cerulean blue shield of magic—which buzzed with energy. He touched the Devari blade at his back. Dimitri's. *Be true. Help me win this. For his memory. For Farhaven.*

He couldn't be certain, but he felt as if the blade listened. He'd left Morrowil back on the balcony since magical weapons, with the exception of the Ronin's relics, were prohibited until the last rounds.

A strange feeling came over him...

Where was his opponent?

From the balcony, the queen stepped forward. "My dear and beloved subjects, I have a special announcement for you! I'm certain you can agree, the games this year have been quite *entertaining*, have they not?"

The crowd roared.

"What if I told you that there is so much more to come...what would you say to that, my dear Covians?"

Again, shouts and cheers that surely Renalin above could hear.

Gray's stomach dropped.

What's she planning? Ayva sent. *I don't like this.*

Imala stilled the cheering crowd by raising her arms, the fat of them jiggling as she did. "Oh, really? I'm so glad you agree. Ask, and you shall receive! As you are my beloved subjects, you deserve not only to be entertained, but enthralled!" On the terrace a man with colorful patchwork attire strode to the queen's side. Ayva had mentioned something about a jester pulling cards for Sasha's place. Cards...deciding his fate? He hated it.

Imala looked down at him, mirth and haughty superiority in her gaze.

Draw your cards, Gray sent with his eyes. *Do your best.*

The jester spoke, his voice filling the amphitheater with the same resonance the queen's held. "Sand is all well and good, but so is snow, lake, mountain, and forest!" With masterful grace, the jester shuffled the cards. They flew from one hand to another in a dazzling display of skill. "With these cards I draw for luck, I endeavor to make you all awestruck!" Flipping, twirling, the man danced the cards back and forth, eyes entranced as if by magic. "Witness now, elements so true: red, green, gold, and blue! What comes next, it all depends on hue..." With a final flourish, he proffered the hand to Queen Imala, showing several dozen cards.

Too many for just the elements, Gray knew. *It must be more specific.*

A smile on her face, Queen Imala drew a card, then flipped it, and Gray's eyes, keener than ever, took in the card's face: a frozen, harsh terrain.

"Asteria Tundra!" the announcer boomed.

All around, Gray saw spark rise into the air. Nefrin and his ilk, along with dozens of other Reavers, raised their hands. Focused as he was, Gray hadn't noticed the red-robed threaders of spark encircling the arena on the lower level. Layers of water and ice battled the oppressive heat. Eventually they won out, and thick white-and-blue threads sank into the colosseum's floor. The whole of the arena was transformed.

Crowds gasped.

Gray took in the treeless landscape of hard-packed snow. Patches of grass tried vainly to poke through, as well as moss, lichen, herbs, and small shrubs. A narrow frozen stream divided the arena.

Icy cold wind pierced Gray, and he shivered against it.

Whoa, Helix sent. *That's a twist.*

Tell me about it, Ayva agreed.

Helix folded his arms. *Of course Gray gets the best setting.*

Snow and ice? Zane grunted, shivering. *No, thank you.*

Uh, water? Helix replied. *That'd be an easy win for me!*

Ignore them. Focus, Gray, Ayva sent.

Breath fogging, Gray nodded as the announcer spoke again.

"Covai, witness now a fight for the ages! In the east corner comes a warrior whose infamy tried to remain hidden, but such notoriety does not stay clandestine for long! She made a name for herself in the Battle of the Sands, and is feared throughout the nine Great Kingdoms! I give you, the Tyrant of the Tournament, Mistress of Shadows, leader of the Darkeye Clan, Faye, Thieflord of Fire!"

Every muscle tensed in Gray's body.

He should have known it was coming, but still... *I have to kill Faye?*

The others made similar reactions through the bond, and he felt their gazes on him.

"Seven hells..." he cursed. Faye...why Faye? Would she try to kill him? Could he possibly fight back with enough willful vehemence to end her? He needed to get stronger to save Farhaven, but Faye? Why'd it have to be her? Gray glanced up to the queen's elegant balcony and cursed again. He was half tempted to use a gust of wind and knock the woman's bloated body over the railing. He could do it too, if it didn't mean being murdered by a hundred Reavers, hundreds of archers, or a thousand soldiers of the Covian Legion. Which also meant dooming Farhaven.

He snarled.

The crowds thundered.

"*Tyrant!*"

"*Tyrant!*"

"*Tyrant!*"

Their chants were even louder than they'd been for him.

So much for you being the famed Ronin of Wind, Helix sent.

Are you going to kill her, Gray? Ayva directed to him alone.

Only, Gray had no answer…

More crowds roared as the gate on the far side grated open, and then…

Nothing.

Nothing came out of the tunnel.

The crowds booed, growing restless, throwing food onto the sands.

The announcer cursed and spoke again, "I said…I give you, the Mistress of Shadows, Faye, Thieflord of Fire!"

This time, no shouts, just poignant silence.

The tunnel remained empty.

Gray looked to the balcony and watched as a nervous messenger delivered news to the red-faced queen. She raged. Then with a gesture and a word, the messenger's head was cleanly severed off.

Oh gods, that can't be good news, Helix sent. *Wait, bad news for Imala is great news for us.*

Not for the messenger, Zane sent darkly.

Ayva's eyes were full of fury. *Imala…She will pay.*

Get in line, Helix replied.

Then the news was transmitted to the announcer, in a small pulpit of his own, and Gray grasped the words to his ear from the new messenger.

"Apparently she…declined…and killed—"

That's all he heard.

Seven hells, Gray thought. *That is so Faye.*

Mustering his rattled voice, the announcer declared, "Winner by default, leader of the Ronin! Gray!"

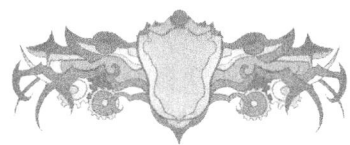

A Wolf Among Sheep

Standing on the Queen's Terrace, surrounded by nobles and sycophants, Merrick's blood boiled. The simpering and bickering, hateful gazes and snide comments of the nobles around him ate at him like a poison. He tried his best to ignore everything, standing farther away, close to the railing, while he watched the battle—eyes riveted to the now-icy tundra, a barren frozen wasteland of sparse vegetation created by the Reavers' magic.

Thinking of the Ronin, Merrick's fist tightened at his side.

Are you getting concerned, dark Ronin of Metal? Osmium said, trying to get a rise out of him.

Merrick snorted. *Hardly. I will say, they've been...interesting, so far. Illuminating, even.*

Osmium laughed sharply, or the sword's approximation of a laugh—more of a mental image. *Sometimes I forget how truly young you are.* Merrick's anger rose, and the blade sighed, as if explaining calmly to a child before he threw a toy to the ground. *You may try to hide from others your hesitation, your uncertainty, but I sense what they cannot...your counterparts are strong. Stronger than you anticipated.*

Yet, they've failed to conquer all of their own Nexus—the source of our power, Merrick replied. *That is a lesson that I fought for with my life. A lesson that took the previous Ronin a thousand years to tap into, to unveil. For that reason alone, they will fail. And you will help me.*

Osmium had no response to his demand.

Then he shrugged. *If anything, I'm glad they won't disappoint. I like the challenge.*

Perhaps more than a challenge, Osmium replied.

Merrick sighed, feigning indifference—almost bored as he leaned on the balcony. Behind him, the nobles laughed sharply. One made a snide remark about offering their servant to "the blood gods." The others took bets. Two of their servants were goaded into fighting one another right there on the balcony, until one smashed the other's head in with a silver pitcher and they all cheered. He ignored the bloodthirsty nobles. *Sometimes, you really get on my frayed nerves,* he told the blade.

Osmium sighed like an ever-patient father. *You don't hate me, Merrick. You hate them,* the blade said, indicating those behind him. *That, and you hate yourself.*

The words stabbed at Merrick. *What did I tell you about sermons?*

I am not trying to lecture. I am simply hoping to show you the light, and in time, let you walk toward it yourself.

Merrick's teeth gnashed. On the arena floor, the frozen grounds remained—clearly waiting to be used for the next contestants. *No, you're trying to antagonize me, and it's working.*

Just as you antagonized them?

I gave them an offer to save themselves.

To forfeit? the sword mocked, and the nobles again tittered nearby. *You and I both know that was an insult. An offer they'd never accept.*

Then their deaths are on them.

You would like that, wouldn't you? To clear your conscience. If you kill them, you know there is only you to blame.

It was Merrick's turn not to answer. He looked away, to the stands filled with people—laughing, eating, waiting impatiently for the next match on the icy ground below. For a moment, his eyes fell upon the Earthstone that sat atop its towering pillar, and the blue shield that glowed around it, fed by a dozen Reavers. He'd come for that. It'd be his once he won the tournament...that and solved the mystery of the arena. *Those are my objectives,* he thought. *Nothing else.*

He watched Reaver Nefrin, the scar-faced man who'd clashed with Zane and lost, nearby. The Reaver whispered something to the queen. She waved him off, and he took his leave.

Osmium spoke again, *I know why else you approached them, because you feel the draw—*

Merrick snapped, *Enough!* He severed the connection to the sword in his mind, and looked down to see his whole arm trembling with barely restrained rage. Why was he so angry? Normally he could tolerate Osmium's jabs *and* the blade's preaching with no issue. Merrick knew why. He was on edge, not just from the Ronin and their battles. It was also because of where he was—standing among these people like another one of their sycophants.

A noble with a snake symbol on her royal-green dress gave a loud, obnoxious laugh. Glancing over his shoulder, he took in the nobles, who all wore different colors: gold, red, blue, and green. Men and women of all shapes and sizes, including an obese man whose legs were kicked up on an ottoman as he puffed merrily on a pipe. The smoke filled the terrace with a sickly sweet stench—which servants with palm fronds tried to fan away. Others too, caught his eye: an axe-faced woman with a calm, calculating look; an irate man who paced back and forth; and a servant—a gray-haired older gentleman who'd been called "Howard," watching it all with discerning eyes.

Merrick hated almost all of them.

If he had his way he'd burn down this whole balcony. He would let Osmium flay their hides or pierce them with a thousand black arrows.

The one who had laughed was Larissa, head of House Hisan Viper. He took her in, with her sharp-featured face and cruel eyes. She sat in an emerald cushioned chair, her inept husband at her side—a balding, dull-eyed man with a lecherous look. She swirled her drink and nibbled on a plate of roasted nuts that a servant, kneeling at her feet, held on a platter, his arms raised and shaking. The man had been kneeling there for an hour with that tray. The godforsaken woman had a table she refused to use.

Everything about her, about all of them, rubbed Merrick wrong. He was a wolf among sheep.

"I say," Larissa said, wearing that smug smile of hers and popping a nut into her mouth with a crunch, "you're a fool, Jaron! For only a fool would have trusted that woman with their coin." She laughed her shrill cackle again. "I swear you are as bad with your coin as you are with women!"

Jaron, a plain-looking man wearing the badge of an orange-tailed bird, a noble of Copper Falcon, stalked the balcony among the other nobles. Anger contorted his face into an ugly mask. "Cursing blood and ash! I lost five hundred silver on that stupid wench! Who calls themself the Tyrant of the Tournament?"

Another noble, Jima'ra, replied, "They did. The people. Or did you forget?" She was the axe-faced woman wearing a wine-colored dress with a red fox stitched onto the lapel. Merrick had overhead the others refer to her as head of House Red Fox. "Your champions keep rising, my queen, despite your best efforts."

Queen Imala, sitting on her throne of bones lacquered in gold, made a sour face. She sucked the sauce off a bone, throwing it aside for a servant to pick up. "Careful with your implications, Jima'ra."

"Why should she be careful?" Larissa added. "You're the bold one, Your Majesty! Trying to pit the Ronin against one another. Their despising eyes are always upon you! They'll abandon their matches and come for you at this rate."

All the nobles laughed at this, several going so far as agreeing.

Queen Imala's heavy chest heaved with sudden ire. Her bulbous eyes fanned wide as she flicked a finger, and all around the balcony nearby guards cleared swords an inch from their sheaths. Imala waved her hand, stopping them. "Don't dare speak ill again, you fork-tongued hag!"

Larissa gulped.

The queen's face quivered with rage. "You all grow too insolent! Too indulgent, suckling upon my teat! No longer will you mistake my kindness and good graces for weakness," she seethed, bloodshot eyes panning over all the nobles. "Your houses exist because I *allow* it! *Everything* can be replaced. Even you." They settled on Larissa, last and longest.

For a while, a sharp, painful silence enveloped the large terrace.

The queen seemed to relish this response, and her eyes danced with content as she picked up another wing of meat.

Larissa fumed, her rage like billowing steam needing to vent, to expel its excess fury. Her eyes roved the balcony, until they fell upon Merrick. "Curious…" Larissa said in her sharp tenor, gaining back some of her confidence. "A Ronin of Metal. I've heard so many stories of that fallen kingdom, filled with terrible beasts." She shivered. "Saeroks and vergs, of misting black nameless, yet to see you here. You have a brooding, ominous look to you, do you not?"

"Was that a question?" Merrick asked.

Larissa grimaced. "An observation…"

The queen stepped in. "As I said before, Merrick is an advisor, sent by the grand Patriarch himself, Lord of the Citadel. You would be wise to watch your forked tongue with him as well, Larissa."

"She can say what she wants," Merrick replied. "I prefer when poison is offered openly, rather than given in the shadows behind one's back."

Larissa tittered. "Oh, it seems our Merrick is handsome, dark, *and* keen of wit."

Her eyes glittered with intent, as if coy, but interested.

The notion turned his stomach.

She was hideous. Perhaps not outwardly, despite the other nobles' jabs. She had large ice-blue eyes, sharp features, and a shapely form: skinny, but she flaunted her…assets in her low-necklined dress. Clearly something she'd used to work her way higher, judging by her worthless, empty-eyed husband, who gobbled a leg of meat and occasionally tried to grope her or any female servants who got too near. Larissa, for her part, paid it no mind, casually dismissing him.

On the icy cold wasteland below, a battle was ending…a big man buried his axe into his smaller opponent. In response, the dying fighter sent a spike of ice that drove its way through the big man's chest. They both fell over, staining the white snow red.

"Well, that doesn't happen often…" said a noble, laughing.

Reavers rushed to heal them.

They were too slow, and both bled out on the ice, blood running into the slowly thawing stream.

Their spark…it floated into the air.

Merrick's gaze tightened, watching.

A portion always returned back into the sands, but it was hard to see…This time, he watched closely. He was under orders from the Patriarch to understand the true nature of the arena's magic. Tendrils of orange, like a thousand writhing snakes, buried deep into the icy snow, and then were gone.

Absorbed.

It's below… He had figured as much, but this confirmed it. Something below the arena.

What was underneath? Whatever it was, it could power a spell that even the Patriarch couldn't mimic. A spell that could absorb and redistribute spark. A spell that seemed alive.

A burning curiosity grew inside of him.

Merrick made a mental note.

He'd need to investigate further.

The others on the terrace didn't seem to care. As if this was a mystery they'd long ago dismissed. Or more likely, blood and coin took precedence.

"I must say I am most curious for your match, our Ronin of Metal," Larissa said, drawing him back.

"I am not your anything," Merrick replied.

Her eyes flared, lips pursing. "Oh, really? Delusions of grandeur? It's really quite understandable, if terribly misguided. You see, if you are in the queen's pocket, then you are in ours as well."

Merrick turned to face her fully and sighed. His fingers curled into a fist, and the metal cup in Larissa's hand suddenly crumpled as if made of parchment. "I am not what you think I am. Play your nobles' games elsewhere."

This woman stood for everything he hated.

Born into power. Lording it over others.

For a moment, Larissa seemed torn. Drawn to his sudden power, yet spurned by his harsh tone. Merrick had a feeling it was the others' eyes on her, judging her, that made her decision. Larissa sneered, setting the twisted metal mug down on the platter as if it were a trophy he'd made her. "Oh, dear Ronin. You think you're special, don't you? You're not the first legend we've had in our midst. We had that petulant little brat of Sun here earlier."

"Ha!" Otto, head of House Belegrun, barked. His feet were still kicked up on his ottoman, and he stopped his pipe puffing to chortle, "Ignore her, Merrick! Larissa's simply bitter because the young Ronin of Sun put her in her place! Made her spill her own drink, then took her own slave! Posing as the young Sasha — which you, of course, enlightened us to."

Merrick mused, having witnessed the queen's irate reaction to Ayva posing as Sasha. Then the foul woman had smiled, clearly plans evolving in her twisted mind. She'd attempted to use the knowledge against Ayva, pitting her against Zane, Ronin of Fire. Only it...hadn't worked. Ayva had defeated Zane and while the two had looked like they wanted to kill one another, it had ended without any real blood spilled. In a way, the queen had looked satisfied. Her twisted kind always enjoyed a spectacle, bloody or otherwise. Merrick was certain she had other conniving plans up her richly brocaded sleeves.

"That little—" Larissa said, chest puffing with thoughts of Ayva. Then she cut herself short. "The point is, Ronin of Metal," she said, ice-blue eyes looking up at him once again. A new drink was brought to her, and she swirled it. Below her, the servant holding the platter trembled, his muscles clearly aching from remaining in a kneeling position with the tray raised for so long. "The point," she repeated, "is that you are just a child, a boy legend, one with a dark streak—that I like—but in the end, you are simply a pet of the Patriarch. We, on the other hand, are nobility. In essence, you represent nothing."

Merrick sighed. Again, he flitted his fingers. "You don't learn, do you?" The metal chalice in her hand melted in the air, then became a longer thick band floating before her eyes.

Larissa watched it curiously, then her gaze widened in understanding, in horror. She squealed in fury, "Guards—"

Guards rushed forth.

Reavers readied spells.

They were all too slow.

Casually tapping into only a quarter of his Nexus, the swirling metal ball of liquid steel fed his power and he waved a hand. All their weapons flew into the air—swords, spears, daggers—placed within a hairsbreadth of their throats, ready to kill. Most notably the Reavers, as they were the only true threat.

The queen raged, "Enough!"

Merrick put a band of metal over Queen Imala's mouth, as well as a sword to her throat. "No," he told her.

Then he turned his attention back to Larissa.

The metal band still floated in the air before the noblewoman. With a flick of his fingers, he wrapped the collar about Larissa's throat and tightened it. She choked, her face turning beet red. He squeezed his hand into a fist, the hot band of steel choking further. "What's that look for? You don't enjoy being collared? Interesting, because when it's on others, you seem to delight in their demise while they struggle and die…" He sneered as she fell off her chair, grasping blindly. Blood vessels ruptured on her neck and face, and she struggled to speak, desperately clamoring for help.

The other nobles just watched, frozen in their own horror and fear.

"Y…you can't do this!" Otto spoke, sweat streaming down his portly jowls.

Larissa's husband suddenly leapt from his chair, raging at him and drawing his sword.

Merrick released a heavy breath. He flattened the platter that the servant held to a razor-sharp disk, then let it fly with a dismissive wave of his hand. It sliced open the husband's throat. The nobleman grasped at his neck as if trying to hold the blood in, then fell over, his eyes staring into the beyond.

Larissa still choked, turning from scarlet to purple, her whole body convulsing now as she groped around the floor, looking up at him, struggling vainly to free herself from the collar. Merrick's gaze held no mercy. Seeing the futility of her appeal, she grasped at the servant who'd been holding the tray. He shook his head. "My lady, there's nothing I can—"

Eyes bloodshot, terror in her expression.

The other nobles watched in horror, too afraid to move and incur Merrick's wrath as well.

In a final attempt, Larissa threw herself on Merrick, clawing at his legs. He merely looked down at her.

"P-p-pl—" She tried to form the word "please."

Merrick released the grip of the collar.

Larissa gasped, sucking in precious air, putting trembling hands to her neck. For a moment, she took in the scene, the panicked nobles, and even spared a glance to her dead husband. That was it...a glance. He'd attempted to save her, and she saw him as no more than fodder. Merrick felt his heart darken. When she finally spoke, it was somehow mirthful, if rattled. "I...gods...you almost made me think you were going to kill me." She managed a pained laugh. "What a foolish mistake that would have—"

With a clean swipe from Osmium, Merrick cut off her head.

Larissa's head, mouth agape, tumbled to Otto's feet and the fat man trembled in horror, dropping his pipe. A chorus of terrified gasps escaped all the nobles as they staggered back, stares fixed to Larissa's headless corpse in sheer dread of what would happen next.

"You don't understand yet, do you?" Merrick's gaze passed over the nobles, the servants, the guards, the Reavers. "*None* of you are in charge here." Then he turned on the queen and released the metal band over her mouth.

Imala raged, "You fool! You will die for this, I will flay your hide and—"

Merrick sighed again. Osmium melted to morph over his hand as a katar, a short, wide triangular blade, its handle engulfing his wrist. A perfect pushing or stabbing weapon. "Do you really think it's wise to threaten me, here, *now?*"

The queen's eyes, normally full of haughty superiority, suddenly grew conflicted, even confused, and her evident fear won over her arrogance. He dug the sharp katar toward her flabby throat, drawing a pinpoint of blood.

"See, you've gotten too used to taking life with a simple command. You don't even understand what it's like when that power is taken from you. Your power is an illusion. You rule humans as your birthright, but you're just a worm in silks, wielding power you don't deserve."

"And you…" she seethed, "you are doing the very thing you profess to hate! Lording your power over us! How are you any better?"

Merrick sighed. "Mine is for a greater purpose, something you suckled swine wouldn't understand. Still," He eyed the flows of metal churning above his hand—unquestionable power at his fingertips. "It's a contradiction I battle with daily. If it helps any, my sword says I hate myself," he said with a small laugh that elicited only more terror in the nobles' eyes, as if they truly feared him to be mad. *Now is as good a time as any,* he supposed. "If you all do not know already, I am here on a mission from the Patriarch. The moment I arrived here, Covai became his. You became his. You can try to resist. Try to kill me behind my back, but more will follow. I am just his messenger." Merrick turned, looking out over the arena, south—as if he could see all of Farhaven—and he spoke to the terrified nobles with his back turned, "You may think I'm dreadful, but you have no idea what's coming…"

Merrick's Match

"My Lord Merrick," a messenger said, arriving at the balcony. He then stopped short, mouth parting as he took in the dreadful scene—from the decapitated woman's body to the dead servants and the swords still suspended in the air before the guards' and Reavers' throats.

"Yes?" Merrick inquired calmly.

"Y-your m-match…" the messenger stammered.

"Thank you." Merrick dipped his head to the queen. "Your Majesty, thank you for the lively…entertainment." Then he left the group of stunned nobles and dropped the weapons, which clattered to the balcony floor. Merrick followed the messenger, only to pause at the door and look back. "Remember, you may try to kill me, but I would think twice. I am but a shadow of the darkness you all know has been rising. You have been willfully ignoring it as you carry on in denial. If you wish to see tomorrow, you should seriously consider the price of your pride over your lives."

Then he left them.

After reaching the tunnel entrance, he moved two fingers, raising the metal gate.

Let's get this over with, he thought.

Osmium was silent. Why? Was it because he put those horrid nobles in their place?

Merrick tried to step onto the frozen landscape when—

A shiver of pain rooted him in place.

The arena forbids magical weapons until the final rounds, Osmium explained. Growling, Merrick transformed the katar in his grip to a long thin sword, then stabbed it deep into the wall, burying the blade to its hilt. "Stay put."

I have no intention of walking off, Osmium replied.

Merrick snorted. The blade's personality seemed to be growing, or at least unveiling itself, of late. Stalking onto the ice, snow crunching beneath his boots, Merrick listened as the announcer began his usual bombastic preludes. "In the west corner, hailing from the rough and wild Cloudfellian region, we have a combatant who is more mystery than man! Born and raised in inns and taverns full of cloak-and-dagger, where wrestling and scuffling with your neighbors is commonplace. He has won the most recent of his matches without even suffering a scratch! I give you a brawler of much notoriety…Zemrin Halrit of Cloudfell!"

The gate opened, and out stepped a man who seemed…unimpressive at first glance. He was roughly Merrick's build, and he was a brawler. His once handsome face was smashed almost beyond recognition, with an obvious broken nose, depressed cheekbones, and dozens of scars. He had a thick protruding brow hooding deeply set eyes that were a strange, very pale gray-green and burned with conviction. The man seemed built for tavern brawls. At first, Merrick dismissed him. Upon closer inspection, however, he saw the man's fists. They were wrapped in cloth, over which he wore brass knuckles, but that wasn't what drew his attention. Zemrin's fists were glowing with a faint magical aura that he was trying to conceal. But Merrick, with his heightened Nexus, could see it clearly.

The tattooed, bony announcer flung out his hand in Merrick's direction. "In the east corner…hailing from Yronia, the twisted scrap pile that was once the Great Kingdom of Metal, now infested with saeroks, vergs, and nameless…He is a legend of legends, a terrifying menace! His predecessor, Baro, was known to have no equal in a duel! No weapon he couldn't master. Known by many as the Unmatched Blade, Darksteel, Black Blood—now, his progeny has entered with a shadow in his eyes and a darkness in his heart! Will our challenger conquer all his foes, including his own brethren? I give you Merrick, Ronin of Metal!"

Merrick sighed, trying not to roll his eyes. *All this fanfare…*

The crowds' gaze intense on his back, Merrick stalked forward. One step closer to finishing this, and accomplishing his goal.

Then he looked about.

All the pillars were now coated in hoary frost, but they were empty. The metal weapons they had held were missing.

He looked up to the balcony.

The queen…

Her eyes glittered with malevolence, and a small smile played on her red-smeared lips. Her stare said it all. It was clever. Not an outright opposition after his stunt, but enough to show him that his defiance had a price. Her eyes said everything: *What will you do now?*

Merrick's glare darkened, and he turned back to his opponent.

On the balcony, Gray watched with the others as Merrick took the frozen tundra opposite the Cloudfellian man, a brawler sort with spiked knuckles and a faint aura of concealed magic. Only Gray could sense it, and it felt…strangely familiar?

"This is going to be brutal…" Helix said.

"Tell me when it's over," Ayva agreed, covering her eyes.

Helix covered his eyes as well, but then fanned his fingers. "Me too."

She elbowed him. "You're cheating."

"So are you!"

Zane interrupted their banter. "There's magic to the Cloudfell man."

Ayva's hands fell. "You're right…I sense it, too. An Untamed? He's clearly strong if we can sense it all the way from here, especially if he's trying to hide it."

Before Gray could say anything, the announcer shouted, *"Fight!"*

The match began.

Zemrin, the Cloudfellian man, didn't charge. Instead, the first thing he did was throw his brass knuckles into a snowbank against the wall. As far away as he could. Then he ripped the buckle of his belt off, and did the same, throwing it into the crowds. Men and women fought like wild dogs over the souvenir.

Clever, Gray knew.

"Merrick has no metal, what's he going to do?" Helix asked. "Wait, can…can he pull it from the air?"

"I haven't seen him do that before," Gray replied. "I'm not sure he's there yet."

"Then he's done for!" Helix exclaimed.

Zemrin grinned, and ran across the hard-packed snow.

Merrick just stood his ground.

Zemrin leapt and unleashed a flurry of blows. Merrick backpedaled, showing his fighting prowess by slipping, blocking, and evading most of the strikes. Zemrin was quick, and a punch Merrick couldn't slip in time clipped the side of his head, rocking the Ronin of Metal backward. He shook his head, in a daze.

Helix cheered loudly, spilling some of the drink at his side. "Get him!" The crowds bellowed as well.

"How was the Cloudfellian man so quick?" Ayva asked, leaning forward in her chair.

"He's Cloudfell!" Helix exclaimed. "They're fighters, my da—" He cut short. "I always heard they were the best in a scrap. 'Cloudfellians are tougher than old oak and twice as stubborn!' or something like that."

"No," Gray said, and his friend's eyes fell on him.

Helix snorted. "What do you mean, no? That's *definitely* a well-known saying."

Ayva rolled her eyes. "Pretty sure you made that up."

Gray shook his head. "Not the phrase, there's just something off about that man."

"Like what?" Helix asked as Zemrin attacked faster and faster.

Zane was silent, grip tightening on his mug.

"I don't know," Gray said slowly, eyes squinting. "It's—"

Then he saw it.

His heart stopped.

"What? *Gray?*" Ayva asked.

Magic swirled about Zemrin's hands. Only it wasn't water, or fire, or moon, or stone, or even metal…not even flesh…but wind. Zemrin ducked a punch from Merrick, then roared and sent a gust of wind, knocking Merrick back.

The crowds gasped.

Whispers flooded across the stands, taking the arena by storm.

"*Wind?*"

"*Not the Ronin of Wind?*"

"*How?*"

"*Who is he?*"

Gray understood now. That's how Zemrin was attacking so fast.

"Wait, what in the Tranquil Seas is going on?" Helix asked. "Did…did he just use wind?" He looked to Gray. "I thought only you could wield wind…"

Ayva stammered. "That's what the stories say. Wait, where was he from?"

"Cloudfell," Zane answered.

Gray felt as if he'd been dunked in an icy lake, his whole mind numb. Memories returned, not from him, but Kail.

Morrow, a city suspended on rising air currents—the most grand and majestic of all the Great Kingdoms—said to be destroyed and lost to time. Its citizens were forced to flee to all corners of the world. Then came images of saeroks, vergs, and nameless. The monsters scoured the land. Hunting. Burning. Methodically eradicating every last denizen of Morrow, as if fearing Kail's progeny. Fearing the return and the reprisal from the next Ronin of Wind.

Gray's reprisal.

More images scoured his mind fast and hard.

Pale-eyed men and women, fleeing, hiding. Many going east. Abandoning their given names, their old ways, blending into society once more and mixing their lines until...

Zemrin.

On the snowy arena floor, the Cloudfellian brawler leapt. His jump was powered by zephyrs of wind as he crossed a twenty-foot gap like it was nothing more than stepping over a puddle. Merrick retreated as the brawler struck with lightning speed, until his punches were a blur.

"He's doing it!" Helix exclaimed. "He's going to win!"

Gray's hand trembled where it clutched his mug.

Again and again, Zemrin scored a hit, smashing a fist into Merrick's gut, his jaw, his chin, and—

Merrick staggered back, then bellowed, as if he'd had enough.

The Ronin of Metal slammed his foot into Zemrin's chest, sending the man sprawling back, kicking up snow and chunks of dead grass. With a breath, Zemrin stood, more wind rising about him.

Zemrin's deformed face was full of vengeance.

"Why does he look so angry?" Helix asked. "I mean, I know Merrick's evil, but what's his deal?"

Zemrin abruptly shouted, voice filtering over the crowds as he addressed the Ronin of Metal, "I can smell their tainted presence on you... You're rank with it... saeroks, vergs... creatures that killed my ancestors. My family scattered to the Seven Winds because of that evil. They wanted us all dead. All my life, I've lived in constant fear, hiding, *running*, concealing myself, but I will hide no longer. I will make them fear us." A vortex of wind rose all about Zemrin.

Is he... Helix sent through the bond. *Is he... one of us? Two Ronins of Wind? Is that possible?*

Zane shook his head. *No. He's just an Untamed, but a strong one. He's using spark, not flow. Wind is just that powerful. It's everywhere, and clearly he's had a lifetime to forge his retribution.*

He was right.

After all, Zane knew vengeance. Gray could sense it too, the haunted look in Zemrin's pale eyes, a wild expression on his battered face that teetered between fury and sorrow. As if a thousand years of torment and suffering were only now breaking to the surface.

Merrick snarled, "I did not kill your brothers, but I would have." Faint steely gray mist wreathed the Ronin of Metal's frame.

Zemrin roared, charging, wind forming—

Merrick lifted his hands. From the hard-packed mud beneath the snow, tiny particles, flakes of gold and iron, lifted into the air—a *cloud of metal.*

Metal in the ground, Gray realized.

From the cloud, Merrick condensed the flakes into three metal spikes, then he flung out a hand just as Zemrin's wind-coated fist raced to end him. The three spikes flew—two were displaced by the man's wind, but the third found its mark, piercing Zemrin's heart in a coin-sized hole.

Zemrin's wind vanished, like a gust repelled by a metal wall, and he fell to his knees on the ice.

Slowly, he looked down. His eyes went wide in horror, then fury, then despair, and finally... sorrow. Such deep sorrow Gray felt it shudder through him as well. As if all his life's ambitions poured out onto the snow along with his blood. He uttered something Gray couldn't hear, then he fell forward, dead.

Gray's breath was ripped from his lungs. "No..." He'd only just seen the man, witnessed his brief fight, but he felt one with him. A citizen of Morrow, Great Kingdom of Wind. Or at least an ancient descendant. Now he was dead. Killed by Merrick. Sudden, profound grief filled Gray.

Merrick turned to their balcony, smirking as he wiped away a trickle of blood on his mouth from Zemrin's strikes. *You look upset. Was that your brother?* the Ronin of Metal asked. *All this time, I thought I was.*

Gray rose, seething, and before he knew it, the others were pinning him down, keeping him in place. *I will end you!*

Merrick's face was empty of emotion. *You will try.* Zemrin's corpse vanished into an orange mist. Merrick absorbed it, the spark flowing into his mouth, into his pores, growing him even stronger.

Gray let wind rise over his body, seeking to leap off the balcony and—

Ayva's shouts finally broke through. "Gray! You can't! They'll kill you if you try!" She gestured to the Reavers and archers.

After a while, too long, Gray's muscles uncoiled, and with a deep shuddering breath, he exhaled his unspent rage. He let his friends pull him back from the railing. Returning back to the moment, back to the world, seeing their small balcony, glancing down to his shaking hands. "I'm fine," he reassured them. "I think you were all correct, and I was wrong."

"As much as I like to hear those words..." Ayva said, "what are you talking about?"

"Merrick," Zane said.

Every part of Gray raged against this, hated the next words that came out of his mouth, as the announcer roared, calling the winner. Merrick stalked off the frozen wasteland, casting a final look over his shoulder.

"I have to end him," Gray said in a dark rasp. "I have to kill Merrick."

The last match of the third round was Jian versus Drega.

That alone had drawn Gray out of his dark thoughts.

Of course, Ayva, Zane, and Helix had responded very differently to Gray's sudden declaration of *I have to kill Merrick.* Helix had agreed. Ayva had been conflicted. Zane contemplative. Before they could say anything else, Jian and Drega were announced, and the two men walked onto the icy plains. Gray was torn. Both men felt strangely like mentors to him.

Yet, he yearned to watch this match.

Helix had left their balcony and returned with arms laden with food. "Did I miss anything?"

"Where are you getting the coin for this?" Ayva asked.

Helix flashed his one red sword on his forearm, wagging it. "Who needs coin? Primarian-basaeri, thank you very much! Fighting in the tournament was a great idea, pretty much everything is free!"

Ayva rubbed her brow. "You would abuse it."

"Abuse it?" Helix scoffed. "They are honored! You should see how excited they get." Waddling to his seat, he set down the armload of nuts, fruits, and meat upon a nearby wooden table. "Anyway, what'd I miss?"

"Jian and Drega are about to fight," Zane said, leaning forward in his seat. So far Zane had mostly just watched the fights with riveted interest, taking mental notes. Turns out, he had a keen eye for fighting forms.

The announcer finished his declaration. "…I give you two titans of the sword…Masters, each terrifying in their own regard! They will—"

"Gods, I can't wait to watch this one," Helix said. "Two leaders of their elite warrior clan?"

"It should be a hard-won fight," Zane agreed.

Gray rubbed his neck. He was eager to see the outcome too, yet…it felt wrong. The announcer boomed, "To the east, a man who has sustained ten thousand cuts! With the innate ability to heal quickly, faster, he is less man and more tempest of blades! Having nearly won the last tournament, losing to Nalia in the fifth round, he is a strong contender for Grand Primus! I give you our very own leader of the Fleshguard, Drega!"

Drega, his dark braids tight to his head, looked immaculately armored, his Fleshguard cloak with its symbol of a heart nearly brushing the ground as he turned in a circle, smiling broadly with that affable look of his, waving to the crowd. Gray saw through the smile that the man was ready for violence, ready for blood, as his eyes focused back on Jian.

"To the west," the tattooed announcer proclaimed, "I give you a man who has fought fifty Devari back-to-back and won every match. Who can sense others' emotions down to each soul's intent! So much so, it's said he can anticipate every move his opponent will make! Famed from the Citadel and the world over, I give you, leader of the Devari, Jian!"

Jian was blade thin and far smaller. Every ounce of fat had been burned off him, replaced with muscle and sinew. He had tan skin and long, shaggy hair. Normally, a fervor filled his eyes. Not today, however. Gray saw that wild light was absent.

Instead, the man scanned the cheering crowds, until—Jian's eyes found his.

From here, Gray opened his ki.

Jian's ki sifted into him.

Gray reeled, shocked by its speed and intensity.

It was powerful, incredibly so. Far more than he remembered.

There was no chance he could stop it from sensing his emotions even if he wanted. *How can he do it from so far away, and so fast?* Then the ki retreated. A faint smile came to Jian's lips.

"Gray?" Ayva asked.

Before Gray could say anything, Jian stepped forward, then made a gesture of prayer and knelt.

The sign of surrender.

The announcer floundered for a moment, then called out, "Winner by surrender, Drega!"

The roaring of the crowds suddenly halted, then turned to jeers.

Drega's brows furrowed. He looked confused and dissatisfied, as if he'd been robbed of a fight.

Jian didn't seem to care.

With a final nod to Gray, the leader of the Devari turned and walked off the icy terrain.

All three looked to Gray.

"What…what was that all about?" Helix asked.

Back to The Red Blacksmith

With the third round finished, again Covai celebrated, the streets alive with chaos, debauchery, and revelry.

The Ronin found themselves in a familiar tavern: The Red Blacksmith.

The portly innkeeper, Archibald Brinwall, looked nervous at first upon their entry, probably remembering their previous visit. Then his eyes widened as if he'd witnessed the fights and the Ronin's sudden rise in fame. After that, he practically gave them the shirt off his back, offering his own bedroom and his finest ales.

Archibald's rich voice echoed through the room as they slowly moved toward their table, the innkeeper following, lavishing praise on them. "I can't believe you won again! You glorious Primarians!" He wrapped his arm around Helix's shoulder, until the Ronin of Water politely extricated himself from Archibald's enthusiastic embrace. "Ronin! Ha! Some doubted, but ole Archibald never did! Legends, the lot of you! Whatever I can get you, just say it, and it's yours! My room, my wife…" He barked a laugh. "Mind you, I don't have one, but ha! I'd get one just for you! Please, sit here, my dearest and most favorite guests." He tried to kick a few people out of the best seats—ones with better views of the stage—but Gray declined, choosing their previous table, which had been replaced after it was broken. They shooed the innkeeper away. Men and women approached their table, wanting to shake their hands, wish them well, tell them they'd won a hefty bit of coin, or just stare wide-eyed at them. It was all baffling to Gray, but the interactions caught him off guard more than anything.

Ayva nudged Gray. "Don't look now, but I think you have an admirer."

Gray looked over. He expected a barmaid or young woman. After all, a few had batted their eyelashes at him, and all the barmaids had been far more flirtatious than before. Only as he turned, he found himself staring eye to eye with a boy.

Perhaps seven or eight-years-old, the boy had curly brown hair, dark round eyes, and a faint scar on his lip. A wood sword was stuffed through his belt. Gray looked about for his parents and saw a man and woman smiling from a nearby table.

"Hello," Gray greeted.

The boy gulped. "I'm Hamish."

"I'm Gray, this is Ayva, Helix, and Zane."

The boy bobbed his head, eyeing them all nervously, then looked as if he had something he needed to say, finally uttering, "Are…are you really the Ronin of Wind?"

Gray grinned. "I am."

Hamish gawked, then asked, "C-can I be a Ronin?"

"Uh…" Gray looked to the others, who were absolutely no help whatsoever.

Zane just watched, then grunted and looked away, as if wanting no part of the conversation.

Helix choked on his drink.

Ayva smiled, saying nothing, clearly reveling in Gray's discomfort.

"Maybe?" Gray cleared his throat. "We all have spark inside of us. Do you sense yours?"

"What does it feel like?" the boy asked.

"Like a small flame," Gray said, "and if you feed it, it will grow."

Hamish's already large eyes grew even wider as he leaned forward onto his tiptoes. "How do I do that?"

Gray scratched his head. He hadn't thought this far.

Thankfully, Ayva, in the chair beside him, swooped in to save him. She was closest to the boy and lightly touched his cloth shirt, where his heart was. "Simple! You breathe and focus, drawing deep within, like this," she said, and demonstrated a deep breath, then exhaled. "When you do that, you should feel a tiny little flame." She gestured with a pinch of her two fingers. She focused on it, pretending it was in the air before her eyes. "Then, concentrating, you pour all your emotion into it, never your fear or hate, but goodness. Kindness. Love. Truth. Do that, and your flame should grow big and strong. Then who knows"—she gave a little shrug and smirk—"you may be a Ronin one day."

Hamish's mouth parted, eyes growing wider and wider with every word she said. Finally, he nodded. "Okay!" Then he summoned his nerve again. "You're my favorite by the way." He was sort of looking at Gray. Gray opened his mouth to thank the boy, when Hamish shook his head. "Not you, you." He looked to Zane.

Gray looked befuddled.

Helix laughed.

"Uh, thanks?" the Ronin of Fire replied.

"Fire, and then you were a bear! It was amazing! That light thing you did," he said to Ayva, "and…" After a few more words recounting their fight, he heard his father call to him. Hamish thanked them, practically trembling in excitement. Then ran off, back to his parents, enthusiastically repeating their entire encounter.

Helix snickered. "That was great. Much better than kissing babies."

"Thanks for the save," Gray told Ayva.

She sniffed. "Anytime."

Moments later, food was piled high on their table, and music sifted toward them from the stage. Gray found some of the horrors and the mysteries of the tournament slowly replaying in his mind.

Helix slammed his drink down. "I still can't believe it! Ole Archibald is right. You two are Primarians! That sounds way fancier and more impressive, or whatever. After this, it's just Primus and Grand Primus…Abyss take me, I think we can actually win this!"

Gray looked down at the three red swords on his forearm that had appeared after his last fight, or lack of a fight, against Faye. He still wondered what she was up to. Part of him was fairly certain she would suddenly show up again, and he occasionally glanced at the door to the inn, expecting her and the giant Jivran.

"You doubted we could?" Ayva asked.

"Well, no," Helix said, then shrugged. "And yes. Hells, they've been the best warriors in all of Farhaven!"

Zane grunted, "You two are rightfully among them." He raised his glass. "Cheers, well done."

"I'll drink to that!" Helix exclaimed, clinking mugs, as the rest did the same.

"You fought well," Gray said, "you all did. I said we had to prove ourselves to the people of Farhaven, and so far we have... I don't think we're there yet, but we're well on our way. I can feel it."

Ayva cleared her throat. "Speaking of Zane, you know if you'd fought anyone else, it would have also been you on the Primarian stage."

Zane leaned back in his chair, and it creaked as he rolled his shoulders. "Maybe."

"Definitely!" Helix said. "If it was Jian, or Faye obviously, since Gray lucked out there."

Gray snorted. "Lucked out, eh?"

"I was looking forward to your fight with Faye," Zane replied.

"Me too," Ayva said, picking up a carrot, dipping it into a sauce, and taking a bite.

"Speaking of which, where is our Mistress of Shadows?" Helix asked.

Ayva replied, "Oh, knowing her, I'm sure she'll pop up somewhere when we least want or expect her."

Gray drew their gaze back to him. "There's so much happening. This all started with trying to find the next Ronin, then an unexpected dragon, then rising through the ranks... Now things are moving even quicker."

"Yeah," Helix agreed. "Jian surrendering was strange, then that look he gave you? You said he used the ki on you, but what could he have sensed that would have made him surrender his fight?"

"That's not all," Zane said. He held a mug in his hands, though he hadn't really drunk from it. Mostly his thumbs played over the pattern of Flesh on the mug's surface, seeming lost in thought. "Did you see the stone pillars? They've always been full of weapons, but just before Merrick took the stage, servants came out and cleared them of anything metal."

Helix scoffed. "Why would the queen sabotage Merrick? Those two are in league."

Gray rubbed his new bracers. He'd changed them back to leather. "Zane's right. I'm not sure what's happening now. Everything's conjecture, but if there is a crack forming between the queen and all these people, we can use it against her. I'm hoping that we can plant a seed. Helix, if you have the opportunity, try and convince Jian to join us."

"Done!" Helix said, popping a grape into his mouth. "I'll use all my charm."

Ayva lifted a brow and held up two fingers barely spaced apart. "So, this much?"

Helix glowered.

Zane chuckled.

"Zane—" Gray began.

Across the table, the Ronin of Fire's orange eyes fixed on him. Gray had forgotten just how much Zane had changed. He remembered a past encounter: Gray had been trying to find a way to save his grandfather, Ezrah, from torture. Zane had barged in with fury in his eyes, searching for Hannah. She'd been kidnapped, and the Underbelly—his home—had been attacked, ravaged. He'd lost everything. Understandably, Zane had been angry all the time, only calming with Hannah's guidance and urging.

Then, when she'd been killed, the constraint keeping Zane in check was gone.

They'd lost him to his rage.

Gray believed he had come back now. He wasn't certain, but he hoped so. When his friend returned right before the tournament began, while there was still a shadow hanging over him, a new seed had been planted: a passion, a desire for life. Then, after Zane's fight with Helix, he transformed again, as if his lone wolf mentality and his notion of strength had altered. Still, Zane seemed to be changing.

Looking at him now, he saw the same burning passion in the man. Reading him with the ki, he sensed more temperance, like a blade cooling, changing shape, and gaining strength—slowly taking its final form.

Gray continued, "Ayva told me you're searching for something. During the next round, I want you to find it. You said it involved becoming the Grand Primus, but clearly now that is not an option. I believe you'll find another way."

"I...do have some ideas," Zane mulled, gripping his mug tighter. Like an arrow given a target, some of the man's uncertainty was banished.

Ayva cleared her throat, broaching the next topic cautiously. Gray knew what she was going to say before she said it. "Are we going to talk about the wind element coming back?"

"Oh, right," Helix said around a mouthful of cake. He swallowed "Yeah, about that. Gray's whole ancestry and heritage just came back to life."

Zane grunted. "How are you feeling?"

Gray felt their looks, and he drew a long breath. "Strange. Conflicted."

"That seems natural. Next topic!" Helix said.

Ayva poked him in the ribs, eliciting a squawk from the Ronin of Water. "Go on," she insisted.

Gray sighed. "I just wanted to ask him questions and get to know him. To understand what it was like…I had memories when he appeared. Visions I think were more Kail's. About the citizens of Morrow fleeing, being hunted." Flashes returned even as he said it.

Men, women, and children chased down by monsters. Rooted out of their homes. Slaughtered like animals. He heard their screams. Gray felt a rage building. So many dead…Their eyes pale gray-green, like his, staring into the empty void. They used wind, just like him. But it was more than that. Something connected them—as if they were his blood, his family. Gray felt each death as every single Morrow citizen was annihilated from the face of Farhaven. They wanted to kill us all.

He closed his eyes against the visions, forcefully shutting them out. Ayva's hand was on his arm. Slowly, Gray returned back to the soft music of the amber-lit inn. "I…felt connected to him, to all of them. Zemrin chose to fight, as did everyone else on that field of battle. Merrick, as much as I dislike who he is, or has become, fought fairly. It was a battle to the death, after all. I think pinning all my anger on Merrick…Well, that's clearly some ancestral pain. It also made me remember that I'm not alone." He looked up into their eyes and saw their concern.

"Right. Surely there's more Wind guys out there!" Helix commented, gulping down a spoonful of mashed potatoes with his ale.

"Not them," Ayva said. "He's talking about us. Wait, you are talking about us, right?"

Gray chuckled. "Yes." Then he grew serious. "Anyway, we need a battle plan for tomorrow. More than anything, we need to eat, and rest. It's going to be a long day. Zane, whatever you find regarding your search, report back to us. Maybe the source of the arena's power can aid us in all of this. Helix—"

"Jian, got it!" Helix said.

"Drega and Captain Leanna too," Ayva said. "I don't think they're as loyal as the queen would like. We might need them before we're done here."

"You guys must think I'm pretty charming."

"Channel your inner Darius," Gray said.

"Never in my life have I heard such sweet words," Helix replied, chewing, mouth filled with food. So it sounded more like, "*Nev in mah ho wife ha I her shush swee wods.*"

"Oh gods, Helix, please chew and swallow, for light's sake!" Ayva replied. "Maybe I should do this."

"No," Gray said. "You and I? We have the hardest job yet."

"What's that?" she asked.

"Not die," Gray replied.

Zane and Helix grinned.

Ayva sighed.

Helix rose from his chair. "I've got an idea. How about we all find a different tavern? One with less history? I keep watching my back here. Shall we?"

"No, Helix. Not for us," Ayva said. "Early night, remember? You know, having to fight the strongest warriors in all of Farhaven."

Dejected, Helix sat back down and put his face in his hands. "Oh, right."

Ayva made a face, looking confused. "To be clear, Helix…you won't be fighting tomorrow, you know that, right? You can go celebrate if you want. I was just saying *we* have to be responsible."

"Wait, I can? Gray? Is this true? I can go?"

Gray raised his brow. "Helix, I'm not your father."

"No, thank the Tranquil Seas. You're something far more important," Helix said. "You're our leader. What you say goes. If you say we need to be clearheaded for tomorrow?" Shoving his cider aside, Helix gave a shrug. "Then that's what I'll do."

Gray exchanged a look with Ayva. When he realized the Ronin of Water *wasn't* being sarcastic, he replied, "I appreciate that. I know I can rely on you, but I won't ever control you that much. You can make your own decisions."

"Right, completely," Helix said, then winced. "Wait, so…is that a yes? I can drink?"

Gray laughed. "Fine, yes, one more. Then sleep, and a clear head."

Helix nodded. "Sold!"

"Whatever I said about you being like Darius, I take back," Ayva replied.

Zane shifted, eyes flickering up. Gray followed his gaze to a candlelit corridor in the back, but saw nothing save a few doddering patrons complaining about losing at cards, and going to relieve themselves. "I, uh, have to go—" Zane hesitated, as if searching for a lie.

"Bah! We all know you're going to see your mystery girl, lover boy," Helix said.

"Go," Gray agreed. "Come back tonight, or not. You earned some rest. But tomorrow?"

Zane nodded. "I'm going to find a relic that can change the world, and you're going to win a tournament for all of us. Don't let me down, fearless leader."

Gray snorted. "I'll try not to."

"What about me?" Ayva asked, scoffing.

Zane shrugged. "I never worry about you. I worry more about your opponents."

Ayva laughed. "Well, you don't have to worry too much about Nalia."

Zane looked serious. "Tomorrow."

"Tomorrow," Gray said. After Zane left, he half expected Faye to barge in again, or Merrick; instead, they were left alone.

Ayva must have noticed Gray staring at the inn's door. "Gray, they're not coming tonight. I'm sure we'll see them soon, fortunately or unfortunately."

"I've an idea," Gray said. "After all, the night's still young."

"Uh-oh," Helix replied.

"Yeah, where are you going with this?"

Gray shrugged. "We need to be prepared for tomorrow. That means getting stronger. Not to mention, I didn't get my match today so…Who's up for a little evening sparring?"

"Wait," Helix said, "I thought you said we had to take it easy. I know it's still early, and I don't mind a little fight"—he rolled his shoulders—"but won't you two be exhausted?"

Ayva cleared her throat. "That's not exactly true." Her eyes glittered. "I think I know just the place."

Zane thought he spotted a familiar face in the shadows of the back hallway of the inn, and he slipped away from the others. He reached the corridor lit by flickering candles. A few old men playing Elements mumbled curses as he squeezed by, and he scratched his head. "Where in the—"

A hand clasped over his mouth, and the scent of her immediately filled Zane's nose. Sweet, spicy—something like cinnamon with a hint of orange. Hells, when had he ever cared that much about the scent of a woman?

She rested her head on his shoulder, whispering in his ear, "Miss me?"

Zane glanced over his shoulder and saw she'd slipped out from a closed door—inside looked a quaint library, with musty old tomes and a long reading table. He chuckled.

"That's not a yes."

Immediately, he turned and kissed her, and she wrapped her arms around him. Zane pulled her into the room, kicking the door closed with his heel, and pressed her against the bookshelves. Only when they both grew short of breath, and she went a little limp in his arms with a moan, did he pull back.

"Guessing that's a yes…" Raina said, catching her breath, her voice soft and sultry.

He shrugged, feigning a yawn. "A little."

"Oh, okay, then I'll just go," Raina said, trying to slip under his arm, but he pinned her again, kissing her, and she returned it, moaning in satisfaction until he pulled away. Long lashes batted up at him as she gave him a mischievous look. "You really did miss me, didn't you? I guess last night was that good?"

Looking into her eyes, Zane replied firmly, "*Yes*."

A sly smile emerged on Raina's face. "It was, wasn't it?"

Zane pulled away, putting his hand to a window frame, gazing out on the busy dusky city. People were still reveling in the night, drinking, eating, laughing, basking in the moon's pale light. Only he felt sour.

"Everything all right?" Raina asked, nearing to lean against him, lightly tracing his arm with a finger. "Didn't wear you out that badly last night, did I?"

"No... well, you did but, in a good way."

"Then what's with the big pouting look?"

Zane sighed, admitting, "I... I didn't win."

She snorted. "I watched your fight with Ayva. You both fought like legends." The word triggered something in Zane, but he suppressed it. "Gods, the whole arena practically rioted in excitement when you started casting those crimson fireballs. Ayva had to pull a rabbit out of her hat by exploding a bomb in your face to win!"

Zane grunted. "You're right. Ayva was amazing."

Raina lifted a brow, scratching her temple. "Yeah, definitely not what I just said."

He sighed. "I don't know how to explain it. All this time, I think deep down I believed I might be the strongest. I still sense something I haven't quite uncovered, something about my true potential, but on that arena floor, I felt her power. I may have looked impressive, but I couldn't hold a candle to Ayva. It was like staring into the sun. I had to turn away."

Raina grabbed his face in her hands. "Listen to me. You both were amazing."

He snorted.

"Fine, that was my first approach. Should I just smack you around until grumpy, doubting, pouting Zane is replaced by gruff, confident Zane?" Tendrils of flesh—ruddy filaments of ephemeral light—floated just above her palm. "You know I will. Don't make me."

He huffed a laugh. "Fair enough."

"There's something else, isn't there?" She tugged on his arm as he grunted. "Well go on, you big lug. You've opened up this much. What's a little bigger crack in that tough, stony exterior?"

Zane sighed. "I... was told to find something. Now I'm worried I won't be able to find it."

"Why?"

"I was told that I needed to become Grand Primus to get it."

Raina shrugged. "Well, then I don't see the issue. When the others become Grand Primus, they'll help you find this incredibly mysterious and vague thing you want. Speaking of which, can you be a little more circumspect and unclear? Seriously," she said, "It's like trying to draw blood from a stone. A fiery, handsome stone, but still."

Zane complained, "That's just it, I don't even know what it is myself."

She planted her hands on her hips. "You're saying they told you to go to an unknown place, to find an unknown thing, and you just said…yes? How in the bone and blood does that make any sense?"

Zane replied, "They did hint it has to do with the magic of the arena, and that it lies below the colosseum."

"Huh…the flesh-consuming power that liberates the spark? That is pretty interesting. I've always been curious about it. Seems too strong for anything a Reaver or Arbiter can do in this age. At least they gave you a little direction. Wait, who's they?"

With a heavy breath, Zane admitted, "Dragons."

"Oh, right. Dragons told you. That's fair. The other day I was riding on a unicorn and stumbled across a chimera. It told me I should find—"

He interrupted her. "I'm being serious."

Seeing his look, her eyes narrowed. "You are, aren't you? Seven hells, Zane, who are you? Talking with dragons, wooing women?" He opened his mouth, and she stopped him with a hand on his chest. "Okay, okay, no need to growl again, though I like it when you do. Still, tell me, if it's 'below' the colosseum, did you already check the halls under the arena?"

"I did," Zane said, "everywhere. I saw nothing."

"Maybe you need another set of eyes," she offered. "Aside from it being linked to the magic of the arena, did they give you any hint as to what you're trying to find? Like a key, or a sword?"

Zane answered, "No. Whatever it is, it can change the future of Farhaven." His grip tightened on the window frame, and wood creaked beneath his fingers. "I'm certain of it."

"Then it sounds like we need to find it. Also," she said tentatively, hand on his tense arm, "maybe losing was a good thing. You've got to choose your battles, right? Now your friends can compete for that fancy Earthstone and the Covian Legion while you and I…" Her fingers stroked his forearm with its two swords. "With your newfound status, I've a feeling we'll be able to open some doors."

Zane grinned. "I like where your head's at."

Raina's lips twisted, and one eyebrow rose. "Oh, that's not where my head is." She eyed the table, jumping to sit on it with a wicked, mischievous smile, "Round two?"

Zane neared her, putting his hands on her waist. "Gods, yes, but…"

She looked up at him. "What?" Then she tapped her soft lips in thought, and winked. "Oh, right, more like round five or six."

"No, that's not what I was going to say." His mind fuzzed, his blood getting hot, and he forcefully returned back to the moment by shaking his head. *Burn me, I need Helix to conjure a cold lake whenever Raina's around. Is it flesh powers she's using?* "Raina…"

"Is it the innkeeper's family portraits?" Raina asked, nodding to the walls behind her head. Portraits of others resembling the portly Archibald, male and female, stared down on them. "We can take them down."

"No, it's just…well, yes, that is a little uncomfortable." Holding her waist, he gently lifted her off the table and back to the ground. It took everything in him.

She raised a brow. "Losing lust for me already?"

"Hardly. It's just…" Zane hesitated, took a few steps away, trying to compose his thoughts.

She followed, leaning back against the musty bookshelf. She batted her eyelashes up at him. "Go on. I'm listening."

He growled, looking away.

"Have I mentioned I like when you get all brooding and contemplative? I get this feeling like you have a maelstrom of thoughts inside your head."

Looking down into her inquisitive wheat-colored irises, Zane ventured, "Join us, Raina."

She narrowed her eyes. "Are you saying 'Raina, join us,' or are you saying 'join us, join us'?" She nodded her head, as if indicating Gray and the others in the common room. "Like that *us*?"

"The second one," Zane said. Then, "Just to be clear, as one of us."

Raina rolled her eyes. "Yeah, I got that."

He shrugged. "Always better to be direct." Looking at her, he pressed, "So?" His heart was strangely pounding. Why was he so nervous? Did her joining the Ronin mean that much to him? It did. Why? Because she'd stay near him, or because Farhaven needed her? Zane wasn't sure, only that he hung on her silence, yearning for her to say yes.

Raina bit her lip, looking away. At last she sighed, moving to a small window, watching the people of Covai in the dusky lit streets. "You know that can't happen, Zane."

He neared, wrapping his arms around her. "Why?"

"You know why," Raina said softly, almost sadly. "I can't just leave Sasha. Not when I've just got him back."

"Bring him—"

Her big eyes looked up at him. "You also know I can't do that. Sasha has spark inside of him, but he's not strong enough. What's coming is going to try to break the world, Zane. I can't lose him, not like…" Her voice trailed to a whisper.

"Not like I lost Hannah," Zane finished, his voice a hollow rasp.

"I didn't—"

Zane shook his head, pulling back a little. "No, it's all right. I understand. I get it." He sighed, then chuckled. "Ash and fire, they would like you, though."

She flipped her chestnut hair. Wait, it was brown now? "Who wouldn't?"

Zane hesitated. *Those words…*

"What, is it the hair? Honestly, I don't even know when it changes anymore. I think it's a subconscious thing. It's normally dark, but I'm pretty sure last night it was mostly a fiery red."

"No, for a moment you reminded me of someone."

"Are you trying make me jealous?" she teased. "She better not be as pretty."

Zane lifted a brow. "No offense, but isn't that an unfair advantage? You can quite literally change your features to anything. I'm curious. Were you—"

"Always like this? You mean, is this my normal face?" Raina asked and shrugged. "I could say yes, but you may never know. Also, does it matter?"

Zane supposed it didn't matter to him, not really, and he said as much. Again, there was something about her that was…unchanging and perfect, even in its imperfection. The little wrinkle at her brow, the crease in the corner of her mouth. The sharpness of her laugh softened when he pulled out a genuine chuckle. "I annoyingly like everything about you."

"Well, so far," she said, "you gotta hide the crazy for as long as possible."

He chuckled and wrapped his arms around her.

She pressed her cheek against his chest. "I like this part of you. The softer side."

"Soft?" Zane replied.

"Yeah"—she tapped his chest—"you seem all fire and brimstone with that brooding gaze of yours, those muscles, and your anger, but I know you, Zane. Inside you're a big ol' softy." Zane grumbled, knowing she was just trying to get a rise out of him. "Oh." She looked up at him, eyes tapering in amusement. "And for the record, this is my real face. Just thought you should know."

Midnight Meetings

After they left the inn, Ayva led them to a courtyard where one's vitality would be slowly restored, a benefit of the arena's magic. Ayva had picked up word about these training grounds while entertaining the queen and her nobles. The way she bit off every word of her explanation, however, made Gray not want to press the topic too deeply. With a touch of sun, Ayva lit the grounds with a hundred tiny orbs of light. "There."

"Oooh, setting the mood," Helix commented. "I like it."

Ayva pulled a training sword from a nearby weapons rack, pointing it at Helix. "You first."

Helix held up his hands. "Oh, I'm quaking in my boots!"

"You will," she replied.

Then they fought with sun and ice, crashing against one another in a dazzling display. However, it was clear both held back. Next, Gray fought Helix. They all sparred lightly, exchanging ideas and moves more than serious blows. They agreed it wouldn't do to rip each other apart before the final battles. Mostly, they strategized for their next fights.

After the sparring session, returning back to his rooms, Gray's mind was set—his resolve ironclad. He or Ayva would win the tournament, gain the Covian Legion, and save Farhaven from impending doom.

Unfortunately, his body didn't agree.

That night, Gray's nightmares grew worse, plagued with thoughts of Merrick and his black bow, of Queen Imala's cruel smile, and of the Earthstone falling into the hands of the enemy…This time, he was forced to watch Ayva die on the sands as Nalia's crimson sword ran her through the stomach, Zane's and Helix's bellies torn open by a saerok's long claws as the city was overrun by beasts. Sitting up with a gasp, sweat covering his body, Gray caught his breath.

It was only a nightmare.

The images clung like spiderwebs he couldn't scrub free. On his right, the balcony doors were ajar to let in the cool night air, and a breeze rustled the white drapes. With a sigh, Gray washed sweat off his face from the water basin, threw on a loose pair of cotton pants and a shirt, then moved to the balcony.

Sitting on the floor, Gray leaned against the wall again and stared out over a desert city.

The people still celebrated, intoxicated on the tournament and well... drunk in general, judging by the raucous laughter, cheer, shouts, and general hum of life below. He stared out, seeing the barren sands beyond, now entrenched in night. The city was like a glowing torch, beating back the darkness. That made his mind wander to the other cities: Vaster, city of Sun, of Narim, Moon, Eldas, Leaf... all of them, churning with their own political machinations, all the while the evil liking festering just beyond reach. Gray realized his hand had become a fist and was shaking at his side. Suddenly, music filled his ears from the lively city below and he unfurled his fist, taking a deep breath.

"So much is happening," Gray whispered into the desert sky.

Morrowil was in his lap. He hadn't even remembered picking up the blade. But he knew it was listening.

"Why does it feel like the calm before the storm?"

It's always this way, Morrowil replied.

It was good to have the sword with him, and it banished some of the darkness weighing on his mind. *Kail felt this way, too?*

Always.

Gray realized now. *It's the same evil... I suppose that makes sense. Despite centuries dividing us, and an age of legends, we're still up against the same threat.*

Indeed. An evil whose depravity knows no bounds.

Gray gulped. *I'm... not sure if that's helping.*

Morrowil made a thoughtful sound, then said hesitantly, *Sometimes, the best way through, is not running from the feelings, but embracing them.*

All of them? Gray felt the jitters in his stomach, the hope, the fear, the doubt. *That's... a lot of emotions.*

Morrowil snorted in amusement. *Perhaps so. Humans do love their emotions.*

Gray watched a few flickering lights, and then he gazed east, into the distance. While seeing only shifting dunes, he knew what was out there. Creatures, giant sandworms, who made their home in the endless desert surrounding Covai. A greater evil lurked beyond that. Median and the shadow's armies. Rounds of shouts, of laughter, echoed from the city below. Gray thought he might have actually heard his name. *What was Kail's downfall, then? Truly,* he asked the sword.

Morrowil was contemplative. *I have thought on this long and hard and have only one answer distilled down to a single word.*

That is?

Trust.

Trust?

The sword in his lap made a humming sound of agreement. *Trust in himself, trust in the other Ronin. Kail doubted and he turned toward darker ways to gain power. Then, well… We all know that part of the tale.*

He went mad, Gray replied. He knew the titles well, all the world did. Kail the Madman. Kail the Betrayer. Kail the Broken.

Morrowil made a sound like a sigh in his head. *Yes. Sadly, he became what he feared most.*

You don't think I'll do the same? I know he wasn't all evil, Gray said, remembering the Ronin of Wind at the altar when he'd helped Gray end the Kage. Gray could still see that final look on Kail, his predecessor's face. Those rugged features softening, a gleam in his eyes, holding a faint hint of a smile. At the time, Gray read it as a man who'd faced a lifetime of pain and suffering, finally knowing a glimmer of peace… Now though, he wondered, feeling like that man's look was misleading, as if had some sort of secret. Gray added, *I know in the end, Kail did the right thing. But he also helped break the world. How am I supposed to do this when even Kail, a legend, centuries older and wiser than me, fell to his own fear?*

Morrowil was quiet for a long moment. For so long Gray didn't think the sword would answer. A lilting musical instrument—he'd discovered it was called a *sansan*—filtered its way to his ears. Finally, Morrowil spoke. *Do you see the people below?*

In the street, men and women began to dance. *There is hope in them,* Gray thought. *They want something more than death and bloodshed.*

You see it, do you not?

I do, but what's it have to do with me?

You fear the shadow within you. That fear holds you back. They too, have a darkness inside of them, only their fear does not paralyze them. Fear is always there. Sometimes more, sometimes less. You must simply dance with it, until it is not the demon you thought it was. They have yet to be shown the light... until then, they dance.

Gray squinted. *So you're saying I should dance?*

Morrowil snorted. *You're avoiding my valid point.*

Gray had a feeling he knew where the sword was going—it was the reason his hands were shaking—but he asked anyway, *Which is?*

On the opposite side of your fear and your darkness... isn't joy, kindness, and love, like for them. It's power. You fear your own power. If you run from it, you run from Kail's legacy, you will never become what you could be. What Farhaven needs you to be.

Gray looked down at his palms. *Accept my fear. Accept my own power...* Was he really that afraid of his own legacy? While clean and calloused, Gray saw blood on his hands. So much blood. From Vera's blood to now the blood if the arena. More laughter rose from below, and the words sank into his mind: *Win the tournament, win the people.* "I need this city."

"They need you." This time it wasn't Morrowil.

He turned, jumping to his feet, and saw Hati standing in the doorway of the balcony. She wore loose tan cloth pants and a baggy shirt. Her head, shaved to show only a bit of hair, was growing out, revealing more of her blond roots; her light green almond eyes arrested him.

"Sorry," Hati said, "I... saw the light on and worried I forgot to blow out a candle. Then I heard you talking."

How long have I been talking aloud? Gray asked Morrowil.

Almost the whole time, the sword responded.

"To whom were you talking?" Hati asked, taking a step nearer.

Gray debated lying. Then, perhaps because he was partly delirious from sleep exhaustion, or perhaps because he wanted to tell someone, he just shrugged and lifted Morrowil by its bone-white hilt. "My sword."

"I see," Hati said, as if that was perfectly logical. She glanced to his side. "Mind if I..."

"Please," he offered, gesturing as he sat once more.

Hati joined him, watching the lights together—both taking in the amber-lit taverns, and wandering citizens through the web of dirty streets—before she asked, "So, your sword... what insights did it have? Anything interesting?"

"You could say that." Gray rubbed a hand through his hair. "Apparently, I'm afraid of my own power."

Hati snorted. "Well, I could have told you that."

Gray chuckled, his eyes on the city. "Am I that easy to read, or are you that perceptive?"

"A little of both." Her eyes flickered to him and she smiled.

Gray suddenly realized her loose clothes were sleeping attire. Her comment about the flame and candle now sounded a little...suspicious. Why was she coming to check on him so late anyway? He cleared his throat. "Hati, you said you were checking on me?"

"Yes, I..." Hati flushed red. "I tried sleeping. It didn't go so well."

"Why not?"

"When I close my eyes I see..." Her brow wrinkled, eyes full of pain and memory. "All that blood and fighting." He opened his mouth, but she continued, "Watching you was worth it."

He chuckled. "Hati, I...I didn't even fight. My opponent never showed up."

She snorted. "You almost sound glad about it."

Gray rubbed his forearm. Having to fight Faye? Being here with Hati put his feelings for Faye in a confusing light. He'd always been drawn to Faye. For a long time, he thought it was because her darkness matched his own. Over time, he started to realize it was because her light was similar. She took on the responsibility of others, others followed her, and she'd help those who needed help. As much as he'd like to deny it, Faye was equally stunning—in an "I might kiss or kill you" sort of way. Now, with Hati here, he wasn't thinking about Faye so much.

Hati's large eyes took him in. *Seven hells*, Gray thought. That alluring shape, her gleaming intelligence...like a still lake with faint moss coloring its water. Or the first bud of spring. He could drown in those eyes, and he realized he was.

She spoke, breaking his trance. "What are you thinking?"

Gray's cheeks heated a little. His pulse raced as he cleared his throat. "I was thinking...how you were avoiding the question." He gave her an impish smile. "Why are you here again?"

Instead of blushing, or turning away, however, Hati boldly looked into his eyes. She leaned in closer. Her breaths made her chest rise and fall, and he felt his pulse quicken. Despite his recent nightmares, he felt drawn to her. She bit her lower lip. They were only a few inches away now. Lights from the city flickered within her eyes. Her breaths came faster.

Finally, she shook herself, rising. "I should go…"

Gray grabbed her wrist. It was almost instinct. He rose as well.

Hati looked back at him, eyes wide. Yet, she didn't pull away. "I…this is wrong…" She cast her gaze to the marble floor. "You're a Ronin, my lord…"

He laughed. "You know, up until recently, no one believed that. Even when they finally did, I promise no one thought it was a good thing. Feared, hated. Only you don't view me that way."

"No."

Gray felt read to the core, incredibly vulnerable beneath her gaze. As much as he wanted to close himself off, to turn away, he also reveled in the intensity of her look. "Why?"

She looked up at him. "I saw it from the first moment I met you…" She gave a small laugh. "I saw it on the sands, too. The way you walked out. No anger, no hatred. It's the look of a man who wants to change the world, even when he's afraid. Even when the world fears him. I believe you can."

Gray took another step closer.

Hati's breath came faster. "My lord…"

"Gray," he corrected, and his hand slipped behind her neck. He pulled her in and kissed her deeply. At first her lips were soft, supple, as she seemed to savor it. Then firmer, as she kissed him back. That was all it took. Gray let go. Pain, darkness, the growing shadow… fights to the death in an arena…pressures to save a world… to not succumb to his own doubts, his own darkness. All of it vanished beneath her kiss. He pressed Hati against the wall and she moaned in response. He bit the nape of her neck, and she gasped. She tried to rip off his shirt, but the cloth resisted, so he tore it off himself. Her hands caressed his body, pulling him to her. So he obliged, and pressed her tight to the wall.

Losing himself to the moment, to her.

An Ancient Secret (Part 1)

"This way," Zane said, as he and Raina wove their way into the bowels of the colosseum, deeper and deeper, passing messengers, guards, and servants in their Covian tans and reds. They were in a secret network of tunnels beneath the arena. Zane's gaze was fixed ahead. Fire in his gut, he tried to keep the flames from rising up his arm. He hunted for an object that could change Farhaven forever.

Beside him, Raina wore her tan jacket with the sigil of the healers—a snake wrapped around a cross. While it had gotten them entrance to certain places, including the dungeons with the Vile Ones, she'd informed him it wouldn't work everywhere. They passed a group of courtesans in colorful, gauzy attire, showing copious amounts of skin. Raina cast him an eye. "Your gaze just skipped right over them, didn't it?"

Zane shrugged. "Why wouldn't it?"

Raina made a little sound.

"What?"

"Nothing."

He raised a brow. "'*Nothing*' usually never means that. Tell me the truth," he said, taking another turn, passing a few Reavers, though none of Nefrin's ilk.

"I'm just surprised you're not taken by now," she said, then clarified. "Not already a handsome, brooding husband, that is."

"Some have tried. Said they couldn't handle my...'edges.'"

Another little thoughtful sound. "Huh. That's where they're wrong. I would never tame the wild edges." He smiled, and she chuckled. "C'mon, we can flirt later." She pulled his arm, "This way." They turned and found themselves in a long empty hallway with double-wide doors that led down, deeper, closer to their goal. Unfortunately, two grim-faced guards with polearms blocked their path, roughly forty paces away. These soldiers were larger, stronger, more muscled, as if whatever was being guarded down here beneath the sands was vital and precious.

Both guards narrowed their gazes.

Zane stepped forward.

Raina whispered, "Zane, remember, *my* way first."

"I thought you didn't want to tame my wild edges," he replied under his breath, now thirty paces away from the guards.

She grumbled, "If you kill these guards, and we get lost, forced to double back, and the halls are suddenly crawling with soldiers, what then, huh? Are you just going to step over their dead bodies and say '*oops, not us*'?"

He shrugged, now twenty paces away from them. "I'd play it by ear."

Raina flicked a finger and a sharp pinch on his rear got Zane's attention. He rubbed his backside as she replied, this time through the bond, *No killing. Not unless we must. Just act natural and do what we discussed. Show your wrist. Trust me. It's going to work.*

Wait, you're just going to casually talk through the bond and act like it's nothing?

She flashed him a look. *I like surprising you. Your face is cute when you're shocked.*

You're talking through the light-blinded bond! This is too strange.

Get over it, we're almost to them.

Zane rolled his eyes.

Ten paces.

Five.

Both guards gripped their polearms more tightly, and the bigger guard called out, "Halt! These are the restricted halls save for only—"

Zane lifted his forearm showing the two thin red swords with cross guards, like crimson claw marks.

Primarian-hadus.

The guards bowed their thick necks. "My Lord Primarian-hadus," the bigger man said, and both pulled back their halberds and opened the door. Zane cleared his throat, letting the fire in his fist dim, then nodded, and Raina followed him through the doorway.

On the other side, she ribbed him, saying, "See? Told you."

Zane sighed.

Six more guards, three more doorways, and an iron gate later, he realized Raina was correct. "You were right. This is far easier than I expected."

"That's Covai. Coin is great and all, but fame is a far better currency." At the next juncture, they came to a four-way intersection. It was empty. Raina froze. "Okay, I have no idea where to go now."

Zane glanced down the long hallways, narrowing his gaze when something tickled his nostrils. He breathed in deeper.

Magic...

His flame pendant around his neck glowed a little. He gripped the relic, trusting some innate part of himself, and—

"This way," Zane declared.

Raina's wheat-colored eyes narrowed, though she followed. After another two times of Zane leading them in a new direction, she finally asked, "Right, what's going on? How do you know where we're going? Are you sniffing it out? Do you have some sort of power of smell I'm not aware of? Which should be mine, if you do."

"I have a secret," Zane replied, giving her a sly smile.

She huffed. "Mind telling me what it is? Or do I have to pry it out of you?" Little wisps of tan flesh hovered over her fingertips.

After another turn, passing ancient corridors, layers of dust having long ago coated all surfaces, he replied, "Open yourself up to your Nexus. You'll sense it."

"Nexus?"

Zane looked over at her, seeing her raised brows. "Right." He realized she probably never had formal Ronin training. None of them really had. They'd pieced fragments together like a tattered quilt, one patch at a time. Still, he clearly knew far more than she did. "The Nexus is the magical source of our power. It's what you sense in your mind when you need to access your *flow*. I'm guessing your Nexus probably looks like a sphere of flesh?"

"Yes, how did you...?"

"Mine is a swirling sphere of orange fire."

"I see."

"How much do you see of your Nexus?" he asked.

"For a long time, it was just a vague shadow in my mind—"

"But recently you've been able to tap into it more, right?"

Raina's gaze narrowed further. "It's kind of eerie how much you know, but yes."

Zane was eager, fascinated that her powers were opening up just like this. "How much have you seen of your Nexus?"

"Like I said, before I could see just a faint outline. Now? Maybe a little more than a quarter."

"When did it change?" he asked, taking another corridor, feeling the hair on the back of his neck rise, like they were getting closer.

Raina looked away, as if pained by the memory. "Sasha was being dragged away by the queen's guards with a Reaver in the lead. I know not all Reavers are evil, but this one was poison to the core. He clearly had some underlying hatred for Untamed."

"What'd you do?"

She shrugged. "I made sure he'd never hurt anyone again. He was strong, however. To stop him, I had to go deeper, access something more. In the process, I think that's when more of my Nexus got unlocked. What about you?"

"Same," Zane admitted. Even now, he touched the orange sphere in his mind, like a crescent moon, glowing orange, slightly less than a quarter full was illuminated.

Raina glanced down a pair of hallways they passed as Zane led them deeper. "What's this have to do with you knowing these halls like you built them?"

"Touch your Nexus, feel its power," Zane replied.

Raina's eyes tightened, and she concentrated. For a flickering moment, a faint light, like bronze smoke, wreathed her arms. She gasped.

"You sensed it?"

"Yes, it's like a tingle at the base of my spine."

"Good, then keep up."

Together, they delved deeper and deeper into the underground hallways below the colosseum, until they reached a large, wide corridor, twice as tall as the others—a strange, red-clay stone covered all the walls. They slowed, marveling.

"What is this place?" Raina breathed.

Zane put his hand to the walls. Something trickled up his arm, feeding him. He opened his mind to the Nexus and saw it. All about, the walls glowed orange as if lit with fire. No, not fire. *Spark.* Endless amounts of it, as if blood had seeped from the many dead bodies high above, through the sands—finally infusing itself into these hallways, within the strange red-clay walls. The red-orange lit the way, better than any torch.

"Ash and brimstone," Zane cursed. "It's spark."

Raina cried out.

Zane's heart leapt into his throat as he saw Raina's knees buckle. In a flash, he was at her side, holding her limp body. Her lids fluttered like she'd suddenly been clubbed in the back of the head. "Raina! What happened?"

With a hand to her temple, she replied, "I was just opening myself to the Nexus, and…" She looked up into his eyes. "Let's just say, it's not a small tingling anymore."

Zane squinted. Warily, he opened his Nexus. Sure enough, the faint tingling sensation in his neck was now a pinching sensation. "For the record, I don't like this."

"Noted, but time is short."

She was right.

He couldn't hear the drums, but he felt them.

Far above, Zane knew the next fight would be starting soon.

They needed that distraction. Somehow he doubted they'd be alone down here for too long. "C'mon, I'm starting to get the hang of this," Raina said, a tan mist again swirling about her body as she guided them onward. Only with the next turn, she stopped short. Zane's heart fell. They were in a hall with corridors that forked in a dozen different directions. Worse still, when Zane tapped into the Nexus, the pressure was everywhere, as if the magic engulfed it all. "Burn me," he snarled, fire coating his fist, "I can't sense where we need to go. It's too much."

"I've an idea," Raina said, taking a deep breath and closing her eyes. "Make sure I don't bump into anything, will you?" She held out her hand, eyes still closed.

Zane sighed. He took it.

"I can feel how grumpy you are even with my eyes closed. You better not let me stub my toe."

"That's not what scares me. You collapsed earlier. This presence, whatever it is, is hurting you."

"I'll be fine," she said, cracking an eyelid to wink at him. "Now hush your handsome face and come on."

Zane had no choice but to follow, while ensuring she didn't bump into any walls. She walked the corridors as if her eyes were open, taking a left, then a right turn. The halls were strangely bright with the red essence, like plunging into the heart of some hellish demon's lair. Here and there, she'd wince against sudden pain. Raina abruptly staggered, and he grabbed her arm. "Raina, enough of this—"

"I'm fine!" she insisted, pushing him back.

"No, you're not," he replied in a dark growl. He wiped at the trickle of blood that was running from her nose.

Eyes fanning wide for a moment, Raina scrubbed at it, shaking it off. "It's nothing."

"No," Zane said, grabbing her shoulders. "This is too much. I won't let you."

"You won't let me?" Raina turned on him, the subtle curve of her ever-present smirk absent as she fixed him with a look that could have snuffed even the strongest flame. Her eyes blazed, her jaw was set, and her fists trembled at her side. "Listen, Fire Boy, you want to find this thing? Then this is how we do it."

"Raina—"

"Before you say anything, Zane, I like you, a lot. You know that, but this is my choice. Not yours, and there's nothing you can say that's going to change my mind. If you respect me, then you'll let me do this."

He growled and opened his mouth, then closed it. She was right. Eventually, he was only able to give a reluctant nod under the intensity of her glare. She nodded back and they pressed onward, down another hall, taking turn after turn. Zane questioned, "I don't get it. Why do you think it pains you more?"

She shrugged as they walked, wincing from time to time, though now she was clearly trying to hide the pain. "Maybe because I'm a Flesh denizen? Something with the city? It doesn't feel evil. At the same time, it doesn't feel good. I…I don't know."

Zane grunted. She was right. He felt the same thing…the sharp stabbing on the back of his neck, it felt *powerful*, though not evil or good. What was it? Finally, they reached a giant pair of red doors. Even Zane, with his conflicted feelings, experienced a wave of amazement. His throat tightened, and jaw went slack. "Ash and fire…"

"You're telling me," Raina breathed.

Each giant door was made out of a strange glossy red metal. They were massive, and looked impossibly heavy; he imagined it took magic to get them down here. It would have required dozens of men to lift a single door. Each door's face was an intricate masterpiece like nothing he'd ever seen before.

It depicted a battle of nine titans fighting dragons. On one door, a Dragon of Fire unleashed a wave of flame that would have engulfed a city. On the other door, a Dragon of Wind blew a tornado to uproot a forest. There were other creatures too, but the image of the Dragon of Flesh formed where the doors met in the center. *Sinew*, Zane knew. Just like he'd seen it in person, the dragon was made of bone, tendon, and red muscles. Sinew had conjured white-bone spikes out of the earth that could have impaled...well, a dragon. The other dragon images all used torrential levels of magic. All of them fighting the nine titans. The titans themselves were depicted just like the stories. Giant, towering godlike creatures made of stone, fire, moon, and the other elements—each the size of mountains, weathering the dragons' blows.

Dragons...

A memory returned.

Zane had just finished his counsel with the nine primordial dragons, and his mind was still reeling. Nine ancient beings...In truth, he felt as if it would take a lifetime to reconcile the entire ordeal. After the meeting, the dragons withdrew to confer, so he'd wandered off, needing to clear his head. Spotting a hill, he hiked to the rise. Now he found himself on a wide hilltop that sat above the tree line. He looked out over the vast wilderness that was Drymaus Forest. The woods looked just as intimidating from up here, a nearly impenetrable dark green canopy—but he caught glimpses of enchanted meadows, majestic waterfalls, a labyrinth brimming with ancient magic and terrifying creatures.

Zane's mind was elsewhere, however, churning with thoughts of Hannah, Sithel, and vengeance.

Suddenly, the ground shuddered with footsteps.

Zane had felt him far before his arrival, like a giant inferno approaching.

Pyre, the massive Fire dragon, lowered himself to Zane's side. While the hilltop was wide enough to fit a large house, the dragon took up most of it, his red-and-black tail curled around boulders and trees. "How'd the meeting go?" Zane asked.

"GOOD. WE ARE IN AGREEMENT."

Zane swallowed. "What kind of agreement?"

Pyre's wagon wheel–sized orange eye fixed him. "THAT WE WILL NOT EAT YOU…YET."

Zane laughed.

Pyre didn't.

He had been pretty sure it was a joke, though now he realized dragons probably didn't have a similar sense of humor. He swallowed. "That's good," he said absently. "Though to be fair, if you wanted to eat me, that's fine too. At this point, I don't really care."

Pyre made a thoughtful sound. "HMMM. I SEE. SUCH LITTLE CONCERN FOR YOUR OWN LIFE?" His large eye peered at him as if it could see into Zane. "WHAT TROUBLES YOU, LITTLE EMBER?"

Zane stared at his own fists. "I thought killing Sithel would give me some sort of peace. I knew it was a lie. Hannah was right. It meant nothing. All I feel now is anger, all the time," he said, and fire roared, coating his fists. It seared the grass all about and left scorched earth behind. "Hannah was the only good in me. The only thing that could keep the anger at bay. With her gone, I'm nothing. For a while, even my vengeance toward Sithel sustained me. Now he's dead, and I'm more lost than ever. I don't know what to do. I just feel angry all the time, a hunger I can't satisfy."

Pyre was thoughtful for a long moment, then asked, "WHAT FEEDS YOUR POWER?"

Zane looked to his trembling fist, watching the flame rise higher, burn hotter. "Anger gives me power."

Pyre blew a jettison of hot steam, and Zane tumbled over from the blast of burning moist air. If he wasn't the Ronin of Fire, he was pretty sure it would have killed him, or at least burned him. Once he righted himself, Pyre continued, "FOOLISH, EMBER. FIRE IS NOT JUST ANGER. THE FURNACE OF THE SOUL IS STOKED BY ONE THING, AND ONE THING ALONE. PASSION. WITHOUT PASSION, ANGER IS MEANINGLESS, AN EMPTY VESSEL WITH NO PURPOSE. ANGER HAS ITS ROLE AS WELL, AS

DO ALL EMOTIONS. HOWEVER, YOU MUST NOT LET IT CONTROL YOU."

"How do I do that?" Zane asked, looking up. He realized his voice was almost pleading.

For a moment, Pyre's wide dragon mouth and terrifying eyes looked contemplative, then the ancient beast replied, "A VALID QUESTION. I HAVE FOUND IN MY LONG YEARS, THERE IS ONLY ONE WAY TO MASTER YOUR HEART. YOU MUST FOCUS ON WHAT MATTERS MOST. YOU HAVE OTHERS THAT CARE FOR YOU, DO YOU NOT?"

Gray, Ayva, Darius…even Helix. Despite his anger, Zane couldn't deny he cared for them deeply. Even now, he missed them. If he was being honest, beneath his self-righteous loathing, he wasn't only worried about them, he was also wracked with an intense pit of guilt in the bottom of his stomach. "I do, but I…I abandoned them. I left them. I'm not a Ronin any longer, Pyre. They'll never forgive me."

"NO," Pyre rumbled. "ONLY YOU HAVE ABANDONED YOURSELF, LITTLE EMBER."

The words stabbed like a dagger, though the truth was necessary. He'd been avoiding it, now he was ripping out the dagger so the wound could heal. "You're right. So, what? I just go back to them and say 'sorry I left'? Then my anger will vanish?"

Pyre blew a torrent of smoke and ash into Zane's face.

Zane coughed and gasped. When he could finally breathe, he asked, still choking, "I-is-is that"—he coughed—"is that a no?"

Pyre growled. "FOOLISH MORTAL." He turned away, as if hesitating to answer.

"Please," Zane said, growing serious. "How do I let it go?"

"YOU CANNOT LET GO OF YOUR ANGER UNTIL YOU LET GO OF YOUR FEAR."

Zane snorted and stared into the giant eye of the dragon, trying not to flinch or look away. "What could I possibly be afraid of?"

Pyre gave a bemused puff of fire, somehow singeing a few hairs on his cheeks. Huh. Zane never had felt the pain of flames before. "WHAT AREN'T YOU AFRAID OF, LITTLE EMBER?"

He growled. "What's that supposed to mean?"

Pyre rumbled, "I AM A DRAGON OF FIRE, I AM WHAT YOU SEE BEFORE YOU. YOU, LITTLE EMBER, MAY BE A RONIN,

BUT YOU SCURRY LIKE A MOUSE, HIDING IN YOUR PAIN, YOUR LOSS. DROWNING IN ANGER AND VENGEANCE. ENOUGH FLEEING, LITTLE MOUSE! FACE YOUR FEARS, OR THEY WILL CONSUME YOU."

"Hiding?" Zane wanted to snarl, to rage, then…he realized Pyre was right. He'd been running all this time, and he knew why, just as the dragon did. Flames burned higher up his arms. "I…I can't lose another person."

"YET, YOU WILL. MORE WILL FALL TO SHADOW BEFORE THE END."

"Then what do I do?" The question seemed to hold the key to everything.

Pyre's lipless maw peeled back, revealing more terrifying rows of orange teeth as tall as Zane. *"WHEN ALL SEEMS DARKEST, THAT IS WHEN FIRE BURNS BRIGHTEST. BURN. RAGE. PROTECT. NOT FOR LOSS, BUT FOR LIFE. YOU MUST FEEL, IN ORDER TO LET GO."*

Feel…

Then Zane felt.

Instead of shielding his heart with his anger, he let his sorrow and anguish wash over him like a wave, nearly drowning him. He sobbed. The dragon merely waited in silence, as if content to be in his company. After a while — Zane wasn't sure how long — his weeping ended, and his breathing eased. He realized he was still alive. Still breathing. A dull, deep ache remained all the same. "I miss her so…"

Pyre made a thoughtful sound, looking north. *"YES, LITTLE EMBER. AS YOU SHOULD. KNOW, HOWEVER, GRIEF IS ONLY LOVE WITH NOWHERE TO GO."*

Zane nodded, feeling the wisdom in the words, and took a steadying breath, looking in the distance over the endless green canopy. "What am I supposed to do, then?"

"REMEMBER HER. LOVE HER. HONOR HER. IN SO DOING, YOUR SORROW WILL LINGER, A FAINT CINDER, BUT THE FLAME OF LOVE WILL BURN MORE BRIGHTLY." Pyre continued, *"AS FOR YOUR FRIENDS, TRUST, AS YOU ONCE DID, LITTLE EMBER. ONLY THEN WILL YOU DISCOVER YOUR TRUE POWER."*

Another voice sounded behind them, deep like Pyre's, but with a distinct dry rasp. He hadn't sensed Sinew's presence like Pyre's, but he recognized the flesh dragon's bony-clawed talons as his earth-shuddering steps brought him up the hill. With a beat of his wings, the dragon opened earth, and a pile of bones sprang out of it—like a massive crypt coming to life. When it was done, Sinew had a platform of bone to rest upon. The dragon bowed his fleshy and muscled head in greeting and rumbled something to Pyre, which made the dragon grumble back. What were they saying? Why did Zane get the distinct impression Pyre was almost…sheepish? Impossible.

"WE HAVE COME WITH A REQUEST," Pyre said.

Then they told him.

"YOUR FRIENDS AWAIT." The Dragon of Fire looked north, massive head swiveling to look beyond the forest, as if past the Rehlias Desert, past Farbs…farther still.

He knew, sensing the dragon's meaning.

Covai, Great Kingdom of Flesh.

"How do I get there?" Zane asked.

At this, Pyre revealed his spear-like teeth, flames and smoke sifting between the jagged fangs. Zane gulped. He was starting to understand the ancient beast, as if he could read the dragon's mind. He grinned back at him, blood growing hot.

Zane returned to the moment, still standing before the red metal doors.

Their words, his mission, echoed in his mind: *"Enter the tournament, and win the Heart of Flesh. Then, your debt will be fulfilled."* He hadn't won the tournament as he thought they'd meant, though he was here, with Raina…and it felt right. He took a moment to gather himself, memories of Pyre slowly fading but the ancient being's words resonating in him.

Raina was still staring at the door. Reliving his memory had taken only a moment. "This is a little ominous," she said. "Titans and dragons? What'd you get me into, brooding eyes?"

He shook himself and answered, "What did Farhaven get us both into?" His hands played over the images of Pyre and Sinew. "They're a lot more intimidating in person."

"Wow, what a line." She gave him a flat look and said in a deep growl, imitating him, "*Look at me, I'm Zane, and I'm friends with a dragon.*"

"Dragons," Zane clarified, then added, "You're just jealous."

"*Obviously!*" Raina replied, rolling her eyes. "Now let's get this door open."

Laughing, Zane searched the door. He shoved it to no avail. Tugging on the spike of a dragon or the curve of another's flames did nothing either. It was closed tight as a Landerian seal, though he saw no latches or handles. "Well, that's not great."

Raina snorted. "I'm bad at puzzles. Any ideas?"

Zane stared at it for a long moment, then words drifted back into his mind: *You need to win the Heart of Flesh.*

All this time, Zane thought what was important was winning the tournament, or perhaps the Earthstone…that was the element of Stone. Only now did he realize maybe that's not what the dragons had been saying at all.

Win the Heart of Flesh.

He looked to Raina, saw the fire in her eyes, her potential power.

His heart skipped a beat.

It was her. She was the missing piece in the puzzle.

"I have an idea," Zane said slowly. "Open yourself to your power."

"Then what?"

"Feed your power into the Dragon of Flesh," he instructed.

She shrugged. "If you say so." She did, and suddenly the whole door began to glow. Raina staggered, and he reached out for her. "I'm good! It's just…something behind the door…it's making it hard to concentrate my power…"

"Then I'll help," Zane said, and tapping into his Nexus, he sent thick threads of fire into the Dragon of Fire on the door. The beast grew orange, a vibrant molten lava-like color. Then Raina's Dragon of Flesh, Sinew, turned a deep ruddy red.

"It's working!"

Inside, he could hear gears clicking, and then—

Nothing.

"You think that worked?" Raina asked, breathing hard.

Zane released a breath of his own. He hadn't realized he'd been holding it. "Only one way to find out." He gave the doors a good shove. One opened just a fraction.

"Well, shall we?" Raina asked. "Not sure how long we have here, or when a patrol of guards is going to stumble upon us entering an ancient chamber that's been sealed for several thousand years. They probably won't like that."

He nodded.

Raina spoke, "Wait. Whatever is in there, if it kills us—"

"At least we die together."

"Well, that's much more romantic," Raina said, shrugging. "I was going to say, it's your fault for getting me into this mess."

He chuckled. She was joking, even though there seemed to be pain in her eyes and her other hand unconsciously glided to her chest, her heart. He felt pain, worry…Gods, he couldn't see her hurt. That alone allowed the veil to slip, revealing more of his power, the burning orange sphere. Fire flooded his body, racing over his arms. Power filling his limbs, Zane smashed his foot into the door, opening the chamber and revealing the ancient power within.

Left Standing

In the morning when Gray awoke, Hati was no longer there. He heaved a heavy breath. Memories of the night returned in a series of amazing and vivid flashbacks. After donning fresh clothes and pulling on his boots, he made his way to the living area, hoping to see her. It was empty, save for a surprise that made Gray's jaw drop.

The table was decked with sliced fruit of all varieties, a fluffy bowl of scrambled eggs, glistening browned sausages, piles of still-steaming vegetables, and more. Somehow, she'd timed the meal perfectly with his awakening. Unable to stifle a small chuckle, he called out, "Hati?"

She was nowhere to be found. He spotted a note scrawled in fine penmanship on the table: *Good luck. You know where I will be.*

Then the drums of war sounded in the distance.

Gray's grin vanished. He devoured the meal, his mind distracted by what lay ahead. Satiated, he left Morrowil and Dimitri's Devari blade in the chest, strapped on his new wind bracers, and found his friends on their private balcony once again. No Zane. *Good*, Gray thought. Hopefully he was finding the secrets of the arena. He saw the rest weren't alone this time, and he smiled. "Drega! Leanna!" Then Gray saw the grave looks on his friends' faces, as if someone had just died. "Wait, what's going on? What'd I miss?"

Ayva's clear blue eyes held a mixture of worry and determination.

Helix sat with his head in his hands, muttering to himself and running his fingers through his wild blond hair, making it a disheveled mess. A plate of eggs thick with red-peppered sauce sat before him, untouched. That was more disconcerting than anything else.

Drega, however, grinned and boomed, as usual, "Good morning, my Lord Ronin!" The man clapped his shoulder, his wide frame occupying a good portion of their small balcony. He wore his warrior leather armor, but now, in contrast to his charcoal skin, he had inked across his cheeks and forehead swirling red tribal patterns that made him look even more fearsome. "We've come with some news."

Leanna said nothing, her face somber.

"What's Helix done?" Gray asked.

Helix squawked, "What? Me?"

"Ha!" Drega boomed. "If you're commenting on your good Ronin of Water's expression, I just told them about the coming match! I believe he's worried for you and our dear Ronin of Sun! Though he shouldn't be. You are each a force with which to be reckoned."

Captain Leanna explained, "There's been a change of plans. The queen has decided to alter the fourth round from one-on-one to a group match."

Gray swallowed, processing this news. "Wait, that's great news! Ayva and I won't have to fight then—"

"She didn't finish," Helix said, looking up from his seat, his eyes bloodshot. "It's a free-for-all, Gray."

"That's—" Gray began to say that wasn't awful.

"A free-for-all to the death," Helix interrupted. "There's no surrender."

Ayva spoke, her expression still warring between worry and resolve. "Drega says only four can live."

Gray's whole body felt dunked in ice. The balcony seemed to teeter, and he gripped a nearby table for balance, taking a moment to catch his breath. It all made sense. He knew the queen was going to try something, but this? When he found his voice, it was hoarse, and the words scraped out, "She can't do that, can she?"

Drega nodded grimly. "Afraid so. As monarch of the Great Kingdom of Flesh, it's her games. The arena gives Imala permission to make changes, as long as the colosseum deems it fair."

"Wait..." Ayva interrupted, "the colosseum is sentient? This is the first I've heard of that."

Drega smiled. "Some believe it's alive, with a will and mind of its own; others believe it's simply a magical spell created by Reavers of old."

"Which do you think it is?" she asked him.

"I'm inclined to believe Farhaven works in mysterious ways."

Helix sent through the bond, *Most evasive answer I've ever heard.*

Gray interrupted with more of a snarl than he'd intended. "Can we get back to the more pressing matter? That is, how is this fight fair? To the death with no option for surrender?"

Leanna replied, sighing, "Unfortunately, it is legal. Whether it's right or moral is another question. Consider your Ronin of Water's battle to the death. Was the Noxii Bloodbath any more or less fair?" She was right, of course. The Bloodbath was a free-for-all to the death, and it was brutal. Leanna continued, "All the arena cares about, at this stage of the fights, is that it fits within the confines of an even match. You all are entering under equal footing, with no magical swords allowed, so the queen's sudden change is acceptable."

The more Gray heard about the arena, the more he realized it was starting to sound alive.

"What about our artifacts?" Ayva asked, twisting the golden ring on her finger, and then she nodded at his bracers.

Gray rubbed at the silver bracers with wind-scroll engravings, which were now in their smooth leather form. He was beginning to get accustomed to them, feeling more connected to Kail. He still had no idea how to use them, though he felt strong magic flowing through them. Something powerful.

Leanna exchanged a look with Drega.

Drega shrugged. "What artifacts?"

Helix spoke, "The items that—"

Ayva cleared her throat, jabbing the Ronin of Water in the ribs.

"Ohhh," Helix said, "right. I get it." He winked. "What artifacts, indeed?"

Ayva rolled her eyes.

Gray looked to his friends. Despite Helix's attempt at humor, he still looked like he was going to be sick. "If you'll excuse us," Gray told Drega and Leanna, then pulled his friends aside. "Anyone have any ideas?"

"Kill the queen?" Helix posed.

Ayva shook her head. "That won't change anything. It might even make a martyr out of her, and the tournament will continue." She looked at him. "This doesn't change anything, Gray. We still need to win. Only this time, we can do it together. Just because it's a free-for-all, doesn't mean we can't team up. I asked Drega about the rules. He told me the arena doesn't forbid people from forming groups, just like Helix did in the Bloodbath." She looked at him for a long moment, a radiant conviction in her blue eyes. "We can do this, Gray."

Her look spoke of hope.

Beyond, the drums grew louder.

The crowds cheered.

Gray took a deep breath, nodding. "You're right, it changes nothing. If anything, we'll be far stronger united."

Ayva nodded, then turned to Drega. "You'll be fighting, too, won't you?"

"I will be, young legend of Sun," Drega said, folding his arms across his strapping chest.

"Join us," Ayva suggested. "Together, no one could take us down."

Drega made a long thoughtful sound, rubbing his cliff-like jaw. "I am honored, my Lady Ronin." Then he heaved a breath, shaking his head. "Alas, for now, I must decline. I fear I must remain neutral, and see how the battle plays out. However, I do not wish for your deaths."

"That means…" Helix said.

Drega shrugged. "I will direct my fury toward others first."

Helix pumped a hand into the air. "Perfect! Think you can make Merrick and Nalia first on that list?"

Drega laughed. "Ha! I like your attitude as always, young legend! I shall do my best!"

Gray sighed. "I've got to admit, I really don't want to fight you."

Drega's smile was broad. "I, for one, can't wait to see what you're capable of doing, my friend," he said, gripping Gray's shoulder tightly, fingers digging into his muscles like iron claws, as always. "Win or lose, it shall be a great fight! After all, all we can do is play the cards we are dealt. Isn't that right, my dear Captain Leanna?"

Leanna's gaze tightened. She dipped her head. "Yes, that's all we can do."

What was that all about? Helix sent to the others.

Ayva answered, *I think this kingdom is coming apart from within itself.*

Gray stepped forward. "I have something to ask of you two." They both looked at one another. "I need to know where you stand."

Drega's face could have been carved from granite. "My Lord Ronin…"

Gray continued, undaunted, "A shadow is coming. I hope the queen still plans to abide by the bargain." His hand curled into a fist. "However, I need to be prepared. I need to know, can I rely on you?"

Leanna spoke, "We both knew this request was coming. It's true. We've made a few moves that would not be viewed as loyal by those in power. Despite that, while this kingdom might be held together by fraying strings, we still have a duty."

Gray took a deep breath and nodded. "I see…"

Then she added, smirking faintly, "However…if someone were to cut those threads allowing us to act? Well, that would be a different story. For now, I am still Leanna, Captain of the Guard."

"I am still the leader of the Fleshguard," Drega agreed. "How you sway the hearts of the people, well that is another matter."

While Gray appreciated their words, he still didn't want to kill the huge, affable, and intimidating leader of the Fleshguard. Only, the man was right. There was no way around what came next. Gray turned to Helix.

The Ronin of Water threw his arms around Gray and Ayva, then said, "Stick to the corners. That worked best when I was out there." He wagged a finger at Ayva. "Watch over Gray, will you? He tends to get lost without you."

Ayva nodded. "Of course."

Gray looked to Leanna, waiting behind them, and sent to Helix. *You remember your goal?*

Don't worry about me! Helix replied with a wink, as if to cover his fear. *Charm and charisma. I got this!*

Not long after, Ayva and Gray were on the vast expanse of the colosseum sand.

"Welcome all of you!" the queen announced to the stands packed with a record number of attendees, her voice amplified by the Reavers' spells. "Today is a special day! I have decided to gather our great warriors together so you could witness a spectacle that has never before been seen! One-on-one fights are quite the display, but all our great warriors fighting for survival? This will truly be a battle for the ages! As you all know, only four can survive to the next round…our gladiators must fight with all of their strength. With skill and luck, they might remain standing. One step closer to the title that all the world covets…Grand Primus!"

The crowd's roar was deafening.

Gray stood beside Ayva and considered the two dozen warriors. With his Devari senses, he assessed the strongest foes. Drega was several paces away, looking stoic, eyes on the crowd. Then the Dryad, Warden Eras Barkblood, a dozen feet from him. She wore ephemeral green armor that resembled leaves, covering her bark-like skin. A crown of roses and thorns sat upon her head, the hair of which was now golden foliage. Next to her was Egrin the Barbarian, staring directly at Gray, covered in black and brown pelts and wearing a bone necklace.

There were other warriors, all powerful in their own right.

Of course, each of them paled to one.

Nalia.

She was decked out in dark tan leather. Even weaponless, she was terrifying, with an aura like an inferno as the spark raged inside of her. All the eyes of the warriors flickered about the arena, though most darted back to her, like moths to the flame.

Gray ignored her and looked to the stands, searching.

Finally, he spotted her beneath the banner of flesh once more, and his heart fluttered. Hati was dressed in fine clay-colored cloth, and a deep kohl rimmed her eyes. She waved. Gray couldn't help the smile that came to his face.

Hati beamed.

Ayva looked at him. "Hati?"

Gray cleared his throat and returned his gaze to the warrior-filled battlefield, feeling as if he'd just been caught.

She snorted. "No need to look so guilty, Gray. You're allowed to like someone."

Gray felt...strange. Still, she was right.

Ayva raised a brow. "So you do like her?"

Rubbing his neck, a bit chagrined, he nodded firmly. "I do. She's...different."

"Agreed. Too smart for you, of course," she teased, making Gray chuckle, "and *annoyingly* smarter than me, but I like her, too. I'm happy for you."

Gray thanked her, then looked about again, realizing something was missing. "Where's Merrick?"

Renalin has blessed us, maybe he died in his sleep, choking on his own self-righteous drivel, Helix sent.

As he said this, another gate rattled open.

Out stepped Merrick, Ronin of Metal.

Great, I just had to say something, Helix sent.

Gray felt a cold wind sink into his bones.

Merrick, dressed in his light and dark gray cloth and leather, met Gray's eyes. Rings, bracers, and other metal pieces adorned the man's body. All of them deadly weapons in Merrick's hands. Clearly he wasn't going to make the same mistake twice. With his appearance, the stands erupted, the people cheering louder than for Gray's arrival onto the arena floor.

A dozen paces away, Egrin called to Gray, "You're going to die today, boy!" The barbarian's muscles flexed as he folded his brawny arms across his broad chest. "I hope you've prayed to whatever gods you hold dear, for I will end you, *and* your little girlfriend! Too bad she's going to die with you. You'll have no one to cry over your corpse."

Helix sent, *What's the big barbarian saying? Something cruel and stupid?*

Pretty much, Ayva replied.

"What? Nothing to say, Wind Boy? Or should I call you by your real title, Blightseeker? The Broken... *Betrayer of Humanity.*"

Anger erupted from Gray's core. "You'd be wise to watch your tongue, pet of Nefrin."

"Or what? You'll hurt me? I saw what your wind brother did... he died, like a dog."

Gray's rage flared. Wind coated his fist.

Ayva put a hand to his arm. "Don't. You're better than him."

"Am I?" Gray asked, fury flowing through his veins.

Ayva glanced at the first row of the colosseum, nodding to the many archers with arrows nocked. "That's what he wants. Remember?"

Egrin was intentionally stoking Gray's ire, so, taking a breath, he let the zephyrs curling around his hand vanish.

Egrin cackled. "Ha! How pitiful! The betrayer of men, the Blightseeker himself, cowed by a woman!" Then he pointed to Ayva and leered. "You, girl! If I let you live, what say you join my harem? With that fire of yours, you'd be a worthy addition to my bedchamber. Hmm, little Ronin of Sun? Would you like that?"

Ayva turned on the man, sun burning in her eyes. A golden glow engulfed her fist as she pointed at him. "You die first."

The conviction in her voice even impressed Gray.

It was the collar around Ayva's neck that surprised him.

Despite wielding magic, her collar didn't glow red, not even a little bit.

Egrin must have noticed this, too.

She's mastering her power fast, Gray realized.

Egrin's grin wilted to a frown, and the large apple in his throat bobbed as he swallowed nervously. Then he sneered, turning back to two barbarians at his side.

Drega warned, "Easy, young legends. Don't let your tempers get the best of you."

Ayva shrugged. "Why not? It's not like we can gain any more enemies." Her gaze spoke for her as it panned over Merrick, who watched them with deadly intent, then Nalia, whose cold gaze was fixed on Gray. Then the other combatants. Many of the warriors cast wary looks about, but their eyes settled on Gray and Ayva.

Suddenly, Reavers fanned out across the lower wall, and thick threads of blue, purple, gold, red, and tan filled the air, slowly forming a giant protective bubble over the whole of the arena.

The crowds whispered in awe.

Whoa, Helix sent. *A shield spell. I've never seen anything quite like it. It's massive.* More and more, the spell formed itself like a spider weaving its web. *What's it made out of?*

If I'm not mistaken, moon primarily, Ayva replied, *which can redirect spells, but I sense some sun, flesh, fire, and water, too.*

Whatever it is, it's strong, Gray sent, then indicated, *Look there.*

On the Queen's Terrace, Nefrin was leading it, working complicated threads from his palms. His maniacal face was fixed with concentration.

Well, at least he's good for something, Helix sent as the spell was formed, then added, *Hey, where's Zane again? He should be watching this.*

Gray reached out, feeling a faint ball of orange in his mind. It was below them. *He's after something equally important,* Gray sent.

Helix replied, *What's more important than cheering for your two friends so they can become Grand Primus, then win a magical stone and an army to stop an evil that's taking over the world?*

Don't worry. We have our mission. He has his.

Thanks for cheering for us, Ayva sent.

Of course! Helix replied, sounding as if he had his mouth full even in his mind somehow. *Gods, I'm so nervous for you guys that I can barely eat.*

Ayva glowered. *You're eating right now, aren't you?*

I said barely! Helix sent back.

The announcer spoke, his grandiose voice reverberating throughout the colosseum, "Welcome all, to the fourth round of the Great Tournament of Flesh! Today is a momentous day! Our queen, in her infinite wisdom, has decided to bestow an event of epic proportions upon you. Witness two dozen of the most powerful warriors in Farhaven fighting to the death! There is no surrender, no yielding, no capitulation, and only four will survive. Spark will fill the air! Blood will flow! Bones will break! Legends will be created!"

The crowds went wild.

"With no further ado, I give you..."

Gray tuned the announcer out as he turned to Ayva. "Listen to me, we stick to the sides. Open battles are always chaotic, so things will change quickly. As soon as we engage, we will likely be attacked from the flank. With this many combatants, the only good fight is a quick and easy one." Much of this was Devari memory. Gray remembered he used to excel in the mad scrum, knowing patience and timing was everything.

"Agreed," Ayva said. "Also, Drega said the pillars with weapons will rise after the fight begins. Let's move to a pillar, grab a weapon, and use the column as a barricade until we get our bearings."

Gray raised his brows. "You know, with tactics like that, you'd make a great Devari."

Ayva grinned. "I'd rather make Grand Primus."

Gray nodded. "Then let's see what we can do."

The drums thundered, slowing.

All the warriors tensed, facing one another, backing away.

The tension practically crackled the air.

Powers were summoned, and collars grew red.

Thump.

Thump.

Thump.

The drums slowed, Gray's heart quickened, and—

"Fight!" the announcer cried.

The arena exploded into chaos.

Fighters launched themselves at one another as the pillars ground upward from the floor, sand spilling to either side of each plinth as they rose. Men and women raced for weapons. Meanwhile, spells filled the air in a wild cacophony, and cries of battle consumed the sands.

Gray turned and a dozen silver arrows flew through the air with impossible speed toward his head. He tapped deep into his Nexus and halted their flight in midair. They hung suspended, encased in wind. Gray grinned wolfishly.

Then he sent them back.

Not at Merrick, however, who was expecting this.

Two Moonguard charged from the right, near the first pillar, having grabbed swords from it. The thin silver arrows penetrated the first Moonguard, piercing his heart. The second leapt. Ayva sent a shackle of gold that pinned the man to the pillar.

Gray looked back to Merrick and sent, *Have to do better than that.*

"Gray!" Ayva called, crashing into him.

A massive fireball crackled over their heads, searing hairs on Gray's scalp.

He pulled her to her feet and saw a Reaver advancing toward him.

He flung out a hand, sending the man flying, but two Terma took his place, a female and a male, flanking him and Ayva, both with swords in hand. "You are a wanted man, legend of Wind! We were sent by our Lord Dryan to kill the legend," said the male with an inky black swirl in his eyes. "He'll be most pleased when we return with a burlap sack bearing both your heads!"

Beyond, Merrick stalked toward them through a barrage of weapons and spells—blocking them with flying axes, stabbing with thin sheets of metal or spikes—striding as if there was nothing in the world but Gray. "You take the Terma on the left," Gray said, "I'll take the other one."

"Deal," Ayva replied.

Both Terma edged closer, now only paces away.

Abruptly, the female Terma, green eyes clouded with inky evil, howled and attacked, cutting for Ayva's head. Ayva blocked with a shield of sun, the sword cracking beneath it. The male Terma stabbed. Gray coated his hands in wind and grabbed the sword. The Terma's eyes widened in surprise, and Gray slammed his foot into the Terma's chest, trying to rip the sword free. The man was strong, however, and his sword grip held. The Terma tried to break his kneecap with a kick, only Gray knew this move from his Devari training. Instead of trying to block or retreat, with wind rushing over his arms—giving him strength, the collar warming against his neck—Gray yanked on the sword. The Terma, because he was kicking, pivoted on only one leg for balance.

As a result, with Gray's added momentum, the man flew, smashing into another warrior who was just rising to his feet.

"Duck!" Ayva called.

Gray fell flat to the sands.

A beam of light, thin and focused, flew over him and melted more silver arrows from the air.

Merrick.

The man was getting closer.

Two dozen paces away, and nearer still.

Gray stood up and saw Drega leap at Merrick with a clashing whirlwind of steel from Drega's two swords, and Merrick's blades. The crowds gasped and cheered. *He's buying us time,* Gray realized.

Just then, Gray felt the wind disturbed.

He turned and two more daggers flew straight for his heart.

Again, a beam from Ayva of white-hot light burned them from the air, melting them to slag. A boom rattled the sands, sending many fans to their feet, and another chorus of cries erupted from the stands. One of the pillars teetered and collapsed to a pile of rubble and dust. *What in the seven hells was that from?* He saw across the way, and his jaw dropped.

Eras Barkblood was wreathed in vines, like giant tentacles writhing all about her, while her eyes blazed a deep forest green. Gray looked about, assessing the field. Ayva spoke the words before he could. "Gray, don't look now, but we're not at the outskirts of the fighting anymore…"

Seven hells, Gray thought. Somehow they were now in the heart of the battle.

A group of six warriors stalked toward Gray and Ayva.

Gray understood. He growled and sent through the bond, *I should have figured. We're the strongest, aside from Nalia. If they take us down now, they don't have to fight us later.* The six charged. Gray sent out a gust of wind, sending three of them flying, and his collar turned hot on his neck.

"Well, that was easy," Ayva said, hands still glowing. "I—"

Gray turned, panic flaring. "Ayva!"

Egrin roared. The bastard had used the others' attacks as a distraction. Now the massive barbarian charged, flanking them with his two other warriors. Dual war axes, gripped in his meaty fists, cleaved toward Ayva's neck, seeking to sever her head from her shoulders. Gray launched wind. Out of instinct, Ayva erected a golden shield in the nick of time. Both axes assaulted the glowing barrier. Egrin's face was wild, primal. "Die! You must die!" he bellowed.

Gray growled.

Wind rose up around him.

Again, his collar burned, but he pushed through it.

Ayva was between him and Egrin. Gray couldn't hurt him without hurting her.

So, breathing in, more eddies swirled higher up, and…

He *shifted.*

One moment, he was a dozen paces away, the next he was behind Egrin, sword arcing toward the man's head. As if expecting this, Egrin had already moved his axes away from Ayva's golden shield, then he slammed a heel into Ayva's barrier, shoving her back as he pivoted, hacking at Gray.

Axe met sword, clanging steel sounding across the arena.

The crowds cheered.

Behind Gray, the two warriors charged, cutting for his back.

Whirls of wind reinforced Gray's arms. Then, with one arm, he held Egrin's parry, and with his other, without looking, he directed it behind him and let the wind flow. His collar burned, and a massive gust of wind slammed into the two men, flying them across the arena and into the barrier of magic. They collapsed to the ground like broken dolls. Gray turned his fury on Egrin, who leapt back from a slash.

Keep him busy, Ayva sent. He felt her power brewing.

Gray laughed. "Afraid of me now that you know what I can do?" He realized it wasn't the best taunt, but it was all he could come up with.

"Fool! You think you are strong because you took out my pawns?" Egrin roared with laughter. "They were nothing. Just like you." His eyes flicked to the side, and he leapt, sensing it before a white-hot beam of light shot from Ayva's hands, searing the dry air. It smashed harmlessly into the barrier. Dazzling colors lit up the protective sphere. Egrin rose to his feet, pelts covered with sand. "Cowards! Little worms, trying to stab me in the back!"

Ayva scoffed. "Are you cracked in the head? You literally attacked me while I was distracted!" She sent another blast of sun that he sidestepped. Egrin charged with bloodshot eyes, ducking and dodging, getting closer.

Why can't I hit him?

Then he realized.

The feeling he had, that sensation…

Egrin has the ki, Gray sent to Ayva as she sent a blast of sun that knocked the man back, though he avoided the majority of the blast once more.

You sure? Ayva sent, breathing hard. *How? He's not a Devari!*

He's got it, Gray sent. *A strong one too,* he added. *That's how he's evading our attacks. He's sensing our emotions and thoughts, down to each attack's intent. That's how he faced the Lightguard before, and how he's now avoiding our strikes.* Only, Gray had an idea. He attacked. This time, without any intention to hurt Egrin. Instead, he focused his mind not at Nefrin's champion but behind him, toward the wall. He then simply sent a spear of wind with no malice, no purpose, toward Egrin who was still focused on Ayva. Egrin never saw it coming. The wind smashed into him and he slammed into the wall, head cracking against the hard stone. He fell limp, blood oozing from his skull.

They didn't have time to celebrate, however, as a Moonguard who Ayva had wounded, but not killed, attacked from the shadows of another pillar. He stepped out of the shade as if materializing from thin air. Gray readied wind. Ayva, sun. They were both too slow. From the sands, hundreds of roots burst out of the ground, encircling the Moonguard like wrist-thick snakes. The Moonguard struggled, trying to slash and claw and—

The roots pulled. They shredded and ripped, and the man roared in agony, blood creating a fine mist in the air as he was torn to pieces. When it was over, the roots sank back into the sands, leaving the man's lifeless corpse behind.

The crowds roared.

Gray looked to the Dryad, who was clearly responsible, spark flowing into her.

She was now enveloped in torso-thick dark green vines that writhed in the air like a sea monster's tentacles. She eyed them, her eyes burning emerald green, though Gray saw no fury, just cold, raw power.

Ayva swallowed. "Is…is she on our side?"

"I've no idea," Gray replied, "but I hope so."

A sudden presence, brimming with menace, drew his gaze.

Merrick strode across the arena floor, his infamous ebony-black bow now a sword the color of seething darkness. Gray's rage peaked, his teeth grinding.

"That's not fair! The rules say we're not allowed our legendary blades yet," Ayva said.

She was right, but something told him that Merrick was 'above' some of the arena's edicts, and he eyed the balcony, seeing the Queen's oily grin. Gray replied, his teeth grinding. "So much for the rules."

Merrick's eyes were a terrifying gray-white. His white hair had streaks of blood in it. He seemed to have taken at least a few strikes. He picked finger-sized thorns from his chest, throwing them aside. A few slashes and burns marred his steel gray clothes, showing bloody cuts beneath.

Gray snarled, hungering to face and end Merrick, though half a dozen men still stood between them.

Before he could even finish the thought, Merrick lifted a hand. Weapons in each of the warriors' hands suddenly turned on their wielders. Swords, axes, and daggers stabbed, cut, or gutted the men, leaving them in pools of blood.

A chorus of wild cheers erupted from the tens of thousands in the stands.

Gods, he's a monster, Helix sent.

"No more hiding or running," Merrick bellowed, as he lifted the metal weapons into the air, aimed at him and Ayva. "Let us end this, once and for all."

Gray readied himself, wind flowing in curling eddies over his body. Ayva's fists glowed with smoldering sun.

Merrick snarled, waving a hand, and the dozen swords flew.

Gray batted them aside, then slashed down with a gust of wind. Ayva followed it with a blazing beam of sun. Merrick pulled a hunk of black metal from a pouch at his side. Yronia plate. It formed into a small shield, deflecting Ayva's beam of light, causing it to ricochet and smash into the barrier that the Reavers maintained. The barrier lit up like a globe of multihued brilliance, as Reavers broke out in a sweat, struggling to maintain the barrier under such a powerful spell.

Ayva was blown back from the collision, sliding across the sand.

Crowds gasped, then cheered.

Merrick dropped his shield with a cocky smile. "You are no match—"

Gray roared, pulling deep from his Nexus, and a torrent of wind shot from his palm. Merrick stabbed his ebony sword into the sand, but Gray sent more, demanding it from his soul, and the wind uprooted the Ronin of Metal tossing him through the air to smack with a crack against the arena wall.

The crowd cheered with feverish delight.

Helix sent, *You did it!*

Not yet, Gray sent, helping Ayva to her feet, wiping sand. A small gash was on her forehead, dripping into her eye. Before he could ask, she wiped it away and nodded to him that she was okay. "Not out of the woods yet," Ayva grimaced.

In the distance, Drega, Eras Barkblood, and Nalia clashed.

Vines and swords dealt devastating damage, also causing fractures in the stone walls. Gray had no time to take in their battle, aside from a glimpse of Nalia cutting thick vines to the ground as if trimming hedges while parrying Drega's flashing blades as if he were just a nuisance. Though once or twice, the man's howls peaked and his sword nearly clipped her chest or arm. Nalia seemed more focused on Eras, the Dryad. Eras's eyes dazzled like emeralds, her hands moving in complicated patterns, controlling the giant vines like they were her own arms. Gray saw Eras was reaching the limit of her power, a note of strain, terror even, in her stunning eyes as Nalia hacked her way through the vine and bramble thicket, getting closer to the Dryad with every slash.

Gray, Ayva sent. *He's not done yet.*

Gray focused back on Merrick.

The Ronin of Metal staggered to his feet, wiping blood from his mouth. "You cannot kill me! I am the Ronin's end. *I am magic's end...*" He raised a hand, and a dozen metal swords, spears, and axes from fallen warriors rose into the air.

There was a horrendous cry of agony, a bloody sound of death.

Then voices shouted.

The crowds, Gray realized. They were...cheering?

The announcer bellowed, "The fourth round is finished! The four winners stand before you!" Gray and Ayva froze where they stood. Merrick's gaze went up to the thousands of archers with arrows, most capped with stone heads, trained on him, ready to shoot if he tried anything. The battle was finished. The eruption of cheers rolled over them like a tidal wave.

A Fleshguard's Fight

Drega's whole life he'd been born and bred for battle. It was his soul, in his flesh. From the time he was a child, he'd wanted to wield a blade. His mother had slapped his hand, telling him he wasn't old enough. Whereas his father had grinned widely, sneaking him to the back of their house, where he trained in secret in the empty alley behind it. To most, it wasn't a glorious first training ground. Shattered boxes and barrels lined a dusty street between dark clay walls. It stank of wine and vomit from the drunkards who came from the nearby taverns, staggering out after a night of drinking and emptying their bellies in the alley.

But to Drega, it had been a great battlefield.

There, under his father's tutelage, he was made a man.

Then, after he was ten, once his father had declared he'd nothing else to teach Drega, Drega had found another mentor. Had pledged his sword to Jarus, a Covian guard, the best in the city. Also a drunk. He'd hit Drega when Drega was too slow to block, parry, evade, or execute one of the hundred different forms the man had learned, picked up from a Cloudfellian blademaster. Slowly, he'd grown stronger. Again, he'd found purpose, and pride in the dusty training ground full of old, rotting haystacks and broken wooden dummies, limbs all shattered, no more than simple wooden poles. Two years into training, he'd sent Jarus to the ground in a duel. The Covian guard had raged, demanding another duel. Again, Drega had smacked the wooden sword from Jarus's hands and sent him skidding across the sand. Jarus had fumed, but Drega knew his time training with the man was over. He'd learned all he could. Taking his meager belongings, he found himself before the austere, unwelcoming gates of the Fleshguard, a series of low, windowless squat buildings. A dozen Fleshguards, elite warriors had been training in the yard, when they turned to see Drega, eyeing him like a fresh piece of meat. There, a long history had unfolded: he'd scrapped his way to the height of most elite warriors in Covai, killed when he had to, and nearly died a thousand times over again, but in the end, he'd become something of a legend in Covai. His boyhood self would have been proud, and perhaps, admittedly, a little afraid of the man he'd become.

Nevertheless, now he was here, in his third tournament.

Some part of him felt he was growing old, yet he also knew all his years of experience were like thick layers, coating his body in armor that none could match. Blood dripped from a thousand cuts across his limbs. Tiny thorns dug into his skin, and they popped out, falling to the sand, as he healed himself, wounds knitting together. Flesh-knitting, fast-healing, regeneration—the many terms others used for a Fleshguard's powers to heal themselves quicker than the average man. Though now his body's healing was slowing.

Before him stood two terrifying opponents.

One he'd faced many times, though not in a fight to the death.

Instead, in the training grounds of the Fleshguard.

Nalia.

Power blazed from her.

Her body was a weapon; scars crisscrossed her forearms, rippling with muscle beneath. She was tall, though he still towered over her. That wasn't where her strength came from. Instead, the hundred souls she'd imbibed made her seem like a glowing inferno.

The other was a woman of enchanting beauty, and nearly just as deadly.

Eras Barkblood. Leaf-green armor coated the Dryad's slender frame. A radiant emerald color emanated from her body, while her hair, like golden leaves, now turned a shade of deep crimson. She stood in the middle of a forest of massive green vines, each barbed with finger-length thorns that could cut just as deeply as any blade. Only, after dealing devastating damage to most of the opponents, she'd engaged in a four-way battle with him, Merrick, and Nalia. The battle hadn't lasted long; Nalia had sheared vines like chopping down old foliage, all while fending off Merrick and Drega. Their blows had been equally exchanged, though now Merrick faced Gray and Ayva. He'd hoped to buy the two Ronin some time. He grinned, happy they'd made it this far.

Legends, indeed, he thought. A new age was coming, he knew, and he was proud that if it was going to be led by anyone, it would be by them.

Only Eras, the Dryad, was breathing hard, her collar slowly growing bright red.

Nalia, on the other hand, standing between them, hadn't broken a sweat.

Worse still, her collar was a cool steel gray.

Nalia was flanked by Eras and Drega.

Drega had positioned it this way.

Nalia didn't seem to care. She looked up at him, a flicker of a smile ghosting across her face—a face that rarely showed anything but cold apathy. She sighed. "So you seek to take my title, old man?" Her words, as always, sent a chill into him. Rarely had he heard her speak. Few had. Now he almost wished she hadn't. Her voice was like the chilling breath of death, soft enough one almost had to strain to hear the menacing words.

Drega chuckled, his laughter echoing across the sands. "Ha! I seek only a good battle."

Her frozen blue eyes narrowed, her smirk deepening. "You mean, you seek a good death."

He rolled his heavy shoulders. "Don't we all?" He sighed. "In truth, I knew this day would come," he said, looking at the tens of thousands of spectators, feeling the eyes of Covai hot on him. "I think we were always meant to fight upon the sands. Fate." He looked back with a broad smile.

Jaw muscles twitched on Nalia's face, her fist tightened on her sword. "You've never bested me in a duel, old man. What makes you think you can now?"

Drega laughed, remembering Jarus's words as he boomed, "I had an old master once! A real bastard of a man." He felt his own fist tighten on his leather handle. "But he said a lot of truths. One which always stuck with me. '*A battle isn't real unless a man's life is on the line. Everything else matters not.*'"

Nalia cackled. "I like that." She turned to the Dryad. "And you?"

Eras Barkblood spoke, and her voice was both enchanting and ethereal, like the whisper of wind in a forbidden woods, carried by magic. "I seek only the power to save those worthy of life. You are not worthy."

Nalia sighed, gaze flickering between the Dryad and him. "Come, then. Let us see what you are made of."

He knew he couldn't take Nalia alone.

But together?

Drega looked to Eras Barkblood.

She nodded to him.

As one, they attacked. Nalia's blade met his, while giant vines shot out from Eras. His blade flickered faster, and faster, and her sword clashed with it while at the same time slicing at the massive roots. Slowly, spark flowed out of Nalia's body, like a well overflowing.

The Grand Primus's power—were they burning through it?

Drega parried an attack and slipped a blow that would have taken his head, barely skimming Nalia's throat with his own blade. The slight cut to her body made Nalia's eyes fan wide.

She touched her skin, eyeing a scarlet droplet of blood, and her voice was shocked as she said, "My own blood…" Then her lips peeled in a rictus snarl, orange vapor rising from all about her body. "You made me bleed. You will regret that." Seizing on her distraction, her own hubris, Eras flung out a hand and a gnarled root from deep within the sands shot upward. The root wrapped around Nalia's waist, trapping her arms to her side. Eras, seeing Nalia pinned, raced forward, out of her barricade of vines, crying out and holding a blade of emerald light.

"End her now!" Eras cried, sword raised.

Drega's own blade moved to cut as well. Even as his weapon arced, however, he saw it was wrong. All wrong. Wrapped in barbed roots, Nalia's skin didn't puncture, her face was still calm. A fury burned in her eyes. "No…" Drega bellowed.

Spark erupted from Nalia's core, disintegrating the roots into a fine mist. Her sword rose and fell.

An arc of…something, split the air, aimed at Eras.

Eras froze in mid-stride. Her mouth parted, eyes wide in horror and confusion as she looked down at her body. A thin red line formed on her skin. Then it deepened, and she was cut from head to toe, and the two sides of her body collapsed to the ground in a pool of blood. Nalia's arm shook, as if trying to restrain the mountain of spark threatening to explode from within her as she turned to face Drega. "You should never have faced me."

Drega had never really felt fear.

All his life, it was a distant concept.

Perhaps he'd felt a little flicker from time to time, yet always he'd treated it with equal parts amusement and excitement. As if the fear was his body telling him he was more alive. Now, Drega was afraid. No, it wasn't fear. It was dread.

He understood what this woman was.

Death.

Still, he faced it.

Blade flashing faster and faster, he lunged at Nalia.

Spark fumed from her body as she matched him.

Faster, more, Drega demanded of himself, his body, his limbs. His every muscle was on fire. For a moment, Nalia's eyes widened. A trickle of sweat ran down her temple, her teeth gnashing as her sword danced, nearly missing a parry. Drega's heart buoyed. *I can do this.* All the many years of training came flooding through him. Countless hours of sweat and toil. Calluses on his hands until they bled and ripped, only to pick the blade back up.

Nalia might've consumed a thousand souls, and was driven by some strange, dark purpose. She might've been death, but luckily for Drega, he was good friends with the reaper. As he lost himself to their swords clashing, everything fell away. The thundering of the crowds, the doubt, even the pain from his countless bloody wounds.

None of it mattered.

Drega was one with the blade, his familiar leather handle held tightly in his grip—he knew each indent and small bump perfectly worn into the leather to fit his fingers. The sword was an appendage every bit as much as his own arm. As Drega flickered between forms, his muscles burned, but each slice, cut, riposte, and thrust resembled a master painter before his canvas.

Sweat dripped from her temple, and Nalia's advance faltered.

Her foot stepped back.

I can do this, Drega thought inwardly, the words like a dark growl in his mind, in his soul, and he pushed further. Moving as if he was a storm of swords, Drega advanced.

He cut a line across Nalia's cheek.

Then another, slipping between folds of her armor to carve a bloody gash across her forearm, and she snarled. Orange mist coalesced around her. Spark. It healed her cuts. So Drega created more. Chest. Shoulder. Hip. Little cuts. Finally, her thrust was too slow. His blade bit deep, creating a bloody furrow across her thigh.

Nalia cried out, staggering back.

It was her first sound of anguish.

Both seemed shocked by it.

A momentary pause held them. They stood a dozen paces apart as she eyed the bleeding gash on her leg. Drega realized his chest rose and fell quickly; he was breathing far harder than the woman before him. She saw this too, and a smirk creased her thin lips.

"You're pushing yourself too far, old man. You're only mortal after all. The leader of the Fleshguard has limits. I am stronger than you."

"Who cares about limits?" Drega said with a deep laugh. Despite this, every muscle in his body burned as if he'd just stepped into a bonfire. Weakness crept into his limbs. Nalia, though being on the back foot, had orange mist rising from her body, as if she held a deep reservoir to pull from. He'd have to finish this fast.

He leapt at her.

Again, swords flashed.

As they pulled away, him gaining a few more cuts, Nalia hissed, "You will not take my title, old man! Grand Primus is mine!

"I'm just a warrior seeking a good fight," he replied, a tired grin on his face.

Nalia flicked the blood on her blade to the sands. "A good fight? You don't see yourself, do you?" Standing a handful of paces away, she eyed him up and down, her lip curling. "You…Time and again, I've seen you let your enemies surrender. As such, your sword has slowed, along with your wits. Whereas, I have drunk upon the souls of hundreds, growing stronger than any Grand Primus before me."

Drega yawned. "An interesting tactic. I presume you're trying to bore me to death?"

Nalia's eyes flared and she lunged again. He dipped under a cut that would have taken his head. As he'd hoped, enraged by his taunts she reacted too slowly and his sword bit into her arm.

She cried out, grabbing the bloody wound.

Drega smiled.

Yes, he thought, hope rising. He could win this. He could defeat her.

Nalia sneered. "I see that look in your eyes. You think you can still beat me, don't you?" She sighed, then her expression shifted. True terror wormed its way into Drega, fear at that look. "Witness the truth. You are not my equal, Fleshguard. You are nothing." Her eyes closing, a hum emanated from her throat, and spark flowed all about her. Not just from her, but rising out of the sands, like a thousand writhing snakes. She lunged.

Fast.

Much too fast.

Drega felt a prick of pain, sharp. It spread, radiating throughout his gut.

He looked down and saw her sword embedded there to the hilt. She ripped it free, grinning. Blood gushed out and he gripped his middle, trying to keep his innards from spilling out.

"I almost pity you. Clinging to that faint ray of hope, when all the while your death was inevitable." She stalked forward.

"All death…is inevitable…" Drega growled, swallowing back blood as it filled his throat. "Even for you, Grand Primus. Legacy is another matter. Yours will die with you."

Nalia stalked forward as Drega looked to Gray and the others. They were fighting with Merrick, the Ronin of Metal. He'd wanted to join them, to fight side by side in their grand battle against the shadow. Too late for that now.

Legacy. At least theirs would continue.

"Farewell, Ronin," Drega said. "May we meet again in this life or the next."

Nalia now stood over him, wreathed in immeasurable spark, seething with hatred. She kicked his shoulder, throwing him onto his back. Distantly, he heard the crowds roar, and he smiled. She snarled, as if his grin infuriated her.

Nalia stabbed down.

Pain erupted, then faded, as the crowd's roars became a whisper, his vision constricting in a field of black. The memories were the last to depart…the simple tavern alley from his youth…the warmth of his father's smile as Drega hefted his first real sword.

The pride in a boy's heart.

A good death, Drega thought as the world faded to shadow.

An Ancient Secret (Part 2)

Raina watched as the red metal doors opened to reveal a circular room with a vaulted ceiling.

All her life Raina had witnessed incredible things. The cruelty of men with no bounds, a man on death's door healed with only three drops from a vial, obsidian-skinned Darkwalkers in the Oasis, and gangly-limbed saeroks and trollish vergs. Even her powers were unnerving and had taken her some time to understand. She knew she was no Reaver, no Untamed. As a child, she felt the essence, the life force that burned inside a person. Despite all those experiences, nothing could've prepared Raina for this moment, and what existed inside that chamber.

Every inch of the room was covered in blood. Red snakes slithered at her feet. Not snakes, more like tendrils of flesh. Eyeless little creatures, some as thin as her finger, others like giant pythons, crawling across the floor. The floor was a thin red membrane that pulsed as if alive. In fact, the whole room was vibrating.

A long series of curses escaped her lips.

Zane, at her side, let go of her hand in shock. "Burn and bury me…"

Raina's eyes fixed on one object.

In the center of the room on a black marble pedestal rested a black metal chest wrapped with red glowing chains of pure bloodstone.

"Raina—" Zane said. "If those chains and chest are bloodstone, that means they are failing to seal whatever magic is inside." She knew he was right. If magic was everywhere, then the bloodstone was doing a piss-poor job at containing it. Which meant a crack had developed, or the object within was just that powerful.

Either way, it was bad. Very bad.

Raina took a step forward.

Zane grabbed her hand. "Raina…it's too dangerous…"

"Really? What gave it away?" Raina asked, glancing at the room as if it had been made for demons.

He grumbled. "I can't lose you."

She sighed. "Then it's a good thing you won't. C'mon. We've come this far." What Raina didn't tell him, however, is that her heart pounded like a drum, wanting to burst through her ribcage. She knew why. Whatever was in that chest was calling to her. Whispering a soundless song that spoke to her very soul. *She* needed to open it. Every fiber of her being demanded it, as much as she feared it. Raina tightened her grip on his hand. Zane followed as she strode toward the pedestal, the room emanating life.

The pedestal was wrapped with thick, pulsing veins of green, red, and blue.

Looking closer, it was obvious everything—the membrane, the tendons, the skin—seeped out from whatever was in that chest. Raina drew closer. Another step. The floor felt soft beneath their feet, as they walked across the living flesh. Perspiration beaded across her skin. Another step. Her head swam and her throat tightened. Another step.

She reached it. Zane was squeezing her hand painfully tight. "Mind letting go? That is, before you break my fingers."

He released her hand.

Raina followed her instinct and pulled on the Nexus in her mind—the swirling orb of flesh—and thick tendrils of flow filled her limbs and sank into the chest. The chains…shattered, as if they'd been deteriorating for millennia and only needed just the right nudge. She touched the lid, her whole body breaking out in sweat. Zane grabbed her hand again.

She turned to him, "Zane—

"Together."

She nodded and gave him a small smile. And, as one, they lifted the chest's lid.

"Gods and Abyss…" Zane cursed.

Sun and Water's Retribution

Ayva knew something was wrong as soon as the group battle concluded. She sensed it in her heart.

Gray was at her side, facing off with Merrick.

Beyond the Ronin of Metal, she saw Nalia standing over Drega.

"No…" she breathed. Before she knew it, she was racing across the field, barely aware of the bodies, the stone rubble, and the vines, shriveling now under the hot sun. Ayva fell to Drega's side, holding him, and…blood soaked her hands. So much blood. "No, no, no, no…"she uttered in horror. In desperation, she cried out to the stands, to the Reavers on the first row, "Heal him, for light's sake! Gods above, you're ready to kill us all, but where are you now? Heal him, you light-cursed bastards!" She realized she was glowing, and the crowds were mesmerized, tens of thousands of eyes all fixed on her with a mixture of sorrow, confusion, and a little fear of her radiant power.

No one cheered.

She felt a warm hand on her shoulder.

Looking up, she knew she'd find Gray's eyes—while there was sympathy in them and sadness, there was rage too. That fire nearly equaled her own. He knelt at her side, looking at the leader of the Fleshguard. Drega, even in death, still held a faint glimmer of a smile, as if he knew a secret. A secret now never to be revealed.

"He'd been looking at us…" she whispered in realization, in horror. *Had he been wanting us to save him? Is this our fault?* Could she have done more?

His eyes—they stared out but not seeing.

Gray gently, reverently closed the man's lids. "A good death my brother," Gray said, *"Reklah forhas."*

Ayva knew that phrase.

She'd heard Gray say it was a code of the Devari and some of the other elite warriors.

Old tongue, which translated to "*With honor, until death.*"

The words felt so fitting now.

Gray looked up, rising. He stared at Nalia.

The woman hadn't moved.

Even now, under his inferno of anger, her face was aloof, though a cold mirth resided behind that aloofness. Nalia sighed, stretching her strong neck, revealing taut muscles. "Shame. It seems like the Fleshguard are in need of a new leader."

Ayva felt her power roar, despite her collar. The next thing she knew, sun bloomed in her mind and she was on her feet, preparing to burn the woman before her in a bonfire. "Take me on," she threatened the woman. "I will incinerate your arrogant indifference."

Nalia smirked, looking down at her. Their height difference was significant. Ayva didn't care if the woman was a giant. "Go ahead, little legend. Hopefully you'll be more of a challenge than him."

Ayva summoned sun. Before she could obliterate the Grand Primus, Gray appeared. He grabbed her, wrapping her in eddies of wind. *Ayva...* He warned. *You cautioned me, remember?* He glanced to the archers and Reavers on the wall.

Damn the archers, we can take them, she sent.

Gray gave her a hard look. *What about the tournament?*

She scoffed. *Don't be a fool, Gray. You and I both know the queen won't keep her promise.*

I'm not relying on the queen.

Nalia chuckled. "As entertaining as this is, if we're not fighting, then I'm done here. Save your sun, little legend. Your turn is soon enough." Then she threw her sword aside, spat blood to the sand, turned, and left them.

Ayva looked about with more horror than awe.

Egrin's decapitated corpse.

Moonguard. The body of Eras Barkblood, split in two.

So many dead. *Yet somehow we survived.*

Suddenly, the twenty corpses all around the field of battle turned to orange mist. Merrick grimaced, still staring at Gray and Ayva. Ayva hesitated. Drega's corpse was one of the last to disintegrate. But it, too, slowly faded, along with his spilled blood, to a fiery vapor. The crowds made sounds of reverence. She looked to Gray. *Are you sure about this?*

Gray sent, *We need every advantage we can get.*

A part of Ayva abhorred the idea of absorbing Drega's spark, yet...

She breathed, filling her lungs. Her skin absorbed it as well, spark flowing into her soul, and power roared through her, like an expanding sun inside her chest, growing more and more. The result was a tingling sensation that made every hair on her body stand on end.

Gray did likewise. Infused with power, wind flowed around him with more velocity and force than ever before. She felt Gray's strength grow like a tangible thing, as if she were standing near a bonfire.

How much spark did we just imbibe?

Unfortunately, she saw Merrick several dozen paces away as he breathed in his share of the spark. He smoldered with power, a sinister silverish-black. She ignored him, ignored the crowds, and closed her eyes again, picturing Drega's affable smile and his booming voice. She placed her hand over her heart, then knelt to touch the sand where Drega had lain, his body gone, even his blood just a fading memory. But not to Ayva.

"I will always remember you," she whispered.

Gray's hand on her shoulder was a warm assurance.

Gates opened and slaves flooded the field, gathering weapons, and guards stormed onto the sands after them, creating a long corridor to escort them off the arena floor to a rising chorus of cheers.

Helix sent them a message from the balcony. *I'm here, guys.* His voice was heavy with empathy.

Gray nodded.

Only after they were off the field, away from the crowds, did Ayva turn to Gray, throw her arms around him, bury her face into his chest, and cry. For a long while, Gray just held her, firmly embracing her as if to shield her from an invisible storm. She sniffled, at last pulling back and looking into his eyes, which were equally wet with tears. "I'm sorry...I think I needed that. It's just...it's been a lot."

"You're telling me," he said, thumbing away a tear from her cheek.

She continued, "All this blood and death was taking its toll, but until now I've been able to justify it. All of it for the greater good. But Drega"—she wiped another tear—"he just seemed larger than life. And strong...Nalia is—"

"A monster," Gray agreed.

"She didn't even take in any of the spark on the field."

Gray rubbed the back of his neck. "I wondered that too. Part of me doesn't believe it. She wants to look invincible, but I suspect she got her share of spark. "

"I wouldn't put it past her," Ayva agreed. "I can't help thinking—"

Gray held up a hand. "It wasn't your fault, and there wasn't anything you could do. Drega, as much as anyone in the world, knew the risks. Besides, the man, from what I could tell, loved fighting in battle more than anything in Farhaven. You could never have stopped him, or saved him. Remember that."

She gave a nod.

"Are you ready?"

"Not really," she admitted, chuckling, "but I can face anything with you."

Gray smiled. "Couldn't have said it better myself." Then together, with a breath, they left the lower hallway and walked up the corridors. As they did, they had quite the surprise. The halls were filled with people, who cheered as they saw them enter the hall. Guards, servants, and messengers were in attendance. Ayva was briefly aware of them taking note of the four red swords on her wrist. Some chanted their names in celebration of their victory.

You'd think they'd just witnessed Renalin fight, Ayva sent, as they were swarmed from all sides.

Gray grabbed her wrist, speaking over the noise, "C'mon, this way."

He pushed, using wind to part the crowds, though it was like moving through thick syrup. They hadn't gotten far when a dozen Fleshguard in tan-colored cloaks with red heart emblems on the back appeared, moving with conviction. Ayva hesitated, but they filed in, pushing others aside. "Need an escort?" the biggest man asked. He had blond hair and pale scars like Drega's on his cheeks and arms.

Ayva and Gray both nodded, confused.

With a dozen Fleshguard leading the way, the masses parted like the sea, and they reached their rooms. Before they could say anything, the big man spoke. "Name is Karis Aligar," the man said. "Drega told me about you two. Saw what he did for you, and you for him." He nodded his thanks. "The Fleshguard honor their own. If there's anything we can do for you, let us know. We'll be there." The other Fleshguard made nods or grunts, echoing his sentiment.

Gray exchanged a look with Ayva. "Same for us."

"You have an ally with the Ronin," Ayva agreed.

Karis's gruff face gave only a nod, as he reached out a forearm. "*Reklah forhas.*"

They returned the gesture.

The battle-hardened warriors turned to leave, and Ayva called out, "Drega, he—" Her voice broke.

The man seemed to understand. "He would have been honored to have fought and died at your side. Same as any one of us..." His head bowed. "My Lady Ronin."

Ayva, throat constricted with emotion, could only nod. This appeared to be enough. Karis smiled, turned, and with long purposeful strides, hurried away with his men, leaving her feeling like the pieces were falling into place.

As she returned to the private balcony, power still flowed through Ayva's veins. She felt as if she could level a mountain. Gray's presence at her side was comforting.

He looked at his hands, flexing them. *Do you feel—*

Crackling with power? she finished.

Good, glad it's not just me.

All this time, flow seemed so different. I know it's the soul of magic, yet there's clearly some deeper connection.

Gray grunted his agreement. *Whatever the connection, I'm sure you'll discover it.* He moved to open the door with a puff of wind, though Helix cracked it wide first, his face brimming with a smile but sorrow in his eyes. Before Ayva could say anything, the Ronin of Water lunged, wrapping his arms around Ayva and lifting her into a hug. She squawked, protesting that he was hugging too hard, but Helix released her only to rush Gray and squeeze him just as hard. "Tranquil Seas! You did it!" He pulled back, running his hands through his hair, which stuck up at all angles. "I can't believe what I just saw. I wanted to say something, but I didn't want to distract you. I think I held my breath for that whole fight..." He took a big breath as if for emphasis, leaning on a nearby table. "Gray, how you moved with wind, and those Devari forms? Then Ayva, you did those shields, and…Oh gods, Egrin tried to backstab you and—"

"Helix, pretty sure we were there," Ayva said.

Helix winced. "Ah, right." He scrubbed at his wild blond head of hair, then questioned, "I gotta ask, all that spark…how do you feel?"

Ayva eyed her hands, speaking softly, "Brimming."

Gray rubbed his palms together, as if also feeling them tingle with power. "Couldn't have said it better."

A moment of silence held the three, clearly all thinking the same thing.

"I…" Helix searched for words, rubbing his neck, tears in his eyes. "I…"

Ayva hugged Helix this time. "I know. Drega was a good man."

Gray looked away with a hard expression. "Better than most."

Helix wiped away a tear, sitting down with a heavy slump, absently chewing on a carrot. "He banished my fear when I was afraid. Abyss take me, nothing scared him. I didn't think he could—"

"I said the same thing," Ayva replied.

Helix's jaw tightened as his fist pounded the table. "Nalia," he cursed. "She'll pay. Now she has to fight either one of you, or you have to fight each other? Or she has to fight Merrick." He scratched his head. "I didn't think about that."

Ayva moved to the balcony's railing.

Gray and Helix joined her. "Ayva?" Gray asked. "What's wrong?"

Something Helix said nettled her, but she couldn't put her finger on it. She looked west. "I don't know, something feels off."

"Oh, what feels off?" Helix asked, a chalice now in his hand. "The fact that the queen wants to betray us? Or that the Ronin of Metal, our own supposed brother, wants to spill our guts for some nefarious nameless evil we don't even know? Also, did we forget about our quest for the next Ronin?"

"It's not like we're not looking, Helix," Ayva replied, "but finding a Ronin requires someone to reveal their hand. I haven't seen anyone standing out in feats of flesh or stone. Not yet, at least."

Gray replied, "We'll find them, Helix, or they'll find us."

"How are you so certain?" Helix asked. "And you have yet to answer what we're going to do about Imala. I feel like she's a giant axe hanging above our head by a fraying string, waiting for one wrong turn of the tournament to come chopping us in two." He worriedly touched his skull, as if already feeling the axe's bite. "Even if we win, you think she's just gonna give up her army?"

Gray's eyes churned with purpose. "I've told you. We don't need to win the queen, we need to win the people. They hold the key to the kingdom."

"Oh, right," Helix replied, draining the last of the mead in the chalice he held, then wiping his mouth with the back of his hand. "So you just need to convince a mob of blood-hungry, morally depraved men and women, who've based their entire economy on a system of subjugation of others, and dominance as a whole, to what…join the side of good? Might I remind you—people might be good, but societies? They grow corrupt. And this one is as corrupt as they come."

Helix was making sense, and Ayva didn't like it.

"You're right, but we just have to keep moving," Gray said. "Trust Zane to find what he's searching for. Meanwhile, we have to win the tournament. That's all we can do."

Helix rolled his shoulders and poured another glass as he heaved a heavy sigh. "Suppose you're right. It just feels like gambling with Darius, and everyone's got a loaded dice, and a sword unsheathed beneath the table, waiting to draw blood. You know what confuses me most? Faye. Where in the seven hells is she?" He scratched his head and looked about the balcony as if she would appear any moment. "She loves a chance to point out how we're wrong, or to flirt with Gray. I figured she'd show up by now and either lead us into a trap or salvation. Or both."

Gray raised a brow.

"Raise your brows all you want, Wind Boy, it's true. Ayva, back me up."

Ayva shrugged. "He's right."

Gray groaned. "Great, you too."

Ayva winced. "This is also going to sound strange, but I'm actually a little worried about her."

"Knowing Faye, she's got her reasons," Gray said. "But you still haven't answered what's troubling you."

Ayva sighed. She felt…strange. Like there was a dark shadow, and she couldn't banish the foreboding. "I can't put a finger on it, but I think it has to do with what's coming for us…"

The dark army.

Gray inclined his head, looking as if he wanted to ask more questions. Instead, he said, "I know. Again, let's focus on one thing at a time. We win today, then deal with the shadow in the west."

Ayva gave a nod, though she knew Gray saw her lack of conviction. Then she turned at the sound of a low rumble. "It's starting…"

The drums thundered.

"Dearest citizens of Covai, let your hearts roil with anticipation and your eyes prepare to feast upon bloodshed and death, as the next battle will be starting soon!" the announcer called. "The semifinals, the much anticipated Primus round!"

The crowds roared, and Ayva saw the arched hallways were crammed with people, pushing and shoving their way into the stands. They were practically on top of one another at this point.

A hard rap sounded on the door to their balcony and Helix answered it.

Covian guards stood at the doorway. "Your battle will begin shortly, my Lord Primus, my Lady Primus," the guard said, with a bow to each. Ayva found that amusing. It seemed their title of Ronin was supplanted by Primus. Of course, only in Covai was a Ronin somehow inferior to the vaunted champions of the tournament.

Gray turned to Ayva, sending through the bond, *Are you ready?*

Still with that unsettled feeling, she sent back, *I'm ready to end this.*

Together, they followed the guards through the halls. People tried to get a glimpse of the current Primuses, and possible future Grand Primus. Helix chatted away, giving them advice, and then he noticed all the attention they were receiving. "Gods, you're famous."

A familiar face parted the crowds. Howard, Queen Imala's steward. His kind eyes now looked stern, his expression troubled. "My Lady Ronin," he said, dipping his head, voice a little rattled.

"Howard? What're you doing here?" Ayva asked, touching his arm warmly. "What's going on?"

"I have urgent news," he said gravely.

"News?"

"Most dire. You must come with me at once."

Ayva's heart skipped, but before she could say anything, from within the crowds Hati appeared, pushing her way to the front.

Beautiful as ever with her shaved head and entrancing green gaze, she fixed her eyes on Gray. A smile lit her face as she rushed to wrap her arms around him. Then the two realized all were staring. "Uh, I have to—" Gray started.

"Go ahead, I need to talk with Howard. I'll see you out there."

"It's going to be all right," Gray said, though he looked as if he wasn't entirely sure himself. Still, it was clear he was trying to reassure her earlier doubts. She gave a brief dip of her head.

"Come, my Lady Ronin," Howard urged.

"Helix too," Ayva said.

Helix grunted, joining them. "Yeah, I definitely thought that was implied. Ayva's not going anywhere without me."

"Of course, my Lord Ronin," Howard replied, then together, they followed him away from the crowds, leaving behind Gray and their flock of guards. As they walked, she glimpsed Howard's face again. A dark shadow was deeply etched into his features, something he tried to hide, but couldn't. "This way, quickly."

"What's going on, Howard? You're worrying me."

"Easier to show you, my lady," Howard said, a crack of dread entering his voice, and they followed him up a series of staircases, higher and higher, into a minaret that looked out over the city and beyond. A spyglass used for perhaps seeing stars was positioned inside, and Howard peered into it, adjusting it slightly, then nodded. "See for yourself."

Ayva leaned down to look through it, and at first...she spotted only a city, far to the west, on a desert bank—Harikus, she believed was its name. It sat on the Ker Stream, a magical river that cut straight through the heart of the Covian Desert. Again, "stream" was an understatement. The rushing body of water was wide and wild, too tempestuous to cross—like an ocean in a storm. The very thing the queen was hoping would keep the dark army at bay. Through the glass, her eyes raced across the distance, and she spotted plumes of dust.

Then she saw it.

Her breath was ripped from her lungs.

A massive bridge—so wide and long, it looked as if it should have been impossible to construct.

Then she saw a hundred Reavers and other magic wielders standing at the far end, employing colossal amounts of spark, adding stone and metal. They were building the bridge over the raging rapids, she realized. Then a feeling of dread filled her as she saw what was on the bridge itself. Occupying the massive stone structure, and flooding the western bank for miles on end, were creatures.

Saeroks, vergs, nameless…

The dark army.

They were coming, and they were close.

Ayva staggered, knees growing weak for a moment, gripping the spyglass to keep herself standing. "Light save us…"

Helix gulped, "Ayva? Okay, you're scaring me now. What's going on?"

She moved to let Helix take in the sight himself. He gasped and stumbled back to lean against a crenellation on the minaret. "Abyss take me…" he said, repeating the phrase over and over.

Ayva turned to Howard, throat dry, rasping as she grabbed his arm, "How?"

Howard's face, normally unbreakable, was now stricken with panic, as if he'd let the dam of indifference finally crack and his terror was evident. A trickle of sweat ran down his brow. "Her Majesty knows if word got out that there'd be panic…perhaps even riots. She has something planned. She needs the tournament to finish, I believe. At this point, she fears a call to war without finishing you three will lead to an insurrection."

"Very likely," Ayva agreed.

"With damned good reason!" Helix said.

"Have you told anyone else?" she asked.

Howard shook his head. "No. I came to you first."

She gripped his arm. "How long do we have?"

"If they finish construction of the bridge soon? By my calculations, they could be here before nightfall," he answered.

"What can we do?" Helix breathed, turning to Ayva.

"*If* they finish construction…" Ayva repeated. She looked up, meeting Helix's gaze. "I think my chance at facing Nalia or Merrick is going to have to wait. Are you ready to do something that'll probably get us killed?"

"I haven't seen Darius in a while, so I've been missing my near-death, insane suicide missions." Helix laughed, though his voice was shaky. He nodded and said, unequivocally, "I'm in."

"How can I assist?" Howard asked, brows furrowed. "Whatever I can do, tell me."

Ayva gripped his shoulder. "I need you to keep the city running smoothly. Inform Captain Leanna of what's happening. She wants what's best for the city. Perhaps there's something she can do without drawing the ire of Her Majesty. In the meantime, watch over Gray. Make sure he doesn't die, at least from Imala's machinations."

Howard bowed his head. "By my word, my Lady Ronin. I'll do my best."

Abruptly, she hugged the man, wrapping her arms around his bony frame, clearly surprising him. "Thank you, Howard. When this is all done, you're going to tell me more about the mystery of the steward that saved a kingdom."

"I shall be happy to divulge, dear Primus," Howard replied.

Ayva smiled, then snatched Helix's hand, and they took off.

"Where are we going?" Helix called as they rushed through the busy halls. Ayva wrapped her white veil around her face, hoping to attract a little less attention.

"You'll see," she replied back, and soon enough they found themselves in a rookery, a giant tower that housed all manner of flying creatures: gryphons roosting in huge hay beds, giant membrane-winged bats hanging from posts, and a host of other magical or rare flying mounts.

A bald man in Covian attire with an emblem of a bird on his tabard—a Roost Watcher—oversaw the rookery. After seeing her four swords, he practically tangled his tongue into a knot, throwing himself into a bow that scraped the floor. "Flesh and bone, a Primus in my midst! What can I possibly—"

She cut him off. "I need a mount. Now."

"But of course, my Lady Primus! Why didn't you say so?" He spread his hands magnanimously. "By the gods, any one of your choosing, you name it, and it shall be yours!"

Helix gulped. "Which one?"

Ayva chose without hesitation.

A moment later, they were in the sky on the back of a giant owl, clutching reins made out of gold chains, the magnificent creature's feathered wings fluttering as they soared through the air over the city of Covai, heading west.

"First off, love the owl, great call. Heard they used to be second to only archwolves for Vasterian flying mounts!"

She glanced over her shoulder, a brow raised, heart pounding. She knew he was panic talking, his habit when he was anxious, or perhaps trying to calm her nerves, but knowing the history of mounts?

"Don't look at me like that, I can read! More importantly, what's our plan?" Helix called over the rush of wind. "You know, how we're going to take out an endless evil army?"

"You let me handle that," Ayva replied. "You just protect me."

"I can do that!" A shield of ice rose to either side of them as they raced through the sky. Desert passed beneath them in a blur, and soon Harikus grew larger still, the teaming clay river town churning with pandemonium as men and women fled the city in panic, strapping belongings on camels and horses. Other residents were halfway into the desert, running. How many would die? "Get ready!" Ayva cried as the bridge grew larger in her field of vision, the nightmarish army becoming terribly real.

"Oh gods," Helix cried. "Ready!"

Power swirled inside of her, and she summoned a glowing golden ball of light. She sent it toward the bridge, but the ball's descent slowed as a Reaver flung out a hand, bursting the sun orb before she could pull the thread. Ayva growled, "I need to get closer!" Helix gripped her tightly as she guided the giant owl lower.

Monsters looked up at them, pointing.

Arrows flew, and she waved a hand of sun, turning them to ash.

Helix roared, summoning water—and thick spikes of ice raced toward the archers. Monsters fell in droves. It was working. She just needed time to form her spell—

Half the Reavers stopped their bridge building to attack, and a deluge of spells—sun, ice, moonbolts, and fireballs—rushed toward them.

"Helix!" she cried.

"On it!" he called back, and a transparent, crystalline-blue structure of ice formed ahead of them. Magic crashed against it, cracking the surface, though it didn't shatter. She cried out in awe, but Helix replied, sounding strained, "Love the encouragement, but this spell isn't exactly easy to hold. Don't want to rush you, but if you're going to do your thing, now would be a great time!"

Again, spells crashed against the shield. It cracked further.

Ayva summoned more of her Nexus.

Half the swirling sun in her mind unfolded, and an orb of radiant sun formed in one outstretched palm while her other hand gripped the reins for dear life. The orb was powerful, crackling with energy, shooting out flares of light and sun, but it wasn't enough.

More, she demanded.

The spells still slammed into the icy barrier, sending deep fissures, ready to burst.

Cries sounded from below. "Take them down!" called a nameless, a giant, terrifying nightmare in black plate and rotting cloth, pointing with a corroded sword. "Now!"

All the Reavers abandoned their building to attack.

The spells redoubled, slamming into the ice, cracking it even more. It would shatter at any moment. Helix called out, "Ayva!"

She felt the same urgency, burning in her blood. However, if she rushed the spell, it wouldn't work. They had one shot. So she demanded more. Three-quarters of her Nexus was unveiled, and she was aware that her body glowed. Her arms shook. With all the spark she'd imbibed, her whole being quivered with energy. She needed more. Only, with her collar on, she'd never have enough. She'd gathered hints from the nobles that the collars were used in all but the Grand Primus battle. Hers still remained around her neck.

The dark army teemed, roiling with unrest, seeking her death…

She knew the town would be the first to burn, innocents slaughtered, bellies opened to the sands. It was just like back in Lakewood, and anguish filled her at the searing memories of the town burning, torn apart by the evil's reckoning. These people weren't willing participants in a tournament of death, just defenseless men and women seeking to live their lives and find love and prosperity. Those lives would be snuffed out.

Ayva would change that fate.

Hope spiraled inside of her.

In the moment before the shield broke, the ring on her hand burned with luminescence. Ayva gripped her collar. The Yronia metal infused with bloodstone at first resisted—absorbing her magic—but Ayva poured more into it. Red metal turned white, and with a final tug, she ripped the metal collar off.

Power flooded her.

The orb of light in her palm suddenly flared with unmatched brilliance.

Helix cried out as his shield shattered.

Spells came roaring forth.

It didn't matter.

Ayva flung out her hand, and the giant orb of sun flew.

Every single spell from the Reavers—every ball of fire, sun, moon, and water—everything in the orb's vicinity evaporated like water on a hot pan, consumed by the great ball of sun. Saeroks and vergs covered their eyes, though others stared directly at it, as if they couldn't look away. Most fled. Some moved forward, pushing Reavers off the bridge. Others scrambled backward, clawing other monsters in their desperate attempt to flee. Yet, as crowded as the massive bridge was, most had nowhere to go, aside from falling into the deadly currents.

The sun descended.

In the last moment, Ayva reached out, frantically searching—like trying to find a single piece of thread in a ball of yarn the size of a boulder. Where was it? She knew the effort would be useless without that. The bridge would be rebuilt. The army would advance. All would be lost, they wouldn't have time to rally, and—

There!

She found it.

Ayva pulled the thread of sun in the heart of the orb.

The spell coalesced.

Collapsing Star.

The orb burst.

Even from this distance, the explosion was deafening, and the rush of air was overwhelming.

Helix created a massive blue-white shield. It cracked and shattered. He created another behind it in an instant. This one cracked, but didn't shatter. Wind raged on either side of the protective blue barrier. Without it, they would have been blown to pieces.

Finally, the wind settled, and Helix let the shield drop.

Below, destruction reigned.

The bridge groaned, and she watched it crumble and collapse into the Ker.

Saeroks, vergs, nameless—thousands had evaporated to nothing.

The rest had fallen into the fatal rapids, their bodies carried downriver.

Helix let loose a long, low string of curses. Finally, when he could speak, he breathed, "Remind me to never upset you…Also, I'm very glad I didn't have to fight you in the tournament."

Inwardly, she chuckled.

Outwardly, Ayva was silent, watching the destruction, as more chunks of stone and dark metal from the bridge tumbled into the turbulent waters. The last few survivors clawed at the water, gasping for air, before being sucked into a watery grave. Silence followed.

"It's over," Helix breathed.

"For now," Ayva replied. "That won't hold them forever." She looked up and saw the western shore. Nightmares crawled out of the river; the rest of the bank teamed with monsters, like a kicked anthill. More streamed in from Median—the long line of the rest of the army. It was growing. "At least we bought a little time, but they'll rebuild it, or find another way. We need to get back and warn the others."

"I hope Gray's okay. Think he's wondering about us? Gods, better question, you think anyone's going to believe us?"

Now Ayva chuckled, and lightly, she pulled on the giant owl's reins, steering them east, back toward Covai. She glanced at her hand, the radiant glow still emanating from the burnished gold ring. "Honestly, I'm not sure I believe it myself." She peered over her shoulder at Helix. His wild hair and blue eyes were full of conflicting emotions. "I couldn't have done it without you," she called over the rush of wind.

"I know!" Helix replied.

Wind's Fury

Stepping up to the gate, seeing the arena beyond, Gray steeled himself for blood.

I must win, Gray thought. *Failure is not an option.*

The announcer began to rally the crowds.

Morrowil was at Gray's hip.

The people roared, the ground rumbled, and the announcer began his speech. "Oh, my dearest citizens of Covai, are you ready to witness the most epic clashes ever to take the sands? Once bonded by a legend as old as time, now blood must be spilled, as a red day dawns!"

More relentless cheering.

It's Ayva or Merrick, Gray thought, heart pounding.

Helix? Ayva? he sent. *Are you two there?*

There was no response.

Panic flooded him.

Where were they? Were they too far away from the bond? How could that be? Earlier, from the balcony, Helix had always been able to send him messages.

Before his worry could consume him, Morrowil sent, *Relax. Just breathe. Focus on this match. Nothing more.*

Gray did, though it didn't calm the fire in his veins.

He saw Hati again in the stands.

A memory took him.

Ayva and Helix had just gone to speak with Howard. Before the steward whisked them away, Gray had sensed the older gentlemen with the ki and felt a wave of dread. He tried to shove it aside, knowing the man's fears could be anything, as Gray took Hati into a hallway, trying to get away from the crowds. From out of nowhere, a half-dozen Fleshguard spotted them, and they made a barrier for him and Hati to keep the onlookers at a distance.

Quickly becoming our new bodyguards, *Gray thought gratefully. Their intimidating looks and scarred faces were frightening enough that most gave them a good bit of space.*

"Aren't I going to get a 'good luck'?" Gray asked Hati.

She shrugged. "Happily, if you need it."

He snorted, then looked down.

She gripped his hands, sage-green eyes narrowing with discernment. "I know what you fear…Do you think he can be saved?" she asked, as if reading his thoughts.

"I don't know," Gray admitted honestly.

"I saw the look in his eyes, Gray. Be careful."

"But not good luck?"

She winked. "It's like good luck, but sweeter."

"My lord—" a guard called, trying to break through the wall of Fleshguard.

Gray sighed.

Hati wrapped her arms around him, giving him a final kiss, and—

The memory broke, and he was back on the sands.

The announcer continued and Gray caught snippets of his words. "…as before…a battle to the death! There is no surrender! If one admits defeat, our archers will ensure he does not survive—" Gray stopped listening, focusing on the battle ahead. The announcer must have finished his speech because the gate opened.

Gray had taken a step when the gruff clearing of a man's throat sounded behind him.

He looked back, having almost forgotten about the two guards who had escorted him down to the gates. They were both surly-looking men. The bigger guard looked like a tavern bruiser, with a large smashed nose, ragged scars, and cauliflower ears. He seemed more suited to throwing drunkards to the street than the duties of a Covian guard wearing a regal tabard of flesh and chainmail. Avoiding Gray's eyes, as if uncomfortable with speaking or expressing his emotions, the man grumbled, "Good luck, my Lord Ronin. We're rooting for you."

The other guard grunted his agreement.

Gray was taken aback. "Thanks," he said and nodded. He moved to leave, only to pause, looking back. "What's your name?"

"Gmit, my lord." Then, hesitantly, Gmit added, "If I may, my lord, I've seen my fair share of battles. I've seen the heart of men. Yours speaks true. Farhaven would be dimmer without you."

"That's...kind of you, Gmit. Though I have no intention of dying today."

Gmit made a thoughtful sound, rubbing his stubbled, broad jaw. "No man intends to die."

Gray raised a brow. Then he said, "True enough." He glanced back at the sands, listening to the roar of the crowds. *Let them wait*, he thought. "Gmit, you said you've seen your share of blood. Any advice?"

Gmit made a low grumble as he pondered. Then he replied, "I know when a man is backed into a corner, he fights like the devil. Like he's ten men in one. He grows claws, and fangs, turns into a wild thing, possessed with the singular need to survive."

"You think I'm backed into a corner?"

Gmit snorted in amusement, lifting a furry brow over a hooded eye. There was a keenness there that Gray hadn't seen before, belied by the man's rough looks. "I think you both might be," Gmit said.

"I see..."

"All I'm saying, my lord, is be wary of his claws, and don't be afraid to lean into yours." He nodded, as if he'd said his piece and was content.

"Thank you. I'll try not to disappoint."

The surly scar-faced man gave a grunt, then both men placed fists to heart, like a warrior to a general.

It's beginning, Morrowil said, a note of pride in the sword's tone.

With a last look to the two men, Gray turned and strode onto the empty sands.

The crowd roared their approval, the feeling of their cries crashing down on Gray from every angle, a violent, hopeful tempest.

A moment later, from the shadows of the far tunnel, Merrick appeared, walking out onto the colosseum's floor, metal threads swirling about his body appearing like silver mist.

Gray felt a cold wind sink into his bones. Merrick was attired in immaculate dark plate—like armor straight out of the stories—and he had an inkling it was...Was that Baro's armor? Some part of Gray hoped Merrick's movements would be hindered by it. Unfortunately, the man strutted forward with perfect grace and the arrogance of a king-killer. He should have figured—Merrick was the Ronin of Metal.

With *his* appearance, the stands erupted, cheering louder than for Gray's arrival into the arena.

In his mind, the refrain echoed, *Win the crowd, win the tournament.*

Gray called out through the bond in one final attempt: *I'm only going to say it once more. You don't have to do this.*

Merrick's grin told him everything. The man lifted a finger to point at him, and smoothly, the bow on his back shifted into liquid and then reformed as a gleaming black blade in his hand. *Are you ready to die, brother? Don't worry, your death won't be in vain. It'll prove to the world that magic is a stain upon the land. That there is no such thing as a valiant champion.*

How can you not see that you're becoming the very thing you hate?

Merrick's armor grew larger spikes, his expression empty. *It's the only way to tear it all down.*

Morrowil sent, *Focus. Don't listen to his twisted logic.*

The blade was right.

Gray's breathing was already faster. His blood was hot. A pain remained in Merrick's eyes that Gray wished he could have healed. Now it was too late.

Some wounds are old and run too deep, Morrowil sent.

So all hope is lost? I refuse to believe that.

Refuse all you want, Morrowil replied. *The will of Farhaven has spoken.*

Sure enough, the thundering drums now slowed. Tension built. The crowds quieted. The people of Covai leaned forward in their seats with bated breath.

On his pulpit, the announcer, all bone and sinew, seized the railing, straining forward as if savoring the tension in the air.

Thump
Thump
Thump.

The drumbeat slowed further.

In opposition, Gray's heart hammered faster, sweat breaking out across his body. Clouds of metallic silver and bronze slowly formed and swirled around Merrick's limbs like ribbons of steel.

Are you ready? Gray asked Morrowil.

Ready, Morrowil replied.

Thump.

Thump.
Thump.
The drums silenced.
An eerie hush filled the colosseum.
"FIGHT!" the announcer roared.
Gray, the power of a tempest within and Morrowil in hand, charged.

Merrick ran. From the opposite side of the arena, Gray raced toward him, wind rising. Dozens of metal arrows hovered all about Merrick, and with a wave of his hand, they flew. Gray knocked them aside with a giant tempest of wind, his collar glowing vibrant red.

Pouncing, Gray slashed downward at Merrick.

Merrick morphed Osmium into a spiked tower shield.

Sword and shield collided.

Boom.

A thunderclap echoed, wind rushing over the sands and shaking the entire colosseum.

As Merrick recovered, Gray slashed again.

Merrick switched Osmium back to a black blade. The two weapons clanged, ebony steel opposing Morrowil's silvery-white metal, creating a fireworks of sparks. Gray didn't slow, appearing driven by some internal force. Changing tactics to complicated Devari forms, he advanced on Merrick, who had no choice but to fall back beneath the onslaught. Morrowil cut a groove across Baro's breastplate. Merrick growled, though the black metal was merely scratched.

Gray wasn't done.

Morrowil flashed again.

Cold fury churned in his gray-green eyes. Merrick flung out a hand, sending more black arrows toward him. Gray waved his own hand, and the arrows froze again in midair. "Two can play that game," Gray said as he exhaled, and with a flick of his fingers, he turned the arrows back on Merrick.

Faster than Merrick anticipated.

A metal arrow grazed his cheek, causing a shallow laceration. Stunned, Merrick touched his face, feeling blood. He lifted his hand to send more arrows, except Gray swung Morrowil. His sword, enforced with wind, smashed into Merrick. He quickly raised a shield, but the force still catapulted him through the air, and he landed, hard, bone bruising and head smacking the sands as he tumbled across the arena floor. The world swam. The crowds were a dull roar through his rattled senses. Slowly, the tumultuous cries resumed, and Merrick heard a familiar voice.

You are losing, Osmium sent calmly.

With the metallic taste of blood in his mouth, Merrick grumbled, *Shut it.*

He looked across the sands—Gray stood in the center of the battlefield, wind swirling about him as he waited. He was not advancing. The Ronin of Wind wore an expression of sorrow mixed with unyielding determination as he raised Morrowil and pointed the tip at Merrick. *Well?* he sent. *Is that all you have?*

Spitting blood to the sand, Merrick rose, muscles twitching. *Cursing wind.*

What, did you underestimate my ability and skill? More currents of air swirled about Gray's fist. His expression was one of vengeance. *You didn't go so easy on the last man who wielded wind...It's always that way, isn't it? Dominating those weaker than you. The very thing you profess to hate so much.*

Merrick showed teeth. *Talk all you want. I am simply a weapon for the greater good.*

Gray gave a sound of rising frustration. *The greater good? How can you possibly believe that when you are working for an evil that wants to dominate everything? When hundreds of thousands will die because of your actions!*

The end will justify my deeds, Merrick roared back. *Magic is a dark stain on this land that infects everything it touches, and only when it's gone will we know peace. Only I can end it.*

Gray's fury reached a peak, then, abruptly, the leader of the Ronin let out a breath. His face changed, rage slipping, replaced by an expression of...pity? Which only infuriated Merrick more. Gray shook his head sadly, as if dealing with a madman. *If only you could hear yourself...*

Merrick stalked forward, blade growing longer. *Enough talk.*

Remember, Gray sent, *you chose this path.*

Merrick reached up and grabbed the metal collar about his neck, ripping it off, as if it were tin and not solid Yronia steel. As soon as the collar was free, he tossed it to the sand, followed by a rush of dark black and gray magic that pulsed out from his core, rushing over the arena, over Gray.

The crowds gasped.

He extended one hand, and Osmium reformed within his grip. The pitch-black sword came to life with spine- and thorn-like protrusions.

Then he raised his other hand.

Another black blade filled it.

Both were long, jagged obsidian swords, each seething with charcoal-like mist. They were stronger than anything he'd summoned before, and judging by Gray's wide eyes, the Ronin of Wind was well aware of that. Merrick cracked his neck. "Come, brother. Let me show you the power of a true Ronin."

Gray felt a chill in his bones. Whatever Merrick had just done had unlocked something else inside the man.

Gray knew he was witnessing something more…What a Ronin was truly meant to be.

He wished the others were watching the match. He feared for them—

Focus, Morrowil sent.

Morrowil was right. "Win the crowds," he muttered to himself, seeing Merrick's black blade and dark armored form stalk toward him. *I have to show them what I'm capable of.* Already, however, the pain of the collar was like warm coals on his bare skin. Gray shoved the sensation down. *More*, he demanded, as wind rose higher around him. He knew he had an ocean of power at his disposal, a roiling sea of flow wanting, *needing* to be used. However, the collar was holding him back.

No. Not just the collar.

His own body.

He needed to push himself beyond those limits.

He needed to prove himself the leader of the Ronin.

The dark intent in Merrick's eyes was clear as he advanced another step, then another.

The Ronin of Metal wouldn't stop until one of them was dead.

With Merrick's new display of power, Gray knew he couldn't hold back. If he did, it would be his own demise. Pain in his heart, Gray understood what he had to do. He let wind stir inside his soul, thick white swirls coating his limbs. The collar seared, burning his flesh.
None of that mattered.
Gray would win.
Even if it meant Merrick's death.

Inky black smoke swirled about Merrick's body as he stalked toward Gray.
He had opened his Nexus wider, revealing more than half of the swirling sphere of metal. Now, he poured flow into his greaves, the infused metal holding a charged force. Powered by his magic, Merrick leapt. The crowds gasped. Air rushed around him as he flew through the air, twin black blades slicing downward.
Gray swept a hand out, trying to bat him from the air with wind, but with a slash from Osmium's dual blades, Merrick cut the spell, dissolving it.
Gray's eyes went wide, and he raised Morrowil just in time. Their blades clashed. Wind rushed outward. Through their locked swords, their eyes met, and Merrick spoke through gritted teeth, "I was hoping to save this for the Grand Primus, but I suppose I can show you a hint of my true power." With that, he poured *flow* into all parts of his armor, enhancing his strength. He attacked, his arms reinforced, and Osmium slammed into Morrowil.
Gray's leg buckled. He was sent to one knee by the force of the monstrous blow and barely held his parry with trembling arms. "You…don't have to do this…"
"Oh, but I do," Merrick said with a sneer, and—

Flash.
Endless pain, chains rattling, the slow drip of water. Screams sounded—his own, Neveaha's, and others'—sometimes echoing for hours, until time lost meaning. Fire, moon, sun, flesh—every element his captors used, and in endless creative ways for their infliction of

agony. He whimpered and she tried to console him. Time and again, he'd awake, screaming, not knowing if the blade was on his skin. One long nightmare bleeding together. Deep down, however, something was brewing inside of Merrick.

Something was coming to the surface.

The door to the dungeon creaked open, as the masked man returned.

Merrick shook his head, thrust back into the moment. Only the pain of the memory remained, and his fury redoubled as he laid into Gray, his obsidian swords seeking to end the Ronin of Wind. Again and again, he struck. In truth, the Ronin of Wind might have been a better blademaster, but he was still at a disadvantage.

Merrick had learned to harness the true power of his potential.

He breathed in, letting the metal sphere in his mind unveil another segment of his Nexus. Almost three-quarters of the sphere.

The clashes of Osmium and Morrowil rang through the arena. *Slice.* He cut a thin line in Gray's torso, making the Ronin grunt in pain. Blood flowed from his wound. Another. A cut to his shoulder, slashing cloth, flesh, and muscle. Again and again, Gray was forced to retreat against the strength of Merrick's fury. An opening appeared. Merrick felt triumph, and slammed a foot into Gray's chest, making the Ronin fly backward. Gray caught himself on a gust of wind, cushioning his tumble, though he lay in a heap on the sand, unmoving.

Merrick advanced on the fallen Ronin.

He raised his swords, preparing to finish him.

The crowds did a strange thing then…

Their roaring slowed.

A few jeers sounded, but many faces looked…sad, almost pained.

Some even cried out, begging for him to stop.

Merrick was baffled. He gazed up at the tens of thousands as he turned in a circle. "What is this? You wanted blood, I am giving it to you! That's all you care about!" he roared to the stands.

"You don't understand them," Gray said through gritted teeth. Planting Morrowil into the sand, he rose. "Power isn't everything. At least, not the way you think it is. They don't want only blood."

"Then what do they want? Oh, wise Ronin," Merrick snarled.

Gray stood straight, wind lightly whipping at his blood-streaked hair. Looking about, he seemed to take in the masses, who were now strangely quiet, leaning forward as if straining to hear. "They want to believe."

Merrick's heart skipped a beat. It wasn't anything he'd expected the man to say. "Believe?" Before Gray could answer, Merrick shook his head and cackled. "You can't be serious! You want me to think that this horde of mongrels who howl at every drop of blood suddenly want you to live because of what? Some misguided notion of hope?"

Gray smiled. "Yes." The so-called leader of the Ronin gave him a penetrating look. "You weren't always this way, were you? You had hope once, didn't you? What happened?"

Merrick was stunned into silence, anger rising higher, though it warred with a strange sensation in his chest. Suddenly, he felt something running down his cheeks. Tears. He scrubbed at them, as if confused. Osmium whispered, *listen to him*. Merrick shut the sword out of his mind and steeled himself as he looked back to Gray with a snarl. "Don't…

The man looked at him sorrowfully. "What did you lose, Merrick?"

Merrick snarled. "Enough!" He roared. "Stop trying to soften my heart, heal my wounds…" He shut his eyes against the pain, realizing his body was shaking. "You *can't* fix this." He raised his sword. "I will end you, and usher in a new age."

Gray sighed. He closed his eyes, a look of calm coming over his face. "Come then."

Eager for death? Merrick thought. *Then I'll grant him his wish.* He roared as his black blades cleaved the air. Only, as his swords descended to cut Gray in two, he was met with nothing but wind, which puffed out. Gray was gone and Merrick assaulted the ground where the Ronin of Wind had been only a moment before.

How? Merrick asked his blade.

Shifting, Osmium replied, a bit in awe himself.

The crowd roared.

He turned and saw Gray behind him, Morrowil raised.

"Come," Gray beckoned. "Let's finish this."

Roaring, Merrick slashed with his two blades, striking a gust of wind at his back that formed into Gray. As the blades cut, they sliced harmlessly at white wind. Gray *shifted* again, reappearing on his left.

Morrowil slashed, scoring a blow on Merrick's black armor that sent him staggering. Merrick bellowed, attacking. Again, Gray vanished, blade flashing, slicing from every side, and he cried out.

Gray was winning...

How?

Merrick had ripped the collar off and Gray hadn't, so there was no feasible way they should be on the same plane. "How are you doing this! I am stronger than you!" Merrick roared.

Then he caught glimpses of Gray. His collar was bloodred. He was pushing past his limitations. Merrick on the other hand wasn't held back by the same issues, freed of the band holding back his magic. He grinned. *I only have to keep going.*

Then, from the stands, a chant arose.

Ro-nin.

Ro-nin.

Ro-nin.

Were they chanting for him? No. He knew the truth.

Merrick's fury rose. *I will silence them all. Prove they are just bloodhungry beasts. This world needs to be burned down before it can be built again.* He pulled back more of his veil. Another portion. Nearly all of his swirling silver Nexus was revealed now.

He sent metal arrows in all directions, dozens, hundreds, flying toward Gray, the zephyr of wind that was his foe.

Gray moved faster and faster.

Shifting, he misted through arrows, through swords, over and over, appearing and reappearing all over the arena to the thunder of the crowds.

At the same time, Gray knew it was killing him.

The collar burned like a hot vise on his neck. He feared if he pulled it away, it would leave raw and blistered flesh. If he stopped, however, Merrick's metal arrows would pierce him, bringing certain death. *I will not lose,* Gray growled in his mind, barely becoming wind in time before a sword made for a titan cut him in half. *I will win, no matter what.*

So he pushed harder...

Hoping his body wouldn't break before his mind did, or the collar wouldn't kill him first.

Merrick bellowed, slashing with Osmium.

The Ronin of Wind found another level, and his blade slammed into Merrick's shoulder, his hip, his back, cutting at him, but his blows bounced off his armor. He cut to sever Merrick's hand, but Osmium created a shield by turning to liquid and then hardening over his wrist. Merrick was still losing…even with all his power. How? How could he lose? No…he couldn't. He wouldn't. So he pushed harder. Blood streamed from his many wounds, and his bones wanted to snap beneath the power of the Ronin of Wind's blows. Still he fought.

"Stop this!" Gray shouted, sword gnashing against Osmium's black steel.

Merrick snarled, slashing.

Gray disappeared, slamming Morrowil into Merrick's back, then his hip, then shoulder. Merrick would have suffered catastrophic blows if it wasn't for Baro's armor. Still, Merrick slashed back, growing bloody. Eventually, one of Gray's blows would crack the armor. Once that happened, Merrick was done. He'd have to finish it before that happened…But how? His eyes searched, mind thinking frantically. "I don't want to kill you!" Gray's voice called over the gales that buffeted the arena.

"You have no choice!" Merrick roared. Then he saw it.

A crack had formed in the magical barrier protecting the citizens. A weak spot.

Merrick raised his hand, creating a hail of black-fletched metal arrows, and directed it toward the crowds. His heart darkened, his mind shouted that this was wrong. Osmium cried out too, but he was already committed. He had to win. Had to end the stain that was magic.

Gray's eyes went wide.

The crowds shrieked, recognizing what was coming.

Merrick loosed the metal volley of arrows at the crowds.

Suddenly, Gray disappeared.

Faster.

Far faster than before.

Merrick had no chance to react, as Morrowil slashed at his throat and then Gray's swing stopped, his muscles flexed, drawing a thin line of blood but keeping Merrick's head attached.

Merrick looked over and saw…

The dozens of black arrows aimed at the crowds were suspended in midair.

Gray had both crossed the distance and stopped Merrick's volley.

That much power? It was impossible.

"How?" Merrick croaked.

Then he saw: Gray's collar was gone.

Blur, Osmium whispered. The ability to move through objects. Gray heaved breaths, his eyes were pure white, and his body shuddered with exhaustion and pain. Still, he held the blade to Merrick's throat. "What are you waiting for? There is no surrender, brother. We both knew one of us was going to die today." His eyes flickered to the archers in the distance, bowstrings taut.

Gray shook his head. "No."

Merrick's gaze narrowed. "What do you mean? There is no other choice."

Gray threw his blade to the ground.

The crowds gasped.

"What are you doing?" Merrick snarled, heart suddenly hammering.

Gray knelt in the sand.

"Fool, they'll kill us both! Pick up your blade!"

Gray replied, giving a small shrug, "You're going to have to kill me."

The words echoed in Merrick's mind.

He was lost.

Those words…

Neveaha's voice rang in his head: *You're going to have to kill me.*

Pain roared through Merrick. He gripped his skull, fingers digging in as if he could pry the agony from his brain. "Stop it! You're wrong! You're all wrong! This world is broken! It needs to be reborn!" He felt something hot and wet streaming down his cheeks. His voice ragged, he said, "It…it can't continue like this…"

Gray rose to his feet. "You're right." Before him, Gray's features were calm despite the burning white of his eyes—as if storms brewed within his gaze. "Change is coming, and we are that change, Merrick." Morrowil floated to his hand on a current of air. "I know something broke you. But you don't have to remain broken forever. None of us do. You have a choice."

Merrick's body shook—whether in rage or sorrow, he wasn't sure. He gazed up at the man who was his so-called leader, seeing him in a different light with the sun high above them. The crowds, everything, faded to a dull blur. Still, there was a pain he couldn't banish. "You don't know what happened to me. Something I can't fix—"

Gray replied, "Then show me."

The Ki sifted into Merrick, tendrils that pulled at his mind.

A memory filled Gray's mind.

Shadows…a dungeon…
Torture tools on a table.
Merrick. Gray was inside the body of the Ronin of Metal, now only a youth. Merrick was bloodied from head to toe and chained to a rack, arms outstretched. Long ago, he'd lost the pain of the metal digging into his wrist and ankles. Rank mildew suffused the air, and the slow drip of water filled the cavernous silence of the dank dungeon.

"You have to…" a woman said.

She was likely around age twenty, and she looked…on the verge of death. Ragged clothes that had once been white now were threadbare and stained in red. Gray's—or Merrick's—heart broke with profound anguish at seeing the woman's suffering. "I-I can't," Merrick stammered, shaking his head. "Please don't ask this of me."

Neveaha.

That was her name.

"I can't do it," Merrick replied.

Neveaha pleaded, "If you don't, they're going to keep torturing you and you're going to break. You'll tell them where the Stone is."

Merrick shook his head. "No, I'd never! I swear, I'll never tell them!"

She gave a sly curve of her lips. "My sweet Merrick, you already almost did…This way, it's painless. Just a simple spell. I know you can do it," she begged. Her chains rattled as she gave a cough, her frail body shivering in pain and despair. Merrick's heart filled with rage and sorrow.

"That's what Father told us. We mustn't let it fall into their hands." She smiled, tears in her amber eyes. "I'm not afraid anymore…"

Again, she coughed, and her body sagged against the chains.

Merrick summoned metal. The bonds holding them were Yronia bloodstone. He couldn't break it, yet he dug deep. Found that strange swirling ball of power in his mind. He pulled it into him, and a gray mist coiled up his arms. Then he took up one of the instruments of torture on the splintered wood table nearby, letting it float into the air.

"That's it," Neveaha pleaded.

Merrick shook his head. "I can't do it."

"Yes, you can," she said, and her eyes fixed him. "It's going to be okay. You're going to make it out of this. You're going to survive, and one day, you'll find a way to change the world. So nothing like this can ever happen again. Not to me, not to you, not to anyone."

Tears flowed down Merrick's face.

Footsteps sounded beyond their cell.

They were coming.

Her eyes said it all. It was now or never. If they saw he'd discovered his magic, they'd find a way to stop him.

The tool hovered closer to her.

She smiled. "I told you, it's okay. I'm not afraid anymore." She nodded. "Go ahead. I'm ready."

Sniffling back a sob, Merrick stammered, "I love you, Neveaha."

"I love you too, Merrick."

Heart breaking, Merrick sent a flicker of his power, and he stabbed the sharp instrument into Neveaha's heart. She gasped. Then, with a last smile, Neveaha's lids fluttered and her head slumped forward as she released a final dying breath.

Sorrow tore through Merrick. He wailed. All his anger, all his pain surfaced like an erupting volcano.

Something broke inside him and the swirling ball in his mind unveiled itself.

True power filled Merrick.

At the same time, Neveaha's words echoed, sinking into his marrow, into his soul.

"One day, you'll find a way to change the world. So nothing like this can ever happen again. Not to me, not to you, not to anyone."

Leaving Merrick's mind, Gray came back into his body.

Merrick fell to his knees. Metal arrows, dozens of them, which had been floating in the air, ready to impale Gray, fell harmlessly to the sand. Merrick stared at his palms as if the blood of innocents was on them. Soft sobs wracked his body. The war within the Ronin of Metal was gone. Gray turned and glared up at the queen on her balcony, wind rising about his arms, curling in his fist as he planted Morrowil into the ground.

Imala's face, still caked with makeup, including a garish purple on her lips, glared down at them. Archers on the walls, ready to answer the call of their queen, held taut strings.

She waved a hand. "Kill them!"

The crowds gasped as bowstrings *twanged*.

Hundreds of arrows flew.

With Gray's collar gone, power filled him like a tempest. He raised his hands. A roaring storm, Wind's Fury, a spell of violent gales. He swatted the arrows aside like an errant swarm of bugs. The arrows clattered into piles to the sand.

The crowds roared.

He grinned up at the queen on her balcony full of nobles. "Your move."

Every single fiber of Imala's being fumed with enough fury that she felt as if she were going to burst. Behind her, the shocked stares of the nobles burned into her back. They had just witnessed that cursing Ronin of Wind challenge her, flaunting his power.

I never should have trusted him!

Naturally, she'd had a little trick up her sleeves, but they'd contested her authority at every turn. The fight itself had been a spectacle she couldn't pry her eyes away from. Merrick, that dark Ronin of Metal sent by the Patriarch, had been terrifyingly impressive. Enough that she worried about his fight with Nalia—for surely, that bastard Ronin would reach the top. And then the Ronin of Wind…

"*Shifting*," her servant, Howard, standing by her side, had whispered into her ear.

That's what he'd called it.

A power Kail, once leader of the Ronin, had wielded.

All of that would have been acceptable had Merrick finished Gray and solved her little dilemma. That had been her plan, after all. Her pact with Gray would be final, and she'd have the other Ronin as slaves. On the other hand, if Gray won, he'd put an end to the Patriarch's hound. She couldn't have lost. It had been a perfect plan, expertly devised by her and Nefrin. With Merrick gone, she'd have her freedom to rule her city as she wished.

However, the idiot Ronin of Wind *hadn't* killed the Ronin of Metal.

Instead, he'd made her look weak, pathetic, by not playing her trump card.

Now both were still alive.

By her own rules, she knew she had to kill Merrick, or both of them. She had an idea. Imala rose from her throne and approached the balcony's edge, all eyes on her. Her arm outstretched, thumb extended, the crowds hung on her next move.

Her hand hesitated.

But every part of her knew what she had to do.

She turned her thumb upward, gesturing for life. "A spectacular showing!" she called. "I will make an exception and grant mercy. Congratulations to our winner, the Ronin of Wind."

The crowds went wild.

Gray's eyes said everything, though he dipped his head. She dipped hers in return, then sat once more, seething with barely restrained anger.

"You let him live?" one of the nobles squawked from behind her. "You broke your own rules!"

The fools. Couldn't they see? She didn't exactly have a choice. She could have ordered out the Covian Legion, but against one man? She'd look like a tyrant. Or, worse, make Gray even more of a legend, the very thing she feared was already happening.

Imala said none of this, however, needing to maintain the illusion of control. "Better to break my rules than face my own death."

Whispers spread among those on the balcony.

They seemed to be reaching a consensus.

Patiently, she waited.

Imala thought, *Come now, little snakes, one of you will be brave enough to say it. But who?*

She thought it might be axe-faced Jim'ara when—

Otto Gromin guffawed.

She looked back over her shoulder. "Something to say, Otto of House Belegrun?"

The rotund man's House Belegrun-blue attire was stained with wine and food from indulging all day. Smoke still lingered from the pipe in his hand. "Enough of this!" he groused, moving across the span to face her, gathering the others' attention.

Good, Imala thought, *at least I won't have to crane my neck.*

Otto stood at the front of the balcony, red-faced from more than a little bit of wine. She folded her arms, giving him an indulgent look, a quirk of amusement to her lips. Otto spoke loudly, with passion in his voice, as if he were performing in a play, "As House Belegrun, the strongest house of the nobles, I declare enough is enough! We've been patient and loyal, but no longer. Majesty, your weakness infects us, and this was the final straw. When you let Merrick, that bastard, run over you, killing Larissa and Jaris, I watched in horror and disgust, but said nothing. Now, you let a young Ronin and a foreign ruler push you around? How can any one of us respect you? More importantly, how can your own people expect to follow such an impotent ruler? No longer!" He made a gesture, looking to his dozen guards in deep blue livery, wearing the golden bear on their chests, as well as two Reavers. He had the majority of the guards on the balcony, as if he'd been planning this move. She had a few of hers, but the rest belonged to the other nobles. "Seize her at once!"

A handful of nobles mumbled agreement, looking as if they wished it was their idea. A few seemed hesitant. The rest, the majority, said nothing, as if fearing to take a side.

Otto's guards didn't budge. "What are you buffoons doing?" he roared at them, now purple-faced. "Seize her now! I order you, you're my men!"

Imala sighed.

Then she made a gesture, a flick of her fingers.

One of Otto's Reavers, in a dark blue robe with three stripes, whisked out a hand and a violent orange fire shot forth from it. Otto loosed a shriek before he was reduced to a pile of ash. His pipe, the only thing remaining of him, clattered to the terrace's floor.

Imala rose and turned to face the quivering mass of men and women who stared at the remains of the once portly man. "You fools, you think these Reavers and guards are yours?" She snorted contemptuously. "I have put my hand in every one of your coffers. Turns out soldiers, like Reavers, have families. Loved ones they care about very much…" Her eyes glinted, a sinister smile forming on her purple lips, as the guards gave worried looks or showed their restrained rage. Imala continued, "A little incentive has allowed them all to see the light. Thus every soldier you think is loyal to you has sworn to me first. Covai is *mine*. If you think for a second I'm going to let a cowardly bunch of sycophants, or even those pathetic legends, take the city from me, then you are woefully mistaken." She felt her jowls shaking with rage, her eyes wanting to pop from her head, as her chalice trembled in her grip.

Her speech garnered the reaction she'd hoped.

The rest of the nobles trembled beneath her fury.

It was a shame—Otto at least had the courage to stand up to her. More of a backbone than she'd imagined. But dead all the same. Jim'ara, head of the second strongest house, bowed her head.

With a calm breath, purging her sudden ire, she smiled. "Now, does anyone else have any further objections?"

The quivering mass of nobles, including Jim'ara, shook their heads—silence the loudest of answers. Then Imala turned back to the colosseum, watching as Gray helped Merrick to his feet. She cursed; things were moving faster now. She'd have to make her final moves. Luckily, those were her strongest. Her lips curled into a grin.

In the distance, and to the west, Imala thought she could hear the cry of war.

Time is running out. Imala's mouth soured. *I must finish this, and fast.*

Before they all drowned in their own blood.

Shadowbane

After leaving the dark warrens near Pickpocket Lane, Faye followed Irasa, the Thieflord of Flesh, and her thieves toward a sprawling complex on the hill. Jivran, King Falla, who recently revealed he was a ruler of a large Covian tribe to the east, moved at her side. He was apparently following Farhaven's whispers. Two thieves of Irasa's opened the gates to the compound and Faye's jaw dropped, words failing.

From the outside, the building had been unassuming.

It turned out, as is often true with life, looks were deceiving.

Behind the gates, expansive grounds overflowed with lush foliage, ponds, trickling rivers, white sand beds with intricate patterns, and all varieties of creatures. The sounds of the compound came alive—hundreds of colorful songbirds warbled on trees, bees buzzed, squirrels scampered up trees, while butterflies of gold, silver, and blue flitted among beds of flowers, colors too vivid to be real.

At her side, Jivran fell short. "*Harisa maril*," the man cursed his own native language.

Irasa looked back. "Welcome to my humble abode."

Faye gulped, but hid it with a yawn.

"Come, we don't have much time," Irasa said, with a bemused twist of her stern features. Her company of a dozen thieves walked off and took up guard positions around the complex. Faye glanced at the woman as they moved through her magnificent grounds. She was tall, straight-backed, with blond dreadlocks flowing down her back, arms covered in bangles. Her proud face was beautiful, if a tad stern.

Faye found her voice, following in step with Jivran beside her. "Nice garden."

Irasa replied, "It's the finest garden in Covai. Perhaps even in all of the northern kingdoms. There are flowers and plants from every part of Farhaven. The queen has curated monsters, I have curated life."

A butterfly the size of her hand whisked in front of her face, trailing gold dust. Faye reached out a finger, but it landed on Jivran's nose, nearly covering his whole face.

Faye grumbled.

Jivran smiled. "Likes me more."

"Probably senses weakness," she replied.

Jivran laughed. "Sore winner. Worse than sore loser."

Faye ignored him and asked Irasa, "How did you do all this?"

Irasa continued, "Many years, and one creature and one plant at a time. There are thousands of different life forms within these walls, large trees down to the tiniest bug. Some"—she lifted the petals of a plant with bright blue and green leaves—"are extinct species from the Lieon, many with medicinal or other powerful properties. We lost much, but I seek to gain it all back."

That was a fascinating notion.

Jivran reached out and a toothy-looking plant snapped to bite his finger off.

Faye sliced it with her small dagger.

Jivran pulled back his arm and mumbled his thanks.

"You see," Irasa continued, "I imagine a world where magic can do anything. Cure any disease, solve any problem, heal blight or end famine." She bent over to smell a green rose as she passed. "Ultimately, perhaps fix our broken world."

Faye kind of liked the woman. Which was annoying. *I really hope I don't have to kill her.* "I think we have very different views on the true nature of Farhaven."

Irasa chuckled softly. "Perhaps."

"This is all very lovely, a stroll through enchanted gardens, but why are we here?"

"I'll show you. This way." She led them into the palace.

Faye ignored the opulence of rich Asterian rugs, Serian vases, and other treasures.

She froze.

The others all turned. "Faye?" Jivran called.

She stood before a painting of the Lieon, containing the nine Ronin. Aurelius, Ronin of Flesh, was prominent, casting giant spires of bone. A figure she assumed was Renalin, the Creator, was floating down on a ray of light. Two other deities were at his side, one cast in shadow, the other in sun, each resplendent. The rest of the painting was filled with titans and elemental dragons, as well as scores of armies, in a battle for the ages.

Irasa returned to her side and said, "It's a favorite of mine, too. I always found the timeline strange, however. Titans and dragons didn't rule at the same time as the Ronin…I think the artist took some liberties."

Faye breathed, "Right…" She realized she was stretching out to touch the painting. She pulled her hand away. "But it's just a painting. Why are we here again?"

"I'll show you. We're late. They're waiting."

"Who's waiting?"

"The Thieflords."

They stopped before a pair of double doors, and Faye felt powerful magic within.

Faye hesitated. "They're in there?"

"Be patient," Irasa instructed, reaching for the door handle.

"Wait," Faye called out, holding up a hand, "I like you. Annoyingly so. But the big giant and I aren't going another step until you tell me what this is all about."

"It's better if I show you," Irasa replied.

She opened the door.

If Faye had been in awe of the garden of life, this…took her breath away and left her speechless.

The vast room was filled with marble pedestals holding magical artifacts, weapons and armor, and even ordinary items such as a quill, a worn leather tome, and more.

Items worth a mountain of gold.

Faye admired the treasures while Jivran moved through the room in awe.

"You asked why I brought you here?" Irasa said, walking toward a pedestal. "A new order is coming. The Great Kingdoms are broken. With luck, your Ronin will assemble at least a few kingdoms. However, many are siding with the shadow in the west."

Faye faced Irasa. "And where do you side?"

Irasa sighed. "I've grown sick and tired of bloated monarchs. The new ruler, this shadow, promises to abolish the current establishment. To end those who have gained power unjustly and wielded it with impunity. To burn the world and build it again, better, stronger. The other Thieflords are choosing sides…"

Again, Faye repeated, "Where do you side?" She was well aware of the heat in her voice, just as she knew of the threats from the coming evil.

Subtly, Jivran moved nearer, hand to the axe at his hip, ready to aid her.

"Fear not, Mistress of Shadows, my allegiance has been and always will be to Farhaven. I know, as do you, the shadow cares only for itself, using honeyed words to pull us in, then swallow us whole."

Faye released a pent-up breath, hand falling from her sword's hilt. "What does any of this have to do with me?"

"Oh, I think you know. You're a Thieflord."

She snorted. "So I'm another vote."

Irasa turned to look at her face-to-face. Her eyes held mischief. "Oh, you're so much more than that…"

The way she said it.

Faye felt a chill in her bones.

Irasa continued, "Have you heard the legacy of Renalin's daughter?" They stopped at a pedestal with gold and silver veins in it. Irasa circled it. Faye saw a dagger displayed on a stand. It was etched, made of a metal she'd never seen before. Not Yronia metal. It had distinct banding and a pattern like flowing water. A faint magic emanated from it, an otherworldly violet glow.

Faye had heard the stories. All thieves had. A thief goddess. A dark deity who worked not for evil, but for those who were forgotten, outside the confines of established "law" and strict morality, to accomplish what needed to be done. To save the world. As a little girl, Faye had loved those stories. A dark goddess, as beautiful as she was powerful. When the titans went wild, Renalin's daughter, Fenarin, had forced them back in line. When relics were stolen, she recovered them…reforged them for the Ronins of Moon, Metal, Flesh, and Fire…the half often considered the "dark Ronin."

Irasa continued, "According to the stories, Fenarin gave up her power, offering it to her descendants. Ones who had the allegiance of the nine Thiefdoms. However, only a descendant can claim the title of Master of Shadows."

"What's this have to do with the dagger?"

"It's hers..." Irasa replied. "Renalin's daughter's, that is. A god's weapon. *Shadowbane.*"

Faye gulped. "Tad ominous, don't you think?"

Irasa snorted. "More so than you know. According to the stories, only her descendants can touch this dagger. The rightful wielder then gains the power of a fallen god. Those who are not descendants? Well, even a faint touch causes excruciating pain."

Faye eyed the dagger.

So did Jivran, as they neared.

For a moment, Faye felt as if the dagger whispered something to her. *Power.*

No, that was just her mind.

Faye laughed, breaking the tension in the room. "Now that was a story. I like your use of suspense. Building it up, slowly stringing us along. Really, masterfully done. Ever thought about becoming a court bard? Anyway, it's a dagger," she said, eyeing the purple glowing blade, "likely a fake."

"But it's not, is it?" Irasa said, smiling. "You sense it, don't you?"

A chill ran down her spine. "What are you getting at?"

"It's you, Faye," Irasa said. "You're the chosen one. I've heard the stories of what you can do. That's no power of a mere Thieflord, and believe me... I know what we are capable of. Besides, I read the ancient texts. There's two passages that are most telling of her future bloodline, one claiming they'll be 'born of fire and flame' and another saying 'the heart of a Thieflord and the blood of a gladiator.'"

"You're leaping to conclusions," Faye said, though her throat was dry.

Jivran looked at her. "Sense truth. You legend..."

"You don't know that," Faye said, then looked to Irasa. "Neither do you. You're both just guessing!"

"So prove me wrong." Irasa eyed the dagger. "If it pains you, then you're right, and I was wrong. If it bonds..."

Faye snorted, folding her arms across her chest. "This is a waste of time. I'm sure anyone can touch that."

Irasa reached forth. As she did, the Thieflord of Flesh's hand paled, then trembled, spark rising, leaching from her body. Irasa's skin began to burn like parchment. Her veins turned black as if filled with inky poison. At last, gasping, Irasa pulled her hand away, then cradled the shaking fist. "Rest assured, I've tried. Many times. I'm not above seizing power for the sake of humanity. But I cannot touch it. No one can, aside from the descendants of Renalin's daughter."

Faye gulped and nodded to Jivran. "Maybe it's a trick. You try."

Jivran shook his head. "No try."

"Why not?"

He grunted. "Different. Magic. *Powerful.*"

She glared at him.

Then she reached out her hand. It trembled…power emanated from her soul.

The object.

Looking at it deeply, into the swirls and etchings, she somehow could see every minute detail—there was an impossibly intricate pattern worked into the steel. The metal was black, and it had a multi-hued glint like oil, the colors shifting as if alive. In its cross guard, a brilliant gem, clear and round like a marble—in its depths, a constellation of stars, as if it truly was forged by a god.

Faye's fingers stretched outward, wanting to wrap her hand around the hilt. She hesitated, pulling back a little. Faye looked to Irasa. "If I can touch this thing...then what? You want me to lead some sort of army?"

"Yes."

"Whose?"

"Whom do you think?"

The Thieflords, Faye knew.

Irasa gave a small shrug. "That is," she added, warily, "if the others deem you worthy. I imagine, however, wielding the celestial blade will go a long way."

Grumbling, Faye's fingers stretched farther, reaching for the gleaming handle.

Her heart pounded, wanting to crash through her ribcage.

Sweat broke out across her brow.

Jivran seemed to hold his breath.

Irasa's eyes grew wide, then narrowed as Faye's fingers crept closer and closer and—

A hairsbreadth away from the dagger, Faye clenched her shaking hand. "Take me to the Thieflords."

Irasa's eyes narrowed. "What are you planning?"

Faye shrugged. "I don't want to know yet. I want to hear what the other Thieflords have to say, see if they're even worthy of leading."

Irasa's arms flexed at her side as she eased a tense breath. "You know if we don't stand up against this tide, your Ronin are all that are saving us from utter annihilation."

"I know," Faye said. "Not really an incentive for me. I'm not the white-knight type. That's more Gray's style."

"You will need to convince them. The dagger is a powerful ally"

Faye shrugged. "I have other ways."

Irasa sighed. She moved to the far wall where a rich brocade tapestry hung. She pulled it aside, revealing a stone carving with nine gems embedded in its surface, each clearly representing the nine elements. She shifted the colorful gems into a certain pattern, and the carving abruptly glowed green. A shimmering portal came to life in the center of the room, like a pane of melted emeralds.

"Right..." Faye breathed. "We're not going to ask how you have one of the legendary portals?"

Irasa snorted. "All Thiefdoms have one. You forget, the Great Kingdoms and Thiefdoms were once equals, after all."

She rolled her shoulders. "That's fair." Faye looked at Jivran. "Well, big guy, care to join?"

Jivran folded his brawny arms across his wide chest. "I follow until I can follow no more."

"You know, your common is getting really good."

"I told you, I'm not dumb. I'm King Falla for reason. Besides, Farhaven says she curious what you do next."

Faye chuckled. "Tell Farhaven, I've no idea what I'm doing."

Irasa cleared her throat, nodding to the green portal. "Shall we? Time is wasting."

Faye rubbed her jaw. "You know I'm missing being crowned Grand Primus for this, right?"

Irasa's smile was full of intrigue. "If you play your cards right, you might just be crowned the Goddess of Shadow."

Faye shrugged. "A decent substitute."

Irasa stepped into the portal, disappearing.

With a heavy breath, Jivran followed.

Faye hesitated. Then she grinned, looking back at the dagger. "Just because *they* don't know, doesn't mean *I* can't know." She moved back to the blade, reached out, and touched the dagger.

Grand Primus

Raising the gate with a gust of wind, Gray walked out onto the sands.

The announcer began his spiel. "Enough!" Gray bellowed. He pointed to the Queen's Terrace with Morrowil, wind rising about his form. Queen Imala watched from her balcony, mouth twisted ruefully as if trying to hide her loathing, especially at suddenly being called out.

Gray... Morrowil cautioned. *Temperance.*

No, Gray replied in a growl through their shared bond, *I'm done playing nice.* Tapping into his Nexus, he let it reinforce his next words. "Bring out your champion. Time to finish what you started!" Threads of wind carried his demand, and the crowd went silent for a moment, then redoubled their cheers.

Morrowil advised, sighing, *I know you're worried about them, but you need to focus. Don't let your anger get the best of you. Nalia is a formidable foe.*

It was true. He was not in the best of moods. The reason was obvious. He was worried. Ayva hadn't shown up for her battle with Nalia. When he'd gone searching for her and Helix, he'd gotten only a cryptic letter from Howard, the queen's steward, telling him to "not worry." That had only made him worry more. He'd searched for Leanna too, but then had been called back for the final fight. *Imala's up to something,* Gray sent, practically trembling with anger. *She's pushing to finish the tournament. Why?*

Then finish it, Morrowil replied.

I intend to. But where are they? Why would they just leave?

I don't know, Morrowil answered. *But Sun is wise, and Water is cleverer than he looks.*

Gray snorted. *I didn't know you liked them.*

You like them, so I do too. As I have told you before, I am an extension of you. Besides, they are Ronin. In many ways, their personalities change, but their natures remain the same. One could argue I have more of a connection to them than you do.

That's fair, he thought. *All the more reason to end this and find them. If they're in danger...* His fist shook at his side, wind curling in visible zephyrs that made the crowds whisper and gasp.

On the other side of the arena, a silhouette appeared from the long hall, appearing like a shadow of death. Without slowing, the silhouette gave a casual wave of her hand, the heavy gate lifted, and Nalia stepped onto the sands to the fanfare of thousands. Gray took in her shaved head, save for the long black braid that ran down her back, the arrogant thrust of her chin, the narrowed eyes, and the new red ink that swirled across her nose, cheeks, and forehead. She was dressed in layers of thick leather. A crimson sword was at her hip.

But more than anything, even aside from the sword, power burned from her like a hundred suns dwelling inside a single body, and that same aura washed over him like a tangible thing that, he admitted, a week ago might have frozen him in place.

Grand Primus. Now Gray felt her title. He'd seen her eyeing others on the sands, but now was the victim of her gaze.

Nalia smiled, crossing the arena floor like a hunter on the prowl.

Then imagining Ayva and Helix in danger, Gray's anger fought back against the visceral feeling, finally swallowing it, and his power flared.

His own smile showed teeth as he marched to meet her. *No,* he thought, *I am the predator.*

They stopped in the center of the colosseum, standing just paces away.

Nalia relaxed her shoulders. "So eager to die, are we?"

Gray said nothing, his blood hot in his veins, though he knew his expression spoke for him.

She snorted. "I see. You know, I've never killed a legend before," she said, shrugging. "Suppose there's a first time for everything."

The announcer spoke, "The Grand Primus battle begins...legends clash...names are burned into the annals of time for all eternity—"

He looked up to the tattooed and bony man. No longer wearing a collar, Gray was well aware that his gaze burned with unbridled power.

The announcer stammered at the sight and then closed his mouth.

Nalia chuckled. "Shall we? There is one thing I want to make clear, before we fight...I took no pleasure in ending Drega's life. He was a good man. But he was growing weak, old. Such is the nature of—"

"You should stop talking," Gray interrupted her, voice filled with cold fury. "I *really* don't need another reason to kill you." He turned, stalking away, giving her space, his breaths coming faster and harder, controlling the urge to not slay her before the drums stopped thundering.

Gray... Morrowil sent.

I know. I know. I'm trying to calm down.

It's not working.

Well aware, Gray replied in a growl. *So be it. If I can't be calm and focused, I'll use it to my favor. Or I'll just be something else.* He turned, looking back.

Nalia still stood in the center of the arena wearing a small, satisfied smile.

On the balcony, Imala wore a similar smug expression, seeing his rattled visage.

Why? he wondered. *Perhaps because they know I'll lose if I can't focus. Nalia's too strong.*

Gray took slow, deep breaths, feeling all eyes as the drumbeats thundered, slowing. The call to fight drawing closer. Out of instinct, he touched his wind bracers.

For a moment he was lost to a memory.

Kail stood on the windy heights of a great snow-white keep, in the center of a breathtaking city, looking out over Morrow, Great Kingdom of Wind. It was... inspiring... Pinnacles, towers, alabaster castles dotting a rolling green landscape. Buildings suspended amid the clouds. Thousands of windmills, windcatchers, and strange gadgets that used wind to power countless devices. Flags flew high bearing the symbol of wind. And the people... so many of them... Gray-green-eyed men and women. Living peacefully, laughing, loving.

All of it, ripped away.

The image shattered, and he was back on the sands.

Why am I getting that image? Because of the bracers?

Morrowil answered, *I believe it's trying to tell you something about your powers.*

Like what?

That is for you to figure out. Last I checked, I am not the Ronin of Wind.

Great, a sentient, cheeky sword. Just what I need.

The drums slowed further.

The crowds shouted and cheered, their cries rattling his bones with their fervor. As if they were trying to tear down the colosseum with noise alone. Stuffing tiny bits of wind in his ears, Gray stared at Nalia.

Ready? he asked Morrowil.

Ready, said the Sword of Wind.

Thump.

Thump.

Thump.

It matched the pounding of his heart.

The drums stopped.

"Fight!" the announcer bellowed.

Gray charged. With a leap powered by vast threads of wind, he slammed his blade down. She drew her crimson sword and their blades violently clashed, a boom echoing with the force of it. Sand flew back, crashing against the magical barrier.

He saw her sword in full display. A crimson blade, faceted with gemstones. *Bloodstone,* Gray knew. Her blade was made entirely of the rare, magic-nullifying gem. It severed the spells from the air as if they'd never existed.

The crowds cried out as he was blown back.

Nalia grinned.

But Gray was just getting started…

He pulled from memory, from Kail's soul, and a spell took form.

Cyclone of the Fallen.

A furious gust with tiny, blade-like wind particles grew in the air before his hand, rising higher and higher. He roared and sent the gale of wind at Nalia. She cut it down, but with visible effort, staggering back from the powerful spell. So he sent another and another, each one making her backpedal. Half of his Nexus showed now. His muscles burned like fire.

She's cutting our spells from the air, Morrowil warned.

Well aware! Gray growled.

Then use me.

What?

Use me! She can cancel spells, but I am no spell.
Gray understood.
Under the guise of a spell, Gray flung Morrowil.
Nalia sliced the spell from the air, only to see the sword too late. It slammed home, piercing the Grand Primus through the shoulder, pinning her to the arena's wall with a sudden fountain of blood. Nalia gasped, screaming in pain and anger.
The crowds were frozen in shock.
So quick...A tremor of triumph, of hope rose inside Gray at such a quick victory until...
Nalia's scream grew and abruptly, spark like a bonfire erupted from her body, as if hundreds of souls trapped inside of her were being released. The sheer force of it propelled a wave of energy toward Gray, throwing him backward. The force of it slammed against the protective barrier shielding the crowds, sending small fissures through it. Gray flew, but caught himself with a gust of wind, landing dozens of feet away.
Nalia grabbed Morrowil's hilt—crying out in agony—and tossed the Sword of Wind to the sand, coated in blood that soaked into the ground, while more bled from her shoulder until...The blood stopped, and the gory wound...knit itself. Gray growled. Nalia's eyes fixed on him. She snarled and leapt, fists blazing, the spark coating her arms and making them look as if they were wreathed in flames. She landed on him, fists slamming down. He deflected burning fists with shields of wind, but she kept punching, cracking one after another. "No weapon, you fool!"
Gray slipped a strike that punched into the ground, creating a crater, then rolled to his feet and extended his hand.
Morrowil flew to his grip.
"Who said I had no weapon?"
Again, he struck, slashing with Morrowil, but Nalia leapt back, dodging and snatching her sword once more. She began to breathe, and Nalia's inferno, the spark around her body, grew greater still... "You don't have any idea of what you face, do you, little legend?" Nalia said with a growl.
Gray's grip tightened around Morrowil's haft, watching.
Still, the inferno grew, a living bonfire, as the crowds shied away.

Even the nobles in the stands seemed terrified. Imala's eyes were wide and bulging.

Gray understood. If he didn't truly know Nalia was mortal, he would've believed he was fighting a god. Still, he wouldn't lose here. He couldn't. Not when everything he cared about hung in the balance. So Gray let wind rise, and beckoned the Grand Primus.

Nalia attacked. A tremor rippled up her arm as her corded muscles bulged with spark. She breathed, focusing, keeping her swelling spark contained—magic from the hundreds, if not thousands, of souls she'd imbibed. Yet the fool legend had the audacity to think he was her equal. He had no idea the pain she'd suffered, or how many bodies she'd felled, or how far she'd climbed to get to this point.

All of it, to get to the top.

She was Grand Primus.

Her, not him.

Despite this, the Ronin of Wind was irritatingly strong.

The entire colosseum shook with their blows as they fought like two titans of old. White wind and orange spark billowed into the air. She released spark from her body faster than ever, cutting his spells down as if she were swatting flies. He sent more spears of wind and gusts of air as he shifted around the colosseum. It'd been years since she'd even had to use more than a fraction of her power. Now it erupted from her like steam from a hot vent.

Gray's muscles burned like fire. His arms grew leaden.

I will not lose this fight.

Win the crowd, win the tournament. But how?

The moment he flagged, shifting a little too slow, Nalia struck. She flicked a finger and muscles seized in Gray's leg. A spell...Gray was suddenly frozen in place.

In that moment, he understood.

Nalia had been biding her time, holding a trump card, and waiting all this time to reveal...she didn't just have power. She had *magic*.

Gray was held by threads of flesh. Nalia bellowed, kicking him in the chest, and the wind was knocked from him, pain exploding in his body. The next thing he knew, he hit the sands, bouncing across the arena floor. Then he caught himself on a zephyr of wind.

Get up, Morrowil called, on the ground near his face. *Get up!*

Images filled his mind: Drega's affable smile and booming voice, followed by his worry for Ayva, Helix, Zane, and Darius.

Nalia stood over him, stabbing down.

It was over.

He couldn't raise Morrowil in time, couldn't summon enough power to shift...

She'd won, he'd failed. His death would spark the beginning of the end.

His hand was still raised protectively, the bright sun shining between his fingers, Nalia's face twisted with rage. His white bracers glinted in the light as her sword arced down to end him.

Fear was there...and yet, a small flicker of hope and an idea.

In that final moment before his end, Gray breathed, sending a trickle of flow into the bracers.

Nalia's sword cut and—

Clanged.

The sound echoed across the arena floor. The bracers were no longer leather. Instead, the legendary artifacts worn by Kail himself had transformed into silver metal that had extended up his arm. *More flow*, Gray demanded, pouring into the bracers, until it was complete. Thin, perfect, iridescent plate molded over his arms, legs, chest. When it was done, Gray was now attired in resplendent armor made for a king. Etched patterns of wind scrawled all across the celestial-forged metal, burning like silver fire. It was lightweight, yet he knew it could stop a titan's sword.

The crowds gave a collective sigh of relief, whispers rising.

I was wondering when you'd figure it out, Morrowil sent.

You knew this whole time?

Morrowil gave the equivalent of a shrug. *Kail's armor is triggered by need, not want. If I told you there was a risk you'd never unlock its power.*

Gray grumbled, *We're going to have a long talk about this later.*

Nalia had been taken aback by the transformation of his armor. Now she rose, her rage practically venting off her like steam. *Probably not the right time.*

Later, Morrowil agreed. *For now, finish this, would you?*

Gladly.

Wiping blood from his mouth, he crossed the distance toward her. She cut with her sword, and instead of blocking it, he let the sword connect. The crimson blade harmlessly clashed against his breastplate. Gray, three-quarters of his Nexus burning in his mind, sent thick flows of wind that slammed her against a pillar. "Surrender and I will let you live," Gray demanded.

"Let me live?" Nalia cackled, stuck as she was. "You don't get it. That's not how this world works." Her words dripped with disdain. "The strong survive—strength is *all* that matters…" Her laughter grew even more unhinged, pressed against the pillar, wind flowing about her, "Just like these people you fight for… You poor misguided fool. Why? Why do you do it when they are pathetic! They aspire for nothing! Instead, wallowing in their miserable *lives.*"

Instead of anger, Gray felt pity seeing her restrained by flows of air, furious and… crying.

Nalia didn't even seem to be aware of the hot wet tears streaming down her face, smearing her black warpaint.

Gray whispered, "What made you this way?"

Her teeth gnashed, her eyes rolling wildly in her head trying to break his bonds of wind as she bellowed in rage. Spittle flew from her lips, and her muscles strained. *"I will kill you! I will sever your—"*

He stuffed wind in her mouth, making her gag, and cutting her tirade short.

"So be it, then I'll find out myself," Gray said, and breathing out, he sent a powerful tendril of ki into Nalia. In reply, the Grand Primus screamed in rebellion, eyes bulging, as if wishing for anything else, clearly terrified what he'd find.

Gray didn't relent, however, the ki slamming home—and her memories filled him.

Thatched houses burned. Men and women screamed. Little Nalia kicked and fought as she'd been taught, raging against her attackers. They carted her off, taking her away from the flames, moving toward the cage led by strange bearlike creatures. A thick, sweaty man had his arm wrapped around her. She grabbed his finger and bit hard. Cursing, he threw her to the ground and kicked her in the gut, driving the air from her lungs.

Finally, she gasped.

"What the hell's going on here?" another brute asked.

"Little wench bit me!" snarled her captor.

Another gave a sharp bark of a laugh. "What do you expect? You gutted her whole family!"

The first brutish, sweat-smelling man growled, "Family? They ain't humans. Tribes like theirs are no more than wild dogs."

Dazed and still on the ground, Nalia took a chance while they were still yammering away. She got to her feet, staggering, then running for the dunes, only black silhouettes in the night, her legs pumping with fire, with need, with terror.

She'd be lost in there.

She knew how to survive in the desert better than anyone.

They'd never find her, then she'd come back…and…and what? No, what she needed was to wake from this nightmare. Still, nightmare or not, she bolted. Something whispered to her within, an urgent, deep-seeded voice that echoed in her soul:

Survive, it commanded.

She only made it a dozen paces before threads of magic grabbed her—muscles and small limbs suddenly frozen against her will.

Threads of flesh, she knew.

"What do we have here?" a venomous voice asked.

With more magic, he made her neck twist painfully to face him.

The other brutes were just shadows, faceless, nameless.

But this man had a name, and a face.

He wore scarlet robes with four red stripes.

A Reaver? She'd heard of them. Magical denizens from the Great Kingdom of Fire… her people feared them, told her to avoid them at all costs, but others said they peacekeepers.

He bent down to her level. His hood hid most of his features, but she saw his thin lips and they gave a smile empty of any emotion. Like something her dolls would show. Then she caught a glimmer of his eyes. Eerie, cold blue eyes that shone even in the dark light, the fire's light from her burning home, her destroyed life reflected in his eyes. "Easy now, little one," the Reaver crooned, "I won't let them hurt you. What's your name, girl?"

She waited until the Reaver got close, then as he reached out to cup her face with a hand, Nalia lunged. She tried to bite his hand, his nose, anything, only for her jaw muscles to lock tight. More threads of flesh.

"You have fire in you, don't you? I like that. My name is Nefrin. What's yours?"

She snarled.

"Foster that fire. It'll keep you alive." He smirked. "How about this? I'll train you, make you stronger than anything the world has ever known. You'll be mine and the queen's champion. Then, one day, if you still desire it, you can try to kill me, take your revenge for your lost family. You'll be strong enough then. If not, you and I, we can change the world."

He let go of the threads holding her jaw.

Nalia only snarled, biting the air.

Nefrin smiled, rising and flicking a hand, releasing her bonds. "Careful with her. Harm a hair on her head, and I'll turn you all to ash."

Nalia was thrown into an iron-barred wagon with others of her tribe. They clutched at her, gripped by sorrow and terror, though none were her family. Nalia pulled away, grabbing the bars of the cage, fire burning in her eyes as the wagon traveled over the rolling dark dunes.

A single thought resonated in her mind.

I must get power, so I can never be hurt again.

The memory faded and Gray understood it all, the origin of her power.

Only, when he looked into the depths of her soul, he saw her past had tainted her so deeply that there was no coming back. The little girl was gone. A word had twisted her to the point of perversion: *survive.* Gray let her go, and she sagged, falling to the ground. Slowly, she rose, and Gray watched the woman's fury dim, her madness ebbing as she replaced it with the cool, aloof mask of the Grand Primus once more. Nalia gave a bloody smile. "Don't look at me like that," she said, panting, raising her sword. "Whatever you're thinking, you're wrong. If you must know, I used to loathe that day. Now I'm thankful for it." She looked up at the Queen's Terrace. "If Nefrin hadn't found me, I would have lived a small, pathetic life."

"And now?"

She grinned. "Now I am a goddess among men, and what does a goddess care about good and evil?" Then, suddenly, she bellowed, sending out threads of flesh to lock him in place. He was frozen in place, this time with all her power. "See? Even a legend can't stop me. In the end, you're too weak to do what was required. What was necessary to become stronger.... To save those you love. That's why you lost." She raised her ruby blade, gleaming in the sun, the crowds crying out.

Imala's eyes were wide, all held upon the edge of their seat.

Gray looked into Nalia, seeing her pain, her past, her need to control and get stronger so she could never be hurt again, and he understood. He yearned for those things too. And yet...the more Nalia seemed to cling to power, the more she had lost, until she'd lost herself, and Gray finally understood.

"Goodbye, Ronin," Nalia said and slashed.

Instead of watching the blade, Gray closed his eyes, and a voice entered his head, a familiar one...

Not Morrowil's, not Mura's, or Ayva's or Darius...

But Kail's, as if speaking from the past, or from another realm, those red eyes staring into him, a small smile on the man's gruff visage, "*You see it now, don't you, boy? The secret of wind...Wind is ephemeral, everywhere, and nowhere all at once, like the strings that guide our fate. You can't control life, you can simply ride its currents to the best of your ability. So let go. Let go of your pain, your anger, your fear, and accept that you can't wrangle the world. If you can truly let go, truly trust in the currents...you'll gain control of everything that matters. Yourself. Your mind. Your soul.*" Up until now, Gray had only had access to three-fourths of his Nexus. The truth of wind seeped into his soul, and Gray tapped into his Nexus, fully revealed save for a final sliver.

It was more than enough. Power suffused him.

The threads binding him snapped.

Wind erupted from his core, and air bent around him as he moved, faster than ever. Nalia's eyes went wide with horror at his impossible speed.

She tried to change her attack to a block.

It was no use. He cut her bloodstone sword in two and the gemstones shattered.

He held it for a moment, seeing the look in her eyes. The little girl was gone. Only hatred burned behind the fear. Morrowil's slice continued until Nalia's head rolled along the sand—that wide-eyed, fury-filled expression still plastered across her face.

Just like that, it was over.

The Covian Legion

It was over. Gray had won.

Yet he felt rage. Nalia…those memories. The horrors of being torn away from her home. His jaw clenched until he felt as if it would crack. Deep down, he knew she hadn't been redeemable—her corruption ran too deep. Even if wished he could have saved her, he knew he couldn't save them all. How many had she killed? How many cut down for her climb to power? And yet, he didn't blame her entirely. He reserved a good portion of his wrath for another who had made her that way.

On the sands, Nalia's body dissolved, and a river of spark erupted, bursting into the air to the gasp of many. So much…Gray opened himself to imbibe that mountain of spark knowing how much power it contained. Then he hesitated. He looked at the people, at the queen, and with a wave of his hand, wind gusted and he let the essence of a thousand souls drift into the masses and the air. Back into Farhaven.

The crowds let the spark fill them, murmuring in disbelief.

They were quiet for a moment.

Then the subsequent roar shook the colosseum.

Breathing raggedly, Gray gazed up to the queen's balcony.

Imala rose from her throne, the nobles clapping quietly behind her looking afraid. The queen approached the balcony's railing, listening to the thunderous applause. She opened her mouth and spoke, but was unable to be heard over the crowd. She called for silence.

They didn't hear. The cheers continued.

Gray smirked.

She roared for them to quiet, growing red-faced, to no avail.

Gray, wearing a small smile, lifted a hand.

The crowds stilled to a hush, almost as one.

Dread entered the queen's bulbous eyes like he hadn't seen before. *Good*, he thought, and then pointed Morrowil at the balcony, his voice booming with threads of wind. "I want what's mine."

Imala ignored him, speaking words that seemed well-rehearsed, "Congratulations, Ronin of Wind! You are our new Grand Primus! As promised, you are entitled to your prizes, including a thousand Farbian gold, all titles and honor, as well as…the Earthstone." From above, sitting at the height of the pillar nearest the Queen's Terrace, the blue magical barrier dissipated as several Reavers on the balcony worked threads.

Cupping a hand, the Nexus still full in his mind, Gray pulled the Earthstone from its pedestal and let it float down before him. It remained there, hovering in the air.

Relief flooded him.

The Earthstone was theirs… But that was only half the battle.

"Go now, rest, rejoice! You fought well this day, and your name will be remembered," Imala said, a smirk growing on her face. Then she turned to the spectators. "My beloved citizens—"

"We're not done here," Gray called, voice booming, cutting her off.

Her face soured as she looked back to him, as if she'd already forgotten him.

Gray's voice was growl, but with threads of wind, he made it thunder, bouncing off the walls of the arena for all to hear, "It's time for you to honor your side of the bargain."

"Bargain?" The queen's thin, painted brows arched in confusion. "What bargain?"

A cold wash of rage rolled over him. She was going to lie. More threads laced his voice and he bit off every word, "No, *Queen*," he said it with derision. "We made a pact, you and I. If I won your little tournament, I would lead your armies against the coming shadow. An evil that wants to destroy all life." He said this more for the crowd's benefit. It had the appropriate reaction, their fear tangible, whispers spreading like wildfire.

Imala's waxy purple lips puckered. "Yes… baseless claims, we've heard it before." She looked to the whispering, fearful crowds and said in a sickly-sweet tone, "Come, my beloved citizens, we *all* know the shadow is far in the west, a harsh desert, and a raging river that no monster can pass sits between us. Covai is safe as can be!" Her furious eyes fixed Gray once more. "So, please, keep your fearmongering to yourself. As for your supposed promise, well, what monarch in her right mind would promise her legions to a foreign entity? Not to mention, one so young and unproven..."

Gray couldn't help but scoff. "Unproven? I won your little game! I am Grand Primus."

Imala laughed, gaining traction, as if twisting lies was *her* field of battle. "Don't get me wrong, you are quite powerful, Grand Primus. But how do we know your skills extend beyond the arena? More importantly, how can the world trust the very Ronin that destroyed us once before?"

Gray's knuckles cracked at his side, fist tightening. She was pulling the strings of age-old fears.

All about, he saw the crowds muttering, as if in agreement, their minds slowly swaying.

No, they have to be wiser than that. Can't they hear the lies for what they are? Gray realized banding words with a snake was fruitless. "You will honor your pact," Gray demanded, his voice a clear command, booming enough that she almost rocked back from her terrace as if it was physical gust.

Imala visibly straightened and regained her composure. "Or what?" the tyrant queen asked, eyes flaring with sudden ire.

Gray felt the heat of conviction enter his voice, his eyes, his bones as he answered, *"Or I will make you."*

"How dare you threaten a queen!" Imala roared and slammed down a jeweled hand—a clear order.

Abruptly, a rumbling shook the arena.

A moment later, like a dam bursting, not guards, but soldiers poured out of the gates. Each in heavy armor, bearing tabards of a deeper, ruddy red. Helmets winged. All from the different houses: Bear, Hawk, Falcon, Snake.

Hundreds, no... Gray realized, as they continued to pour into the arena.

Thousands.

The Covian Legion, hardened from battle, adorned in gleaming armor marched like the drums of war, their precision and cohesion daunting, as they surrounded him in a semicircle.

Crowds gasped.

Gray's insides boiled in rage.

Deep down, he knew this was coming—knew she'd betray him—but seeing her wield the very army that was promised to him like puppets upon her strings, made his blood boil. This was an army that was meant to help save Farhaven, not destroy it.

Imala's jowls shook with unrestrained wrath. "You might be Grand Primus, but this kingdom is *mine!*"

Gray took a deep breath. Wind flowed over his body. His power felt like a hurricane in his mind, wanting—no, *yearning*—to be unleashed. *With nearly all of my Nexus unveiled, how many could I take out before I'm killed?* A part of him even felt a heady sense of power, almost arrogance, as he wondered… *could I maybe win?*

It wasn't that simple though.

These were the very men he needed if he was to win the war against evil.

More than that, Gray was trying to win this city, not destroy it.

Having surrounded her prey, Imala's bulging eyes widened. As if salivating with thoughts of his demise, spittle flew from her mouth as she commanded, "*Seize him!*"

Soldiers marched, clanking forward as one, the rattle of their steps jarring as they raised heavy tower shields, and aimed hundreds of spear tips.

Gray let more wind rise. "You don't want to do this…"

The men hesitated, the hundreds of faces inside their gleaming helmets looked stricken with expressions caught between uncertainty and fear? He realized: how many had just watched him kill the current Grand Primus? Or knew of Kail, his predecessor? Still, Gray's mind was aflame. *I'm bluffing. I can't fight these men. What in the seven hells am I doing?*

Their footsteps thundered, sand arena rumbling as they continued their advance.

Gray's mind raced, frantic to stop the soon-to-be-slaughter.

Abruptly, behind him, a grating sound, like gears grinding.

He looked back and his breath caught.

From the dark tunnels, figures emerged.

The Fleshguard, dozens of them, flowed out of the arena's gates, moving with deadly purpose to file in at Gray's side.

"My Lord Ronin," said a voice, as Karis Aligar appeared from his ranks of men. It was the blond, scarred man who'd addressed him earlier, after Drega's final battle. He was a blade-slender man—though the muscles on his lean sword arm rippled with strength. Karis's cloak seemed different, a little more threadbare. Gray realized... It was Drega's cloak. He had a knot of rank on his shoulder. The new leader of the Fleshguard. Karis bowed his head, hand on his sword's hilt as he eyed the Covian Legion. "Seems you need some assistance." A smirk puckered the corner of his scarred face.

Gray was so relieved he wanted to hug the man, though he doubted the hardened Fleshguard would know how to react. He settled for a grip of Karis's muscled shoulder. "You are a welcome sight for weary eyes," he said, breathing heavily. He looked back to the Legions, seeing more Covian soldiers filling the halls and tunnels, knowing they likely extended throughout the entire colosseum, and far out into the streets. Despite his relief, Gray knew that was too many to face, even with the elite warriors at his side. "I will say, I think we're a little outnumbered."

Karis snorted. "They say the Covian Legion is a million strong."

"So save some for us, Grand Primus!" said another Fleshguard.

The others laughed, pulling swords.

Again the legion faltered, seeing the blademasters forming ranks, though they still advanced. A moment later, there was a cry. "Halt!" a familiar voice called, clear as a bell. This time, guards, not soldiers, poured onto the sands from the gates behind, joining their ranks. While not as well trained, these men held a glint in their eye, and had been forged daily by controlling skirmishes and other Covian scuffles. They looked fearless. A man joined his side, and Gray saw it was the guard from before. The broken-nosed, tavern bruiser of a man. He dipped his head. "My lord."

Captain Leanna strode through her men's ranks, joining Gray. "Seems you made our mad queen a tad upset." Her eyes panned over the thousands of well-armored soldiers who had stopped their advance for a moment, taking in the change. "I don't think I've ever seen an army sent to kill one man."

"I guess I should take that as a compliment," Gray replied. "For the record, wind and heavens, I am happy to see you."

She nodded, her gruffness breaking a little, then she eyed Imala. "I really hate that woman."

"That makes two of us," Gray said.

"Three," Karis added.

"For Drega," Leanna said.

He grinned. "For Drega."

"What is this nonsense?" Imala roared. "I said seize them, you fools!"

Staring at one another as if for confirmation, the legions advanced again, hesitantly.

Just then, from above, there was a birdlike screech.

Gray looked up.

An…owl?

All eyes panned to the sky as a brilliant gold light flared. A moment later, a giant owl the size of a draft horse, with huge plate-sized eyes, landed in the center of the arena, blowing sand. It hooted, head twisting in a swivel as it took in the scene. On a ramp of ice, Helix and Ayva slid off its back.

Ayva embraced Gray, then pulled away, tears in her eyes.

Helix grinned. "Are we late?"

Gray breathed a heavy sigh, and so much of the fear and tension in his body released. "Yes, yes, you are."

They took in the Fleshguard—still in the center of the arena—then the Earthstone, floating on a zephyr of wind. Gray debated using the stone, though he had no idea of its potential. Again, power wasn't his issue. "Whoa, seven hells," Helix replied, "seems like we definitely missed some things."

"So did I," Gray said. "Also, an owl? Where did you—"

"Long story," Ayva said. Sun roared to life in her palm and Aurora blazed, as if made of molten gold. "Well, this is a bit of a predicament."

"What are you fools doing!" Imala gripped the railing, her whole body shaking with rage. "I am your queen! You will listen to me. Attack them, kill them all, now! They are traitors to Covai, betrayers of the highest order! Might I remind you of the crime of refusing your queen."

The Covian Legion strode forward.

"There's too many of them," Helix said, ice rising to his hands.

"Not the issue, Helix," Ayva said. "Killing our own future army is a very bad idea."

"Definitely not the issue right now!" Helix said. "We can't stop any evil if we're killed by our supposed future army."

Boots clanked, almost as one, as the army took measured steps forward. Thousands of spears, their armor moving. *Clang. Clang.*

Clang. Their shields were raised high, gazes locked on them. Fear still broiled in their eyes. Gray felt it through the ki, yet the lash at their backs was strong.

Imala.

Ayva strode forth, lowering Aurora and addressed the tens of thousands in the stands. "The queen is lying to you..." Until now, the crowds had simply watched, their whispers filling the arena; now they listened, leaning forward, confusion in their faces. "There is a war out there beyond those walls!" She pointed. "I, with the Ronin of Water, destroyed a bridge that would have spanned the Ker Stream."

"*Not possible...*" said some.

"*It's too wide,*" others whispered.

"*The dark army...*"

"*It can't be...*"

"*Saeroks and vergs...*"

Ayva cut them off. "It's true!" She neared the owl, grabbed something out of a sack, and threw it to the ground. A verg's troll-like head rolled onto the arena floor, sand sticking to its gore and dried blood. The crowds gasped, eyeing the monstrous head with its flat nose, wide eyes, leathery-gray skin and wide mouth filled with sharp teeth. With a hoot, the owl flew into the air, landing on a nearby weapons pillar to watch. Ayva continued, "Some survived, many did not. But the enemy will be coming. With vengeance. The queen hopes to keep you in the dark. We ask only for the strength of your army to keep the shadow at bay."

Imala, from her balcony, snickered. "Foolish girl! Did you learn nothing in my company? They do not care for politics or war. Your words fall on deaf ears. As I told the Ronin of Wind, I will not give you my kingdom!"

"Then we will take it," Ayva called.

Imala grinned. "You will try."

Nefrin and his dozen Reavers suddenly appeared, standing on the wall, surrounding them from above in a wide semicircle. The man's face split by burned scarred skin from Zane's flames, his eyes smoldering with rage. From his place on the wall, Nefrin's gaze looked down to where Nalia had died. He trembled with anger. "She deserved better than you, Ronin," Nefrin said, and magic burned in his palms, growing. "You will beg for death before the end, and Covai will rejoice, perfect and whole once more." Spells of fire, ice, moon, sun, and more coalesced into the air.

Gray opened his mind, his Nexus nearly completely revealed, ready to annihilate the spells from the air.

Helix and Ayva did the same, ice and sun roaring to life.

Spells flew, only—

Black arrows rained down, piercing Reavers on one side of the wall. The red-robed men and women cried out as they were riddled with obsidian-fletched bolts. It looked like Osmium's doing.

Merrick?

On the other side of the colosseum, a man was cleaving through the ranks of Reavers, sword flashing with impossible skill.

Jian?

He finished off a Reaver and a few guards, mowing them down like stalks of wheat. His Devari cloak wavered. Then he gave Gray a glance, putting a fist to his heart. Even from this distance, Gray could feel the emotion he sent through the ki.

Honor and duty.

With a final look, the leader of the Devari dipped into a tunnel, as if his job was done.

Nefrin seethed as he blocked the metal arrows, until the four-stripe Reaver's bony fingers curled. The column of stone on Gray's left groaned, leaning, near collapse, when a black blade abruptly sprouted from Nefrin's stomach. Nefrin gasped, peering down at the blade now sticking out of his gut and coated in his own blood. Then he fell to the arena floor with a sickening thud.

Merrick coolly leapt from the wall, black blade in his hand, now coated red, an aloof expression on his face. His white hair was wind-swept back. A dark, haunted look still burned in his eyes. He flicked the scarlet blood on his sword to the sand and joined them, keeping his distance. Merrick's glance back to Gray was quick. At his side Osmium swirled back into a bow, black mist wreathing its form, before Merrick turned to gaze with hatred at Queen Imala, as if a part of their crew.

Helix's jaw dropped, then he exclaimed throwing up his hands, "Okay! What in the seven hells of Remwar did we miss?"

Ayva looked equally baffled.

Gray scrubbed his hand through his hair with a wince. "Yeah…long story. I'll have to fill you in."

Two more figures leapt from the wall.

"Zane?" Ayva breathed.

Zane walked onto the battlefield—along with a woman with clay-colored eyes—in Covian attire, moving with a sort of Darius swagger. They held a blackened, chain-covered chest in their hands that even from this distance Gray could tell it pulsed with power. They'd only taken a few steps when two of Nefrin's Reavers who hadn't been defeated by the arrows launched flaming balls of molten fire their way. Zane's eyes flared, but the young woman at his side was faster. Bone materialized from thin air. A wall of it, wider and thicker than anything Gray could possibly imagine. The fire collided with the bone wall, bursting harmlessly. She turned to the two men who readied more spells. Before they could, she flicked a hand, and both of their necks snapped as if made of brittle twigs. She gave a sigh, turning back to Gray and company. All of it had happened in flash of a moment. Casually, the woman let the bonewall behind her dissolved to fine powder, and blow away on the wind. Gray felt his whole body tense, along with the others. It was clear as day, an aura of power surrounded her—like a halo of tan and faint red.

Helix gawked.

Ayva breathed, "You're..."

"Are you..." Helix stammered.

She yawned, then extended a hand. "Raina, Ronin of Flesh, pleasure to meet you."

Helix shook her hand dumbly.

They all looked at Zane.

The Ronin of Fire just shrugged, as if he'd just found a stray diamond amid a haystack.

"*That's* who you've been going to see?" Helix asked.

"I was meaning to tell you. Never felt like a good time."

"Don't blame it on him," Raina said. "I like flashy introductions."

Helix's jaw was still hanging. "Also, Tranquil Seas, Zane! It's not fair! She's stunning, you lucky—"

Zane grumbled, flames rising.

"*Helix*, not the time." Ayva's words cut them all short.

"Oh, right," Helix said sheepishly. "Giant army of an evil queen wanting to cut us to pieces."

Imala had witnessed all of this, looking increasingly irate and baffled by each defeat, from Nefrin, to her private army of Reavers—now her sausage-like fingers dug into the railing as he bulk leaned over—eyes bloodshot and fixed on Gray and the others. "KILL THEM!" Imala bellowed from her balcony. "NOW! OR I'LL SEE YOU AND ALL YOUR FAMILIES SUFFER!"

Gray raised his voice. "You have a choice!"

The Covian Legion, as if finally making up their mind, advanced to attack one last time.

When a boy raced onto the sands, crying out, "No!"

His mother chased after him.

The boy was no more than ten or eleven, with large brown eyes, curly hair, and a wooden sword in his belt. He turned, facing the army, clutching his training sword. "If you want them dead, you're going to have to go through me!" His mother wrapped her arms around him, trying to tug him away, but he fought against her. Then a young woman raced onto the sands. Then an old man. And more, like a dam bursting, as the crowds flooded the colosseum floor.

"No more!" cried a woman. "Enough of this…"

They advanced, nearly upon the legion, paces away, two forces about to clash.

At the head of the Covian Legion, a commander with a red plume on his helmet saw the blood about to be shed and grimaced in horror. "*Legions!*" the commander called. "Stand down!"

Almost as one, the Covian Legion sheathed their blades.

Their advance halted, boots clanking to a stop.

The queen raged, "NO, YOU FOOLS! I AM YOUR QUEEN! YOU WILL—"

In a flash, Gray pulled wind into his soul.

Imala was on the balcony, then he was there, beside her. Wind wrapped around her, and they both shifted again, back to the arena's floor. Wind fell from Gray's form and Imala, clearly staggered by the sudden transition, crumbled in a heap before them, jeweled hands upon the sandy ground that had once been stained with endless blood. He leveled Morrowil to her throat, and she stared up at Gray, wide-eyed, breathing hard. Then her gaze panned to the Fleshguard, Captain Leanna, the soldiers, the people.

All of them, surrounding her.

Imala uttered, "I...I don't understand. You could have done that the whole time, couldn't you?"

Gray shrugged. "I couldn't simply kill you." He looked to the many people. "They needed to believe they could defend themselves first. That they could make a difference. You would just be replaced by another. I needed the heart of the kingdom to change."

Imala stared at the citizens who hemmed in, realizing his words, her face fell. "No..."

"Yes," Ayva said, "You thought of them as just as mindless subjects, but you're wrong."

"Well, that and being an evil conniving witch," Helix added.

Ayva looked to Gray. "'Win the people, win the tournament,'" she repeated Gray's phrase. "You knew the whole time?"

Gray shrugged. "Gut feeling."

Imala just stared, bulging eyes now hollow, expression shocked.

Leanna stepped forward. "I'll handle this." She tossed a look to Zane; seeing Raina, she gave a little smirk. "Glad to see you found your fire, ca'ran," the Captain said, and Zane returned a small smile.

Gray and Ayva exchanged a look.

What is going on? Raina sent through the bond.

Don't ask, Ayva replied. *Just Zane things.*

Captain Leanna gestured and several guards neared, clapping chains on Queen Imala and dragging her to her feet. Makeup ran down her face, and she howled, vacillating between despair and rage as they dragged her off. "You fools, this will change nothing! I am Covai! I built this city with my own blood! I am your queen and you are nothing! Cowards, dull-eyed beasts that take the form of men and women! I should have put the lot of you in chains! You all are beneath me!" When the crowds only parted for her passing, watching pitifully, others spitting or laughing, she changed her shrieks. "The shadow is coming and it will end you all! You will fall to the darkness without me!"

"Oof," Helix said. The shouts dwindled as the deposed queen was hauled away. "She was a delight." Then he dusted his hands, smiling. "Welp, good riddance!"

Ayva, at Gray's side, watched the mad queen go with a strange mixture of emotions on her face. "What are you going to do with her?" she asked.

Captain Leanna replied, "We'll hold a tribunal to determine her crimes. She'll be met with justice. The way Covai was meant to be."

Ayva gave a breath, looking content at this.

Gray nodded, knowing that meant death or a life in the dungeon. For once, he felt no room for pity. There were more important things at hand. He looked at the people and the Covian Legion when sudden shouts of joy filled the air, cries for the Ronin.

Hope, like a wave, suffused the crowds as men and women embraced, the turbulence and tension suddenly shattered. Karis, the Fleshguard, clapped Gray on the shoulder, much like Drega used to. "Happy to have been the swords at your side. Hopefully next time, I'll get to actually dance blades with you, brother." With that, he and his Fleshguard marched off the fields.

"Gods…it's really over," Ayva breathed. "What is it really over?"

"Don't jinx it," Helix said.

"I don't want to be the one to address the Ronin in the room but…" Zane eyed the Ronin of Metal. "Merrick is—"

"—One of us," Gray finished firmly.

Merrick folded his arms across his chest, looking away.

Gray noticed he didn't protest, even if he didn't agree. That at least was a step in the right direction.

Helix rubbed his wild blond hair. "Am I the only one who feels like they're going crazy? Didn't he try to kill us? Like…quite a few times? What in the seven hells did we miss? Is this a different world where bad guys are good?" Helix laughed, "Ah, no wait, now I get it! I hit my head and I'm the crazy one, right? Riding on a giant owl and saving Covai should have been the first hint."

Ayva playfully shoved him. "I didn't save your hide just for you to call it a dream."

He snorted. "Saved whose hide? And you should trust Merrick least of all. You saw what he did in Median."

She turned her gaze on Merrick, who remained half-turned. Ayva glanced to Zane for a moment, and smiled. "People can change." She raised a brow at Helix. "You should know that better than anyone, Ronin of Impetuousness."

Helix folded his arms with a glare. "One clear distinction, I never killed anyone."

"Did you not?" Merrick asked, eyeing the sands and the blood.

"Helix—" Ayva began.

Helix growled. "You want to say that's the same?"

Merrick's slate-grey eyes looked ready for violence.

"You haven't changed have you? Prove to me you're not the killer, the madman, and I might just not turn you to an ice sculpture," Helix said, frost crawling up his arm.

Ayva snarled, "Helix! He came to our aid!"

Zane growled, fire rising, sensing the brittle tension. "No, Ayva, I want to hear it from him!" Helix snapped.

Gray said nothing.

The others looked to him, but he merely watched.

Not going to intervene? Morrowil asked through their bond.

I can't make them bond. They need to resolve this without me, or I'll just always be stepping in.

You are learning.

Gray shrugged, eyeing Merrick, who seemed to be wrestling with himself internally. *That, and I'm curious for his answer too.*

Merrick's jaw tensed, looking as if it was going to crack, his eyes roving, as if he wished to be anywhere but here, before he finally said with a heavy breath, "I have done things. Horrible things. Most of them to bad people. Everything else, I could try to rationalize, tell you how I was manipulated by an evil you could scarcely understand, but the truth is…I am far from good. And yet, I don't want to be that any longer. I know that may not be enough, but it's all I have. It's a start at least… I want to be different." He looked up, unshed tears in his eyes, both filled with rage and sorrow. Merrick held Helix's gaze, who returned it in kind. He dropped his shoulders, then he let Osmium melt, then dropped to one knee, bowing his head. "I will join you, if you will have me."

Helix's eyes narrowed, silence stretching for a long moment, and then… "Good enough for me!"

"What?" Ayva gawked. "That's it? You just wanted to kill him a second ago."

"Testing him," Helix corrected. "I'm a great actor."

Merrick looked up. "You're not… angry at me?"

"Eh." Helix shrugged. "I don't think you've got a heart of gold yet, if that's what you're asking. But anyone who can bow their head and admit their wrong, well… they're not all evil. Besides, if I can forgive ol' fire-brains over here for nearly turning me into a living torch, then I can maybe forgive metal-brains as well. I mean, he didn't even try to light me on fire."

"I like you already, but we really gotta work on your nicknames," Raina remarked.

Gray spoke, drawing their eyes, his gaze turned to the wood and chain box in Zane's hand that was consuming his thoughts. "Are you going to tell us what's in the chest?"

Zane exchanged a meaningful look with Raina. "It's…well, I guess we should just show you."

Again, Gray felt supernatural power emanating from within.

Others must have sensed it, too.

Then it made a sound.

Thump.

A pulse resonated through the air.

As if drawn by a magnet, the others came closer, including Captain Leanna, as Raina grabbed the lid.

"You all…might wanna take a step back," Raina remarked.

No one did.

Raina shrugged. "All right, don't say I didn't warn you." She cracked the lid.

Gray's breath was ripped from his lungs.

A collection of gasps from the others nearby.

"Abyss take me," Helix cursed.

"Light above, is that…" Ayva breathed.

Within the chest, thumping rhythmically, clearly alive, was a heart. Or at least a sizable chunk of it. Pale, ghostly white it had thick red ventricles and arteries, and glowed with an otherworldly light.

Helix gulped. "Abyss take me, is that…gods, is that what I think it is?"

Raina lifted, then dropped her shoulders. "That depends. If you think it's the heart of a primordial dragon? Then…yes. Or at least a good portion of it."

Gray's own heart hammered, thumping against his ribcage.

"That…that's what was powering the arena, wasn't it?" Ayva asked.

Zane nodded. "Held in an ancient vault beneath the colosseum. Something no one but a Ronin can access."

Raina chuckled. "It gave me one killer headache while calling to me. It's a piece of the heart of the Dragon of Flesh. I don't know who put it there, but it's clear it's been imbibing spark from thousands of warriors in the arena. I don't know about you all, but I think this thing is strong enough to give life to a titan."

Zane grunted in agreement, and he glanced to Merrick. "If I'm right, I think that's what our menacing Ronin of Metal was sent here for, isn't it?"

Merrick, however, was silent. He had been for a while. Now his breath came faster, and he stepped back as if the heart was cursed. In fact, he'd been looking terrified since the object was revealed. "No…" Merrick said in horror, "You must hide that. Now! Put it back in the vault!" His gaze panned upward, terror in his eyes. "Gods above, it's too late…He's already here."

There was a strange, eerie silence in the air. Everything shifted. The world seemed to slow. Gray's heart crashed against his ribcage, and dread rose like a tidal wave. "Something's wrong…" Judging by the others' looks, they sensed it, too.

A brittleness that crackled with power.

BOOM!

A deafening crack of thunder split the sky and lightning flashed in their midst—a single thick, white bolt arced downward, crashing in the center of the arena and the colosseum quaked. Crowds of men and women, soldiers, and guards cried out, shielding their eyes.

With a buffet of wind, Gray guarded those closest from the eruption of power, as a smell like that after a thunderstorm stung his nostrils.

Thick mist filled the air where the lightning had struck.

When it cleared, a man stood on the sands, turning, taking in the scene before him.

No, not just a man.

Dressed in immaculate black robes, with a single band of red on his cuffs and hem, stood the Patriarch, Lord of the Citadel, and the most powerful man in Farhaven.

Epilogue: A Leafbug's Fancy

Darius loved flying. Oddly enough, the scent of it was perhaps his favorite part, and he had a feeling that had something to do with his element of nature. Of course, the heart-pounding exhilaration was a close second.

As he soared, wind rushed about his body, making his hair whip, his cheeks flap, and his eyes water. Darius guided Leafy, his elven mount, with white-knuckled hands on the reins. The mount, for all intents and purposes, was just a giant bug with colossal translucent, green-veined wings, huge multifaceted bulbous eyes, large feathery feelers, and a chitinous body big enough to swallow a draft horse. But he was also much more than a simple insect. A rare-as-gold mount from the city of elves, he was a powerhouse of strength, nimbleness, and essentially a giant puppy housed in a bug's body.

They performed rolls, twists, and spins, whooping and hollering with each one. Leafy's wings, sheer as paper, shone in the morning light, fluttering as the massive leafbug followed his every command.

It was here in the air that Darius felt truly alive.

He circled above his three glum companions. "Hurry up, won't ya! Ha ha!"

Below, the three rode on elven cormacs.

Rydel was at their head—their leader. He rode straight-backed, sword-calloused hands loosely holding his reins as he stared ahead, as if seeing the battle far beyond. The intimidating broad-shouldered elf always gave Darius a bit of the shivers. Not because the elf was evil, but because he felt like Rydel's penetrating green gaze saw through his antics to the heart of his fear… and because the man could likely gut a saerok with his pinky finger.

He wore as usual his scarlet robes—his three stripes evident on his cuff. But now he'd split it down the middle, making it more of a red overcoat. Beneath, he wore a black shirt with stitched red flames.

As usual, Alandra wore an exasperated look, staring ahead, pretending not to hear him. The new head of the Lando was a real sore thumb, and an attempt to warm her obsidian heart was met with grumbling, a hard gaze, or a lecture on "what responsibility meant." Darius just grinned through it all. He was determined to win her over.

"Alandra!" Darius called out, swooping down to hover over her head. "I know you want a turn on Leafy. Just say the word! I'm guessing you've got a sensitive stomach, but I promise not to do too many barrel rolls!"

Alandra looked up at him. "Keep it up, Leaf Boy. I will shoot you out of the air."

"You wouldn't—"

She reached for her bow, as if she meant it. He gulped and pulled Leafy higher, figuring it was a bluff but not entirely willing to bet on it. "I'm going to win you over!" He called down. "You play tough, but deep down we both know you're a big ol' soft—"

An arrow whizzed and Darius *felt* a flash of green in his mind.

Out of instinct, he reached out and... *caught* the arrow.

Darius stared at his outstretched hand dumbly. Dead wood? That was the second time he'd felt unalive wood. Normally, he could only manipulate what was living. Still, it'd only been out of impulse. Not intentional. He needed to learn to manipulate it on command.

"You almost hit me!" He shouted down to the grinning elf.

She hadn't. It'd been barely in arm's reach.

He huffed. Little did she know he was stubborn if nothing else.

Darius lost himself once more to the joy of flight.

He banked left, narrowly avoiding a puffy white cloud that would've dampened his clothes. He breathed in the cornucopia of scents. First was the sharp, crisp pine, then earthy moss, then the musk of cedar. They passed over a field of wildflowers, a sea of gold and amethyst. Darius gasped as the intoxicating floral blast nearly knocked him off his saddle.

Right, nature powers.

Beyond the endless farmlands, his heart thumped, yearning to reach their destination, to go faster. "Eldas." He said the name aloud, tasting the sound of it, and letting it be carried by the rushing winds.

Leafy chirped.

"What do you mean, why are we going? To stop a mad tyrant king and save a pretty elven queen to reclaim her kingdom. It's the stuff of stories, my dear insectoid companion! A kingdom that just so happens to be nature, which I bet is also your home, and mine too." His hands tightened on the reins. "If we win the battle, we'll have Eldas on our side, and we're going to need every army we can get if we're to crush this rising evil, Leafy."

Leafy made a sound.

"Right you are, buddy! The shadow never stood a chance. Sure, our predecessors with infinitely more power and knowledge might have failed against a thousand-year-old, supremely powerful evil with unerring patience..." He shrugged. "But you know, that's them, and we're... us. I think a little levity was probably their missing ingredient, and we can all agree Maris isn't nearly as handsome as I am."

Leafy chirped again, louder, more questioning.

"You think I'm rambling because I'm afraid?" Darius snorted. "Hardly!"

Leafy's reply was low, almost a grunt.

Darius gasped. "Wow, uncalled for. I am *not* a liar. A fabricator of inventive alternate realties, sure, but liar feels a tad harsh." Then he gazed north, spotting the blackened range of the Mountains of Soot. Nestled in those ridges was Yronia, Great Kingdom of Metal. He could just glimpse the towering black gates, now ruined to little more than scrap metal, and he saw plumes of smoke. He gulped.

Right. Maybe I'm a little afraid.

He swooped down to the others, informing them of what he saw.

Riding with a soldier's ease on her white cormac, Alandra answered, "Yronia's dark forges have been burning day and night for several moons now."

"Right," Darius said, flying above them. "Evil like that, I'm sure it'll just decide to keep to itself and play nice. Nothing sinister about that at all."

Alandra made a sour expression, her jaw tightening.

Rydel interrupted, "One battle at a time, Darius. For now, focus on what lies ahead. We can't do anything about Yronia until we save Eldas."

Darius grumbled, but he knew that was true enough.

After another few hours of flying, the sun dipped toward the horizon, and Rydel called out for Darius to land.

The giant bug's immense translucent wings flapped a slower rhythm as Darius guided it to the ground alongside the three on cormacs. He didn't dismount. The bug skittered forward, easily able to keep up with the three steeds. The cormacs seemed fairly nonplussed by the giant creature, despite dwarfing them nearly two times over. They only occasionally nickered if Leafy got too near. "Yes, can I help you?" Darius asked Rydel. "We still have another hour or two of daylight. I thought we wanted to cover as much ground as possible."

"We need the light," Rydel explained, guiding his cormac to a patch of land with clumps of dry, brittle grass near a thicket of trees. Rydel leapt off his mount but made no move to tie the cormac. The intelligent elven beasts were too well trained to wander off.

Finn and Alandra also dismounted, making camp.

Darius pulled Leafy short. "Light? For what?"

Rydel tossed him an object, and Darius examined it. A training sword, little more than a bundle of reeds tightly wound. Rydel let a faint smile crack his craggy exterior. "If you're going to defeat Dryan, I'm going to teach you how."

Darius grinned. "Right, sounds fun."

"I don't think you'll be saying that when I'm finished," Rydel replied.

"You'll find I'm surprisingly tenacious," Darius hefted his training sword.

"We shall see. Let's begin."

Without wasting any time, they trained.

Finn stopped his duties and sat down to watch. Even Alandra cast curious glances despite herself.

For several hours, Darius showed how much he knew about a blade. It turned out, after the countless bruises and Rydel moving almost at a snail's pace, not a lot. True to his word, however, when his legs were swept from him, and he landed hard enough to almost break his tailbone—even Finn had winced and asked if he'd needed a heal—Darius had thrown a smile, and picked up the blade again.

I will get stronger.

Rydel's hard visage cracked just a little.

Not a smile, or a gleam of pride, but that would come.

The days passed, and training progressed as one would expect.

Darius got smacked left, right, and center by Rydel's sword, until every part of his body hurt. Reaver Finn would heal him, but the memories of the injuries started to take their toll. Rydel taught him to push through that as well. With each passing hour, his body slowly transformed. He'd always been lean and athletic. Agile, one could say, but under Rydel's instruction, Darius changed.

After two weeks of rigorous training, Darius's saw the definition across his body—muscles grew stronger, his legs faster, his lungs expanded. One day he'd tested it, and he could easily jog for hours beside one of the cormacs or Leafy while they cantered, and not lose his breath.

One night, while massaging his aching muscles, he realized they felt as hard as rock.

"That's called getting stronger," Reaver Finn said around a mouthful of potatoes, the hot steam rising into the night.

"This is more than stronger. I feel like I could bench press a boulder."

Alandra huffed. "I'd be willing to watch that."

He glared at her, ignoring her little smirk. "Anyway, in Daerval I could never get this strong. I feel superhuman. How?"

"Farhaven allows you to imbibe its spark, if you can handle it," Rydel explained. "It's a slow process, but we're trying to accelerate what would normally take decades."

"They say Hidden's bodies, as well as Fleshguard's, can withstand a sword's cut," Finn said.

Darius glanced over to Rydel who was once again staring into the flames. "Is that true?"

"I'd recommend trying not to get cut first," Rydel said. "But yes, a standard slash or jab won't normally break the skin. Spark reinforces muscle. With time, it can be more dense than steel."

"So...I'm going to become immortal?"

Rydel gave him a flat look. "That's most definitely not what I said."

Darius smirked. "I got the gist."

Sitting across from the fire, Alandra gave a disdainful snort as she whittled a stick with a dagger.

"What's with Miss Grumpy Pants?"

Alandra sighed. "You don't see it, do you?"

"Well, do explain, as I'm sure you're about to in a really non-condescending way."

"Rydel's just been giving you glimpses of a Hidden's training. If he truly showed you what it took to become him, you wouldn't survive. You're barely scratching the surface."

"Is that true?" Darius asked Rydel.

Rydel looked away. "It is. I can't go killing our legendary Ronin of Leaf just—"

"Then stop holding back," Darius interrupted.

"I just said—"

"I know what you said," Darius replied, "and I know it's dangerous. Eternal spirits, everything is about to become far more terrifying. I need to be prepared." His eyes hardened as he stared at Rydel over the flames. "Please…" For the first time in a long time, there was no mirth in his tone, no light joviality. Just a burning desire to get stronger. Darius looked down into the flames. "If I'm going to get stronger, if I'm going to save my friends, then I need to become something more than what I am currently, much more. If that means becoming a Hidden, or getting as close as I can, then I'll do it. I'll do whatever it takes, or I will die trying."

For a moment, even Alandra's face in the firelight lost its sneer, her face softening. Then she sighed, looked away, and returned to her whittling.

Rydel considered him for a long moment, then took a heavy breath, his broad shoulders rising, then falling. He gave a slow nod. "So be it. I will make you a Hidden, or you will die in the attempt."

Darius nodded. "Thank you."

The moment lingered.

Darius couldn't help himself. "Oh, man, this is exciting. Hidden Darius! Ronin of Leaf! Man, how many titles do you think I can get? Really a shame I couldn't join the others and try to tack on the title of Grand Primus." The other two groaned, but Reaver Finn just grinned. That was the reaction Darius was hoping to get out of him. "How do you think they're doing, by the way? They better have won that tournament by now. My silver is on Helix to win. The card up the sleeve is always the best bet."

They all looked north.

"Nalia always wins," Alandra replied.

"Well, I know you don't know me, but you clearly don't know them either," Darius replied.

She eyed him, not challenging him, only giving a quirk of her lips. "Perhaps."

"Either way," Finn said, "Let's hope they are safe."

Darius slept restlessly, and when training came again, Alandra proved more right than he'd like to admit. Rydel nearly killed him. He broke his arm, leg, and nearly lost his eye, if it wasn't for Finn. After gasping from healing, he was given an hour to recover, but the man strapped rocks on his back and Darius was forced to run until his legs threatened to shatter and his feet bled. Three more awful nights like that, and Darius thought he might break. But he forced himself to rise again.

Time lost meaning.

He just remembered pain, until he blacked out, or until he gasped awake from Reaver Finn's healing. Suddenly, a week, a month, a year, he wasn't sure, but he was following Rydel for another round of torture when the man stopped in a field full of golden leaf litter, in the shadow of an abandoned farm and a giant old oak.

Darius swallowed, facing Rydel who turned to face him.

"You ready?"

"I won't break," Darius said. *Even if I want to.*

Rydel folded his brawny arms, and for the first time, gave him the smallest glimmer of a pride in his eyes. "Good. But no sword tonight. You're ready for the next round."

"Next round?" Darius asked.

Finn stepped up, smiling. "We decided to make your training more than a Hidden. A Hidden both with the powers of magic and sword. A new rank, if you will." He grinned. "Something *more.*"

Darius shivered at that look. "Right, terrifying, love it, no offense, but you're a Reaver Finn…"

"Yes, and?"

"A Ronin's power is flow. You wield spark. How are you supposed to teach me?"

Finn nodded thoughtfully. "True, however, spark and flow have more overlap than you might think. Also, I'll have you know, I was considered a protégé in my day," he said, snapping his fingers. Blue, green, and red flames burst above his hand, rising high into the sky in a dazzling display. Darius was slack-jawed. Then Finn added, "It's not going to be easy. If I'm right, it'll be even harder than training to become a Hidden."

Darius grinned, his body and mind battered, but his spirit found a new surge of energy in the thought of becoming *more* than a Hidden—or maybe it was the wild gleam in Finn's eyes—but he straightened. "Well? What are we waiting for?"

Just like that, they trained.

It turned out Finn's notion of drawing out the true extent of Darius's power was inventive, bordering on cruel.

One idea of Finn's was for Darius to put his hand over their campfire, instructing him to move the dead logs, before his skin blistered and bubbled. That one had even Alandra's sour face creasing with worry. Finn showed him "Defense Drills", which basically was hurling sizable chunks of rock, wood, or ice, while Darius was forced to duck, dodge or use his surroundings. Sometimes it would go on for hours. His rationale? 'If you can't be hit, you can't be hurt'. Twice, when Darius had won out, grinning in victory, Finn would send a final barrage telling him to 'always be prepared'. He'd push him from heights, and Darius was forced create ramps of wood to cushion his fall to prevent breaking every bone in his body. Each experiment was worse than the last, leaving Darius burnt, bruised, and bloodied.

But the worst was the Ker Stream.

Darius hated swimming.

Once Finn found this out, he'd forced Darius to jump into the fast currents of the southern Ker and try to access his power.

Darius had nearly drowned, but this had made him tap deeper into the burning green sphere in his mind—his Nexus—still not fully revealed.

Yet, after the first week, he unveiled a quarter, his power deepening.

On the second week, after a particularly brutal 'Defense Drill', he'd accessed half his Nexus.

During the latest 'swimming session', Finn had started barraging him with fire.

Darius had been forced to dive and breathe in a belly full of water through his nose and mouth.

The currents had sucked him under and he'd smacked his head against a rock.

You can't die. Not yet.

He wasn't sure whose voice it was, but it sounded feminine, ancient, yet familiar...

Not yet, he snarled to himself, water swirling about him, bubbles and currents making it a maelstrom.

The nexus flared.

Darius seized it.

Three-quarters unveiled—a burning green sphere.

On the verge of death, his eyes snapped wide, and he drew on thick ancient roots from deep beneath the rocky bed of water—they wrapped around his waist and flung him to the mossy shore like a flopping fish where he gasped for air.

Finn had stood over him, hands on his robed hips. "Not bad, but still using nature around you."

Darius, half-dead, gasped, and groaned. With muscles like wet noodles, he pushed himself to rise, feeling like a soggy piece of driftwood, and snarled, "Again."

"That's my boy." Finn's eyes were like dark flint and he grinned. "We're not stopping until the shadow flees at the mere sight of you."

Darius chuckled, then he saw Finn's look and gulped. He had an image in his head of Dryan stepping outside the gates, then fleeing for his life. "You know you're a little terrifying, right?" Then he smiled. "But I like it. Best part? After all this training, I'll be able to rub how much stronger I am in Zane's face."

Finn chuckled. "That's the spirit."

The next night, in a forest, Darius felt something weighing on him as he collapsed to his knees in the leaflitter.

The Reaver neared, folding his arms in his robes, "What is it?"

Darius sighed. "I'm getting stronger. I can feel it in my bones," he said, feeling as if he could see green pulsing in his veins. With a flick of his fingers, roots buried deep, sprang up from the ground nearby, dancing to his tune. "If I'm being honest, what I really want is to be able to use my power from thin air. To summon a tree from nothing." He'd felt it before, a few times—he'd moved a dartboard in Farbs, and even thrown a cart in Median—but it was sporadic and he didn't know how to do it on command.

Finn snapped and Darius's roots burned then shriveled to ash on the forest floor.

"Hey! What was that for?"

Finn's eyes bored into him, the unnerving look on his face deepening. "Oh, you're going to be able to do much more than that when I'm done."

Darius gulped again. "Why do I get the feeling that sentence should end with 'if you don't die.'"

Finn smiled. "I won't let you. Farhaven needs you."

With that, training resumed, hours on end, until Darius flopped down on the ground beside the others, every muscle ragged and his mind spent.

Day in and day out, Finn's training never relented, but after a while, he both feared and relished it.

Finally, he felt like he was becoming a Ronin.

When flying the next day, Darius had an idea, a plan for another little backspin. He called out, "*Etras—*" The command was only halfway out of his mouth before the leafbug, with his massive shimmering wings, did a somersault in midair. Darius squinted. "Did you just read my mind?"

Leafy chirped.

That was happening more often of late. The rare flying mount seemed to know where Darius was going before he did. Even more fascinating, Leafy seemed to be growing stronger and faster as well.

Darius put his hand to the leafbug's chitinous bright green flank, patting it and paused. Was Leafy…bigger? Through his connection, the leafbug *felt* stronger. "Are you doing little bug push-ups when I'm not watching, buddy?"

Leafy chirped happily.

"Ha! Well, we're both getting stronger, then!"

Rydel's impossibly fast sword, and Finn's brutal, and terribly creative, magic was hardening his body and soul. While the days nearly broke him, he reveled in it. He wanted, no he needed to be stronger, to save his friends, to save others.

One night, alone by the fire—his turn to stand guard—Leafy settled to his side, the giant bug slumping down in the grass with a loud harrumph. Staring into the flickering flames, Darius whispered, "I wonder if they're thinking about me."

Leafy chirped.

"You're right, of course they are. They're prolly pining over me as we speak. *Seriously, Darius,*" Darius said, imitating Gray's gruffer, dry tone, though it always held a hint of mirth that few could hear but him, "*without you, the day is so dull.*"

Then he made his voice a few octaves higher, impersonating Ayva. "*Oh, I agree, Gray. You're great and all as our leader, but Darius always finds a way to add a little sunshine to our day.*"

"Ha. Sun pun," Darius said to himself, before leaping back into his fictive dialogue.

Darius cleared his throat. "*I'm Helix, and I'm not so annoying now that I've shed some of my dark past. I sure do miss my banter buddy. Sure, he nearly gets us killed over and over, but what's a little adventure without harrowing, near-death heroism!*"

Darius sighed, eyeing Leafy. "Whattya think, spot on?"

Leafy chirped, eyes shining with the fire's light.

"Well, of course I wish I was with them! A city that bases its whole economy on drinking, gambling, fighting, and revelry?" He made a wistful sound, leaning back onto a pile of plush moss that grew up from the ground. "Covai is supposed to have the most beautiful women and the best taverns in all of Farhaven. Well, aside from maybe Cloudfell." He groaned. "Literally, every flap of your big green wings that brings us farther away is actually painful. But…" He sighed. "I'm a man of action and duty now, and Karil's counting on me." He patted Leafy who gave another chirp. "Us."

In the morning, Darius awoke with a renewed vigor.

As he looked at the sky, low sweeping clouds passed over, he spotted a trail of smoke rising miles high. *No…* He breathed with a gut-sinking terror. Something told him this was no mere forest fire. He alerted the others, and Rydel instructed him to scout ahead. As he flew, his dread grew. In the distance, he saw massive billowing plumes of smoke and below… a city on fire. Horror filled him and he told Leafy to fly faster. As he neared, it hit him. The stench, like putrid flesh rotting in the high sun, made him nearly lose his lunch. As he got closer, he saw the aftermath.

Bodies burned beyond the outer walls, while inside behind a large wall was practically a torch. Men and women had tried to flee, or fight, and their corpses were strewn across the land.

Thousands dead.

He felt like he was going to be sick.

Then he saw the evil, the cause… the blight.

Monsters teemed over the land, saeroks and vergs, a long trail of them leading all the way back to the shattered and torn gates of Yronia. Anger threatened to consume Darius. His jaw clenched in pain at the horror below.

Leafy, beneath him, made a plaintive, mourning chirp as they circled over the endless dead—his sight blurred, tears streaking down his cheeks.

Worse, Darius knew what this meant.

The true war, the final battles, had begun.

Suddenly, he felt his vision race towards Eldas, the vast forests—he saw the battle looming, the one that would decide the fate of the Great Kingdom of Leaf. More than that, he *felt* the elves and their worry. *His* people. Karil's plight was a vise on his heart, her need palpable. Darius felt it all and his Nexus replied in kind, burning brighter, like an emerald sun. It coursed through his veins like fire.

Darius breathed it in, ignoring the pain, giving into the feeling. His fist tightened on the reins of Leafy until his knuckles cracked, and a green glow suffused his entire body.

"I'm coming for you," Darius vowed to Dryan, to the shadow.

His power listened, and below, the woods quaked with a Ronin's fury.

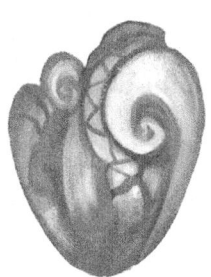

GLOSSARY

Arbiter: A supreme wielder of magic, born of the Citadel. There are only three and some say ever were. Their power is equivalent to their rank.

Arbiter Fera: the third most powerful wielder of the spark Arbiter Fera is a force to be reckoned with. Enigmatic and playing behind the scenes her nature and ultimate plans are hidden to almost all. She is also one of the few spark users who attempts to understand the flow, and researches and experiments with magical creatures. Her half Darkwalker half phox pet is always at her side.

Aurelious: A Ronin, also known as the Confessor. His element is that of flesh and his home the Kingdom of Covai. He is brother to Aundevoriä and known for having a small temper, but a fierce love for his brother, and loyalty for his Ronin brothers.

Aundevoriä: A Ronin, also known as the Protector. He wields Durendil, the stone blade and his home is the Great Kingdom of Lander within the impenetrable crags, a fortress of stone; it's walls thicker than most cities. He is known for his willingness to sacrifice all for the sake of humanity.

Aurora: Fable Sword of Sun belonging to the Ronin of Sun, name given by Avya

Ayva: Ayva is the tomboyish friend of Gray and Darius. She and her father run The Golden Horn in Lakewood. Ayva is an avid reader of the world that lies outside Lakewood.

Balder (Jiro): A man who claims to be the leader of the Stonemason Guild (a well reputed guild), and he lives in the Shining City. Gray befriends him just outside the Dipping Tsugi.

Baro: A Ronin, also called the Bull, the Bladeslinger and Slayer of Giants. His element is that of Metal, and his home is the Great Kingdom of Yronia — a city that is a mass of steel and steam. Its forges were once lit with undying fires but now it is one of the "forgotten kingdoms". Baro wields the blade *Iridal*, a giant sword made of unbreakable steel. In all the stories, he is larger than any man known, described as having a waist like an oak trunk, and shoulders as broad as an ox, often known as the one who led the vanguard of the Ronin into battle.

Belegrun: A rare Covian bearlike mounted beast worth a fortune

Bloody Blacksmith: Inn in the city of Covai

Burai Mountains: Endlessly tall mountains that reach towards the heavens, and are often called the spine, or back of the world. Deaths Gate is nestled between these impassible peaks.

Cerabul: A bulllike beast of burden

Calad: One of Hiron's famous twin swords.

Citadel: A great keep of black stone within the Kingdom of Fire, and home to both Devari and Reavers.

Cloudfell Lake: Lake beside Cloudfell, turquoise waters and low-lying mist make the lake look like it hovers just beneath the clouds.

Cormacs: Cormacs are elven steeds. They have long legs and broad, powerful chests which makes them formidable sprinters. They have shorter muzzles than a horse, long silken tails, and slopping backs. Karil also mentions they are attuned to the spark.

Covai: Kingdom of Flesh, the city of men, women and beast, land of the mortals, and the largest spiritual sect of all the lands.

Covai Riders: A vast horse tribe from the Kingdom of Flesh that control much of the plains of Farhaven.

Covian Legion: The rank-and-file troops of Covai

Curtana: Dared's twin daggers, thin with broken tips.

Cyn: (pronounced 'kin') A game played with small, carved figurines, consisting of followers and a mark.

Daerval: A land without magic, on the other side of Deaths Gate.

Dared: A Ronin, also known as the Shadow. His element is that of moon and his home is the Great Kingdom of Narim — a vast subterranean gem located in the dark hills, half above the land, half below.

The least is known about Dared. He is said to never have spoken. Rumors of his powers include the ability to turn completely invisible in the night even under the brightest moon.

Dared (the statue): Dared the silent Ronin in statue form.

Darius: Darius is a wiry young man of seventeen who is from Lakewood. Darius is perhaps most well-known for his love of gambling and tomfoolery.

Death's Gate: The infamous gates that divide the two lands. The origin of the name is said to come from all those that died during the Great War which divided the lands, specifically during the final battle that stained the White Plains red.

Desiccating: To remove one forever from their innate spark. It is a dreaded occurrence that is often worse than death to any wielder of the spark.

Devari: An elite group of warriors who live within the Citadel, and they are masters of the blade. Using "Ki" they hold certain powers, including inhabiting another's body and feeling their sensations.

Dipping Tsugi: Mistress Hitomi's inn in the Shining City.

Drega: Leader of the Fleshguard

Dryads: Fabled magical creatures of the forest of Drymaus, a great mythical forest to the north of Eldas.

Dryan: High Councilor and elf who assumes the throne when Karil's father, the old king, is murdered.

Drymaus: Home of the mythical dryads.

Dun Varis: An offshoot and fragment of Lander, the Great Kingdom of Stone, rumored to exist again within Daerval, and Aundevoriä's homeland.

Durendil: Aundevoriä's famed sword. It has a wire-wrapped handle, and turns to stone.

Eldas: Home of the Elves, one of the nine Great Kingdoms, also the Kingdom of Forest.

Elementals: Magical beings of Farhaven.

Elements: A game of Farhaven that Ezrah and Kirin used to play.

Eminas: The name for Gray used by the elves, and literally means eminent one, but its variant meaning is harbinger.

Ester: A city once bound together with Menalas in what was called a "false kingdom".

Ethelwin: A powerful Reaver and lecturer who is only a few below in rank and prestige of the female Arbiter.

Ezrah: Arbiter of the second rank who lives in the Citadel, and Gray's grandfather.

Farbs: The sprawling desert city wherein the Citadel resides.

Farhaven: A land full of magic, on the opposite side of Deaths Gate.

Fendary: Also called the Storm-breaker, or the Sentinel. He is Fendary Aquius, a high general during the Lieon who supposedly fought the Ronin. The legend says he had a hundred men to the Ronin's nine.

Fleshguard: Covian solders that heal faster than normal

Flow: What is often called the source of all magic, or the "essence." It is what the Ronin wield.

Frizzian Coast: Located in Farhaven, full of peaceful towns and villages along the coast and in the Northern provinces.

Frostfall: Legendary sword of Water, formally known as Calad and Laidir

Fusing: A bond between magic users that wields even greater power. It is said hundreds of Reavers were used in ancient times to forge epic creations, including the transporters.

Grand Primus: Title bestowed on the winner of the Grand Tournament of Flesh

Great Tree: The tree that is at the center of Eldas, and bears the spire; the great buildings where all nobility reside.

Guard Captain Leanna: Guard Captain of the Fleshguard of Covai

Gryphons: mounts of Farbs, half eagle and half lion.

Hall of Wind: Within the legendary Morrow, Great Kingdom of Wind. Mura claims Kail stashed his most precious of weapons in the "Hall of Wind."

Hando Cloak: A black and forest green cloak Rydel wears. It signifies that he is one of the *Hidden*.

Haori: Colored vests, each matches the powers the Ronin hold, and the color of the Kingdom they represent.

Hati: Servant of Queen Ilama, attendant to Grey

Heartgard: The name for Seth's famed sword; meaning brave, enclosed.

Heartwood: Harder than most human metals, most of Eldas is constructed out of it.

Herbwort: An herb that aids with shivers and insomnia.

High Council: The council of elves in Eldas that oversee affairs; they are also known *see also* Elders of Eldas.

Hiras Uga: Tribe of people the live in the desert east of Covai

Hitomi: Often called "Mistress" Hitomi. Hitomi is the proprietor of the Dipping Tsugi in the Shining City. When the others stumble upon several rare books in her packed library, they discover her obsession for books.

Hiron: A Ronin, also known as the Kingslayer. His element is that of water, and the Great Kingdom of Seria. He is known as the peace-keeper, and the Ronin of wisdom and serenity.

House of Belegrun: One of the four great noble houses in Covai. Houses color is Gold and symbol is a bear with scales. Richest of the noble houses

House of Copper Falcon: One of the four great noble houses in Covai. Houses color is orange and symbol is a orange-tailed falcon

House of Hisan Viper: One of the four great noble houses in Covai. Houses color is Green and symbol is a two-headed snake

House of Red Fox: One of the four great noble houses in Covai. Houses color is Red and symbol is a desert fox with red fur

Howard: Presider over the schedule of events

Irasa: Theiflord of Flesh

Iridal: Baro's famed sword, rumored to be impossible to shatter.

Jiryn: A high elf healer from Eldas.

Jivran: Fought in the Bloodbath, Leader of the Hiras Uga

Kage: The nine nameless evils who pose as the Ronin and hold equal powers.

Kagehass: The saeroks and verg's name for what others refer to as the Nameless (the Shadow's Hand).

Kail: The once leader of the fabled Ronin. He is known by many names, from many eras including the blight seeker, betrayer of men, and the wanderer. He is rumored to have survived the Lieon, and still exists, told in fearful tales for the past two thousand years.

Karil: Karil is the queen of Eldas, home and kingdom of the Elves. She is half-human and half-elf. Karil is tall and beautiful, with silver eyes, and white-blonde hair. Her beauty is only equaled by her intelligence.

Ki: The source and power of a Devari.

Kin: Dark men and women who are agents of the "shadow", specifically the Kage. Gray runs into one in Lakewood when trying to retrieve the sword.

King Gias: Karil's father and the King of Eldas.

King Katsu: King of the Shining City.

Komai tail: The braided hairstyle of the Devari; the longer the braid, the higher the rank.

Koru Village: The town Gray and the others run across. It is just north of Lakewood.

Laidir: The second of Hiron's famous twin swords.

Lair of the Beast: the home of the Darkeye clan within the Underbelly.

Lakewood: A peaceful town, but resides close to the ill-famed Lost Woods. It is the home of Ayva and Darius.

Lander: One of the "forgotten kingdoms". Lander was the Great Kingdom of Stone. It was a city that had walls purported to be thicker than small cities.

Lando: Translates as "redeemers" or "liberators" in the common tongue. They are the group that saves Karil in the woods of Eldas.

Lieon: The Great War during the Final Age that lasted over a thousand years.

Lokai: The god Darius evokes; the god of "luck".

Lost Woods: The infamous dark forest where Gray and Mura live, and said to be full of direbears and other nefarious beasts. Villagers say the woods come alive at night, and travelers who venture in are rarely ever seen again.

Malgar: Overseer of the Bloodbath

Malik: Leader of the Kage. He has a spiked pauldron and is bigger than his brethren. He speaks to Vera and is the voice of the dark army.

Maris: A Ronin. He is also called the Trickster, a Ronin of many names and faces. He wields Masamune, the leaf blade — its powers unknown. His element is that of tree, and his homeland is the Great Kingdom of Eldas.

Mark of the Gladiator: Red swords along the forearm indicating rank in tournament

Masamune: Maris' famed sword.

Mashiro: Guard captain of the Shining City.

Menalas: A southern city of Farhaven that was once part of Ester, together they were deemed a false kingdom denied the position of power as one of the nine Great Kingdoms. They were forced to split and divide up their power. Many of their inhabitants, however, still lust for a crown and throne that no longer exists. Moreover, they share an iron mine with Ester that was too difficult to upend in the Lieon.

Merai's: Servants of elven royalty, not elves but humans of a small, but ancient lineage when wars were fought and slaves were taken as servants.

Mirkal: Darius' cormac.

Mistral: A Polearm gifted to Kail made of Yronia Steel, darkstone, and infused with Bloodstone

Mistress Sophi: Darius' aunt, she owns an inn in Lakewood, and taught Darius how to dance.

Morrow: A city upon the windy high cliffs of Ren Nar that oversaw the world. It is the Great Kingdom of Wind. It is the last of the three lost Great Kingdoms and the most famous. It is Kail's homeland.

It contains the Hall of Wind, as well — the famous meeting place for the great kings, queens, and generals who fought for the armies of Sanctity and against the Alliance of Righteous in the Great War of the *Lieon*.

Morrowil: The infamous sword that Gray inherits from Kail.

Mortal Being: a religion of Covai which often encourages self-inflicted bodily harm to achieve a higher spiritual state.

Motri: Gray's hawk and companion, who also seems to have a mysterious alliance with Karil.

Mura: Mura is a charming, but irascible hermit of unknown age. He lives in a cabin in the middle of Lost Woods where Gray stumbles upon him. Mura is wiry with thick gray brows and an often stern, heavily-lined face, and black and gray peppered hair. He is Karil's uncle.

Nalia: Current Grand Primus of Four tournaments

Nameless: Created from Reavers, a horrible evil that mists from thin air, and is rumored to be invincible to "mortal blades." Their armor is made from overlapping dark plates. Gray and Darius fight them in the back alleys of Lakewood, behind the Golden Horn.

Narim: The Kingdom of Moon in the dark hills, half above, half beneath the land, and is a vast subterranean gem.

Neophyte: A threader of the spark, a rank below a Reaver. They reside in the Neophyte Palace and wear gray robes.

Nexus: The source of Gray's power. It is a swirling ball of air that he focuses on to tap into his power.

Niux: A unit of twelve, that consists of vergs and saeroks.

Noxii: Title for the criminals, degenerates, and ones that obtains a refused scroll, fight in this first round of the tournament (The Bloodbath)

Omni: A Ronin, also known as the Deceiver. Omni's element is that of Sun, and from the Great Kingdom of Vaster. Omni leads the Ronin in Kail's absence.

Osmium: Famed sword of Metal, formerly called Iridal

Oval Hall: Where the Seven Trials takes place in the Citadel. It is beautiful and ancient.

Patriarch: the well-known benevolent ruler of Farbs, Great Kingdom of fire. The most powerful wielder of the spark and first rank Arbiter.

Primarian: Winners of the third round of fights are awarded this title, Marked with 3 swords on forearm

Primarian-Basaeri: Winners of the first round are granted this title, Marked with 1 swords on forearm

Primarian-hadus: Winners of the second round of fights are awarded this title, Marked with 2 swords on forearm

Primus: Ones in the semi finals of the tournament are awarded this title

Pyre: Primordial Dragon of Fire

Queen Ilama: Ruler of Covai and collector of Ronin artifacts

Raina: The new Ronin of Flesh

Reaver: A powerful wielder of magic born of the Citadel.

Reaver Nelfin: Four striped Reaver, High Counselor of Magic to Queen Ilama

Rekdala Forhas: "Honor and duty" in the Yorin tongue.

Reliahs Desert: The desert surrounding Farbs, sometimes called the Farbian desert.

Relnas Forest: The forest of Eldas, home of the elves.

Ren: Close friend of Kirin's and leader of the Devari. He wears a graying Komai tail, a long braid, and is described as ageless. Most characteristically, he is a man hardened from years of training and battle, both mentally and physically.

Right of Innoctus: To refuse the sealed contract and release the magical seal allowing another to take their place

Rimdel: Trader's paradise or jewel of the Eastern Kingdoms: capital with no central rule, inhabited by only thieves, ruffians and traders as hard as stone, destroyed by the Kage.

Ronin: The legends of the *Lieon*, nine warriors who each holds a supreme power. According to the stories, they are dreaded and the bane of mankind.

Rydel: An elf of the rank of *Hidden*, the most elite of guards that protect the royal family of Eldas, the Great Kingdom and home of the elves. He is Karil's ever-present companion and guard. He has shoulder-length dark hair and piercing eyes.

Sa Hira: "I see", in Yorin.

Saeroks: Creatures in the Kage's dark army. They are tall beasts with thin, patchy fur, sinewy muscled frames, and long gangly arms and legs with long claws. They walk on two legs, but can run on all fours for greater speed.

Sasha: Younger brother to Raina

Seth: A Ronin, also called the Firebrand. Seth's element is fire, and his home is the Great Kingdom of the Citadel, a dark keep whose fires light the night sky. Seth is known for his fiery temper, and proud spirit.

Sevia: green lands known for their wine, silk, and, unfortunately, bandits.

Shadow's Bane: A God Weapon, Dagger forged of mysterious metal. Used by the Thief Goddess or "Dark Ronin"

Shifting: Kail's rumored ability to transport great lengths of space in a short amount of time.

Shining City: The great city in the mountains. It is a part of a massive kingdom, and the last remnant of the Kingdom of Ice.

Silverroot: A tree of both Farhaven and Daerval. Within Farhaven it is described as having veins of glowing silver that flow visibly beneath its bark, and bark that glows like fish's scaled bellies. Within Daerval, where there is no magic, it is simply a large evergreen, producing nut-sized fruits.

Silvas River: A magnificent river that flows south and divides much of Daerval.

Sinew: Primordial Dragon of Flesh

Spark: The magic that all but the Ronin wield, including Reavers, Neophytes and Arbiters, and the majority of Farhaven's magical beings. It is said to be derived from the Flow.

Spire: The highest building of Eldas where the council, king, queen and their family reside.

Sprites: Magical beings that have no form.

Star of Magha: The famous insignia that symbolizes the eight recognized kingdoms.

Stice: Aurelious' famed sword.

Taer: a land within Farhaven.

Tales of the Great Schism: Stories about the end of the Lieon and the Devari's split from old alliances to new ones, including their origin in the Citadel.

Tales of the Ronin: One of most famous books about the infamous deeds of the Ronin.

Tanglevine: A thorny root of the Lost Woods.

Temian: An elf with long golden hair, and strange golden eyes. Gray befriends the elf in the encampment beyond the Gates at the border of the woods.

The Great Kingdoms: The legendary cities. There were nine. Stone, Ice, Leaf, Fire, Flesh, Moon, Sun, Metal, and Wind. Each kingdom was the home of one of the Ronin, and coincides with their powers.

The Lost Road: The road to the forgotten kingdom of the Shining City.

The Red Moon: A mythical event that is said to coincide with "The Return" of the Ronin.

The Return: The fated return of the Ronin; an event the world fears. It is said they will finish the destruction of the lands they were rumored to nearly destroy during the *Lieon*.

The Eight Trials: The trials that a Neophyte must pass to become a Reaver.

The Sodden Tunnels: The tunnels that lead out of the Shining City; a dark and dismal place with no light, full of thousands of misleading paths. At one point, Mura says darkness called his name within the Tunnels. Karil also refers to them as the "Endless Tunnels".

The Terma: Elite elven warriors, the second highest in rank and skill in the armies of Eldas.

Tir Re' Dol: Often called The First City. Appropriately named as it was the first city to rise from the ashes of the Lieon, and soon became the capital of Daerval for millennia.

Transporter: A device that transports its wielder to a specific place by use of magic. They are hidden around the Citadel. Ren says they were created by a hundred Reavers working as one through the use of a "link."

Yorin: The old human tongue for all of Farhaven.

Yronia: Great Kingdom of Metal once known for their gleaming steel and mountainous walls of iron, and home to the Ronin Baro. Also home of the Great Forge and the Deep Mines. However, its "unbreakable" walls were shattered during the Lieon and it now lies as one of the forgotten kingdoms.

Vaster: The Great Kingdom of the rising Sun, named for the shining keeps that gleam like alabaster jewels, always in the dawn's light. Omni's homeland.

Vera: A woman, originally from the Citadel and connected to Kirin. She is beautiful, but equally dark and would gladly use her looks as a tool to gain even more power.

Vergs: Brutish, behemoth like creatures with leathery gray skin and flat snub-nosed faces; they are said to vaguely resemble childhood tales of trolls, though are considered more intelligent.

Vile Ones: The first mortal Race, Crafted after the titans and dragons

Zephyr: Primordial Dragon of Wind, True nme is Mali'cor.

ACKNOWLEDGEMENTS

To my grand God Tiers (a *very* special thank you)—Rob Falla, and John Lloyd

To my devoted (and epically awesome) Dragons—Alexa Loper, Cheri Heune, Craig Suiter, Dan Risse, James, Jason Kobylarz, Joshua Gray, Leanna Velotta, Michael Gonzales, Michelle Sharley, Tiffany Burton and Matt Sopha—*a collection of dragons is a thunder, and you make yourself heard, thank you, truly.*

To my remarkable Ronin—Laura A, and Sonjia Clemens

To my awesome Arbiters—Annette Polsky, Christian Juel, Jennifer Graff, Joe Desiderio, Mike Leaich, Paul Gmitter, Zach Teters

To my dashing Devari—Christie W., David Tolbert, Flavio Bolla, Gordon Hitt, Jeremy Minor, Julia Barbi, Kyleen McHenry, LordKaiju_2, Riley

To my respectable Reavers—Shelby Langdon

To my noteworthy Neophytes—DragonSindurZ, John Idlor, Littleninjabooks, Mikael Monnier, Nic Davis, Samuri, Terri Connor

Join the Patreon army and get insider info on the next books as well as Max's famous pancake recipes:

www.patreon.com/writerwolf

ABOUT THE AUTHOR

MATTHEW WOLF was born on March 14, 1986 in San Diego, California. He graduated from UC Santa Barbara as a literature major with a specialization in medieval studies and Japanese. Throughout college, he studied Old English and Japanese extensively, both of which are strongly tied to the languages of the book. He has also traveled considerably, from Switzerland and Scotland to Bonaire, and these sights inspire much of the land of Daerval.

Aside from the book (which is his main passion), he is also a Kung Fu instructor. His hobbies include woodcraft, archery, and of course, writing. He has several works of poetry published with *Leafnotes* in June 2010, a UCSB publication. And as of Spring 2013, *The Knife's Edge* is available to readers worldwide. Matt Wolf is currently building the brand of the Ronin Saga, giving rousing speeches, and encouraging others on the exciting path of writing.

MATTHEW WOLF

www.mattwolfauthor.com

Made in the USA
Coppell, TX
19 February 2026

71819812R00341